BEAUTY AND THE BEAST

L. STEELE

PART I

MAFIA KING

1

Karma

"Morn came and went—and came, and brought no day..."

Tears prick the backs of my eyes. Goddamn Byron. His words creep up on me when I am at my weakest. Not that I am a poetry addict, by any measure, but words are my jam. The one consolation I have is that, when everything else in the world is wrong, I can turn to them, and they'll be there, friendly, steady, waiting with open arms.

And this particular poem had laced my blood, crawled into my gut when I'd first read it. Darkness had folded within me like an insidious snake, that raises its head when I least expect it. Like now, when I look out on the still sleeping city of London, from the grassy slope of Waterlow Park.

Somewhere out there, the Mafia is hunting me, apparently. It's why my sister Summer and her new husband Sinclair Sterling had insisted that I have my own security detail. I had agreed...only to appease them...then given my bodyguard the slip this morning. I had decided to come running here because it's not a place I'd normally go... Not so early in the morning, anyway. They won't think to look for me here. At least, not for a while longer.

I purse my lips, close my eyes. Silence. The rustle of the wind between the leaves. The faint tinkle of the water from the nearby spring.

I could be the last person on this planet, alone, unsung, bound for the grave.

Ugh! Stop. Right there. I drag the back of my hand across my nose. Try it again, focus, get the words out, one after the other, like the steps of my sorry life.

"Morn came and went—and came, and... and..." My voice breaks. "Bloody asinine hell." I dig my fingers into the grass and grab a handful and fling it out. Again. From the top.

"Morn came and went—and came, and—"

"...brought no day."

A gravelly voice completes my sentence.

I whip my head around. His silhouette fills my line of sight. He's sitting on the same knoll as me, yet I have to crane my neck back to see his profile. The sun is at his back, so I can't make out his features. Can't see his eyes... Can only take in his dark hair, combed back by a ruthless hand that brooked no measure.

My throat dries.

Thick dark hair, shot through with grey at the temples. He wears his age like a badge. I don't know why, but I know his years have not been easy. That he's seen more, indulged in more, reveled in the consequences of his actions, however extreme they might have been. He's not a normal, everyday person, this man. Not a nine-to-fiver, not someone who lives an average life. Definitely not a man who returns home to his wife and home at the end of the day. He is...different, unique, evil... Monstrous. Yes, he is a beast, one who sports the face of a man but who harbors the kind of darkness inside that speaks to me. I gulp.

His face boasts a hooked nose, a thin upper lip, a fleshy lower lip. One that hints at hidden desires, Heat. Lust. The sensuous scrape of that whiskered jaw over my innermost places. Across my inner thigh, reaching toward that core of me that throbs, clenches, melts to feel the stab of his tongue, the thrust of his hardness as he impales me, takes me, makes me his. Goosebumps pop on my skin.

I drag my gaze away from his mouth down to the scar that slashes across his throat. A cold sensation coils in my chest. What or who had hurt him in such a cruel fashion?

"Of this their desolation; and all hearts
Were chill'd into a selfish prayer for light..."

He continues in that rasping guttural tone. Is it the wound that caused that scar that makes his voice so…gravelly… So deep…so… so, hot?

Sweat beads my palms and the hairs on my nape rise. "Who are you?"

He stares ahead as his lips move,

"Forests were set on fire—but hour by hour
They fell and faded—and the crackling trunks
Extinguish'd with a crash—and all was black."

I swallow, moisture gathers in my core. How can I be wet by the mere cadence of this stranger's voice?

I spring up to my feet.

"Sit down," he commands.

His voice is unhurried, lazy even, his spine erect. The cut of his black jacket stretches across the width of his massive shoulders. His hair… I was mistaken—there are threads of dark gold woven between the darkness that pours down to brush the nape of his neck. A strand of hair falls over his brow. As I watch, he raises his hand and brushes it away. Somehow, the gesture lends an air of vulnerability to him. Something so at odds with the rest of his persona that, surely, I am mistaken?

My scalp itches. I take in a breath and my lungs burn. This man… He's sucked up all the oxygen in this open space as if he owns it, the master of all he surveys. The master of me. My death. My life. A shiver ladders along my spine. *Get away, get away now, while you still can.*

I angle my body, ready to spring away from him.

"I won't ask again."

Ask. Command. Force me to do as he wants. He'll have me on my back, bent over, on my side, on my knees, over him, under him. He'll surround me, overwhelm me, pin me down with the force of his personality. His charisma, his larger-than-life essence will crush everything else out of me and I… I'll love it.

"No."

"Yes."

A fact. A statement of intent, spoken aloud. So true. So real. Too real. Too much. Too fast. All of my nightmares…my dreams come to life. Everything I've wanted is here in front of me. I'll die a thousand deaths before he'll be done with me… And then? Will I be reborn? For him. For me. For myself.

I live, first and foremost, to be the woman I was…am meant to be.

"You want to run?"

No.

No.

I nod my head.

He turns his, and all the breath leaves my lungs. Blue eyes—cerulean, dark like the morning skies, deep like the nighttime...hidden corners, secrets that I don't dare uncover. He'll destroy me, have my heart, and break it so casually.

My throat burns and a boiling sensation squeezes my chest.

"Go then, my beauty, fly. You have until I count to five. If I catch you, you are mine."

"If you don't?"

"Then I'll come after you, stalk your every living moment, possess your nightmares, and steal you away in the dead of night, and then..."

I draw in a shuddering breath as liquid heat drips from between my legs. "Then?" I whisper.

"Then, I'll ensure you'll never belong to anyone else, you'll never see the light of day again, for your every breath, your every waking second, your thoughts, your actions...and all your words, every single last one, will belong to me." He peels back his lips, and his teeth glint in the first rays of the morning light. "Only me." He straightens to his feet and rises, and rises.

This man... He is massive. A monster who always gets his way. My guts churn. My toes curl. Something primeval inside of me insists I hold my own. I cannot give in to him. Cannot let him win whatever this is. I need to stake my ground, in some form. *Say something. Anything. Show him you're not afraid of this.*

"Why?" I tilt my head back, all the way back. "Why are you doing this?"

He tilts his head, his ears almost canine in the way they are silhouetted against his profile.

"Is it because you can? Is it a...a," I blink, "a debt of some kind?"

He stills.

"My father, this is about how he betrayed the Mafia, right? You're one of them?"

"Lucky guess." His lips twist, "It is about your father, and how he promised you to me. He reneged on his promise, and now, I am here to collect."

"No." I swallow... *No, no, no.*

"Yes." His jaw hardens.

All expression is wiped clean of his face, and I know then, that he speaks the truth. It's always about the past. My sorry shambles of a past... Why does it always catch up with me? *You can run, but you can never hide.*

"Tick-tock, Beauty." He angles his body and his shoulders shut out the sight of the sun, the dawn skies, the horizon, the city in the distance, the rustle of the grass, the trees, the rustle of the leaves. All of it fades and leaves just me and him. Us. *Run.*

"Five." He jerks his chin, straightens the cuffs of his sleeves.

My knees wobble.

"Four."

My pulse rate spikes. I should go. Leave. But my feet are planted in this earth. This piece of land where we first met. What am I, but a speck in the larger scheme of things? To be hurt. To be forgotten. To be taken without an ounce of retribution. To be punished...by him.

"Three." He thrusts out his chest, widens his stance, every muscle in his body relaxed. "Two."

I swallow. The pulse beats at my temples. My blood thrums.

"One."

2

Michael

"Go."

She pivots and races down the slope. Her dark hair streams behind her. Her scent, sexy femininity and silver moonflowers, clings to my nose, then recedes. It's so familiar, that scent.

I had smelled it before, had reveled in it. Had drawn in it into my lungs as she had peeked up at me from under her thick eyelashes. Her green gaze had fixed on mine, her lips parted as she welcomed my kiss. As she had wound her arms about my neck, pushed up those sweet breasts and flattened them against my chest. As she had parted her legs when I had planted my thigh between them. I had seen her before...in my dreams. I stiffen. She can't be the same girl though, can she?

I reach forward, thrust out my chin and sniff the air, but there's only the damp scent of dawn, mixed with the foul tang of exhaust fumes, as she races away from me.

She stumbles and I jump forward, pause when she straightens. Wait. Wait. Give her a lead. Let her think she has almost escaped, that she's gotten the better of me... As if.

I clench my fists at my sides, force myself to relax. Wait. Wait. She reaches the bottom of the incline, turns. I surge forward. One foot in front of the other. My heels dig into the grassy surface and mud flies up, clings to the hem of my £4000 Italian pants. Like I care? Plenty more where that came from. An entire walk-in closet, full of clothes made to measure, to suit every occasion, with every possible accessory needed by a man in my position to impress...

Everything... Except the one thing that I had coveted from the moment I had laid eyes on her. Sitting there on the grassy slope, unshed tears in her eyes, and reciting... Byron? For hell's sake. Of all the poets in the world, she had to choose the Lord of Darkness.

I huff. All a ploy. Clearly, she knew I was sitting next to her... No, not possible. I had walked toward her and she hadn't stirred. Hadn't been aware. Yeah, I am that good. I've been known to slit a man's throat from ear-to-ear while he was awake and in his full senses. Alive one second, dead the next. That's how it is in my world. You want it, you take it. And I... I want her.

I increase my pace, eat up the distance between myself and the girl... That's all she is. A slip of a thing, a slim blur of motion. Beauty in hiding. A diamond, waiting for me to get my hands on her, polish her, show her what it means to be...

Dead. She is dead. That's why I am here.

A flash of skin, a creamy length of thigh. My groin hardens and my legs wobble. I lurch over a bump in the ground. The hell? I right myself, leap forward, inching closer, closer. She reaches a curve in the path, disappears out of sight.

My heart hammers in my chest. I will not lose her, will not. *Here, Beauty, come to Daddy.* The wind whistles past my ears. I pump my legs, lengthen my strides, turn the corner. There's no one there. Huh?

My heart hammers and the blood pounds at my wrists, my temples; adrenaline thrums in my veins. I slow down, come to a stop. Scan the clearing.

The hairs on my forearms prickle. She's here. Not far, but where? Where is she? I prowl across to the edge of the clearing, under the tree with its spreading branches.

When I get my hands on you, Beauty, I'll spread your legs like the pages of a poem. Dip into your honeyed sweetness, like a quill pen in ink. Drag my aching shaft across that melting, weeping entrance. My balls throb. My groin tightens. The crack of a branch above shivers across my stretched nerve endings. I swoop forward, hold out my arms, and close my grasp around the trembling, squirming mass of precious humanity. I cradle her close to my chest, heart beating thud-thud-thud, overwhelming any other thought.

Mine. All mine. The hell is wrong with me? She wriggles her little body, and her curves slide across my forearms. My shoulders bunch and my fingers tingle. She kicks out with her legs and arches her back, thrusting her breasts up so her nipples are outlined against the fabric of her sports bra. She dared to come out dressed like that? In that scrap of fabric that barely covers her luscious flesh?

"Let me go." She whips her head toward me and her hair flows around her shoulders, across her face. She blows it out of the way. "You monster, get away from me."

Anger drums at the backs of my eyes and desire tugs at my groin. The scent of her is sheer torture, something I had dreamed of in the wee hours of twilight when dusk turned into night.

She's not real. She's not the woman I think she is. She is my downfall. My sweet poison. The bitter medicine I must partake of to cure the ills that plague my company,

"Fine." I lower my arms and she tumbles to the grass, hits the ground butt first.

"How dare you." She huffs out a breath, her hair messily arranged across her face.

I shove my hands into the pockets of my fitted pants, knees slightly bent, legs apart. Tip my chin down and watch her as she sprawls at my feet.

"You…dropped me?" She makes a sound deep in her throat.

So damn adorable.

"Your wish is my command." I quirk my lips.

"You don't mean it."

"You're right." I lean my weight forward on the balls of my feet and she flinches.

"What…what do you want?"

"You."

She pales. "You want to…to rob me? I have nothing of consequence,

"Oh, but you do, Beauty."

I lean in and every muscle in her body tenses. Good. She's wary. She should be. She should have been alert enough to have run as soon as she sensed my presence. But she hadn't.

I should spare her because she's the woman from my dreams…but I won't. She's a debt I intend to collect. She owes me, and I've delayed what was meant to happen long enough.

I pull the gun from my holster, point it at her.

Her gaze widens and her breath hitches. I expect her to plead with me for her life, but she doesn't. She stares back at me with her huge dilated pupils. She licks her lips and the blood drains to my groin. *Che cazzo!* Why does her lack of fear turn me on so?

"Your phone," I murmur, "take out your phone."

She draws in a breath, then reaches into her pocket and pulls out her phone.

"Call your sister."

"What?"

"Dial your sister, Beauty. Tell her you are going away on a long trip to Sicily with your new male friend."

"What?"

"You heard me." I curl my lips, "Do it, now!'

She blinks, looks like she is about to protest, then her fingers fly over the phone.

Damn, and I had been looking forward to coaxing her into doing my bidding.

She holds her phone to her ear. I can hear the phone ring on the other side, before it goes to voicemail. She glances at me and I jerk my chin. She looks away, takes a deep breath, then speaks in a cheerful voice, "Hi Summer, it's me, Karma. I, ah, have to go away for a bit. This new...ah, friend of mine... He has an extra ticket and he has invited me to Sicily to spend some time with him. I...ah, I don't know when, exactly, I'll be back, but I'll message you and let you know. Take care. Love ya sis, I—"

I snatch the phone from her, disconnect the call, then hold the gun to her temple, "Goodbye, Beauty."

3

Karma

The whoop-whoop-whump grows louder, infiltrates my mind. Darkness, so dark, I'm floating. The back of my head hits something hard. Red and white sparks flare behind my eyeballs. I crack my eyelids open and pain slices through my brain. I groan, and the sound echoes back at me. Sweat beads my neck, my palms. My sports bra is sticking to my back. Booty shorts? Check. My running shoes—I wriggle my feet—I still have them on. What happened? What—? The ringing in my ears whooshes up, engulfs me.

He shot me. The bastard shot me?

A trembling grips me; my arms and legs grow numb. The blood beats in my ears. My pulse rate ratchets up and my guts churn. Bile rushes up my throat and I cough. No, I will not be sick. Not now. I take in a breath, another. Focus, focus on the now, as Ma used to say. She was a hippie, who'd hitched a ride with my businessman father. Then married him and given birth to me and my sister. Bequeathed us quirky nicknames, which had ultimately made it to our passports…talk about fate, huh?

As to why she called me Karma? It was a joke, on me. Bad luck seems to dog my footsteps. How else do you explain this...this situation? Me being kidnapped by...tall, dark and dangerous?

My stomach flutters, my scalp tingles. No, no, I am insane. That brooding gaze, that mean glare? Damn it, what is it about me that I seem to attract the assholes, huh? I fumble around, shove my hand in the pocket of my shorts... No! My phone is gone. Of course, bastard had kept it, and then he had pushed the barrel of his gun into my temple. I had squeezed my eyes shut, the blood roaring in my ears, and then I'd heard the bang. Then nothing. But he hadn't shot me. No he hadn't. If he had, I wouldn't be alive. And I'm pretty sure I am.

I run a mental check across my body... No, I don't seem to be hurt anywhere. Which means, he had pretended to shoot me... Likely, shot into the air next to my head... Asshole. Clearly, he'd done it to frighten me...to get me to comply. What a bastard. My pulse begins to drum. Why? Why did he do that? What is he going to do with me?

Whoomp-whoomp-thump. The hell? I stiffen. The container I am in rocks from side to side...very gently. Not a boat... I am in a... I glance around the enclosed space. There's room for, maybe, one more person, a very small person... My foot grazes something. I feel around with my sneaker. There's something springy—made of rubber. A tire? A car honks, muffled, as if coming from a distance or through a layer of metal. A car. I am in a vehicle? In the trunk, probably.

I snake my fist out and into the curved barrier around me. "Ow!" Pain glances down my arm. "Let me the hell out!"

The vehicle seems to speed up. My heart begins to hammer so fast, I am sure it's going to break out of my ribcage. This is not good... I really shouldn't put so much stress on my heart... I was born with a hole in my heart, which hadn't been discovered until a few years ago. It isn't life-threatening, yet. But it could be, if left untreated. The doctors had warned that I would need a procedure soon, but for the time-being, they had put me on medication to see if it would help.

Meanwhile, I'd been told not to exert myself... Instructions which I hadn't adhered to, of course. It's why my sister Summer is overly-protective of me. It's why I had gone running in the park, and why I have refused to take the medicines; because I hate feeling less than anyone else. I had wanted to prove to myself that I was fine.

Damn it, if I hadn't gone running, he wouldn't have come across me and kidnapped me. OMG, he's kidnapping me. Adrenaline laces my blood. My heart beat instantly spikes. That's not good, not good at all.

Calm down, take another breath, and another. I manage to calm myself down somewhat.

Where is he taking me? Why did he kidnap me? I have to get the hell out of here. Have to. I join my fists, draw in a breath, then yank them up. Connect with the overhead covering. The loud thunk fills the space. I cry out. Pain slices down my arms and my shoulders hurt. There's a screeching sound, audible even through the layer of metal. I am thrown forward, then back. All movement stops. Hell. I've done it now. I've gotten their attention. Jesus H. Christ, are you somewhere around? I'd never prayed when the nuns had held mass, but damn it, if you are there... Please, please... I bring my knuckles to my mouth, suck on the throbbing flesh. Help me, God.

The cover flies up and light pours over me. I squeeze my eyes shut, then crack them open, just a tad. Wide shoulders, a massive chest that blocks out the daylight. His features are in repose, the sun to his back. I can't see his face, but I know who it is. Him.

"Move over." His hard baritone whips through the space.

"What?"

He swoops out his hand, grabs my shoulder and pushes me back. Then swings a leg over and inside the boot.

The hell?

He sinks down. *No, no, no. He can't be doing this.*

"I am."

He lowers his big body and I scoot back, all the way back in that enclosed space, until my back is flat against the barrier of the car... He sinks down into the space I vacated. If he gets in here with me, we'll be face to face, chest to breasts, thigh to thigh, crotch to— I turn my back on him, as he lowers the last of his bulk into the already cramped space.

"Good thinking." His voice rumbles down my back.

"At least one of us is," I growl, "because, clearly, you're not in your right senses... You—"

The cover of the boot slams down and a tiny light bulb flicks on just above us.

"What the—?" I blink, stare up at the illumination. It's not much, but at least, I can see my nose in front of my face.

"Say thank you, Beauty."

"Go fly a kite."

"You can do better than that."

The vehicle roars forward, slamming me back and into the wall of his body. Every hard, corded, coiled inch of him surrounds me. I gulp. Dense waves of heat sear my back, sink into my blood, snake into the hollow between my thighs. Oh, hell!

Goosebumps flare on my skin; moisture laces my palms, my brow. My throat is so dry that I swear my tongue is stuck to the roof of my mouth. Not good. This is not good.

"Where are you taking me?"

"You're hardly in a position to ask questions."

The hard planes of his chest graze my shoulders. I gulp. Freeze. Every muscle in my body goes rigid. His powerful thighs fit in the V of where I have folded up my legs. He slides his arm under my neck, wraps the other around my waist, and pulls me close.

Something thick and long stabs at the curve of my backside, OMG! Is that…is it…? I squeeze my thighs together, try to scoot away. His grip tightens.

"Stop that," he growls.

As if I am going to jump to his every command. I huff, wriggle forward, but end up brushing my butt against his turgid length.

"See what happens when you don't obey?"

I freeze.

"You can't…do this."

"I already am."

"My sister will be worried when she can't reach me."

"You already called her."

"I…what?" I turn my head, glower at him.

"You told her you were going on a long holiday with a friend."

Oh, right. "She'll never believe that," I huff.

Besides, Summer's so overprotective. She wouldn't just let me take off like that without suspecting something, right?

"She has a new husband, a future… She's not going to miss you for a while."

"How did you…?" I shut my mouth. "You…you stalked me?"

"You aren't that important."

Anger coats my tongue. How dare he insult me? "I mean something, because you didn't kill me…"

"Yet." I hear the amusement in his voice.

Bet all this is just one long walk in the park for him. Which is where he found me. How long had he been following me? Did he know my routine? Is that how he marked out the best time to abduct me? My heart begins to thud. This is not good. This is really happening.

"Why me?" I say in a low tone. "Why did you kidnap me?"

"The eternal question." He yawns. The bastard yawns, as if he's bored with this conversation.

"Tell me," I insist, "what do you want in exchange?"

"What makes you think I am interested in getting anything in exchange?"

"What do you mean?" I glance sideways and up at what I can see of that gorgeous face. Those high cheekbones, the hooked nose, that pouty lower lip of his that was made for sinking my teeth into, swiping my tongue across the seam, as I nibble on that delectable mouth… Gah! My face heats and a pulse flares to life between my legs. "What do you mean, you are not interested in an exchange? You must want something in return."

"I have everything."

"Then why take me?"

"That's what I am trying to figure out."

What the—? I frown, "That makes no sense. You must have had a plan when you decided to steal me away from my everyday life. I mean, people don't just see someone else and decide, on the spur of the moment, 'oh, I want that person, so I am going to kidnap him or her,' you know?"

"No," he shakes his head, "I don't, actually."

I blink, open my mouth and shut it again. "I see." I bob my head. "I understand what you are trying to do here."

He arches an eyebrow, "Pray, do tell."

"You're trying to confuse me with your cryptic words, and you're trying to keep me off balance with your stupid domineering ways."

"You meant controlling ways."

I snarl, "What's the bloody difference anyway?"

"To control means to command, to have mastery over, to—"

"Forget I asked," I mutter.

"You, on the other hand, clearly love to be subjugated."

"No I don't," I snap.

"Sure, you do."

"Not."

"Want me to prove it to you?" He lowers his voice to a hush, and instantly my toes curl. A shiver ripples down my spine. Every cell in my body opens, all my nerve endings go on alert…and my synapses…they seem to fire all at once. *Oh, hell, what is this man doing to me?*

I strain away, try to put distance between us once. He hauls me even closer, throws his leg over both of mine, so I can't move.

I try to draw in a breath and my lungs burn. I am having a nervous breakdown. In the boot of a car, with my kidnapper.

No, no no, this can't be happening. I can't breathe. My heart beats so fast, I am sure it's going to jump out of my ribcage.

"Shh!" His warm breath grazes my cheek. "Relax, I promise I won't harm you."

Says the man who almost shot me. A chuckle bubbles up and my entire body shakes.

"What's so funny?" he rumbles.

"You…" I choke out, "you, asshole. Have you heard yourself? You sound like a psycho bastard—"

Cold metal pushes against the curve of my neck. My breath hitches. My pulse rate ratchets up, even as my limbs tremble.

"Shh." His warm breath raises the hair at my temples. My skin prickles and my scalp feels too tight. I open my mouth, but no words come out. *Is that a knife?* It's a knife. A bloody knife. OMG. How many freakin' weapons does this man carry on him, anyway?

He drags the tip of the blade down the side of my throat. The tip pricks my skin. Not enough to hurt, just enough for me to go still. My breath hitches and a trembling grips me. Even as my core clenches. What the hell is wrong with me? Do I find the idea of him holding a weapon against my skin such a turn on? Am I such a sucker for punishment? One who hankers for something darker, deeper, more violent that the usual overtures than a normal woman would enjoy.

"Now, Beauty, don't freak out on me, not after that very promising start."

He removes the knife. I sense him move away as he tucks the knife back from wherever he'd pulled it out, then he grips my chin. He forces my head toward him and my gaze meets his.

Those blue eyes are piercing, a beacon in the darkness. My light at the end of the tunnel. *What? No.* Anger squeezes my guts and fear bubbles up, a tangy, bitter taste on my tongue.

I open my mouth to scream, but he's already there. He lowers his chin, slants his lips over mine.

4

———————

Michael

Heat, sweetness. The taste of her, like strawberries and sunshine, punches me in the gut. My head spins. I need her, want her. I pull her up until she crashes into my chest, her body twisted against mine. I slide my leg, between hers, apply pressure until her body curves further.

Bend for me, Beauty. Break for me. Open. I swipe my tongue across the seam of her lips and her mouth parts further. I swoop in, because… that's my second nature. I take what I want. Use weakness to my advantage. Rush in to consolidate my position when I have the upper hand. I flatten my palm over the flatness of her belly, graze my fingers over the core of her. She moans low in her throat, the sound so soft I'd have missed it, except I've plastered her to me. Her every breath, her every inhale, the trembling that sweeps up her spine… It's mine. I tilt my head, deepen the kiss even further. Thrust my tongue inside the honeyed spring of her mouth and drink from her. Suck on her tongue and a whine bleeds from her. I swallow it. Bring my fingers up to cup her breast and she arches her spine. Pushes her flesh into the hollow of my palm. I pinch her nipple and her entire body bucks. Against me. Into me. Her hair slaps against my chin, coils around my neck, binding me to her, tugging at me, connecting us... *No.* I tear my lips from her mouth and she tips up her chin, reaches up, seeking my touch, my essence, what only I can give her.

"Beauty?" I clear my throat.

She peers at me from between the fringe of her eyelashes, pupils blown from the pleasure I'd drawn from her. She blinks; her lips part, swollen from my ministrations.

"Wanna shag?" I allow my lips to curl in a smirk. Rake my gaze down her flushed cheeks, her heaving chest. "You're a bit on the heavy side for me, but you'll do for a quickie."

Her cheeks redden; a spark lights in her eyes. *There, you are.*

"Fuck you."

"If you insist."

She pulls away from me, and I loosen my grip. Not that she's going anywhere, considering we were trapped here in the confines of this car for a little while longer. Why the hell did I crawl in here with her? A temporary loss of sanity, that's what it was. I'd heard her beat her fists against the car and...knew it would attract attention. Didn't want that. Couldn't bring her up front so... I'd done the logical thing. I'd climbed in.

"Get away from me, you obnoxious jerk."

"I'm sure you're aware that's not possible, considering." I jerk my chin towards the space around us.

"And who's fault is that?"

"Yours."

"What?"

"If you hadn't quoted Byron, you wouldn't be here."

"Yeah, I would be dead." She glowers.

"Right on your first guess." I nod. "Impressive you recognized that."

"So, what's your plan?"

"Plan?" I frown.

"You know, the hell are you thinking, transporting me to God knows where? Why didn't you kill me like you should have?"

"I'm the one asking the questions, *piccolina.*"

"Your Italian insults suck, you know that?"

I blow out a breath. "You English think a word in any other language is an insult."

"Wasn't it."

"Nope."

"Then?"

"It doesn't matter."

"What about what you called me earlier?"

"What?"

"Beauty. You called me Beauty."

"You are fucking annoying. I liked you better with my tongue in your mouth." I lower my head and she arches away. She tugs at my grasp. I release her chin and she faces forward.

"Don't kiss me again."

"You liked it, hmm?"

"No."

"Don't lie."

"I'm not.

"Wanna bet. I am more than happy to go another round." I allow my lips to curve, "It's as good a way as any to pass the time."

I coil a strand of her hair around my fingers, bring it to my nose. Cinnamon and sugar, with a dash of hot spice. My mouth waters, and I release the silken length.

"So, what do you say?"

"Go to hell."

"Been there, and I'm not in a hurry to repeat the experience."

"Do you have a rejoinder for every insult?" She huffs.

"Do you always mouth off your captors?"

"I've never been kidnapped before.'

"I've never..." my voice trails off. I don't lie, ever. And the fact is, she's not the first I have abducted. She's the first whose life I've spared, and hell... Why? Why would I do that? Just a few mumbled words and boom... I'm the bitch in this equation. Nope. No way. I need to take control of this situation. Of whatever it is that stretches between us. Need to snap this connection.

"Never been at a loss of words before, huh?" Triumph tinges her tone, and warmth curls in my chest.

My heart begins to thud, my pulse rate ratchets up, and even before the words are out of my mouth, I know I am going to regret it... But fuck that. I am Italian enough to not mess with forces beyond my comprehension. When I had set out this morning to take her life, I hadn't realized that it would be mine I was forfeiting. Too little, too late. I am helpless, and I have to take the next step. Else we'll both be left hanging between the devil and a dark place, and to hell with that. I'll make the decision and be damned. Pay the consequences; no choices. This is it. It has to be this way. There is no other option.

"I've never had to choke a woman into complying before."

"What the hell?" She yells, whips her head around.

I wrap an arm around her neck then grab the bicep of my other arm.

She struggles, kicks out, manages to free a leg and sinks her knee into my thigh. Pain laces my nerve endings, lengthens my cock even further. Don't judge. My tastes have always been on the edge…and this... This has pushed them past a point of no return.

I manage to slide my other hand behind her head, apply pressure to the sides of her neck and she goes limp.

"Sleep, Beauty."

Her breathing deepens.

"Good girl." I cradle her close, whisper my knuckles over her cheek. "When you awake, it will be the start."

5

Karma

Whispers, the scrape of something smooth against the back of my thighs. I rub my cheek against the silky-hard sensations. The masculine scent of testosterone, musky, like leather with a hint of woodsmoke. Fresh snow on fallen earth. The cold rush of a winter's wind. The snap and crackle of a fireplace. Warmth creeps up my fingers, my toes. I turn toward it, snuggle in against the hard unrelenting surface. Thud-thud-thud-thud; the beats sink into my blood. My core clenches in perfect rhythm. Him. He is near. He had crawled into the back of the car with me, had wound his big body around mine and he'd choked me until I'd fainted. I crack open my eyelids and the world swims in my line of sight.

"How dare you?" I cough. "You knocked me out, you obnoxious jackaloupe."

"Sleep hasn't improved your disposition, huh?" A lean arm appears in front of me, holding a glass of water. "Drink."

I purse my lips, gulp, glare from the glass of water to his handsome, gorgeous, ugly-mean features.

"Do it or I'll pour it down your throat myself." His tone is soft but he doesn't fool me. Bastard would do it, too. I reach for the glass. The water slides between my parched lips. I drain it. My swollen tongue thanks me, and the drumming behind my temples seems to recede. I lower the glass, take stock of my surroundings. I'm in a leather chair, and a seatbelt is strapped across my lap. I also have my running clothes on. I glance down and find my feet are still clad in my sneakers. The low hum of engines, hushed voices soaked up by thick carpeting, and the kind of luxury only the filthy rich or the filthy—period—can buy, reaches me.

"We're on a plane?"

I glance up at the face of my kidnapper. He sits in the chair opposite me. Elbows on the armrests, fingers steepled together in front of him, his legs are spread apart, powerful thighs stretching the soft fabric of his tailor-made pants, and between them, the unmistakable bulge of— I jerk my chin up, meet his gaze. "Private jet, huh? I guess crime really does pay well. How did you acquire it? Did you kill the owner?"

"Tortured him, actually. By the time I was done with him, there was no blood left in his sorry-ass body."

I blanche.

He laughs and I can't tell if it's because it's true or he just likes the look on my face and wants to torment me.

"Do you want more water?"

Maybe both. *Jerk.*

"What I want..." I tighten my grip on the glass, "is to smash your face in." I pull my arm back and hurl the glass at him. It catches him at the side of the temple, then falls to the carpet with a soft thud. Blood blooms from the gash, a trickle of scarlet that rolls down his temple, over the razor-sharp, high cheekbone.

There's a sudden movement, then the barrel of gun is pushed against my temple. "Want me to kill her, Michael?" A hard male voice sounds from somewhere to the side and above me. I swallow; my pulse begins to race.

Michael rubs his chin as he considers me.

The barrel of the gun digs deeper into my temple. I wince, but don't take my gaze off the asshole opposite.

Finally, Michael tilts his head. "Not yet," he rumbles, and I stiffen.

The cold metal disappears from my skin, and I am not ashamed to say that the tension drains from my body.

"Oh, and Antonio?"

Antonio tilts his head.

"No one gets to pull a gun on her, except me. No one hurts her, but me." His lips curl.

I set my jaw and his grin widens. "Now leave us," he growls and Antonio retreats to the far end of the cabin. Shit, now we are alone. Maybe it would be better if Antonio were still here. So what, if he held a gun to my temple? I'd rather face a weapon head-on, than the shark-faced, Mafia asshole who eyes me like I am the tastiest morsel ever. I tip up my chin, grip the handles of my seat, "If that was meant to frighten me—"

"Shut up."

My breath hitches.

"Don't talk to me like—"

He swoops forward so fast that the blood from his temple splashes onto my dress. "I mean it, Beauty. Keep those pretty lips zipped or I'll stuff your mouth, and it won't be with your favorite cupcake."

My shoulder muscles lock, my core puckers. I squeeze my thighs together to stop the insidious moisture that drip-drip-drips from my treacherous core.

"Unless." He taps his fingertips together, peruses my features. "Unless that's what you want?"

No.

"Maybe that's why you've been barking at me, scratching at me, demanding my attention, making it difficult for me to concentrate on anything but your face, your legs, the hard nipples of your breasts that tremble in anticipation of my touch, hmm?"

Of course, not. What the hell is he talking about?

"Is this what gets you off?" I drop my gaze to his crotch, where his bulge has grown noticeably bigger in the last few seconds. "Lording it over those helpless in front of you, those weaker than you? Does that make you feel more macho? Does it feed your manliness, you obnoxious bastard?"

"No, but this will."

He grabs the hardness between his legs and squeezes it. I flinch. My toes curl. I should look away from how he cups the thick girth between those powerful thighs. My throat closes, my ribcage tightens, and moisture pools at my core.

"Down."

"What?" I jerk my chin up.

He nods towards the space between his legs.

"No."

"You have two choices."

Oh?

"You get down on your knees and blow me or..."

Or?

"I get down on my knees, pull your legs apart and eat you out. And then I let you blow me."

I squeeze my thighs together. *No way.* If he touches me now, he'll know how…how wet I am. And I shouldn't be. I hate him; hate him for how he pulls a response from me, by just being…himself. I blink. What I see with him is what I get, and that's refreshing. In a way, he's more decent than any other man I've encountered in my life. The hell am I thinking about?

"Which one's it going to be, my Beauty?"

"I'm not your anything," I snarl.

"Wrong, you're my captive."

I chuckle. "You don't say?"

"Choose fast and choose wisely, for this sets the course of our future relationship."

"Relationship?" I glower. "You are more deluded than what I first thought."

"No more than what your father was."

"The son shall not bear the iniquity of the father…" I stutter. A quote from the Bible? That's the best I could do? Guess I was paying more attention than I realized to the daily, evening readings by the nuns. God bless their souls, they'd done their best for us. If it weren't for them… I wouldn't be alive.

I wouldn't be here, facing down this absolute brute who, clearly, will not listen to reason, so why am I even trying?

"And the daughter? What is the daughter going to do, hmm?" The blood drips down his cheek and onto his shirt, smearing it scarlet.

"This daughter sure doesn't owe her old man a single ounce of respect. What I do, I do out of choice." I set my jaw.

"Which is…?

I draw in a breath, then unhook the seatbelt from around me and drop down to my knees.

6

Michael

She peers up at me from under her lashes. Her dark hair about her shoulders, her cheeks flushed, she chews on her lower lip and all the blood rushes to my groin. As if I weren't hard enough already. I drag my arm to the side, force my fingers to relax.

"Tick-Tock, Beauty."

She makes a sound deep in her throat, one I am already coming to recognize. That almost subvocal note half-way between a snarl and frustration. My dick lengthens further. At this rate, I am going to jizz myself in my pants, and before she's even touched that part of my body. *Focus, focus.* I draw in a breath, pull back my shoulders.

"Perhaps I should take the lead—"

"No." She scuttles forward, undoes my belt, then seizes the zipper on my pants and lowers it, along with my briefs. My dick springs free.

"Oh." Her mouth forms a circle; her pale lips shorn of lipstick beckon. My balls tighten. My fingers tingle. I'd told her to blow me; doesn't mean I am going to let her control the proceedings.

"Drop your head, take me down your throat."

She swallows.

"Do it."

She folds her fingers around the base of my shaft and sparks explode behind my eyeballs. This was a mistake. I shouldn't have told her to do this. I am revealing too much of myself, in just how my body responds to her.

I grab the armrests, dig my fingers in.

"That all you got?"

She tips her chin up and her green eyes spark fire. Something hot stabs at my chest. This woman, she's a fighter. A survivor, like me. Who will break first? Me or her? It has to be her. It will be her, if it's the last thing I do.

"Maybe you're scared, huh? Maybe you're just like your old man, all talk, no—" She lowers her chin, licks my dick from base to head. Lust slams into my groin.

She swirls her pink tongue around the swollen appendage, licks off the precum oozing from the slit. I hold her gaze, lower my chin. One side of my mouth curls and a deep red stains the creamy skin of her neck. Fascinating. I could spend hours...days exploring every millimeter of that gorgeous expanse of womanhood, wring orgasm after orgasm from her, play her body like it's a finely-tuned musical instrument...

But I want more. I need her open and thirsting for what only I can give her. I have to own her, body and soul, until her every emotion is mine to read. Her every thought is mine to foresee. Her every wish... mine...only mine to grant. If I so deem it.

Hmm. A fierce sensation fans to life deep in my groin. I track it as it spreads up my spine, to my extremities, until it seems to envelope every inch of my body. What would it take for this woman to give up all her secrets to me...willingly? That would be a first. A different challenge. Something I've been searching for...for quite a while.

I widen my legs even more, pump my hips forward. My swollen shaft slaps her across her lips. She flinches. I glare at her and she pales. I tilt my head. She stiffens her shoulders, squeezes the base of my cock. Then she opens her mouth, drops her chin and takes me down her throat...in one go.

The fuck? It's clearly not her first blowjob... And I had thought, what? That she was innocent? No way. I had been fooled by her youth, her feistiness. Well, no more. It works better this way, for both of us. I don't have to feel guilty for what I am going to put her through, hmm?

She sucks in her cheeks, and I feel the pull all the way down to my balls.

She pulls back, saliva drooling down her chin, dragging the rough edge of her tongue across the underside of my shaft. The pulse thrums to life at my wrists, my temples, even at the backs of my eyelids. Goddam her. She pauses, with her lips framing my cock, and my balls draw up. I can't hold out any more. Damn her.

I swoop down, dig my fingers into her hair. I tug and her neck arches. I wrap my other hand around her neck. She swallows. Every hesitant vibration strums over my palm, sinks into my blood. My heart begins to thud. This is too carnal, too real. This isn't how I intended it to be. I thought I was in control? I was wrong. As long as she is near me, I'll never be able to manage my reactions. I pull her back until my dick slips from her mouth with a wet sound that has me instantly twitching again. Hell. I release her.

She sits back on her knees. A tear trickles from the corner of her eyes. I reach forward to swipe it away, and she flinches. Anger squeezes my guts. I tuck myself back in, zip my pants.

She blinks.

"Go," I jerk my chin toward the seat.

"But." She scowls at me.

"Do it, before I change my mind."

She scrambles back and sinks into her seat, snaps her seatbelt back on. What an obedient little girl. Was she as willing to please whoever she had administered blowjobs to earlier? I squeeze my fingers at my sides. The blood throbs in my veins. Why am I so angry at the thought of her with any other man? I had no claim over her…yet. I need to keep it that way. I need to find a way to keep my distance until I have decided what to do with her.

I spring up to my feet, stalk away from her.

"Michael?"

I freeze, turn on her. "You haven't earned the right to call me by my name."

She huffs. "So, what should I call you? Asshole?"

"Lord or Master will do well enough."

"Okay, Lord Asshole it is, unless you prefer Master Asshole?"

I chuckle, then firm my lips. "You have a sense of humor. Good. You are going to need it over the next few days."

She pales, then squares her shoulders, "If you think you are going to scare me into doing what you want, you have another think coming, buster." Her green eyes flare with a hidden fire. Color smears her cheeks. She's truly magnificent. And I need to get my head examined for finding her so attractive.

She's the woman from your dreams, you asshole. You've been looking for her. And now I found her...and all she is, is a debt I intend to reclaim.

I curl my lips, then turn and stalk away, hellbent on finding a way to take care of the raging hardness that tents my pants.

"Wait," she calls out.

Now what? I glare at her over my shoulder.

She twists her fingers in front of her. "Why did you...stop?"

I tilt my head, "Didn't you want me to?"

"N...no, that's not what I meant. I thought that..."

"I wanted you?"

She stiffens, then jerks her chin.

"You thought wrong. I wanted to see how willing you'd be to fulfill my wishes. Seems you are ready and able to do my bidding... Too willing. It's not enough of a challenge." I yawn. "I don't play with little girls, Beauty."

Her face pales. "I'm nineteen, you prick."

And I'm a full twenty years older than her. I'd known it, of course, when I had taken her... But having her throw her age in my face... makes the age gap even more of a reality. Of course, twenty years is nothing in the Mafia world. There are other Capos who've married girls thirty years their junior. They swear by the fact that a younger wife keeps them young at heart, too. Only, I hadn't ever thought I'd be one of them. Hell, knowing the age gap hadn't stopped me from being attracted to her from the moment I saw her. Besides, she's here as an asset. All I have to do is use her as I see fit to consolidate my plans. That's all this is —a means to an end. There is no reason to attach any other significance to it.

I shake my head. "What you are, is pathetic."

"You didn't think so when you kidnapped me." She snaps her teeth at me. Cute. I almost smile, then school my features into a semblance of seriousness.

"I kidnapped you because you owe me."

"My father owes you."

"Same thing."

"It's not the same thing." She draws herself up to her full height.

"Frankly I found the entire experience boring."

Her chin wobbles. *Fuck, I hurt her.* But that was the idea, right? It's why I took her in the first place. So she can pay for the sins of her father. I squeeze my hands at my side, then look her in the eye, "Figured I'd find a woman, a real woman, to take care of my needs. Know what I mean?"

She pales.

A hot sensation stabs at my chest. I glance away, then up as the stewardess approaches me. I snap my fingers and her eyes light up. "On your knees; you know what to do."

7

Karma

Why that arrogant, emotionally unstable prick. He wouldn't. No way.
Michael props his hands on his waist and widens his stance. His jacket
pulls tightly across his butt and I gulp. This man? He is the epitome of a
wet dream. *Look away, look away now.* I lean forward and my breathing
heightens. The stewardess sinks to her knees. I can see her framed by
the inverted V of Michael's legs and it should be voyeuristic, should
make me feel dirty to watch her pleasure him. And it does. And that is
part of the appeal.

I swallow hard and slickness coats the space between my thighs. The
planes of his broad back flex, then I hear her gasp. His shoulders flex,
his arm moves in a forward motion. No doubt, he's grabbed her head,
then pulled her forward so he can feed his cock to her. That's the alphahole for you. There's no way she is in control here. No doubt it's him
who's *taking* the blowjob from her.

She must have her mouth open as she swallows him, takes that dark,
hot, throbbing length down her throat. As I just had. And he'd hated it,
when I'd done that. But with her? His shoulders blades pull back and
his entire body tenses.

I bend lower, watch as her body jerks, and again. She's moving her lips across his hard length, taking him in, sucking, licking... The sound of slurping fills the air and my mouth waters. This is insane. The dark taste of him coats my palate, the edgy scent of testosterone lingers in my nostrils. I wriggle around in the seat, but can't find a comfortable position. Dig my sneaker clad feet into the carpeted floor, grasp the armrests, watch as his thigh muscles clench.

Her body jerks faster, no doubt as he uses her mouth. As he crams his dick between her lips. I hear the sounds of gagging and my belly flip-flops. I squeeze my thighs together as he thrusts his hips forward. His butt muscles tighten, then he throws back his head and a groan fills the air.

I glance around the space but none of the other men—there are five men other than Michael on the plane; how had I not noticed that before? That's how wrapped up in him I've been—and none of them are paying attention to the spectacle unfolding. Does he do this often? Get the stewardess to jerk him off? Every time he gets on the plane, maybe? He'll whistle and she'll come running? Something hot stabs in my chest. *Bitch.* Not her, but me, for wanting...what? To be her... No, it's not that. I want his attention.

A gasp leaves my lips. I want to have his full and complete focus, to be the cynosure of all that smoldering, melting scrutiny. To have his fingers dig into my skin, my breasts, my aching core. *The hell is wrong with me?* I straighten, force myself to watch as his muscles coil with tension. His spine is straight, his feet planted on the floor as if he owns the goddam space... Which he does... And every molecule of air in this infernal enclosed area has been sucked in by the heat generated by the sexual hunger that flows from him. Unrequited.

He'd wanted me. Despite what he'd said earlier, he'd enjoyed what I'd done to him. Perhaps, too much?

Had I scared him away? A low chuckle catches in my throat. Am I being delusional? Me, the woman who had practiced blowjobs by watching them on porn hub...and the erotic novels I've been reading since I turned fifteen. Don't judge. A direct consequence of being surrounded by nuns—God bless their souls. I loved each and every one of them, but their singular preoccupation with sacrifice and sin—the two words that had etched themselves in my mind—had perversely driven me to seek out the forbidden. Well, as much as a teenage girl had been able to access, that is. God bless the internet.

I tilt my head, squeeze my thighs together, scrutinize his movements as he swoops up his free hand to press it to the curved ceiling overhead, then renews his pleasure seeking, as he yanks her head back and forth, at least I assume so from the sucking, mewling noises that emerge from their direction. My heart begins to race and my fingers tingle. I shouldn't…shouldn't. *What the hell!* I press the heel of my hand into my core and grind down, just as Michael speeds up.

His entire body goes solid, a vertical column of desire that swells and flows, and I can't take my gaze off those solid, tight hips of his.

As he thrusts forward, backward…forward. My hips catch the rhythm, as I push up and into the heel of my hand, then back. I mirror that frantic rush up the slope toward that distant horizon, where the silver lining of the sun shines against the clouds, the wind blows hard, shoves the darkness away. And for a second, I am there, right there with him, soaring up, up. A low growl rips from his chest, his butt clenches, his thighs tighten, stretching the material of his pants, his elbow seizes, then he groans. And I splatter right there in my panties.

I throw my head back, my eyes half-closed, panting. A bead of sweat slides down the valley between my breasts. *Jesus, what's wrong with me? Why did I find the sight of him using another woman to pleasure himself so…hot?*

I lower my hand to my side, cross one leg over the other as he pulls out a handkerchief from his pocket and hands it to her. She glances around him to meet my gaze. Her lips curve up, wet, gleaming from the evidence of his cum.

How dare he do this to me?

She licks her lips, then pats them with his handkerchief before shoving the piece of cloth down her breasts. He gave her a part of himself to keep. *Jerk!* He knew exactly how that would make me feel.

She rises to her feet, turns and saunters away.

He glances over his shoulder at me. "Did you enjoy that, Beauty?"

My nails dig into the cloth at the apex of my thighs. *No. Of course, not.* I glare at him.

One side of his lips turns up. "Remember the feeling, for it's the last time you come without my permission."

8

Michael

"The fuck are you up to, *Stronzo*?"

I don't look up from the screen. The camera is pointed at the bed in the center of the room. More specifically, at the woman sleeping on it. She hasn't moved since we arrived on my island a few hours ago. I'd left it to my men to escort her there. She'd tried to speak with them and they'd ignored her…as they had been instructed. They hadn't looked at her, or met her gaze—they knew the consequences of disobeying my orders. She'd glanced around the room, walked up to the window, which was open… And I knew what she'd see—sheer drop to the ocean below. Her shoulders had sagged, and she'd flounced around, examined every corner of the room, before she'd staggered to the bed and thrown herself on it. She'd fallen asleep in seconds, like the child that she is.

Except, when it had come to sucking my dick…she'd known her way around that particular appendage. Or bringing herself to climax… Should I be insulted that she jacked off to me? I tighten my fingers into fists. It should have been my fingers, my lips, my cock on which she came… If I let her… Which I won't. Not for a while. She'll have to pay for the mistakes she made me commit. Once I figure out exactly what I am going to do with her.

"You lose your tongue along with your ability to think coherently?" Luca prowls into the room.

My brother can be a real fucking pain in the ass at the best of times. And right now, when he is in a foul mood... Which, admittedly, he is entitled to, considering I had broken the one pact we had strictly adhered to since purchasing this island—no women. It's a hideout, which only our closest *famiglia* know about, and a few of our associates.... And strictly on a need-to-know basis.

"Maybe it's your balls that are bothering you?" Luca smirks. "No, now wait, did you replace your brain with your dick? Is that why you brought her...here?"

I draw in a breath, stare at the sleeping figure. She hadn't stirred in the last—I glance at my watch—in the last half an hour. She's okay, right? I lean in closer to the screen. Breathe Beauty, breathe for me. Her chest rises and falls. My shoulders slump. The tension drains, leaving... a strange tightness in my chest.

"No, don't tell me, maybe she has a magic pussy or something?" Luca murmurs, "That why you can't take your gaze off of her?

My left eyelid twitches. *How dare he talk about her in that tone?* And what the hell is wrong with me that I am taking this entire conversation so personally? It's no different from how my siblings and I kid each other all the time.

I push back from the table so fast that my chair screeches against the floor. "Or something," I keep my voice casual.

"You don't fool me, *fratellone*." There's a sly edge to his voice. "Clearly, she means something to you."

"You're right about that."

"I am?"

"She's an asset, one who will help me claim what's rightfully mine."

"The title of the Don?"

"That too." I smirk. It's no secret that I am ambitious, that I want to become the next Boss of Cosa Nostra. But that's assuming our current Don decides, at some point, to retire. Not that I am in a hurry, but every step I take is calculated to get me there. Except her.

She's the wild card. The one that came into my possession by chance, and now I am figuring out the best way to play her.

"That's wise," Luca nods. "Then you wouldn't mind if I—" he nods his chin toward the screen, "tried my luck with her?"

Red tints my vision. Only when my fingers hurt, do I realize that I've crossed the floor and have hauled him up by his collar.

"So, it's like that, huh?" One side of his lips curls, the expression so fucking similar to mine. His gaze narrows, calculating. He glances past me at the screen, then back to my face. "You want me to guess, or you going to come clean about her?"

Her? There is no her. She's a prisoner... She belongs to me and her fate is mine to decide. Period. I release him. He doesn't move. I pivot, walk to the bar in the corner of the room, pour myself a whiskey.

"Want one?" I pour without waiting for his reply. Then walk back and offer it to him.

"She's mine." I declare.

His eyebrows shoot up. "Oh?"

I toss back the drink. It burns its way down my throat. My stomach clenches. My dick hurts. Fuck. This entire sequence of events since I'd heard her voice those fucking words is...a nightmare. Confusing. And that's not something I am used to dealing with. I have to convince myself she means nothing... More importantly, I have to ensure that Luca's attention is focused away from her.

"Mine to leverage," I clarify.

"She's better off if you kill her."

My guts twist. The thought of her not breathing, not sighing, not mouthing off at me, as she's done so often since we met... No, I have to convince him that it doesn't matter either way to me.

"She has her uses," I drawl. "I plan to use her to get the Seven to back off from enquiring after the Mafia."

I prowl back to the bar, pour myself another drink.

"Only..." Luca murmurs and I stiffen, cap the bottle of Macallan.

I raise the glass, wet my lips with the dram. Rich cloves and the taste of ginger spices explodes on my tongue. As lush as figs, as moist as her cunt will surely be. I tighten my fingers around the glass. "Only?" I turn.

"That's not your style. Are you planning something that you're not letting me in on?"

"Would I ever do that?" I tilt my head.

"Only all the time." He chuckles, "We may stop the Seven from coming after us right now, but it's only a matter of time before they resume their efforts."

"What if I find a way to buy us time, on a more permanent basis?"

"What do you mean?"

"What if I secure an alliance with the Seven?"

"They'd never agree to it."

"Not unless they don't have a choice."

"What do you mean?" He tilts his head.

I hold his gaze, and his forehead clears, "Ah, I see." He rolls his shoulders, "You mean to—" he jerks his chin toward the screen.

"I am thinking of it," I murmur slowly.

"Of course, you'd be killing two birds with one stone. Alliances which help further our business are not new." Luca strokes his chin, "But in this case, you'd be sleeping with the enemy, literally."

"Stranger things have happened."

"Not that she is hard on the eyes or anything."

I growl low in my throat and Luca throws up a hand, "Fine, I'll back off. But you know it's risky. What if the Seven don't agree to it? After all, money is a powerful motivation. More important than saving the life of a loved one, sometimes."

"What if I don't give them a choice?"

"You mean wed her and bed her first, and then take her help in winning them over to your side?"

"I mean giving neither of them a choice. She'll do as I say."

"You're assuming that you'll be able to control her."

"What's wrong with that?"

"Don't underestimate women."

"Don't underestimate my way with women."

"Hmm." He purses his lips in that annoying way he's had from when we were little. I am the older one here, and yet, Luca is the one who has a wise head on his shoulders. It's why I use him as a sounding board more than any of my other brothers.

"What?" I scowl, "What's on your mind, *stronzo*?"

"It's risky."

"It's better than killing her, which is what I had in mind when I came upon her."

"What changed your mind?"

Her eyes, her lips, the scent of her skin, the way she looked at me with her bright green eyes, so curious, so full of life that it had sparked a yearning deep inside.

"I need to consolidate my position at the earliest possible time," I murmur.

"Maybe you're attracted to her?"

"I need to send a message to the other four families that we have some strong powers aligned behind us."

"There are easier ways to do that."

"How?"

"You could deploy our men and shoot them."

I laugh, "And start an outright war?" I shake my head, "There's a time for violence and a time for..."

"Romance?"

"An arrangement." I frown.

"With her or with yourself."

"What the fuck are you talking about?" I growl, "Whatever is on your mind, just come out and say it already."

"Just that this seems a very long and contrived way of consolidating our position."

"She's already here with us," I point out. "Half the job is done."

"You're hellbent on this?" He scowls, "There's nothing I can say to change your mind?"

"Why should I?" I widen my stance, "She's the key. Don't you see it? Her sister is married to the fourth richest man in the UK, one who is part of a close-knit circle of powerful men who hold the ability to open up not only the British Isles, but also Silicon Valley."

"So, in one stroke, we not only send out a message to the other families, we also widen our sphere of influence geographically."

One of our father's stipulations: I have to marry and produce an heir before I turn forty in order to secure the role of Don. Else it will open the line of succession as a free-for-all. Anyone from the four other ruling families could challenge me to a fight, and if they won, I'd lose everything I have worked toward. Not that they can't attack me now. The only thing stopping them is the fact that my team and I are too strong. However, like most things, power ebbs and flows. I need to marry and quickly consolidate my position.

A sound comes from the direction of the screen. I turn to it. Beauty yawns, sits up, and the cover falls to her waist. Her breasts, encased in that stretchy sports bra, fills the screen.

"I see you've been keeping close watch on your assets." Luca smirks.

I wave my hand and the screen shuts off.

"Hold on… It was just getting interesting." Luca walks toward the screen, but I plant myself in his path.

"I see." He bares his teeth.

"No, you don't."

"You sweet on her, hmm?" He scratches his jaw.

"Fuck off."

"Your American roots are showing, *cazzo*." He clicks his tongue.

"The fuck I care about that?" I rub the back of my neck. "You're half-American too, or have you forgotten?"

"Tried my best, but it's a stain that doesn't wash off easily, and neither will the mistake you've made by bringing her here."

"Bringing who here?" A new voice sounds. I glance up to find my second brother Massimo, followed by my youngest twin siblings Christian and Alessandro walking into the room.

Antonio, my right-hand man, stands to attention by the open door. He's been told not to let anyone except family inside. Doesn't mean he ever lets his guard down. Since he fell in love with one of the women that we'd saved from being trafficked, and married her—with my blessing—his loyalty has been unshakeable. Not that he had been anything but faithful before that. But finding his woman had made him even more faithful, something for which I am appreciative. He meets my gaze and I wave him off. He steps back, shuts the door behind him, and I turn to my brothers, "The fuck you guys doing here?"

"Someone's pissed," Christian murmurs.

"Think big brother, here, isn't getting enough?" Alessandro smirks.

"Or maybe he's getting too much and it's not satisfying enough? After all, quality over quantity, and all that," Massimo drawls as he precedes the other two further into the room.

I scowl as the three of them prowl around the space. Christian sinks into a couch, then promptly turns sideways and stretches out. Alessandro lowers his bulk into a chair, and props his feet on the coffee table, "Thought you were supposed to be in London?" He jerks his chin at me.

"I was," I mutter.

"Is it a woman who had you returning so quickly?"

I hold his gaze, don't say anything else.

"Knew it," Christian crows. "It has to be a woman who's put him in such a filthy mood."

"It's not only my mood which is going to be filthy soon," I growl. "What the hell are you three *stronzi* doing here, anyway?"

"You're repeating yourself, *fratellone.*" Massimo smirks.

"Fuck off." I rub the back of my neck.

"Now he's taking refuge in insults." Christian chuckles, "And it was you who'd asked us over for a meeting."

Of course, I had. How could I have forgotten that? I walk over to stand over the three of them. Luca follows me. "Get your foot off the table, Xander," I growl at my youngest brother.

"Seriously?" He grimaces, "What's wrong with where my foot is?"

"Want me to show you?" I pull my knife from my belt, flip it over in my hand. I glare at him, and he grimaces.

"You're such a bore, Mika." Xander lowers his foot to the floor anyway.

"Why did you call us?" Massimo straightens in his seat. "It has to be something serious that had you summoning all of us here."

Goddam it to hell. I can't believe I forgot about that. Shows just how much she's addled my mind that I can't recollect half the orders I've issued in the last few days. I glance between them, "Can't I ask my own brothers to join me? After all, we are a family, aren't we?"

"We met just before you went to London, so I take it there have been developments?" Massimo tips his chin up at me.

"You could say that." I rake my fingers through my hair, then survey them, "I'm getting married."

"Married?" Xander slowly bats his eyelids, then bursts out laughing, *"Che cazzo?"* He snickers, "You sure have a strange sense of humor, Michelangelo."

"I hate that name," I say through gritted teeth, "and what's wrong with my getting married?"

"Everything." He tries to school his features into some semblance of seriousness, then bursts out laughing. Again.

"And here I thought Xander would be the first to get married, considering he's had a lifelong crush on Theresa." Massimo leans forward on the balls of his feet.

"Hey," Xander protests, "I don't have a crush on her."

"Oh, please," Christian scoffs, "whenever you see her you go all googly-eyed."

"Googly-eyed?" Xander sputters, "What does that even mean?"

"Why is it that the two of you still squabble like you are ten?" I rub the back of my neck.

"Guess they never grew up, unlike you, Mika," Massimo smirks, "though I can't help but think that London's polluted air got to you. Maybe that's why you decided to get married?"

"You may have a point, " Christian turns to Massimo. "Think we need to call the doctor to have him checked out?"

"Fuck off, *testa di cazzo,*" I growl.

"Oooh," Christian mock shivers, "I am so afraid."

"I am your Capo, dumbass," I say mildly, "better show me some respect, or I'll be asking for your pinky finger next."

"Sometimes," Luca sighs, "you sound like an actor from a bad Hollywood Mafia movie."

"I don't watch movies."

"More's the pity." He looks me up and down, "If you did, you'd know that your story has the makings of a chick flick."

"A chick flick?"

"A romantic comedy," he clarifies, "where the hero and the heroine meet and are attracted to each other, only to realize—"

"I know what a romantic comedy is," I say dryly.

"Do you now?" Christian pretends to do a double take. "Next you'll be telling me that you are in love."

I laugh, "Good one." I smirk. "I see you've been polishing up your comedic skills."

"And you're going to have to polish up your role as a husband."

"Only until I get an heir." I raise a shoulder.

"Surely, there are fringe benefits," Xander murmurs. "Who's the lucky woman, by the way?"

"Someone none of you know."

"*Fantastico.*" Christian rubs his hands, "Is she so beautiful that you don't want us to meet her before the wedding?"

"Yes, she is, and no, that's not the reason I don't want you to meet her before the big day. It's purely because she is currently unaware that's the plan I have in store for her."

"So, you what, kidnapped her?" He fixes me with his shrewd gaze, "What else are you not telling us, Michael?"

"I am telling you everything you need to know at this stage."

"You know that, as your lawyer, I do need to know everything, if I am supposed to help you on this in the future."

"And what makes you think I will be needing your help on this?"

He laughs, "You and I both know that almost everything you do needs my expert touch to steer it along at some point."

"Don't remind me." I scowl.

"Not that I am not grateful for it."

"You better be." I glower at all three of my younger siblings, "It's why I gave you three roles in which you didn't have to get your hands dirty." Massimo's my lawyer, Christian takes care of our finances, and Alessandro? He's the artist among us. My youngest brother—he's younger than Christian by two minutes, has the softest heart, the face of a fallen angel, and the talent of a Renaissance artist.

The joke among us growing up had been that he should have been called Michaelangelo, not me—the oldest, the most cynical brother, on whom the responsibility falls to keep the family business going. One way or the other, though, all of us have our lives intertwined with the firm. Once you're born into a Mafia family, really, there's no way out, particularly for the males. Even if you are as prodigiously talented as Xander, who paints masterpieces... We use his growing fame in the art world to identify potential new targets we can kidnap and hold for ransom in return, not for money—that would be too crass—but for influence, power, and the ability to infiltrate governments and those in the higher echelons of power. It had long ago ceased to be about wealth. Our focus now is to build up our network, to ensure we have the means to influence governments and heads of organizations.

"And I, for one, am grateful that I don't need to be directly involved with the day-to-day business," Massimo murmurs.

"Enough to back me up in what I am going to say next?"

"Which is?"

"That you support my wedding and the consolidation with the other families that I am aiming for."

"But that's not the only reason you are marrying her, is it?"

Luca and I exchange glances. Massimo has always been quick on the uptake. If it weren't for the fact that he's too smart a lawyer and very good at what he does, which is to ensure that my men don't land in prison, I'd have him more involved in the strategizing and planning of our operations.

It helps that our parents had sent all seven of us—including Seb and Adrian—to the US to receive top-class education. It's what came of having a mother who was American. Although, the way she'd taken to the Mafia way of life, and subsumed herself in the old ways, you'd often forget that she was Texan by birth.

"Well?" Massimo scowls, "What's behind this sudden rush to marry? What kind of alliance are you actually seeking through it?"

"It's something Luca and I talked over before you got here."

"Good thing, then, that I got in here before you spilled all your secrets." A new voice interrupts me. I turn to watch Adrian my half-brother, and only one of the two other people outside of my immediate family whom I trust, walk in. "What did I miss?"

"Nothing," I murmur. "Now, all that's needed is for Sebastian-asshole-Sovrano to join us and—"

"Someone mention my name?" Seb walks into the room and I groan. I walk over to the bar, seize the whiskey bottle and top up my glass.

"Drinking alone, *stronzo*?" Seb prowls over to the bar. He bypasses the bottle on the counter, to walk around to the other side. Then, he bends down, and when he straightens, he holds a bottle of only my most expensive whiskey. He opens it, then snatches a glass and is about to pour when I caution him.

"That will cost you, *testa di cazzo*," I growl.

"Why? Aren't celebrations in order?" He smirks, "I am just getting started, is all."

Of course, he'd overheard our previous conversation.

"Eavesdropping again, *fratellastro?*" I address him by the Italian word for stepbrother, hoping it will irk him, but this time, he doesn't take the bait.

"The door was open, *fratellastro.*" He smirks.

"Why are you here anyway?" I glower at him.

"Family meeting." He glances around the space, "Surely, you didn't think I would stay away."

"You weren't invited."

"I am here now, aren't I?" He pours liquor into a tumbler, then grabs five more and places them on the table. He proceeds to top them up. With my whiskey. Mine.

A growl rumbles up my chest.

He fills up the glasses, then glances around the assembled faces. "What, no one joining in the festivities?"

Next to me, Luca shifts restlessly. "Seb..." he warns, but I throw up a hand.

"No, let him be. He's right, after all."

"He is?" Luca glances between us, his gaze wary. Seb and I don't agree on much. It's not only because he is the closest in age to me, older than even Luca, while being my stepbrother. My father had had a mistress, a woman much younger than him who had borne him two sons. When she had died in an accident, he had brought Seb and Adrian over to our house. Seb had been five, and Adrian only three when my father had asked my mother to take them in and take care of them. She hadn't refused. Whatever her thoughts were about the situation, she had kept them to herself. But she'd had a big heart, and not once, had she allowed Seb or Adrian to feel like they weren't her own sons. But while Adrian had bonded with us instantly, Seb is...one of us and yet, he isn't. Maybe because he was older than Adrian when he joined us, so it was more difficult for him to adjust to living with us. Or perhaps, he is conscious of the fact that he grew up dependent on us. And then there's the fact that he is my father's bastard son, which means my father will never accept him as the next Don. Something he resents, even as he acknowledges that he couldn't have survived without us.

"You are part of the family, Seb," I murmur. "You always have been."

"Just not good enough to ever have a chance at becoming the Don, though?"

"There is only one Capo," I lower my voice to a hush, "and that's me."

He raises his glass. "To the wedding of the one and only Capo," he says in a voice which sounds sincere. Fucking *stronzo*. Not that he means it.

I move forward and tip some of the alcohol into my glass. The others crowd around the bar as each of them reaches for their own glass and raises it.

"To the Capo," Luca fixes his gaze on mine, "and to the alliance with the Seven."

"The Seven?" Seb turns to me, "That's who your new bride is related to?"

I tilt my head, "Is that a problem?"

He scratches his chin, "Amongst them all, they own most of the UK and parts of Silicon Valley too, I hear." He fixes his gaze on me, "Ambitious, are we?"

"Disbelieving, are we?"

"It's not my life, *fratellone*." He raises a shoulder. "And I assume this has to do with getting access to enough connections to consolidate your position with the other families?"

Seb really is smart. As intelligent as Massimo, as hungry as Luca, with the rakish charm of Christian and the beauty of Xander...

All of it, rolled into one ambitious, cynical, man who'd do anything to take over as Capo one day. It's what makes Seb so dangerous, and yet also, the one with the most promise. It's why he's the only one of all my family who can stand up to me. Precisely why I trust him the least and kept him as close as I can. The only way to keep track of someone who poses a threat to you is to keep them in your inner circle.

Do I trust Seb? That's an interesting question. I don't think he'd do anything to hurt my family, but given the right motivation and circumstances, could he turn on me?

"So," Christian glances between us, "when do we get to meet your new bride?"

"At the wedding," I murmur

"What?" Xander blinks. "We don't get to meet her before?"

"No."

"Don't you trust us with her?" Massimo drawls.

"Never." I fold my arms across my chest.

"Aww shucks." Seb smirks. "The way you're acting, you'd think you have her hidden away here and want us to get the hell away so you can spend time with her."

I glare at him and a look of understanding dawns on his features, "So you do have her here with you?"

Of course, Seb would have to figure it out. Not that I am hiding anything from them or anything. "And if I do?"

"*'Sto cazzo!*" Seb exclaims. "Why, you old coot, you kidnapped her and brought her here, eh?"

"Fuck off," I growl.

"You did, didn't you?"

I glare at him. Asshat is seriously getting on my nerves.

He places his elbows on the bar, and leans forward, "Was it love at first sight?" He smirks, "You saw her and it was the proverbial *colpo di fulmine*?" He's referring to the thunderbolt that Italians use as a term for describing love at first sight. Like most things, my people are prone to exaggeration. Hence, love at first sight needs to be described literally as being unexpected and as powerful as a lightning strike.

I snort. "Next you'll be telling me that you've experienced it yourself, the way you talk passionately about it."

"Me?" Seb laughs, the sound without mirth, "Would I be standing here if I had?"

I peer into his features, take in the tightness of the skin around his eyes, the slight slump to his shoulders, which is a surprise. I've never seen Seb anything but on the offensive. Apparently, the *testa di cazzo* has his share of secrets. Something I intend to worm out of him someday. Just not right now.

One thing he's right about... I am anxious to meet with my bride-to-be, but not for any of the reasons he thinks. Fucking her is out of the question, at least, until the wedding. On that much, I am clear. There, however, remains the task of breaking the news to her... Something I need to mull over. I need to figure out a way to get her to willingly agree. This entire plan which I had hatched on the spur of the moment is, clearly, more complicated than I expected.

But how hard could it be, anyway, to get her to see things my way, hmm?

I place the glass back on the bar counter, then step back, "I am sure you can see yourselves out."

I shut down the camera, then turn to leave.

Seb chuckles. "So anxious to see your woman?" he calls after me.

"Vaffanculo," I hold up a middle finger above my shoulder, "not that it's any of your business."

"Everything you do is our business," he retorts. "Considering you're the Capo... Capo."

I pause, turn to glare at him over my shoulder, "It's because I am Capo, I am asking you for the first and last time to never talk about her, *capisci?"*

I hold his gaze, and he finally lowers it. Good. Seb may be as alpha as they come, but he knows I am the one in charge. And I intend to be for a long time. If he thinks he can displace me from my hard-won position, he can think again. No doubt, one day, he is going to challenge me, too. I know that as well as I know my name... It's why the next move I make is going to be very important, one on which hinges the future of me and my *famiglia.*

"I am leaving, and when I return, I want the lot of you to have cleared out." I glance around the faces of my siblings, "You feel me?"

9

―――――

Karma

The domed ceiling far above the bed has an ornate pattern. How old is this building? From the outside, it had a baroque architecture… The kind I've seen in magazines. It was beautiful. Does he own it? He must. Just like he owns the private jet we'd flown in that had landed on the private airstrip on the other side of the island.

He'd stalked off the flight and driven off in a car. His men had directed us to the second car. There had been two more following us as our little procession had made its way here.

Is this the only building on the island? Where is this island, anyway? Somewhere in Italy, given the language his men had been speaking. Michael himself, though, spoke with an odd accent, something between American and Italian.

Michael, huh? As if knowing his name means I know anything about him? He is, clearly, Mafia… If he hadn't given himself away when I had mentioned my father…the proceedings after that had given away his identity. I stand up and stretch.

The hair on the back of my neck prickles. I glance around the room, but there's no one. A shiver runs down my spine. I wrap my arms around my waist, take stock of my surroundings. There's a closet in the corner, an old-fashioned dressing table pushed up against one wall. Beyond that, a door. I walk to it, push it, and step inside a bathroom that's spacious enough to have a clawed bathtub in the center. Beyond that, a large window allows light inside. On the other side is a sink. I walk over, catch my reflection and flinch.

Dirt streaks my face and my hair has bits of... I pull at it—dried leaves? There are towels on a chair nearby. I strip out of my clothes, ignore the bath and walk over to the shower stall at the far corner. The shampoo and the shower gel smell of moonflowers. Whoa! How did he know that this is my preferred scent? I step under the water, which is hot... Thank god.

I let it flow over me, sink into my tired muscles, allow my muscles to unwind. When the hot water runs out. I step out, dry myself, survey my clothes. My sports bra has flecks of blood...his blood. Hmm. I wrap the towel around my torso, cinching it in under my arms. I step out of the bathroom and my breath leaves me.

"What are you doing here?"

Michael turns from the window. The light haloes him, and for a second, the shadows mask the lower part of his face. His blue gaze burns into mine. I flinch. He peruses me from head to toe and his eyes gleam. Then he lowers his eyelashes, jerks his chin toward the bed. A new change of clothes is folded on the bed. "You're welcome." He smirks.

Fuck you, very much. I snarl low in my throat. "How did you...?" I frown, then turn on him. "You were watching me?"

He tilts his head.

"You...you creep."

"You really do need to get more inventive with your insults, Beauty."

"Stop calling me that."

"Stop trying to resist every step of the way, it's...annoying."

"What's annoying is you haunting me, turning up at every corner, insinuating yourself into my life, making it a living hell, taking me away from everything and everyone that—"

"Made you unhappy."

I still. "What are you talking about?"

"You hated your life."

Yes.

"You know nothing about me."

"On the contrary." He drums his fingers on his thigh. "Karma West. Birth name: Karma Rhodes. Born twenty years ago to Charlotte and Adam Rhodes. Mother died when you were a young, leaving you in the care of your father. Who promptly threw himself into his work, then fell into debt. He then abandoned you and your sister to the foster care system, and left the UK to escape the wrath of the Mafia. Your sister made it out of the foster care system when she came of age, then took you on as your legal guardian. Just a few weeks ago, she married Sinclair Sterling, one of the richest men in the UK. You attended their sham wedding… Then drank the night away with your two friends at the pub two streets down from their residence in Primrose Hill. Wanted to go home with a man…but didn't. Along the way, you also dropped out of a graduate course in fine arts at Goldsmiths, where you had received a full scholarship, instead preferring to spend the days at your pop-up shop in Camden Market where you hawk your wares."

"I don't hawk. I share my designs," I snap.

"You mean the clothes you sew?"

"They are dress creations that I fashion," I sniff, "and sell under my independent label."

"What-fucking-ever." He smirks. "That's…when you are not haunting your local pub or dancing to electronica with fellow goths who pretend to understand you. But really, no one does."

"And you do?"

"You have to admit, I know far more about you than anyone else." He rubs his knuckles across his thigh, and I shiver.

No, he doesn't. He has no idea that I have a heart problem or that I'd been seeing a specialist about it before he took me captive… Or that…in a way, I am glad that he took me away from my life because, while my sister Summer means well, she is stifling me with all of that attention. In a way, he set me free. Does he know that? Now, all I have to do is take back the ability to make my own choices. I tilt up my chin, "You've barely scratched the surface of who I am."

"Hmm." He draws his gaze down my features, over my chest, "And what a thing of beauty that is, too."

My nipples grow erect. "Get out."

His smile widens.

"I need to change."

"Go right ahead."

Bastard. Of course, he'd taunt me about that. I march up to the clothes folded on the bed. There's a pale yellow dress, and next to it, underwear—a matching bra and panties set. My cheeks flush. Did he choose my underwear? Nah, he probably had it ordered or something for me, not that I am going to ask him. That will simply reveal just how nervous I am. I take in the comfortable ballet pumps next to the bed on the floor. Not my style, but at least they look comfortable.

His gaze bores into mine and the skin around his eyes tightens. A strange nervousness seems to roll off of him as he flexes his shoulders. He can't be nervous. Can he? Nah, it's my imagination. Alphahole here isn't afraid of anything…or anyone. All of this is just a ruse to get me naked. If he thinks I am going to shrink away from it…he's…mistaken. I tip up my chin, drop the towel.

His entire body stiffens. A breeze blows in from the window and I shiver. *Look at the clothes. Reach for them. Put them on. Do it. Cover yourself.* I grip my fingers at my side, try to glance away from his perusal, but I can't. He walks over, until he's right in front of me. So big, so tall. I have to tilt my head back, and then further back, to meet his gaze. Blue eyes deepened to an azure steel reflect back every single one of my emotions. Uncertainty. Lust. Desire. His gaze rests on my features, down to my lips. A moan wells up my throat. Down to my nipples which instantly pebble, across my trembling belly, to the slippery core between my thighs.

"Open your legs."

No.

No.

"Yes." He jerks his chin. I shuffle my feet apart. Draw in a breath. Another. Dense clouds of heat spool off of his massive body, and slam into my chest. I pant. His gaze rolls down my thighs to my feet. My toes curl. Then back to my pussy. Liquid heat thrums low in my belly. Blood engorges my nub. Hell. Is it my own audacity that's turning me on as much as the fact that he can't seem to take his gaze off my cunt?

"*Che cazzo*," he exclaims, "is that what I think it is?"

"What do you think it is?"

"When did you get your clit pierced?"

"None of your bloody business." I'd have had my nipples pierced too, but that would have been too obvious, and if my sister had picked up on it? Gah, Summer would have had a cow about it.

Maybe, once I escape this asshole, and I've told Summer that I am safe, I'll figure out a way to be independent and stand on my own two feet without having to be dependent on anyone else... Then I can pierce any bloody part of my body and I won't have to explain it to anyone.

His lips twist, "You're wrong, Beauty. Everything about you is my business. You're my property now, you understand?"

"I'm a woman, a person, you bastard. I am not a possession."

"Wrong." He yawns. "When you left your life behind, you gave up all rights. Now you'll do everything I tell you to, when I tell you to, how I..." he leans forward on his heels, "tell you to."

"I didn't leave my life behind. You took me," I object.

"Tomayto, tomahto; potayto, potahto."

"Let's call the whole thing off," I retort.

He raises his eyebrow. "As I was saying, you're mine now, and you'll do as I say..."

"No."

"Yes." He nods, "Starting with that." He jerks his chin toward my core.

"What the hell do you mean?" I scowl.

"You need to shave."

I blink. "Excuse me?"

"I'll send someone to help you clean up the hair." He pivots, then begins to walk toward the door. "I prefer it completely bare."

Anger explodes in my chest. My gaze narrows. All of my senses seem to pop. A low cry spills from my lips. I close the distance between us and throw myself at him.

10

Michael

The hair on my forearms rises. All of my senses jangle. I swivel around and catch her around the waist, lift her off of the ground.

"I hate you. I fucking hate you," she snarls, then swings her fists. I duck. I must be losing my touch, for her knuckles graze my jaw, and my dick, which had stood up and saluted her bare bottom the moment she'd bared it, is sure it's found heaven. My groin tightens and my balls ache. I tighten my grip around her. "Stop."

"How dare you insult me...you...you...pig?"

A chuckle trembles up my throat and I swallow it. "Calm down."

"Let go of me."

"No."

She goes still.

"No?"

"Not until your blood pressure drops back to normal."

"The only person I see having a bloody cardiac is you." She brings up her knee. I twist my body to the side, she catches me in the thigh, and damn it, but my cock instantly lengthens. The fuck is wrong with my reactions, that I can't control myself around her?

"Back off, Beauty or you'll regret it."

She makes that noise deep in her throat, that sound of anger and frustration that sends sparks down my spine, engages all of my nerve endings so that all my brain cells seem to shut down, then flare all at once.

"Last. Chance."

"Oh, sod off." She strains in my embrace, and her breasts thrust into my chest, her nipples sharp enough to stab me through my jacket and my shirt.

Fuck. I squeeze my arms, haul her even closer. I'm not copping a feel… Okay…so maybe I am, but can you blame me? This tiny soaked-with-bath-water-and-desire female…is…simply the most delectable piece of femininity that I have ever come across and..

My breath leaves me.

"You didn't just do that," I growl.

"What, you mean this?" She slips her palm between us and squeezes my balls… Again… Fuck. A growl tears from my lips. My thighs spasm and sweat breaks out on my brow. "You're going to regret that, Beauty."

She bares her teeth. "Oh yeah? What are you gonna do? Spank me."

Hmm.

Her gaze widens, her breath hitches, her pupils dilate and…fuck this shit! I am only a man. There's only so much I can take.

I bend my knees, peer into her eyes. "How many?"

"What?"

"How many slaps?"

"Fuck off."

"You choose or I will, and I promise you, the number will not be one you like."

"Bet you won't like this either." She clears her throat and spits. A gob of warm saliva slashes across my lips.

She freezes.

So, do I.

The warmth drips down my chin, and something snaps inside of me. I scoop her up, twist her and throw her over my shoulder. She screams, struggles, and I throw an arm over the back of her thighs, squeeze her close enough for her knees to dig into my side. She beats at my back, down my side. Nice. My muscles warm, lengthen. I reach the bed, seat myself, then drape her across my lap.

"Let me go." She huffs.

"No." I bring my arm down and my palm connects with her butt.

She yells, "You bastard, how dare you!"

"Don't challenge me, baby girl."

"Let me, the fuck go, this moment!" she howls.

"Or?"

"Or I'll scream."

"Is that a promise?" I spank her left butt cheek and she screams. Slap her right and she gasps, sputters. Bring my palm down again on her left and her entire body bucks.

"Fuck you, asshole."

"Not just yet, and I do prefer alphahole."

"You conceited, obnoxious, swollen-headed—"

"Love it when you talk dirty, darling." I take aim, lower my palm across the curve of her ass, right over the reddened palm print I'd left there, and she squeals. And again. And again. My palm tingles, my forearm muscles hurt, and still, I don't stop. *Eight, nine, ten.*

A sob bubbles up from her, "I'll never forgive you for this."

"Good."

"I'll get back at you."

"Hope you're keeping count, hmm?"

Twelve, thirteen, fifteen. She squeals, digs her fists into the bed and growls.

"Had enough?"

"I'll never beg you to stop. Never apologize… Never," she retorts.

I slide my fingers between her swollen lower lips and she hiccups.

"Fuck, Beauty, you are soaking wet," I growl

"From the bath, you idiot." She snarls, "I took a shower not ten minutes ago."

"Let's put that to the test, hmm?" I drag my knuckles down her slit and she moans. Slip a finger inside her slippery channel and she wheezes. "Please."

"Please what?"

"Please stop."

I draw her slickness up her cunt, into the valley between her butt cheeks and she freezes.

"Anyone taken you here, Beauty?"

She makes a low noise at the back of her throat.

"That's what I thought." My groin hardens. The blood begins to thud at my temples.

I press my wet middle finger into her back hole and her butt clenches; her spine arches.

"How does that feel?"

"How do you think, you jerk?" She yells, "I'll push something up your ass and ask you the same question!"

I laugh. I can't help it. The laughter just bursts out.

She turns her face, peers at me from between the strands of hair that fall over her face. "It's not bloody funny."

"You're right." I wipe the smile from my face. "It's boring. I've wasted enough of my time." I stand up and she falls to the ground on her ass.

She mewls, and I hesitate. I should take care of her...make sure I soothe the reddened skin that bears my marks. No. What am I thinking? She is...my captive. An experiment, perhaps, to find out how long I can hold out before my control snaps. She is nothing. Nothing. And I am trying too hard to convince myself.

"Get dressed." I pivot, stalk to the door.

"Michael."

I keep walking.

"Stop."

I reach the door, shove it open.

"Goddamn you, you can't ignore me. You can't keep me here."

I step through.

"Master," she calls out to me.

I pause.

There's silence for a beat.

I turn, glare at her over my shoulder.

She pales, tips her chin up. Brings her arms to her sides so the full beautiful expanse of her body is bared to my gaze.

I peruse her face, the flushed features, the trail of tears down her cheeks. This woman... She is magnificent. Unclothed, naked as nature intended, with that dyed black hair of hers in disarray around her shoulders. She is...dangerous.

I should keep away from her... I should...punish her for how she brought out the base part of me, for how her nearness has unhinged me. I should break her. Only, in this fight between us there will be no winners. There is only way forward... And it leads into darkness. Fuck her, and fuck me for what I am going to have to do to her.

I drum my fingers on my thigh, "I don't have all day, Beauty."

"How long," she squeezes her fingers together in front of her, "how long do you plan on keeping me here?"

"For as long as it takes."

11

Karma

He spanked me. I shift my weight from foot to foot as I stare out of the window. After Michael left, I had taken a quick shower, then ignored the clothes he had left out for me, because... Yeah, as if I am going to obey that prick after what he did to me.

And if you defy him, will he spank you again?

My thighs clench. *Oh, my god, what the hell is wrong with me?* I did not just think that, did not.

I had marched over to the closet, then pulled on the first dress I had come across—this knee-length dress in pink, which I absolutely hate, but whatever. It's something to cover myself up with. There had been enough clothes in the walk-in closet... Most of them seemed new, along with underclothes that were made of the finest laces...and decadently cut.

And all the clothes fit me... no doubt about it, they were to my measurements, how the hell had he managed that? How had he gotten them delivered here so quickly?

I'd run my fingers over the fabric of the dresses in the closet. Everything is exquisite. Even if they have been bought off the shelf they are of the finest quality. The undergarments are as seductive as the outerwear is modest. It's as if he wants me to appear docile to the world, but under my clothes, appear every bit the whore he, no doubt, regards me as. Whore... Yeah, he definitely thinks of me as his possession.

It's why he'd taken me across this knee, then taken his palm to me like I was an errant child and I... I'd loved it. *Damn it.*

I grip the window frame with my fingers. Damn the obnoxious brute of a man. He hadn't hurt me, to be honest. The slaps had stopped just this side of being hard...unlike him. He'd been aroused from the beating he'd given me, too.

My belly trembles. I'd felt his length thrust up and into my sensitive center. The faster he'd beaten me, the more I'd tried not to scream, and the less I'd succeeded.... And the harder he had become under me. It had been... Strangely arousing. How could it be?

I swipe the hair from my eyes. His wide palms had seared me with each contact. His fingers cupping my flesh, leaving drums beats of fire in their wake. I squeeze my thighs together. There's no denying the arousal that coats my core as the images cling to my subconscious mind.

How would it be to have him spank me again, then turn me over and part my thighs and swipe me from backhole to my clit, the way he'd used his fingers earlier? My bottom throbs and my pussy clenches. *No, no, no.* I am not going to let him crawl into my head and play with my fantasies.

The man kidnapped you, held a gun to your forehead, then knocked you out and you... All you can think is how hot he is, how sexy, how completely ovary-exploding that smirk of his is. If he looks at me one more time and drawls some insult... I'm going to lose it.

I'm going to throw myself at him again and lose every last shred of my dignity. I stalk to the center of the room, look around the space. The hair on the back of my neck stiffens. I glance around the space again. It looks like a normal bedroom, but appearances can be deceptive, right? Why can't I get rid of the feeling that I am being watched, even now? I bite the inside of my cheek.

Has he hidden a camera in this room? Would he do that? Is he watching me, even now? I shiver. Wriggle my hips. It's creepy as fuck. But...when had I last been the single-minded focus of someone's attention to this extent? Not my mother or my father, not the nuns at the school that I had attended, not my older sister Summer, who—well, okay, so she fussed over me, worried about me. She is my substitute parent, after all.

But Michael... He is intrigued by me. Maybe that's too complimentary a word... More likely, I am something to pass his time. His newest shiny plaything, to toy with. He looks at me like a boy would a captured butterfly when he has no idea what to do with it. He could imprison me in a bell jar, watch as I flutter my wings and try to escape, or he could pluck my wings out. I shiver.

Ugh, that is not comforting. I rub my fingers over my goosebump ridden arms.

Whoever this man is, he's not kidding around. Every time he's seen me, he's had a plan, an agenda... To put me down. To strip me of all of my dignity, to make me crawl and... I won't. No. No way, am I going to give in to him. The moment I do, I'll lose his interest, and then he'll kill me. I swallow. Or...or worse. *No, don't go there. Focus on the now.* I am here, alive and — the door opens — apparently, I have a visitor.

A woman stands silhouetted in the doorway.

I blink. "Who're you?"

"I'm Cassandra." She smiles, "I am the Capo's housekeeper."

"Capo?" I scowl, "You mean Michael?"

She nods, her dark eyes wide, her face pleasant. She's in her thirties, hair scraped back in a bun that makes her seem older than her years. Her starched black dress comes to below her knees and is shapeless in the way women who don't want to draw attention to themselves tend to dress. She has sensible shoes, which don't detract at all from her shapely, fair legs. In her hands she holds a vanity kit.

"What do you want?" I frown. Okay, so I am being belligerent, but can you blame me? I don't trust anyone in this house.

"I'm here to help you shave your vagina," she murmurs.

"What the hell?" I choke out, "I can't believe that asshole actually went through with this."

She moves toward me and I throw up my hands, "Whoa, hold on, I can shave myself, thank you very much."

She hesitates, "Are you sure? I can help you —"

"No," I snap, "Just...hand over the stuff I need and you can leave."

She blinks, then holds out the vanity kit. "As you wish."

I grab the bag from her. "Is this what you do? Shave the women he brings here?" I snap.

"He hasn't brought any other woman here before."

"Oh!" I gape. O-k-a-y. What the hell does that even mean? Nothing... Don't go attaching meaning to actions where there are none, bitch. Fine. Okay. I blow out a breath. "Whatever," I murmur, then stare at her. "Was there anything else?"

"The Capo asks for your presence at dinner." She half smiles, then beckons "Whenever you are ready, please come down to the dining room on the ground floor."

I toss the kit onto the bed, "I am ready now."

"The Capo insists that you shave first."

"And if I refuse?"

Her eyes widen. "I don't think you want to do that."

My backside throbs. No, of course, I don't want to disobey Lord Alphaholington himself. A snicker catches in my throat. Whatever. It would be nice to be away from this room, even if it is a meal with his obnoxious alphaholeness.

"Fine," I sniff, "I'll be down once I've..." I wave the bag in the air.

She smiles, then turns and heads for the doorway.

"Wait, Cassandra."

She stops.

"Michael kidnapped me, you know. Is he holding you against your will too?"

She turns, fixes me with an inscrutable gaze, "The Capo gave me a job when I needed it most. He saved me and my family."

What the — ? Not what I had expected to hear, but makes sense. The jerkass is smart enough to surround himself with people who owe him. What better way to gain their complete loyalty than by making sure that you provide for them and their families?

She half bows again, "Best not to keep the Capo waiting, signorina."

Turning, she leaves.

❋ ❋

An hour later, I leave the room, freshly shaved—and no it's not because I want to please the asshole. It's only because... I feel much cleaner after shaving myself all over. My panties stick to my freshly-shaved pussy as I walk. Shit, the skin there feels so much more sensitive than usual, now that it is exposed. It's hard not to be constantly aware of it. Bet he wanted me to feel this way. That's why he'd insisted that I remove all hair from there. *Jerk.*

I walk down two flights of stairs, then head past double doors that have been flung open. I peek out to see a grassy lawn sloping down. Trees fringe the sides of a path that curves and disappears. In the distance, the wide-open sea beckons.

I keep walking until I stop at another set of double doors. This should be it. I shove open the door, walk in and come to a halt. Michael is standing at the window with two men I have not seen before.

Michael turns to me. He looks me up and down. His nostrils flare and his eyes gleam. Asshole looks almost pleased that I defied his orders. Holy shit. Did he know that I would ignore the clothes he'd laid out and opt for something of my own choosing?

His lips curl and I resist the urge to stamp my foot. Walked right into that one, didn't I? *Sneaky bastard.* I glance away, just as one of the other men turns to me.

My breath catches. Oh, wow, this guy is beautiful. Face like an angel, piercing blue eyes similar to Michael's, but darker in color. High forehead, sharp cheekbones, that same hooked nose. He's as tall as Michael, is dressed similarly in a dark fitted suit that hugs his corded length. His jacket stretches across shoulders that are bulked up as if he lifts weights every day. Light pours over him, catches the golden lights in his dark blonde hair.

The overall effect is that of lightness. Where Michael carries a dark, edgy, dangerous aura, this man…has an electricity that sparks off of him. It seems to light up the space as he walks toward me.

I blink.

He holds out his hand, "Karma?"

I put out my hand to take his when there's a snarl from the direction of the window, "Get away from her."

12

Michael

"Forgive my stepbrother, he can be an impolite motherfucker."

Seb grabs her palm and brings it up to his lips.

The *stronzo* kisses the back of her fingers. I stiffen. How dare he? And after I warned him to stay away from her. I'd told them all to leave, but Seb had stayed back. Next to him, Adrian shuffles his feet.

Clearly, Seb had coerced him to wait, as well. Now, he glances between us, uncomfortable. "Seb," he says in a low voice, "we should leave."

"What's the hurry?" Seb drawls in a tone that ensures that I can hear it.

Clearly, he is testing me. I roll my shoulders, take a step forward. Then stop. It won't do to give away what I feel...*which is...a confusing set of emotions that sits heavy in my gut.*

I take in her face, her gaze alight as she glances up at him. No doubt, her attention is captured by the bastard's beautiful countenance. It's what makes people trust him, that is, until he pulls the rug out from under them.

Seb's smile widens. His gaze dips to her lips, down the slope of her breasts—and I snarl low in my throat.

He laughs. "Why, *principesa*, I believe it's going to be delightful to get to know you."

Anger laces my blood.

"Didn't I tell you to leave?" I growl.

"How could I? Especially after you mentioned that you have a guest. It was but polite to stay on and introduce myself to her. Though I understand, now, why you prefer to keep her to yourself. She is stunning." He peers down at her, and his face alights with a smile, "Your beauty is breathtaking, *principessa*."

Karma giggles. I glance sideways, watch the blush rise to her cheeks. Anger crawls at my gut. She isn't allowed to respond to any other man, to react to their flirtation, to have them hook her arm in the crook of their elbow and allow them to lead her to the table.

Seb pulls back the chair and she drops into it. He places his hand on the back of her chair and his fingers graze her shoulders. My vision tunnels. I stalk up to them, grab him by the back of his collar and haul him back.

"Whoa!" He swings around, fists raised.

"Leave," I snarl. "Get the fuck off this island and don't come back until I send for you."

His eyebrows furrow; his breathing is ragged, "You should know better than to step up behind a man."

"You should know better than touch what is mine..."

"Interesting choice of words." His smile twists, "I do believe this is the first time I've seen you lose your composure, *fratellastro*."

"Fuck off." I jerk my chin toward the exit.

"Or what? "

The blood begins to thud at my temples. I step up until we are toe to toe, "You don't want to find out."

A chair scrapes, and she appears between us. "Stop it."

"Stay out of this," I growl without taking my gaze off of the *stronzo* in front of me.

Seb shoots me a glance from under hooded eyebrows. "You threatening me?"

"What do you think?"

She thrusts her face closer, "I think you guys are hangry."

I glower at the man in front of me.

"It happens to men and babies. When they are hungry, they can't think straight, and often, end up fighting. So why don't we sit down and eat, huh?"

Her stomach rumbles, the sound loud in the silence. She giggles, the sound a little nervous. "If I don't eat soon enough, I am going to faint."

"No, you're not." I glance at her sideways.

She turns her face up, "I really am starving."

I frown.

"It's not a ploy or anything. I mean, I'd love to see the two of you beat the shit out of each other, but it's easier on a full stomach, huh?"

The door opens and one of my staff walks in with a tray of food. He stops, glances between us.

"Ah, food." Seb rubs his hands together, "Dinner does seem like a good idea."

"We are going to eat." I turn to Seb, "You, on the other hand..." I jerk my chin toward the exit.

He dips his chin, then turns to Beauty. "Another time, my lady. I look forward to deepening our acquaintance."

Not if I have anything to do with it. I grab his shoulder, shove him toward the exit. Adrian turns to me, "I'm sorry, Michael. Seb can sometimes be a dick."

I tilt my head, "You're a good brother, and an even better made man." I widen my stance, "It's one of the reasons I have tolerated Seb, so far. But his time is running out."

Adrian firms his lips.

"Next time, I won't be so lenient."

Adrian nods. "I'll talk to him," he mutters, "you have my word." He follows Seb out, and the door clicks shut behind him.

I glare at Beauty then jerk my chin toward the table. Her jaw firms but she doesn't say a word. Thank fuck. She marches around and drops into the chair at the center of the table.

I stalk back to my chair opposite her, hold up my arm.

Emanuel places the dishes of food before us.

"*Buon appetito.*"

"*Grazie,* Emanuel." I wave him off.

The scent of garlic and parmigiana fills the air. Opposite me, Beauty stares at the dish, picks up her fork and hesitates.

"It's not seafood."

She shoots me a glance from under her eyelashes. "How did you know that I am allergic to..." Her features tighten. "I don't want to know."

"You're learning quickly."

I twirl strands of spaghetti and bring the fork to my mouth. She watches me as I close my mouth around the fork, wipe it clean. Her pupils dilate and her breathing deepens.

"Like what you see?" I smirk.

She reddens, lowers her gaze to the plate. She cuts the pasta with her knife—a fucking knife—and I stare. She scoops it up with a spoon, and—*Che cazzo!*—I drop my fork on my plate with a clatter.

"What the fuck are you doing?"

"What?" She scowls at me, "What did I do now?"

I glance at the strands of pasta hanging off of her spoon, then back at her face.

"What is it?" Her frown deepens, "You going to tell me, or are you simply going to glare at me like I committed an act of treason?"

"It's worse than that."

"It is?"

I nod. "You cut your spaghetti with a *knife*... Then proceeded to eat it with a *spoon*," I growl.

"So?"

"So?" I glower, "That's...a fucking crime."

"Umm... *That's* a crime?" Her lips tremble. "You are the Mafia and you call *that* a crime?" She snorts, tries to control herself, then laughs, turns it into a cough, which turns into a real coughing fit. She places her knife and spoon down—finally, fuck—reaches for the glass of water and drinks it.

When she's calmed herself down, and wiped away the tears which had run down her face, she glances at me.

I scowl at her, and she giggles, snorts again. I glare at her. "What the fuck is so funny?"

"N...nothing." She chuckles, then manages to get a hold of herself. "So...you were saying—"

"Nothing," I say through gritted teeth, "if you want to continue to eat your pasta like a philistine, be my guest."

"But I don't." She giggles again, then firms her lips. "No, really Michael, show me how I am supposed to eat pasta."

My glare intensifies and she raises both of her hands, palms face up, "No, I mean it. I want to learn. Promise."

"Hmm." I take in her features, her pink cheeks, her bright eyes, and fuck me, she looks beautiful. No, she always looks beautiful. Now, she looks full of life, happy, relaxed, the way she's always meant to be. My scowl deepens.

The fuck am I thinking along those lines? One shared meal and I am harboring thoughts of what...? Wanting her in my life for a longer period of time? Fuck that. That's not why I brought her here. She's here to fulfill a purpose, that's all.

I pick up my fork. "You are supposed to pull aside a small amount of pasta, maybe two or three strands, twirl it on the plate, then carefully lift the fork." I demonstrate to her, "The big mistake people always make is to try to pick up too much at once. It takes practice to get it right." I twirl a few pasta strands with my fork then nod toward her plate. "Now, your turn."

She looks like she is about to protest, and I shoot her a warning glance, "If you are going to eat Italian food, learn to do it properly."

"Fine, fine," she huffs, "don't get your knickers in a twist."

She twirls some of the pasta around her fork, then reaches for her spoon. *Porca cane!* I make a warning sound at the back of my throat and she glances at me, "Now what?"

I glare at her spoon, then back at her face.

She rolls her eyes, but lowers the spoon back to her plate. She twirls the pasta, then raises the fork with the pasta strands wrapped around the tines. Before she can get it to her mouth, the strands unravel and she lets out a groan of frustration. She looks at me and I nod at her fork.

"Pazienza. Try again."

She lets out a sigh before turning her attention back to her fork. This time, she grabs fewer strands of pasta, carefully twirls the fork, and slowly lifts it to her mouth. "Happy, now?" She pretends to be irritated with me, but I can tell she's feeling proud of herself.

"I'll be happier when you taste the food."

She tries the forkful and her expression lights up.

"Good, eh?"

"It's incredible." She scoops up another forkful, following my instructions to the letter, and wipes the tines of the fork clean, then closes her eyes, chews. A moan spills from her mouth. She swallows and my belly tightens; my dick lengthens, tenting my pants. Fuck. Is everything with this woman an orgasmic experience?

She cracks open her eyes and her gaze locks with mine. She reddens, then scowls, "Like what you see?"

My lips quirk and I firm them. So much sass, so much fire. Why does this girl always seem to get to me?

I rake my gaze across her mouth, down the flushed skin of her throat. "Every bit of it," I murmur.

Her blush deepens. "I love eating." She frowns.

And I'd love to eat you. I twirl more pasta onto my fork, bring it to my mouth and close my lips around the fork. "Don't let me keep you from your food."

She swallows, lowers her gaze to her own plate, then digs in with a relish that is fascinating to watch. Her every movement so immersed in taking full enjoyment from the moment. Everything she does, she puts her heart, her passion into it. When was the last time I was that… involved with what I do? Be it my work, my people, the things in my life that I took forward to… When had I begun to take it all for granted? When had I become so cynical that everything had begun to blur into a meaningless mess? A patchwork of black and white and grey, sometimes interlaced with crimson.

Then she'd splashed right into the center, a joyous rainbow. Something… Someone to be savored and held and stroked. Caressed until blood swells her skin, thrums at her fingertips, pours into her veins and engorges her pussy. As I drag my fingers up her curves to her neck, across the creamy expanse of her chest, where I squeeze her nipples, tease them into hard peaks of delight to be nibbled on, sucked on.

Her fork hits the plate with a clatter, and I look up.

She leans back with a sigh. "That was the best meal I've had in… forever."

Good. I take another leisurely mouthful.

"Who is the chef? I'd love to pass on my compliments to him."

"Her," I murmur.

"What?"

"Larissa cooks all of my meals."

"Oh," she tilts her head, "I'd love to meet her."

"You will."

As I place my fork on my plate, there's a knock on the door.

13

Karma

The door opens and Emanuel strides in. He picks up Michael's now empty plate and sets a crystal creamer next to him, then walks over, collects my plate as well.

"*Grazie,* Emanuel," I smile at him.

"Prego, signorina." He walks out just as another women enters the dining room.

She's wearing a chef's apron and a scarf around her neck. Her black dress reaches to just above her knees, and on her feet are six-inch heels. Hangonasecond. Who cooks wearing stilettos? I sit up, stalk her as she walks to the far end of the table. She glances from me to Michael.

Her eyes flare and her lips turn up.

Michael jerks his chin toward the woman, who nods. She takes off her scarf, places it on the table. Then unties the apron and lets it drop on the floor.

Umm, what?

She flips around a chair, steps onto it, then onto the table.

I scowl, "What's she doing?"

Michael doesn't reply. I glance toward him and find that he's watching her progress with a single-minded focus. The kind I thought he'd reserve only for me. My heart begins to thud. It can't be; this can't be happening....

"You...you don't mean to..." My voice sounds too loud. I cringe.

She glides across the table to stand in the space between us.

Michael makes a swirling motion with his finger.

"I... I don't understand." I fold my fingers together in my lap, take a steadying breath. "What's for dessert?"

"She is."

"What?" My pulse thuds at my temples.

She reaches behind her neck and unhooks the clasp of the dress she's wearing. It slides down to the surface of the table and pools around her ankles before she kicks it aside. Underneath, she's completely naked. *Look away, look away.* I trace the line of her spine down to the curve of her smooth ass...her smooth, perfect butt cheeks. She sinks down onto the table on her back, then lowers her head until it touches the table not a few inches away from me. Her legs are toward Michael.

He rises to his feet, raises the small crystal pitcher and leans over her. He tilts the glass container and a trail of white pours out across the tops of her thighs, across her pussy—completely bare, just the way he likes it. He draws the liquid down one leg, up to the arch of her ankle. Then he places it aside.

"Why...why are you doing this?" My voice comes out too thin, too high.

"You defied me, Beauty; you need to be punished for it."

"What do you mean?" I scowl, "How did I defy you?"

He glances at my dress and I draw in a breath. He means the outfit he laid out, the one which I'd ignored. The asshole. I went against his stupid order and now he wants to what? Put me in my place?

He hangs over the other woman, one hand pressed to the table near her hips for support. He dips his finger into the cream then trails it down her inner thigh. The darkness of his skin against the white of the cream is...obscene. My throat closes. I curl my fingers into fists, dig my nails into the palms of my hands and pain shoots up my arms.

He peers up at me from under sooty lashes and I gasp. His nostrils flare; the skin around his lips is stretched tight. His gaze clashes with mine and I can't look away. The band around my chest pulls in further. A burning sensation builds behind my eyes. How dare he touch her that way? How dare he try to pull off this exhibitionism in front of me?

I straighten my shoulders; the skin around his eyes creases. He rakes his gaze down my features, over my lips. He stares at my mouth and holy hell, it's like he's touching me right there. A moan bubbles up and I swallow it back. I clench my thighs together.

"Look at her."

I shake my head.

"Do it." He lowers that deep voice of his to a hush and I shiver. I drop my gaze to where the cream drips down her inner thigh.

He snaps his fingers and I jerk my face toward him. *"Vieni qui."* He crooks a finger.

A snarl ripples up my throat. How dare he order me around like I am some kind of dog…or a bitch…on leash? Gah!

"Now, Beauty." He lowers his voice to a hush and I shiver. Only when my feet hit the ground do I realize that I am walking toward him. What the hell—?! My body seems to have a mind of its own where this alphahole is concerned. It can't help but obey him when he commands. How dare he be able to wield so much power over me?

I pause in front of him and he smirks. *Jerk.* He dips a finger into the bowl of cream then holds the cream-coated finger out to me. "Open," he growls.

You've gotta be kidding me.

I purse my lips together and he arches an eyebrow.

"Open. Your. Mouth," he orders. "Do it, Beauty."

I part my lips and he slides his finger inside my mouth.

"Suck it off."

No.

"Now."

I curl my tongue around his finger and his breath catches. A hot feeling flares to life in my chest, at the backs of my eyes. He wants me to suck his fingers, huh? Fine. I'll do just as he says, obedient woman that I am. I open my mouth, lean forward and take in his other fingers. His chest heaves. I pull back until his fingertips are poised at the edge of my lips, then move in again. I close my mouth, swallowing his fingers.

His shoulders tense.

I curl my tongue around the underside of his fingers, licking it to the top as I pull out, only to lean forward again. I claim his fingers, let him finger fuck my mouth, my gaze never wavering from his. Wetness pools between my legs, my core clenches, and my toes curl. I wriggle my hips, needing something more to relieve the yawning emptiness between my thighs. I want more. I'm overcome by a yearning for the emptiness between my legs to be filled. By him. *No.* I pull away so fast that I stumble, the popping sound of his fingers leaving my mouth echoing around the room.

His eyebrows draw down, his jaw tics, and he opens his mouth, but I don't wait. No way, am I allowing him to seduce me with his voice, his words, that rich timber of his subvocals which curl around me, coax me, seduce me into doing as he wants.

I pull away, then run around the table.

"Stop."

I keep going.

"Don't leave this room."

Are you fucking kidding me? You think I'm going to stay here and watch as you...you...finger-fuck that woman? As he had just done to my mouth. And I had let him. I had encouraged it. Enjoyed it. My chest heaves and my breath comes in short pants. I twist the handle of the door.

"You are going to regret this."

I'll regret it more if I stay. No way, am I giving in to whatever twisted plan he's set in motion for me. I pull open the door and rush out. Down the corridor, to a large room, cross it, pass a large fireplace, a comfortable leather settee on the other side, to the massive double doors at the far end. I shove open the doors, race across the lawn.

Footsteps sound behind me and I increase my pace. I have to get away from him.

"Karma, don't go any further."

"Fuck you," I glance over my shoulder. He's a few feet behind me. His features are contorted, his gaze narrowed. He's racing toward me so fast he blurs.

He shoves out his hand, "Stop!"

"No way." I turn, spring forward through the undergrowth, and my feet touch air. I throw my hands out and scream.

14

Michael

She disappears over the edge and my heart slams against my rib cage.

I see sparks behind my eyes. No, this can't be happening. I propel my body through the undergrowth, thrust out my arm. My fingers graze her skin and I grab at her wrist. Hold.

She screams, and the sound is torn away by the wind.

"I've got you."

Her body dangles, sways. One of her pumps slips off her foot. She screams again, and the blood thuds at my temples, at my wrists. The weight of her body drags me forward. *No, no, no, I am not going to let her die. No way, am I ready to go over the edge either.* I dig the toes of my shoes into the ground, hook them around a protuberance and come to a halt. Stay there for a beat, another. Sweat streams down my forehead, down my nose. She glances up at me as the moisture trails down to splash onto her cheek.

She blinks, her green eyes dilated with terror, her pupils so large, I can see myself reflected in them.

"I am not letting you go.

"P...promise?" Her chin quivers and her teeth chatter.

"You bet, not until I have exacted my revenge for this stupid stunt."

Her gaze narrows and some of the color returns to her cheeks. There's my Beauty, my Huntress.

"It's your fault I landed here, in the first place."

"Oh?"

A gust of wind blows against us. Her body sways, I skid down further, and she yells, "Don't you fucking let go of me, you motherfucker!"

"Never thought I'd hear you say the words, baby girl."

"Fuck you."

"Time for that later." Pain shoots up my arm. It feels like it is being torn out of the socket. I grit my teeth so hard that pain shoots up my jaw. *Not letting her go. Not letting her go. No.* I shove my other arm out. "Take it."

"No."

"Not the time to act prissy."

"Not until you tell me what this is all about."

"Huh?" *The woman is one hair's breadth away from falling to her death, and here she is, arguing with me?* "The fuck you talking about?"

"You know." She swallows. "I want to know, why?"

"Why?"

"The real reason you saved my life."

"I'll do one better."

She frowns.

"I'll show you at dinner tomorrow."

Her mouth opens and closes. Her other shoe slides off. She whimpers. Color fades from her cheeks again.

"Work with me here, Beauty." I glare at her and she blinks. A tear drop makes it way down her cheek.

"Didn't think you'd be the kind to resort to tears."

"I'm not." She sets her jaw.

"Or that you wanted to die without living fully?"

"Is that what you are doing?" She scowls; her dark hair flows around her shoulders.

"I've only been half alive... Until I met you."

"What?" She blinks.

The fuck am I talking about? "Your arm, give me your arm first."

"Only if you promise to complete that statement."

"Now," I growl, and she winces.

"Do it." I infuse all of my dominance into that phrase. She holds up her other arm. *Thank fuck*. I grab her hand, slide forward a bit further. She screams.

"Trust me," I implore.

"I did and look where that got me."

I grit my teeth, lock my muscles and haul her up...an inch, another. The wind seems to pick up. She bites down on her lower lip.

"I am not letting you die that easily."

I pull her up another inch.

"I'm sure that's not out of any sense of compassion or a conscience. It's not like you have one anyway, right?"

"You done insulting me?" I blink away a drop of sweat.

"Just getting started."

"Good, so am I." My shoulder muscles knot and a burning sensation crawls up my forearms as I drag her up, until her arms are just over the ledge. "When I get you on firm ground—and believe me, I will—I am going to teach you a lesson—one you won't forget."

"You don't scare me."

"Good." I haul her body toward me. "Then you won't mind when I show you exactly what I have in mind for you." She huffs, digs her feet into the curve of the ledge and pushes herself up. I brace myself, bend my legs and pull her over the edge. She falls on her front next to me, her breathing loud. I sit up and haul her into my arms. "I am going to fucking kill you for what you did to me."

She trembles, her shoulders shake. "I... I thought... You said you wanted to save my life to teach me a lesson."

Her features crumple.

"No," I growl. "Not now."

A tear slides down her cheek and my heart stutters. Fuck this. Fuck her. Fuck everything that brought me to this exact moment, when I have my end in plain sight.

"Why do you have to be so fucking annoying?" I growl.

"Why do you have to be so—"

I lower my head, close my lips over hers. I thrust my tongue inside her mouth. A moan swells up from her and I swallow it. I suck from her, draw her breath, bite down on her lower lip, and she shudders. I tilt my head, haul her even closer, wrap my arms around her and yank her to me. Her entire body trembles. Her breasts are flattened against me, and her nipples harden. The blood rushes to my groin. I dig my fingers through her hair and tug her head back. Grip her chin, tilt it up and lower my lips to hers. She throws her arms around my neck and strains in my hold. Another hoarse whine bleeds from her and something inside of me shatters.

I tear my mouth from hers, chest heaving, blood buzzing, my nostrils filled with her scent. Her taste is heavy in my mouth, her melting core drawing me in. She raises her eyelids and those green eyes stare back at me, dilated...this time, with passion. She licks her lips, raises her chin.

"No." I unknot her hands from around me, stagger to my feet and pull her up with me. I head for the house, pulling her along, and her legs seem to give way from under her.

"For fuck's sake." I turn, swing her up in my arms.

"I can walk." Her voice is hoarse; her frame is too light. Anger boils up my spine. Why does she always have to complicate everything? Why is it that everywhere I turn, she is there, turning my world upside down? If she had gone over the ledge, if I had reached her one second later ... My arms tighten around her.

She winces, shoves at me, "You're hurting me."

"Good."

"Why are you upset?"

"I'm not."

"You could have fooled me." She purses her lips.

"You are too much trouble, you know that?" I growl.

She huffs, "Your mistake for having kidnapped me."

"You're right."

"I am?" She scowls up at me.

"Abso-fucking-lutely," I drawl, "I can't wait to get you back to your room so I can get on with the rest of my evening. Larissa is waiting for me."

15

Karma

"You ass, I almost died and now you shove your...your floozie in my face? You're a real piece of work, you know that?" I struggle in his arms and he tightens his grasp.

"Stay still," he orders, "or I might drop you."

Jerk! "Don't you dare," I shove at his shoulder, and my palm encounters the hard muscles of his body. Goosebumps rise on my skin. Shit, why does he draw such a primal response from me?

He continues walking and I glance up at the jut of his chin. For a second there, when he'd kissed me, I was sure I'd been wrong about him. That he isn't the kind of monster I'd thought him to be. He saved my life, didn't he? He'd come after me after that...that show that he'd put on for me. Why did he do that?

"Why wouldn't I?"

"You are scared about how I make you feel?"

His jaw tenses.

"You are worried that you are attracted to me?"

"You?" His lip curls. He stares straight ahead, lengthens his stride. "Is that what you think?"

"Why else would you have left behind that…that…?"

"Beautiful woman, who is actually the kind of female I go for. I promise you, girls with little to no experience are not my type."

"How do you know I have no experience?"

"Are you telling me that you have had experience?"

I tip up my chin, "Are you trying to ask me if I am a virgin?"

"Are you?" He lowers his chin.

I gape. "Seriously, like, is that even a thing anymore?"

He holds my gaze and the blood rushes to my cheeks.

"What?" I scowl. "Didn't think you were the kind to worship at the altar of the hymen."

His gaze intensifies.

"But then you are Mafia, so I guess you forget that the rest of the world has progressed enough to recognize that the hymen is a myth. Many girls aren't born with one, and most lose it thanks to exercise or when we use tampons."

He arches an eyebrow and I feel the blood rush to my face.

"What?" I snap. "Why are you looking at me like that?"

"Answer the question." He lowers his voice to a hush, "Are you, Karma?"

"Yes," I murmur, "I am Karma."

He scowls. "Are you a virgin, Karma?"

"None of your bloody business."

"It is, actually." His arms around me tighten and I gasp as he pulls me closer into his chest. The heat of him seems to increase in intensity. The planes of his chest seem to harden until they dig into the flesh of my arms.

"You're hurting me," I protest.

"Tell me." He growls, "Are you a virgin?"

"No," I snap, and his scowl deepens.

"Are you lying to me, because if you are…"

"No, I am not." I set my jaw. "Why would I lie to you about that anyway?"

"Good," he growls, "because I am tired of your impertinence."

"Impertinence?" I scowl. "I am simply trying to show you just how backward you are in your thinking."

"Take a good look around you. Where do you think you are?"

"Somewhere in Italy, with someone who kidnapped me and brought me here and is holding me captive and not even telling me what he wants from me."

He pauses so suddenly that the breath catches in my chest.

I sense his gaze on my face deepen and glance up, then wish I hadn't. Blue eyes, bottomless and cold. In their depths is something unfeeling, something inhumane, something that causes my muscles to stiffen, my pores to pop. The hair on the nape of my neck rises.

"Wh...what?" I clear my throat. "What is it?" I force out the words through a throat gone dry, "What do you want from me?"

"I told you," he drawls, "your father owed me, I took you in payment."

"And what are you going to do with me?"

His lips twist, and I flinch.

I tilt up my chin, keep my gaze trained on that cruel, beautiful, gorgeous face of my captor. "I mean, other than that..."

"Other than what?"

"Of course, you want that. It's why you brought me here."

"Want what?" His lips curl.

"You know," I scoff.

"No, I don't." He holds my gaze, "Why don't you tell me?"

"Sex," I snap, "you want sex with me."

"That's too easy."

"What do you mean?" I scowl. "Obviously, it's why you took me and brought me here and are now trying to impress me with your wealth, and power and control, and your stupid dominance—"

"You think I am dominant?"

"Unfortunately, while I wish I could say otherwise, I have to concede that much to you."

"At least, you are honest."

"At least, you are..." I search for a suitable adjective. "Not bad look-ing, for a kidnapper."

He blinks. "I wasn't aware that was a quality one needed to have to suit the role."

"It's important." I bob my head up and down, "Very important. I mean, if you were old and fat and had onion breath..." I shudder, "it would be so much more worse."

"You taking the piss, Drama?"

"It's Karma, you asshole."

"Maybe I'll call you Llama."

"Don't you fucking dare."

"Language…" he says in a mild tone.

"Oh, fuck off." I hunch my shoulders and turn my head away from him. Tears prick the backs of my eyes, and honestly, that's just stupid. Why do I care what he calls me? Hell, he can call me Destiny, for all I care. Not that it is insulting or anything. Actually, I'd take Destiny over Karma anyway, considering the number of times I've been teased for having been called that. It's a stupid name. Why did my mother have to call me by that name. Being a flower child is all well and good, but why couldn't she have called me by some other new age easily pronounceable name instead? And why did she have to die on us, anyway?

I had been a baby when she'd passed on. The only things I remember about her come from the photographs of her that we have. I don't remember anything about her in real life. If it hadn't been for my sister Summer, who became the de facto maternal figure in my life, well, I'd have never had any inkling of what it would be like to have a mother. Thanks to Summer, though, I've always felt loved. She's done a lot for me, my sister.

Surely, she'll be missing me. Despite the messages that this man says he's been sending her from my phone, surely, she'll know that something is wrong and she'll come in search of me? Surely.

I sniffle, and to my horror, a tear makes its way down my cheek. Shit, shit, shit. The last thing I want is to be seen as being weak by this man. I don't want him to see just how defeated I feel right now. That the true horror of my predicament is finally sinking in.

Shit. I have been kidnapped by this monster and he is not letting me leave. I can't even try to jump off a cliff without his somehow snatching me back from the jaws of whatever fate had in store for me. How the hell am I going to find a way out of here? Why the hell had he come after me in the first place?

"Why?" I demand, my voice hoarse. "Why the hell did you have to turn my bloody life upside down?"

"Why did you have to turn my life upside down?"

I blink.

"Wh…what?"

"You heard me." He lowers his face until his lips are right above mine. Until that hooked nose of his bumps mine, until those long thick eyelashes of his kiss mine. "It's you who's turned my plans upside down."

"I… I have?"

He nods, "I was supposed to kill you, not bring you here and spare your life and—"

"Wait, what?" My heart gallops so hard in my chest, I am sure it's going to break through my rib cage. "What do you mean kill me?"

His lips twist, "Off you, shoot you in the head, or did you forget that I did hold the gun to your forehead? If you've forgotten, I don't mind reminding you."

"No," I snap, "I remember."

"Good," he nods, "so you can understand how crazy it seems that I'm standing here, carrying you in my arms, and after saving you from throwing yourself down the side of the cliff into the sea—"

"My foot slipped," I snap. "I would never kill myself."

"Sure didn't seem like that to me."

"Believe me, I love my life. Or rather, I loved it before you came along."

"Did you?" He peers into my face.

"What's that supposed to mean?"

"You may have told yourself that you were happy, but the woman I saw that day on the hillside of the park was lonely and quoting Byron in the hopes of finding a reason to live."

I open my mouth to retort, but he tilts his head, "Am I wrong?"

I glance away.

"Thought not."

He straightens, then heads off, once more, in the direction of the house. He retraces my earlier steps, back across the lawn, through the front door, then up the stairs. He walks down the corridor, enters my room, and lays me down on my bed. I turn away from him, wrap my arms about my waist. The softness of the pillow under my cheek, that masculine scent of his that surrounds me, all of it confirms that I am safe. Safe.

A trembling grips me. Maybe it's the fact that I almost went over the side of the cliff. *OMG, OMG... I almost died. Gah.* My arms and legs feel too weak. A ball of emotion clogs my throat. What the hell? I had been fine this far, so why am I breaking down now? A tear slides down my cheek. *Stop that, you idiot. What's wrong with you? Why are you crying now?*

Say something. Protest again. Ask him to let you go. As if any of that is going to work. Face it, I am here as his captive and I'll stay here until he lets me go... Which is never. Unless he kills me... But he's never gonna release me and I am going to spend the rest of my life in this stupid room, on this stupid island, playing stupid word games with this over-the-top, mean, growly, grumpy, way-too-handsome, egoistical, controlling, arrogant tyrant.

Another tear slides down my cheek and I can't stop shaking. Gah.

The bed dips, and the next second, the heat of his body sears my back.

16

Michael

"What are you doing?" Her voice is shrill. "Why did you get into bed with me?"

Good question. Something I am asking myself, since I'd sworn I wouldn't bed her until we are married. Not something I am going to let her know. Especially since I haven't told her what my plans are for her yet, either. Why am I so hesitant? Since when have I needed a woman, or anyone else for that matter, to be willing before deciding to go through with a plan. Nothing stops me from marrying her without her consent. Hell, nothing stops me from sleeping with her without her consent, either. And ultimately, I am going to marry her, whether she agrees to it or not. So why does it feel so important that she submit to her fate willingly?

Why do I want her to want me? Want her to *want* to marry me? Why do I need her to feel something more than the resentment she so clearly bears for me? Why do I crave her…devotion?

Her body in submission to me, her will in subjugation to mine, her heart in my grasp, her attention on me, her arms and her legs tied back as she spreads herself open to my ministrations; with her pussy in readiness and wet for my penetration, as she gives herself over to me. Willingly, over and over again. As she allows me to fulfill every depraved, filthy craving that has painted my mind from the moment that I first laid eyes on her.

Fuck. The blood drains to my cock. My pants suddenly feel too tight.

I stay there, with the length of my front plastered to the soft curvaceousness that is her body.

Gradually, her trembling stops, and her muscles tense as she grows aware of me. I know the exact moment she feels the arousal that tents my crotch, for she stiffens.

Every part of her goes rigid, her curves tightened in attention. Every single pore in her body seems to be tuned into me, and for a moment, I enjoy that. The fact that she is so tuned into my presence. That she's so hyper-aware of everything, anything that I am going to say and do next.

I close my eyes, draw in a breath, and the lush moonflowers fragrance of her skin reaches me... Laced with that unmistakable, sugary-sweet scent of her arousal. My cock throbs and my groin hardens further. Hell, if I stay here a second more, I am going to turn her on her back, cover her with my weight, hold her down, and close my mouth over hers, Right before I slide down to rest my head on her creamy thigh as I take my time familiarizing myself with that succulent flesh between her legs.

She gulps, the sound heavy in the space. I should move. I should simply get out of here. I should return to Larissa. Better still, I should leave Beauty be as I attend to the rest of my business for the day: the war with the Russian Bratva that is heating up again, the rivalry with the Kane Company that's proving to be a pain in the ass; the upcoming talks with the Five Families and the Don that could, likely, mark the turning point in my career and everything that I've worked for to-date; my errant stepbrother, Seb, whose loyalties I need to test... Hell, the many things that I need to address as the Capo... All of which are crucially important to ensure that things stay on plan. None of which seems as vital as the woman lying in front of me.

I draw a finger down the shape of her hip and she shivers.

I reach the edge of the skirt of her dress, slip a finger under it, and she chafes her thighs together. The scent of her arousal deepens and my mouth goes dry. Jesus. How could she smell so luscious, so juicy, so ready for the picking, like the flesh between her legs needs me, wants me, yearns for me to do whatever I want with her.

"M… Michael." Her voice trembles, "Michael… I have something to tell you?"

"What?"

"I am dirty."

"Excuse me?" I blink, pause in the action of slipping another finger under her skirt, "What do you mean?"

"My clothes, I mean," she murmurs, "they are filthy from that head-long dive I took off the side of the cliff."

"So?"

"So I am making the bedclothes dirty," she explains.

"I'll have it cleaned up."

"Uh, I need to get out of these clothes. They are uncomfortable, and itchy and—"

"Fine." Once she sets her mind on something, nothing can stop her, can it? I roll off the bed, then bend and scoop her up in my arms.

"What are you doing?" She huffs.

"What does it look like?"

"Why do you have to answer every question with a question?"

"Why do you have to ask so many questions?" I sneer.

"What kind of an answer is that?"

"Exactly."

"You're impossible," she cries. If she'd been standing, bet she'd have stamped her little foot.

"You're too easy to tease."

"Were you teasing me?" She snarls.

So cute.

"Not really." A chuckle rolls up my throat and I swallow it down. Bet if I showed her just how amused I am right now, she wouldn't be very happy about it. For that matter, nothing I've done so far has made her happy. Not that I have tried to make her happy or shit like that. Hell, she is my captive, not my guest. Not that I have had any guests here on this island. I haven't had anyone else over, period, except for my close family.

She is the first—other than my very close circle of confidants, who I can count on my fingers—who I've allowed such close access. I pause half way to the bathroom. What does that mean? Do I trust her enough to allow her such proximity to me so quickly? For that matter, from the moment I first saw her, I haven't allowed her too far from me. It's why I'd brought her to this island. So I could observe her without any distractions. What the hell is wrong with me? Why am I acting like a man possessed? Why do I feel so out of sorts? Probably because I haven't fucked her yet…

Okay, assuming that explains the shortness in my breath, the tenseness of my shoulders, the knot that seems to have lodged itself permanently at the base of my spine—let's say that's why I feel so goddamn on edge… It still doesn't explain why I am standing here in the middle of her room, with her in my arms, about to run a bath for her.

"Michael?"

Since when did I get so solicitous? Since when did I…put another's needs before my own? Since when did I…want to fight the world and anyone who'd dare stand between us? Since when did I want to pluck the stars from the skies and lay them at her feet? *Che cazzo*, I am turning into a complete cliché, if there ever was one.

"Michael!"

I draw in a sharp breath.

"Hey, Michael!" She punches my shoulder and I glance down at her upturned face.

What the hell is she doing to me? Since she came into my life, everything really has been turned upside down. It's time to get things back on track. To show her who is the fucking boss here. Which is me, by the way. Not the curvy, tiny sprite who scowls up at me as if everything that had happened today was my fault. Which it was…but that's beside the point.

I will not feel sorry for taunting her with what I'd done to the other woman. I will not feel guilty about the fact that I pushed her to the end of her tether, so she ran out and almost fell over the side of the cliff. If I had lost her… If anything had happened to her—

"Michael, hey, what's wrong?"

"Why the fuck should anything be wrong?"

"You're trembling."

"I am not," I say through gritted teeth.

"Yes, you are."

"No, I am not," I growl, "and you'd best shut the fuck up before I do something that both of us will regret later."

"Oh, you'll do something, will you?" She sets her jaw. "Of all the moronic, bloody, asinine things to say," she snarls and I snap my teeth.

"Enough!"

She stiffens. "Stop talking to me like I am some stupid, brainless twit who you can yank around with a lasso around my neck."

"Then stop acting like one," I retort. "Though, come to think of it," I eye her slender throat, "a collar around your neck may not be a bad idea, actually."

She pales, "Stop trying to frighten me."

"Am I succeeding?"

"No." She blinks rapidly.

"Liar."

"Asshole."

"Alphahole to you, doll." I smirk.

She gapes at me. "You have such a big ego, you know that?"

"Not the only thing that's big, by the way." I head toward the bathroom door as she opens and shuts her mouth.

"Honestly, that was cringeworthy," she complains.

"You disagree?"

"I have no opinion on it, either way."

"Lying again, Beauty?" I lower her to the counter near the sink, then point a finger at her, "Stay." I growl, and she rolls her eyes.

"Like, where would I go? I am on a stupid island, you dummy."

"At least, learn to insult effectively."

"Just callin' it as I see it, buster."

I arch an eyebrow, "If you are going to curse, do so in Italian."

"You offering to teach me?" She tilts her head at me.

I fold my arms across my chest, look her up and down, "You sure you want to learn?"

"I asked, didn't I?"

"Remember, once you start down this path, there's no going back."

"From what?"

"Wanting to not just curse, but taste, bite into, suck on, lick up…" I lean in closer to her, "chew on, slurp, kiss, rub," I bend my knees, peer into her eyes, "fondle, squeeze, pet, fuck—"

"Stop." She slaps her palm over my mouth, "Please, stop."

I allow my lips to curve up, "Scared, Beauty?"

"Never."

"Let's put that to the test, shall we?"

17

____

Karma

"What…what's that supposed to mean?" My voice quivers. Hell, I hate that. I so don't want to appear weak in front of this man. I bite down on my lower lip and his gaze drops there.

"Scared, Beauty?"

"Of course, not."

"You should be." He bends his elbow behind his back, and when he straightens his arm the light catches a flash of silver in his hand. "Wh… what's that?"

He swoops out his arm and the front of my dress loosens. I glance down to find he's cut through the straps holding up the dress. "What did you do?"

"What does it look like?"

"Do you have to answer every question with a question?"

He arches an eyebrow, then swoops out his hand again. His movements are so fast, they seem like a blur. I blink. He retreats, then surveys his handiwork. I glance down as the dress falls apart. Oh. He cut enough slashes in the front of the dress for it to literally deflate in on itself. Whoa. I glance up at his face, "Was that supposed to impress?" I murmur, "I mean, all you had to do was ask me to get undressed—"

"What's the fun in that, hmm?"

He hooks his left forefinger in the neckline of my dress and tugs. With a whisper, the entire front of the dress separates. He throws it aside, as the back of the dress falls away, leaving me clad in my bra and panties. I raise my hands to cover myself, then stop. Damn it, I am not going to act like a shrinking violet. I have seen worse. I survived the foster care system, I survived dropping out of Goldsmiths and forging my own creative path. And look where that got me? Sitting in my underwear on the counter of the bathroom of a Mafia Capo in Sicily. Jeez, at least my life is not boring, I have to admit.

I place my arms in my lap, stare up at me, "What now?"

His lips curl. He reaches out, slides the flat edge of his knife under the strap of my bra, tugs. The thin material snaps. He does the same on the other side, then slides the tip of the blade under the strap between my breasts. He twists the blade and the tense material snaps. My bra falls away and cool air assails my heated flesh. My nipples instantly harden and my breasts swell. He doesn't look down at my chest; neither do I.

His gaze intensifies; the darkness in those blue eyes swirls, coils in on itself. He seems both relaxed and on edge. Bored and turned on. Intensely focused, as always, and yet also, strangely, disconnected from everything. This mass of contradictions about him is what attracts me and challenges me and makes me want to do everything possible to get a rise out of him; get under his skin, break his control, watch him as he finally shattered. Or maybe that would be me. What will he do when he finally gives into those emotions that writhe and twist under his skin? Will he hurt me? And why does that thought not scare me?

"That all you got?" I allow my lips to curl. "The big, bad, alphahole Capo who loves to keep his men in check... That all you going to do to me?"

"You don't have any sense of self-preservation, do you?"

I shake my head.

"That makes two of us."

He steps back from the edge of the sink. "On your feet."

I frown and he arches an eyebrow. "Do it," he growls, "now."

I slide down so my feet touch the floor, and my dress and the remnants of my bra fall away. I tip up my chin, hold his gaze. He reaches down, his arm moves, and I don't need to look down to know that he's cut through the straps holding up my panties. The fabric falls away, exposing my pussy to the air. I hold my elbows at my sides, not daring to glance down at myself.

He glances down at my core and his breathing grows ragged. "You shaved."

"Like I had a choice?" I scoff.

"You didn't," he agrees. "Part your legs for me, *Belleza*."

"And if I say no?"

"I'll do it for you." His grin widens, "And trust me, I'll enjoy it, too."

"Bastard." I slide my feet apart, and he thrusts his massive thigh between them, forcing my legs further apart.

The thick muscles feel like a column of iron against my most tender place. My core clenches and my lower belly ties itself in knots. I lock my thighs around the muscle, press my core into the rigid pillar.

His breath catches and his dark pupils seem to grow even blacker. One side of his lips twists, as he raises his knife and places the flat edge against my cheek.

I freeze, watch as he slides the blade under a lock of hair. He flicks his wrist and the strand slices clean through before it drifts to the floor. Heat flushes my skin; my core clenches. My nipples grow impossibly hard, and damn it, I can't understand this crazy response to his screwed-up gesture. I mean, I've always known my tastes are a bit out there. They would have to be to mesh with the goth side of me, the one that is attracted to everything dark and beautiful. Like him.

He flattens the blade against the side of my face, draws it down without breaking skin, down my neck, down to the valley between my breasts.

My nipples continue to tighten, until they are painful points. My breasts seem to swell. Moisture gathers between my legs, and his nostrils flare.

"That turns you on, hmm?"

"Of course, not." My voice cracks and his grin widens.

"If I were to check between your legs, would I find you wet, Beauty?

Yes. Yes. "No." I shake my head.

"You know what?" he says in a conversational tone. "I am tired of you lying to me, sweetheart."

He retracts his hand, flips his knife so he's holding it with the handle face up, the blade pinched between his fingers. He pulls back his thigh, only to replace it with the handle of the blade.

"Wh…what are you doing?" I squeak.

"What do you think?" He nudges the handle of the blade against my entrance and goosebumps pop on my skin.

"Michael," I whisper, "don't."

"Tell me you don't want this, Beauty. Tell me that depraved part of you inside that I've sensed does not want to know how it feels to ride a knife handle."

No. No. I nod and his entire body tenses. His jaw tightens, his chest planes seem to harden, and his shoulders seem to grow wider, filling my line of sight.

Heat flushes my skin and my toes curl. I curve my fingers into fists at my sides, hold his gaze as he fits the handle of the knife into my melting slit. He thrusts up and into me and I gasp. My heart begins to race and my pulse pounds at my temples. Why is this very obscene, very kinky action of his such a turn on? It shouldn't be. I should be repulsed. I should be crying out, asking him to stop. Telling him he can't insert a weapon into the most delicate part of me. I open my mouth, but the words don't come out. Instead, I part my legs wider, bend my knees, and push down on the handle. Too much, too thick. My lips part, a groan trembles from my mouth, and I wheeze.

His gaze intensifies and the skin around eyes tightens. "Fuck." He groans, "F-u-ck, Beauty. "

He winds his fingers around the nape of my neck, brings me close enough for my breasts to press into the fabric of his shirt. He urges me to tip my chin up, as he glares into my eyes. His pupils are dilated, the black filling his iris until only a dark blue circle remains around the circumference. A lock of his dark hair falls over his forehead. A strand of grass clings to the thick strands, reminding me of the fall I had taken so very recently. He looks like someone on the verge of coming undone, and somehow, the thought fills me with a gnawing need. The emptiness swells in my belly, crawls up my spine, and I raise my palm, press it into his cheek.

"Michael," I whisper, "fuck me with your knife handle."

Embers spark in his eyes. He bares his teeth, grips the back of my neck even harder, then he pulls the knife handle out, only to slide it back inside. A groan spills from my lips. He dips his head, places his mouth so close to mine, his nose bumps mine, his eyelashes brush mine.

Jesus… This… When he does this. When he watches me with so much intensity that it feels like he's crawling his way inside me, when he peers into my eyes as if he's searching for my hidden depths, as if he means to solve me, decimate me, rip me apart and put me back together in a fashion that makes so much more sense to him, to me.

He pulls out the knife, then slides it up inside me again, deeper, deeper, and my thighs tremble. My breasts swell further. My knees seem to almost give way and I grip his biceps, feeling the rock-hard muscle push back, unyielding to my touch. And it's so damn erotic. The heat of his body around me, the toughness of his body under my palms, the hard length that he's inserted up between my legs—that somehow symbolizes exactly how screwed up this…whatever connection is there between us, is.

He continues to fuck me with the knife handle, and heat crawls up my spine. Sweat breaks out on my forehead, dampens my palms at the point of contact of where I am still holding onto his shirt sleeve covered biceps.

He glances down his nose at my mouth as he weaves the knife handle in and out of me, in and out. The trembling begins at my toes, sweeps up my thighs, coils in my belly. "Oh," I gasp, "oh, my god."

My eyelids flutter as I tense, my muscles lock in preparation as I hurl faster, closer, to that edge.

"Michael," I gasp, "please…."

"Eyes on me," he snaps and I crack open my eyelids to stare into that blackness that swirls in his eyes. The blue, like chipped ice around the edges, promises me that, even if I manage to conquer his blackness, I'll slip and fall through the icy surface, to an uncertain end, from which I won't return without being changed.

"What are you doing to me?" I whisper as his lips twist.

He pulls out the knife, slides it up and into me one last time, hitting a spot deep inside that I didn't know existed. A moan bleeds from my lips, and he bares his teeth, "Come for me, Beauty. Come all over my knife."

18

Michael

She snaps her head back, her spine curves, her lips part and she shatters. The orgasm sweeps up her body and she tenses, stretches, green eyes a tormented, coiling mass of storm clouds that boil over as she screams. I fit my mouth over hers, absorb the sound as she slumps into me. I pull out the knife, place it on the counter behind her, then tear my mouth from hers and slide to my knees. I lick my tongue up the moisture dripping down her inner thigh, to her damp pussy. I tug on her clit ring and she groans. I slurp at her cunt and she shudders.

"Michael," she chants, "Michael. Michael."

"Mika," I growl against her sweet, scented pussy, "call me Mika."

"Oh, Mika." She grips my hair as I ease my tongue inside her channel. "Mic-ah!" She gasps, tugs on my hair. My scalp tightens and my shoulders go rock hard. I grip the backs of her thighs, yank her closer as I proceed to fuck her with my tongue. In-out-in. I squeeze her asscheeks, position her hips just right as I proceed to eat her out.

"Jesus," she whines, "please, Mika, please —"

I pull my tongue out of her, only to close my mouth around her cunt.

She groans, pushes her hips forward, chasing the release that only I can give her.

"Oh, my god. Oh, my god," she warbles.

I can't stop the rumble that rolls up my chest, as I glance up at her to find her breasts jutting out, nipples pebbled, head flung back and her dark hair flowing down the curve of her back. A goddess, a huntress, a Beauty about to come apart on the tongue of this Beast, the one who is going to show her why she shouldn't trust anyone so easily with her pleasure. I slide my finger in between her buttcheeks, down to her back-hole. She tenses, a ripple shudders up her spine. She parts her legs further, allowing me to slide a finger inside her backchannel, as I continue to fuck her with my tongue, in and out, in and out of her.

Her entire body, seems to vibrate with tension as she grabs handfuls of my hair, and presses herself closer to where my I am eating her out. Her back bends, her breasts jiggle as she pants and gasps and throws her head back, and that's when I pull back. I release her, rise to my feet, grab my knife by the blade and freeze. "What the fuck?"

She cracks open her eyelids and blinks, "Wh…what's wrong?"

I stare at the blood that stains the handle of the knife, then glance up at her.

"So, you're not a virgin, huh?"

She lowers her gaze to the knife handle and color leaches from her cheek, "Guess I am not now."

"What the hell, Karma?" I growl, "Why the hell did you lie to me?"

"How did I know that you'd put it to the test so quickly?"

Shit, shit, shit. I squeeze my fingers around the blade and pain slides up my arm. The knife cuts through my fingers; blood drips down my fingers and drips to the floor.

"You…you're bleeding," she whispers.

"Look at me, Karma."

She glances away, shakes her head.

"I swear, look at me or—"

"Or what? You'll make me? Is that it?" She firms her lips. "Look, being a virgin is hardly the kind of thing you want to confess to, okay."

"So you lied to me?"

"I am nineteen and never been with a man." She squares her shoulders. "How the hell do you think that makes me feel?"

"I'll tell you how that makes me feel." I bend my knees, peer into her face, "It makes me want to make sure no one else touches you but me. It makes me want to hide you away and protect you and take care of you and ensure that your innocence belongs to me. It makes me want to—"

"What, marry me?" she says lightly and I stiffen.

She searches my features and the color leaves her face, "Oh, my god! You really think because you took my virginity you should marry me?"

"Yes."

She blinks and her jaw drops. "What the fuck?"

"Language." I scowl, and she merely stares back at me.

"You're kidding, right?"

I straighten and she shakes her head. "You *are* kidding." She laughs uncertainly. "You really have a rotten sense of humor."

"I am not laughing."

She presses her lower lip between her teeth and my dick twitches. She folds her arms about her waist, calling attention to her beautiful tits, the hourglass figure that has her tiny waist, flaring out to meet those fleshy hips, sleek thighs, down to those upturned ankles that beg me to fall at her feet and worship at those gorgeous toes.

Oддio! I really have it bad, if all I can think of is sucking on her toes, before moving my way up her body, pausing only to take a bite of that scrumptious pussy, before I fasten my mouth on those luscious nipples and suck and lap and slurp on them until they are full and heavy and trembling in my grasp.

"I… I don't understand." She murmurs, "Are you serious?"

"Have I ever been anything else but?"

She looks at me, then glances away. "What do you want?"

"I told you already, sweetheart. You are going to marry me."

"And if I refuse?"

I tilt my head.

She opens and shuts her mouth, "Look, you don't have to do that. I mean, virginity is overrated anyway and—"

"Shut up." I bring the handle of the knife to my mouth, and without taking my eyes off of her, I lick the blood—her blood—off the grip."

She draws in a breath, her gaze widens, and her pupils dilate. "Wh… what are you doing?"

"What do you think?" I step back, pass the knife to my other hand, then wipe the blood from the blade—my blood this time—on the sleeve of my shirt. More blood drips from my fingertips from where I'd wrapped it around the blade earlier.

She makes a sound of distress, turns, grabs a towel and reaches for my injured hand. She wraps the towel around it, folds my fingers over it. "There, that should help," she murmurs.

"Why did you lie to me?" I glance down at her bent head, "I would have been gentle with you your first time."

"Maybe I didn't want you to be?" She peers up at me from under her eyelids, and her green eyes are filled with uncertainty, "Look, I couldn't bring myself to confess that, okay? It just felt like I would be handing you an advantage of some kind..." She raises a shoulder.

"So instead, you let me fuck you with a knife handle."

"Kinky, huh?" Her lips twist. "Not that I didn't enjoy it."

That's what I am afraid of. My tastes are far gone enough, and the longer I stay with her, the more I am going to reveal just how depraved I am when it comes to taking my pleasure.

I hadn't intended for things to get this out of hand with her... But something about this woman makes me want to drop all the veneer of civility and bare the animal I am inside to her. I want to scare her, shock her... Fuck the hell out of her. I want to take her pussy and imprint myself inside of her, so she'll never forget what it is to belong to me.

It's precisely why I am going to keep my distance from her. I'll marry her, I'll use her to get to the Seven, and then I'll set her free. Until then, I am going to restrict my interactions with her to the bare minimum. It's the only way I am going to survive this unscathed.

I pivot, head for the door and she calls out, "Wait, Michael."

I pause.

"What you said about marrying me... You... You really mean that?"

I nod.

"You don't have to do it, you know. I mean, just because there is something between us..."

I turn, glare at her over my shoulder, "So you admit, there is something between us?"

"I admit no such thing."

"You just said so."

"I meant..." She draws in a breath, "Okay, yes, so there's some kind of weird chemistry between us. Doesn't mean we have to get married." Her lips draw up in a parody of a smile. She's smart, this woman, and quick-witted and able to think on her feet. Exactly the kind of woman I have been searching for. The kind I want by my side...

Wait, what? I don't need anyone else. I have myself and my siblings. They are all I need to consolidate my position.

Oh, well, I do need her...but only as a means of getting to the Seven. That, and the fact that her father did promise her to me. It would be crazy to not use that to my benefit. So, I will... And then I'll release her.

"Your father promised you to me in return for his life. I am just making sure you honor the debt. Also" I look her up and down, "I took your virginity."

"Oh, please, let's get past that, okay?" She takes a step forward, "And my father may have pledged me to you, but we don't have to fulfill it."

"No?"

She nods, "You and I both know you could do much better than me."

"Is that right?"

"Yes." She folds her arms around her waist. "Don't you want to marry a nice, shy, demure bride who'll do as you tell her to?"

No.

No.

"Yes." I jerk my chin.

"You do?"

"It's how you are going to be by the time I marry you."

"Oh, pfft." She waves her hand in the air, "Have you met me? I am wild, evil-tempered, I swear like a trooper—"

Everything I find fascinating about you.

"I'll never stop standing up to you."

Something I look forward to.

"You'll never be able to tame me."

My cock instantly lengthens. "Is that a challenge?"

"What?" She frowns, "Of course, not. I am merely pointing out why I am so wrong for you."

And yet, why do you feel so right?

"Nice try," I allow my lips to curl, "but it's not working."

"No?"

I shake my head. "Your father gave his word. Now you are going to keep it."

"And if I refuse?"

His grin widens. "I look forward to changing your mind."

19

Karma

Shit, shit, shit. This is not how it's supposed to be. I guess I was holding out some hope that he would let me go eventually. Then, I had made that stupid suggestion, as a joke, and he was supposed to laugh it off, or merely ignore it. Instead, he'd informed me that's his plan. Bloody hell, that's the last thing I want. What sane person would want to marry the person who kidnapped her?

He'd told me my father owed him. And I'd thought…that he'd hold me captive, probably threaten me, maybe contact Summer for some kind of ransom… And, to be honest, there has been a part of me afraid to admit my ultimate fear—that he plans to kill me. Although, he could have done that a long time ago, so maybe not…

Okay, the simmering chemistry between us could have something to do with it. It is hard to ignore. And I'd even thought, perhaps, at some point, I'd give in to that temptation… But marriage? What the hell? Why would my jerk of a father promise me to someone in the Mafia without telling me? And why did he wait until now to find me?

Shit. I pace the length of my room, back-forth-back.

After Michael had left yesterday, I'd showered, then emerged to find

Cassandra waiting for me. She'd changed the bed clothes and had a first aid kit with her. She'd treated the few scratches I'd gotten from my accident, and helped me dress for bed.

Frankly, I had been so affected by what had happened after my fall that I had all but forgotten about that incident, let alone checked for any scrapes or bumps. It's a miracle I escaped without any serious injury. In fact, it's nothing but a freakin' marvel that he'd managed to get to me in time and haul me back.

As long as he is near me, it seems I'll always be safe. Shit, why am I thinking that way? I wrap my arms about myself. Maybe it has to do with the way he'd held me close and carried me back and gotten into bed with me... I could have sworn he'd felt... Something? Remorse at having pushed me that far? Relief that I was safe? Or maybe it's my imagination playing tricks on me.

One thing is for sure, though. I am *not* going to marry him. Nope, nah, no way.

I have to think of a way out. I walk to the window once more, survey the steep drop to the sea below. The dress I'd pulled out of the closet billows around my knees. This is another creation that fits me, and the quality of the material is soft and, clearly, expensive. Only, it's a pale pink. So not my color.

I curl my fingers around the window sill. How the hell am I going to get away from him? He is never going to let me go. No way, can I break out of this stupid building, and even if I could, we are on an island. I need to find a way to get to the mainland. Need to get to a place with a phone, or with other people, normal people. Surely, someone could help me then. They'd see that I was being held against my will and would be able to get a message to my sister or to the cops or something?

Surely, there has to be a way out of being married to this...this... alphahole.. This...man who is gorgeous and hot as hell, and dominant, and such a fucking commanding presence that simply being near him makes my pussy clench on itself, makes me as horny as hell, makes my panties so wet, my core so empty, that I'll do anything for any part of him inside of me... Even his knife handle... Hell.

What the hell is wrong with me? Not that I am not aware of kinks and knife play, but really, I never thought I'd be into it. But then, I never thought I'd be so drawn to a man who is so completely wrong. Wrong side of the law, wrong attitude, wrong mindset, wrong fucking idea on what it means to be attracted to a woman. I mean, you do not first take your knife and use it to fuck her, just because you feel a connection to her.

Or maybe that's it. Maybe he doesn't feel anything, he just sees me as a possession—something he can own and possess and shag when the need overtakes him. But seriously, why would he do that? Use his knife like that? Not that it hadn't been hot as hell, not that I hadn't come all over his knife handle, and gah! What does it say about me, that I had found it such a turn on? Clearly, that darkness inside of me is more pervasive than I'd realized.

That's the only reason I am so freakin' attracted to the man who resembles the Lord of Darkness himself. And that voice of his? OMG, whatever happened to him must have been really painful, considering the scars on his throat, but hell, if it hadn't given him that hoarse burr that completely kills me every time he speaks.

I am screwed... I am way too attracted to him to marry him. Any more time spent in proximity to him is going to completely do my head in. As it is, when I close my eyes, I hear him, sense his touch on my skin, scent his dark, edgy, masculine scent, feel how it had been when he'd fucked me with his knife... My core clenches, my pussy flutters, and moisture laces my center. I am in so much trouble. I simply have to find a way to beat him at his own game.

But how?

I can't defy him... I can't obey him... But maybe I can pretend? I can find a way to win a modicum of his trust... Just until I find a way off of this island, at least.

The door opens and I turn to find Cassandra waiting for me.

"The Capo is waiting to have breakfast with you."

She beckons to me and I follow her down the stairs. She walks past the dining room where I had my last meal, past the door leading to the study, and past the main living room, to a small alcove that looks out onto the lawns, and beyond that, the sea. The small table is set for two and Michael is seated in a chair, reading something on his phone. He's, once again, dressed in a black suit, with a black tie. Does the man not have anything else in his wardrobe? He glances up and spots me, rising to his feet. He nods at Cassandra, who pauses, then comes around and pulls up a chair for me. I sit down and he eases the chair in, before going around to take his seat again.

He takes in my features, "How are you feeling?"

"Fine." I place my hands in my lap, "I am good."

"No lasting impact from the fall?"

"Told you, it was an accident," I murmur, "and you got to me in time...so...." I shuffle my feet, glance up at him to find him perusing my features.

A blush steals up my cheeks, "What?" I mutter, "You're beginning to creep me out with the way you're looking at me."

"And what about the other thing?" He seems to hesitate, and I stare. First, he actually seemed regretful yesterday that he'd fucked me with the knife handle. And this morning? He's being exceedingly polite and coming across as unsure? Wow.

"Karma?" he urges me. "You sure you're okay?"

"If you mean are there any aftereffects of being fucked by the blunt end of a knife handle, then no." I tip up my chin, "I am fine." My pussy clenches. *Except for that.* My stupid cunt wants more, and ideally, it would rather he replace the knife with the bigger blade...the one that he wields between his legs, I mean. Argh, I didn't just think that. My cheeks heat, and he arches an eyebrow. He stares into my face a while longer, then nods.

Just then, Cassandra arrives, this time with our breakfast. She places a large cup with what seems like a crunchy, frozen slushy in front of each of us. There is also a bowl of what looks like croissants between us, along with fresh fruit, muesli and a massive plate of fresh pastries. She places a small bowl of fresh-cut fruit before me, then adds the tiniest cups of espresso next to each of us. She leaves and I glance down at the frozen slushy in front of me.

"What's this?"

"A granita," he replies as he breaks off a piece of the croissant, dips it in the dark brown slushy, then brings it up to his mouth and closes his lips around it.

I can't stop myself from flicking my tongue as I watch him crunch down on the ice, swallow, then reach for another piece of croissant.

He glances up and I flush, look away, then back to his mouth. Watch as he repeats the action, making a slight humming sound. My clit instantly throbs. Shit. How would it be to feel those vibrations against the most sensitive part of me? Why is it that everything he does seems to have a one-way connection to my pussy?

He looks up at me, then at my plate. "Eat," he gestures.

"Can you pass me a croissant," I murmur.

"It's a brioche," he corrects me.

"Oh," I frown, "it looks like a croissant."

"It's similar, but different. This," he offers me the plate of brioches and I take one, "is a soft sweet bread made using Marsala wine and honey. It's uniquely Sicilian."

I break off a piece of the brioche, dip it in the slushy, then pop the entire thing into my mouth. The complementary flavors of coffee and chocolate burst on my tongue. I chew, crunch down on a few pieces of ice and swallow. "Wow," I breathe, then lick my lips, "what was that?"

He doesn't take his gaze off of my mouth. "That was a traditional Sicilian breakfast," he murmurs.

"I get that." I scowl, "But what did you say the slushy thingy is called?"

"A granita." He raises those deep blue eyes to mine, "The Arabs brought it with them. They called it *Sarbut*, the Brits call it *Sherbet*.... The Arabs left Sicily, but their influence in food and in architecture stayed on."

"It's yummy." The heat of his gaze sinks into my blood. The tension between us ratchets up. My heart begins to beat hard in my chest. I swallow, reach for a piece of fruit and pop it in my mouth. The juicy sweet flavors burst in my mouth. "This orange is delicious."

I pop another slice into my mouth, then jerk my chin in the direction of the fruit, "You're not having any of it?"

He chuckles, "I hope not, considering I am allergic to them."

I blink. "You're allergic to oranges?"

He tilts his head. "Surprised?"

"You mean the big, bad alphahole actually has a weakness?" I lower my chin, "Yeah, I am surprised."

"I am human, Beauty." He smirks, "Though you can be forgiven for thinking otherwise."

"Ha, ha." I laugh without humor, then reach for my espresso. "You really have a big opinion about yourself, don't you?"

"Nothing that's not warranted." His grin widens, "Eat up, Beauty, we have a packed day."

20

Karma

The packed day, as it turned out to be, was Michael taking me shopping in Palermo. We'd taken a motorboat across to the big island which Michael had piloted, then he had guided me to a gleaming red Maserati that had been parked not far from the pier. He'd told me to snap on my seatbelt before roaring out. A half hour later, we'd walked into this gorgeous boutique… Which had been closed off for the pleasure of the Capo, as the woman who ran the place had informed us.

She'd taken me inside, to a large changing room, complete with a sprawling couch, a large mirror that took up one wall, and next to it, a changing cubicle, where I now stand. I run my fingers down the pale green dress that dips modestly in the front, plunges at the back, and flows in an 'A' line to just below my knees. It's all right, I guess. The cut is awesome, the fabric is beautiful, but the color is all wrong. I blow out a breath.

How weird that he'd offered to take me shopping anyway, and after I'd been so grumpy about the earlier pink dress I'd had to wear. There hadn't been many options in terms of color in the closet. It was either the cream-colored dress…or the beige skirt with the matching top, or the pink pant-suit — no seriously, it was a pink pantsuit — more suited to my sister Summer's tastes, really. I hunch my shoulders.

How is Summer, anyway? Is she enjoying her married life with her new husband? Has she missed me yet? Even if she does, I have no way of knowing, considering Alphahole had commandeered my phone. Most likely, he is putting up a good front with her, probably answering her text messages with enough alacrity that she doesn't suspect a thing.

Anyway, why would she miss me? I have always been the annoying, younger sibling who was critical of her innocent, trusting ways. She's older than me, but I've often felt more worldly-wise than her, more cynical... In many ways, I am darker than her. My tastes have always run to the extremes, while Summer is all pink roses and glittery unicorns and shit. I bow my head. A hot sensation stabs at my chest.

Shit, now I am feeling sorry for myself. I mean, things aren't that bad. I am standing here, trying on a dress that costs... I search for a price tag and realize there isn't one on the dress. Hmm, so it's that kind of a place. Not that I blame them. The dresses are exquisite and I am the first to not begrudge an artiste the value of their creations... It's just, this really is not my style. I take in the shimmering, silvery green of the dress. Guess the color's not too bad. I blow out a breath, then turn, just as Michael steps through the door that separates the changing cubicle from the rest of the room.

"What are you doing here?" I frown.

He drags his gaze down my face, my chest, the skirt of the dress, to my feet, still clad in the pink ballet flats — ugh! — that I had found in the closet at my room — I mean, the room at the place where he's holding me captive.

He raises his gaze to my face and those deep blue eyes gleam. "I came to check if you were okay."

"You mean, you came to check that your little captive hadn't escaped?"

"You couldn't escape me, even if you tried."

"Is that a challenge?" I set my jaw. "I could leave anytime I want."

He laughs, "The lies we tell ourselves."

"Better small lies than big ones."

The smile drops from his face. "I told you I am sorry for what I did yesterday."

"What did you do earlier?"

"You know what I mean," he says through gritted teeth, "I am trying to be nice."

"This is you being nice?" I scoff. "Please, save it for Clarissa—"

"Larissa."

"Whatever," I snap. "Like I care what her stupid name is."

"Jealous, Beauty?" He smirks and my traitorous pussy instantly throbs. Gah! Enough, already.

"I am not jealous." I draw myself up to my full height, which still means I have to tilt my head back, way back, to meet his indigo gaze. "In fact, I think you can fuck her day and night and I wouldn't care."

"Hmm." His grin widens, "I think you're lying."

"Oh, go to hell." I turn, face my reflection in the mirror, then gasp. He's right behind me.

He holds my gaze in the mirror, then runs his finger down my spine. I shiver and his lips curl. "Don't you like it?" he rumbles.

"It'll do, I suppose."

"What's that supposed to mean?"

"Well, firstly, I am not sure what I am doing here shopping for clothes. Secondly, even if I did decide to accept them from you, this is not my style."

"We are shopping for clothes because it was a chance for you to get out. And secondly, what do you mean it's not your style?"

"Don't do me any favors by planning an outing for me." I frown up at him, "And secondly, just that. This is not the style of clothing I wear."

"Surely, you must be able to find something in this shop that's to your taste?" He frowns.

"I suppose I might find a thing or two, if I look hard enough," I murmur.

"Hmm." He firms his lips, "So you don't like the one you are wearing now, either?"

I shake my head and his smile widens, "Then you won't mind if I do this?" He hooks his finger in the 'V' of the dress and tugs. The delicate fabric tears. I gasp as he rips the cloth all the way to the hem. The dress stays poised over my breasts, then with a whisper, it falls away. Leaving me clad only in my panties—I'd taken off my bra earlier to try on the dress—and in the stupid pink ballet flats.

His gaze eats me up as he slides it down to my breasts. My nipples pucker, and he lowers his gaze down to the shadowy cleft that can be seen through my panties.

"*Oddio,*" he growls, "you're fucking beautiful."

My thighs clench and moisture pools between my legs. More of this and he'll be able to make out the damp spot that I am sure is currently gracing the inside of my knickers.

Heat flushes my skin. I want to throw my arms around myself and hide from his gaze, but I don't. Instead, I tuck my elbows into my sides and watch as he drinks his fill of me.

He slides his palm around and flattens it against my belly. The dark skin on the back of his palm is a startling comparison to the ivory of my skin. He brings this other hand around to cup my pussy. Through the thin cloth of my panties the heat of his touch sinks right into my core. Without meaning to, I widen my legs. A low rumble of approval vibrates up his massive chest. He slips his finger under the gusset of my underwear. He brushes against my weeping slit and I can't stop the moan that bubbles up my throat. I lean back into that hard chest of his, thrust up my breasts, tip up my chin, and watch from under hooded eyelids as he slips his finger inside my opening.

Goosebumps pop on my skin. I bite down on my lower lip and his gaze instantly goes there. His lips part as if he's remembering how it'd been to eat me out. The thought sends a shiver down my spine. More moisture slides down from between my thighs. His breath catches. He slips in a second finger, then a third. A groan bleeds from me. I slide my arm up and around, hold onto his shoulder as he begins to finger fuck me. He doesn't take his gaze from mine in the mirror, and I swallow, watch as those darkening eyes grow blacker, more unfathomable. As if there is a fire deep inside that he's hiding from me. As he speeds ups and saws his fingers in and out of me, in and out, my breasts jiggle and my belly trembles. My entire body seems to be participating in this carnal exercise. I wind my fingers around his thick wrist, not so much to stop him as to hold on as he continues to weave his magic fingers in and out of me. The climax bursts upon me. I throw my head back and into his chest. My eyelids flutter down and he clicks his tongue. "Eyes on me, Beauty."

I raise my gaze to his again, and somehow, the intimacy of watching him jerking me off—of the very erotic picture we make, with me almost naked and him fully dressed, his fingers inside me, as he brings his other hand up to cup my breast, before he pinches my nipple with callous disregard—makes me throw my head back and scream as I fall apart. I black out for a few seconds, and when I open my eyes again, I am still in the same position, leaning into him, held up by his fingers in my cunt, that he pulls out.

"I screamed," I say in a dazed voice.

"Indeed." He smirks and my pussy clenches again. Argh. Stupid pussy.

"So, the rest of the people in the boutique would have heard too?" I frown.

"Since when did you start caring about what others think of you?" He tilts his head and something hot stabs at my chest. How the hell does this man know me so well? I really don't give a shit about what others think of me. But society dictates I should. And sometimes I give in to that pressure. And this man... My captor had cut through to the heart of my quandry with a few careless words.

He proceeds to lick his glistening fingers one by one, before he holds them to my mouth.

"Open," he commands and I part my lips. He thrusts his fingers in my mouth, and the sweet taste of my cum, the darker, edgier taste of him, crowds my sense. My core dampens all over again. Hell, I want him. I need him inside of me.

"Mika," I whisper, "please."

He curls his lips, removes his fingers from my mouth, then wipes them on my stomach. "Get dressed." He steps back, holding my shoulder for a few seconds while I regain my balance. "I'll be outside," he murmurs, not unkindly...just...without much emotion, as if he is simply attending to a chore. Is that all I am to him? A captive, a possession, an asset, someone he wants to wed out of some stupid sense of ownership.

"Michael, why—"

He shakes his head, "I'll see you outside."

21

Michael

What the hell is wrong with me? Why the hell can't I keep away from her? And after what I did to her yesterday, you'd think I'd have the decency to give her a wide berth? Apparently, not. Apparently, taking her virginity with a knife handle is not enough. Now, I have to jump her in a changing room cubicle and make her come all over my fingers.

I had planned this excursion with the purpose of trying to make up, somewhat, for what I had done. I'd thought a quick outing, doing what women seem to love most—shopping, buying new clothes—would take her mind off of what had happened, off of what a sick fuck I am. And maybe, in some way, I hoped to make amends for what I had done. Okay... I had been shamelessly trying to buy my way into her good books. The plan had been to leave her alone, to let her browse and choose the clothes she loved, but the situation had backfired on me.

I hadn't been able to wait while she changed her clothes. All I had been conscious of was that she was behind closed doors slipping out of what she had been wearing... She was probably naked and stepping into one of the new outfits. She'd pull it up and over her breasts, cover her flat belly with it, allow it to flow around her knees. I had tortured myself with visions of how the silent cloth would feel against her skin, as it caressed her nipples and slithered in between her legs, slipping across the newly-exposed and extra-sensitive skin there.

Before I'd realized it, I had made my way to the changing cubicle and stepped in. The thought of making her come in a public place had only added to the excitement. It had been hot and so damn sexy, seeing her respond to my ministrations. Clad in that green dress that had enhanced the emerald of her eyes... I had taken great pleasure in tearing it off of her body.

And she had shattered and wanted more. I had seen the need in her eyes, knew if I threw her down on the floor of the changing room, she'd have parted her legs and welcomed me into her weeping cunt. And I had wanted to take her right then and there. Make her mine, tie her to me, ensure I'd imprinted myself on every cell in her body. And it was precisely that overwhelming compulsion which had made me pull away.

This woman is like crack. Every time I see her, touch her, smell her fragrance, I want more. When I am with her, I lose sight of everything else... Everything except this need to bury myself between her legs and taste her, sniff her, absorb her essence into my body. It's crazy, the intensity with which I want her, and that urge only grows with every encounter.

When I am with her, I lose sight of everything that I have worked so hard to achieve. I am perilously close to throwing it all away for one more hour with her and that...is dangerous. For me, for my family, for my men who depend on me for survival. For the way of life that I chose a long time ago. How can I let one slip of a woman sweep in and displace all of that?

No, I have to keep my distance from her. I have to rush through this wedding, then ensure I use her to get to the Seven. Secure my empire and my position within the Cosa Nostra, and then I'll be free of her.

I thought I could, with a few more weeks, give her time to adjust to the idea of a wedding, but I guess I don't have that luxury. I need to get on with it. No more wasting time. She simply has to get on board with what is going to happen to her.

I watch from my position against my Maserati as she walks out wearing another dress. A dark blue, almost black colored, outfit that clings to her like a second skin. It stops just above her knees, and the neckline is high, except for the heart-shaped cut-out just above her breasts that shows off the shadowy valley between the mounds.

It is very different from the outfit she'd been trying on earlier, the one I destroyed. It is also much more her. More complex, more in keeping with the feisty personality that she has.

Have I bitten off more than I can chew with her? Did I make a mistake in taking her, in the first place? If I'd known just how much she'd turn my life upside down, would I have kidnapped her? Did I even have a choice in the matter?

As soon as I had seen her reciting Byron to herself in that moody voice as she gazed out over London... I knew that I had to have her. And here she is, within my grasp. So why am I still hesitating to make her mine? What is stopping me from taking what rightfully already belongs to me?

I track her progress as she walks over to the car, she holds a bag in each hand. I take them from her and she slides inside the car with a whisper of fabric and that luscious scent that is so very Beauty.

I shut the door, dropping the bags in the trunk—*Gesù Christo*, the woman's turning me into a chauffeur—before rounding the car to the driver's seat.

I fold my length inside. "Thought you didn't like anything you saw in there." I jerk my chin toward the shop.

"Guess I saw a few things which could suffice." She sniffs, "Besides, they are a step up from what's in the closet back at the house." She shudders.

"I take it the outfits in the closet back home are not to your liking?" I say dryly.

"Let's just say, they leave a lot to be desired, especially in terms of color."

I scowl. "What's wrong, in terms of their color?"

"They're all pink and beige and shit."

"So?"

"So?" She turns to me, "Hello, take a look at me." She waves a hand at herself, "Do I look like someone who wears those girlie colors? And their fitting..." She scoffs. "Not that they are not of good quality. That's their only redeeming factor, but seriously, they have this ladylike air about them—"

"And you're not a lady, are you, Beauty?" I lean in closer to her and her breath hitches. "You're someone who wants to be treated like a queen in real life and like a whore in bed, isn't that right, *Belleza*?"

Color reddens her cheeks and her pupils dilate. *Merda,* that turns her on, all right. Beauty has no idea just how depraved her tastes really are, does she? My cock tightens and my belly hardens. She opens her mouth, no doubt, to protest and I raise a hand. "Don't bother to deny it," I drawl, "we both know that's true."

She folds her hands over her chest. "You don't have a clue, what I like."

"And we both know that's a lie."

She scowls, then shifts in her seat. The pulse at her throat speeds up. *Porca miseria.* At this rate, I am going to pull her over, and have her riding my cock in no time. And I don't want to do that, not yet. Not until I have her married to me.

"So," I widen my legs, trying to make myself more comfortable, "what kinds of clothing would you rather wear?"

She firms her lips, "Doesn't matter."

I frown. "Tell me," I insist. "I want to know."

She blows out a breath, then shoots me a sideways glance, "I'd rather stitch my own clothing, if you really want to know."

"You would?" Then I nod, "Of course, you would, you are a tailor."

"A fashion designer."

"A seamstress."

"I'm a couturier, you ass."

"What-fucking-ever," I mutter. "You want to create your own clothing; I am sure we can arrange that."

Half an hour later, I watch from the comfort of yet another couch that I have draped myself on in a corner of a well-known fabric shop that also carries any tools she may need for stitching her wedding dress. I had my men talk to the owner, who was only too happy to shut down the shop to the rest of the public so my woman could shop in privacy.

Holdonasecond. Did I just think of her as my woman? I drag my fingers through my hair. Shit, shit, shit. When you start slipping up like that, and your subconscious mind insists on playing tricks on you, then you know you're really in trouble.

I follow her with my eyes as she literally vibrates with excitement as she examines the fabrics in front of her. Shades of black and gray, and a blue so dark that it could be mistaken for black in low light, a green so deep that it calls to mind the depths of the sea, a purple on the spectrum of—you guessed it, black. Doesn't the woman like any other color?

Her dark hair dances about her shoulders as she leans in closer to the man behind the counter. She says something to him and he nods. She lowers her head to examine the cloth, whispers something else and he bursts out laughing. He whispers something back to her, eliciting a smile, before he pivots, heads inside the shop, only to appear moments later with an armful of ribbons and fabrics in shades of— See if you can guess. Yes, black.

Together, they examine the cloth. The man glances at her bent head, a positively adoring look on his features.

Something hot stabs at my chest. Damn it, I knew it had been a bad idea to let her off the island.

It's only a matter of time before everyone else sees what I already know. She's special. She's different. Nothing, and no-one else, can hold a candle to her. She is unique, a magnificent creature who seems to breathe life into everything around her. There is something so luminescent about this girl, I wonder how has she survived this far without anyone else recognizing how unique she is?

I had, of course, from the moment I had spotted her. I haven't been able to let her go since, and look where that has gotten me. Skulking about in the periphery, stalking her like a creepy-ass motherfucker, while nursing a bad case of blue balls, and all because I can't bring myself to own up to just how drawn to her I am.

I had taken her with the intention of making her pay her father's debt. I had realized her links to the Seven make her a key asset. I should go through with my original plan of killing her... Instead, here I am, contemplating marrying her. Except, I can never allow for that to be real. If, for one second, I allow myself to think of how it would be to really be married to her... Hell... My groin hardens and my heart begins to race. I'd never be able to let go of her. I'd, forever, have handed over my power to her... And that, I cannot allow.

I am my own man. I built up the authority I wield with great effort and I cannot let anything or anyone get in the way of the empire I have envisioned for myself. It's all I have —the promise I made to myself that I will be the most powerful of all the Five Families—and I can't stop until I have achieved that.

I rise to my feet and stalk over to her. I loom behind her, and she glances up at me, "Hey, Michael," her face lights up, "this is incredible. The warp, the weft, the velvets and the chiffons... They are gorgeous. Look at the sheer variety of these decorative ribbons. And this lace—"

She holds up a length of an antique, cream-colored mesh-like fabric, "It's incredible. It's so old, there are very few of this left anywhere in the world, and Roberto, here, is happy for me to have it."

I glance from her to the middle-aged man who watches her with stars in his eyes. Fucker. I can't stop the growl that rumbles from my chest.

Roberto pales; his throat moves as he swallows. He looks up at me, blinks rapidly. "Signor Capo," he mumbles, "I am more than happy for the Signorina to have whatever she so desires."

"The Signorina desires that you wrap up everything—" I rake my gaze across the heaps of fabric, and the various other sewing tools and other odds and ends that she's chosen. "—Everything that she has liked so far, and have them delivered to my place on the island." I jerk my chin toward the door, "Now, get out of the shop and leave us alone."

"But," he glances down at the heaps of fabric, then back up at me, "Signor, Capo…" He swallows, "Uh, the payment."

"Oh, for fuck's sake." I shove my hand in my pocket, pull out my credit card and hand it over. "Charge the whole damned thing, and anything else she'll need for creating her trousseau, to it."

"Yessir." The man grabs the card, turns to Beauty and smiles, as I fight the urge to bash his head in. He nods, "Signorina," then scampers off. The door shuts behind him as Beauty whirls on me.

"What the hell are you thinking? You gave him your credit card?"

"So?"

"And you're not going to check what he's charging to it."

"He won't dare pull a fast one on me. Besides," I smirk, "it's just money."

She scowls, "I can't accept all of this."

"You will."

"I don't want it." She all but stamps her foot.

Aww, how cute. "You do want it," I murmur. "You just don't know it."

"What will I do with so much fabric?" A line appears between her eyebrows. "It's more than I have bought in my entire life."

"Good," I bare my teeth, "you can use it to stitch your wedding gown."

"No." She shakes her head, "No, no, no."

"Yes." I allow my grin to widen, "You can and you will."

"I will not."

"Is that right?"

She folds her arms across her chest, "I refuse to participate in this sham of a wedding that you keep threatening me with. I refuse to give in and act all helpless."

"Pity, you'd make a great damsel in distress."

"But you are no knight in shining armor."

"I am glad you recognize that." I bend my knees, peer into her face, "You will do as I say."

"And if I don't?"

I glare into those bright green eyes. Eyes I can lose myself in, eyes that are angry and frustrated, and yet, so filled with life that they take my breath away. "If you don't, I will—"

The phone in my pocket buzzes. She glances down at my pocket just as I whip her phone out, stare at the message. "If you don't, I won't let you see the message that your sister sent you."

"My sister?" She cries, "Summer? That's a message from Summer?" She stretches out her hand for the phone and I hold it up and out of her reach.

"Give it to me," she huffs.

"First, agree that you will stitch your wedding dress."

"No."

"Then you won't see this message from your sister."

She hesitates and I glance at the screen. "Don't you want to find out how she is doing? How her husband is treating her after the wedding? Where they are going for their honeymoon—"

"Bastard," she snarls.

I arch an eyebrow, "Now, you are definitely not going to see her message."

I swipe the screen and she frowns.

"Hold on. My phone is profile protected. How the hell did you unlock it?"

I lower my chin, "Really, that's all you are concerned about? How I hacked your phone?"

"Jerk." She sets her jaw, "Guess you got someone to get around the security."

I tilt my head, and her color deepens. "Show me the message."

"Apologize first, for being so impolite."

"I won't."

"Fine."

I dance my finger across the screen, reach for the delete button, and she snaps, "Okay, fine, I apologize."

"That didn't seem like much of an apology."

"What the hell?" she snarls. "Do you want me to get on my knees?"

I arch an eyebrow and she pales.

"No," she says through gritted teeth. "Of all the annoying, stupid, humiliating things, you'd ask me to do that?"

I yawn and she snaps her teeth shut. Then she lowers herself to her knees, tips her chin up and purses her lips together, "Happy?"

"Not yet," I tilt my head, "open your mouth."

She pales.

I glare at her and she swallows, then parts her lips.

"Good girl." I slide my thumb inside her mouth, then lower my voice to a hush, "Suck on it." She doesn't take her gaze off of me as she curls her warm tongue around my digit.

The blood rushes to my groin. *Fuck.* I press down her tongue, as she parts her lips further. The thought of those lips wrapped around my cock... *Goddamn it to hell.* A surge of need races up my spine. To think, I'd thought I'd be able to stay away from her. I pull my fingers out, then jerk my chin, "Get up."

She rises to her feet and I flip the phone so she can peruse the screen. She reads the message, once, twice, then swallows. I lower the phone, frown down at her, "Well?"

"What?" She glowers back, "What do you want now?"

"What's your reply?"

"Oh," she blinks, "you're going to let me answer her message?"

"I am going to allow you to tell me what you want to say and I am going to type it out for you."

"Don't trust me, Capo?"

My vision tunnels and my balls harden. Shit, the sound of my title from her lips... It's so damn erotic. I toss the phone at her and she catches it.

"Go on, answer the message."

She blinks. "So, you do trust me?"

"I trust you...to say the right thing, Karma. If you don't, I know exactly where your sister and her new husband are right now, and trust me, they'll pay for your impertinence."

She scowls, "Fine, fine, you don't have to go all Godfather on my arse. I know you're too clever to simply hand the phone over to me to reply without having your own checks and balances in place."

She glances down and her fingers race across the screen. The sound of the message being sent fills the space. She straightens, then hands the phone over to me.

"That wasn't too bad, was it?"

"If you mean my having to beg to use the phone which, honestly, is as crucial as breathing…then yeah, it sucked balls."

"I need to wash out your mouth," I fix my gaze on her lips, "and it's not going to be with water."

"Whatever." She flips her hair over her shoulder, "You're all talk and no action, you know that?"

"Are you trying to get under my skin or are you trying to get under my skin?" I slide the phone into my pocket.

She tosses her head, "If that was a joke, I don't get it."

"Good," I widen my stance, "because by the time I am done with you, you won't be laughing."

"What's that supposed to mean?" She twists her fingers together, "I mean, seriously, you are worse than a B-grade Hollywood flick, Capo. Have you heard yourself lately?"

"How about we settle for hearing you as you come?"

"What?" She glances around the space, "Here?"

I twirl my finger in the air. She huffs. I glare at her and she pales.

"Do it, Beauty," I murmur. She spins around and faces the counter.

I press my palm into the small of her back and a shiver trembles down her spine. I push forward and she leans over beautifully. I glide my palm up her spine and fix my fingers around the nape of her neck. The length is so slender that my fingers meet around the front. She turns her head, and I urge her to press her cheek into the glass counter. Another trembling grips her. I increase the pressure around her neck and she subsides.

"Relax," I murmur, "I am not going to hurt you."

"No, you did that already."

I glance down at her face, at where she's staring up at me from the corner of her eyes, "And you enjoyed it."

She shakes her head, and I increase the pressure around her throat, "Don't lie to me." I lean in close enough for my breath to raise the tendrils of hair at her temple. "You loved every minute of riding my knife handle; you enjoyed coming on my fingers in the changing cubicle.

Even now, bent over the counter with your arse up in the air and at my mercy, you can't stop your cunt from dripping for my touch, for my fingers to be crammed inside of you, for my mouth pushed up against your slit as you ride my tongue."

"N...no..." she stutters, "that's not true."

"It is." I close the distance between us so my pelvis is pushed up against her curvy rear end, so my dick nestles in the valley between her ass cheeks. So there is no doubt about just how turned on I am. How at my disposal she is. All I have to do is yank up the fabric of her dress, lower my zipper and—"

"If you're going to fuck me, why don't you simply do it and get it over with?" she huffs.

"Because that would be too easy?" I bend and place my mouth so close to hers that we share breath, "Because I am not going to put you out of your misery that easily. Because you can fool yourself all you want, Beauty, but the fact is, under that innocent exterior beats a heart that is every bit as perverted as mine, a soul that yearns for every depraved thing I can do to you, a mind that is, even now, racing ahead with the possibilities of exactly in what positions I can tie you down, how I can restrain you, how I can render you helpless and willing to take my cock in any position that I choose to give it to you...or not."

A low moan bleeds from her lips, and my dick instantly lengthens. I cup her ass cheek and her entire body grows rigid. I drag my finger down the fabric that clings to the cleft between her butt cheeks and her thighs clench.

"Shh!" I slip my hand under the slit that runs up the back of her dress, my fingers brush the back of her thigh, and a whine spills from her lips. I thrust my thigh between her legs, pry them apart as I slip my fingers in between them and freeze.

"You didn't wear panties?"

22

Karma

"The dress was too tight," I snap, even as a trembling begins in my core. I try to rise up but the grip on my neck holds my immobile. Also, his massive trunk-like thigh between mine has me pinned. Shit, how can this guy be so big? Not that I can forget his height, considering how he towers over me, but when he holds me down like this, exactly how much weaker than him I am is brought home to me. I am in his power. His to be played with. His to be used. His to own. His to…be brought to the edge of pleasure with the kind of sweet pain only he can bestow on me. I open my mouth to tell him just that, then snap my jaws shut.

No way, am I making that tactical error. If he knows how close I am to throwing caution to the wind, to forgetting who I am, and what my life used to look like, how the future I had envisaged for myself is slowly fading away… Poof... how it's all gone under the mesmerizing influence of his touch. Crushed under the overwhelming force of his dominance that demands that I lay here and watch him as he surveys my backside.

"Or maybe you wanted to tease me…?" He raises those unfathomable eyes to mine, "Tell me, Beauty, is this your way of telling me that you'd rather not wait for the holy union of our marriage, and that you'd rather that I fuck you right here and now?"

"Exactly," I murmur, "now you get it. The faster you shag me, the faster we can put this…chemistry we have, behind us. Then, you can send me back home and—"

"No."

"What?" I frown. "What do you mean, no?"

"No, I am not letting you go."

"But if you fuck me, you don't have to marry me, right?"

He laughs, "Whatever gave you that idea? This entire exercise is so I can make our arrangement official, remember?"

"But what benefit do you get out of it? I mean, sure you get a wife and someone to breed for you. But as we've already established, I am not the kind of woman you want."

"That's your conclusion, not mine."

"But seriously, Michael," I lift my head but he pushes me back down.

"Less talk, more action," he growls.

"You mean, more pretending to make me come without actual penetration?" I scoff.

His entire body goes solid. That's the only warning I get before he grips the sides of the slit in my dress and tugs. The fabric tears up the middle. He rips it all the way to the neckline and the dress falls apart around me. Cool air assails my skin and I shiver. "If you wanted to get me out of the dress, you only had to ask."

"And you'd have agreed?"

"Of course not, but maybe, I could have saved this dress. Not that I like the outfit or anything, but it was new, and someone had put time and effort into creating it, so… I just like to be respectful of other people's work. After all, I know what it takes to produce a design… And by the way, are you going to make this a habit? Ripping apart the dresses I am wearing? Because when I wear my own creations, I promise you, I won't take lightly to that, I won't…"

"Shh." He puts a finger to his lips and I bite the inside of my cheek.

One word from him and I am ready to do his bidding. One glare from him and all I want to do is roll over and open my legs, my mouth, my arms, and accept him into my body, my soul…my mind.

Am I a feminist? I'd like to think so.

Would I ever let a man tell me what to do? Never.

But would I bow down to this man and let him disrespect and

degrade me? Absolutely. A-n-d, that folks, is all you need to know. For I am hopelessly drawn to this alphahole, and hell, if I can understand why. Is it his dominance, his complete confidence that is so attractive? Is it his self-assured approach to most things that is a turn on?

All he's done since I've met him is hold a gun to my temple, then make me come on his knife's handle, then all over his fingers in a semi-public place, and now... He reaches around, yanks up a length of the decorative ribbon that I had been examining earlier.

He pulls my arm behind my back, then the other. He ties the swath around my wrists, once, twice, thrice, knots it, then tugs. The soft material rustles against my skin. A shiver slithers down my back

He brings the ribbon up until just below the elbows, then wraps it around. He puts one arm around both of my arms to hold them together while he wraps the length up until just below the elbows.

Then he wraps it under both of my hands, before pulling it back up to form a cinch. He uses the exact same process to create another band above the elbows.

He pulls the swath up over a shoulder, pulls me forward, then loops the ribbon down on the inside of one breast.

He takes the material beneath the other arm and up again on the inside of the other breast. Shit. He is, in effect, creating straps. Then he brings the ribbon back and around horizontally beneath the arm, wrapping between the two straps. I tug and realize he has, very effectively, tied me down in a matter of seconds.

"What are you doing?" I scowl.

"What does it look like?" He murmurs, "I am tying you down."

"You into Shibari, or something?"

"Or something," he agrees. "Let's just say, finding creative ways of restraining people happens to be one of my hobbies."

"Oh?" I wriggle around and find, while the fabric is loosely tied, it does a very good job of restraining my movement. He's pulled my shoulders back, so my breasts are thrust forward and into the glass counter and my arms are immobilized. All in all, while it's not uncomfortable, there's something very vulnerable in the position. It ensures that I feel exposed, laid out for his delectation.

"Michael," I frown, "undo me."

"Not yet." He steps back and I sense him surveying his handiwork.

"Hmm," he makes a sound of approval deep in his throat, and instantly, my nipples pucker. Hell, it's as if there's a direct line from his voice to all the erogenous zones in my body. He leans over me and heat surrounds me, pulls on me, swirls about me, and pins me down to the counter. I can't move and he isn't even holding me down any more.

"Look at you." His voice is low and melting. "All tied up and laid out like a buffet." His tone dips another octave and a pulse flares to life between my legs. I chafe my thighs together, clench my core in the hope of plugging the emptiness that yawns in my center.

"Michael," I groan, "what are you doing?"

"Admiring my handiwork, of course," he retorts at once.

Jerk.

"Please, Michael, please."

"What do you want, Beauty?"

"Fuck me, Michael."

"Not happening."

"What the—?" I try to rise up but he, once more, wraps his fingers around my neck to hold me in place. "What the hell are you playing at?" I snap. "Seriously, I am done with how you keep toying with me and then making me come—"

"So, you'd rather not come?"

"That's not what I said."

"So, you do want me to touch you."

"Argh, stop putting words in my mouth, asshole." I stare up at him from the corner of my eyes, "Honestly, what are you up to?"

"I think I need to stuff some of the fabric in your mouth."

"Don't you dare, you jerk."

"Then stay quiet, *Belleza.*"

He slides his fingers between my legs, drags the edge of his hand against my pussy. My core clenches and my toes curl. Moisture pools in my center, slides down my inner thigh.

"*Dio cane,*" he growls, "you are soaking, Beauty."

"Oh, fuck off." I mutter. "How about this? Next time, I'll be the one to tie you down, and play with your balls, and then we'll see how you respond.

"You can play with my balls even without tying me down, baby."

I snort then quickly turn it into a gagging noise, "Seriously, that was a terrible attempt at banter."

"So why are you laughing?"

"I'm not."

"Yes, you are."

Her reaches for the curved ruler that I'd been examining earlier. He picks it up and I frown. "That's a French curve," I explain. "It's used to create the perfect curved line for pants and skirts."

"I can think of a perfect curved line I'd like to use it on."

I blink rapidly, "Wh...what do you mean?"

He releases his hold on me, steps back, no doubt, to admire his handiwork one more time. *Jerk!* Then he positions himself at right angles to my body, widens his stance, raises the ruler, much like the position of a golf player raising his club. My throat closes. My scalp tingles and a hot sensation coils in my belly. "Wh...what are you doing, Michael?" I gulp

"One guess." He smirks down at me, "Go on, surely you have an inkling by now."

"Are you..." I clear my throat, "going to use it on me?"

"Right on one." He brings it down and taps it against my naked backside. My breathing hitches. My core clenches. I lick my lips and his gaze drops to my mouth. His blue eyes blaze. His muscles uncoil.

He raises the French ruler again, swipes it against my arsecheek, and I yelp, "What the hell? Stop that!"

He chuckles. The asshole chuckles. "Come on, it didn't even hurt, Beauty."

"Fuck you," I snarl. "Why don't we exchange places and I'll spank your tight ass and then we'll —"

He brings the curved part of the ruler down on my other arsecheek and goosebumps pop on my skin. I huff, try to pull away, but of course, the bastard doesn't allow me to move. He places his free hand on the middle of my back, leans enough weight on me so I can't pull free, then he brings the ruler down on my other arsecheek. Fire sears my butt and I yell, "Goddam you, you...you jerk."

Whack! He brings down the ruler again and I howl. Again, and my entire body jerks. My nipples pebble, my toes curl, moisture laces my core and I squeeze my legs together. A groan bubbles up, and I bury my teeth in my lower lip to stop it from escaping. He pauses, and I glance up to find his gaze arrested by my expression.

His shoulders bunch; his chest rises and falls. I lower my gaze to the front of his pants, which is tented, showing just how much he is aroused. He drops the ruler on the counter, and the sound chafes across my already sensitized nerve-endings.

He massages my backside and pinpricks of pleasure crawl up my spine. He slides his fingers between my thighs, scoops up some of the cum from my core, then drags it up between my arsecheeks to my backhole.

"What the hell are you d...doing?" I stammer.

"What does it feel like?"

I hear the smirk in his voice. *Bastard.* He plays with my puckered hole and I tense.

"Shh." He brings his other hand up to massage the back of my neck. He digs his fingertips into the knotted muscles there and moves them in small circles. The tension instantly drains out of my flesh. My shoulders relax and a delicious warmth seeps into my blood. He slides his finger inside my backhole and I can't bring myself to protest. He pulls out his finger, slips it in again, works his way inside my channel. I wriggle around, dig my heels into the ground. He curves his finger inside and a trembling grips me. *Shit, shit, shit.* I shouldn't find what he's doing so much of a turn on.

He removes his hand from my neck. There's a whisper of fabric, the rasp of metal, then a thump. I snap my eyes open to find his knife laid out on the counter next to my face. Goosebumps pop on my skin. "Wh...what are you going to do with that?"

"Nothing you don't want me to."

I take in the handle of the knife and my heart begins to race. "Michael," I whisper, "you wouldn't..."

"No, I wouldn't."

"Huh?" I glance up from the side of my eyes, "So you agree that you are not going to...use it?"

"Is that what you want, Beauty?" His blue eyes are hard, all emotion wiped from his face. He seems cold and unreachable. Like he's putting me to the test. Like he's already decided about the outcome. Like he knows that I am going to refuse what he wants to do next.

I swallow, draw in a breath. I can't let him know just how afraid I am. How much I want what he can do to me, and yet, how scared I am that I will like it. What does that say about me? That dark side of me that I have always suspected I have. Which is the reason I had been down for becoming a goth... Which still hadn't satisfied that deep nothingness inside of me. The place where there is no judgment, where I can indulge my appetites, can allow myself to be used the way I want, for it seems to satisfy that need inside of me to become someone's fucktoy.

There, I said it. Well, in my head, anyway. Something I've known but which I've never admitted, even to myself. I know, it's me being judgmental about myself... Then, I'd met him and he'd ripped off my mask. He'd laid that kinky fucked-up part of himself out there and I had recognized it... Only, I have yet to come to terms with what that means... Still, I want to own it.

I want to be able to wear my smutty heart on my sleeve. I want to be free to be myself. No judgement. It's what he's offering me. A safe space in which to embrace my own fucked-up-ness. It took a beast to bring out the monster in me. I wonder what that means?

"No," I whisper, "that's not what I want."

His features seem to freeze. His gaze widens. Then, those blue eyes seem to catch fire. Cold fire that sweeps through my skin, heats my blood, and lodges somewhere deep in my gut. My heartbeat ratchets up and moistures slicks my core.

"Tell me," he rumbles, "tell me what you need."

23

Michael

"You," she whispers, "I want you, Michael. I want every depraved, dirty thing that you want to do to me."

My balls harden. Fuck me. How can she say that? How can she lay her innermost desires at my feet? How dare she trust me to do what I want with her? Doesn't she realize how dangerous that would be? How it would ensnare me, trap me into wanting her, feeling for her, tying her to my side and never letting her go? It would make me want to own her, to make her mine. Mine. And that, I can't afford. No distractions. Nothing that could touch my heart. That could infiltrate the walls I've built around myself.

The fact that she wants everything I can do to her… That she aches for my possession as much I want to own her. That she yearns to be at the receiving end of every filthy, fucked-up, obscene one of my actions… It shows just how well-matched she is for me.

It's why I must turn away from her. Why I must never be alone with her. Why I must kill her as soon as she's outlived her usefulness. It's why I must walk away from her. Just...not yet. Not when she's tied up and laid out in front of me, asking me to fulfill the perverted fantasies I've had ever since I met her the first time.

And if I do, I am a goner. I'll never be able to leave her. It's why I need to stay away from her as I had originally planned. A promise I have broken many times over. It's why I am going to walk away from her right now, before I take that final step that will bind me to her irrevocably.

I grab the knife then slide it back in its sheath.

"What are you doing?" She frowns

I step back, reach for the ribbon that I knotted around her wrist. I tug on it, and it comes free. That's the beauty of knowing how to tie someone. The process of unbinding takes, maybe, one fourth of the time that it took to truss them up. If only it were that easy to loosen the ties she's already wrapped around me.

I tug on the fabric and it falls away. I step back and she straightens, then turns on me.

"What's wrong?" She glances between my eyes, "What happened, Michael?"

I school my features into a mask, "We're going to be late for our lunch. That's what happened."

"Lunch?"

I nod.

"But I thought that you —"

"Wanted to fuck your ass?"

She winces, "You had to put that out there, didn't you?"

"Just saying what's on your mind, sweetheart."

"If you think that's going to make me feel embarrassed, think again." She firms her lips, "You went to all that trouble of tying me up. You wouldn't have done that if you hadn't meant to…uh, fuck me."

"Told you, I enjoy tying people up. It's a skill of mine. Doesn't mean I fuck everyone I tie up."

"And those who you tie up and fuck, do you use your knife on them too?"

I draw myself up to my full height. "That's none of your business."

I turn and walk toward the exit.

"Michael," she calls out, "one of these days, you are going to have to tell me why you keep running away from me."

"You're mistaken." I glance over my shoulder and brush away a loose thread from the ribbon. "You need to care about someone enough to have any reaction to them, none of which pertains to this situation."

She pushes her shoulders back and glares at me. "You're an unfeeling asshole."

"Now that we have established that," I glance at her over my shoulder, "wait here while I get you an outfit from the car, so you can get dressed."

Half an hour later, I sit across from her as she glances around the space.

"Capo." Paolo walks up with his usual glower on his face. You'd expect a man of his girth, who runs the most popular restaurant in Palermo, to be the quintessential happy, jowly-faced proprietor who'd go out of his way to keep his clients happy. The reality couldn't be further from that. Paulo is the most ill-tempered man I know. He was just born that way, apparently. But his *Spaghetti alle vongole* is to die for.

He begins to talk to me in Italian and I gesture to Beauty. "English, please," I murmur.

He glances at Karma, then at me, "The usual, Capo?"

"For me, yes. For her…" I tilt my head, "She's allergic to seafood."

"Spaghetti *Aglio Olio e Pepperoncino* for the lady then," he states. "And a carafe of the house white?"

"Please." I nod as Karma opens her mouth, likely to protest. But Paulo has already turned to leave.

"Before you ask," I turn to her, "there is no menu here. You get whatever Paulo has made for the day."

"Huh?" She blinks, "So he decides what you are going to eat?"

"He's the expert, and whatever he cooks is the best you can find in the city on that day, so yeah, you get what he's cooked."

She takes in the tables and chairs in the small space, all packed to capacity. The dining hall opens onto the sea on one side. On the other is the kitchen, open to the guests, so you can see the chefs cooking while Paulo assembles the plates behind one of the counters.

"You come here often?" she asks with her head still turned away.

"Often enough."

"Is Paulo a friend?"

I chuckle. "That asshole is nobody's friend."

"So why do you come here, then?"

I tilt my head, "You still don't get it, do you?"

"What?"

"The food, Beauty, the food."

She scowls, "Still, you could have, at least, let me ask him what the options were."

I simply shake my head. "That's not how it works."

"What do you mean?"

"Firstly, you don't get a choice. You eat what he gets you. Secondly, even if there were a choice, I would have ordered for you."

She gapes. "Is that presumptuous, or what?"

"Be thankful I allowed you out of the house on this outing." I smirk.

"Big-fucking-deal," she murmurs under her breath.

"What did you say?"

"I meant," she clears her throat, "thank you." She coughs.

"That's what I'm talking about."

Just then, Giorgio arrives with our food. He places a plate of the Vongole in front of me and the *Aglio Olio* in front of Karma. He pours the wine into glasses, then sets out glasses of water, and fresh bread with a little receptacle containing olive oil. "*Buon Appetito.*" He steps back, then leaves.

The scent of the pepper, parmigiana, and the intense fresh aroma of the vongole permeates the air. My mouth waters. I reach for my fork, twirl the pasta and take a bite. The plump, briny taste of the clams fills my mouth. The fresh pasta crowns the experience. I break off a piece of the fresh bread, dip it in the white wine sauce, and pop it inside my mouth. So fucking good. A groan rumbles from my chest. I glance up to find her staring at me. She hasn't touched her food.

"Eat," I gesture to her spaghetti.

She twirls some of the strands around her fork, just like I had taught her, and brings it up to her mouth. She wraps her tongue around the tines and wipes it clean. My dick twitches and blood drains to my groin. I watch as she closes her eyes, chews, then a moan bleeds from her lips. She snaps her eyelids open, stares down at her plate, "Wow… That was…"

"Almost as good as an orgasm?"

"Yep," she nods, "I have to say, on this occasion, I agree."

She scoops up more of the pasta, and I do the same. We eat in relative silence until our plates are wiped clean.

"That was incredible." She licks her lips, as she reaches for her wine glass and drains it. Warmth suffuses my chest. The sight of her content and radiating satisfaction does strange things to me. I want to always take care of her, feed her good food, take her to my other favorite restaurants... Be with her as she explores the culinary delights of my heritage...

Hold on, what the hell am I thinking about here? What the hell is wrong with me that I am suddenly envisioning a future with her?

Paolo ambles over to stand between us. He surveys our now empty plates, places his palms over his wide girth, "*Dolce*, Capo?"

"Yes," she says eagerly, "I'd love to eat whatever dessert you have made today."

"No," I snap, "we're done here."

He turns to me, a frown on his face, "You are leaving without having my dessert?"

Yeah, I know. Sacrilege. Not something I'd do on any other day. But right now, I need to get this scrumptious piece of temptation away from me and back in the cage I have created for her. Before I do anything else I am going to regret.

I rise to my feet. "*Grazi*e Paolo." I add in a conciliatory tone, "Maybe next time."

He glances between us, then turns to Beauty, "*Buongiorno, Principessa*." He half bows to her, "Did you enjoy your meal?"

"It was..." she searches for the right word, "incredible. The best pasta I have ever eaten. And such a simple dish... I can't believe you put all those ingredients together and came up with something so amazing."

Paolo's features light up. "I am so pleased that you liked it. You come back anytime." He turns to me, "Make sure you bring her back with you, Capo."

I stare. Paolo actually smiling, and being civil, and to someone he's never met before? That has to be a first. Clearly, I am not the only one who is falling under her spell. I scowl up at him, but he doesn't seem to notice. "You take good care of her, Capo." He holds my gaze.

I nod and he seems satisfied.

A young man scurries up to him with a paper packet which he hands to Karma. "Dolce for the dolce." He grins down at her and my jaw falls open. What the hell? Paolo actually allowed a take-away of his precious dolce? Unheard off. He treats his food with too much respect to do that. In fact, I can't recall a single instance before this when he's actually packed his food in a take-away container. But he did it for her?

Che cazzo!

I jerk my chin, dismissing Paolo, who glances between us again. A sly look comes into his eyes, but he doesn't say anything else. He nods once more to both of us, then turning, he saunters off.

"Well, that was rude." Karma scowls, "You all but told him to fuck off, and after he was being so nice to us."

"It's Paolo," I raise a shoulder, "he can handle it."

"What set you off now?" She glowers up at me. "Seriously, your moods are worse than a woman on her period."

"That was an incredibly sexist remark to make," I chide her.

She laughs. "You should talk. The most misogynistic, most toxic, meanest man I have ever encountered."

I tip an imaginary hat down at her.

"Only you would take it as a compliment."

I smirk, "Don't tell me you don't find it attractive?"

"Certainly, not." She scowls.

"Don't lie to me, Beauty." I widen my stance, "There's something inside of you that relishes the fact that I don't hide behind meaningless niceties. That you see me and you know what you get. That I don't conceal exactly how perverted I am." I lower my chin to my chest as I hold her gaze, "That you know exactly how sordid my thoughts are, and that my actions are even more debauched... And something within you is relieved that my warped tastes give you the permission to unlock all the lustful emotions you have kept to yourself. That—" I place my hands on the chair on either side of her and bracket her in, "the corrupt truth inside of you feeds off of my deviance, indeed wants to embrace my every obscene act... If I let you. Only, I won't."

"You won't?" She blinks.

"I won't," I reiterate. "For you see, you are an asset, first and foremost. A gorgeous one, one with the kind of baseness that I hadn't expected...but an asset, nevertheless. One I am in no mood to break in, regardless of how tempting that may be. No, you, Beauty, are my property, and I intend to ensure that I leverage you for the purpose for which I kidnapped you in the first place. You're my captive, nothing more, and it you would do well to remember that."

"As if you'll ever let me forget," she mutters.

"Good, we understand each other then." I jerk my chin, "You should know that it's time for you to fulfill your role, Beauty."

24

Karma

My role… My stupid role, as it turns out, is to play the part of his bride. Why the hell does he have to marry me, though? If I ask him again, he'll pull that line of the fact that my father owes him, blah, blah, blah. But surely, that's not the only reason he's marrying me? There has to be something more, something else, some other reason why he's going through with his wedding. It can't be because he finds me attractive, right? Though he does… I mean, he must, considering how he can't seem to keep his hands off of me every time we are together. And yet, he also pulls back before he can complete what he started. Like, at the fabric shop. It's as if there's an internal war he's waging with himself every time he sees me. He wants me, but he hates himself for wanting me…

And well, the feeling's mutual. I hate myself for how my body responds to him. For how I understand those dark desires inside of him. Everything that I have tried to lock up inside of myself, from the time I had first been aware of the edginess inside of me, seems to respond to his presence. It's as if I can't keep my innermost feelings hidden around him anymore. His corruption attracts the filth I'd thought I had buried deep inside of myself; which I had never dared to acknowledge, to be fair, before him.

That coarseness inside of me which had spurred me on to stitch the kind of wedding dress in which I had always hoped to be married. I run my fingers down the black silk dress that I crafted in just forty-eight hours. It's amazing what you can accomplish when you cannot access the internet or talk to any of your friends and family.

On our way back from the shopping trip, Michael had informed me that we were getting married in three days. He had told me that he would have a dress delivered to me if I didn't promise to stitch my own dress. He had seemed uncertain I'd have the time to do it myself, but I had assured him I could work quickly. After all, I already knew the design I wanted. Then, I had reminded him of all the fabric he had purchased for me and that it would be wrong to let that go waste. I had asked him for a sewing machine, and to my surprise, he had told me it was already on its way.

How strange that he hadn't refused me. If anything, he seemed more than happy to indulge me on this. Like he had in taking me to the fabric shop. He knows I am a designer, but has he guessed just how much I need to create? It's a passion so deeply embedded in my cells it's as vital as breathing. As intrinsic as that filth that resides in the core of me. Something I, in fact, channeled when I designed and stitched and gave shape to fabric.

Creating a dress, somehow, eases that heaviness that resides within me. Almost as much as getting myself off does. Well, okay, not quite, but the sensation is similar. It's like I am channeling all of those forbidden desires inside of me and giving shape to something concrete, something I can wear and feel and touch, something that, on some level, feels as real as the shadows that crawl inside of me.

I haven't made it out of the room in the last few days, pausing only long enough to eat. That's how it is for me. Once the muse takes over, I can't stop for anything. All I have to do is get out of the way and let the creativity pour through me.

So, I'd measured and pinned and cut and sewn, and adjusted, and hand-stitched the final embellishments. I'd tried on the dress earlier and known it was almost there… Almost… Something was missing. A last adornment, a final trimming… Something to just push it over the edge.

My brain feels too tired, my fingers begin to cramp from the amount of time I had held the needle between them. Not to mention, the headache that has been building up behind my eyes. Shit. I need a break. I stare at my reflection in the mirror and my knees threaten to buckle. I yawn so loudly that my jaw cracks. The cool night air blowing in through the open window makes me shiver. I peel the dress off, carefully lay it over a chair. Then, clad only in my panties, I crawl into bed and under the covers to close my eyes.

The next thing I know, something infiltrates my consciousness. I come awake, but don't open my eyes. There's someone in the room; I am sure of it. Someone who's not moving, but standing over me, watching me. The hair on my forearms rises. My heart begins to thud.

Ever since Michael brought me here, I've been unable to shake the sensation of being watched. I assume he has eyes on the room, that he's watching me… Hell, of course, he is.

I'm not naive enough to think he'd, for one second, take his attention off of his asset. But this is different. This is not the eye of a camera on me. This is someone watching me, in real time.

My left leg cramps. I want to shake it out, but resist the effort. I draw in a breath, force myself to stay silent. A gust of wind blows in from the open window. I smell the brine of the sea, before it fades away, leaving behind that unmistakable masculine scent of testosterone, musky like leather with a hint of woodsmoke, that fills my senses. My belly trembles and my thighs clench. Moisture laces my core and I know then, it is him. Fucking Michael. He's in my room. What the hell is he doing, creeping around here in the middle of the night… Or is it early morning?

Fucking stalker. I regulate my breathing, force myself to stay still. Force my muscles to unwind, one by one, as he remains motionless. The minutes stretch. My pulse rate ratchets up, as it always does when he's anywhere close to me.

He stands there watching me, not moving, not saying anything. Gah, what the hell is he up to? His breathing seems to deepen. I sense him shift closer, the heat of his body sears my arm, and I know he is leaning over me. I sense the warmth of his breath on my cheek, then the hair on my forehead rises. I sense him sniff at my throat…

What the—? Is he smelling me? The heat of his body recedes, I sense him straighten, then the unmistakable sound of flesh hitting flesh. Wait, what? Is he getting off? Is he actually masturbating here in my bedroom? Watching me?! Why the hell couldn't he do so when he was watching me via the cameras? Why did he have to come in and watch me in real time?

I sense his breathing grow ragged, and my heart slams against my rib cage. His actions seem to intensify, the sound of him pleasuring himself growing more frantic. My belly flip-flops and moisture laces my core. I resist the urge to squeeze my thighs together. To slide my fingers inside my panties and shove them inside my aching core. Damn it, I should not be turned on, should not find this—whatever it is he is indulging in—so much of a turn on. A low groan rumbles from him, then I hear his breathing catch, sense him shudder as he climaxes. Heat sluices my veins and my toes curl. My core clenches on itself. I want to come so badly, as well. Why the hell do I find this so much of a turn on?

Then heat envelops me, the scent of him grows deeper as he leans over me. Something wet touches my lips, such a whisper of a touch that if I hadn't been awake and attuned to him, I wouldn't have caught it. I resist the urge to flick my tongue out and sample it. I sense him hesitate, then he touches his lips to mine, but before I can react, he's moving away. I hear his footsteps recede, then the door softly closes.

I crack my eyes open, but of course, the room is empty. I flick my tongue out and the taste of him—musky, dark and salty—trickles over my tongue. Did he...is that...did he dab his cum onto my lips and then kiss me to rub it into my mouth? Oh, my god!

I run my tongue across my lips, and the salty, dark taste of him fills my palate. I swallow down every last drop of his arousal, then slide my fingers under my panties, inside my wet channel and proceed to work them in and out of me. In and out, I increase the intensity of my movements, add a third finger, then a fourth. Shit, it's no substitute for the thickness I really want between my legs... Or the closeness of his skin on mine, his breath on my cheek, his lips on mine, his tongue playing with mine... As he grinds his heel into my swollen clit and makes me come. Heat suffuses my skin. My toes curl, my thighs clench, as I continue to pleasure myself with my fingers, chasing that elusive climax. No way, can I go back to sleep when I feel so empty inside and yearning, and... strangely, very aroused after that bizarre performance from Michael.

Had he sensed that I was awake? Did he know just how much of a need that would kindle inside of me? Had he realized just how horny it would make me to sense him come by just watching me? The thought of his long fingers around his fat dick as he grasped his thick length and got himself off sends me over the edge. The trembling overwhelms me and I climax around my fingers. I collapse into the bed, rub my cheek into the pillow and blow out a breath. Then, I bring my fingers to my mouth and suck on them. If I pretend hard enough, I can taste the dark flavor of his mixed with the sweeter tang of my cum. A heaviness grips my limbs and my eyes flutter shut.

When I open them next, light is streaming in through the window.

I sit up, glance around the room. Had I imagined it all? Did he really come into my room last night? Had he actually jerked off watching me sleep? Shit. I drag my fingers through my hair. Why the hell am I not more shocked, more grossed out by what happened?

I swing my legs over the side of the bed, when there's a knock on the door. Cassandra walks in.

"*Buongiorno*," she smiles at me, "it's such a beautiful day for a wedding."

I stare at her. Seriously, did she just say that? I brush past her and walk to the dressing table, sitting down. "I assume you are here to help me with my hair and make-up."

"I am here to help you get dressed for your wedding." She beams at me, her face all bright and happy, like this is actually some honest-to-god, real wedding, or some such shit.

"You and I both know, this wedding is a sham," I murmur, "so you can cut the act."

Some of the cheeriness fades from her face. Shit, now I feel bad for having burst her bubble, but c'mon. Why is she so happy? I don't feel cheerful or anything.

It feels weird, strange that I am going to get married to a man who is, not only my kidnapper, but is also, most likely, a criminal of the worst kind. Someone who may be achingly handsome, but is also so dangerous that you don't want to cross his path in the middle of the night. Or during the day, for that matter, considering that's when I met him.

I chuckle to myself and she frowns. I rise to my feet, head inside the bathroom, and take a quick shower, taking care not to wet my hair. When I walk out dressed in a bathrobe, she's standing by the dressing table.

I cross the room and seat myself at the stool in front of the mirror.

She comes over to stand behind me. "May I?" She gestures to my hair.

"Have at it," I murmur. "Only, I have to warn you that I have a certain look in mind."

"I am happy to help you."

"Good." I meet her gaze in the mirror, "I plan to wear my hair down so it flows around my shoulders."

"Keeping it simple." She nods. "That's good."

"After you dye it red."

"Red?" She blinks, "You want to dye your hair, red?"

"You heard me." I nod. "I need the color bright enough that it shows up against the black."

"Black?" She looks confused, then swallows. "May I suggest that—?"

"No." I slash my palm through the air. "I told you, I want to dress a certain way. And in fact, your Capo is on board with it."

"He is?"

"He bought me the fabric and did not refuse me when I told him that I wanted to wear my own creation."

"But.." she gulps, "it's your wedding."

"Is it, now?"

"It is, and the Capo would not appreciate it if you made a fool of him in front of everyone else."

"Well then, he should have picked someone else to be his bride."

"But he wants you." She frowns at my reflection in the mirror.

"Does he?" I snort, "He's only using me to further his plan, something he hasn't even revealed to me yet, by the way."

"Would it have made a difference if he had?"

I scowl, "I suppose not. Still, it might have helped me understand a little bit more about why he's gone to all this effort of bringing me here, and why he insists on going through with this charade."

"The Capo has his reasons."

"Yeah, yeah." I wave my hand in the air. "Whatever they may be." I raise a shoulder, "Not that it matters to me." I tie the bathrobe more securely around myself. "Now, are you going to help me or not?"

"How are you going to get hold of the hair dye?"

I can't stop my lips from curving. "I had Roberto deliver it to me, along with the materials for the wedding gown."

"Roberto?" She blinks, "You mean the man who runs the cloth shop in Palermo?"

"Fabric store," I correct her, "and yes, the same guy."

"The Capo won't be happy when he finds out about him."

"Then you'd better not tell him, huh?"

She firms her lips.

"Right, then," I rub my hands together, "are you going to help me or what?"

"Yes." She nods. "I'll help you." She reaches for the comb, runs it through my hair, "If you want to dye it, we'd better get started right away."

25

Michael

I stand facing forward, at the top of the aisle in the chapel. Aside from my residence, it's the only other building on this inland.

Next to me, Luca shuffles his feet.

Sebastian stands next to him, his dark blonde hair a contrast to the darker looks of the rest of my siblings bringing up the rear. Massimo, Christian and Xander are all clad in black tuxes and black ties…similar to mine. Hair combed back and gelled, and with their similar scowling visages, broad shoulders and towering height, the three resemble a American football team. Our parents certainly bequeathed their best features to them. Too bad, my father is a fucking *stronzo*.

Adrian brings up the rear of the group.

From the other side of the aisle, the Don folds his arms across his chest. I meet his gaze, hold it. I slide my fingers to my side, and my fingertips brush the knife in its sheath that I have tucked into my cross draw sheath; even as I play the fucking power game of who blinks first with my boss.

After a few seconds, he finally nods. "Good to see you finally settling down, son," he murmurs. His voice, low and deep, echoes in the empty church. Yeah... There are no other invitees. Just family. Which, sadly, includes the Don.

"I didn't invite you to hear your opinion on the matter, Father," I growl. "You are here simply because—"

"Of her." He nods. "I understand; you'll never forgive me for what happened to her."

"It's your fault she's dead." I scowl. "Because you couldn't control your temper," I say in a hard voice. Not one of us had been spared being beaten by him growing up. As the oldest, I had taken it on myself to shield my brothers and my mother whenever I could. More often than not, though, he took it out on her behind closed doors... And my mother never protested. It was her burden to bear, she'd say. She'd borne the almost daily beatings silently.

The day I had turned eighteen, she'd called me into the kitchen. Had fed me my favorite *lasagne al forno*. Then, she'd told me how I was now the man of the family and she made me promise to take care of my siblings, including my stepbrothers, when she was gone. A week after that, she had dropped dead of a heart attack. And with that, any gentleness in my life had gone out of the window...

Until I'd caught sight of *her*. Why is it that seeing Karma had awakened the kind of protectiveness I had felt for my mother? Not that there is anything similar between the two of them. My mother had been blonde, slim, so tiny that seeing her boys all grown up and standing here today, it's difficult to imagine them having come out of her.

The side door to the church opens, then an older woman steps inside the church. She wears her flowing mane of almost completely gray hair about her shoulders. She's barely five-feet four-inches, but her erect posture makes her seem larger than life. She's clad in a pale pink trouser suit and heels which, while fashionable, are also comfortable for walking. That's my grandmother, who, at almost eighty is still agile, independent and doesn't suffer nonsense from anyone. Not even my father.

I glance from her to him and my father raises his shoulder. "You know, I couldn't have stopped her from coming, even if I had tried."

I walk forward to meet her. "Nonna," I bend and kiss her cheek, "you needn't have come all the way here."

"My oldest grandson is getting married, and you thought I'd stay away?" She scowls up at me. "How could you, Michelangelo?" She scolds me, "I have been hoping for you to get married and have grandkids since you turned eighteen. You finally oblige me, twenty-one years later, and you think I wouldn't come to witness it with my own eyes?"

"I'd have brought my new bride to visit you," I murmur.

"And when would that have been?" She glowers at me, "If, indeed, you did get around to doing it. You think I don't how hard you work at building the business, that I am not aware of how ambitious you are, about succeeding," she jerks her head to the side, "him."

"I am still alive, Mother." The Don growls, "I'd thank you to remember that."

"What you haven't learned, Byron," she says without looking at him, "is that respect is earned, not demanded."

"Who cares, how you get it. Respect is respect, Mother." The Don folds his arms across his chest. "One way or the other, I'll get it, even from my own sons." He stares at me meaningfully.

I glare back at him. What a prick. How is it possible that he is my father? More to the point, how could he have come from someone as gracious and as caring as my Nonna?

She had been the one steady influence all through the turmoil of our growing years. And after our mother's passing, she had insisted on being a part of our lives. And yet, not even that had stopped him from beating us up. If anything, after mother's passing, his predilection to hit us had escalated. By then, I'd been strong enough to stop him. I'd managed to hold him back from hitting my younger brothers, though not even I could stop him fully.

When I had finally confessed to Nonna, she had been horrified. She had immediately moved us in with her...and confessed that she'd suspected but had no idea it had been so bad. I hadn't been sure if I should forgive her, but she had intervened, and insisted that my father get help for his issues. Something my father had grudgingly agreed to do. I owed that much to her—that my siblings had been spared the torture of being around him. She had, at least, managed to salvage some of their growing up years.

Me, on the other hand... The damage had been done. Perhaps it's the reason I've turned out so twisted, in my own way. Perhaps blood is thicker than water... Perhaps his violent tendencies were imprinted on me more than I realized. It is the only reason I can think of to explain my twisted needs when it comes to sex. Something I'd hope to keep in check with Karma, except every time I see her, my base instincts seem to emerge. Something inside of me insists that I claim her, that I show her what it means to be possessed by that darkness inside of me. My cock instantly thickens. Shit. That's the last thing I need—sporting a hard-on while I am surrounded by family, and in church.

"Michelangelo," Nonna's voice intrudes in my thoughts. "I hope you'll forgive me," she says in a tone low enough that only I can hear.

I tip down my chin, gaze into her midnight-blue eyes, so like mine.

"If I had known, if I'd had even an inkling of how far he'd go with her, I would have stepped in," she adds.

I set my jaw.

"So you have told me before, Nonna," I say stiffly. "I understand you want to find a way of alleviating the guilt you are carrying inside, but you know, I can't forgive you."

She blanches.

"You had a ringside view of the marriage; you knew about your son's temper; you must have known that she was being abused; you must have guessed, when we turned up with bruises, that he was hitting us. Yet you never asked any questions. Not once."

A stricken look comes into her eyes before she wipes all emotion from her face. "I guess, much as I think I am moving with the times, perhaps in this, I am more old-fashioned than I realized." She swallows, "It was their marriage and I didn't want to interfere..." She glances away, then back at me, "Something I will never forgive myself for, Mika." Her voice softens, "But perhaps your father was preparing you for your future. Look how you turned out after all that—"

"Nonna," I say through gritted teeth, "is that what you think? That his abuse of me and my brothers was a way of building character? That just because his father beat him, he should also be allowed to hit us? Do you really think that this is the natural progression of things?"

She looks away

Silence stretches for a beat, then another.

"I.." she swallows, "I don't condone what he did." She looks in my eyes and says, "But you have to admit, it played a part in making you so driven to succeed."

I step back from her, and her hand falls away.

"Mika," she murmurs, "I was brought up never to question the man of the house. First, my husband, then," she glances at the Don, "my son." She folds her fingers together in front of herself, and I notice that they are trembling.

Nonna always comes across as so strong, I forget sometimes, what she has been through. My grandfather had not only abused my father, but also her. He had beaten her and she had borne it all without a complaint and emerged stronger. She had been through it first-hand— all the more reason that she could have done something to stop the abuse of my mother and us at the hands of our father. But she hadn't... And here we are. An emotionally broken, facsimile of a family, trying to project a strong, unified front, lest our rivals find out just how tenuous the bond between us really is.

"Perhaps, if I had been less traditional, things would have been different. I have been trying to change, but it's not easy." She swallows, "I know I have my faults, but you have to believe me when I say that I did what I thought was best in the situation."

"The scars he left on my skin may have healed, but there are others…more emotional ones that changed me in ways you can't even recognize."

"Mika—" Her chin wobbles, "Please, don't block me out of your life."

"I have never done so, Nonna, you know that." I draw myself up to my full height. "But you will also never have my complete trust, either." I hold my grandmother's gaze. She tips up her chin, and I recognize the stubborn set to her features. That iron resolve is something I share with her.

Once I want something, I go after it—like her. From the moment I saw her, I knew that she would turn my life upside down. All the more reason to get through this ceremony, then get on with the plan I have in place to consolidate my position with the Seven.

"I understand." Nonna, nods once, then steps back. She turns and walks slowly across the stone floor to the first pew. She sits down, and my father takes his place next to her.

The main church doors open just then.

I turn, watch her framed in the doorway.

"What the—" Luca exclaims next to me, "what the hell is she wearing?"

26

Karma

I stay there, poised at the threshold of the church. At the far end of the aisle, he turns to glance at me, then freezes. Even across the distance, there's no mistaking the tension that radiates off every inch of his powerful body.

Next to him, a man who is, clearly, his brother, and Seb, as well as several other men, who also look like brothers—I wonder how many he has—turn toward me, and a collective ripple of shock seems to run through them. I take a step forward, then another.

The cool interior of the church wraps around me like a shroud. I shiver, tighten my grasp around the bouquet of white zagara flowers from the orange trees, that Cassandra had managed to rustle up for me this morning.

My large train drags behind me, the weight of it tugging at my shoulders so it feels like I am physically dragging along at least three times my body weight as I place one foot in front of the other. My footsteps echo through the completely silent church. It seems I have struck my audience dumb. A giggle bubbles up and I swallow it back. It won't do to get hysterical. Not now, not after I've come this far.

With Cassandra's help, I'd managed to don my wedding gown… And when I had seen myself in the mirror… The contrast of my red hair with the black silk and lace and my pale creamy skin, all set off with the white roses…ah! Let's just say, I knew I had outdone myself.

I begin to move forward, when the church door snicks shut behind me. I resist the urge to turn, shove open the door and tear out of there.

Firstly, I am not going to drown myself… The last time really had been an accident, but either way, I am not going to risk running over the edge of a cliff again. Besides if I did that, it would show him that I am afraid. That I had lost my nerve. And no way, can I allow that.

My heart begins to race and my pulse pounds at my temples. A bead of sweat trickles down my back and another shiver grips me. Shit, I will not give in to my fear. Not now. I set my jaw, square my shoulders, then continue to walk down the aisle.

With every step, the rustle of my gown, the swish of my skirt against my skin, the susurration of the train against the stone floor… All of the sounds seem to grow louder, more amplified.

There's no music. Why the hell isn't there any music? Don't weddings typically play the wedding march, or whatever shit tune that accompanies a bride walking up the aisle to meet her end? I mean, her husband-to-be.

Maybe Sicilians do it differently? Bloody hell, maybe I should have specified that he play music for the ceremony. A chuckle bubbles up and I swallow it down. As if he would listen to anything I have to say, huh?

My blood begins to thud in my ears. My throat goes dry. All of their gazes are fixed on me, on my black wedding gown, that I had fashioned as an amalgamation of the most grotesque designs that I had come across. The sleeves are made of lace and encase my arms, so the cream of my skin is visible through the gaps. The actual gown is cut deep at the bosom, so the curves of my breasts are on display, almost until the nipples. The waist cinches in, before flowing into a full princess skirt, except it's ripped and hung with black pearls and hooks which jingle as I walk. My feet are clad in red velvet shoes, the only accessory that I had chosen from the clothes I had tried in the boutique the other day.

My nails are painted red, as are my lips, the color set off by the red of my hair. The overall effect, I know, is over-the-top, almost steampunkish in presentation. I resemble a twisted goth princess… Exactly what I am inside. In many ways, this dress is also the truest I have been to myself. A no-holds-barred representation of the rebel that I truly am.

It's the culmination of my emotions, my feelings, all the designs I had studied over the past many years… From the time I had realized that being a fashion designer was my calling. I have invested all of it into this dress. This is me. This is what I am. Outrageous, audacious, scandalous, and borderline offensive. This is what he gets for daring to seize me from my life and try to turn me into a pawn in his game.

He thinks I am simply going to turn the other cheek and allow him to walk over me? Well, he's wrong. This is me — unvarnished, unhidden, uncensored. This is me being truthful to myself, to what I truly am. A feisty girl on the cusp of womanhood, on the verge of making the world her bitch, who will never give in to anyone. Certainly not, to my captor, who thought he could make me pay for the sins of a parent I'd been sure was dead until not too long ago.

I square my shoulders, tip my chin up, then stride up the aisle. Closer, closer to the devil waiting at the end of my journey. With every step I take, I sense the tension that vibrates off of him. The way his shoulders bunch, how he widens his stance, how he tilts his head, stalking me as I draw nearer. His jaw flexes, a vein drums at his temple, yet his gaze is clear. Brooding, deep enough to lose myself in again.

I grab hold of that nothingness inside of him which seems to mirror the worry coiling in the pit of my stomach. Somehow, that lack of feeling in his eyes grounds me. What's the worst that he can do, eh? Kill me? I have already resigned myself to the fact that I may not get out of here alive. And somehow, that gives me the courage to close the distance between us. To pause in front of him. Even in my six-inch heels, I barely come up to his shoulder.

I tilt my head back, all the way back, making sure not to sever the connection between us. He drags his gaze down my face, to my mouth, to my breasts, down to where my skirt grazes the floor. When he lifts his chin and claps his gaze back on mine, his eyes are alight with an emotion I can't place. Anger? Hate? A combination of the two, maybe? Then his lips curl and I know it's neither. He's amused with me. Asshole, is laughing at me? I grit my teeth and his grin widens. He holds out his hand.

I stare at his proffered palm, then ignoring it, I step up to stand next to him.

I hear a slight gasp… Probably from the older woman I had spotted seated in the pew. Who is she? His grandmother? Like I care.

I stare straight ahead at the priest who begins to speak. His mouth moves, I am sure he is saying something, but I can't hear him. The blood thuds in my ears; my heart beats so loudly in my chest that I am sure it's going to break through my rib cage. Spots of back flicker at the corners of my eyes, and I must sway, for a grip on my arm brings me back into my body. I blink, become aware that the priest is staring at me.

I swallow and my throat is so dry that I can't form the words that tremble at the tip of my tongue.

The priest looks at me with a resigned air. He seems to be waiting for me to say something. What? What the hell am I supposed to say?

"Ask her again." Michael growls.

The priest draws in a breath, "Do you Karma West take Michael Byron Domenico Sovrano to be your husband, and promise to be faithful to him always, in joy and in pain, in health and in sickness, and to love him and honor him and obey him every day for the rest of your life?"

His voice slices through the nothingness in my head. Anger thrums through my veins. Be faithful to him? Obey him? Love him? Are you freakin' kidding me?

I firm my lips as I stare back at him.

The priest glances from me to Michael who turns to me. He steps in front of me, then lowers his knees and thrusts his face into mine. "Answer the question," he growls.

"Fuck you," I say in a low voice, and his features brighten. His eyes gleam. Fuck, how sick is this man that when I insult him in front of everyone, he positively seems to relish it?

He places his big palms on my cheeks, and he squeezes down so my lips purse. He increases the pressure until a tear drop leaks from the corner of my eyes. "Say it," he snaps. "Tell me what I want to hear, Beauty."

Anger sluices a path through my veins. My vision tunnels and all my senses seem to pop. You want it, asshole? I am going to give you the answer you are looking for. "Yes," I force out the word. "Yes, I will."

"Good."

He straightens, steps back to stand next to me.

"Uh, do we have rings?" The priest blinks rapidly.

Michael turns to me. "Her bouquet." He frowns. "Someone take the blasted thing from her."

Sebastian walks over, holds out his hand. When I don't move, he whispers in a soft voice, "Please, *principessa,* hand it over."

I glare up into his blue eyes. So similar to the alphahole standing next to me, yet so much warmer.

"*Principessa*," he urges me and I extend the bouquet. He takes it, steps aside.

Michael grips my shoulder, applies enough pressure so I turn to face him. He slips a ring from his pocket and slides it over my left hand. A plain gold band, with a black diamond set in the center, surrounded by red sapphires. Huh. It fits… Of course, it does…

But the colors of the diamonds… They match my dress. How the hell had he guessed what colors I was going to wear? Of course, he may have seen me stitch the black dress on the closed-circuit cameras, but I'd only dyed my hair red this morning. How strange.

I glance up, in time to intercept an expression of… Possessiveness? Lust? A strange look filled with heat that he wipes off of his face instantly. I blink, captured by what I'd seen there for a second. Naked want… A yearning that struck me to my core. My pussy clenches and my fingers tremble as the priest asks, "What about the ring for the bridegroom?"

"Not for this bridegroom," Michael retorts.

I jerk my chin up, hold his once-more vacant gaze.

The priest clears his throat, "This...this is...ah...highly irregular, Capo."

No kidding. Like, of all the things that have happened so far, this particular aspect is the most shocking. A chuckle bubbles up and I stifle it.

Of course, the alphahole doesn't want to be constrained by a ring. While me... The bride must wear his mark of ownership at all times. Typical.

"Ah," the priest shuffles his feet, "in that case...you may now kiss the bride."

Michael steps forward. He notches a finger under my chin, angles it up as he lowers his face to mine. Closer, closer, the scent of him envelops me and a cloud of heat spools off of his body and crashes into me. I gasp, draw in a breath and the scent of him seems to infiltrate every cell in my body. His lips brush mine once. It's so soft, so unexpected, that I part my lips and he sweeps his tongue inside. He swipes his tongue across the seam of my lips, across my teeth, tangles with mine. His mouth closes over mine and he slurps from me like he's thirsty and I am his only sustenance. A moan bleeds from me and an answering groan rumbles up his chest. I step into him so my breasts are crushed into his chest. His entire body hardens, then a trembling grips him. He wraps his arm around my waist haul me to him as I slide my hand around his waist.

My fingers brush the dagger he wears at his waistband. I play with the sheath, then close my fingers around the handle of the knife. I draw it out as he winds his arm around my shoulder, the other slipping down over the curve of my hip. "Beauty," he breathes against my lips, "you're killing me—" He gasps. His eyelids snap open, his mouth parted slightly. He stares into my gaze. "You…you…" he growls, "you—"

I nod, "I stabbed you, and I am going to do it again." I pull back and he releases me. I raise the dagger, and this time, bring it down squarely in the middle of his chest.

27

Michael

I glance down at the dagger protruding from my chest, then up at her. The train of her black dress streams behind her. Her hair flows about her shoulders. She raises the dagger and the blood—my blood drips from her fingers. Her green eyes blaze at me, the look in them triumphant and stricken, at the same time. I hold her gaze, and in the depths of her eyes, I see myself reflected. I reach for her and she holds out her hand—the one without the dagger. Our fingers touch, cling together. Her lips part and my gaze drops to her mouth. The redness of her lipstick matches the scarlet that runs down the blade of the dagger.

"Beauty," I whisper, "what have you done?"

"I…" she swallows, "I didn't have a choice… I didn't mean to—" Her shoulders shudder. "I—"

Her beautiful features sway in front of my eyes. Black spots flicker at the sides of my vision. My knees seem to give way from under me.

I hear her scream and her fingers tighten around mine. The dagger slips from her fingers and clatters to the ground. The world tilts. Arms grab me from behind, and I shake them off. I steady myself, glance past her to find my brothers crowding in around us.

Sebastian reaches for her and I growl, "Don't fucking touch her."

I glance over their shocked faces until my gaze connects with Luca's. I glare at him, then lower my gaze to her face, then back to him. He nods. And a breath I hadn't been aware I was holding leaves me. I take in her pale features, her green eyes pooling with tears that run down her cheeks. I raise my palm, brush away the moisture on her delicate features.

"Shh," I bare my teeth at her, "you didn't think that I would die that easily did you?"

I tear at the front of the shirt and my buttons bounce to the floor. I glance down at the bleeding cut, then back at her. "You barely broke the skin," I drawl. "Seems I am going to not only discipline you but also instruct you on how to use weapons."

"Fuck you." Her chin wobbles, "I managed to hurt you. In my books, that's a win."

"You barely wounded me. You showed your cards too soon, Beauty."

Her breath heaves.

"I am afraid I am going to enjoy teaching you your place."

She stiffens. "You can go to hell," she snaps.

"Only if you'll come with me. Now that we are husband and wife, and all that."

"Fuck your sham of a marriage."

"It was very real, *mia cara*," I smile at her broadly, "don't forget you still wear my ring."

She raises her left hand then begins to struggle with the ring on her finger. "Fuck, fuck, fuck," she snarls, "it won't come off."

"Of course, not." I smirk, "You didn't think I was going to leave anything to chance, did you?" I drum my fingers on my thigh, in part to distract from the pain in my chest. "It's half a size smaller, easy to push onto the finger, much more difficult to get off."

She stills, then raises her gaze to mine. "Bastard," she spits out, "how dare you?"

Behind me, the priest winces.

"Now you've shocked the Father."

Her cheeks tinge red. "The fuck I care?"

I click my tongue. "You're spirited, I give you that." I smirk, "I'll enjoy teaching you your place."

"Argh!" She makes a sound deep in her throat that seems to tug on my nerve-endings. The blood drains to my groin.

Then, Luca wraps his arm around her shoulders and urges her away from me. Her fingers drag against mine, as she pulls away. A shiver runs down my spine.

Nonna steps in front of her. I see her hand move, then the thud of a slap echoes around the church as her palm connects with Beauty's face.

"Stop," I call out. "She's my wife, mine to punish as I see fit."

Nonna's shoulders rise and fall. She turns, tips up her chin at me. Her features are flushed. She seems to compose herself, then nods at me, "See that you do." My grandmother pivots and walks out the way she came, through the side entrance of the church where, no doubt, her bodyguards are waiting for her.

"Take her to the basement." I jerk my chin at Luca.

Around me, my brothers stiffen, but none of them say anything. They wouldn't. They know better than to question my authority in front of the Don.

Beauty stares at me over her shoulder as Luca guides her away, Adrian in tow.

I don't take my attention off of her, until she's out of sight, out of the main door. My chest twinges, but I dismiss it. I glance down to find the front of my shirt sodden with blood.

I shrug off my jacket, then I tear off my shirt and press it into the wound.

"You need stitches." Christian murmurs, "I am calling for the doctor."

I am tempted to say I don't need to see a doctor, but I know better than taking foolish risks. I nod, as my father prowls over to me. "I hope you are not going to let this go unpunished." He looks me up and down, "She spilled the blood of a Capo; you know what that means."

I stiffen, "She's my wife. I decide how I am going to make her pay for what she did."

He chuckles, "No doubt, you can turn the consummation of the marriage into something that she will never forget."

I whip my chin up, glare at him. "Mind how you speak about her," I say through gritted teeth. "She's still mine."

"Not questioning that, son," he says in a soothing voice. "Just making sure you realize that this cannot be overlooked. When word of what happened gets out..." He shakes his head, "It will seriously undermine your position as being in the running as successor of the Don."

"And who will let news of this leak out?"

My father glances at the priest. I pull out the gun from the back of my waistband and shoot him in the forehead. The man collapses to the floor.

I turn to the Don, "That only leaves you as the weak point in this entire proceeding."

"You threatening me, son?" he asks in a mild tone. "Not even you would be foolish enough to do that."

"It was merely an observation." I tilt my head.

"As long as that's all it was." He bares his lips in the semblance of a smile, which is almost as sharklike as mine. Fuck! Apparently there is more of him in me than I'd like.

He glances around at the faces of my brothers, "I'll see the lot of you at our next meeting then."

Turning, he begins to walk away, then stops, "By the way, Michelangelo." He glances at me over his shoulder, "Congratulations."

He leaves by the side entrance. The door slams shut, the sound echoing around the space.

"Fucking fuck," I growl as I pull the shirt away from my chest. I glance down to where the blood flow seems to have lessened, then ball up my shirt and throw it on the floor. "What a fucking mess."

"Was that necessary?" Xander glances sideways at the priest's body, "Did you have to kill a man of god."

"I didn't have a choice."

"The man would have taken what happened here to the grave with him," he protests.

"And I made sure he did."

Xander grimaces, "And her... Did you have to send her to the basement?"

"It's where anyone who commits a crime against any of the *famiglia* is sent." I tilt my head.

"She's part of the *famiglia* now," Xander argues.

"She needs to prove herself first." Christian jerks his chin in my direction, "I agree with *fratellone,* here."

"You were very lucky," Massimo rumbles. "She missed your heart.

"She wasn't aiming for it," I retort.

Silence descends as the guys glance at me.

"You sure of that?" Sebastian drawls, "because from where I was standing, she sure seemed to be aiming to kill."

"To injure, at the very least," I agree, "but did she want to kill me?" I raise a shoulder, "I am not so sure."

"So why send her to the basement?" Christian frowns.

"Why not?"

"Because she's your wife?" Xander offers.

"And she stabbed me."

"As you said, she wasn't aiming for your heart," he retorts. "In fact, the wound isn't that deep; you've lost blood but you'll recover."

"She attacked me in front of the Don," I say steadily. "I don't need him seeing me as weak, no matter that it was my own wife who took a dagger to me."

"Bullshit." Xander scowls, "Since when do you let father steer your actions?" He prowls over to me, "No Mika, you are up to something else here."

I look him and down, "Are you going to tell me how I am supposed to treat my wife?"

Xander hesitates, "I don't presume to tell you anything, *fratellone*." He murmurs, "I am merely pointing out that she is entitled to basic human rights."

"Is she though, after what she did?" I hold his gaze steadily and he glances away.

"I know you are angry, and I am not condoning what she did," he murmurs. "Still she is a woman, and she is the one you love…"

"Love?" I chuckle aloud, "You really think I am in love with her?"

"Why else would you marry her?"

I open my mouth to protest and Xander holds up his hand. "The way you look at her, Mika," his gaze softens, "it's the glance of a man obsessed."

"Obsessed with ensuring that I get the respect that is due to me from my own wife." I bare my teeth, "And that is the last I will entertain on this issue."

Xander hesitates, and Christian walks over to him. He claps a hand on Xander's shoulder, "Let the Capo handle this the way he thinks best."

Xander scowls at him, "You are a harsh man, but you are not heartless, Mika."

I tilt my head. "Not looking for a character reference." I glance around the assembled faces. "And that's the last I will entertain in this regard, do I make myself clear?"

The rest of them keep silent.

"Do I?"

They nod. "Yes, *fratel*—Capo," Sebastian replies.

"Yes, Capo." Christian adds.

"You got it, Capo." Massimo rumbles.

Xander draws in a breath. I hold his gaze and he nods. "As you wish," he says stiffly.

"Good." I walk over to where she had dropped the knife, then scoop it up. I wipe it on my shirt then slide it back into the sheath at my waist. "When does the doctor get here?" I glance at Christian.

"I sent the chopper for her; she won't be long."

"Good." I turn to Sebastian, "Take care of the body."

An hour and a half later, I've been stitched up by the doctor who had departed after administering an antibiotic shot. I change into a fresh pair of slacks and a shirt, then head down the stairs of my mansion. As I descend, it gets cooler. When I hit the lower ground level, it's at least ten degrees cooler than what I had left behind. That's the architecture of these old homes for you. The basements were always cool enough so you could use the space as a natural refrigerator to store food… Or temporarily keep dead bodies… As I have done in the past.

I head down the corridor to the door at the far end. I grab the handle, twist it and shove the door open. Step inside the gloom that's illuminated by the light streaming in from the lone window near the ceiling.

On the far side, there is a single bed and on it, Beauty is curled up. Her black dress slashes across the white of the mattress. The train flows behind her and trails on the floor. Her red hair flows about her shoulders and over the side of the bed. Her body is curved into the fetal position. Her slender fingers pillow her cheek.

I let the door slam shut behind me. The sound echoes through the cell and she visibly jolts. Her eyelids snap open. She spots me but doesn't move. I prowl over to stand over her. She tips her chin up, meets my gaze.

"What do you want?" she snarls, and a chuckle boils up. This woman… She, seriously, has some gumption. After stabbing me in the chest, at our wedding, she acts as if she's the injured party. Fuck, if that isn't hot. I swallow down my mirth, school all emotion from my face.

"On your knees."

28

Karma

"What the hell does that mean?" I scowl up at the man who towers over me. Michael's a tall guy, at least six-feet four-inches in height, but in this light, and with the angle at which he is poised over me, he looks positively massive. His shoulders block out my line of sight, his dark eyes seem to merge with the blackness around him. My heart beat ratchets up. Shit, this is not good. I am in a cell, on my own, with the man—okay, technically, with my husband—who is not in the least bit happy with me. I glance around the cell and he shakes his head.

"Don't even think about it." His lips curl, "If by some miracle, you get out of the cell, the only way out is up and my brothers are standing guard as we speak."

"So the entire family is on this?" I swallow. "Why am I not surprised? After all, torturing helpless women must be your family's past time."

"Hmm." He drums his fingers on his massive chest, then winces.

My stomach tightens. So, I had managed to wound him, after all, though you can't see it, with how he's standing with his spine straight, and dressed in clean clothes. You wouldn't guess I had had my dagger—okay, his dagger —buried in his chest less than a few hours ago. Again, that may be a gross exaggeration, considering he is nowhere near death's door. Bastard looks like he's ready for an evening out in those tailored pants and shirt.

He lowers his arm to his side, then jerks his chin. "You heard me," he drawls, "Get on your knees, Beauty."

"And if I refuse?"

"I'll make you," he props his massive hands on his lean waist, "and trust me, you don't want that to happen."

I glower back at him.

"Do it, Beauty." He lowers his tone to a hush, "Now."

His voice slices through the thoughts in my head. Only when the room rights do I realize that I am sitting up on the bed. Without taking my gaze off of his, I swing my legs up on the bed, then behind me as I push up to kneeling position.

"Happy?" I snap.

He shakes my head, "You know that's not what I meant." He stares down at the floor then back at me.

"What, you expect me to read your mind?" I huff.

"Don't try my patience," he murmurs.

"Or what?"

"Or." He moves so quickly, I blink. The next second, he's grabbed me by the back of my neck and hauled me up to my feet, on the bed. My heels, which I still hadn't removed, dig into the mattress and I totter. With his other hand, he grabs me at the apex of my thighs. His big palm closes around my pussy and he lifts me down to the floor

I totter on my heels and he holds me there for a few seconds until I've regained my balance. Then he releases his hold on me, only to clamp a heavy hand on my shoulder. He applies enough pressure that I have to sink down on my knees. Good thing the dress is so thick that it cushions them from the dirty floor. My poor dress, it's never going to recover from this assault… First, by the droplets of his blood which had splashed onto the bodice, and now, from the filth on the floor. Ugh! And this is so not the time to be thinking about the state of my dress. Not that I intend to wear this one again. No, it's served its purpose and it is expendable. Like me.

Stop it, stop it. Don't give up even before you've started fighting. After all you've only begun this… Whatever it is, for which he brought you down here. If he had thought that he would intimidate me... He is succeeding.

My heart slams into my ribcage as I kneel there, while he looms over me like some stupid medieval knight... Only, he's not a knight. He is a devil, a monster, a man with no remorse, no emotions, no feelings. A brute who takes what he wants, when he wants, and there is no reasoning with him.

I'd known all this when I had reached for his dagger. Call it impulsive; call it a sense of inevitability which had gripped me. When I'd realized that he was tracking my sister and her new husband; that he wouldn't hesitate to hurt them; that nothing I said or did would, ultimately, help me in any way; that once I was married to him, he'd take full advantage of me... And then kill me...

I'd known then, that this is a fight to the finish. My life is already in danger. Likely, I am never walking away from this. No way, am I also going to endanger Summer's life. No, I had to do something about it. I had seen my opportunity and seized it. I hadn't even realized what I intended to do; not until my fingers had brushed the handle of the dagger. I had pulled it out, and I had not hesitated. Had I meant to kill him? Honestly, I don't know. Had I, for one second, thought that I would actually succeed in hurting him? I'd hoped so.

At least, I had managed to cause him some pain... Had put a halt to the sham of the proceedings. My fingers brush the palm on my left ring finger. Yeah, except for the stupid wedding ring that refuses to come off, which insists the wedding ceremony was, unfortunately, very real. I swallow, tip up my chin at him. Damn, if I am going to let him break my spirit... At least, not that easily. "What are you going to do?" I demand.

"That's what I am trying to figure out." He stares down at me, an expression of something—curiosity, a certain interest even in his glance as if he's trying to figure me out. Shit, that's the last thing I want, to be seen as a challenge by him.

And yet.. I can't stand down, I can't. Something inside of me... That same darkness that has crawled at the edges of my consciousness all this while, insists that I stand up to him. That I confront him, defy him, make him realize that he can't just bend me to his will that easily.

I pretend to yawn, then pat my fingers to my lips. "Well whatever it is, you'd best get on with it." I look him up and down, "My knees are already beginning to ache."

"It's not only your knees which will be hurting by the time I'm through with you." His lips curl, "Unless that's your plan, hmm?" He circles around me and I sense him sizing me up... For what? What could he possibly have in mind that could be worse than anything he's done to me so far?

"Maybe you think that if you goad me enough, I'll lose my control, that I'll do something to slip up, something that you can take advantage of and try to escape, hmm?"

"You've already told me your family is guarding the entrance to the dungeon —"

"Basement," he corrects me.

"Funny, from where I am, it resembles a torture chamber."

He laughs, "You think this is a torture chamber?" His grin widens, "Wonder what you'll think when I take you into the real torture room."

"Oh," I swallow, "you're joking right?"

He arches an eyebrow. "Have I ever joked with you?"

Of course, he hasn't. The alphahole doesn't have a single funny bone in his entire body. Hell, even if I were to tickle him, he'd probably just respond with that glowering expression, before telling me that I bore him.

My pulse begins to race and sweat laces my palms. Shit, shit, shit. Had I actually thought that this man was going to let go of me that easily? Wait, actually, I hadn't thought much at all. But the fact that he has an honest-to-god torture chamber down here, one that he plans to use on me... Shit, I am not ready for that. Seriously, not.

"So what..." my voice cracks and I clear my throat, "what are you going to do next?"

"It's more about what you are going to do next, Beauty."

How I hate that nickname. I am going to find a way to get back at him for this. For making me feel so helpless, like I am completely at his mercy, which I am... But hell, does he have to rub it in this way? Of course, he holds the power here, doesn't mean he has to go all villainous on me and threaten me without saying anything. Argh!

I fold my fingers in front to stop them from trembling, then force myself to meet his gaze. *Don't say it, don't say it.* But there's no other way out. Best I pretend to play along... At least, for the time being. At least, until I have figured out a plan of action.

I set my jaw, "What...what do you want me to do?"

His pauses, taps a finger against his chin, then nods, "Strip."

"Excuse me?"

"You heard me. Take off your wedding dress, wife."

I grit my teeth, hating the fact that I can't tell him off for calling me that. Loathing the fact that he is, on this account, at least accurate. I am his wife…technically.

"Don't make me wait," he says in a casual voice, "and don't even think of disobeying me. You know I can strip you of this dress very easily, I am giving you a choice here."

"Oh, yeah?" I scoff, "What's that?"

"You can strip your dress on your own steam and then I can fuck you, or *I* can strip off your dress and then..." He bares his teeth, "I can fuck you."

29

Michael

A trembling grips her. A shudder runs down her spine. She squares her shoulders, then shoves her hair back from her face, with trembling fingers. Hmm, my Beauty is all sass, but deep down, she's scared. Good. She should be. Right now, I am not sure, exactly, what I am going to do to her, but anticipation is half the enjoyment, after all. Besides, I love it when I surprise myself... I relish it even more when my opponent surprises me. And make no mistake, Beauty here, is the deadliest enemy I have ever faced. I'd underestimated her once and she'd drawn my dagger on me... I am not gonna let her pull a fast one on me again.

I snap my fingers, "Don't keep me waiting." I fold my arms across my chest, stare down my nose at her.

She sets her jaw, then draws in a breath. Her chest rises and falls and the peaks of her breasts threaten to overflow the low neck of her gown. I widen my stance, watch as she tips her chin up.

"You'll have to help me." She scowls at me.

"What do you mean?"

"My zipper," she snaps. "I can't reach it; you'll have to help me with it."

Che cazzo! "Are you serious? You want me to help you with the zipper?"

"You want me out of this dress?" She arches an eyebrow, "Then you'll have to help me."

"If this is a joke of some kind…"

"It's not a joke, you asshole," she snaps. "I had help putting it on, and now I need help taking it off." Her cheeks heat. She glances away, then up at me. "Trust me, I don't feel like asking for your help on anything either, but it's not like I have a choice."

Perhaps it's the ring of truth I hear in her tone, or the fact that, clearly, she is uncomfortable asking me to help… Or the very feminine blush on her cheeks that, somehow, touches a place deep inside of me.

Either way, I find myself moving around to sink down behind her, and onto the train of her dress that is piled around her. She pulls her hair over one shoulder as I reach for the zipper and begin to lower it. The rasp seems to echo around the empty space. The fabric parts, revealing the ivory of her skin. Goosebumps rise as the cool air touches her back. I lower the zipper all the way down to the small of her back.

The dress slides down one side, revealing the curve of her shoulder. I take in the graceful arch, the tendrils of hair that cling to the column of her neck, the ridges of her spine and ribcage under the ivory of her skin. Something hot stabs at my chest. My heart stutters. My groin hardens. I lean in, touch my lips to the exposed shoulder and she shivers. I press tiny kisses up the curve of her shoulder, push aside the ringlets on the nape of her neck and kiss the soft skin there. A moan bleeds from her and she lowers her chin, giving me further access. I push aside the dress, down her other shoulder. It slides down, then stops when it catches over her breast. I shove the dress and it falls to the crook of her elbows. I slide one hand around to cup her breast, and she shudders. I bring my forefinger and thumb to her nipple and squeeze. A soft cry falls from her lips and I am instantly hard. I slip my other hand around to squeeze her other breast. I massage them, pinch the nipples and she leans back into me.

"Michael," she pants, "oh, my god, Michael."

I continue to knead her breasts, pausing only to pinch her nipples, again and again. Her entire body trembles. She arches her spine, throws her head back and into my chest as she stares up at me from under heavy eyelids.

"Michael, please, please…" she cries, "please, Michael."

I release one breast, slide my hand down her belly to cup her pussy. "Part your legs," I command, and she instantly widens her stance. I pinch her clit ring and she shudders.

"Oh, fuck." She writhes in my arms, "Oh, my fucking god."

"Your mouth, Beauty," I murmur. "Your dirty mouth is a fucking turn on, you know that?"

I thrust two fingers inside her soaking channel and her pussy instantly clamps down on the intrusion. I push my fingers in and out of her, even as I continue to massage her breast. I pinch down on the nipple again and twist, and her entire body bucks. "Your breasts are so fucking sensitive." I lean into her as I slide a third finger inside of her. I continue to fuck her with my fingers as I twist her nipple. She screams and her shoulders shake.

She thrusts up her chin, opens her mouth. "Kiss me," she demands. "Fucking kiss me, already."

"*Gesù Cristo*," I swear, "you're something else, you know that?" I lower my face, then close my mouth over hers. I tangle my tongue with hers, swipe it across her teeth, across the seam of her inner lips, as I bury my fingers deep inside her, then curve them.

A groan bleeds from her and her entire body quakes. The scent of her arousal surrounds me, sinks into my skin, coils around me, and threatens to bind me to her. My belly knots and my groin hardens. My dick lengthens and my balls draw up, and I know if I don't bury myself inside her sweet, hot center, I am going to come in my pants.

Fuck me. I did not mean for it to get this far, did not come here to lose control. I meant to punish her, to show her that she could not simply disregard my rules and do as she wants. That, no way, will she disobey me again, let alone pull a knife on me. The same dagger that I had held over a flame, and allowed to cool before sliding it into the sheath at my hip.

I release her breast, reach for the knife and pull it out, then hold the blade to her throat.

I sense her stiffen, even as she continues to kiss me back. I draw the blade down to her breast, circle her nipple with it. She shivers, tries to speak, but I absorb the sounds. I continue to finger fuck her, even as I thrust my tongue in and out of her mouth, drag the blade down the curve of her breast to rest it in the space between the mounds.

Her entire body trembles, her pussy clenches around my fingers, and I know she's close, so very close. She pushes down with her hips, chasing her release, and I pull my fingers out of her and release her mouth at the same time.

She blinks, stares up at me as I press the edge of my knife into her chest. A trickle of blood runs down her belly, streaking across the black of her dress. It's fucking arousing, watching that combination. So similar to the red of her hair.

"Why the hell did you stop?" She pants, "I was so close."

I smile and she flushes. "You better finish what you started, *stronzo.*"

I chuckle, "I see you've been brushing up on your Italian."

"I see you've been brushing up on your alphaholeness." She bares her teeth, and fuck me, but her anger is such a turn on.

I wrap my fingers about the nape of her neck, then rise to my feet and pull her up with me. The dress falls to the floor and she stands there, clad only in her lacy thong, surrounded by the yards of fabric that make up her dress.

She trembles and her eyes gleam. "How dare you?" she snarls. "How dare you withhold my orgasm?"

"Because I can?" I keep my fingers around the nape of her neck as I circle to stand in front of her, "Because I'd prefer to mark you first; because you need to earn every single orgasm, from now on."

"Fuck you." She tosses her head, "If you think I am going to do a single thing that you ask of me, then you are sadly mistaken."

"We'll see." I press the tip of the knife into the skin between her breasts, and she shivers. "You may deny it, but everything in you yearns for my touch, for me to etch my sign of ownership into your skin, for me to tattoo the symbol of my possession onto you, to own you, to dominate you, as only I can."

Her pupils dilate and her breathing grows more ragged. She wants everything I can do to her. I have no doubt about it. She wants my body, wants the pleasure I can wring from her, yet she resists me, resists submitting to me, resists allowing herself to trust me. Not that I have given her any reason to do so, but if she wants me to complete what I started then she is going to put herself in my hands completely. I step back, wipe the blade on my sleeve, then slip it into my sheath.

Turning I head for the exit, when she calls out, "Wait."

I keep walking.

"Damnit, Michael, stop."

I reach the door, and she draws in a breath. "Please," she whispers, "please stop."

"What's that?" I pause, but don't turn, "I don't think I heard you."

"Bastard," she bites out, and I push open the door.

"Please," she begs, "please stop, Michael."

I turn to glance at her over my shoulder.

"Are you going to leave me here?"

"It would seem that way."

"But…but…it's freezing."

"Those yards of fabric," I glance down at the dress strewn about her feet, "I am sure they can finally be put to good use."

She pales. "I hate you," she declares. "I fucking hate you."

I tilt my head, "Which doesn't matter to me one bit, you understand?"

"What do you want from me?" She folds her fingers at her sides, "Why are you doing this to me?"

"You brought this on yourself, Beauty, when you tried to kill me."

"You kidnapped me first."

"So?" I look her up and down, "I am the one who holds the power here."

"Like you'll ever let me forget that."

"No, but it's time you realize how serious I am about you acknowledging it too."

"And if I don't?"

I bare my teeth, "I am looking forward to convincing you otherwise."

Turning, I head out of the door, then stop. "There's one more thing," I stare at her over my shoulder, "you will not come until I give you permission."

30

Karma

I pull the train of my dress around my shoulders, and huddle into the mattress of the narrow single bed. Seriously, this entire thing sucks. Why the hell had he left me behind? I mean, who leaves their wife in the basement of his house on their wedding night? Michael fucking Byron does.

Yeah, yeah, I know what you are thinking. When it suits me, I am his wife, and when it doesn't, I am not. And isn't that the truth of it? I bring up my hand, stare at the ring on my finger. The black diamond in the center is smooth enough that I can see myself reflected in it. And the rubies surrounding it… Wow!

Honestly, if I had chosen a ring for myself, it would be this. Not that I had spent much time thinking about my wedding… Considering I had been too busy trying to focus on my fledgling career as a designer. And then there was that little issue that I had been in the foster care system until my sister Summer had turned eighteen and found a way to become my legal guardian.

So no, weddings and wedding dresses and wedding rings weren't exactly the kinds of dreams I went to sleep with every night. And yet, I had known exactly the kind of gown I'd wanted. I hadn't hesitated when I had stitched it. And the ring… OMG, the ring… Fact is, I love it. And I hate myself for it. And I hate that he knows exactly what I like. And the fact that he knows how to play my body, and that he knows that holding back my orgasms is a surefire way to break me down.

He had given me a taste of how good it could be between us, and yet, he hadn't yet fucked me. I squeeze my thighs together. The way it had felt to have his fingers in me as he had twisted my nipples… Goosebumps pop on my skin and it's not only because it's cold. The thick fabric of the train of my dress is actually quite a comfortable blanket… It's annoying how he'd been right about that as well.

Is there anything that over-the-top, control freak isn't right about? I turn on my back, pull up the skirts of my dress. I had worn it after he'd left because it had felt like the quickest way to stay warm, and to a certain extent, that was true too. Except, it's uncomfortable to sleep in it… Or wait, maybe I am uncomfortable because the bastard hadn't let me come. He hadn't let me orgasm, damn him. And he'd told me I can't climax until he tells me to, but hell, if I am not going to try.

I pull up the skirt of my dress, and making sure I am still covered by the train, I slide my fingers into my panties. I thrust a digit inside my sensitized channel and gasp when I find myself wet. Pinpricks of pleasure radiate out from my touch, and I add a second finger, then a third.

It's not enough, damn it. Nothing will be enough to plug that nothingness that yawns in my core, but this will have to do for now. I begin to fuck myself, weave my fingers in and out, as the tension begins to build at the base of my spine. I increase the intensity of my movements, and my entire body shakes. I squeeze my legs together, close my eyes as I shove my fingers in and out of my melting channel. And again. And again. The waves build up from my core, radiate out and up my spine, I don't stop, I keep going. Come on. Come on. I am so close now. The waves spiral upward, and just as the climax threatens to spill over, his command echoes in my ears, *You will not come until I give you permission.*

I yank the fingers from my core and the orgasm recedes. The emptiness inside of me seems to grow bigger, thicker, until it envelops all of me, consumes me. Sweat beads my upper lip, sticks to my palms. Heat flushes my skin and I throw off my cover… I mean, the goddamn train. I swing my legs over the side of the bed, glance about the space.

He must have cameras here…somewhere, right? I stare at the walls, glance up at the ceiling… There! Above the doorway is the unmistakable eye of a camera. Aha… So he does have eyes on me, after all… Had he just seen my performance? Had he taken in how I'd almost orgasmed?

Does he realize just how close I am to losing my freakin' mind? My stomach rumbles and my tongue sticks to the roof of my mouth. Bet my hair is a rat's nest, given how I had writhed on the goddamn bed earlier, too. Not that it is my most pressing concern, but a girl has a right to be concerned about her looks, right? So what, if I am his stupid prisoner? Surely, he won't deny me my basic rights… Like using a goddam, proper bathroom.

I stare at the bucket in the corner of the room. If he thinks I am going to be using that, he has another think coming. I have my dignity, goddamn it. I am not peeing in a stupid bucket, no bloody way.

I shuffle my weight from foot to foot. What the hell can I use to get his attention? Something that will ensure he comes back here…?

I take in the space, the light from the single bulb in the ceiling that came on earlier. At least, he hadn't switched that off. It would have been goddamn creepy if he had, not that I am afraid of the dark… But still, I prefer not to think about this space with the lights off. I shudder.

I glance about the space again… Nothing… There is no piece of wood, or a nail…or anything I can use… And the goddam bucket… I refuse to touch it. Ugh. No, he has to come for me. He has to get me out of here… And there is only way I can think of to force his hand.

I stare up at the unmistakable eye of the camera above the door, then I begin to undress.

31

Michael

"What the hell is she doing?" I glare at the screen which is linked to the camera that's trained on the cell. Karma stares into the lens — of course, she'd figured out where the camera is. Not that I had tried to hide it from her or anything. It had been an interesting experiment, on my part, to see how long it would take her to spot the camera… And clearly, she hadn't realized she was being watched when she had writhed under the train of her dress as she had tried to make herself come.

That had been hot, and so fucking erotic… I am not ashamed to say that I had grabbed my dick and jerked off in tandem. And when she had stopped just short of actually orgasming…that's when I had stopped too… And fuck, if that hadn't been a surprise. Why the hell hadn't I let myself come? Not out of some twisted sense of wanting to keep her company as she stayed unsatisfied, that's for damn sure.

Of course, I could have taken her earlier… I had had her in my arms, my dick nestled in the valley between her ass cheeks, and though I had been fully dressed, it hadn't stopped me from rubbing myself against her curves. Like the pervert that I am.

And I had opted to walk away from her. I had thought I was

denying her... Turns out I was denying myself, as well. As she had worked her fingers in and out of her cunt—not that I had been able to see her sweet pussy, but my imagination had filled in the gaps—I had mirrored her rhythm. Speeding up when she had and pausing with her. I hadn't been able to take my eyes off of her; had watched as she had jumped out of bed, glanced around the space, then turned to face the camera, as if coming to a decision.

Then, she had begun to strip.

And *maledizione*, I can't stop myself from taking in every inch of exposed skin—as she pushes the dress down her shoulders, then down her flat stomach, as she wriggles her hips and eases the dress down her legs, letting it fall about her ankles, along with her panties. She straightens, kicks aside her clothes, and the breath whooshes out of me.

Fuck me, but she is naked. Absolutely, completely naked. Except for her gorgeous hair that flows about her shoulders and curtains her breasts so the pink nipples peek out from between the strands. Her hips are rounded, her belly flat, before it leans into the dip of her sweet slit, encased in the fleshy folds of her luscious pussy. I tap on the screen, zoom in to her core and spot the glint of metal—fuck me, it's that damn clit ring of hers, the one that drives me crazy. That makes me want to thrust my head between her legs and bite down on that ring and tug so she feels the pull all the way to her nipples—yeah, that ring. Except for that adornment, her skin is completely bare.

I had touched her there, so I knew she had done as instructed and shaved between her legs... Hell, I had instructed Cassandra to make sure that she did it. So, I knew that she had followed my instructions, but to see her like this—full frontal, fully nude, bared to my gaze as she props her palm on her hip, bends a knee and strikes a pose, as if daring me to take in her glorious nakedness.

And I do... I zoom out again, so I can see her in totality. Those high cheekbones, parted rosebud lips, her slender throat, those high pointed breasts, curvy hips, fleshy thighs that I want to mark with my blade, before I run the tip around her pussy, then trail it down her clit, down her inner thighs, to those narrow ankles and tapered feet. I want to suck on her toes as I draw lazy circles up her calves, until I reached her plump behind... Which I, absolutely, want to bite down on as I slide my fingers inside her forbidden back channel, opening her up, readying her for my intrusion. First with the handle of my knife, then with my dick. I drag my fingers up the handle of my knife and my dick lengthens.

Transferring the knife to my left hand, I reach down between my legs and grasp myself again. I pump myself once, twice. My cock elongates...but it's not enough. Fucker knows it's my hand that's doing the work and it wants more... So much more. It wants her cunt, her pussy, her tight, melting channel to sink into. Her pussy to clamp down on my cock, her cunt to milk me as I come inside her and fill her up and mark her as mine. Only mine.

The door behind me opens and I clench the knife more tightly. "Michael, what the hell is happening — ?"

"Not now," I snap, without turning around. "Get the fuck out, Luca."

I sense him hesitate, then the door closes and his footsteps recede.

Yeah, so my brother had almost seen me jerking off... Something that hasn't happened since we were teenagers. Not that he had seen me... Not that it would have mattered if he had... As long as he didn't see my queen, naked and exposed to me on the screen.

I squeeze my dick, then drag my fingers up my cock, as she slides her fingers down between her pussy lips. She thrusts one finger, then another, inside her channel, then adds the third. She continues to push her fingers in and out of her cunt, in and out. Her breasts jiggle and her hair sways about her shoulders, as she tips up her chin and holds my gaze. Her mouth opens, and I can almost hear her moan of pleasure as she continues to fuck herself. She licks her lips and I swear I come right then.

The blood drains to my groin and my balls harden. She increases the pace of her movements and so do I, mirroring her rhythm as she thrusts out her chest, brings up a palm to cup one breast. She twists her nipple and lust roars in my veins. I reach forward, glare at the screen as she moves her hand to the other breast, gives it the same treatment.

Fucking fuck. My thigh muscles grow rock hard; the pressure at the base of my spine tightens. I am so fucking close, so on the edge. Heat suffuses my skin and my dick screams for release. I cup my balls and squeeze as, on screen, the witch smiles. Huh?

Her eyes gleam; she tosses her hair as she lowers her hand to her side. She pulls her fingers out of her cunt, holds her hand up. The moisture on it glistens and, fuck me, but my mouth waters. Maintaining eye contact, she licks each of her fingers, one by one, making a meal out of it, and my balls draw up. That's when she bends and draws her dress up over her shoulders. What the hell?

She turns her back on the camera, heads toward the bed. She pulls her train over her body, covering herself from neck to toe completely, then she turns her back on me, and the *strega* falls asleep. I swear, she switches off, just like that, for she doesn't move. Not a peep out of her. She sinks into slumber as I watch her prone figure.

I glance down at my raging hard-on, wanting to get myself off. And I could. I could continue pumping my shaft until I come. Only, it's not going to be anywhere near as satisfying as coming inside of her.

Damn woman had gone toe-to-toe with me, and had defeated me at my own game... I stare at the screen as a chuckle bursts out of me. *Well, well... Beauty, this round is yours. But you had better be prepared for what's coming next.*

I grab my handkerchief, wipe my cock, then tuck it away. I clean my fingers, shove the piece of cloth in my pocket, then rise to my feet.

32

Karma

I rub my cheek into the soft pillow and snuggle in. Warmth surrounds me, cocoons me, sinks into my body. I slide my hand across the mattress and the bed is so comfortable. My muscles are so relaxed, my entire body seems to be floating on some kind of cloud. Hmm. I try to turn and find something heavy around my waist holds me down. I try to pull away, and the weight around my middle intensifies. I crack open my eyes, glance down to find a thick arm about my waist. Huh? Thick fingers that lead to a wide wrist, which is attached to a sculpted forearm.

I manage to turn, enough to take in the tattoo of a knife on his tanned skin. It sports an intricate handle and the blade features a single eye. The blade points toward his fingers and the overall effect screams danger and caution. The corded muscles of his forearm wind up to massive biceps which are twice the size of my neck, at least, so it seems. I gulp, follow the arm to where it is attached to wide shoulders, a chest so broad that it blocks out everything else from my sight. A smattering of hair covers those sculpted pecs...which are demarcated by a white bandage that is taped vertically across his sternum. The contrast of the white against his darker skin is a shock. As is the fact that his chest is decorated with tattoos. Tattoos? Whoa, and there are so many of them.

I take in the design of a knife, the blade of which is painted with fire. Next to that is a design of a knife with the blade featuring roses. Then, another tattoo of a knife, with the blade featuring the sun; another one in which the blade is filled with stars; one in which a snake winds around the blade... Wow... And that's just on the skin I can see. How many more knives does this man have inked on his skin? Why is he so obsessed with them? And P.S. How the hell did I get here? In his bed, with him wrapped around me like a boa constrictor around its prey. Ugh, why the hell did I have to come up with that comparison in my mind?

I tip my chin up, take in that thick hair that falls over his forehead. Those dark eyelashes that fan over his cheekbones, the hooked nose, that thin upper lip, the pouty lower lip, that square jaw of his... And have I told you about his lips? Full, dreamy lips that look so hard but are so soft to kiss.

Again... How the hell did I end up here, anyway? Once more, I try to move out from under his arm, and this time, he hauls me to his chest. "Stop struggling," he rumbles, "I am trying to get some rest."

"*You* are trying to get some rest?"

I stare at his relaxed features. He looks almost content... Asshole. He'd spirited me away from that stupid cell—not that I miss it, by the way... And also, that reminds me, I need to pee... I really have to pee; I wriggle my hips and something stabs into the valley between my butt cheeks.

It can't be... Uh, it's not...uh, his dick? Of course, it is... Bastard's all aroused and I don't think it's only because of morning wood.

"Let go of me," I hiss. "Honestly, how dare you bring me here?"

"Would you rather I'd left you in that cell?"

I still.

"Thought not." His lips curl, "Best get your rest while you can, Beauty."

"I will not."

"Trust me, you are going to need it."

"Oh, yeah, and for what might that be?"

The next moment I squeak as the world tilts. I gasp, then glance up into those deep blue eyes of his. His arms bracket me on either side of my head, and he manages to keep most of his weight off of me, except for his hips, which are flush against mine. His thick length stabs into the soft valley between my thighs, and I almost moan aloud at how good it feels. Oh, yeah, he's naked under the covers. And so am I…for I can feel every thick, fat inch of his cock as it happily nestles against my core.

My belly quivers, my thighs clench, and my cunt…argh! My cunt seems to curl in on itself in anticipation. *Down, stupid pussy, you don't get to be this needy. He's the monster who kidnapped you for revenge, remember? He forced you to marry him. And now he's your husband. And I'm his wife, and uh…! Doesn't that mean I have to indulge in certain wifely duties?* My throat seems to dry up. I lick my lips and his gaze drops to my mouth.

Oh, my god, when he watches me with that single-minded intensity, I can forget that there is a world outside of this cocoon, which is composed of his body, his chest, his scent… His heat, that flows around me, pins me to the bed, the force of his dominance a low-pitched hum that sinks into my blood and coils straight down to my clit. I draw in a breath and he jerks his chin up. His gaze holds mine. Dark, deep, so many secrets and yet, underneath all that there is a vulnerability.

What the fuck? This man has no weaknesses. Besides, any possible empathy he had for me is probably gone, now that I took a knife to him. Gah, what had I been thinking, with that pathetic attempt at trying to wound him? I should have known he was much too strong to be disabled that way. But I had gone with my instinct... And see where that got me? Under him…in his bed, surrounded by him. OMG.

I swallow, then slap my palms against his chest, "Let me the hell go."

"No."

"How the hell did you bring me here?"

"How do you think?"

"How the hell did you bring me here without my even realizing it?"

"It's easy when you sleep like the dead."

My cheeks heat. That much is true. I sleep like the proverbial log… Once I fall asleep, a bomb could go off next to me and I wouldn't realize it. I purse my lips together, "Some of us sleep with a clear conscience, while others…" I scowl at him, "clearly, are haunted by the screams of those they have killed."

His gaze intensifies. For a second, the expression on his face is bleak, then he nods, "That much is true."

I blink. "It is?"

He nods. "I was twelve when I killed my first man. It was my father's idea."

"What do you mean?"

"He put a gun in my hands, told me it was time I became a man. He had his men drag out a traitor from among them, and—"

"It was your job to kill him?" I whisper.

He nods.

"And you did...kill him?"

He nods again, "One shot between the eyes." He forms his fingers into the shape of a gun, places his forefinger and middle finger in the center of my forehead. "Boom." He mimes pulling a trigger and I flinch.

He drags his fingers down my nose, across my lips, to the hollow at the base of my neck. My pulse rate speeds up as he swipes his fingers down to the already healing scratch between my breasts... The tiny wound that he had inflected on me with his knife.

"Does it hurt?"

I shake my head and he digs his fingers into the scratch, reopening it. A sliver of pain fires across my nerve-endings. I wince. He glances down and I follow his gaze to find the blood seeping down my belly. He removes his fingers, only to bend his head and slurp at the open wound. A shiver of something—lust, fear, maybe a mix of the two?—ladders up my spine. He licks the scratch again, then glances up at me, "Does that disgust you, Beauty?" He tilts his head, "Me drinking your blood."

"No." My voice cracks, and I clear my throat. "No." I shake my head, "Strangely, I find it reassuring."

"Reassuring?"

"It confirms to me that you are human, for some reason. It tells me that you don't hide your proclivities. It..." I swallow, "it affirms that you don't shy away from what your heart wants, and that... That is something."

"Is it?"

I nod. "Most people go through life trying to ignore what they really are deep inside, but not you." I peer into his face. "What you see is what you get with you. You wear your likes and dislikes on your sleeve; you don't hesitate to declare what you want and go after it. You are brutally honest about your intentions, and for that, I am grateful."

"You are, huh?" he says in a strange tone. "I kidnapped you, Beauty. Held you to the marriage that your father had promised me."

"And I stabbed you for it."

"I locked you up in a cell as punishment. I withheld orgasms from you—"

"It's called edging," I murmur.

"I'm aware." His eyebrows rise, "Though I am not sure how a nineteen-year-old fashion designer whose claim to fame is hawking her clothes—"

"Designs." I scowl, "Thought I corrected you on that already."

"—at a flea market—"

"Camden Market is a world-renowned space for artists," I counter.

"—knows the term for an S & M technique, is something I am keen to find out more about."

"It's just…stuff I picked up along the way."

"Is that right?"

I nod, "Just like you learned everything about knives… Let's just say, I read up a lot of informative literature about BDSM."

"You did, huh?"

I bite the inside of my lip. "For example, I know that you like to indulge in knife play."

"Oh?"

"And blood play."

"Hmm." He tilts his head, "Tell me more about my depraved, filthy tastes, Beauty."

"What if I told you that I have always wanted to know how it would feel to be at the receiving ends of both of those?"

"I wouldn't think you meant it."

"And what if I said I do?" I tip up my chin.

"Then I would call you a liar."

"Why would you say that?" I frown.

"Because you don't know what you are talking about. You don't know what you really want."

"And I won't know, either. Until I try it." I set my lips.

"And what if it's too painful for you?"

"What if it's exactly what I was waiting for? What if that's why you were attracted to me in the first place? Because you saw me and knew that I was the kind of woman who you wanted to tie up, and deny orgasms, and use your special talents to get me to submit?"

"What if all of this is just you trying to pull a fast one on me?

I blink. My heart begins to race. "Wh…why would you say that?" I flutter my eyelashes. "Haven't I fought you every step of the way? Am I not the one who stabbed you?"

"And then you decided to bring yourself to the brink of orgasm not once, but twice, in front of the cameras, knowing full-well I would be watching."

"Did you like it?" I breathe. *Shit, what the hell am I doing? Pretending to be all worldly-wise and knowing what I am doing, and trying to beard the lion in his den…or in this case, in his bed.* "Did you?" I hold his gaze.

"And if I say I did?"

"Then I'd reply that it doesn't matter what my motives are. I am here, aren't I? Willing and ready to do as you command."

"You think you can throw the right words at me and get me to do what you want?"

"Am I succeeding?"

"No."

"Oh…" I pretend to pout, "So then, why are we still talking?"

"My point exactly."

He pushes off from the bed, stands over to me, only to lean down, then swing me up and over his shoulder.

"Put me down."

He doesn't answer. He marches to the bathroom, shoulders his way past the door, then heads for the toilet and places me on the seat.

He stands above me and I blink. "What fuck are you up to?"

"You needed to pee."

"Says who?"

He raises an eyebrow and I flush.

"So, what if I do? I could have walked here on my own."

"I carried you instead; deal with it."

"And how did you know that I had to, you know —"

"Urinate?" He smirks. "You can say it. It's a bodily function, just like fucking. Or would you prefer if I said fornicating?"

I scowl, "If you think you can throw clinical words my way to fluster me, then you are sadly mistaken."

"Good." His grin widens. He widens his stance and I don't dare look straight ahead…because, uh! I am at the exact same height as his big, fat dick, that I know is standing to attention against his belly right now. Yeah, okay, I peeked. I couldn't help it. It's right there in front of me. Also, since we had woken up, he had pressed that monster shaft against me, so I am well familiar with its length and its—gulp—girth, which is bloody impressive, I'll have you know.

"What are you doing still standing here?" I murmur. "I need to *urinate.*"

"So go."I gape at his smirking face. "Not in front of you."

He folds his arms across his chest, and his stance indicates…he's not moving. Okay, whatever, like I care if he sees me pee.

I close my eyes, try to relax…but hell, I can't go. Not when Mr. Monster Cock is standing over me like Satan himself.

"Turn your back," I say through gritted teeth, "else I won't be able to."

I sense him hesitate, then feel the slight breeze as he pivots around. To my surprise, I hear him move away. I open my eyes, and sure enough, the space is empty. I sigh as I settle into place, and almost instantly, my muscles relax enough so I can let go. I finish my business, flush, wash my hands and face, smooth my hair the best I can, then hesitate. I take in my naked body, so very pale, except for the thin streak of red in between my breasts.

In a way, we match, I suppose. Only, the wound I bestowed on him is much deeper. I raise my hand to touch the scratch and the ring on my finger catches my attention. It picks up the color from my dyed red hair, and damn it… It really does feel like it's already part of me.

Why does he have to be so…so perceptive. Speaking of… I spin around, head for the door. "How did you know that I had to pee?" I demand. "I never told you that I wanted to."

Alphahole finishes stepping into his gray sweatpants, then turns around. "I guessed."

"You guessed?" I scowl. "How could you just guess?"

"It's morning." He shrugs. "It's natural to want to use the facilities after a night's sleep." He grabs a bathrobe, then walks over to me and holds it out.

I stare at it, then up at him. "Shit," I blink, "you removed my clothes last night…"

"You only just realized that?"

"No, I mean, yes, I mean…" I shove my hair over my shoulder. I must have really been out of, it if I hadn't even stirred when he'd undressed me.

"Your dress is safe. I've asked for it to be cleaned."

"Oh?" I blink rapidly at him. That's thoughtful of him. Though why would he do that? Why is he being so nice to me?

"Relax," he laughs, "I know how much your creations mean to you and that dress was so *you*… That I figured you'd want to keep it, and maybe, modify it and wear it again."

My mouth drops open. That's exactly what I had planned to do, but how the hell is he able to read me so easily?

"Fine, fine," I grouse. "It's what most women do—adapt their wedding dresses so they can wear them again."

"Is it?" He frowns, then raises a shoulder, "Good guess, huh?" He jerks his chin toward the dressing gown, and I slide my arms through the sleeves. I knot the tie around the middle as he runs his palms down the shoulders, in a gesture that is both soothing and possessive. Huh. What the hell is this man up to? I turn around and scowl at him, "Out with it, Mister. What are you planning now?"

"Breakfast?" He smirks. "Do you like pancakes?"

33

Karma

I have been transported to some strange, alternate reality. That is the only reason I can imagine for why I am sitting here, at the breakfast counter of the kitchen of this manor on an island somewhere off the coast of Italy…watching a Mafia Capo, clad in only gray sweatpants and an apron, cooking at the stovetop.

OMG! That's so damn hot. His broad back is to me and I can't take my gaze off the play of muscle, the shift of those sculpted planes under his skin as he bustles around the space. He pours out the pancake batter onto one skillet, while in another, he cracks eggs. On a third pan, he's frying bacon and on the fourth burner, he has hash browns sizzling. OMG. My head spins as I watch him manage all four dishes at the same time, and not lose a step. He wipes his hand on the apron… Did I already mention? Yes, the man is wearing a freakin' apron… And honestly, he looks too damn sexy… Gah! My mouth waters, and it's not for the food.

I must have made a noise because he smirks at me over his shoulder, "You all right over there?"

I open my mouth to speak, but all that comes out is a gurgle.

Damn! I reach for the glass of water on the table in front of me, and take a sip to clear my throat. Then scowl back at him, "Of course, I am."

A strand of hair falls across his forehead and he brushes it away. the gesture is so familiar...so very Mika. My heart stutters, and I can't take my gaze off of him.

"You sound like you have a lot on your mind." His grin widens. No doubt, the fact that I am staring at him is inflating his already inflated ego. Jerkass!

I carefully place the glass of water back on the table, then meet his gaze, "I was just wondering how you managed to get all of those clothes, and all in my size, in the closet before I first arrived? Did you order them on your way here, after you knocked me out?"

"I simply pressed down on the carotid artery on either side of your neck, and you lost consciousness."

"Thanks for the medical lesson." I scowl. "If you don't want to tell me about how you acquired the clothes for me —"

"Yes."

I frown. "What do you mean, yes?"

"Yes, I ordered them on the phone to have them delivered before we arrived at the island, while you were unconscious."

"You had all of those clothes, shoes, and underwear delivered in a few hours?" I blink. "How did you manage that?"

He stares at me and I huff, "Yeah, of course, money can solve anything." I hold his gaze, "And what about the shampoo and shower gel in the bathroom?" I tip up my chin, "Did you order that too? How did you know what fragrance I prefer?"

"Your scent, Beauty," his lips twist, "it's a combination of moon-flowers and your essence. It's uniquely you... I found the most highly-rated sources and bought them for you."

Heat flushes my cheeks. Why the hell does that feel so intimate? After everything he's done to me, the fact that he accurately identified the fragrance of the shampoo I use should be the least of my worries. I shuffle my feet as another thought strikes me, "So, does this mean that you had already decided that you were going to —"

"Keep you? Play with you? Marry you?" He raises a shoulder, "Not consciously. All I knew was that I wasn't going to let go of you in a hurry."

I blink rapidly. What the hell does he mean by that? He isn't telling me anything I didn't already know and yet, these words seem very close to a confession of...something. Emotions? Feelings?

Nah, the Capo doesn't feel all that. All he means is that he isn't letting go of me until he gets what he wants from me. Yeah, I lean back in my seat. That's what it means.

My heart flutters and I rub at my chest. Please, please, don't tell me that my stupid heart condition is deciding now is the time to surface again. Not after I've been fine all these years, too. The sensation subsides and I blow out a breath.

He grabs a few slices of bread, pops them in the toaster, then turns to me, "I assume you like your eggs sunny side up."

I blink, then nod. I'm about to ask him how he guessed, but frankly, at this point, it doesn't matter. He's definitely going to have some dumbass explanation about it, and it's not like I want to know, anyway. I mean, the proof of the pudding is in the eating, and in this case, it's in the delicious breakfast that he serves up not ten minutes later. He places a plate piled with pancakes and drizzled with syrup, while on another plate, there are two eggs, sunny side up, with toast, hash browns, and bacon, which he sets down in front of me.

"Um, who is all this food for?"

"You?"

He grins and his face lights up. Oh, dear god, when he smiles like that, he's way too attractive. The bandage over his sternum is a stark contrast to the rest of his sculpted, tanned chest. And I can't take my gaze off it as he sits down in the chair opposite me.

"It doesn't hurt," he murmurs. "You didn't hurt me… Much."

"I don't know if that's good or bad." I fight the urge to apologize, then scowl back at him. "I did intend to cause you harm, you know?"

"No, you didn't." He reaches for the Moka—the Italian version of a coffee pot—and pours out the coffee he's freshly brewed, some into my espresso cup, then some for himself.

"What do you mean, I didn't?" I frown. "You a mind reader or something now?"

He raises his espresso cup to his lips, takes a sip, then sighs, "That's how coffee should be drunk—strong and intense and bitter."

"Just like you."

"What's that?" He smirks and I cough.

"Nothing, and don't change the subject."

"I wasn't."

"Yes, you were." I accuse him, "Here I am, trying to figure out what the hell you are up to, and you are extolling the properties of Italian coffee while making a combination of an all American/British breakfast...or a combination of breakfasts, that is."

"Don't you like it?" He eyes the food on the plates in front of me, "I figured you'd prefer this over a traditional Sicilian breakfast, but if you'd prefer something else..."

"It's not that." I drag my fingers through my hair. "I just wish you'd tell me why you decided to move me from the cell. And now, you are cooking me breakfast and..." I draw in a breath, "and this morning, even though you were, clearly, turned on, you didn't try to —"

"Fuck you?" The alphahole smirks as he reaches for his pancakes and begins to dig into them. As I watch, he inhales a quarter of the stack in seconds. Shit, and I haven't even started on mine.

"As you are well aware, your use of four-letter words doesn't bother me, in the least." I scoff as I cut into my own stack. "And yeah, that's what I mean." I pop the piece of pancake into my mouth and chew. "Whoa." I stare at him. "These are good."

"Surprised?"

"Well, yeah, I wasn't expecting you to cook." I frown, "Speaking of, where's the staff? Did you give them the day off?"

"The week off, actually."

"You did?" I dig into more of the pancakes and chew on them, "Is it some special occasion or something, that you allowed them time off?"

"It is." He nods, then pushes the plate with the eggs and bacon toward me, "You need to eat that too."

"After I finish the pancakes, if I have space, that is." I dig into the remainder of the food on my plate, then polish off the rest of the pancakes. I push my plate aside and he slides the other one in its place. "Eat," he commands, as he reaches for his second plate filled similarly to mine.

"Also," I say with my mouth full, "this is the first time I am seeing you dressed in sweats. Didn't think you owned a pair, considering you are always dressed in suits that seem to be from Saville Row."

He makes a sound deep in his throat, "Wouldn't touch those with a barge pole."

"Huh?" I frown. "Why's that?"

"I get my suits tailor-made by an artisan who has been stitching them for generations for the men in my family."

I resist the urge to roll my eyes. "Of course, you do."

He smirks. "You sassing me, Beauty?"

"Me?" I say crunching my way through the bacon, which is absolutely delicious, by the way, "Of course, not." I widen my gaze, "I wouldn't dare... My Lord." I flutter my eyelashes at him and his grin widens.

"Very good. Keep that up, and I may just be willing to give you your next orgasm."

"And there he is; the alphahole extraordinaire makes an appearance," I raise my eyes skyward, "just as we were getting along, too... Or at least, it seemed that way," I mutter under my breath.

"I heard that." He chuckles, "And to answer your earlier questions, one," he holds up a finger, "I learned to cook when I went to university in the US, and I enjoy American and British style breakfasts and didn't want to presume that the full English was the only kind of food you'd like to eat in the morning so I made both, and two," he holds up a second finger, "the reason I am wearing sweats is because there's no one else in the house."

"Oh." I set down my fork and glance around the space, "That's why the place seems empty. So, the staff is gone, and so are your brothers?"

"That's correct." He finishes off his bacon, then cuts up the eggs and scoops them up with a piece of toast. I watch as he chews his food, the tendons of his throat moving as he swallows. Fuck, but only Michael Byron Dominico Sovrano would make eating into an orgasm-inducing process. My throat goes dry. Somehow, I manage to chew and swallow my food, as he lowers his gaze to mine. He sets down his fork, then reaches for his napkin and dabs at his mouth. I lower my gaze to his lips and heat tugs at my belly. I squeeze my thighs together, mirror his actions and place my fork down.

"So, how come your brothers and the rest of your family and the staff are away?"

"Haven't you figured it out yet?" His eyes gleam, "Come on, Beauty, one guess, why there's no one else in the house..."

"Umm," I wipe my suddenly damp palms on my bathrobe, "because it's your birthday and you've given them all time off?"

"That doesn't explain why my family left the house."

"Because you fought with them and told them to leave?"

"It has happened on occasion, but no, it's not that."

My heart begins to pound in my chest. My pulse rate ratchets up.

Moisture pools between my thighs and I slide my chair back... I try to be discreet but one of the legs catches on the stone floor and a screech fills the space.

I stiffen, but Michael doesn't move a muscle.

"You were saying?" He scratches the area of his chest around the bandage, and bloody hell, my gaze is instantly drawn to those gorgeous sculpted pecs again. What a pity that I had to hurt him. It feels like I have spoiled a work of art designed by God himself.

"Beauty?"

I hear the smirk in his voice and raise my gaze to his, "I was saying that...you gave your staff time off and probably sent your brothers on some Mafia-related job."

"Very good." He lowers his hand. "I knew you were smart."

I paste on a bright smile, even as my stomach flip-flops. This is not good. Not good at all. "So," I grip the edge of the table, "when will they be back?"

"Next week."

"Excuse me?"

"You heard me." His grin widens until he resembles one of those freakin' sharks in that stupid Jaws movie, the one that had made me laugh because the special effects, clearly, hadn't withstood the test of time, but right now there's nothing amusing about this situation, because Michael's shark-smile is infinitely more unnerving.

I gulp. "Wh... What do you mean?" I press the heels of my bare feet into the floor. Shit, why hadn't I thought to, at least, put on some shoes? Well, too late now. I'm just gonna have to face this situation head-on. "Well?" I scowl. "Tell me, Michael, what does it mean that they' re not coming back until next week?"

"It means," he yawns, "that this is our honeymoon, Beauty. You and me, husband and wife, darling." He smirks, "And this is when we consummate our wedding."

34

Michael

She blinks once, twice, I watch as the information sinks in, then color smears her cheeks. Her muscles tense and she draws in a breath, "You have got to be fucking kidding me."

She pushes back the chair and jumps to her feet. But I, too, am ready. I spring up, race around the table as she darts for the kitchen door. I grab her arm, turn her around and into me. "Let go of me, you oaf."

She struggles and I hold onto her, trying not to increase the pressure of my hands on her. I don't want to hurt her. And while I want to mark her, I want it to be intentional, not because I had done so by mistake. "Stop it," I growl.

"Oh, fuck off." I sense her raise her knee and move aside. I grab her around the waist, throw her over my shoulder and she screams, "Bloody hell, what do you think you are trying to do?"

"Only taking what's mine, by right." I pivot, walk around the breakfast bar and to the dining table. I shove the breakfast dishes aside, then lower her onto it. She tries to rise and I fold my body over hers, slam my hands on either side of her and bracket her in.

"I thought you wanted me to fuck you?"

"That was before."

"Before what?"

"Before we were married."

I blink, "So you were willing to shag me before we were married, and now that we legally can fuck, you don't want me?"

She tips up her chin, "That's right."

"Liar." I can't stop the smile that widens my lips. "You want me to overwhelm you. Want me to hold you down, take choice away from you. You want me to take you by force, isn't that right?"

She blinks, then glances away.

I freeze. "*Merda*," I glare at her, "that's what you want, isn't it? You want me to play with you before I bed you, Beauty?"

"No," she sets her jaw, "of course, not."

I take in her heightened breathing, her flushed features, the way she darts her gaze around the room then back at me. She may think that's not what she wants, but I know better. All the signs are there...

Seems this woman is more of my soulmate than I had realized. Every filthy need of mine is reciprocated within her. She wants me to chase her, hunt her down, capture her all over again; she wants me to establish, once and for all, just who is in charge here. The little minx wants me to leave her in no doubt of my dominance. Clearly, the fuckedupedness inside of me has found its match in her. How can she be so...very perfect?

I bare my teeth and she snarls back at me. Goosebumps pop on my skin. Fuck me, but she...is absolutely one-hundred percent in tune with me. She's mine to possess. Mine to own. Mine to claim. Mine to establish just how very much she belongs to me. Only me.

I push away from the table, only to reach for the tie of her bathrobe. I yank it open and she gasps. "What the hell do you think you are doing?"

"Nothing you are not going to enjoy, *piccola mia*."

"Go fuck yourself."

I laugh, "Can't wait to get started, hmm?"

"Buzz off, you ass."

"Gotta stuff that little mouth of yours, and this time it's not going to be with food." I jerk my chin at her, "Get up."

"What?"

"On your feet."

"First, you throw me down here. Now, you tell me to get on my feet. Can't you fucking make up your mind or—"

I hold out my hand and she squeaks. She stares at my proffered arm, then back up at me, "What are you doing?"

"Helping you up."

"Ah, hmm, okay." She grabs my hand, uses the leverage to haul herself up to sitting position. She lets go, then slides off the table.

"Take off your bathrobe."

She scowls and I fold my arms across my chest, "Don't defy me."

She huffs, then shoves the bathrobe off. "Happy?" She props a hand on her hip, thrusts out her chest as I look her up and down.

"Not yet, Beauty." I bend my knees, peer into her face. "Run."

"What?"

"Run, Beauty. I'll even give you a head start."

"What…what does that mean?"

"You heard me." I smirk. "Run now, *Belleza*. If I catch you… *When* I catch you, I intend to have my way with you…."

"And if I evade you."

"You won't."

"So sure of yourself?"

"I am sure of…" I glare into her eyes, "the fact that you want to be caught."

"No, I don't."

"Yes, you do."

"No."

"Yes." I snap my teeth and she jumps. I point my thumb toward the door, "Go, else I'll take this as your giving in without a fight."

She sets her jaw, "No fucking way."

"Good." A chuckle rolls up my throat and I swallow it down. "Go."

She blinks.

I reach for her and she squeals, then pivots and takes off for the door. I can't take my gaze off her pert, little butt as it twitches, as she bolts out the door. I amble over to the doorway, watch as she races down the corridor and up the steps. She flings the door open, bounds outside, and I follow.

I reach the doorway, leap down the steps. I glance around, and spot her running toward the back of the house. I take off in hot pursuit. I am not wearing any shoes…and neither is she. Only difference, I am used to running barefoot. It's how I grew up on the streets of Palermo. Sure, my father was the Don, but my mother was happy to let us boys run wild. She believed it would toughen us up if we went barefoot outside. And so, we had, until my father had found out and put an end to the practice. But that early experience now stands me in good stead as I run around the perimeter of the property. Where is she? Where the hell could she have gone?

Above me, the sun slides behind clouds. The temperature drops suddenly. It's late November, and while the weather is still pleasant, it's also more unpredictable. Sure enough a few drops of rain hit my arm as I pause, getting my bearings... Which way could she have gone? I close my eyes, attune my hearing, trying to catch any sound that would give away her presence... I tilt my head, wait...wait... A slight thud... The sound of bare feet on mud reaches me.

I turn, head across the clearing at the back of the house and toward the treeline. Step onto the muddy edge of the forest that borders the house. The dirt and stones bite into the soles of my feet. I push aside the discomfort, head toward where the sound had come from. Past the first set of trees, deeper into the forest, down the path that leads into a small clearing. I pause at the edge, wait...wait... A tiny sound... Almost an inhalation of surprise...reaches me and I turn. Lunge in the direction of the large oak tree that stands at the edge of the clearing.

Its branches spread out overhead, shielding me from the rain that is turning into a steady drizzle. I reach the massive tree trunk, throw myself around it, and she screams, then darts away from me. The pulse thuds at my temples and adrenaline laces my blood. A growl rips out of me as I lunge toward her, bridge the distance between us as I tackle her around the waist.

She screams as we both go down. I twist my body, make sure that she lands on top of me. She wriggles, yells out, and I throw my arms around her. I roll over so she is on her back on the grass and under me. She tips her chin-up and stares up into my face. I take in her flushed features, her hair flowing about her face, so fucking gorgeous. I lean in closer, wanting to sniff her, to lick her, to kiss those pouty pink lips of hers, then flinch when she lands her fist in my shoulder.

Pain shivers down my chest as the wound she'd inflicted on me protests at the impact.

She swipes out her fist again and this time I duck. "Stop that," I growl.

"No." She brings up her knee and I lean some of the weight of my lower body onto her, effectively arresting her in place. Which also means that my already swelling thickness lodges neatly in between her legs. She freezes; color smears her cheeks. Her chest rises and falls as she glowers back at me.

She throws her fist and I block it. I grab her arm and wrench it over her head. Then do the same with the other. I shackle her wrists together. "Gotcha." I bare my teeth, "I caught you fair and square, *piccola mia.*"

"The fuck I care?" She wriggles in my grasp, writhes under me as she tries to break free, and the friction of her soft core against the tent in my crotch sends shivers of anticipation up my spine. I plant my thigh, then the other between her legs, wrenching them apart. She strains in my grasp, scowls up at me.

"Let me the fuck go."

"No." I bare my teeth and she makes a sound at the back of her throat. "Tell me you want this," I growl. "Tell me you want my cock inside you; tell me you want me to fuck you; tell me you want your swollen hungry cunt clamped around my shaft as I plow into you."

Her pupils dilate until there's only a ring of green left around the black.

The scent of her arousal bleeds into the air, and fuck, if my cock doesn't leap forward right then. I transfer the hold on her wrist to my left hand, then shove the waistband of my pants down with my other hand.

"No," she snarls, "no, no, no."

"Yes, Beauty, yes."

I notch my swollen shaft against her entrance, then pause, "Say you want this." I tease her entrance with the head of my weeping cock and a moan bleeds out of her, even as she fixes me with a scowl.

"Say it," I insist. "Say you want me to own you, to punish you for trying to kill me, to fuck you so hard that my cum seeps out from your pores."

She sets her jaw, then scissors her legs around me. She thrusts her pelvis up so I slip inside her.

35

Karma

What are you doing? What the hell are you doing? Why are you taking him into your body? Why are you allowing him to do exactly what he's been threatening to do? Why do you have your legs wrapped around him as you hold his gaze, as you take in his gorgeous features, that thick corded neck, those broad shoulders that shield you from the rain that patters down from above?

He holds my gaze for a beat, then clucks his tongue. He pulls out of me and I scowl, "What the fuck? Thought you wanted to consummate our marriage?"

"You can't top from the bottom, Beauty."

"What the hell do you mean by that?"

"You know what I mean." He lowers his head until his eyelashes sweep over mine, "Say you want this, tell me you want me to fuck you."

"I want you to..." I swallow, "to nail me," I whisper.

"What's that?" He tilts his head, "Don't think I heard you."

"I want you to...to take me, you asshole."

"Say it like you mean it." He smirks. "Say you want me to fuck you."

"Fine, fine," I yell, "I want you to shag me, you bleeding idiot. I want you to fuck me, you —"

He propels his hips forward and impales me in one smooth move. I gasp and my breath catches in my chest. He's so damn big, so huge; I am so full. Oh, my fucking god. I swallow, open my mouth, but no sound comes out.

"Lost your ability to speak, hmm?" His smirk widens as he pulls out of me. He slides his free hand under my knee, heaves it up, so it's next to my chest, opening me up, then he thrusts forward with such force that my entire body jerks.

A moan bleeds from my lips. Oh, my god. Oh, my god. This is… fucking insane. It feels so fucking good, so right… I can't understand how every part of me feels ready and aching and wants more, so much. I make a sound deep in my throat and he nods.

"I know what you want, Beauty."

You do?

He holds my gaze as he begins to fuck me in earnest. In and out, in and out. I dig my heels into his back just above his tight butt as he plunges into me over and over again. Every time he rams into me, my body jolts. My breath shudders. Pinpricks of pleasure scream up my spine. The climax crashes over me and I scream, as he continues to fuck me through the aftermath that ripples through me in waves. He stares into my eyes, then releases my hand only to cup my cheek, "Fuck, you're beautiful when you come, you know that?"

I stare up into those cold, remorseless eyes of his. I watch myself watch him as he rams into me again and again. His features grow intense, his muscles coil and uncoil as he seems to put all of himself behind the movement. He releases my wrists, only to slide his thumb in between my lips and I suck on it. His gaze narrows as he pulls out, then propels his hips forward and buries himself to the hilt again. He hits that spot deep inside me, and to my shock, I find that shivers start at my feet again.

"No," I moan, "it's too soon. I can't come again."

"You can." He pounds me again, this time, with such force that his balls slap against my inner thighs. He pulls out, then tilts his hips, and nails me again, and I swear, I feel him in my throat.

"No," I whine, "no, no, no."

"We gotta work on your vocabulary, *piccola mia*." He impales me again and again as the rain increases in intensity. The raindrops sting my legs as I lock my ankles around him, as he glares into my eyes, "Come," he commands. "Come all over my cock, wife."

"Oh, my fucking god." I throw my arms around his neck and scream as the orgasm sweeps up my spine to burst behind my eyes. I'm dimly aware of him picking up speed and ramming me over and over and over again. Then, his big body shudders and his dick swells inside me. I feel his butt tense as he comes deep inside me. He slumps down, and I sense him holding his weight off of me and on his arms as the aftershocks ripple over me. I open my eyes and flinch when I am faced with his intense gaze.

"What?" I murmur. "Why are you looking at me like that?"

"You okay?"

I nod, dimly aware that I still have my arms and legs locked around him. He slides his hand under my neck, the other under my waist. The next second, the world tilts as he flips our positions. He places me on his chest, then wraps those big arms around me.

"I need to get you out of the rain," he murmurs as he contemplates the rain that's pouring down on us. We are shielded somewhat by the branches of the tree overhead. Still, we are both completely drenched. And dirty and filthy.

Somehow, it feels right that he chased me down and took me in the open, exposed to the elements like we were animals. He's the most untamed man I have ever met. A beast who wears a tailor-made suit that only enhances that savage part of him that had attracted me from the moment I'd met him.

I raise my hand to his neck, trace the scar there. "How did you get this?" I murmur, "It seems painful."

He wraps his fingers around mine, guides my hand back to his chest. His fingers graze the ring and he freezes. Then he traces the diamond in a slow circle.

"We need to get out of here," he finally says, then pushes himself, and me, up to sitting position.

"Fine, fine," I huff, "if you don't want to tell me about the scar, I'll understand." I toss my hair over my shoulder, "You only have to say so. No need to brush off my question, you know."

He glances down at me, then sets me to the side before tucking himself inside his sweatpants. He rises to his feet, then holds out his hand, "Come," he murmurs, "let's get out of the rain."

. . .

Fifteen minutes later, I scoop up some of the hot water, then pour it over myself as I lean back into his broad chest. He'd carried me up and back into the house, pausing only to rinse the mud off both of us in the outdoor shower attached to the house, before he'd carried me into his bedroom. He'd filled up the bathtub in the ensuite, throwing in salts that had fizzed and bubbled before the space had filled with the scent of roses and lavender. When I had commented that it was a terribly feminine scent, he'd admitted that he'd bought the salts for me. Huh, okay. I hadn't expected to hear that.

I'd decided to keep the rest of my questions to myself for a little longer. Not that I don't want to find out more. It's just, after being freshly fucked, I want to revel in the pleasant buzz that grips my limbs, and the silence that seems to have taken the place of the thoughts that normally buzz around in my head. Apparently, the Capo fucked all thoughts out of my head. I snort, then swallow down the rest of the laugh that bubbles up. Either I am getting lightheaded, or a little hysterical, or both...

He reaches for the shampoo, pours some of it out, then begins to work it into my hair. The complex scent of moonflowers fills the space. "I love this scent." I murmur, and I sense him smile above me.

"I know."

"It really is annoying how you always seem to have all of the answers."

"I don't, actually," he retorts. "For a long time, I had no idea what I was going to do with my life."

I turn my head and he increases the pressure on my hair so I have to glance forward again.

"Thought you were born into the Mafia, so you didn't have a choice but to join the family business?"

"You always have a choice, in everything you do, Beauty." He urges me to tilt my head back as he digs his fingertips into my scalp in slow circles.

A warmth envelops me and the muscles of my neck relax. "Hmm," I sigh, "you sure are good with your fingers, Mr. Capo."

A chuckle rumbles up his chest and the vibrations sink into my blood. The warmth of his body, combined with the heat from the hot water, envelops me fully. I close my eyes and give in to his attention as he begins to wash the suds out of my hair with the hand shower. Then he positions my head against his shoulder, and I sink into him further.

He holds the hand shower over my breasts, then moves it down my belly. He dips the hand shower under water and holds it right over the entrance to my pussy.

"Ooh," I murmur, "that's…ah…nice."

"Nice, hmm?" His breath teases my temple a second before he runs his tongue around the shell of my ear. He bites down on my earlobe at the same time that he pushes the shower head right up against the entrance of my channel.

The pressure of the water is muted, yet it stimulates my clit. I wriggle around and he brings his big hand down onto my hip and holds me in place.

"Relax, Beauty," he murmurs, "I know what you need."

Do you? Do you know how much I love having your hands on me? How much I want you to debase me? How much I need you to degrade me? How I want you to humiliate me, to make me submit, to reach out to the darkness inside of me and bring it to the light so I can see myself through your eyes? Feel my desires as they ripple up your skin, sense how I break you apart, as you shatter me and put me back together in a design that mocks the girl I used to be.

Do you, my Capo, understand what it means that I met you this way? Even though the timing of our encounter is all wrong, even though the nature of our tryst is suspect… Even though you claim that I am your wife…though we both know this marriage is a sham. One that is a means of helping you get what you desire, that allows you to fulfill all of your ambitions… And me…what about me? What about what I want, what I need, what I want to do to you as you pleasure me?

I grip his wrist, applying enough pressure that he pauses. I turn my head, glance at him from the corner of my eye. I urge his hand back and he frowns. I turn around so I am kneeling between his legs, facing him, in the bathtub.

Then I bring his hand back between my legs and position the shower head back at the entrance of my channel. He arches his eyebrow at me and I raise a shoulder, "I can see you this way."

He moves the shower head closer to my clit and a shiver runs up my back. I reach down to grasp his erect cock, as he reaches behind him and increases the pressure of the water. The stream gushes up and against my already sensitive clit and I gasp. I tense my fingers around his cock, and damn it, my fingers don't meet around his girth. I mean, I'd felt him inside of me…as he'd stretched me, and filled me, as he'd pushed his way down my throat…but I hadn't realized just how big he is, in relation to my hand. I swipe my fingers down to the base of his shaft, and he grits his teeth.

A nerve throbs at his temple, as he grips my hip with his other hand, bracketing me in. I part my legs, allowing him to bring the spray even closer. The spray massages my pussy and I can't stop the moan that bleeds from my lips. I hold his gaze as I swipe my fingers up the length of his cock. I drag my thumb across his swollen head and he bares his teeth. I squeeze down his length again and his chest rises and falls. "You're fucking killing me," he growls as he reaches behind to turn off the water before letting the shower head sink to the bottom of the tub. He wraps his fingers about the nape of my neck, and the tips almost meet around the front of my throat. I swallow and I can feel him feel the action.

The skin around his eyes tightens. "Take me in your mouth," he orders.

I glance down, then back at his face. I take a breath, then lower my head to the water. The depth is just enough to cover my mouth, as I close my lips around his cock. A groan rumbles up his massive chest, as he increases the pressure on my throat. "Take me down your throat, I want to feel you swallow." He lowers his voice to a hush, and OMG, that dominance in his voice chafes across my nerve-endings. All of my pores seem to pop. My core clenches and moisture pools between my legs as I open my mouth wider, then drop my chin as I take him down my throat. And promptly gag. He holds me in place as my eyes water.

"Take it all in, Beauty," he growls, his voice hard, his gaze burning into me, a challenge in them, maybe? And fuck it, but I want to show him that I am not some stupid, virginal woman who can't keep up with him. So, I draw in another breath through my nose, hold it, then relax my throat as he pushes me down and I take him in as deep as I can. The water flows over my nose and I don't dare breathe as I lick my tongue up his swollen length.

He presses his thumb into the front of my throat and groans, "Fuck me, but you have no idea how hot that is, Beauty. To feel my cock as it slides down your throat." His breath catches, "It's fucking erotic." His tone deepens, "You're a fucking queen... My goddess."

Umm, okay, is that the blow job speaking, or does he really mean it?

I draw back, so my nose is above water, draw in a breath, then plunge down again. This time his cock slides down my throat easily as I lick down his length, then up again as I pull back. I wrap my lips around the head of his cock, give it a slurp, then again.

"*Dio cane!*" he growls as his fingers tighten around my nape. He urges me to lower my head, as I open my mouth as wide as possible. He applies enough pressure that I take him down my throat, then he pulls me back, allowing me to take a breath, before he once more pushes me down. His dick slides down my throat, and again. The next time he pulls me back, I take in a breath, and he pauses. "You good?" He tilts his head, "If you want me stop, Beauty, you only have to tap my thigh, and I'll release you."

I stare up at him, and he curls his lips. *Bastard.* No doubt, he expects me to tap out. He probably wants me to admit that he's too much for me. That I can't take his rough handling of me. That I am not able to keep pace with him. That I am too weak to bear his proclivities…and… I know, I know… It's stupid that I have to turn this into some kind of competition. I mean, ultimately this is about him manipulating my body to suit his needs. Not that I am not getting any pleasure out of it, but surely, he could be more…gentle on me…

Except, I don't want him to be gentle. I want him to take me as he would any common whore. I want him to use me as his personal fuck-toy… Yeah… I know, I need therapy, surely. Who would want a man to debase her, demean her, use her mouth for his pleasure, use her cunt to bring him satisfaction, use her every hole as it would best suit him? Me… That's who. And no, I am not going to apologize for this anymore.

I have always known my tastes are warped, my preferences extreme, my needs different from what most women want. No pink roses, or candles or soft beds… Okay, maybe the third one is okay… But only so they bring out the contrast to the unyielding body that pushes me into said bed and masters me. So yeah… This is me…unapologetic, uncaring, not in denial for what I want. Not when I've met a man whose tastes, surely, run as much to the extreme as my own.

I wrap my fingers around the base of his dick and squeeze hard.

His breath catches. Color smears his cheeks. I bring my other palm down to cup his balls. I massage them and his chest rises and falls. His shoulders flex. He seems to grow bigger, darker, more dangerous, if that were possible. A cloud of heat spools off of him, and slams into my chest. I gasp and sweat beads my brow.

He bares his teeth, then pushes me down, watching as his cock disappears in my mouth. He pulls me back, then presses me down, again and again. His movements speed up. His gaze intensifies. I don't take my gaze off of him. I keep the connection alive as he fucks my mouth, as tears run down my cheeks, joining the rest of the bath water. Heat flushes my skin and my pulse rate speeds up. I am turned on by how he is using me, and fuck, if I'll do anything to stop myself from relishing how he uses me. How his body reacts to what he's doing to me.

His chest planes flex, his belly clenches. The skin around his mouth tightens as he squeezes my hip with enough pressure that I know I'll bear the imprint of his fingers for days. Hell, if he hasn't marked me already, in ways that may not be visible, but which I will carry inside of me. On my dark soul, which speaks to his. In my mind, which is racing to keep one step ahead of him. In my heart, which is already his... Fuck... No, no, no. No way... I can't allow myself to fall for this beast.

His nostrils flare, he grits his teeth, and I know then, he's coming. A groan rumbles from him as he pulls me back, then urges me down to take his cock all the way down my throat one last time. His entire body tenses, then he throws his head back and growls as he shoots his load down my throat.

36

Michael

Black spots flicker at the edges of my vision. I come with an intensity I have never experienced in all of my thirty-nine years. The orgasm seems to go on and on, then fades away as suddenly. My shoulders relax and I stare down at the witch who did this to me. The water laps over her mouth as she meets my gaze from under half-closed eyelids. I pull her up and off of my cock, watch as she licks her lips. There's no evidence of cum around her mouth, and it's not because the water wiped it clean. I had blown my load down her throat. She had taken me so deep inside that there was no chance of cum spilling from her lips.

I haul her toward me, then close my mouth over hers. The salty taste of my cum, the sweetness of her palate, that sexy feminine scent of her, tinged with moonflowers... All of it overpowers my senses. I pull her into my chest, wrap my arms around her as I ravish her mouth. As I suck on her tongue and drink from her. As I lose myself in her. Fucking only her. I tear my mouth from her, gaze into those green eyes. Pupils blown, color high on her cheeks, her lips are swollen from my attention. I glance down at her creamy breasts, cup one, then bend down and kiss the nipple. She shivers as I similarly anoint the other pebbled tip, then press small kisses back up her throat, to her mouth.

"Michael," she whispers as I brush her lips with mine. I lick her mouth, then rub my nose against hers, before kissing her one eyelid shut, then the other.

"Michael." She wriggles in my hold, and I pause.

"What is it?" I murmur as I press more kisses to her forehead, to her temples, lick the shell of her ears before sucking on the lobes of her ears.

"Michael," she pouts, and this time I lean back.

"What?"

She opens her eyes and scowls up at me, "I need to come."

I blink, then burst out laughing. "*You* need to come?"

"It's not funny." She slaps my shoulder, "You just had the most intense orgasm ever—'

"It was okay," I lie.

"Bullshit." She presses her forefinger into my chest, "You came like you were the last man on earth and this was your very last orgasm, ever, and you hadn't had sex in months before this."

"Days," I raise a shoulder, "but who's counting."

She opens and shuts her mouth. "You're a real piece of work, you know that?" she snarls, tries to pull away and I tighten my grip about her.

"You know I don't try to hide the kind of man I am. It's what you like about me, after all."

"Not." She leans back, trying to put space between us, as if I am going to let her.

"Liar," I murmur. "And you were right."

"I was?"

I nod. "That..." I rub my nose with hers, "was the best orgasm I have ever had."

Her eyes open wide before she schools her features, then sniffs, "You don't have to sound so surprised. When I set my mind to something, I don't back down; and I told myself that I was going to suck your soul through your dick."

"Is that right?"

She tips up her chin, "Are you denying that it was an out-of-body experience for you?"

"It was..." I scan her features, "more than that. It was like dying a little, and much as I am not a fan of the French, la petite mort—the little death, is the best way to summarize how it felt."

"Oh." She blinks, "Okay, that's good."

"It was more than good... It was *eccezionale*, Beauty." I smirk, "And now it's your turn."

I rise to my feet and lift her up with me. I step out of the bath tub, grab a towel and hold my hand out for her. She steps down from the tub, and I pat her shoulders, her breasts, her waist, her hips, the dip between her legs, her ankles, her pretty feet. By the time I straighten, she's staring at me with parted lips. I use the same towel to squeeze the excess water from her hair, then rub myself dry and toss it aside. I bend my knees and lift her up, and throw her over my shoulder.

"Hey," she protests, "what are you doing?"

"Making sure my wife gets the orgasms due to her."

She huffs against my back, "Wish you wouldn't call me that... It feels...too intimate."

I chuckle, "We are in my bedroom, after I came down your throat in my bath tub, and now I am about to put you down on my bed, and make you come all over my tongue, so this, *tesoro, is* intimate."

I slap her bottom and she protests.

I lower her onto the bed, and she sprawls on her back, her long, red hair still dripping and flowing around her shoulders.

She shoves the strands away from her face, then tips her chin up. She pushes up to her elbows, thrusts her chin out, then bends her knees and slides them apart. I rake my gaze down her flushed face, over her heaving breasts to the juicy flesh between her legs.

Fuck me, but she's a temptress, a gorgeous siren, an enchantress come to tempt me from my path.

And apparently, I am more than willing to let her distract me... For now. I walk around the bed, then stretch out next to her with my head on the pillow.

She turns over, braces herself on her elbows. "I thought you owed me an orgasm?" She pouts.

"And you'll get it." I tap my chest, "Come 'ere."

"Huh?" She frowns, "What do you mean?"

"Ride my face, Beauty."

She blinks, then crawls over to me. Throwing a leg over my chest, she positions herself over my face. I stare up and into her most intimate place, the pink lips flushed and swollen, and glistening with evidence of her arousal. The opening of her channel that would be warm and wet and welcoming, and so fucking tight that I could lose myself there for days. The sweet, sugary scent of her arousal, and beneath that, the light trace of moonflowers. Always fucking moonflowers. I am going to have to plant a garden full of them, then roll about in them, so I can always carry her next to my skin.

Fuck, she's truly getting under my skin. I really do need to fuck her out of my system so I can get on with my life.

"This is bullshit," she mutters from above me. "Why are you staring at me like that; it's so embarrassing." She tries to move away and I grasp her hip. "Shh," I glance up at her, "I am studying the lay of the land."

"What?" She scowls, "I am not some stupid, rival gang that you need to plot against and figure out how to overpower."

"But you are as deadly, Beauty," I place my other palm on her hip, and hell, she is so tiny that I could easily span her waist with one palm. She seems fragile, but packs a punch. She looks like a gust of wind would blow her over, but she has a spine of steel. This woman has so much gumption, such strength, such resilience… And if I let her, she could wield so much power over me.

Nope, not happening. Never going to allow someone else to hold sway over me. I am going to fuck her, then use her to get to the Seven… And once I have the alliance locked down formally with them… Well… then I'll decide what to do with her.

I pull her close enough for my nose to nudge against her center. I draw in a lungful of Beauty and my cock instantly thickens.

"Oh, my god." She moans, "Why did you do that?"

"Don't you like it?"

"I… I…"

I sweep my tongue up her slit and she shudders. I slurp at her pussy lips and she shivers. I curl my tongue around the swollen bud of her clit. Her entire body trembles. She tries to close her thighs; I lean in, so the width of my shoulders is in between them. I plunge my tongue inside her sopping wet channel and she squeaks. Her pussy clenches down as she digs her fingers into my hair and tugs on it. My scalp tingles. Pinpricks of heat race down my spine, and my groin hardens. I push my face closer to her core, then begin to fuck her with my tongue. In and out of her, in and out. I lick the cum that dribbles from her channel and a whine bleeds from her lips, "Oh, my god, Mika." She warbles, "Oh, my fucking god."

A chuckle rumbles up my throat. I continue to thrust my tongue in and out of her as she yanks at the hair on my scalp, and holds on.

"Oh, Mika. Mika. Mika," she chants as she thrusts her hips forward, trying to encourage me to bury my tongue deeper inside of her. I curve my tongue inside her channel and she huffs. I hold her upright with one hand as I slip my fingers around and in between her ass cheeks, to play with her back entrance. She stiffens and I lick up and into her, again and again. Her entire body trembles. Her thighs clench. I pull my tongue out of her channel, then slide my thumb inside her backhole, even as I bite down on her pussy, and she screams as she comes. Moisture drips out of her, down her inner thighs, and I lap it up.

I lick up her slit, between her pussy lips as she slumps over me. I lower her to the bed, push her onto her front, then arrange her on her hands and knees. I press my palm into her upper back and she pushes her cheek into the pillow. She thrusts out her hips, and fuck me, but her heart-shaped derrière sends the blood racing to my shaft. I grab my cock, position it between her pussy lips. Then grab her hips, and in one smooth thrust, I impale myself to the hilt. Her entire body jolts and a moan bleeds from her lips as her pussy clamps down on my cock.

All of my sense focus in on her and I begin to fuck her. I slam into her with such force that the headboard slams into the wall. My balls slap against her clit as I set a punishing pace. Sweat beads my shoulders, as I pump into her wet, soft, tight channel. She grabs hold of the headboard, holds on as I plunge into her, over and over again. The pulse beats at my temples, my heartbeat ratchets up, and my muscles tense as the pressure at the base of my spine builds up on itself, and becomes bigger and bigger, until it seems to consume my entire body.

"Fuck," I growl, "f-u-c-k, Beauty." I grip her hips, as she pushes up. She widens her stance, reaches down and between our legs to grip my balls. She squeezes and heat sears my spine. All of my pores pop, and with a growl, I pull out of her, then ram into her once more, so she has no choice but to release me. This time she grips the headboard with both of her hands. "Come with me, Beauty. Come the fuck with me, right now."

I thrust into her and she throws her head back and screams. Her entire body shudders as the orgasm grips her. Moisture floods her channel and I continue to thrust into her over and over again as she collapses. Only then, do I allow myself to come.

37

Karma

When I wake up next, I am alone. I glance around the large bed, at the crumpled sheets, at the darkness gathering outside. Shit, did I sleep the day away? The last I remember, he'd carried me to the bed, and proceeded to fuck me... I mean he hadn't been kidding when he'd said that he'd pump me with so much cum that it'd overflow from my pores. I bring my hand to my nose and sniff. That dark, edgy scent of his, laced with the lighter notes of moonflowers, fills my senses. I smell like a combination of me and him. A combination of me and him.

I sit up so suddenly that the blood drains from my head. Shit. I lean back against the headboard, until the world stops spinning. A combination of me and him.

Fuck, fuck, fuck. I allowed him to fuck me without protection. What had I been thinking? Or rather, I had not been thinking at all. I had been swept away on a sex cloud; lust had addled my brain and turned my thoughts into mush. And he... He hadn't said a word. Fuck, fuck, fuck.

I throw the covers back and begin to pace. That is what he wants...

for me to fall pregnant. To fuck me nonstop until I am carrying his child… And then, I'll have no choice, but to obey him.

As if he doesn't have me under his thumb enough, as if he doesn't control me enough, as if he doesn't already own me, body and soul… And to think, I had thought that I was falling for him. Jeez, give a slut some big dick energy and she instantly thinks she's in love.

Jesus fucking Christ, I am pathetic. No doubt about it… And it's not about the fact that I wanted him to fuck my brains out, which I now suspect he actually did, or that I wanted him to do every filthy possible thing that a man could do to a woman, and things I haven't even read about yet. No, it's the fear that I had been so careless. I had gotten so carried away by everything that had happened, so taken in by his personality, so completely consumed by his charisma, so absolutely owned by his dominance —

And there it is — he had successfully made me submit without my even realizing it. I had not only given him my virginity, but I had also sacrificed my free will at the altar of his arrogance. I had simply rolled over and allowed myself to be taken in by his…cock, his sexual profi-ciency, his…his…larger-than-life presence. I had thrown caution to the winds… Hell, I hadn't even thought about the fact that I could fall pregnant.

As someone who grew up in the foster system, I am well aware of the risks of having a child when you are unable to care for it. And while Summer and I had been lucky in that we had had decent foster parents, still, we had learned very early on to protect ourselves. And I had forgotten all about it. A few days in his presence and I am losing myself, losing my independence and my pride. He's bringing the woman I am deep inside to the surface… And I don't want to deny who I am. I don't want shame to prevent me from being myself. … But, here I am, facing the very real possibility that I might have conceived a child by my captor already, and that is not a part of my life plan right now.

Fucking hell. I grip my hair and tug on it. Think, Karma, think. You have to do something about this. But what? I glance around the bedroom…his bedroom… Shit, I am standing here naked, and he could walk in at any moment. I'll take one look at his delicious body and all other thoughts will leave me. I'll probably throw myself at his feet and ask him to fuck me again.

And would that be so bad? To let him have me, to assuage this hunger deep inside of me. So what, if I fall pregnant? It would mean that he'd have to keep me, he'd have to protect me, he couldn't harm me then, right? And this…this is exactly what he wants. For me to give up my will, and my ability to make decisions, my prerogative to choose… He wants me to lay it all at his feet so he can dominate me absolutely. And that…that I cannot bear.

I want children…eventually. And if I am pregnant, I will keep this kid too… Only, no way, am I going to let his presence taint his or her life.

Either way, I need to get the fuck out of here. Surely, there has to be a way off the island? A boat somewhere…? No way, would his staff and his brothers and the rest of his team leave him without, at least, some way to get off this place. If there is a way off, then I am going to find it.

I pivot, run out of his room, down the corridor into what had been my bedroom. I race across the floor to the closet. Pull out underwear, scrounge around until I find a pair of pink jeans and a white sweater. I pull on the clothes, along with a pair of beige-colored ballet pumps. Ugh! Hate the colors, but they'll have to do. At least, they are comfortable and I can run in these ballet pumps. Too bad the asshole had taken the clothes I'd been wearing when he'd kidnapped me. Guess he'd only wanted me to wear the clothes he bought for me.

My stomach flip-flops. *Oh, hell no, I do not like that gesture of ownership; I do not. Totally, not.*

I glance around the room. Anything else I can take from here? Anything to protect myself? Anything I can defend myself with? His knife. Of course.

I retrace my steps down the corridor, back into his room. As soon as I enter, the scent of sex hits me. My belly quivers. I only have to scent his smell and my entire body seems to go into overdrive. Fuck that. Don't look at the bed. Pretend he didn't just fuck you on those sheets.

I scan the room, spot his knife on the side table. No way. Did he actually leave it behind? He must have been more distracted than usual to do that. Or…he's not far off. Shit, maybe he went to get some food to eat or something? I run over to the side-table, grab the sheathed knife and tuck it into my waistband at the small of my back. Then I race out of the room, to the staircase, down the steps.

I hit the ground floor and hear the sound of his voice from the kitchen. Guess he's speaking to someone. The sound of pots and pans being thunked around reaches me.

Is he cooking again? For me? For us? I pause. I could just walk over to him, hug him and join him for a late lunch... Or an early dinner... Or —I shake my head. Fuck no, this is exactly why I need to leave. All of these thoughts of domesticity and cozy meals and hot, steamy fucking between the sheets... *OMG! Stop it, right now.*

I walk away from the kitchen, across the big main living room, to the front door. I yank it open, slip through, then close it softly behind me. I race down the steps, down the driveway, toward the main jetty, then stop. I can't see any boats there. There has to be another jetty, another boathouse. Another way to get off this island.

I retrace my steps, then run around the perimeter of the house. When I reach the kitchen windows, I duck low, straightening only when I reach the end of the house. I break into a sprint, taking the path that runs through the forest, past the clearing where he had tackled me not too long ago.

The rain has eased off, and while the ground is slushy, it doesn't pose a problem. I run through the trees, emerge on the other side, and spot a boathouse. Yes! I take the steps that lead down to the structure. When I reach the shed, I push the door and it opens. Huh. Okay, I wasn't expecting that.

I step inside the gloom, take in the boat tethered on the water between the two ramps on either side of it. The far side of the boathouse is open, and beyond it, I can see the inlet of water that leads out to the open sea. Shit, how the hell am I going to navigate that? I don't know how to navigate a boat, but I know how to drive. I mean, it can't be that different, right?

I step in, close the door behind me, when a hand clamps down on my mouth.

No, no, no. I begin to struggle, and someone hisses in my ear, "Stop it, I am trying to help you."

It's not his voice. Michael's voice is darker, more...gravelly, deep enough to send a shiver down my back. This man, whoever it is, also has a strong voice. It's just not intense enough to be Michael's.

"I know you are trying to get away from him, and I can help you."

I freeze.

"I am going to take my hand away from your mouth now," he murmurs. "Promise me you won't scream?"

I hesitate and he whispers with more urgency, "Nod your head if you agree."

I comply, and he removes his hand.

I draw in a breath, turn and blink up at him. His features are familiar—that height, the width of his shoulders. He's taller than Michael and more leanly built. Where Michael is all raw power and blatant dominance, this man wears his sophistication like a veneer. His muscles coil and his gaze sweeps over my features...

No, underneath the mask he wears to the world, he is all ruthlessness and authority. Shit, this man is as dangerous. Maybe more so, because he conceals his savagery with refined elegance.

"I... I saw you at the wedding." I murmur. "You're Michael's brother?"

"Younger to him by only a year." His jaw hardens. "Funny how fate determines exactly where you land in life, isn't it? Take birth at the wrong time within a powerful family, and you'll find yourself always in sight of the seat of power but never close enough to grab it."

"Ah," I nod. This man is bitter, maybe aggrieved about the fact that he isn't the eldest in the family. He wants revenge for that? Perhaps he's even upset for something that Michael did to him? No wonder he saw his opportunity and moved in now. "I don't intend to become a pawn in whatever twisted games you and Michael are playing."

"And what about the games he is playing with you?" He tilts his head, "What about the fact that he kidnapped you, then married you to pay your father's debt, then threw you into a cell."

I stiffen. "What are you trying to say?"

"That we can help each other."

I frown, and he chuckles. "Not like that." He steps back, putting space between us. "Not that you are not attractive, but you are married. The two of you exchanged vows in front of a priest, so you are morally his. Also, Michael has filed the marriage papers signed by both of you with the local municipality. So legally, as well, you belong to him."

"Hold on," I scowl, "I didn't sign anything."

He stares at me and I throw up my hands, "Jesus, he forged my signature, didn't he?"

"Do you blame him?" He raises a shoulder. "Even I can see that you'd have never agreed to sign it of your own free will, and seems, he wanted you for his wife, at any cost."

"Which is why you want to help me get away from him," I firm my lips, "because you know it will hurt his ego more than anything to lose his most prized possession."

His gaze widens and he takes in my features with something akin to...respect? Maybe wariness, even. "I can see why he is so taken by you." His lips curl. "Perhaps you are more intelligent than you look."

I scowl. "Perhaps we need to get out of here, before he comes?"

I tip up my chin and he chuckles.

"He really has no idea what he's in for, does he?"

"Oh, I think he must be getting an idea about now." I brush past him, step onto one of the ramps, when I hear the sound of Michael calling my name.

"Che cazzo," Luca growls. "He'll find us. Come." He brushes past me, up the ramp, and begins to undo the tether to the boat. I walk toward him, then clamber onto the boat. He finishes untying the craft, then jumps onto the vessel, which rocks from side to side. I grasp the edge of the boat, hold on as he brushes past me. He reaches the driver's seat, then presses his finger to the ignition button. The engine fires up, then stops.

"Fuck," he growls as he presses down on the ignition again. The engine coughs, roars to life, then dies away again.

"Oh, god," I squeeze my fingers together, "come on, come on, please, start."

He pauses and I shot him a glance, "Why aren't you trying to start it again?"

"Can't flood the engine," he explains. "Just need to give it a few seconds."

"It's time we don't have." I hiss, glance around the boat as the door behind us is flung open. I don't need to glance around to know he's entered the space. Anger thrums off of him, crashes into my back as I gasp. The hair on the back of my neck rises.

"Beauty," his familiar growl rumbles through the space, "what the hell are you doing?"

38

Karma

"What do you think?" I turn toward him. "I am leaving you."

"Not having much success, are you?" He prowls over to me, pauses on the ramp near the motorboat which has begun to drift away from the ramp. "Come back to me," he orders. "Now."

"No." I shake my head, "No, I will not."

"And you?" He glares at Luca. "I trusted you," his jaw hardens, "my brother, my second in command... The man I believed in all these years."

"Excuse me while I play the violin for your woes." Luca laughs.

"Who got to you, Luca?" Michael tilts his head, "This is not you. This bitter, cynical man, who is betraying me... This is not the brother I know."

"You don't know me very well then, do you?" Luca's lips turn down in a sad smile, "You only ever saw what you wanted; you always believed that you knew what was best for all of us."

"What are you talking about?" Michael frowns, "My entire life, to date, has been devoted to protecting all of you."

"If only that were true," Luca says in a low voice, "and you accuse Nonna of turning a blind eye when he beat up mother."

Michael stiffens, "What are you talking about?" He leans forward on the balls of his feet, "What did he do to you, Luca? Tell me what happened."

"Don't worry about it, *fratellone*," Luca's lips twist. "You just worry about how you're going to explain how you let your wife run away from you."

Michael's shoulders stiffen. The skin around his eyes tightens. He glares at Luca a second longer, seems about to say something, then changes his mind.

"Why are you doing this?" He widens his stance, "Turn back, and I'll forget any of this happened."

"I think not." Luca's lips curve, "Not when I am enjoying the sight of the powerful Capo, reduced to begging his woman to stay. If you're not able to keep her, how are you going to take charge as the Don? Clearly, you are not fit to succeed him."

"So that's what this is about? Power?" Michael folds his fingers into fists at his side.

"When is it not about power?" Luca chuckles, then glances toward me. "Oh, I forgot, you think yourself in love, don't you? You think she is the woman who came to redeem you? Too bad, she doesn't feel the same way."

I stiffen, wanting to tell him to shut the hell up, but I don't. He's wrong, though. Michael isn't in love with me. All he wants is to possess me, own me, use me, then discard me. But I'm not going to correct him. Not when he's doing a damn good job of keeping Michael occupied while we wait to re-start the goddamn engine again.

"I would have done anything for you, my brother." Michael lowers his chin, "I would have given up anything for you."

"So, if I had asked you to hand over the title of Capo to me, would you have done so?"

Michael stiffens. A nerve pops at his temple, but he stays silent.

"Thought not," Luca murmurs. "Don't kid yourself, *fratellone*. All these years, you've kept me close just to keep track of my movements." Luca, shakes his head, "No brother, if I had told you how I truly felt, if I'd even breathed a word of the fact that I wanted to be Capo, you'd have killed me —"

"Or not," Michael folds his arms across his chest, "and now we'll never know. Either way," he nods toward me, "let her go. She isn't part of whatever power games you want to indulge in."

"I beg to differ," Luca smirks. He wraps his arm around me and I shoot him a confused glance. What the hell is he up to? And after he told me that he's not interested in me in that way.

On the ramp, I sense Michael tense. "Get the fuck away from her," he says in a voice so hard, so cold, that a shudder runs down my spine. My thighs clench and my belly flutters. Shit, I should not find his anger such a turn on. I should not find the possessiveness that laces his voice so damn sexy. I should not allow myself to turn to him, fix my gaze on his as I lean into Luca and murmur, "I don't want you, Michael. I want him."

Michael's nostrils flare.

Next to me, Luca's muscles bunch. But he must understand that I am playing along with him, for he hauls me closer. "You heard her." I can hear the smirk in his voice as he addresses Michael over my head, "She's not with you anymore."

"She's. My. Wife." Michael's voice whips through the space. The pores on my skin pop. My toes curl. Oh, my god. Michael Byron Domenico Sovrano in a rage...is, surely, one of the most erotic spectacles I have ever seen. It's definitely one of the scariest.

Why the hell does everything about this man turn me on...even as I am trying my best to leave him? I squeeze my thighs together, lift up my chin, "Your wife?" I snarl. "Is that what you call kidnapping me and forcing me to marry you?"

"It's what I call what happened over the last 24 hours between you and me," he snaps and my heart stutters. It bloody stutters. I draw in a breath and Luca's grasp about my shoulder tightens.

I try to pull away from him and he whispers, "Don't let him get to you. Remember, you're doing this because you want to escape him."

I stiffen, then firm my lips. "What happened between us was a mistake." I look Michael up and down, "If you think, for one second, you fooled me by what you did, you're wrong. I hate you." I swallow, "I loathe what you did to me, and if I had the chance, I'd turn back the clock and ensure I was never in the park where you first encountered me."

He pales, then sets his jaw. "We'll talk about that later," he says in a tone that is so soft that there is no mistaking the menace that laces it. Jesus H Christ, I've done it. He's so bloody pissed at me, that the moment we are alone next he is going to... Shag me? Spank me? Both of the above, and maybe not in that order.

I gulp, even as wetness laces my core. Oh, my god, what's wrong with me that, even now, I can't get rid of the images that crowd my mind? Of him cramming his dick inside me, his touch on my skin, his scent in my nostrils, the heat of his gaze as he takes in my features, as he glares at Luca's arm about my shoulders.

"Take your hands off of her or—"

"Or what?" Luca smirks, "From where I am, there's not much you can do."

Michael's jaw tics. He squeezes his massive hands into fists at his sides, then takes a step forward. Luca tries the ignition again. The engine fires up, the boat leaps forward, then the engine dies down.

"Fuck," he swears, takes his arm off of me, then begins to play with the buttons on the dashboard.

"Couldn't you have thought of this before?" I hiss.

"It's a last-ditch resort." He bends, pulls out a panel, then yanks at some wires.

There's a flash of movement to the side. I turn, then scream when Michael dives into the water. He swims toward us and panic squeezes my chest. *Shit, shit, shit.* I need to do something about this, but what?

If he reaches the boat, if he gets on, no way, can we escape. Worse, if he gets his hands on me again… If he takes me captive again… He'll never forgive me. He'll make me regret trying to escape him. *And you'll love every minute of it.* No. I shake my head…

It's this addiction to him that got me into this situation, in the first place. It's because I couldn't stay away from him, that I let my guard down enough to, perhaps, even trust him, that I may now be pregnant with his child and… *No…* If that's the case, I definitely need to get away from him. He reaches the boat, grabs the edge and the craft rocks. I scream again, grab the back of the seat to steady myself. I need to do something, anything, but what?

"The oars," Luca jerks his chin to a corner of the boat. "Grab an oar and fight him off."

"No," I cry, "I don't want to hurt him."

"If you don't, he'll hurt you," he retorts. "You don't want that, do you?"

Do I? How can I tell him that I like it when Michael puts his hands on me? How it turns me on when he treats me like his plaything. How… I lose sight of everything when he's near me.

Oh, my god, I have no choice. I am going to have to do this. If I let him near me again… I am never escaping him… And my child… If I am pregnant, he or she will never know a normal life.

I scramble around the seat, totter toward the end of the boat, where one end of the oar pops out from under the cover of the tarpaulin.

Michael grabs the edge of the boat, begins to haul himself over the side. That's when I spring forward. I grab the oar and raise it. My muscles scream in protest. The oar is heavy enough that my knees almost give way under me. I manage to find my balance, and the oar slips from my hands. The edge slams into the side of his head. I tighten my hold on it, pull back as his gaze widens. Those blue irises flare with… Surprise… No, something else… Hate? No… Love? Not possible. It's lust. It has to be lust. And maybe possession. And anger that I've beat him at his own game.

Blood blooms at his temple and I fight the urge to run to his side and help him. He bares his teeth, swings one leg over the side and I scream. I bring the oar down on him again, just as the boat's engine roars to life. Michael's gaze holds mine. A beat, another. Then his grip loosens, and he falls back into the water. The oar falls from my fingers and hits the bottom of the boat.

I lean over the side, scan the surface of the water, then scream when he surfaces. He thrusts out an arm, and I reach for his hand, only the boat leaps forward as Luca shifts into gear. My fingers brush his, then he's gone, under the water. The wake of the boat fills the space where he'd been.

"No," I scream, "No, no, no."

AND NEXT MAFIA QUEEN

PART II

MAFIA QUEEN

1

____

Karma

"Michael!" I scream as his head disappears under the water, "Oh, my god, Michael!" I spring up, ready to dive into the water, but Luca catches me around my waist.

"Let me go," I yell. "Michael! No! I have to go to him."

"If you jump into the water now, you know what he's going to do to you, right? He'll not only imprison you, he's going to kill you, and then you'll never be able to see your sister again."

Summer. My breath hitches. _Summer._ I need to get out of here so I can return to her. It's what I want, right? It's why I had first stabbed Michael, then run away from him when he'd been occupied with fixing food in the kitchen. Michael... I swallow. What if he doesn't survive though? I stop struggling and Luca releases me. He focuses on steering the motorboat.

I stare back at the receding jetty as the boat pulls away. The wind whips my hair into my face and I shove it back.

"He needs help." I turn to Luca, "Please, call someone. We can't leave him alone."

He hesitates and I clutch at his sleeve, "Please Luca, please, he's your brother."

"It's too damn dangerous," he says through gritted teeth. "It'll place me squarely at the scene of the crime."

"If you don't call someone and have them help, then if he does recover, he'll never forgive you."

"He'll never forgive me anyway." Luca twists his lips, "Asshole will kill me… That is, if he does survive."

"He will survive," I say fiercely. "He has to. Please, Luca, please call somebody and have them send help. You know I am right in asking this."

He stares at me a second longer, then swears aloud. "Steer the boat, will you?" He jerks his chin toward the steering wheel. He steps back and I slide into the space in front of the steering wheel.

I grab it, and when he's sure that I have a firm grip, he releases his hold on it.

He pulls a phone out of his pocket, and presses a few buttons, before holding it to his ear. "Seb?" He snaps, "There's been an accident, at the island. Michael needs help."

He listens for a second, as the other man speaks, before interrupting, "I know because I was there, and now I am not. You'd better send someone before it's too late."

He disconnects, then tosses the phone overboard, before turning to me, "This call was a big mistake."

"It wasn't," I insist. "I don't want him to die, and neither do you."

He laughs, the sound bitter, "Asshole wouldn't die that easily. He's probably clambering onto the beach as we speak and walking toward the house."

"I hope so." I swallow as he crosses over to me and takes the wheel again. I shift to the side, sink down onto the seat next to him. "I didn't mean to…hurt him," I murmur. "I only did it out of instinct. I didn't mean for him to…" I can't say the word aloud. He's not going to die. He cannot die and yet, I can't take my gaze off of the island that's growing smaller by the second. What am I hoping to see? Michael emerging from the water and walking onto the shore? Michael standing there and watching me as I leave him? Michael with his dark gaze, his chiseled features, those massive shoulders, his wide chest… Michael with his edgy, dark scent that I will forever carry with me. *Michael. Michael.*

Michael. A sob bubbles up and I don't stop the tears that run down my cheeks.

"I wish I could go back," I wrap my arms around myself. "I wish I could make sure that he's okay." I am mumbling to myself but Luca hears me.

"He has a harder head than you can imagine." He speaks in a loud enough voice that I can hear him above the sound of the breeze, "Look, I know it's unfortunate that you had to do what you did, but at least, you are free of him now."

"Am I?" I swallow, "He's going to come after me."

He has to come after me. He has to live. He has to survive what I did to him. Surely, he can't have drowned. I didn't hit him that hard, did I?

"You're right," Luca concedes, "it's the first thing he's going to do once he's back on his feet. You likely bought us a little time though."

I keep my gaze focused on the island until it recedes from sight. My heart stutters, a cold sensation stabbing at my chest. *You'll see him again. You have to...* I shake my head. What is wrong with me? I had spent the entire time I was on the island trying to get away from him. And now that I have managed to escape, I can't stop thinking about him.

This is for the best. I am leaving him behind and going to find my way back to my own life, to my home... That's what I want, right? Home... I swallow. Why does it feel like I left my home behind? That house on the island that belongs to Michael...isn't home. Not my home. It's his place. I am... His? *No, no, no.* I rub my fingers across the ring on my left hand. That...is his... The mark of his possession with which he branded me. Just as he imprinted his touch into every cell of my body, engraved his name into my soul, stamped the sensation of his thickness in between my legs. I squeeze my thighs together.

Shit, this is not the time to think about how brutally he had taken me that last time. How he had eaten me out, before positioning me on my hands and knees, then gripped my hips, holding me immobile as he had thrust into me from behind. Oh, my god, he had...taken me, owned me with the sureness of his movements. He had consumed me, imprinted himself into the most intimate parts of me. He had changed how I perceive myself... He had reached deep into the recesses of my soul and forced me to confront who I am. A woman whose tastes are extreme, someone who needs to be challenged, and subdued, someone whose spirit can only be matched by the lord of the underworld himself. A beauty who needs her beast, her master's hand upon her head as he calms her, his fingers around her neck as he chokes her, his tongue inside her soaking wet channel as he licks into her and — "Bloody hell," I swear aloud and Luca glances sideways at me.

"You okay?"

I chuckle. "What do you think? I may have murdered my husband, who I only married a few days ago, after he kidnapped me, by the way," I squeeze my fingers together, "so no, I am not okay."

I stare forward, into the wind that slaps my face. My eyes sting and a pressure knocks at the backs of my eyes. Shit, I've made a complete mess of this. Not only had I fallen for my kidnapper, aka my husband, but now I can't stop thinking that it was a mistake I managed to escape from him. What the hell am I going to do about this? I turn to Luca, "I need to call my sister as soon as possible."

"I am afraid that may not be a good idea."

"What do you mean?"

"It means if you call her, you'll only be putting her in danger."

"What danger?"

"As you said, he's going to come after you. No doubt about it... Unless..." He raises a shoulder, "Unless he didn't make it out of the water."

"He made it out of the water," I snap. "He is alive, dammit."

"Either way, it's best we lay low until we know for sure."

"Shit," I squeeze my eyes shut, "I'm so screwed if he's alive."

"And if he's dead—"

"No," I open my eyes and turn to him, "don't you dare say that."

He blows out a breath, "As you wish. My saying it or not is not going to change the reality though."

"I am aware," I mutter, as I scan the shoreline that's coming up. "Where are we going, by the way?"

"To a safe house in Bagheria."

"Bagheria?" I turn to him, "Where's that?"

"It's the town to the east of Palermo."

"Shouldn't we, maybe, try to move further away from Palermo? I assume he is well known in town and must have contacts around the city. Besides, doesn't he know about all of your safe houses?"

"Not this one." He shoots me a sideways glance, "You're no pushover, are you?"

Only when it comes to him. Oh, Michael, what have I done? If you don't make it out alive I... I'll never forgive myself. My chest hurts and I rub at the space above my left breast.

"You okay?"

I shake my head. "Not really," I mutter. A trembling seizes me and I wrap my arms around myself. If he were here, he'd fold those massive arms around me, he'd pull me into his chest, tuck my head under his chin, and rub my back... Right before turning me over his knee and spanking me for what I did.

Luca shrugs off his coat, and hands it over to me. I glance at it and shake my head. It feels wrong. I shouldn't be wearing another man's jacket. If Michael saw it, he'd kill Luca... Or maybe not. Luca is his brother, after all. Although, after this incident... Yeah, not sure how Michael will treat Luca after this... And shit, why are my thoughts back on him?

"Take it." Luca, places it around my shoulders, "You don't want to catch a cold. Michael would never forgive me if anything happened to you."

He stiffens as if realizing what he's just said. "Not that you'd want to have anything to do with him, now that you've escaped him."

Right. I stare at the shore as Luca continues to steer the boat. Half an hour later we reach a jetty that juts out from the approaching beach. As soon as we draw up next to the wooden platform, he cuts the engine again. Then walks around to the far end of the boat—the end from where I'd raised the oar and brought it down on *his* forehead.

Shit. Unable to process my feelings, with tears welling up in my eyes, I press my face into my palms and feel my body convulse. What the hell have I done? How the hell am I going to live with myself if something happened to him? My heart feels like Michael used his dagger to cut it into pieces and now part of it is missing, and he has it. My belly twists itself up in knots. I gasp for breath as I allow the tears to flow down my cheeks... Until the sobs finally subside. The boat jerks, and I glance up to find Luca's tethered the boat to the jetty. He's watching me with a look of sympathy on his face.

He bends over, holds out his hand, "We need to move fast, Karma, before one of his guys finds us."

Right. I take his hand and he helps me onto the jetty.

. . .

Two hours later, we draw up in front of his safe house on the outskirts of Bagheria. Someone had been waiting for Luca with a car at the jetty.

He'd glanced at me, and had seemed surprised. Following a flurry of conversation in Italian with much gesturing from the other guy, he'd finally seemed pacified and had left. Luca had driven us here.

I glance at the small, single-story cottage. It has white-washed walls and a fence around it. It's no more than a cabin, really. In the distance, I can see the hills, but there is nothing else around the building on either side.

I follow him inside and he scans the space, then points me to one of the bedrooms at the end of the corridor. "That's yours. Why don't you shower and see if you can find some extra clothes in there, left by some of the other guests before us?" I glance at him and he shrugs. "May as well get comfortable; not sure how long we're going to have to stay here."

I strip off my clothes and the knife—Michael's knife that I had taken with me—falls to the ground. I stare at it and tears prick my eyes again. I pick up the knife, still in its sheath, press it to my cheek. The dark, edgy scent of him instantly fills my nostrils. My chest hurts and my heart, what's left of it, feels like it's going to burst. *Oh, Mika, Mika, what have I done? Mika!* Nothing I do will ever make up for what I did to you. How am I going to live with myself after what I did? How am I going to live without you, my darling? My one and only. My...other half. My soul.

My fingers tremble, the knife slips from my hold and I manage to catch it before it hits the floor. I straighten, place it on the small table near the window, then stagger to the bathroom. By the time I shower and change, my tears have dried up somewhat. There is a hollowness in my stomach and it's not only from hunger.

That's how it is...eh? Doesn't matter that you have committed a heinous crime. Your body still needs sustenance to live, apparently. Live for what though? And for whom? A pressure builds again at the backs of my eyes and I swallow down the ball of emotion that has lodged in my throat. I walk into the kitchen to find Luca is heating up something in a saucepan.

He turns when I walk in, "It's stew, the best I could do."

"It smells of..." I walk closer, then pause next to him and peek into the contents, "It has seafood?" I frown, "I'm allergic to it."

"Ah, well." He blows out a breath, "There should be some bread in the bread basket and cheese in the refrigerator."

"That works for me." I pull out the bread and cheese, and make myself a sandwich. By the time I sit down, he's served himself a bowl of stew and poured us both coffee from the *moka* coffee maker he'd had going on the flame.

We tuck into our food, and when I am done, I lean back in the chair. "Any word on…"

He shakes his head, "I put out some feelers earlier, reached out to some old contacts who are in touch with the Cosa Nostra. They've heard nothing."

I frown, "But you dumped your phone—"

"I keep a few spare burners here."

"Right," I shuffle my feet, "so you were saying that they've heard nothing about Michael," I swallow. "Is that good or bad?"

He shakes his head, "I am not sure."

That familiar cold sensation stabs at my chest. My fingers tremble and I place my palms in my lap. "This doesn't feel right." I mutter, "Shit, if something has happened to him, I… I…" I jump up and begin to pace, "maybe I should go back and make sure he's okay. I'm his wife after all, aren't I—"

"Do you think he's going to see you in that role after everything that happened?"

My shoulders slump. "I guess not…but I wish I could do something. Why did I have to hit him that hard? Why did I have to panic? Why couldn't I have just…pushed at him or something instead? Shit, this is not good. This is so not good." I wring my hands together in front of me, "There must be something I can do?"

"The best thing you can do is stay here, until things cool off."

I pause, turn to him, "Can I call my sister?"

He shakes his head, "It would be best not to."

"Maybe I could text her and let her know I am okay, just so she doesn't worry."

"Can you put that off for a little while longer? It's best for you not to communicate with anyone."

"You think Michael and your other brothers could track us?"

"They have access to some of the best hackers, so yeah, that would be correct." He places his spoon down in his bowl and leans back.

"Thanks to me, the Sovrano clan is technologically the most advanced of all of the families."

"Why did you fall out with Michael?"

"Why didn't I fall out with him?" He chuckles without humor, "From the time I was born, I've known that he was the older brother, the heir, the man who would one day be the head of the clan, the one slated to take over from the Don, when the time comes. It's always been all about him… As long as I am in his shadow, I'll never be able to come into my own."

"So, you saw me trying to leave, and seized the opportunity—" I scowl. "What were you doing at the boathouse anyway? I thought Michael asked everyone to leave."

"I don't obey my brother in everything." He smirks.

"So, you stayed on after everyone left?" I tilt my head, "Why would you do that?"

"Let's just say, I had a hunch that not everything would be fine in paradise."

"You thought I'd make a run for it?"

"I thought…that you'd try something." He rubs the back of his neck, "To be honest, I didn't think you'd get as far as you did. Michael is way too sharp, too alert. I didn't think you'd get past him." He regards me with a shrewd gaze, "But then, I don't think he realized how smart you really are."

"Is that a compliment?"

"One-hundred percent." He grins and his face lights up. I blink. Shit, this man is truly handsome, in a very classical kind of way. He has the same kind of presence as Michael. To be fair, all of the Sovrano brothers do, as do their half-brothers. But in terms of charisma, Luca is the closest to Michael. Both fill up the room in a similar way. Both have that determined set to their features, the stubborn tilt to the jaw, that sense of dominance that rolls off of them in waves and which screams that they can be very persuasive and authoritative, and that once they set their minds on something, nothing can deter them. Only he isn't Michael.

I slip back into my seat at the table, and he tilts his head. "I am guessing my brother was so taken in with you, he lowered his guard. It's why you managed to slip by him."

I play with the ring on my left hand. I'd tried to remove it in the shower, but of course, the stupid thing is stuck. It refuses to come off. "I think you are wrong," I murmur. "Michael never lets his guard down.

Not with anyone, and certainly, not with me. It was a lucky break that I found myself alone and decided to risk running out of there."

And the main reason I'd wanted to leave was because I'd thought that I could be pregnant. How had I forgotten about that? Shit, it's too early to test if I am. Probably... I could wait for a week or more at least, right?

And what if I am pregnant and he's dead? Does that mean I would bring up my child without a father? I am keeping the kid, of course. That's assuming I am pregnant. And if I am not... Well then... I'll still be on my own, after Michael... How could I ever be satisfied with anyone else?

Shit, he's the one, isn't he? Why have I taken so long to recognize that? But this doesn't change anything... Even if I had stayed... Even though it felt like he was changing his attitude toward me... Even then, he was a man on the wrong side of the law. He kills people for a living, for hell's sake. He's not the kind of man I'd want as the father of my child, or the type of person, I'd want to stay married to... Right?

And yet... I'll never be able to forget him, or how my body had responded to him. Shit, shit, shit. I lower my chin to my chest. If only things had been different. If only he weren't in the Mafia and I had met him in more normal circumstances. If only I'd had a chance to date him like a normal person, and...

Who am I kidding? Michael would never be a 'normal' anything. That man has too much dominance, too much self-assuredness, too much confidence... Too much everything. He'll always stand apart from others. He'll always be different... And fact is, the sense of danger that clings to him only adds to his allure. The darkness in him... It's what drew me to him. The sense of menace that hovers about him... It's a turn on. The fact he wields instruments of violence like other people employ pens...is what appeals to me.

So why is it that when I thought I was pregnant, my first instinct was to escape from him? Is it because I think I can't trust him when it comes to my child? Because I don't know how he would react when he finds out? Because I know he'll want the child... And then what? Would he forget about me completely after that? Would he want me to conform to the role of wife and mother and lose my individuality completely? Shit. What's wrong with me? A dull headache drums at the backs of my eyes and I draw in a breath. "I think I need to lie down," I murmur.

Luca glances up at me, "Everything okay?"

"Yeah." I swallow. "It's been a long day. I need to get some rest."

I am woken up by the sound of knocking on the door. "Karma," Luca calls out, "you awake?"

I clear my throat, "I am now." I glance around to find the sun's rays slanting through the open window. I reach for the lamp near the bed and turn it on.

"Can I come in?" he calls through the door.

I sit up in bed, glad I had worn all of my clothes when I'd gone to sleep. "You can come in now," I reply.

Luca enters, and his features are set.

"What happened?"

"I'm afraid it's not good news," he murmurs, as he leans a hip by the doorway.

My heart begins to thud and my throat closes. "Wh…what do you mean?"

"I managed to connect with one of my team and…"

"And…?" My voice cracks. I fold my fingers together, narrow my gaze on him, "Tell me, please, what did you find out?"

"It's Michael, he…" Luca swallows, "he didn't make it."

2

Karma

I stare at him, trying to process his words, trying to make sense of what he said. "What do you mean he didn't make it?" I throw the covers off, jump out of bed. "Who did you speak to? Maybe they are lying. He made it out of the water. Of course, he did. He had to... You, yourself, said that he's not easy to kill, that he had a hard head, remember? He has to be alive. He can't be dead."

Luca shakes his head, "I'm sorry," he murmurs, "Seb announced it at a meeting of the family. He is taking over temporarily as Capo."

"No," I shake my head, "no, no, no, it can't be true." The world tilts and my vision narrows as black spots creep into my periphery. I blindly reach behind me, find the edge of the bed, and sink back down. "Please, no. Not M...Michael." My voice breaks and tears flow down my cheeks. I cover my face in shame.

How could this have happened? How could I have killed my...own husband...the possible father of my child? The only man who's ever touched that part deep inside of me, who awoke that darkness in me... Who made me feel so alive. Who...loved me. I know he did. I saw it in his eyes right before he went under. My throat closes, my ribcage tightens and something hot stabs at my chest. Oh, Michael, Michael, what have I done? I grab my pillow and squeeze it tightly as I begin rocking.

How can I make up for this? What can I do to repent for my mistake? For having killed the man I love? My fingers tremble and a cold sensation grips me. I lift my head and glance up at Luca, "I need to go."

"Where?" He frowns.

"To Michael."

"Karma," he squats down in front of me, "Michael's gone."

"His funeral." I clear my throat, "I need to attend his funeral."

"No," he scowls, "that's impossible."

"Why?" I set my jaw. "He was the Mafia Capo. Surely, they'll have a big funeral for him so everyone can pay their respects."

"If you go, if they see you, you're dead."

"I'm dead now," I reply. "I feel like I cannot breathe, cannot live after this. I..." I hunch my shoulders, "How can I live with myself after what I've done? I...need to go see him and apologize to him. I can't go on without seeing him one last time."

"That is a seriously bad idea," he groans. "If, by some miracle, you get near the casket, they will shoot you on sight, or worse."

"I don't care." I firm my lips, "I must see him, so I can tell him..." *How sorry I am for what I did.* Not for having run away, but for having hit him with that oar. He'd been coming after me. He'd wanted to pull me... his wife away from leaving with another man. He hadn't been thinking straight when he'd jumped in the water and swum toward me. He'd lost his control, shown his weakness and I... I had taken advantage of it.

Damn it, I have to see him one last time. See his gorgeous face, kiss...his forehead, say my goodbyes... I'll never get closure for what I did, but... I can, at least, tell him how I feel. Tell him that I love him. I owe him that much, surely. "I..." I swallow, "Please, I need to go to him."

Luca rises to his feet and begins to pace, "Not only are you going to die, but you are going to get me killed with you."

"You don't have to come with me."

He snorts, "What if my brothers stop you?"

"I'll take my chances."

"Shit." He digs his fingers in his hair and pulls at it. "Seems even here, my dear *fratellone* beat me at my own game. I left the clan so I could find a way to challenge him, to show him I could wield more power than him. Just one time, I wanted to sit at the same table as him and show him I was his equal, but the bastard had to go one up on me here, too." He stops, turns to me, "And if I refuse to help you now, he'll probably never forgive me. The *stronzo* will probably come back to haunt me."

He blinks, and I swear, I can see his eyes shining with unshed tears. Guess he loved his brother in his own way. And me... How had I loved him? As a wife, his submissive, his slave...his...captive? All of the above? I bite the inside of my cheek. "So, you'll help me?"

He stares at me, then jerks his chin.

Some of the tension drains out of my muscles. "I'll probably need to get a different set of clothes."

He stares at my red-colored hair, "That's probably a good idea." He tilts his head, "We'll need to get there first thing in the morning."

"So soon?" I stiffen. Not that it would mark a difference, but I'd hoped I could get some kind of a grace period, at least a day to prepare?

"The Mafia prefer to bury their loved ones as quickly as possible. So, we need to get to the vigil before tomorrow evening."

Right. "Will you help get me the clothes I need?"

He blows out a breath, then nods.

"Thank you," I murmur

"You won't be thanking me when my brothers come after you."

I set my jaw. "We'll see about that."

3

Karma

"So, this is it?" I stare through the window of the car. In front of me are the steps to the church and next to it, and tucked a little to the side, is a small chapel, which is where the wake is being held, apparently.

Michael's wake. Mika… My husband's wake. Shit. Is this really happening? Could I have been married and widowed in such a short time? I toy with the ring on my finger, then cover it with my palm. It's the last piece of Michael I have with me and I am never going to let go of it. Unless… I press my palm to my stomach. Unless… I am carrying something else of him.

"You don't have to do this, you know." Luca's voice cuts through my thoughts. I turn to find him staring at me, a concerned look on his features.

"I do." I bite the inside of my cheek. "Thanks for bringing me here."

"I would have come in with you…but—"

"No, that's fine." I clutch at the edges of the thin black veil that covers my face. "This is something I need to do myself."

He looks as if he is about to say something, then stops himself.

"Good luck," he murmurs as I push open the door of the car and step out.

A gust of wind whips my hair about my shoulders. The veil flattens against my features and I run my suddenly damp palms down the skirt of my dress. The handbag in the crook of my arm bumps against my side. Luca had bought it for me, along with these clothes and sensible black shoes. None of which is my style... But at least, the colors are more to my liking. Not that it matters... Where I am going... There's going to be only me and my conscience...and him. The body of my dead husband.

Shit. I stumble, then right myself. I take a step forward as the car drives off, leaving me alone. I glance around the empty street, then move toward the chapel. My heart begins to thud and my pulse rate ratchets up. What am I going to do when I see his body? Will I break down completely? God, I hope not. I simply want his forgiveness, that's all. I mean, what happened wasn't entirely my fault, right? It's he who had wronged me first. If he hadn't kidnapped me...then forced me to marry him... I wouldn't have been pushed into doing what I did. I was right in wanting to escape him... It's just... I hadn't expected my actions to result in such a horrible conclusion, okay?

I square my shoulders, move toward the chapel, push open the door and step into the dimly lit interior. The door shuts behind me with a snick. I glance about the space... Take in the mourners in the pews. It's not as full as I thought it would be.

Two men stand on either side of the coffin. All in dark suits, all with their heads bowed. I recognize Seb, and next to him is the broadest of all the Sovrano brothers. The men on the other side of the coffin are the brothers who resemble each other so closely that I'd placed them to be twins the first time I saw them at my wedding. A motion to the far left draws my attention. Antonio, Michael's bodyguard stands to attention by the side door. I glance to the other side and find another of his brothers by the other exit.

My heart begins to thud. Will they stop me from seeing him? Please, God, please don't let them.

There's a man standing in front of the coffin at the end of the aisle. He bows his head, stands silently for a few seconds. As I near him, he straightens, then makes his way back to his seat.

A woman glances up as I pass, then looks away. The rest of the people face forward, their features solemn.

As I approach the coffin, the biggest of the Sovrano brothers glances up. His jaw stiffens as he watches me approach, but he makes no move to stop me. As if alerted by my presence, Seb, then the twins, turn their gaze on me. The hairs on the back of my neck rise. The tension in the air seems to ratchet up. My stomach ties itself in knots, and I feel light-headed. I force myself to put one foot in front of the other until I draw level with the first pew.

When none of the men stop me, I step up to the coffin. A dull pressure presses down on my temples, and I squeeze my eyes shut. *Oh, Michael, Michael, what have I done?* I tuck my elbows into my side, then force myself to open my eyes.

Strong features, square jaw, that hooked almost aristocratic nose, those thick eyelashes that fan against his cheekbones... The wide forehead with a bruise at his temple... The bruise that I had caused when I had hit him with the oar. I curl my fingers into fists, take in his thick hair that is combed back except for that errant strand in the center that curls over his forehead. No longer will he reach up for it and push it away. No longer will he glare at me with those beautiful blue eyes of his. A sob wells up... Oh, Mika, Mika, I am so sorry for what I did.

A trembling grips me. My legs threaten to give away and I dig my heels into the ground to steady myself. I raise the veil and push it back over my head, then touch my fingers to my lips, and press my fingers to his forehead. I lean over him. A teardrop slides down my cheek, plops on his forehead. That's when his eyelids snap open.

4

Michael

"Hello, Beauty." I bare my teeth, and her fingers tremble. Her gaze widens and color drains from her face.

"No," she shakes her head, "No, no, no."

"Yes." I allow my smile to widen, "Oh, yes, my darling wife."

"It can't be." Her voice wavers and her chin trembles. She looks like she has seen a ghost, which of course, is what I am to her now. It should be almost comical. I should enjoy just how terrified of me she seems to be, except...The throbbing pain at my temple where she had smashed the oar into me insists that she is real, and standing in front of me, arm outstretched. Tears glisten on her cheeks.

She opens and closes her mouth, grows even more pale.

She pulls back her arm and I swoop my hand out and grab her wrist. She sways; her eyes roll back in her head. Her legs seem to give way and she slumps toward the floor. *"Che cazzo!"* I growl as I sit up, then leap over the side of the coffin. I catch her before she hits the floor, then pull her into my arms as I sink to the floor. She's so fucking tiny, and weighs next to nothing. Has she lost even more weight in the last day?

The veil flutters back from her face, the paleness of her skin a stark contrast to the black of the fabric. Dark shadows circle her eyes, her cheekbones seem too prominent in her face. She seems too still, too lifeless. I hold a finger under her nostrils. The warm rush of air flutters across my skin and the tension drains out of me.

Seb approaches us. He squats down next to us, peers up and into my face, "You okay, *brother*?"

His voice is gentle, and fuck, if that doesn't annoy me. "My wife tried to kill me. Do you think I am okay?"

He hesitates and I blow out a breath. "Get them out of here," I jerk my chin toward the gathered crowd, "and the lot of you can leave too."

"But," he frowns, "Mika, you're still in pain."

My heart hurts. And I don't understand why. She hit me on my head, which has no connection with my chest. So why is it that there is a heavy sensation crowding against my ribcage?

"Go," I snap. "Keep watch for Luca. He's bound to turn up again for her."

My grip on her tightens. My own brother had deceived me. He'd helped my wife escape from me. He'd prompted my wife to hit me with the oar, then he'd sped away as I had sunk under the waves. He'd left me for dead. They both had. So why the hell had she returned? To gloat over what she'd done? It doesn't make any sense… And yet, I had counted on it.

A part of me had been confident that she would come. It's why I'd had Seb formally announce my death to my clan. Luca has a mole on my team… Someone leaked the news out to him. I'd had my suspicions… and I had been right. He'd taken the bait and believed the news. He must have told her and she'd asked him to bring her.

I'd vacillated over whether she would show up, but ultimately, I'd been sure she would, just to make sure I was dead. To ensure that she was rid of me… I'd been right. Which also means that she spent the night with my brother. Fucking, fuck. A growl rips out of me, and Seb frowns, "We need to get both of you out of here, before the Don gets wind of how you staged your own death."

"Not now," I snap.

His frown deepens, "Mika, you're not thinking straight. Let's take her and get you both home. Get you looked at by a doctor and —"

"Not-fucking-now." I glare up at him, "Leave."

"But —" He raises a hand and I cut him off.

"That's an order." I glance around to where my brothers watch me with varying expressions of concern on their faces, "All of you, out. Now."

Seb nods, then rises to his feet. He glances at the other men, who exchange glances with him, before they begin gathering up the guests and ushering everyone out the door. Finally, the door closes, leaving me alone with my errant wife. My beautiful wife who'd dared defy me. Who'd spread her legs for me then walked away from me. Who'd taken my brother's help to escape from me. Who'd left me for dead then come back to gloat in my face.

The silence deepens, intensifies… A beat, another, then her eyelids flutter. I take in her features as she opens her eyes. She gazes up at me, and for a second, there's a genuine smile on her face. As if she'd fallen asleep next to me then woken up from a dream. Then a line appears between her eyebrows as her forehead furrows. A look of pain… of helplessness… hopelessness? —taints her gaze.

"Mika…" she whispers, "oh, Mika, is it really you?"

Her green eyes hold mine. She reaches up to touch my cheek and I pull away. She swallows and her frown deepens. "You're alive," she murmurs.

"Are you surprised?" I tilt my head, "Wishing I was dead, Beauty?"

"No." She shakes her head. "No, no, no. If you were dead, I don't know how I would have survived."

"You seemed to have done quite a good job of it, considering you left with my brother."

"Luca?" She frowns.

Anger crowds in on my mind. "You dare say another man's name in front of me?"

"But, it's not like that."

She reaches for me again and I growl, "Don't fucking touch me."

She pauses, bites on her lower lip, and of course, my gaze is drawn to her mouth. Her gorgeous mouth with which she had sucked me off. Her tongue, her lips, the very teeth that she uses to chew on her food… All of it which belong to me, and she had dared turn her back on me. She'd left with another man… And not just any man, with my own brother. She had betrayed me. She had used my own blood to get back at me. My guts twist and heat flushes my skin. My vision narrows. "Did you sleep with him?"

"With who?" She scowls, "What are you talking about?"

"Enough," I roar and my voice echoes through the space. "I have had enough of your act, the way you always use your sassy attitude to disorient me. The way you stand up to me and mislead me."

"Me mislead you?" She sets her jaw, "I've always been straight-talking with you, buster. I have always told you what I wanted, have always been upfront with how I wanted to be able to choose for myself."

"And you chose to leave me for dead."

She pales.

"Tell me, did you enjoy looking into my eyes while I went under the waves and imagine that you'd never see me again? Did that gladden your heart, Karma? Did that make you happy? Did you and your lover laugh about it while he fucked you last night—?"

Her palm connects with my cheek and my face snaps back. The sound of the slap echoes back, enveloping us in a cocoon of rage before it fades away.

She gulps, then covers her mouth with her palm. "I'm sorry," she whispers, "so sorry. I didn't mean that."

"I don't believe you."

"Please, Mika, please believe me when I say that Luca didn't touch me. I left with him, only because he happened to be there and I wanted to escape. He was just a means to get out of there. That's all."

"And you hitting me and leaving me for dead, are you sorry about that too?"

"More than you can imagine." She tries to sit up and I release her. She tips up her chin, gazes into my face, "You have no idea how much I hated myself. How I couldn't believe I'd done that. How I hoped that you would survive. How I prayed that you would be alive."

"Seems your prayers were answered."

"And I am so grateful," she swallows and a tear runs down her cheek. And my heart stutters; it fucking stutters. What the fuck? The woman is barely back for a few minutes, and already, I am softening. Already, I can't wait to take her home, to my bed, to make love to her, and ensure she never leaves me again... And... I am setting myself up for a fall again. The next time my back is turned, what guarantee do I have that she won't do the same thing? How do I know that she won't murder me in my sleep? Why does the thought of clashing with her send all of my senses into overdrive? Adrenaline laces my veins. My groin hardens.

"Turn over," I growl.

She blinks, "Wh…what?"

"On your hands and knees; turn over."

5

———————

Karma

Anger rolls off him in waves, and the hair on the back of my neck rises. I stare up into his blue eyes and shiver. There is no trace of the man who had fucked me… Or of the man who had married me… Who had made pancakes for breakfast for me. This man is closed up and hurting. He is raging at me… At the world. He is wounded, and not just from the physical hurt I had caused him. It's the fact that I had run away from him. That I had taken the little bit of empathy he had begun to show me, and turned it against him. I had left him…had insulted him, had ground his ego underfoot as I had run away from him… With the help of his brother, who had also betrayed him. It probably convicts his brother doubly in his eyes.

I chew the inside of my cheek, "I… I know you are angry with me Mika, but—"

"You know nothing." His voice is low, so hard… So harsh that a shiver runs down my spine. He is shutting down, taking any emotions that he may have once shown me and shoving them so deep down that I might never reach him again. My heart begins to thud in my chest and my pulse rate spikes.

"Mika, please listen to me."

"You may call me Michael," he commands as he takes in my features. Those blue eyes are cold fire, like ice-chips, that glow with the reflection of the northern lights.

A cold sensation coils in my chest. I have to reach him. I can't let him build up these walls between us again. If he does, I'll never be able to get through to him.

"Mika... I mean, Michael," I tip up my chin, "I have something for you." I reach for my bag and he grabs my wrist.

"Don't fucking touch that."

"I just want to return something that I took from you."

"Oh?"

I nod, "If you'll only let me open my handbag."

He releases me, only to snatch my bag from me.

Jerk.

He opens the handbag, pulls out the knife, then throws the bag aside.

"Did you think you could stab me again?"

"No, Michael. It's not that; its —"

"Shut the fuck up," he growls. "I don't believe a word you say. Do you know how much this knife means to me? Is that why you took it?"

"Michael, please. Please, let me explain."

He laughs, "If you think you can tell me what to do, you have another think coming."

"Oh, for heaven's sake!" I curl my fingers into fists, "Will you, for one second, stop posturing and let me explain, you macho asshole?"

He stills, then looks me up and down, "You, clearly, have no attachment to your life. It's why you marched in here, and with my knife on you."

"That's what I am trying to explain to you." I swallow, "I came because —"

"Shut up," he snaps, "just shut the fuck up. I have had enough of your tricks, you pathetic excuse for a woman."

I pale, "Thought I was your Beauty."

"I was, clearly, mistaken."

"I am not, though."

He frowns, "The fuck do you mean?"

"There's a reason I returned, and with your knife." I swallow, "I want you to use it on me."

He sneers. "How many lies can you tell? It's a record, even for you."

"It's not a lie," I say through gritted teeth. "Seriously, haven't you been listening to a word I am saying?

"No more tricks," he growls, "turn around. On your hands and knees, or I'll make you do it."

"I'll do it… Just… I want you to use your knife and —"

He grips my shoulder, applies enough pressure so I am forced to turn around. I push up on my hand and knees, then flinch when he taps the outside of my thigh.

"Spread your legs," he says in a hard voice, and bloody hell my knees go weak. Moisture beads my core and my pussy clenches. I slide my legs apart, or as much as the skirt of my dress will allow.

I hear the sound of him moving, the scrape of metal on metal. I turn, glance at him over my shoulder, in time to see the glint of light off the blade. He swoops down. I flinch, then cry out when I feel him slice through the skirt of my dress. Cool air assails the heated flesh of my thighs.

"Wider," he growls. "Part your thighs."

I obey, slide my legs apart, even as my core dampens further. What the hell is wrong with me? Why do I find his rough handling of me, the thought of him taking me right here in this church… Which is, technically, a blasphemy… Why do I find that so much of a turn on?

I sense him move a second before the blade nicks my skin. I whimper, feel the draft on my pussy lips and know he's cut through my panties.

Silence descends and I can feel the blood pumping in my ears. My heart beat ratchets up further, even as a sinking sensation crowds in on my chest. My belly twists and more moisture slides down my inner thigh.

I hear the jingle of his belt, the rasp of his zipper being lowered, and all of my nerve endings seem to catch fire. I push up my butt, knowing he'll spot the small movement…but I don't care. I am horny for him. I want to feel his thick, fat cock inside me. I want him to take me, to fuck me, to prove to me that he is alive. To show me that I am still worthy of him. Bloody hell. I squeeze my eyes shut. Why am I so ready to degrade myself like this? I lower my chin… Wait… Wait as he grips my hip.

I sense him move closer, the heat of him enveloping me, holding me in a space where there is only me and him.

"Stay still," he commands as his hand moves.

I glance over my shoulder in time to watch him slice through the dress at my hip. He rips the fabric apart, and cool air strikes my hip, a second before a lick of pain slices through me. I huff, crane my neck, to find his hand moving. What the hell? The breath rushes out of me. He's carving something on my hip. Another tingle of pain crawls up my spine.

"Michael," I groan, "what are you doing?"

He doesn't answer, continues to cut into the skin over my left hip. More pain sears through me and I bite down on my lower lip. Whatever he is doing… I deserve it. More than deserve it. At least, it shows that he heard me. At least, this means he cares about me enough that he is marking me.

He digs the knife deeper than the previous times and I stop the cry that bubbles up my throat. I taste blood and realize I have bitten down on my tongue. I swallow down the urge to sob, tilt my chin up. I can do this. I can get through this. If it means, in the end, Michael will forgive me… Can he forgive me? Will he forgive me?

He wipes the blade on my sleeve, and I turn again in time to see him slide it into the sheath.

I draw in a breath, only to cry out when fire slices through me. I dart my gaze to where he scoops up the blood from my freshly cut skin, then he teases my backhole with it.

Fear grips me. "Michael, please," I swallow, "please don't."

He glances up at me, "Are you saying no?" His voice is cold, as remote as his gaze. His shoulders are bunched and his chest planes seem hard enough that if I touched him, I am sure I'd come away hurt... And bleeding… More than I am now.

"Well?" He raises an eyebrow, "Say the word and I'll back off."

I swallow, then jerk my chin.

"What was that? I didn't hear you?"

"I…" I swallow down the ball of emotion that threatens to clog my throat. "Yes," I reply and am glad my voice doesn't waver. "Yes. I say yes."

He instantly slides his finger inside my puckered hole and a groan spills from my lips. I feel myself tense around the intrusion, and draw in a deep breath. In, out, in. I force my muscles to relax as he moves his finger in and out of me. He adds another finger and I stiffen. It's already too much, too soon. Shit, how am I going to take all of him inside. He pulls out of me completely, then slides both fingers back in.

"Open for me," he commands and the sound off his voice shivers over my skin. My pussy clenches and warmth sears my skin. He brings the fingers of his other hand to my pussy, then slips them inside my soaking channel. He scoops up the moisture, drags it up to my backhole, smears it around the entrance. He adds a third finger, and I throw my head back.

"Omigod, omigod," I chant as he thrusts the three fingers in and out of me. In and out. He pulls them out, then a blunt something nudges at my back entrance. "No, not yet, please, Michael," I burst out, and he pauses.

"Do you want me to stop?" His voice is remote, so standoffish, almost bored.

I stiffen, turn to stare at him over my shoulder. He holds my gaze as his features take on an impenetrable look. I have come this far. I can do this. If this is the only way to get through this, then I am going to let him fuck me in the arse. I wince, then steel myself. Tip up my chin, and shake my head. "No," I say in a firm voice, "I want you to take my arse. I want you to bury your thick, hard cock inside my—"

He pumps his hips and breaches my backhole.

Oh, bloody hell. I dig the heels of my palms into the ground, grit my teeth against the strangeness of the sensation. I won't lie, it's painful, and weird...and feels unnatural... It feels like... I have something up my arse... Which I do. I swallow down the stupid giggle that bubbles up. Jeez, that's what comes of having a stupid sense of humor. It takes me by surprise at the most inconvenient of times. He grips my hips, and I sense him stay still as he allows me to adjust to his size.

Then he reaches around and cups my breast. He tweaks my nipple with such ferocity that a groan spills from me. The trembling starts at my toes, creeps up my legs and what the hell? I can't already be coming. Not so soon. He releases my nipple, only to slide his hand down to my clit. He plays with my piercing and my pussy instantly clenches. Jesus, God. I had no idea, that I could respond with such intensity when my piercing was tugged. A warmth builds in my core. I draw in a breath and that's when he slips inside me further. So full. So... Packed... How do I even describe the sensation? A tingling sweeps up my spine as he pulls out of me. He reaches down to play with my pussy lips at the same time that he thrusts forward.

A burning sensation coils deep inside and I yell out as he hits a spot deep inside me. My eyes roll back in my head and oh, my god... What the—what is that? How is it that this is even more intense than the time he fucked me before? My knees protest and pain shivers up my thighs, meets that gnawing, yearning, sensation that coils in my core. He pulls out, then begins to fuck me in earnest. He thrusts into me and I shudder. He pulls out once more, then lunges forward, impales me with such force that my entire body bucks.

"Michael," I groan, "Oh, my god, Michael."

"That's it," he says in a hard voice, "you scream my name, every time you think of coming, you get me?"

I nod.

He thrust into me again, hitting that spot deep inside me again and sparks go off behind my eyes.

"Michael," I whine, "Please, Michael, please."

He propels himself forward with such force that I almost fall over. It's only his grip on my backside that holds me up. A burning sensation radiates out from where he cut into me and heat sears out from where his cock, once more, hits that secret space in my core. The feel of his big hands on me as he impales me, yet again, makes me feel like I am a puppet being moved around in a fashion designed to give him the most pleasure, even as I surge toward my climax.

With each thrust, my breasts jiggle, my muscles coil, and that tension at the base of my spine tightens, hardens into a knot. The trembling grows more intense, sweeping up my thighs, up my back. That's when he pulls out of me.

What the—?

I glance over to find he's already on his feet. He tucks himself inside, zips himself up, and tightens his belt.

"What are you doing?"

"Leaving." He saunters past me and I stare at that tight behind of his. Those powerful thighs, clad in a custom-made suit, those shoes made of the finest leather... H-o-l-d on. "What the hell?" I yell, "Why did you stop?"

"Because I can?" He snaps his fingers in the air, "With me."

I stare, "What do you mean, *with me*?"

He pauses, then turns to rake his gaze over me, "On your feet; walk toward me. You do understand English, don't you?"

Asshole. That prick... That complete, wanker. Here I am, getting all emotional, ready to do anything for him... Hell, I had done everything for him. I let him take me in the arse, in the middle of the goddam church, and this is what he does? He...fucking pulls out before I can come. I scramble up to my feet, aware of the dampness between my thighs, of the sorry state of my dress. I stomp after him as he walks out of the church. There are two cars parked in front of the church.

As we approach them, Seb walks over to Michael, followed by his other brothers.

"Did you get him?" Michael asks.

Seb shakes his head. "He hasn't shown up, not that I blame him. He'd have known that you would shoot him, if he did."

They don't mention him by name, but they have to be talking about Luca.

"Or worse, you could ask him, why he did what he did," I burst out.

Both men turn to me. Seb glances at me, then averts his gaze. I look down at myself and heat flushes my cheeks. The skirt of my dress is in tatters. The bodice is not torn, but it's clear from the creases on it, not to mention how my veil is half off my head, what Michael and I had been up to. And I don't even have an orgasm to show for it, damn it.

Michael... He simply takes in my features, before he turns back to Seb, "Take her home."

"Xander, Christian," he nods toward the twins, "follow me. Massimo," he jerks his chin toward the biggest of his brothers, "I'll meet you at Venom. You too, Adrian."

The remaining brother nods.

Michael walks off in the direction of the Maserati parked on the road.

"Wait!" I call out, "What do you mean *take me home*? Where are you going?"

He ignores me as he opens the door to the Maserati. Anger flushes my skin and I march over to him, "You'd allow someone else to take your wife home?"

He slides into the driver's seat, then glances up at me, "You left me, Beauty, and now you expect me to treat you as my wife?"

"Yes," I snap.

He chuckles. "Your innocence knows no bounds, *amore mio.*"

"I am not innocent."

"And I don't see you as my wife anymore."

"What then?" I scowl. "What do you see me as?"

"My whore."

6

Michael

I lean back in the chair in my office at Venom. By rights, I should be out there in the room that my crew and I use whenever I am here. But that hit to the head did a number on me. Because I refuse to take the painkillers, the pain is a constant heaviness behind my eyes. And the last thing I want to face is the constant throb of the music that pulses through the nightclub. I bring the glass of whiskey to my lips, then hesitate. I am taking antibiotics… And the doctor had warned me not to mix alcohol with it… But fuck that. You only live once… And right now, I need something to take refuge in. Considering I just disowned my darling wife…

I had called her my whore… And that look of absolute shock, and confusion…and sadness on her face… *Merda,* it had almost gutted me. I tighten my grip around my glass, then bring it to my mouth and throw back the contents. The whiskey burns a path down my throat. It hits my stomach and heat explodes in my gut. Too bad it doesn't fill the emptiness that tears at my insides. I place the glass on the table with a thump, just as the door to my office opens. The throbbing of the music instantly fills the space. Seb walks in, followed by Massimo, then Adrian, Christian and Xander. The door shuts, cutting of the music once more.

Porca miseria! "What the hell are you *stronzi* doing here?"

Massimo bypasses Seb and walks over to the bar on the far side of the room. He grabs five glasses, then stalks over to me. He places the glasses on my desk, and fills them up, including mine, before placing the now empty bottle on the surface. "*Salute, fratellone,*" he clinks his glass with mine. Christian and Xander snatch up a glass each. Only Seb folds his arms across his chest as he glowers down at me.

"What?" I frown, "The fuck you looking at me like that?"

"Feeling guilty, yet?" His gaze intensifies.

"Why should I feel guilty?" I take another sip of my whiskey, then survey the contents of my glass, "If this is about her—"

"Of course, it's about her," Seb growls. "The state in which you left her... You should be ashamed of yourself."

I chuckle, "And you are...what? An expert in relationships?"

"More than you, for sure." He rocks forward on the balls of his feet, "I understand you are upset with her. I know you can't get over the fact that she injured you and ran—"

"Injured me and left me for dead."

"You weren't even close to dying." He mutters, "You have too thick a head for that."

The wound at my temple pulses as if in agreement. The headache behind my eyes increases in intensity. "She spent the night alone with Luca," I snap.

"She'd never be unfaithful to you," Xander insists.

"No, she'd only leave with another man." I fold my fingers at my side.

"You need to be more broadminded in your outlook, *fratellone,*" he chides. "Luca would never betray you."

"And yet he did."

Xander grimaces, "Have you asked her if anything happened with Luca?"

I glare at him.

"So, you are just drawing conclusions based on circumstantial evidence?"

"Are you saying I should forget what she did to me?" I retort.

"I am saying that you should treat her with a little more sensitivity."

"Wait until you meet a woman who gets under your skin, and then have her try to kill you and walk away from you, then we'll see how you react."

"You admit that she's gotten under your skin?" Massimo smirks. "Also, are you sure she tried to kill you?"

"I admit to no such thing." I scowl, "I only meant that as a figure of speech, and," I roll my shoulders, "as to the answer to your second question, the intent in her eyes when she took the oar to my head was very much about keeping me away from her."

"Maybe she panicked? Maybe the oar slipped from her hands?" Seb strokes his chin, "Have you considered that?"

"She hit me on the head. Twice." I tip up my chin at him. "Trust me when I say that the second time it was clearly with an intent to hurt."

"Maybe she was simply trying to hold you off. After all, you did kidnap her and force her to marry you."

After which, I had made love to her. Damn it, those couple of days when it had been just the two of us on the island, when we had consummated the wedding… When I had fucked her and poured my heart, my soul…my cum into her. When I had made her mine, and…she…she had walked away from me.

"*Vaffanculo!*" Christian smirks. "The Capo has tied himself up in the proverbial knots."

I glower at the most irritating of all my brothers. Christian has the face of a model and the IQ of a genius. It's one of the reasons he's in charge of my finances. The man keeps all of the figures in his head, never gets his numbers wrong. He's also blessed with eidetic memory, which means he has a nearly perfect photographic memory of most things he sees. Which he often uses to his advantage. Which means he's normally one step ahead of most people. Just not me… Except this time, he, clearly, is.

I reach for the bottle of liquor, then frown. "You guys finished my booze."

"You're on antibiotics, aren't you?" Christian scowls at me, "Should you even be drinking?"

"Mind your own damn business, *fratellino*," I growl.

He raises an eyebrow, "Clearly, fighting with the wife has not improved your disposition." He chuckles.

"Hey," I glance around at their faces, "thought you guys were on my side."

"We are," Adrian murmurs. "It's why we are looking out for you, *fratellastro*."

"Seems more like an intervention," I growl.

"What if it is?" Seb drawls, "It's not every day that our Capo goes a little *pazzo*." He smirks, "I wouldn't miss this chance for anything."

"Fuck off." I snap, and Seb chuckles.

"Seems you're angry enough to use English swear words instead of your favorite Italian ones."

I glare at him and he merely laughs. "*Gesù Cristo*," he drawls. "This entire incident is affecting you more than expected, huh?"

I take in the expression on the faces of all the guys... There's concern and worry, and yeah...love, too. Fuck, I must be completely losing it if I am actually picking up on the emotions from them. Not that I've doubted for one second that my brothers and stepbrothers love me... Okay, so maybe with Seb, I've always been sure that he wouldn't hesitate to betray me. Seems I was wrong. Seems I should have been more worried about my wife...and my own brother. Luca... Damn it, how could Luca do this to me?

"You are thinking about him, aren't you?" Xander's voice interrupts my thoughts. Of course, my youngest sibling picks up on my disquiet. He always has been the most empathetic, the most instinctive of all of us.

I glance toward him, then nod.

"It's okay to share your concerns with us, big brother." His lips curve, "We are family, after all. It's what we do. We talk, we air our worries, we support each other."

"That's what I thought about Luca, then see what he did."

Silence descends, then Seb straightens to his full height. "Take that back," he growls. "Everyone in this room is here because they are concerned about you."

"I don't fucking need it," I snap. "Speaking of, I am tired of this emo shit. Why the hell don't you guys get the hell out of here?"

No one moves. They stare at me, with varying degrees of sympathy. *Merda*, that's all I need, my own family looking on as I fall apart in front of them. To think, I had sworn never to appear weak in front of them. I stare down into the depths of my empty glass, "*Che cazzo*, I need a refill."

Xander steps over to the bar. He leans over, grabs a new bottle, then walks back to my desk. He opens the bottle, tops me up, then places the bottle within reach.

I toss back the liquor and it burns its way down my throat. My stomach protests; my head spins. Shit, maybe I'm weaker than I thought. Guess that blow to the head really has affected me more than I realized.

Xander leans forward on the balls of his feet, "You're hurting, *fratellone*. It's understandable. Losing both your wife and your most trusted confidant and friend in one go, it's not easy. Hell, it would have felled a lesser man."

"But not me," I declare.

"Not you," he agrees, his expression filled with understanding. Shit, that's all I need: Xander's particular brand of empathy that would most definitely prompt me to open up about my fears, my anger, my utter disappointment at having been cast aside… Like I don't mean anything to either of them.

Just like my father has only ever needed me to the extent that he needs an heir, someone to carry on his legacy. He's never seen me as anything else. Not his son, not a child who needed someone to look up to. He had been my hero and he had destroyed me. Abused me until I had begun to look at the world with suspicion, with mistrust. Something that I have never gotten over. No wonder her turning her back on me had sent me into such a spiral. And now, I am psychoanalyzing myself. Shit, enough of this emo shit.

I set down my glass, then rise to my feet, "If you all think I am going to sit around and commiserate about the loss of my wife and brother, you are mistaken."

"They are lost," Xander frowns, "but not in the way you are making it out to be. They just need to be guided back home. You need to only speak to them, Mika. Open your heart to your wife; talk to her. Reach out to Luca; forgive him; talk to him about how the two of you can work together and—"

"Enough," I snap. "You're the youngest, Xander, and in many ways, the most thoughtful of all us. You mean well. It's why I have tolerated your reactions thus far. But don't think you can tell me what I should feel toward what happened. They both betrayed me, and shall be suitably punished."

"But—"

I raise my hand. "I am leaving, now, and I expect the lot of you to track down Luca, and bring him to me." I turn to Seb, "You have ten days."

7

Karma

I raise my face to the shower. The hot water pours over me, down my back. My side twinges. It's where he etched something into my skin. To be honest it hadn't hurt too much — not then, not now... Probably because I have a high pain threshold. Also, because he hadn't pressed down too hard. It's more like he had scratched the surface of the skin enough to draw blood. Bet that had made him happy. He probably wanted to see me bleed. After all, I, too, had drawn blood when I had smashed the oar into the side of his head. I wince. Jesus, we really are all wrong for each other. The way we are hell bent on causing each other pain... It's just plain unhealthy.

I'd tried peeking in the mirror earlier but hadn't been able to make out what he'd etched into my skin. What could that alphahole have written there? The man who had pretended to be dead just so, what...? So he could surprise me with that crazy back-from-the-dead enactment in church? Jesus Christ, the man has a macabre sense of humor. That particular scene was like something out of a horror flick... Or some gangster flick I saw with Summer, who's name I can't quite remember, in which the guy rises from the coffin and proceeds to gun down everything in sight.

Not that Mika had had a gun on him. He didn't need it. Not as long as he had his knife. The knife I returned to him; the one which, clearly, has sentimental value for him, even though he hasn't mentioned anything about it to me. The man has more secrets than the Mafia. Oh, wait, he *is* the Mafia. I shake my head. Seriously, I am losing it.

Seb had driven me here to Michael's house, making sure to keep his gaze averted most of the way. He'd paused only long enough to guide me up the steps of the house and to what looked like a spare bedroom. He'd told me someone would be along shortly with clean clothes for me. Before leaving, he'd also warned me that I shouldn't try to escape because the place is guarded.

Question is, do I want to escape? Frankly, right now I am not sure about anything. I had had my chance to be rid of him, and I had come back. I pause in the act of massaging the shampoo into my hair. If I had stayed on with Luca, it was only a matter of time before I could have gone home. But I hadn't. I'd insisted on returning for Michael's fake funeral. Had I wanted to make sure that he was really dead? Had I wanted to satisfy myself that he was truly gone? Or had my subconscious known that he was alive? That he'd grab me, and make me his prisoner again? Is that what I wanted? To be reunited with my husband?

I lower my hand, stare at the ring on my left ring finger… The ring I have grown attached to, the one that I am not in any hurry to remove. The one I consider mine. Just as he is. All mine. My capo. My captor. My husband. Shit, I really am a goner. I am half-way into falling for him… Or maybe, I am already in love…or at least, in lust with him. It had taken almost killing him to figure that out. What does that say about me, huh? Guess you have to lose something to find out how much it means to you, eh?

I rinse off my hair, shut off the water, then dry and wrap a terrycloth robe around myself. I step out and glance about the bedroom. It's smaller than the room I'd had at the villa on the island, but the view is still breathtaking. I walk to the window, glance at the sea that stretches out in front of me. Clearly, the Capo ensures that all of his homes come equipped with the most spectacular scenery.

As soon as I had stepped into this house, I'd known that this was the alphahole Capo's place. It had to be because his scent had wrapped itself around me like that of a security blanket. I wrap my arms about myself. It's crazy that, despite how horrible he had been to me at the chapel, I still...trust him? Or maybe trust is too strong a word... Let's just say that I still sense the connection I have with him. The attraction I feel for him... That mindless lust that I seem to succumb to every time I am near him. And he feels the same. I know it; I can feel it. Can sense it. Had seen the lust in his gaze when he had told me to turn around and drop to my hands and knees. Had heard the heaviness of his tone when he'd instructed me to part my legs for him.

My core clenches. My nipples bead. Shit, all I have to do is think of him and I am already dripping. Also, because that jerk had denied me my orgasm. Honestly, how dare he? If he thinks he can continue to do that to me... Well... No way, am I standing for it. He has to come to me at some point. Unless... he's fucking someone else? I curl my fingers into fists.

Still, that little encounter in the chapel had confirmed that he wants me. So why had he not escorted me back? Why had he left it to Seb to do so? The Michael I have come to know is so possessive, so primal in his ownership that, no way, would he have allowed anyone else to come near me, let alone hand me over to another man's care, even if it had been only for a little while. I hunch my shoulders, stare at the horizon...

Unless...what I had done to him, had really broken down the trust —tremulous as it had been—between us completely. Unless he really doesn't consider me as his wife anymore. No, not possible. He's not someone who would let go of his possessions. And really, that's what I am. That's what I want to be... His property. His plaything. His.

There's a knock on the door, and I jerk my head around.

A familiar face peeks through the gap between the door and the wall.

"Cassandra?" I exclaim, "OMG!" I pivot, walk over to her as she steps inside the room. I throw my arms around her. "Am I glad to see you, or what?" Okay, maybe I am overdoing the welcome a little bit, but seriously, I am just happy to see a familiar and friendly face. So what, if it's the alphahole's housekeeper?

She steps back, and that's when I notice that she's carrying clothes, and what looks like a first-aid kit in her arms.

"Are those for me?"

She nods, "The Capo instructed me to tend to your wounds."

"Did he?"

She nods, "If you take off your bathrobe, I can attend to them."

I hesitate and she holds out the clothes, "Perhaps you'd be more comfortable wearing a fresh set of clothes first?"

"Whose clothes are they?" I murmur. She opens her mouth to answer and I hold up my hand. "You know what? It doesn't matter. Either it's clothes from someone who's left them behind, or else, he'll have some dumbass explanation of how he ordered them for me or something. Either way, they aren't clothes that I stitched, so it's all the same."

She hands over the clothes, as well as underwear, complete with tags. So, he bought me fresh underwear, huh? Guess I should be grateful, but honestly, it's the least he can do for me. Besides, the thought of him buying lingerie for me feels... Intimate and somehow, right. Okay, maybe a little bit creepy, but hell, he is my husband, he knows my size, and yeah, I definitely need clean underwear right now, so I'll take it.

I accept the clothes from her, murmur my thanks, then walk back into the bathroom to change. Not that I am a prude or anything... But it feels weird just drooping my bathrobe in front of her, you know? Apparently, I have no such qualms when it comes to the Capo. Heat flushes my cheeks. Need to stop thinking about him, seriously. And considering he sent Cassandra to tend to me, he can't be all that angry with me, right?

I pull on the jeans and the T-shirt. It's all in my size, and thankfully, neither is pink in color. Or beige. Or cream. Not even the underwear, which is all black. Hallelujah. I pull on the socks, then walk out into the bedroom, where she's waiting.

"Okay, so while you are applying antiseptic to it, or whatever, can you tell me what it is?" I turn my back to her and pull up my T-shirt.

A gasp fills the air. "What the—!"

I stare at her over my shoulder, "What's wrong?" I frown at her features. She's definitely gone pale.

"What is it?" I ask again as she stares at whatever it is that he drew there.

"It's," she swallows, "it's nothing."

"It's something." I scowl, "Go on, you can tell me."

"No really, it's just, uh, a scratch."

"It didn't seem like a scratch when he drew it onto my skin with his knife."

She walks over to the bed, "Why don't you lie down on your front so I can bandage it?"

"Not before you tell me what it says."

"No," she shakes her head. "Really, Karma, you should let it go."

"You do realize that refusing to tell me what he drew on me is only making me even more determined to find out what it is, right?"

I march back inside the bathroom, turn my back to the mirror, then lift my T-shirt, twist around and try to make out what the hell he carved into my skin. I catch sight of the edge of what looks like a letter. Huh, did he write something on me? What could it be? His name, maybe? Perhaps a declaration of his love?

My heart begins to thud in my chest. Maybe he'd done it and then he'd been upset about it, and that's why he had pushed me away. My capo hates being vulnerable. It's probably why he had asked Seb to drive me here. He probably needed some time to come to terms with having bared his soul to me. That's why he had turned away from me and driven away. Yeah, that's what it is. But why would Cassandra gasp like that?

I arch my neck, trying to sneak a peek. Oh, bloody hell, can't see a thing yet. My spine protests and my side hurts. I turn back, glare toward where she is hovering at the doorway to the bathroom. "Come, on, Cassandra," I whine, "you have to tell me what it is."

"I can't."

"If you don't, I won't let you clean the wound and bandage it, and then the Capo will be angry with you."

Her shoulders slump. "Please, Karma," she says in a low voice, "you are not going to like it."

"Oh, please," I swipe my hair over my shoulder, "I am a big girl; I can take it. Besides, I have an inkling what it could be."

"You do?"

I nod, can't stop myself from smiling. "Sure, he's my husband, remember? We already had a fond reunion," I smirk, "earlier at the chapel. Trust me when I say that it won't be a surprise for me."

She hesitates.

"Come on, please, Cassandra, please," I beg.

She blows out a breath, then walks over with the first-aid kit that she places on the counter near the sink.

She begins to roll up the back of my T-shirt and I turn my head, "Well?" I scowl, "Are you going to tell me, or what?"

"Whore," she mumbles.

"Excuse me?"

"Whore." She grimaces. "He wrote, whore."

8

Karma

"How dare he!" I pace back-forth-back across the floor of my bedroom. How could he do that? After Cassandra had told me what he had scrawled across my lower back I hadn't been able to believe it. She had finally procured another mirror from somewhere in the house and had held it behind me so I could see in the mirror over the sink exactly what he had scrawled on me.

Asshole! What a fucking bastard! How the fuck could he do this? "Aargh!" Anger spikes my veins. Adrenaline laces my blood. I glance around the room, looking for something to break, but can't see anything handy. Damn him. Bet he purposely put me in this room because there's nothing to vent my anger on. I need to do something… Anything…to give vent to this frustration inside of me.

Why the hell did he do this? Is he that angry with me? Not that I don't blame him. Guess I'd be very cheesed off if someone had smashed an oar into my head, and then left me to drown... But he'd pushed me to it.

He kidnapped me first. Surely, I was justified in doing anything and everything to get away from him? I hunch my shoulders… Yeah…

No... I don't believe that rationale myself. I mean, when I had thought that I had lost him, I had pretty much fallen apart. So yeah, facts speak for themselves.

I do regret what I did. Nothing justifies what I did to him... Only, he had survived... Thankfully. So, while I understand that he is pissed off at me....

Seriously though, I still can't condone what he scrawled into my skin. Asshole had marked me...in more ways than one. And I'd thought he tattooed his name onto my body...or professed his love for me? Ha! I pivot and begin to pace again. At least, he'd sent Cassandra to take care of me, so that has to count for something, I suppose. More likely, he wanted to be sure that I don't fall prey to an infection and die. If I did, he won't have anyone to torture. No doubt, that's the only reason he had her clean the scarred skin and bandage it.

That had been two days ago. Since then, the only person I have seen is Cassandra. When I'd asked her where Michael was, she'd said that she didn't know. She'd brought my meals to my room. After the first two, I had insisted on eating at the breakfast counter in the kitchen, and she hadn't dissuaded me. I'd eaten dinner on my own earlier—Cassandra had left, saying she had to run some errands—then I had come up to my room...stared out of the stupid window, gone for a walk around the terrace until it had grown a little too chilly.

I had walked around the huge house... Even peeked into the asshole's bedroom which, holy shit...has a bed which is even bigger than the one at the villa. The bedspread is as blue as his eyes, and the wooden headboard seems to be hand-carved. The entire bed stands on a platform and dominates the room. Other than that, there's a door leading off to a closet, another door that leads to the ensuite, thick carpet on the floor, also blue, a table and two chairs by the window, another table and chair at the far end of the room with a bank of screens that indicates he worked from there.

The scent of him had been so strong and I had filled my lungs with him. Pure, one-hundred percent Capo. My body had instantly switched on—nipples pointed, skin flushed, blood rushing to my cunt, which I admit, is still wet. I had come back to my bedroom, but haven't been able to go to sleep.

Where the hell is he? Why hasn't he returned? Who is he with? Some whore... No wait, that's me, apparently. So, who is he with? Someone else? Someone he is fucking right now, no doubt, trying to get rid of the touch of my skin on his, trying to remove any trace of my scent on him, trying to bury his cock in someone else's pussy, eh? Asshole that he is.

I spin around, stomp to the door, then march down to the library I saw earlier. Maybe I can read some books. That will take my mind off of where my bastard of a husband is.

I grab a book, some stupid strategy book — *SunTzu and the Art of War.* Since when did the Capo read books about war? Though, come to think of it, you could apply the same strategies to Mafia business, I suppose.

I manage to read a few chapters, when the sound of the front door opening reaches me. I hear footsteps approach, then move away. I jump up, run to the door of the study, but can't see anyone. I walk out of the room, down the corridor, peek into the massive living room, which can seat fifty, maybe? Does he use it for his mafia meetings or something? What do they do during that time? Hopefully, not just sit around and shoot at each other. Ugh, I really am going by stereotypes here, huh?

I pivot, walk toward the kitchen, peeking around the doorway to find him standing at the open refrigerator. As I watch, he pulls out a bottle of beer, shuts the refrigerator door, then snaps off the cap and tosses it in the direction of the bin. It misses, hits the floor and rolls away. I step inside the kitchen and realize I am wearing sleep shorts and a T-shirt, along with a thick pair of socks. It's from the pile of clothes that Cassandra had gotten. Huh, not quite the outfit I had in mind for when I'd see him again. Not that I have anything else to wear, anyway. I pad into the kitchen, walk around the island and toward the fallen cap of the beer bottle. I pick it up and he swings around. I straighten, flinch when I stare straight down the barrel of a gun.

"Jeez," I murmur, "it's only me."

Okay, so I had come to chew him out, to rage at him, to maybe slap him, and ask him what he meant by what he did. But now that I am in his presence, surrounded by his overwhelming masculinity, that brooding heat in his eyes as he looks me up and down with no change in expression on his face, and that gun. OMG... There's something about Michael holding a weapon that's so damn sexy. Jeez, it's Summer's fault. I've been watching too many movies with her. That's why I can't do anything but gape as he slides his gun back into his underarm holster.

He tilts the bottle of beer back, chugs down half of it. The tendons of his throat move as he swallows, and I swear, my toes curl. This man, he's a walking, talking orgasm-a-minute, and no, I am not kidding, honest.

He's wearing another suit… Similar to the one he'd been wearing at the chapel, but without a tie. So, he must have changed somewhere else. At his mistress' place maybe? I grimace.

His chin sports a five o'clock shadow… Which would feel scratchy to the touch if he dragged it across the skin of my inner thigh… OMG, bet I'd come just from the friction. My scalp itches. My skin feels too tight for my body. The tanned skin of his neck looks so damn inviting. My fingers tingle and my toes curl. I bite down on my lower lip, watch as he lowers the bottle. The white bandage at his temple stands out against his skin.

"Does it hurt?" I jerk my chin toward his forehead, "It looks like it's healing nicely."

He doesn't answer, simply swallows down the rest of his beer before placing the bottle on the island. Then he pivots and leaves the kitchen. *What the hell?* I follow him up the stairs, and into his bedroom. I stand at the threshold, watch as he takes his jacket off and throws it on the bench at the foot of the bed. He sits to remove his socks and shoes, then reaches for his cufflinks, tries to unhook one.

I walk over to him, "Here let me do that."

I undo the cufflink, pull it off, then turn to the sleeve on his other arm. "Who even wears cufflinks nowadays?" I laugh lightly, "It's quite old-fashioned, actually. But then, you are Mafia. Keep forgetting you guys are still stuck in the sixties." He glowers at me. "Okay, seventies."

He frowns.

"Fine, eighties…"

The furrow in between his eyebrows deepens.

"All right, nineties, okay? Happy now?"

He snorts.

I unhook the cufflink on his other sleeve, and he stands up and steps around me. I turn as my eyes follow him. He begins to undo his shirt, baring more of that glowing tanned gorgeous expanse of his chest. My throat closes and my nipples pebble. He shrugs off his shirt, tosses it on the bench, then rolls his shoulders. I take in the sculpted pecs, the trim waist, the trail of hair disappearing into the waistband of his pants. He reaches for his belt and I swallow. He unfastens the buckle, lowers his zipper. The metallic rasp shivers across my skin. My nerve-endings pop. He shoves down his pants and his boxers in one smooth move, then steps out of them. His full, thick, hard cock stands at attention. A vein runs up the backside, leading to the engorged, angry, purple head.

I salivate, then gulp. Moisture beads my core. My palms begin to sweat and the cufflinks slide from my grasp. "Whoa!" I tighten my grasp on them. When I look up, the full blast of those icy blue eyes of his greets me.

The hair on the nape of my neck rises. Shit, what am I doing? Why had I walked in here? Oh yeah, it was to confront him about what he'd done to me. "How dare you—" I swallow the rest of the words as he wraps his thick fingers around his much thicker, much broader cock. He pumps his shaft once, twice, thrice…and I swear, his dick swells further. A bead of precum oozes from the tip. I step forward, sink to my knees and open my mouth.

9

Michael

What in the name of the *Santa Madre Maria* is she doing? I glare down at where she's positioned on her knees, her fingers still clasped around my cufflinks and linked together in front of her. Her mouth is open in that perfect 'O' that invites me to stuff my cock between her lips. To bury my fingers in her hair, hold her in place as I fuck her mouth, and shoot my load down her throat. She holds my gaze, those green eyes beseeching, pupils dilated enough, breathing ragged enough to indicate that she's turned on.

If I bent down and sank my fingers in her pussy, no doubt, she'd be dripping. Her cunt ready and open and willing to take my cock. She'd tighten her inner walls around my length, milk me, and not let go until I had come inside her, until I had impaled her and fucked her so hard that she'd feel me in her throat. Her chest rises and falls, nipples pebbled against the tiny T-shirt that stretches across her chest. Fuck me.

I begin to jerk off in earnest. Squeezing my cock from base to crown, again and again. In seconds, the tightness at the base of my spine curls in on itself, tighter, higher, until it snaps. The orgasm slams into me with the force of a thirteen-millimeter bullet. My balls draw up and I come, shooting my cum across her face, in her mouth, across her hair, her breasts.

She licks off the white ropy strands without breaking the connection of our gaze. And fuck me, but this woman... She is going to be the death of me... Correction, she had been the death of me... She has tried to kill me, not once, but twice, so far. Will she be lucky the third time? Why do I keep coming back to her?

I had managed to stay away for two full days. Two days in which I had thrown myself into work with a ferocity that had taken my brothers by surprise. Two days in which I had taken meetings separately with the Bratva and the Kane Company, had negotiated deals with both of them which would secure the future of my clan within the Cosa Nostra and cement my bid to be the next Don. Two days in which I had learned that it wasn't the Kane Company which had sent the four unarmed men who had tried to kill me a few months ago. Two days in which I had not stopped thinking about her. In which I had tried to fuck a woman in my apartment above Venom—which is where I had stayed the last two nights. I hadn't been able to get it up then. Couldn't bear the thought of any other woman touching me either. But one glance at her, one sniff of her scent and I had gone rock hard.

Fuck. What the hell is Beauty doing to me? My wife, my would-be-murderer, what kind of magic has she woven around me that I seem to find my way back to her, whether I want to or not?

"Michael," she murmurs, "you okay?"

I lower my hand to my side, brush past her. I head for the ensuite and her footsteps follow me.

"What the fuck?" she yells. "What's wrong with you?"

Something hits me on the back and I freeze. I turn to find the cufflinks on the floor between us. I glance up at her, and the color fades from her cheeks.

She squares her shoulders. "I am not going to apologize for that." She looks down at the cufflinks, then shifts her gaze to me and firms her lips. "You deserved it, the way you've been acting."

I look her up and down and she shuffles her feet. I turn, take a step forward, and she skitters back. Another step and she props her hands on her hips.

"You... " she clears her throat, "you don't scare me."

I bare my teeth, snap at her and she squeaks.

"What the hell?" She jumps back a few more steps, putting distance between us.

"You're the one who carved…that…that horrible word on my back. How could you do it, Michael, how could you?"

"Because it's true."

"What are you talking about?" She gulps, "I am your wife, Michael. Your wife."

"You didn't think about that when you left me for dead?"

"And I've already apologized to you for it."

"You think you can say sorry and it wipes away everything you did, Beauty?" I glare at her, and she pales. My cum drips from her chin, trickles down the valley between her breasts and my dick begins to harden again. Fuck, but as long as I am in her presence, I can't stop myself from wanting to be inside of her again.

"I really am sorry, Michael."

"Not as sorry as I am for having married you."

She inhales sharply, "You don't mean it."

"Don't I?" I growl, "You left with Luca. You spent the night with him."

She frowns. "I spent the night in a safehouse with him."

"Under the same roof as him."

"Yes, but not in the same room," she frowns. "We slept in different rooms."

I set my jaw.

"Is that why you are so pissed at me? You think I slept with him?"

I grit my teeth so hard, pain shoots up the side of my face.

"Nothing happened, Michael." She takes a step forward.

I hold up my hand, " I am not interested in your pathetic excuses."

"I wouldn't do that to you, Michael. You must know that."

I glance away, then back at her.

"It's because, to the outside world, it seems like I slept with him. That's what's got you so riled up, isn't it?"

I curl my fingers into fists at my sides.

"OMG," she gasps, "that's what it is. I mean, you guys are old-fashioned enough that you think you've lost face because I spent the night in the same house as another man."

Heat flushes the back of my neck. Damn her, for guessing that. She's way more perceptive than I gave her credit for.

"I swear, nothing happened between us, Michael." Her features soften. "As for having embarrassed you? I really am sorry about that." She tips up her chin, "How can I make it up to you?"

"You don't want to know."

"Try me." She sets her jaw, "I almost lost you, Michael. You have no idea how relieved I am to find that you are still alive. Let me make amends for what I did. I'll do anything to show you how sorry I am."

"Are you sure?" I fold my arms across my chest and her gaze flits over my biceps. Her lips part, and it's as if she can't stop herself from glancing down at my crotch.

"My face is up here," I drawl.

She flushes, jerks her chin up, "Yeah, yeah I know." She juts out her lower lip, "So what do you say? I'll do anything you want, and in return, you'll forgive me?"

I laugh. This woman… She has too much gumption. Does she actually think that she can manipulate me like this?

"Anything, huh?" I drum my fingers on my chest. "You sure about that?"

She shakes her head, "No, I am not." She swallows, "But I am not going to back down from your challenge, Michael. I need you to believe in me and if this is the only way to do it, then so be it."

I lower my arms to my sides, walk over to her. She flinches, then releases a breath when I pass her. I circle her, coming back to stop in front of her. "So," I drawl, "you think you have the guts to stand up to me, huh? You think I can't punish you the way I do my men."

"Oh, I know you can, and that you will. In fact," she draws herself up to her full height, "I am counting on it."

"You can't take what I have in mind, *Bellezza*."

"Oh?" She tilts her head, "Try me, Capo."

Sant'Iddio! I bunch my fingers into fists. She only has to call me by my title and my entire body strains to cover hers. To throw her down and bury myself inside of her and— I shake my head. "Shut up," I growl. "From now on, you won't speak. Not until I give you permission."

"But—"

I raise an eyebrow and color suffuses her features. "Do you wanna play or do you wanna play?"

She opens her mouth and I shake my head.

She raises her hand and gestures.

"Sorry?" I smirk, "Not sure what you are telling me."

Her green eyes blaze with a combination of anger and frustration, and fuck, if I don't want to subsume that fire inside of me, to have her spirit consume me, even as I draw on the darkness inside of her. But first, I need to find out if she can actually deliver on her word.

"Take off your clothes."

She tosses her head, then grips the bottom of her T-shirt. She tugs it up and over her head, drops it to the floor.

Her breasts, enclosed in her lacy black bra, spill out over the top. Her nipples are outlined against the sheer fabric of her lingerie…that I had bought for her. She's wearing clothes that I had picked out for her, personally. Call it a moment of weakness, but I hadn't been able to resist shutting down yet another shop in Palermo while I had searched through the lingerie on offer and chosen exactly what I wanted her to wear.

Maybe it's the blow to the head that changed my view of the world… Maybe it's that I had known that she would come back to me… Either way, my brothers had thought I was crazy to drag myself out of bed, when I had barely begun to heal, to pick out the clothes for her. But then I had been vindicated, hadn't I? She had turned up at my fake funeral and she had been shocked to see me come to life. The amazement and then the relief in her eyes when she had realized that I was alive... She couldn't hide that.

Her waist is so tiny I can span it with the width of my hands. She seems so strong, this woman, so full of spunk, so always ready to stand up to me, that I forget how fragile she really is.

And she tried to kill you.

But had she meant it? Had she been acting out of instinct…because she was as afraid of what was between us as I am? And now what? I am making excuses for her?

Che cazzo! I am making excuses for her behavior! What the hell is wrong with me? Why is it that every time I am with her, I lose all sense of myself? That I can't stop myself from wanting to wrap my fingers around her throat and pulling her close, and kissing those gorgeous lips as I play with her breasts while I thrust my hips forward so my cock nestles in its real home…between her fleshy thighs? Thighs I can't stop myself from squeezing, and leaving my mark over her creamy skin.

She licks her lips and all thought empties from my head.

"Take off the rest of your clothes." My voice cracks, goddamn it, and I clear my throat. "Do it, Beauty, now!"

She swipes her hair over her shoulder, then reaches for the waist-band of her shorts. She shoves them down, then kicks them aside along with her socks. Straightens to stand in her bra and panties. Color blooms on her cheeks. How sweet. After everything I've done to her, after how she's come apart under my fingers, she still blushes when she stands almost naked in front of me. I jerk my chin and she bites down her lower lip, and fuck me, but my dick instantly twitches. My balls harden.

I close my fingers at my sides, glare at her. "Take it all off," I snap.

She stiffens. then pulls her shoulders back. Without taking her gaze off of mine, she reaches behind to unhook her bra, then tosses it at me.

I snatch up the piece of fabric and she makes a noise deep in her throat. I stare down at her panties and her flush deepens.

"Do it, Beauty," I growl.

She tips up her chin, hooks her fingers in the waistband of her panties, and shoves them down her legs. She throws them at me. I catch them with my other hand, bring them up to my nose and inhale. The scent of Beauty fills my senses. A pulse flares to life at my temples, behind my eyelids, even in my fucking balls. Fucking fuck, this woman is doing me in.

"You are an animal," she scowls, "you know that?"

"No talking," I growl as I toss her underclothes aside, then stalk over to her. "Also that wasn't me being an animal; but this is."

10

Karma

He prowls toward me and I stumble back. He closes the distance between us even as I try to evade him. Which is stupid. I mean, I am the one who initiated this bizarre scenario, and here I am, trying to escape him. Why is it that since I've met him, all I've seemed to do is run from him as he's tried to chase me? There is something wrong with this situation… Something I intend to rectify. I've had enough of always being on the defensive. Enough of always being the one who is trying to get away from him. Why should I be afraid of him? What can he do that he hasn't already done thus far, huh? I do not fear him; I do not. My back hits the wall of the bedroom and I squeak. Jesus, so much for my pep talk.

He pauses in front of me, and my heart hammers in my chest.

One side of his lips kicks up in that smirk I hate…and love…and can't resist. My pussy spasms. Argh, stupid cunt, that's my pussy, not me. Okay, also me, for having put myself at his mercy.

A plume of heat seems to spool off of him and crash into my chest. I gasp. My throat dries. The strength of his dominance is a tangible presence that pushes down on my shoulders and pins me in place. I want to shove at him, raise my knee and bury it in his groin, kick him in the shin and try to escape him, but my arms and legs seem to be frozen in place. My fingers tremble and my toes curl as he leans in close enough for his eyelashes to tangle with mine.

He peers into my face. Those blue eyes of his are ablaze with a fire that seems to come from somewhere deep inside. I've never seen him this...turned on. This...consumed with an emotion that I can't quite place. Does he want revenge? Does he want to punish me, perhaps? Maybe he wants retribution for what I did to him. For heaven's sake, I practically killed the man. It's a wonder he hasn't tried to do the same to me yet—he grabs me by my throat and I gasp.

Oh, hell, maybe I should watch my thoughts? Maybe, that's what he meant when he said I couldn't take what he has in mind. My breath catches, my heartbeat ratchets up, and my pulse rate spikes, even as moisture pools between my legs. Shit, shit, shit. Clearly, my body is all mixed up with the signals it's getting. I am supposed to want to take flight or fight...not... Fuck. Not get turned on. Not wrap my fingers about his thick wrist as he hauls me to him and slams his lips to mine. Not open my mouth and allow him to thrust his tongue inside, tangle with mine, swirl it over my teeth, before he sucks on me as if he wants to consume every last morsel of pleasure that I can offer him.

He growls deep in his chest as he increases the pressure around my throat, even as he plants a massive thigh between my legs and cups my bottom with his free hand as he hitches me up and pulls me even closer to him. The thick length between his legs pushes into my melting core, as he begins to move me up and down the column of his thigh. The ridge of his cock grinds against my pussy as he continues to kiss me, even as he maintains his grasp around my throat.

The trembling starts from somewhere deep inside as he intensifies the action of making me ride his thigh. A moan slips from my lips and he swallows it, snarls low in his throat as if in answer. A primal mating of man and woman, of Beast and Beauty, of a husband and...his whore?

I blink. My muscles stiffen. Every part of me protests that I can't just allow him to do whatever it is that he has in mind. Yeah, so I started it, but it's a woman's prerogative to change her mind, right?

I slap at his shoulder and he only tilts his head. His gaze intensifies as he deepens the kiss until it feels like he's literally sticking his tongue down my throat. I grip his shoulders, try to push him away, but it's like trying to shove at a brick wall. I dig my fingers into his biceps...and that strength of his shimmers, coils, thrums under my fingertips. Oh, hell. I stare into his face, try to pull away, and his grip around my throat tightens. Spots of black flicker at the edges of my vision as he pulls me into him with such force that my breasts are crushed against his massive chest, and his cock stabs against my pussy lips as if seeking entry. *Not yet... No fucking way. Not until I decide I am ready to spread my legs for you, buster.*

I bite down on his tongue with enough pressure that the salty taste of blood fills my mouth. His gaze widens, he tears his mouth from mine and blood drips from the corner of his mouth. The blue of his eyes darkens to nearly black as he bares his teeth. His chest planes flex and his shoulders seem to grow bigger in size, as he slides his hand up my throat so I am forced to tip my chin up.

"Want to play dirty, is that it, Beauty?"

No, you asshole, I want you to tell me what's going on in that dark as Hades mind of yours.

I would open my mouth to answer him, but the jerk still has his fingers wrapped around my throat. Not to mention, he told me that I can't speak until he gives me permission, and annoyingly, my body, at least, seems to respond to his suggestions. Shit. I struggle against him and that shark-like grin of his widens. I swallow and fear skitters up my backside.

"I'd hoped to save this for later, but guess I don't have a choice, eh?"

I scowl at him. What the hell is he talking about? He licks his lips, sucking down the blood that smears his mouth, the blood that I had spilt. Again.

Honestly, I am not a person with violent tendencies. I mean, I fight for what I believe in, but that's only fair, right? You need to stand up for yourself, after all.

I release my grip on his shoulder, only to wrap my fingers around his wrist. I stare at him and he holds my gaze. Without breaking the connection, without letting go of his hold around my throat, he pulls back so I slip off his thigh. He loosens his chokehold just enough to spin me around, so I am pushed up against the wall. He pushes his body into mine and my entire body trembles. Heat from his frame envelops me, as he places his cheek next to mine, "From the moment I saw you, I knew you were trouble. I just didn't realize just how much I'd enjoy also being challenged by you."

I grit my teeth, push my cheek into the cool surface of the wall, as I stare at him from the corner of my eye. "You don't have to say a word, Beauty. I know what you need."

Do you, asshole? Do you have any idea how it feels like you are infiltrating my body, my soul, every part of my mind, my heart? Shit... Do you understand how threatening it is to feel so consumed by your presence, to be overwhelmed by your dominance, to want to surrender and yet not giving in? For something inside me insists that if I do... I'll lose your respect. And that... That is what I crave more than anything. To be your equal. Do you see that? Can you sense how I want to be able to meet you on your level?

He lowers his head and bites down on where my neck meets my shoulder. My pussy instantly clenches even as I throw my head back. A scream boils up, but his hold on my throat stops any noise from escaping. He slides his fingers between me and the wall, and strums my pussy lips. He raises his head, sucks on the skin that he'd just bitten, and a thrill chases down my spine. More moisture laces my core and he scoops it up, steps back, only to bring his hand up and around to slide it between my butt cheeks. I sense his intent a second before he probes my back hole.

I slap my palm against the wall as he slides his finger inside my back channel. I struggle against him, and he brings his mouth near my ear, "Shh, Beauty, trust me."

My heart beat ratchets up. I close my eyelids and a tear squeezes out from the corner of my eye. He licks it up and my heart stutters. Of everything he's done to me, that feels the most intimate. And why the hell am I crying? I never cry.

Not when my father left us. Not when I found out I had a heart condition. Not when I found out that Summer was getting married, that I was going to be alone... Not that Summer would ever forsake me or anything, it's just ... You know what I mean, right? I hadn't even cried when this bastard had kidnapped me...

So why am I feeling so overwhelmed when he licks the shell of my ear, then sucks on my ear lobe as he plants his leg between mine, forcing me to widen my stance? As he adds a second finger to the first and pushes his digits inside my backchannel. I stiffen, clench down on his fingers, and he groans. The sound is so hot, so male, so dominant that my nipples harden. My breasts seem to swell as he curves his fingers inside of me. A groan trembles up my throat. He leans in, kisses the corner of my mouth as he pulls his fingers out of me, only to replace it with something bigger, more blunt. Something that feels awfully like the crown of his monster cock.

I swallow and my throat moves against his fingers. "F-u-c-k," he growls, "do you have any idea how erotic it is to feel you swallow?"

He nudges my back opening and I wriggle against him. He wraps his fingers around my hip, holds me in place as he whispers in my ear, "Do you want me to stop, Beauty? All you have to do is tap out."

A-n-d, there it is. Him telling me to give up. To admit that I can't take what he throws at me. If I ask him to release me now, he will… and…then… I'll know I am not as strong as I think I am. But him taking my arse… Isn't that a test of my strength of character, too? I mean, it does test my arsehole. *An alphahole testing my arsehole.* I snicker, and he licks my cheek.

"I take it that means you are fine to continue?"

I scowl at him, and he kisses the tip of my nose. "Nod, baby," he whispers, "tell me you are going to keep pace with me all the way."

Shit, I am a glutton for punishment, and clearly, my inability to turn down a challenge is going to land me in a lot of pain. Fine, whatever, nothing I can't bear. I nod, and his entire body seems to harden. He kisses me on the mouth, then leans back, and propels his hips forward.

His length breaches my backchannel and a flash of pain slices through me. I squeeze my eyes shut as my muscles tense, as I push my palms into the wall, flatten my forehead against the flat surface. He pauses, allowing me to adjust to his size—as if that's going to happen anytime soon. I sense the tension radiating off of him as he stays where he is, as his cock throbs inside of me. The pain ebbs away, and a shimmer of lust licks my veins. My pussy throbs and my toes curl as he rubs his thumb across the front of my throat. A shiver crawls up my spine and all of my pores seem to pop as he leans in and kisses my cheek.

"I am going to fuck you now."

11

———————

Karma

What the hell! What does he mean by that? I open my mouth to ask, then gasp when he pulls out of me. He pushes forward again, and this time, sinks his cock deeper inside of me. Oh, hell. Oh, bloody hell. He's filling me up, cramming himself into me, throbbing inside of me... It's so real, so vital, so full of the kind of energy that had attracted me to him in the first place. A groan trembles up my throat as he pauses again, allowing me, once more, to accommodate him. Once more, the pain fades away and a trembling starts up somewhere deep inside. Moisture beads my core, slides down my inner thigh. I glance up at him, find his attention is focused on my face as he begins to move. He pulls out, then thrusts forward and impales me with enough pressure that my entire body jerks. He retreats, then lunges forward, buries himself inside to the hilt, and hits that spot deep inside of me.

OMG! OMG! My eyes roll back in my head as he begins to slam into me in earnest. That's my Capo for you. He always fucks like he's throwing the weight of his entire body behind his action, like his very life depends on just how deeply he can ram into me, like his soul is urging him on to possess me, own me, break me. He thrusts forward, once more hitting that spot deep inside, and my belly spasms. My pussy clenches as I push my breasts into the wall, jut out my butt, trying to take him in even deeper.

"*Dio santo,*" he growls as he begins to slam into me with even greater intensity. In and out of me, in and out, he crams his entire length inside me once more and I sense his body go rigid.

My climax threatens, lapping at the edge of my consciousness, and that's when he releases his hold around my neck. The orgasm roars forward just as he pulls out of me, only to retreat. *What the hell?*

I open my mouth to protest, and that's when he turns me around to face him. He drops to his knees in front of me, then buries his head between my legs. *What the —!* I glance down just as he swipes his tongue from my arse crack all the way up to my clit. *Oh, my god!* I throw my head back and pant as he licks around my pussy lips, then curls his tongue around the nub of my clit. I dig my fingers into his hair and tug as he swipes his tongue in between my lower lips, then bites down on my clit. I cry out, feel him smile against my core, right before he plants his shoulders between my thighs, forcing them apart further, then thrusts his tongue inside my sopping wet channel. In and out, in and out, he sucks on me, slurps up the moisture that leaks from me. He laps his tongue inside my core and a moan spills from my lips. He squeezes my arse cheeks as he yanks me even closer until I am riding his face. Until my thighs clench around his ears, until I slam my head back against the wall, as I writhe to get away from him, even as I pull on his hair, trying to urge him closer, closer to my weeping center. *OMG. OMG. I am going to —*

He pulls out of me. He releases his hold on my thighs, and I stagger back against the wall. I open my eyes — uh, when had I shut them? — to find that he's walking away from me. The planes of his back ripple, the muscles of his tight arse flex as he strides away from me.

"What the fuck?" I yell, "You come right back here and finish what you started, you son of a —"

"Don't insult my mother," he warns as he raises one finger above his head, "Also, I don't recall giving you permission to speak, *Bellezza.*"

"Fuck that." I stomp over to him as he enters the bathroom. "What the hell are you playing at, you imbecile, you dithering wanker, you... you...*stronzo.*"

He laughs, the jackalope actually laughs as he prowls over to the spacious shower enclosure and steps inside.

I walk over, yank open the door to the shower as he flicks on the water. The spray pours over him, ripples down his back, down those powerful thighs and all thought spills from my head. Jesus Christ, to see him naked and with the water cascading over him… It's like my favorite wet dream. Well, he is wet, and so am I… I slip my fingers inside my empty channel. I weave my fingers in and out of myself as he turns. His gaze roams over me, then intensifies as he realizes what I am doing.

He tilts his head as I return the gesture, rake my gaze over that gorgeous torso, those to-die-for abs, the V-shaped muscular grooves on the abdominal muscles alongside his hips, which, holy Mother of God, is absolutely perfect, to that fat cock of his, now turgid and standing to attention, with his swollen balls nestled between his legs. Oh wow, this is like my personal pin-up to jerk off to, and trust me, I am going to make the most of it. I grip the edge of the shower door as I thrust a second finger, then a third inside of myself. Damn it, it's still not enough to fill me up, and the asshole knows it.

He bares his teeth as he grabs the shampoo, pours out some of the liquid in his palm and begins to wash his hair. His biceps bulge, the tendons of his forearms tauten as he digs his fingers into his hair. He lowers his gaze to my crotch where I still continue to finger fuck myself. I grind the heel of my palm into my clit and goosebumps rise on my skin.

He leans his head back, so the shower begins to wash away the soapy suds as my core clenches. My backchannel which is still sore from his earlier ministrations protests at the lack of intrusion. What the hell? If his plan is to train me to seek out his touch, then he's doing a damn good job of it. Something I intend to put an end to right now. I manage to fit a fourth finger inside myself, when the climax threatens again. This time I am going to come, I am not going to follow the dictate of any dumbass Capo. So what, if he hasn't given me the permission to come yet. The vibrations shiver up my thighs, to my core, continue upwards, and that's when he switches off the shower.

"Stop," he commands.

My fingers tremble.

"Now, Beauty." He lowers his voice to a hush, and my nerve endings pop. Only when I tuck my elbow into my side, do I realize that I have lowered my arm.

He walks toward me, comes to a stop in front of me. The heat of his body, and the steam from the shower envelops me.

"Why?" I demand, "Explain why you wrote whore."

He merely smiles, then goes to brush past me. I grab his wrist, "Answer me," I snap. "Goddammit, Michael, why did you do that?"

He turns, grabs my throat with his free arm, pushes me up against the frame of the shower door. "Because you are," he growls as he thrusts his face into mine. "You are my whore. Mine to do with as I want. Mine to own. Mine, Beauty. Only mine. Don't forget that."

12

Michael

I pace the length of the conference room in my office above Venom. How dare she question me about my actions? What right does she have to make me feel sorry about what I did? I will not regret it. She deserves it. She is mine to do with as I want, after all. I will do what I want to her, and she'll damn well take it.

After that scene last night Beauty, had returned to my room, picked up her clothes, then stomped out. I had almost called out to her and told her to stay, but thankfully, for once, my brain had won the war over my dick… Okay, not really. My cock had wept to see her go, and I hadn't stopped myself from watching the sway of her butt, or the flow of her hair down her back as she had marched out without a word.

I had gotten dressed, then decided to get the hell out of there. I hadn't wanted to spend the night in my own house. If I had, nothing would have prevented me from going to her room, throwing her down on the bed, and rutting into her… That's the only word for the intensity with which I want to fuck her. Only, I can't, because of some stupid notion that I won't allow her to come. Nor myself, for reasons I cannot begin to articulate.

F-u-c-k! I grab my hair and tug, and the wound at my temple protests. The wound that *she* inflicted on me. The almost healed one on my chest itches and I curl my fingers at my side to stop myself from worrying it. I had spent the night in the apartment adjacent to my office, which I have used in the past when work was so intense that I didn't have the time to make it back home.

Not that it helped my disposition, to be honest... Or my shaft, which still tents my pants. I glare at my crotch. *Get a fucking life, you complete cock.* I frown. *Great, now I am talking to my dick.* Something I would never have done in the past. But then, I never had her to contend with in the past either. This is what she does to me. Ties me up in knots, then twists, just to ensure that I realize how much of a mess my life has become since I chanced upon her.

The door to my office opens and Sebastian saunters in.

"Whatever happened to knocking?" I scowl.

"Whatever happened to your demeanor?" He smirks. "Not that you'd ever be caught dead in a good mood, but this," he looks me up and down, "your frame of mind leaves much to be desired, brother."

"What-fucking-ever," I grunt.

He laughs, "Very eloquent of you, Mika. I take it things are not going well on the home front?"

You can say that again. Clearly, I have backed myself up into a corner, where I won't let myself come and I will not allow her to come either. The result is that not only am I sporting a raging erection since I walked out of my house but I also have no way of alleviating it. No way, am I going to back down from my position of not allowing her to orgasm. But why is it that I am unable to satisfy myself either? Is it out of some sense of solidarity with her? Which, considering I am the one who decided to leave her unsatisfied—is poetic justice. Or is it because I want to punish myself...?

Not that I regret one bit that I took her in the first place. Or that I forced her to marry me. Or that I marked her in a way that I knew would upset her. Make her feel a little bit of what I had gone through when I had realized that she had left me.

Only she returned.

After you pretended you were dead.

And then you had to go screw it up again. Why the hell can't I forgive her for what she did? Why can't I be more normal with her? And that would bore her. My Beauty has a soul as dark as mine, her tastes as perverted as mine. Her need for the extremes that turn me on were clear to me from the first time I looked into her eyes. It had thrilled me as much as it had frightened me.

And in a way, I have been running from facing those thoughts ever since. It had stopped me from sharing all of myself with her... For if I do that, there will be no turning back. I'll be lost to her. I'll be vulnerable in a way that I have never been before. Hell, I am already vulnerable to her. If anything were to happen to her... If I lost her again, I wouldn't be able to take it. It's something I need to figure out how to manage... Just as I need to come up with a solution for the problems that have been plaguing the Cosa Nostra.

"Michael?" Seb frowns, "I asked you a question."

I glance at him. "I heard you," I growl, "doesn't mean I have to answer you."

"But you have to answer to us." The door opens wider to admit Massimo, followed by Christian and Xander. Adrian brings up the rear, as Antonio shuts the door behind him.

"*Figlio di puttana.*" The day hasn't even started and I wish it were over already. Since when had I become so disinterested in work? The one solace that has kept me going all these years, the only focus of my life so far, the one thing that I value more than anything else, the key to underwriting my future... That's what my role as Capo has been to me so far... And now...? I am not so sure.

I stalk toward the bar, grab a fresh bottle of Macallan. I twist open the top, pour out a generous amount in a glass, then toss it back. The liquid burns its way down my gullet, and I slam the glass back on the counter.

"Replacing coffee with whiskey, are we?" Massimo drawls. "Didn't take you for a quitter, *fratellone.*"

"Quitter?" I pivot and level a glare at him. "What do you mean?"

"You're here weeping into your whiskey, while she is there weeping into her pillow, no doubt."

"Weeping?" I scowl. "Who's weeping? Not me, and certainly not her. I promise you, she's undoubtedly figuring out yet another way to bring me down."

"Have you spoken to her yet?" Xander walks over to the coffee station in the corner of the office. He tops up the coffee beans in the machine before switching on the grinder. Once the coffee is ground he taps the handle, tamps down on the coffee powder, before scraping off the excess coffee. He inserts the handle in the brew head and proceeds to extract the espresso. He places the cup on a saucer, then reaches into the jar next to it to and takes out a biscotti that he places on the saucer. He tops off a glass with water, then places it all on a tray. He turns and walks over to the couch, "Sit, *fratellone*," He gestures to the settee.

I walk over, seat myself, and he places the tray in front of me.

"Drink." He stabs a finger at the espresso, and I arch an eyebrow at him.

"No one tells me what to do, not even my favorite brother," I murmur.

He laughs, "At least, you admit that I am your favorite."

"*Che cazzo!*" Christian frowns. "Just because *stronzo* here is the most creative of the lot of us—"

"Also, the most handsome," Xander chuckles.

"If you like the cookie cutter definition of handsome." Christian counters. "I have the rugged good looks, don't forget that."

"And I have—"

"A talent for brewing espresso that tastes better than what I make, and that," I nod in Xander's direction, "is not praise I give lightly."

I take a sip of the espresso and the dark complex notes of coffee laced with chocolate and cinnamon fills my senses. I take another sip, and my sinuses seem to clear. Another and my brain cells finally seem to start firing. I place the espresso cup back in the saucer, dip the biscotti in the coffee and crunch down on it. "These are good." I scowl at the baked item, "Different from what I normally have, but really *eccezionale*."

"New supplier," Massimo, who is also in charge of procurement, offers. "They are homemade, and sold only through our coffee shops."

Yep, we also run a coffee shop chain. One of our many businesses through which I launder the not-so-legit money. The coffee shop chain is one of the more successful ones.

I crunch down the rest of the biscotti, then drain the last of my espresso. My muscles relax, and whether it's the effect of the baked good or the coffee... Or perhaps, a combination of both, I don't know, but I feel almost human.

"So, what are you guys doing here?" I glance between them, "Don't you have enough work to take care of? Do I need to rebalance the systems and make sure you all get more to do?"

"Whoa!" Massimo blinks. "You don't remember?"

"Remember what?"

"You, *fratellone,* who never forgets a work gig. You don't remember why we are here?"

I blink around at them, "I still remember all my work appointments—"

"Except why we are here?" Christian smirks.

"You guys going to spill it, or what?"

"May I?" Seb glances at the rest of the guys, who nod.

"Go right ahead," Massimo acquiesces. "Enlighten *fratellone,* here, about what has slipped his mind completely."

"Enough with the fucking drama." I scowl. "The hell are you guys trying to imply?"

"That you are right." Seb tilts his head.

"I am?"

"You bet." Seb's grin widens, "You don't remember there being a meeting this early in the morning because it wasn't planned."

"It wasn't?"

He shakes his head, "However you did miss a meeting."

"I did?"

"Last night." Adrian adds.

"The fuck you mean?"

"Last night, we had a meeting scheduled with the Russians, which you didn't turn up for," Seb informs me.

"I didn't?" Shit, I am repeating myself, but clearly, these guys are fucking around with me. "Get out of here," I murmur. "You guys could do better if you wanted to play a trick, which by the way, is something so juvenile I'd have expected it of the twins."

"Hey," Both Christian and Xander protest, for once, sounding exactly like the twins they are.

I continue, "It's not something I'd expect the possible future Capo to be after me to say."

Seb blinks, then laughs, "Now, you're the one yanking my chain, *brother.*"

"Am I?" I allow my lips to tilt up. "You stepped in when I was out of commission."

He opens his mouth and I raise my hand, "I know it was only for a couple of hours, but you stepped in, took up the reins like you were born for it. And given Luca is, clearly, not the person we thought him to be—" I raise my shoulder, "I can't think of anyone better succeeding to become Capo after me."

"But," Seb frowns, "I am the bastard child—"

"Who was more loyal to me than my own blood brother." I rise to my feet, walk over and grip his shoulder, "I confess, I doubted your loyalties to me, but you came through for me when it most mattered, Seb."

He opens and shuts his mouth, then shakes his head, "But the rules of the Cosa Nostra—"

"I *am* the Cosa Nostra," I draw myself to my full height, "and as soon as I am Don, I will ensure that these archaic rules are overturned. We need to move with the times if we hope to survive in a fast-changing world."

"And her?" Xander's voice has me glancing at him over my shoulder.

"What about her?" I scowl.

"You want to modernize the Cosa Nostra, but what about your views toward women?"

"What about them?" I draw myself up to my full height, "What are you trying to tell me, *fratellino*?

"That you need to treat her more as your peer and less as your possession."

Silence descends on the gathering. Adrian shifts his weight from foot to foot. Seb glances between us, turns to me, opens his mouth as if to speak, then seems to change his mind. Massimo tenses, and Christian… He's the only one who doesn't seem bothered. He watches his twin with something akin to admiration on his face but he stays silent. Thank fuck.

Bad enough, one brother is trying to tell me something which my subconscious, perhaps, even recognizes as the truth…but fuck that. No one tells me what to do. Not her…and definitely not, my youngest sibling… So what, if he's always been the conscience among the group? Only I decide how I manage my wife, and no one else.

"You advising me on how to run my domestic life?" My voice is soft, yet it seems to echo back from the walls of the room.

"Of course, not." Xander's lips quirk, "All I am saying is that you might want to do the one thing that most couples don't seem to master even after years together, which is tell her the truth."

"Thus says the man who hasn't been able to come out and share his truest feelings for the woman he's spent most of his life loving from afar."

Xander pales. His features take on a stricken look. He glances away, and when he looks back at me, his features are once more composed into that angelic face that all of us associate with him. "You're right." He lowers his chin, "I have never managed to tell her how I feel, probably because I suffer from the same issues as you when it comes to women. Apparently, our father's treatment of our mother screwed all of us over enough that, when it comes to the opposite sex, we have only one use for them."

I stare at him. "Now, that is not what I was expecting from you, I confess. You surprise me often, little brother, with your insight into human nature."

"Not as much as you surprise me with your empathy."

"Me? Empathetic?" I laugh, "Surely, you are talking about someone else?"

"If you weren't, you would have killed her as soon as she showed up in that chapel—which you didn't."

"Thought you said you didn't like how I treated her."

"I wouldn't dare butt into a relationship between a Capo and his wife, but when it comes to my brother and his soulmate..."

"Whoa, hold on." I raise my hand, "Who said anything about a soulmate?"

"It's not what you say as much as your gestures that indicate that you love her."

"No, let's not get ahead of ourselves." I smirk, "All this emo shit is not in my vocabulary."

"Maybe it's time you made it. Maybe it's time you actually shared what's going on in your mind, in your heart, how your soul feels about her. I—"

Seb's phone pings just then. He glances at it, then back at us. "Don't mean to cut in on this touching family scene," he drawls, "but the Russians are here for the meeting."

"Why the fuck are they here for a meeting?"

"As I told you," Seb chides, "you didn't make it to the meeting with them last night."

"A meeting in which the rest of us covered for you, by the way," Massimo adds.

"But, of course, they need to meet the Capo to confirm the deal we struck is legit." Christian raises a shoulder.

"*Merda.*" I rake my fingers through my hair. "How the hell did I miss that meeting?" I walk toward where my jacket is hanging over the back of a chair. I slide my hand in the pocket, pull out my phone, which is dead. "*Porca miseria,*" I growl. My phone had run out of battery at the office, and I hadn't bothered to plug it in when I got home…because I had been otherwise distracted. Nor had I once checked it throughout the night, thanks to my infatuation with one feisty woman who had, clearly, pushed herself to the forefront of my mind. I have never once not made it to a meeting on time in all the years since I joined the Cosa Nostra. Apparently, there is a first time for everything. Apparently, my brain is going to shit because I can't even remember to charge my phone anymore.

"Fucking fuck." I slip the phone back in my pocket, then turn to Seb, "Let's get the Russians in here and get this over with."

13

Karma

He left me. Yet again, he hadn't let me come. Well, neither had he come, to be fair, and then, he'd left. I know because, after I'd gone to my room and showered, I had marched out and back to his room, which had been empty.

I had walked down the stairs, headed to the living room, found it also empty. So was the kitchen…. Apparently, he'd left… And he hasn't returned. Guess he has no intention of coming home anytime soon.

I had come to the kitchen, after smelling the coffee and toast and hash browns searing on the griddle, and for a second, I had thought that it was Michael… But sadly, it wasn't. I finished my breakfast on my own, and wandered around the house, before finding my way back to the library.

I had lingered there, picking out more strategy books like *The Prince* by Niccolo Machiavelli—of course, he'd have Machiavelli in his collection— *Meditations* by Marcus Aurelius, *A Book of Five Rings: The Classic Guide to Strategy* written by someone called Miyamoto Musashi who had been a Samurai centuries ago. OMG, does this man only read books by dead men or what?

Well, he also has more eclectic books in his collection, like *Man's Search for Meaning* by Viktor E. Frankl, the entire collection of *The Hitchhiker's Guide to the Galaxy* by Douglas Adams, *Jonathan Livingston Seagull* by Richard Bach....Apparently, there is a thinking side to the alphahole, not that I had doubted it.

Michael has a streak of cruelty a mile wide, but he also has a lot of depth. Bet if he put aside that simmering resentment for all living things, we could have an interesting conversation on anything under the sun. I move to another shelf, spot some well-thumbed volumes of poetry by Byron, Pablo Neruda, and a few other familiar names. Poems, huh? Does he actually read these books? From the well-used condition of them, I'd say yes. Plus, he quoted Byron the first time we met.

Also... I see Harry Potter. WTF? He reads Harry Potter? Does that mean he's also a romantic and somewhat of a dreamer deep inside? Does that dark soul of his also harbor something as mundane as emotions? At least, that's what his book collection tells me. And books, as we all know, don't lie... Unlike people. They don't go about trying to kill their husband to get away from him, or hold a grudge against their wife, so they end up withholding orgasms.

My pussy instantly spasms in sympathy. *Stupid pussy! You've become such a greedy little thing. Can't stop begging for his fat cock to be buried inside of you, huh? Great, now I am talking to my cunt.* Heat flushes my skin and moisture laces my core. The emptiness inside of me writhes and moans. I squeeze my thighs together, then slide my fingers under the waistband of my jeans. I part my legs, play with my clit and a shiver of pleasure runs up my spine. I press down on the already engorged bud, and goosebumps pop on my skin. I slide my fingers down between my pussy lips, thrust one finger, then another inside my aching channel. I weave my fingers in and out of my melting channel, again and again. The vibrations shiver along my nerve-endings and my toes curl. OMG, a few more seconds of this and I am going to come...

My fingers tremble and I pull them back. I lower my hand, press my elbow into my side, and blow out a breath. My knees tremble and I lean against a book case. Raise my cum-soaked fingers. Shit, why the hell did I stop? I could have gotten myself off so easily. And I hadn't. Just because that stupid douchebag had told me to not to come. And of course, much as my body wants the relief, something inside me insists that I can't come. Not yet. Not until he gives me permission. Argh! I dig my fingers in my hair and tug. *But I wanna come! And right now.*

Which means, there's only one way out. If the alphahole won't come to me, I'll have to go to him, to paraphrase one of those popular sayings. I pivot, walk out of the library, and up to my bedroom. I mean, he hasn't said that I can't leave the house. He hasn't told me that I have to stay here. Which means that it is up for interpretation. Which means, fuck it, I am going in search of him. But first, I have to wear something that reflects the mood I am in. Which is… I am not to be taken for granted. I am not to be pushed aside and made to feel like I am a spare wheel… Or a docile wife who will float around her husband's house waiting for him to come to me.

Nope, no way, no siree, I am going to him and that is that. I head up the stairs, fling open the closet door, and examine my limited options. Unlike the island, alphahole hasn't filled the wardrobe with dresses. Which is good…considering I hadn't exactly liked his taste… But the gesture had been sweet. As much as the lack of his thinking about my needs here is…a little worrying.

Well, what do you expect, after you tried to kill him, not once but twice? Hmm. Okay, guess it's reassuring that he did let me live and he hasn't tried to off me since I stumbled back into his life, so there is that. Also, he had remembered to bring one of the dresses that he'd bought from the boutique in Palermo. I run my fingers down the fabric, then turn to the only other dress in the closet, the one I had been avoiding looking at. My wedding dress. It's freshly laundered, but not in good shape.

The bodice is torn, one of the sleeves is in tatters, and the long train that I had stitched on lovingly takes up a lot of space in the closet. The skirt grazes the floor of the wardrobe, the black of the fabric so dark that it absorbs all of the light in the area. A creation that truly represents what I am… What he is… What we are together. A perfectly black object, a completely clandestine crush, an enigmatic love that is, surely, fated to be doomed before we can start anything together. A gaze, a touch, a fleeting glance, a connection that binds us together for better or for worse. I rub the ring on the finger of my left hand.

Oh, Michael, are we fated to implode? Are we but ships that pass in the night…with a bridge thrown across our decks for a short span of time? Are we lovers? Are we enemies whose chemistry turns our every meeting to kryptonite? Are we…nothing but dust, sparks that fade into the dark, fireflies with a short life that burn out before they even start living? A teardrop rolls down my cheek and I brush it away.

Hell, what's wrong with me? From where did these thoughts tumble into my mind anyway? There can't be anything lasting between us. So what if, I've fallen for that rat's ass of a man. He is a bloody criminal… which only makes him all the more appealing. He is a sadist…who speaks to the masochist in me. He is…a Capo… I am a seamstress… And never the twain shall meet.

So, I have nothing to lose by seeking him out, and insisting that he put me out of my misery. As long as he will give me an orgasm… Or two… Or a whole bunch… Hell, I'll be happy. The answer to all your problems is sex, and don't let them tell you otherwise.

I grab the green dress from the hanger, and turn to find Cassandra in the doorway.

She glances at the dress, then at me, "Want help getting changed?"

Forty-five minutes later, I glance up at the facade of the four-story building…all of which is, apparently, Venom—the nightclub and offices owned by Michael's clan. I push open the door of the car in which Cassandra had driven me here. She had not only helped me get dressed, she'd also handed over an entire bag of cosmetics which she'd, apparently, bought for me when she'd been out of the house yesterday. I'd protested and she'd insisted that I keep it. That it would help me look my best for the Capo, and honestly, I couldn't resist taking it then.

Only, I want to look good not just for him, but for myself, know what I mean? Though, why has she been this generous with me? Maybe she feels sorry for me? Maybe it's because of that word which Michael scrawled on me?

I'd almost told her that it was nothing to feel sorry about. The very fact that Michael had felt angry enough by my actions to do that to me, that he'd etched a part of himself into me, that even though it said 'whore,' it was as close to an endearment as any I'd gotten from him.

Shit, why had I not realized that earlier? Maybe my subconscious mind had known, which is why I hadn't gone completely ballistic in response to what he'd done. I had been enraged but not over the top, tear your hair out, going on a killing rampage like the bride from *Kill Bill* furious. Nor like *Dominic Toretto* in *Fast and the Furious* upset. Ugh, clearly, Summer's movie trivia references are rubbing off on me, if I am taking refuge in Hollywood movies to express my frustration at why I had not realized this earlier. Which means, it is doubly important that I get to him, and confront him and say… Well, I'll think of something to say when I come face-to-face with him.

"So," I turn to the car and Cassandra rolls down the window of the passenger seat. "His office is on the top floor, eh?" I ask.

She nods, "You sure you want to do this, *Signora*?"

She just used the word as a form of address in the Italian language to indicate that I am a married woman. I bite the inside of my cheek. Shit, I am married to him… He is my husband… And I could be pregnant with his child… Something which I have avoided thinking about since I went back to Michael. Not sure why it popped up in my mind now… except… If I am pregnant, it would be a hell of an incredible way to ensure that I change the tone of our relationship into something a bit more…permanent? Another reason to walk up there and confront my husband. I swallow the ball of emotion that crowds my throat.

Shit, my husband. The one person I can actually call mine. I have to find a way to, somehow, get through that cloak of hurt he's donned since my ill-fated attempt to escape him. I need to get through the barriers he's building between us, somehow make him see, just how much I regret what I did to him.

"Yeah," I jerk my chin, "I am sure. Wish me luck?"

14

Michael

"What makes you think I want to do a deal with you?" I glance across the conference room table in my office. The man sprawled out at the foot of the table chuckles.

"Come now Capo, you and I both know that you need allies on your side in your quest to bid for the role of Don."

"I don't need you for that, Nikolai." I yawn. "I am the son, the heir; the title of Don is as good as mine."

"If that were true, you wouldn't be meeting with me." Nikolai's lips twist, "You not only need to show that you have built up your association with the strongest organized crime syndicates in your region, but you also need us in your corner should the Don, for some reason, decide to turn on you."

I stiffen, then force my muscles to relax. Fucker is good. As strategic as me. As ruthless as me. As power-hungry as me... Which is why he hadn't hesitated to accept meeting me on my own turf in my office. Not that it was my idea, but I have to give Seb credit. By asking Nikolai to come here, he'd shown that he was thinking ten steps ahead. Nikolai accepting it? It shows that he needs me as much as I need him.

"The same can be said of you." I tilt my head, "You're here meeting me on my turf, unarmed—"

"But not alone," He spreads his arms wide, drawing my attention to the two men who stand on either side of him. His younger brothers Roman and Victor stare back at me, their faces impassive.

"Brothers, eh?" I jerk my chin toward mine who stand behind me, "Can't live with 'em, can't live without 'em."

"That's family for you." Nikolai chuckles, "In our business, it's all about blood ties. You may not get along with your family, but you can trust them to have your back."

That's what I had thought too. Then Luca decided to turn everything on its head.

"The times are changing," I murmur, "enemies become friends become enemies."

He frowns, "I am not following."

"We've never been on the same side of the fence before—"

"Yet you reached out to us, and offered us a proposal we couldn't resist."

He's referring to our earlier agreement where Nikolai agreed to stop targeting our ships in return for a cut of the money we make on the shipping routes.

"The enemy of your enemy is a friend, too." I allow my lips to kick up.

Niko's forehead creases. "The Kane Company."

"Indeed." I lean back in my chair. "They've become more daring, of late."

"Are they responsible for—" He nods toward the bandage on my forehead.

"No, that was me."

I jerk my head around in the direction of my wife's voice. She stands by the now open door, Antonio, hovering behind her.

"Sorry, Boss," he raises his hands, "she wouldn't take no for an answer, and—"

"You did the right thing," I wave my hand and he steps back.

Beauty walks over to me. She's wearing one of the dresses she'd chosen from the boutique in Palermo, where I had taken her. Where I had pushed her up against the wall of the changing room and ripped the dress she'd been wearing and thrust my fingers inside her sopping wet cunt, and she had come. She had moaned loud enough for everyone in that boutique to hear her. The blood drains to my groin and my balls tighten. I move around in my chair, trying to ease the strain on my pants. That's when I notice that the gaze of every single man in the room is on her. *Che palle.* I rise to my feet, "This meeting is over."

Nikolai glances between my wife and me. "Indeed." His lips curve, "Aren't you going to introduce us to the beautiful *signorina?*"

"*Signora,*" I clarify as Beauty pauses next to me. "This," I wrap my arm around her and pull her stiff body against mine, "is my wife."

"Ah!" Nikolai finally gets up from his seat, "*Ocharovannyy, printsessa,*" He half bows.

Why is it that every man who comes across her seems to be enchanted by her? Can't the fuckers see that she belongs to me?

I yank her even closer and she digs her elbow into my side. My cock instantly jerks. Fuck. Hasn't she realized by now that any hint of violence from her only turns me on? Maybe it's why she's tried to kill me twice, and both times, the connection between us has only grown stronger. What the hell? Why hadn't I realized this before? That the more she tries to hurt me, the more I want her. The more she wants to push me away, the more I need her. The more she tries to prove to me that she can do without me…the more I want to imprint myself on every pore of her body.

"And you are — ?" Beauty holds up her hand.

"Leaving," I snap at the same time that Nikolai walks around the table to take her hand in his.

"Very pleased to meet you…" He tilts his head.

Beauty laughs. "Karma," she murmurs, "call me Karma."

"A fitting name for the woman who has brought the Capo to heel." He kisses her fingers and every muscle in my body goes on alert.

"Relax, Capo," Nikolai drawls, "I pose no threat to you or your family."

"Didn't take you to be a liar," I say through gritted teeth.

He releases her hand and I shove her behind my back.

"Hey," she protests, "what are you doing?" She tries to step around me and I wrap an arm behind and around her, keeping her in place. She digs her fingers into my arm, and a shudder shivers up my spine.

I glare at Nikolai, who meets my gaze. He doesn't back away, doesn't lower his gaze either. For a few seconds our staring match goes on, then he jerks his chin. "You protect what's yours." His lips twist, "I respect that."

"Then you'll also respect when I say that you need to leave now."

"A straight shooter, too." He chuckles, "We are cut from the same cloth, Capo. I do believe we have more in common than we realize."

"We'll see about that."

"Until next time then," he nods at me, then pivots and stalks out, followed by his brothers. The door shuts behind them.

I release Karma who stomps out and around to stand in front of me. "Jesus, all that posturing. It was highly entertaining—not." She fumes, "If you dare try to control me again in front of your acquaintances I will—"

"How are you Karma?" Xander cuts in. "Haven't seen you since your unexpected arrival at the chapel."

Karma scowls in his direction as he walks toward her. Her forehead smoothens out. Typical. No woman can resist the lure of the beauty of my youngest brother.

Karma smiles at him, "You must be..."

"Alessandro, but people call me Xander."

"At his insistence." Christian steps forward, "Personally, I think he does it because it annoys the Capo."

"Does it?" She shoots me a side glance. "And why is that?"

"He claims it's a bastardized version of Sandro, which is, of course, the Italian version of my nickname."

"For the record, I prefer Xander." Her smile widens, "Reminds me of Xander Cage in the xXx series."

"Love action-packed Hollywood movies, eh?" Xander laughs.

"Also, video games."

"SIMS 4?"

"Wha-a-t?" She tosses her head, "Give me some credit, yeah? Call of Duty, all the way here."

"Holy shit, you don't say, you—"

"Okay, that's it," I step between them. "Out, you guys."

"But, *fratellone*," Xander's smirk widens, "we were just talking."

"And now, you've finished talking." I nod my chin toward the door, "Don't call me, I'll call you."

"Aww," Xander chuckles, "and I was only trying to be friendly."

"Well, take your friendliness somewhere else." I fold my arms across my chest, fix him with my most stern gaze. "Now," I say in a low voice and that wipes the smile off of his face.

"You got it, Boss."

He walks past us without saying another word. The rest of the guys file out with him. Antonio closes the door, and I turn to find Beauty staring at me with an incredulous look other face.

"Don't call me, I'll call you?" She huffs, "You really do need to work on your dialogues."

"Is that right?"

"Yeah," She swipes her hair over her shoulder, "I mean, how trite can you get?"

"Trite, eh?"

"Seriously, every part of you is a cliché." She sniffs, "From your dark suits, to your glowering face, to..." She glances around the space, "To this office, on top of a nightclub."

"What's wrong with having an office at the top floor of a nightclub?"

"It's predictable."

"It's convenient."

"Why? So you can have women service you as you are working?"

"Hmm." I stroke my chin, "Now that you mention it, that is a fringe benefit."

"What the hell?" She pushes against my chest. "How dare you say that to me?"

"I'm not the one who brought it up, Beauty; you did. Speaking of," I peer into her face, "what are you doing here?"

"I wasn't aware that I was a prisoner."

"My point, exactly." I hold her gaze, "You could have escaped, Beauty; you could have walked out of the house—"

"Which I did."

"Or called your sister—"

"You didn't give me my cellphone, and if I had called from your home, no doubt, you would have found out about it right away."

"You could have called her from somewhere else, once you left the house.

She blinks, "True."

"But you didn't think of it?"

She shakes her head.

"Why is that?"

"For the same reason that you didn't imprison me in your home, this time," she murmurs.

"What reason is that?" I fold my arms across my chest.

"I know why you carved out the word 'whore' on my back."

"Oh?" I tilt my head.

"It's because you feel something for me."

"You're right about that."

"Oh, yeah?"

"Apathy." I look her up and down. "You're a nice hole to bury my cock in, but considering I've already sampled what you have to offer," I raise a shoulder, "I think it's time I set you free."

"You're lying!" She bursts out.

"Am I?" I round the desk, drop into my seat, then flick on my laptop. I busy myself looking at the figures from last month's sales…which has taken a hit, thanks to the Kane Company hijacking our gun shipments in and out of Eastern Europe. Fuck… Something I need to deal with right away. I glance up at her, "What are you still doing here?"

She opens, then shuts her mouth.

"You're free to leave."

"What will it take for you to realize that this connection between us cannot be broken so easily?"

"There's no connection…and even if there was one, it shattered when you took the oar to my head."

"Oh, my god!" She throws up her hands, "Your stupid ego is going to be the death of me."

"That day can't come soon enough."

"And yet you faked your death so I'd come back to you," she points out.

"I faked my death so I could draw out my brother who betrayed me; you were a fringe benefit."

Her features crumple, hurt writ large across her features. My heart twists and I glance away to stare at the computer screen. The figures fade in and out in front of my eyes.

Cazzo! What's wrong with me? Why does she still affect me so? When she had walked in here, it had felt as if the world had finally tilted right on its axis. Then I had seen the men in the room look at her and had experienced the kind of jealousy that had twisted my guts, that had made me want to whisk her away somewhere, away from all of them, hide her in a place where no one else could see her or talk to her or glance at her.

Then, I'd realized that I have to let her go. If I continue to hold onto her, she'll completely undo me. She'll make me weak, expose my frailties, derail me from the course I have set for myself. Something I can't afford.

As for her relationship with the Seven and how that would have strengthened my own bid to be the next Don... Well, I'll just have to do without it.

"So, this is it?" she whispers. "This is what it's come to? You asking me to leave because you can't deal with your own insecurities?"

"Interesting theory," I drum my fingers on the table, "but I'm afraid I am not in the mood to listen to it."

She stiffens. Anger pours off of her. Then she straightens her back, "You're going to regret this."

"I regret the day I saw you in that park. I should have turned around and left. Sadly, you seemed too easy an opportunity to pass up."

"That's all I am to you, then? After everything we've been through, it's all you view me as?"

"You know the answer to that already." I glance away, pretend to focus on my work.

She stays motionless for a second, then out of the corner of my eyes I sense a flash of movement. I turn to find her pulling off the ring from her finger. "Here." She slams it on the table. Turning, she walks out.

Karma

The ring, which had refused to come off my fingers all this time, had finally slipped off in there. Maybe it was a sign that he's right? Maybe I had been wrong to come back for his fake funeral?

He had written 'whore' on my skin, and I guess he really meant it. He doesn't really want me. In fact, he'd rather let me go than admit that he feels something more than hatred for me. Hell, the *stronzo* is half in love with me. Only, he doesn't want to admit it. And hell, if he hasn't converted me to using Italian words in my vocabulary in a matter of weeks. I have only known him for a fraction of my life, and already, it feels like he is a part of me in a way that nobody else has ever been before. Why am I still so attracted to him? Someone who is a psychopath…and a criminal…probably, a murderer.

I draw in a breath and my lungs burn. I stomp down the steps of the nightclub, past the bar on the ground floor that has two bartenders restocking the shelves behind the bar. I reach the door, push it open, and step into the early afternoon.

A cool breeze blows over me and I shiver. The weather has been so pleasant even for early December. Shit. It's already early December.

Soon it will be Christmas... Will I be home for Christmas? Where is home? Here, with the alphahole Mafia Capo? Or in London with Summer and her new husband, who, I confess, I don't know well at all?

Not like I have a choice. After all, he had thrown me out... Well, he'd kidnapped me, so it was his prerogative to let me go. Hold on... What prerogative? He had taken me and married me... The least he could have done was share his feelings with me. Not to mention, at least, gotten me off.

Now, here I am, walking up the road in the center of Palermo, with nothing but the clothes on my back, and nowhere to go... I need to get to a phone and call Summer. I pause. Maybe if I turn and go back to the nightclub, I can ask to borrow a phone or something? And risk running into my husband—well, my not-husband, to be precise... Nah, no way. It would only give him a chance to smirk. Maybe a chance to tell me to get out, all over again.

Nope. N-a-h. I am going to have to do this without him. Gonna have to find someone with a phone, or someplace which will allow me to make a call. Aren't Italians largely warm-hearted people? Or at least, that's what I had read somewhere. I walk up the road, which features other bars, eating joints... No other nightclubs on this street. Guess when the Mafia runs a nightclub, no-one wants to go head-to-head against them. They'd lose. As I had.

I'd thought I could go toe-to-toe with this man, and see what happened? Asshole really did do a number on me. Why the hell did he have to be so...hot? So sexy... So irresistible. Why did he have to show a glimmer of humanity under all that alphaholeness, eh?

If I were truly convinced that he's evil, I would be jumping for joy right now. The problem is, I now know he isn't as mean as he pretends to be. Nor as unfeeling as he'd like me to believe. Unfortunately, nothing I've said or done so far has convinced him to open up to me either. Jerk.

To think, we actually had a chance to make a go of it. We could have had a future together; a possibility of a life together. Gah! I really have done it now, falling in love with him so completely. I knew I was attracted to him, that I was falling for him, but to be in love with him? Shit, shit, shit. A pressure builds at the backs of my eyes. I am in love with him and he... He, clearly, hates me.

Nice one, Karma. The story of my life. Why do I always realize what I want a little too late?

I had gotten into Goldsmith to study fashion design, then in a fit of rebellion, dropped out… Only to figure out later that I could have done with that little bit of extra guidance… I mean, I was rushing to break the rules without first learning what the rules were. So, in the end, the only person who was hurt by the entire process was me. Just like now, when I am the only person mourning the end of a relationship that wasn't.

I continue walking up the street. The bars and restaurants have given way to shops that look more run down. There is a coffee shop with a group of men standing about it. Some are seated at the tables outside, drinking coffee, talking together. Many are dressed in pants and vests. Their forearms tattooed. One of them raises the espresso cup to his lips. The guy opposite him says something, and the man throws the coffee in his face. The guy screams. The second man jumps to his feet, smashes the cup into the first guy's temple. The cup shatters. Blood pours down his face. Shit, I really am in Mafia land, huh?

I pause, glancing up and down the street. I could turn back…but… nah, I am not conceding defeat. I need to keep going. I cross the street, to the other side, then stay close to the wall. I continue walking, keeping my gaze forward. My palms begin to sweat, and I wipe them on the silk skirt of my dress. Shit, why had I worn this outfit? It had seemed like a good idea then. But on the street and trying not to draw attention to myself…? Yeah, think again.

A wolf whistle rings out from the other side of the street. I wince, but don't look in their direction. Hell, the one thing I know is self-preservation. If I don't pay attention to them, hopefully, they'll lose interest. Another wolf whistle sounds, this one louder and accompanied by kissing noises. Ugh. I draw myself up to my full height, keep my pace even. If I run, they'll know I am scared… And while I am—shitless, to be honest—I am not going to give these assholes the satisfaction of knowing that.

A bead of sweat trickles down my spine. The hair on the nape of my neck rises. The sound of a vehicle accelerating reaches me. I stiffen, turn to find a van overtaking the car in front as it hurtles up the road. The hair on the back of my neck rises. My senses jangle. Somehow, I know the van is headed for me. *Run! Get out of here.* These blasted heels I borrowed from Cassandra are not meant for running. My ankles wobble, I cry out, then kick off my stilettos, and break into a sprint. The soles of my feet hit the hard concrete. Vibrations of pain race up my legs. I wince, but keep going even as the sound of the vehicle's engine draws closer. It draws up next to me and the door slides open. A man jumps out in my path. I careen to a stop, pivot to find another man behind me. *No, no, no.* I throw up a fist, then scream when arms wrap around my center. I am lifted straight off of my feet, and even as I try to kick out, I am flung inside the van. I jump up, but something hits me on the head from behind. Then everything goes dark.

16

Michael

Shit, shit, shit. I shouldn't have let her go. I snatch up the ring that she had flung down on the table. I close my palm around it and the edge of the diamond seems to bite into the flesh of my palm. Shit, what was I thinking, letting her leave like that? I slide the ring inside my pocket, then pull out my knife and flip it, catch it by the handle. I stare at the polished blade. The edge of which I had sunk into her skin when I had carved the mark of my possession of her.

Was she right? Did I do that because I wanted to own her? To make her mine. To have her as my wife to cherish, to protect, to love… No… Not that. I am not capable of that emotion. No, my feelings for her are already way more complex than that. If I had asked her to stay, if I had given in to the temptation she is… In that gorgeous dress which had clung to her like a second skin, outlining the thrust of her breasts, the curves of her hips, and pulled tight across her thigh… I would have never been able to let her go.

And would that have been so bad?

Pain slices my palm. I glance down to find the blade has nicked the flesh at the base of my thumb. *Che diavolo*. I stick the knife into the wooden surface of the desk, then bring my palm to my mouth and suck on the wound.

The door to my office bursts open and Seb stalks in. His features are set in hard lines, his forehead furrowed.

"What is it?"

"Karma." He scowls, "They took her."

My heart slams in my chest. My pulse rate ratchets up. "What do you mean, they took her?"

"That's what he says." Massimo drags in a guy by his collar. The man is bleeding from his mouth; blood stains his vest. A sleeve of tattoos covers one arm and runs up the side of his throat.

"Who is this?" I growl.

"Found him bragging to one of the dancers downstairs, that he saw a woman being kidnapped. She reported it to me, and I got suspicious. I collared him, asked him to describe what he saw, and from his description, I am positive that he witnessed Karma being taken."

I rise to my feet, slam my palm into the table with such force that a glass crashes to the floor. "Will one of you tell me who the fuck would dare come into my territory and take my wife from me?"

"You did let her go," Seb reminds me. "You sent her out there unprotected."

Anger squeezes my guts and pain slams into my chest with such force that my lungs burn. "Shut the fuck up," I growl.

"Am I wrong?" Seb tilts his head.

"Don't fucking talk to me like that."

"Someone needs to, considering you are letting your ego blind you to what's there right in front of you."

"And what's that?"

"That you love her."

Something hot stabs at my chest. I round the table, throw up my fist. He doesn't duck... He had enough time to evade my blow, but he doesn't. My strike hits home. I connect with the side of his face and he grunts. I raise my fist again, but Massimo shoves the man he's holding at Antonio.

He steps between us, holds up his hands, "Enough, Capo, you need to get a grip on yourself."

"I am going to kill him."

"For telling the truth?"

I freeze, "What the hell is wrong with all of you?"

"What is wrong with you?" He snaps. "Your woman has been taken... This time, likely, by our enemy, and you're standing here fighting with your own clan? With people who are on your side, in your corner. You need to rein in your temper, *fratellone,* and focus on what we must do next."

I lurch back, shake my head. Fuck, fuck, fuck. What's happening to me? I drag my fingers through my hair, then jerk my chin at him. "You can step aside," I murmur, "I won't attack him."

Massimo lowers his arms and I brush past both of them. I stalk over to the *figlio di puttana* who's struggling to get away from Antonio. I swipe out my arm, bury my fist in his face. Blood blooms from his nose, drips down his chin.

"What did you see?" I growl.

"I had nothing to do with." His throat moves as he swallows, "I swear, on the holy Virgin Mary, I was minding my own business when she comes along. I only noticed her because... Well, it's difficult not to, the way she was dressed, and her figure, I—"

I bring my fist up, sink it into his stomach this time. He gurgles, bends over, and would have fallen if Antonio hadn't jerked him back upright.

I slam my fist into his shoulder, then raise it again, only to be grabbed and yanked back.

"*Fratellone,* stop." Massimo grips my shoulder, "We need him to tell us what he saw."

"I'll kill him." I say in a low voice. "I'll tear him from limb to limb, then smash all his bones and throw him in a barrel of acid while he's still alive."

"If you did that, we'd never be able to find her."

Find her. Find her. The anger drains away and silence fills my head. I step back, look the *bastardo* in the eye.

"Who took her?"

"I don't know, I swear," he warbles. "I was watching her... Hell, we were all watching her—"

I fold my fingers into fists. I will not kill him. Not yet. Not until he's told me everything he witnessed.

"And then?" Massimo prompts, "What happened after that?"

"A van drove up the road, pulled to a stop in front of her, and they took her."

My vision tunnels and a coldness grips me. "What kind of a van?" I ask in a low voice. "Did you notice the numbers on the license plate?"

"The license plate was c-covered in dirt," he stutters. "It was a white Fiat Ducato," he adds.

"Like that is helpful," Massimo growls. "There must be a million of them on the road."

"Any other distinguishing features?" Seb walks up to stand on my other side, "You'd better come up with something that is going to help us, if you want to live."

The *testa di cazzo* blinks, then glances between us.

"Or maybe, he wants to die right now?" Massimo raises his fist and the man yells.

"Wait, wait, let me think."

"Think fast," Seb prompts him. "Else your insides will be gracing the floor very soon." He pops his knuckles and the man pales.

"A…a…flower."

"What?"

"I saw a design of what looked like a flower on the windscreen."

"Are you sure?" I scowl at him.

"Yes, no, I don't know," he pants. Sweat drips down his temples. "It... lt…looked like it, but I can't be sure."

"What kind of a flower?" I glare at him and he blinks rapidly.

"I am not sure."

He glances between us, "Please, just let me go. I promise never to look at her again."

Fuck, if I don't want to pull his eyes out for daring to look at her in a lascivious way. And if I did, I'd never have witnesses come forward in the future with information. I roll my shoulders, narrow my gaze on him. "Get out while you're still alive," I snap.

The man turns and scampers out.

I fold my arms across my chest, "I am going to find whoever did this, and when I do… I am going to destroy their entire bloodline. Every. Last. One. of them."

Neither Seb nor Massimo contradict me.

"There are only two gangs who would dare do this," Massimo murmurs. "It can't be the Bratva because we've struck a deal with them. Which leaves —"

"The Kane Company." I roll my neck from side to side "Would they dare come right into my territory and do this?"

"They attacked you on your turf." He's referring to an incident a few months ago when four unarmed men had attacked me. I had managed to overpower them, and even brought two of them in for questioning. One of them had swallowed poison and died, the other, I had knifed. We hadn't gotten much from either of them, but it stood to reason that it was the Kane Company who were behind both incidents.

"They are the only ones with enough gumption to attempt something like this." Seb scratches his chin. One of his eyes is half closed, a ring of black already showing up around it, thanks to my hit. "They probably wanted to get your attention," he warns.

"Well, they have it."

"They, clearly, wanted to make you angry enough to commit a mistake." Massimo tilts his head.

I glare back at him. "Fuck that," I growl. "They took what is mine and now they have to face my wrath."

I brush past both of them, head for my desk. Working the knife from the surface of my table, I slide it back in its sheath. Then I pull out my drawer, snatch up my gun, check to make sure it's loaded before I slide it at the back in my waistband holster. I grab another gun, repeat the actions to ensure that it's loaded, then slide it into my underarm holster. I snatch up a third gun, bend and raising my pant leg and slip it into the holster around my ankle.

I straighten to find both of them watching me.

"What?" I snap.

"You don't think you are going in alone, do you?" Seb drawls.

"It's my fight."

"It's our territory," he counters.

"She's our family." Massimo frowns, "And if you think you…our Capo is going there on your own—"

"You are wrong," Christian says from the open door.

"Thought I told the lot of you all to head off and get on with your work."

"This is work," Xander prowls into the room. "Much as I hate bloodshed, I am afraid this is one time I can't help but back you up."

"They dare to raise a hand on our flesh and blood," Christian growls. "They'll answer for this with their lives."

"I can't allow everyone to come with me on this."

"But—" Christian begins to protest, and I raise my hand.

"If this is some kind of trick, and I'm not saying it is, but if it is, then with the lot of us heading out together to confront them, we are playing right into their hands."

Xander nods, "So what would you have us do instead?"

"Stay back," I glance between the twins. "Monitor for any unusual activity within our network. Anyone who could have leaked news of what happened here. They were keeping a close eye on us. There's no doubt about that. It's how they knew the moment she walked out on her own." I widen my stance. "Whoever is leaking information needs to be brought to heel, before any more damage is done." And her... What about her? If my actions led to her being hurt... I'll never be able to forgive myself. I won't stop until she has been avenged. And how will I live after that? How will I continue without her? I roll my shoulders. Only one way out. I need to get to her before anything happens.

I stalk past the men and to the door, then pause to glance over my shoulder at Seb and Massimo, "You two coming?"

17

Karma

Darkness presses in on me. Pain thuds at my temples, between my eyes. I turn on my side and the throbbing in my head ratchets up. Red sparks flare behind my closed eyelids. I groan and the sound seems to echo in the space. I crack my eyelids open, wince when the brightness overwhelms me. I turn on my back, lay still. Take a deep breath, another. Shit, why won't the pain recede? I swallow and my throat hurts. I take a mental inventory of my body, but nothing else seems hurt.

I open my eyes again, slowly, and this time they seem to adjust to the brightness which is sunlight pouring in from a window to my right. I glance around, take in the empty room I am in. Well, except for the bed that I am on. I attempt to sit up, then almost cry out when the headache worsens. I bring my hand to my head, then wince when I feel the bump at the back. No wonder I have a headache… I hit my head. OMG, the van. I had been trying to get away from those men in the cafe, when the van…had drawn up next to me. One of the men had grabbed me and thrown me inside, and then… Someone had hit me on the head, I think. Bloody hell, I've been kidnapped… Again? What the hell?

Is it just my bad luck, or do I walk around with a target painted on my forehead to attract all of the creeps around me to come after me? Not that Michael is a creep… No, he's worse… He's an asshole. A jackalope. A douche canoe of the nth degree. Gah! And here I am, back to being a captive. My freedom had lasted roughly half an hour, if that? And am I going to, once more, lay here waiting for someone to tell me what to do next? Whoever these guys are, they're surely as dangerous as, if not more than, Michael.

Of course, it's also thanks to him that I am in this situation. If he hadn't turned me out, I would never have been kidnapped. A-n-d hold on… If he hadn't kidnapped me in the first place, then I wouldn't have been kidnapped again, either. Yeah, everything that's happened to me is because of him. He's the one to blame. When I see him again, I am going to yell at him, slap him, then…fling myself on him, climb him like a tree and kiss him. The sound of the door being opened reaches me. My heart jackknifes in my chest. My pulse rate ratchets up. I jerk my head toward the doorway, stifle another cry when the headache seems to intensify.

A man walks in. He's tall—as tall as Michael, maybe—and broad, but in a way that hints at him spending too much time in a gym… That, and steroids. He is definitely on something, to have his biceps balloon in that fashion. His shirt strains at the seams and outlines his chest, as well as the making of a flabby belly…which is a weird combination. He stops at the foot of the bed, looks me up and down. My skin crawls. The hair on the nape of my neck rises. Shit, this man, he is up to no good. His gaze comes to rest on my chest—asshole—before moving in a leisurely path down to the apex of my legs.

"You're awake?"

"No, I am sleeping. And clearly, I like to talk in my sleep too."

He blinks, jerks his chin up. "Har, har." His lips kick up, "You have a sense of humor."

"That makes one of us." I scowl at him. "How dare you kidnap me?"

He opens and shuts his mouth. Evidently, I have rendered him speechless, which is a start. I lever my body up, swing my legs over the side of the bed and stand up. My stomach lurches, bile boils up my throat and I swallow it down. My head spins. I draw in a breath, and the world rights itself again. I take a step forward, then another. I walk to the door, grab the handle and twist it. I try to open it and the door resists. Shit. I jiggle the handle, try to pull it back again, "Come on, come on."

I hear his footsteps approach, feel him close enough for his body heat to envelop me. My stomach ties itself in knots. I slide away, just as his heavy hand lands on the door, which shudders. Shit. If he'd grabbed me, he'd probably have broken a bone or two. I turn to face him. He takes a step forward and I stumble back against the door. *Don't show him how scared you are. If you do, it will only make it worse.* And there is no one looking for me.

Alphahole has no idea that I've been kidnapped again, and if he did, would he come for me? My heart stutters. He would. I have no doubt about it. He may be upset with me, enough to have cast me out, but there's no doubt that his ego would not permit him to allow anyone else to take what is his. But does he still consider me his? What if he really is done with me? Shit, what if I am doomed to spend the rest of my days here, in this stupid room, with this horrible, overgrown gorilla of a man, whoever he is? Trying to come on to me... Who definitely wants to do worse than just come on to me. Gross!

He rolls his shoulders, no doubt, to impress upon me just how much bigger than me he is. *Bloody baboon.*

He cracks his knuckles and I pretend to yawn. That wipes the smile off of his face. *Stupid shitstain.* He lunges forward and I bring my knee up and smash it into his center. He roars in pain. I slide aside, as he bends over and grabs his nuts. I race for the door, hammer on it, "Let me out of here. Let me out. Let me out right now." My head throbs each time my fist connects with the door, but I don't let up. I sense him straighten and begin to lumber toward me. I pivot, bring my fist down on the door with such force that the entire frame shakes. Pain ripples up my arm, and I cry out. "Open the goddam door. Please open the door, please—"

He grabs my hair and pulls me back with such force that I scream. He shakes me, and I see sparks behind my eyes. Tears squeeze out from the corners of my eyes and my legs seem to give way from beneath me. He releases me and I sink to the floor. He steps toward me, when the door is wrenched upon.

"The boss wants to see you," someone says from outside the room. The man hesitates when the voice speaks again, "You know how he doesn't like to be kept waiting."

The man grumbles under his breath, then turns and walks out of the door. I lay where I have fallen on the floor. My headache seems to have grown exponentially, now filling the entirety of my head. I groan, then stagger to my feet. I manage to stumble to the bed and sink down onto it. The scent of stale cigarettes and other assorted smells I don't care to identify assails me. I cough, turn my head away, throw my arm over my eyes and curl into myself.

When I open my eyes again, it's dark outside. My headache, at least, seems to have receded. Thank God. I sit up, then groan when every part of my body aches. My tongue seems to be stuck to the roof of my mouth. I swallow and my throat hurts. The soles of my feet throb, probably from that hasty run to get away from my kidnappers earlier. I glance around the empty room again. I hate this… Sitting here, waiting to be rescued. Not that there is anyone coming to get me. I hunch my shoulders as a tear makes its way down my cheek. I sniffle, then wipe the back of my palm against my nose. Goddammit, how the hell am I going to get out of this situation?

I rise up to my feet, then hobble over to the window. I glance outside, and blink. We must be on a hill or something, for the lights of the city stretch out in the distance.

I glance down and realize I am on the second floor.

I reach for the handle on the window frame, try to pull it down but it won't budge. Dammit! I grab it with both of my hands, tense my biceps, then yank it down. Still, no movement. Argh! I draw in a breath, then brace my feet on the floor. I throw the entire weight of my body behind it, and it moves, maybe, just a centimeter. I collapse against the windowsill, panting. A headache knocks behind my eyes, but I ignore it. I grab the handle and twist it. My muscles protest; my arms hurt. My biceps feel like they are being put through a wringer. The handle slides down a little more. Oh, my god! I sink down onto the floor, lean my head into the wall.

I close my eyes, draw in a few deep breaths. Close my eyes and focus inside myself. If my hippie mother were here, she'd tell me to center myself. Zoom in on the intention. Ground myself, draw on the energy of the earth and—I hear the sound of footsteps approaching. I snap open my eyes, then spring up, turn to the window, then grab the handle and yank on it. It moves down a few more millimeters. "Goddam it!" I cry out as I hear the door open behind me.

I throw everything I have into grabbing the handle and hang off of it. Metal against metal screeches and it slips free. I turn around to find the guy from earlier entering the room. My heart slams into my ribcage.

My pulse rate spikes. Adrenaline laces my blood. I turn back to the window, fling it open. Then pull myself onto the window sill.

He reaches for me and I clamber out onto the ledge. He leans out of the window, and I evade him. My feet slip on the ledge and I cry out, then right myself. I slide forward, out of his reach, and plaster myself against the wall. I turn to find the bastard trying to pull himself up. His shoulders fill the window, his frame, clearly, too big for the space. As I watch, he maneuvers himself onto the window sill, then shoves one leg over the frame. Fuck!

Sweat trickles down my spine and my dress sticks to my back. I glance down at the ground which, despite the fact that I am on the second floor, seems way farther down than I'd like, then back to where the gorilla climbs out onto to the ledge. He bares his teeth, and my stomach twists. No way, am I going to be a sitting duck, waiting for him to get his hands on me again. Wait — I am standing; does that make me a standing duck? Ugh, not the time for wordplay, Karma! Just this once, can karma be on my side?

He edges toward me and my heart gallops in my chest. Adrenaline laces my blood. My vision tunnels, I stare down at the ground, then toward the horizon.

He gets closer, close enough for him to swipe out his arm. The tips of his fingers brush my hair. I duck, hold up my middle finger at him, then jump.

18

Karma

I squeeze my eyes shut and prepare for impact. I crash into something hard. Solid. The shock smashes through my system. I groan. This is not going to be pretty. Am I going to look like one of those people who jump from a height and ends up splattered over the sidewalk? Not that I have seen any in real life, thank God... But I have seen enough movies to know it's a gruesome sight.

The ground under me moves... Huh? I snap my eyes open, stare down into blazing blue eyes. Gone is the coldness, the remote look he had worn when I had last seen him. This man is angry...livid with the kind of rage that vibrates off of him and slams into my chest.

"You jumped," he growls, "you fucking jumped."

"It was only from the second story, besides I...I didn't have a choice."

Debris rains down on us and Michael steps aside, his movement so graceful I can only blink as he stares up. I don't take my gaze off of his beautiful face as he growls, "Who the fuck is up there?"

"One of the men who kidnapped me."

His features harden. All emotion drains from his face. His gaze narrows as he walks back a few paces.

"Wh…what are you doing?"

He merely heaves me over his shoulder like I am a sack of potatoes.

"What the fuck?" I yell as I stare at his perfectly hard backside. My hair streams down about my ears and down to cover his gorgeous rear. I sense him move, then hear a shot, and the ground seems to shudder. "Fuck." I close my eyes as a trembling grips me, "Fuck, fuck, fuck."

Footsteps approach us, then Michael snaps, "Make sure you kill every last *figlio di puttana* inside the house."

"Will do," a voice replies.

Seb? Is it one of his other brothers. Michael's body moves, then he lowers me down and back into his arms. I turn my face into his chest, breathe in his dark, edgy essence, fill my lungs with his scent, and burrow into him. His grip tightens around me.

His voice rumbles above me and the vibrations resonate up his chest, sink into my blood. His voice fades in and out as I begin to drift.

"Set fire…send a message…taking her home."

He turns and walks away, as the sound of gunshots reaches me, then wanes as he moves further away. His grip tightens around me, then he brushes his lips over my hair. "I need to lower you to the ground so I can open the car door," he murmurs.

"No," I grip the front of his shirt, "no, no, no."

"Shh!" He presses a kiss to my forehead, "You're safe with me."

Tears fill my eyes and run down my cheeks. How the hell am I ever going to feel safe after what happened? After I was kidnapped, twice, in quick succession, in such a short time? And to think, my once kidnapper is the only person in whose arms I now feel safe. I am such a bloody mess.

"Don't cry," his voice catches, "please don't cry, Beauty."

Of course, that only makes me sob harder.

He walks around the car, then bends and manages to open the door on the driver's side. He slides inside, shuts the door behind him as I cling to him. Gah, shrinking violet, I am not. But right now, if I let go of him… What if someone else tries to take me away? What if he decides, again, that he doesn't want me?

Fuck, I am conforming to every damn stereotype of a damsel in distress that I hate. My throat closes and another wave of trembling grips me. My teeth chatter and my bones feel too brittle for my body.

I draw up my legs, try to conserve what warmth I have left in my body.

He wraps his arms around me, plasters me to his chest, then lowers his head to kiss the skin between my eyebrows, my eyelids, the tip of my nose, my mouth. I moan, part my lips, and he sweeps in. He dances his tongue across mine, closes his mouth over mine in a deep, draining kiss that seems to suck every last thought from my head. His chest heaves, his breath grows shallow, a hardness digs into my side, and when he finally breaks the kiss, I can't think anymore. Maybe that was the point. When he lowers me onto the seat next to his, I don't protest.

He yanks on the safety belt, snaps it into place. Snatches up a bottle of water from the holder between the seats and hands it over to me. I gulp down the water, then close the bottle and hand it over to him. He tosses it back in the holder then reaches over to grab my hand. He places it on his thigh. The strength in that thick, hard column sinks into my blood. A warmth steals up my arm, fills my chest. My head throbs and I lean back into the seat, as he sets the vehicle in motion.

How did I put myself in this position? Since when do I need a man to take care of me? I have navigated life on my own terms since a very young age, yet a few weeks with this guy, and I am dependent on him for my security. When he's the one who kidnapped me in the first place. Since when has my kidnapper become my protector?

"How—" My voice cracks and I clear my throat. "How did you know where to find me?"

"Someone saw you being taken. He was bragging about it at Venom. When Seb heard it, he realized that he was talking about you."

"How did you track me down?"

He turns down a road, and the muscles of his forearms flex as he steers the car. "The man who saw you noticed a symbol on the windshield. One that, as we found out, is associated with the Kane Company. From there, it was a matter of raiding each of their strongholds. If we had gotten to you even a few seconds later—" His jaw tics, "I'll never forgive myself for letting you leave unprotected. If it were up to me, I'd tie you to me and never let you leave my side. If I could, I'd take back everything I said."

"But you can't."

He grimaces, then turns onto another road. "I am going to try my very best to make it up to you."

"I... I'm not sure that's a good idea."

"What's that supposed to mean?" he growls

"We are not good for each other, Michael." I firm my lips, " For heaven's sake, I tried to kill you. Twice… And you forced me to marry you, then turned me out when you felt like you didn't want me around anymore."

"That's not true," he says through gritted teeth, "I turned you out, because…"

"Because?"

"Because I knew if I kept you around, I'd end up falling for you."

"Huh?"

"Surprised?" He peers at me from the corner of his eye, "Didn't think I could admit that to you, huh?"

I swallow, "It still doesn't change the fact that every time we are together, we bring out the worst in each other."

"That's how the best relationships are." He stares through the windshield. "We are not a normal, staid couple meant to have a normal, staid marriage, where the husband holds down a desk job and makes an appointment to have sex with his wife—"

"You're right."

"I am?"

I nod, "We're the kind of couple who needs to steer clear of each other if we want to survive."

"Survival is overrated." His lips curl. "We bring out the darkness in each other. We speak to each other on a primal level. Even now, as we maintain the distance that society asks of us, our bodies hunger for each other, our flesh wants to reach out to the other, and our souls? Our souls recognize the twisted, fuckedupness that each of us has tried to hide from the world, but which we haven't been able to hold back from each other."

"My point, precisely." I pull my hand back from his thigh, but he captures it and imprisons it between his big palm and the solidness of his thigh. My core flutters.

Shit, even as I am trying to put distance between us, I can't stop being aware of him. Can't stop myself from being turned on by his strength. Can't stop myself from wanting to turn to him and crawl into his lap and feel his arms around me as he hides me from the world. Tears prick at the backs of my eyes. Goddammit, since when have I become so needy?

Is it his dominance, his need for control that brings out the feminine side in me? Is that why I veer toward him for safety? Is that why, despite everything in me knowing how wrong it is to want to be with him, I want to trust him?

"We need to have nothing to do with each other."

His fingers tighten on the wheel.

"You did the right thing in turning me out earlier." I set my jaw. "It was my bad luck that I ended up being kidnapped again. But I'm safe now, so there's no reason for you to hold onto me."

He doesn't answer, simply keeps his gaze forward.

"If you return my phone back to me, I can call Summer and have her send someone to help me leave here."

"No."

"What do you mean no?"

"If you think I am letting you go that easily, you are mistaken."

"I thought you said that you were falling for me."

"All the more reason to not let you go."

And there...he is. The big, bad, alphahole Capo. Guess it was too much to hope that he was actually revealing his more sensitive side. Not that I doubt he has it. Not that I want him to share it with me. Somehow, it's easier if he continues to stay in his arrogant, over-the-top, alpha persona. It's much easier to deal with him that way. It's so much easier to hate him when he doesn't reveal the man behind the ruthless Capo. Yeah, I'd much rather he be unreasonable, and inconsiderate, and conceited.

I whip my head toward him. "I thought you said you were going to try to make it up to me."

"Doesn't mean I am going to let you go free."

"Then your idea of making it up to me and my idea of your making it up to me are, clearly, different."

"We'll see."

19

Karma

As it turns out, his idea of making it up to me is to transport me back to his island. He'd first driven me to a house in Palermo where a doctor — one he trusts, apparently — had checked me out. He'd checked out the wound at the back of my head, treated it, then given me a shot to help ease the pain. Guess Michael didn't want to risk taking me to a hospital, though the doctor had been competent and very professional.

Then he had driven straight to the pier and whisked me up in his arms, despite my protesting that I'm not some stupid, helpless female. To which he'd retorted that he had rescued me, so perhaps I am more helpless than I thought. Which had promptly upset me more, but he'd ignored my reaction. He'd marched to his yacht... Yeah, there was a freakin' yacht that he'd had anchored at the pier. He'd carried me aboard, parked me in a chair in the captain's cabin, then had shrugged off his jacket and wrapped it about me. I had shoved one arm, then the other, into the sleeves, pulled it close — even as I had hated myself for snuggling into the comfort it offered, even as I had berated myself for being stupid enough to turn my nose into the collar and sniff, drawing his dark, edgy, masculine scent into my lungs. As he'd started the boat and steered it across the water, I had watched his broad back, his powerful shoulders, the corded strength in his arms as he had steered the boat, and my heart had stuttered. Hell. I had just told him that I wanted nothing to do with him, yet watching him maneuver the boat with that innate confidence that defines my Capo had turned my insides to jelly. I had slipped off the chair, walked up to him, and he had pulled me close to his side.

I had slid my arms about his lean waist and clung to him as he piloted the craft to the island. By the time we had reached it, I could barely keep my eyes open, thanks to whatever it was that the doc had given me, I guess. He had swung me up into his arms again, and I had fallen asleep as he'd carried me inside, only to wake up in the middle of the night screaming.

In my dream, I was back in that room, with that same gorilla of a man on top of me, threatening to…not only kill me, but first, to do much worse. He slapped me about, tore my clothes and… That's when I woke up and found I was clinging to Michael.

His arms around me, he held me close enough for my breasts to be crushed against his massive chest. "Shh!" he soothed me, then rocked me and made these rumbling noises that seemed to emerge from deep within his chest. It soothed me enough to fall asleep, until I woke up this morning, alone…in his bed…in his room. Huh?

I stare about the space, wondering what it means? The last time I was on the island, I was his prisoner. Well, I still am, considering he said that he's not letting me leave, despite my stated desire to do so.

I roll out of bed, trudge to the bathroom, and make the mistake of looking at myself in the mirror. I look terrible, downright frightening. The dark circles under my eyes are almost as dark as my favorite goth make up, which I don't have with me to cover the ravages of my recent ordeal.

I shower, carefully wash my body, then shampoo all of the filth from my hair, wincing only a little when my fingers encounter the bump on my head. When I emerge, I find a set of newly-laundered and folded clothes, along with fresh underwear.

Was it him? More likely, Cassandra, assuming she returned to island as well. I pull on the jeans and T-shirt (both black), along with the socks and the sweatshirt (both grey), and walk down to the kitchen to find Cassandra at the stove cooking.

She turns to me with a smile on her face, "How do you feel?"

"Not too bad," I concede as I take a seat at the breakfast counter. "When did you get here?"

"Earlier this morning." She pours out a glass of orange juice, then places it in front of me.

I glance at it, then fold my hands in my lap.

"The Capo wants you to drink that."

"No doubt." I scowl at the glass of juice, "Where is he, anyway?"

"He had some business to see to."

"Is he still on the island?"

She nods.

"So why isn't he here?" Jesus, why do I sound so whiny, so needy? Everything I had sworn to myself I never would be. Summer had taken good care of me, and had ensured that she had moved me out of the state's foster care system as soon as she was old enough to be able to do so... Still, the time we had spent apart had taught me that, ultimately, the only person I can depend on is myself. "Forget I said that," I clear my throat.

"No need to explain." She slides a plate of pancakes in front of me, then places a jar of honey next to it, along with butter. As well as a cup of espresso. "I'm just glad you are safe."

"So, you heard what happened?"

"The Capo was beside himself. He didn't rest for one second, not until he had found you. He contacted me early this morning and told me to get here so I could help make you more comfortable."

"Oh," I glance down at the pancakes, "maybe that's what he wants you to believe." I raise a shoulder. "Or maybe, it's just that he can't bear the thought of anyone else getting ahold of what he considers his."

"And is that so bad?" She murmurs, "I'd give anything to have a man look at me the way he looks at you."

"What do you mean?" I frown, "I am not exactly his favorite person."

"That's not true, you —"

"Cassandra." His hard voice rings out from the doorway.

Both of us turn to face him. I expect Cassandra to get nervous, or at least be startled at having been interrupted half-way through a conversation, which I am sure would have shed some more enlightening details on the Capo. Instead, there is no change in expression on her features. Huh?

She merely nods at me, "I'll see you later, Karma." She walks over to the doorway and he steps aside to let her pass.

He prowls over to pull up a chair opposite me. "You aren't eating."

"Neither are you," I retort.

"I ate already."

I lean back in my chair, "Why did you bring me here?"

"How's your head?" He rakes his gaze across my features, "No headache or anything?"

"I'm good," I say grudgingly, "and you are avoiding the question."

He quirks his mouth, "I'll make you a trade."

"Huh?"

"One answer to one question that you can ask me for every mouthful of food."

"It's a terrible deal." I purse my lips.

"How do you know without trying it?"

"Sometimes you don't need to try to know you are being set up." I scowl at him, then glance down at the pancakes. My stomach grumbles. My mouth waters. Damn it, they look so good. I pick up my knife and fork, cut a piece and raise it to my lips. I chew on it, then tip up my chin, "So, will you answer my question now? Why did you bring me here?"

"That's two questions," he retorts. "Also, it's safest for you here."

"You mean because you can keep me prisoner?"

He stares at me, looks down at the plate, then back at me.

Yeah, yeah, whatever. I cut into the pancake again, pop it inside my mouth, then glance at him."

"I brought you here to ensure that no one can get to you."

I shoot him an icy look, "So you *are* keeping me prisoner?"

"Does it look like you are a prisoner here?" He raises his hands, "You are free to come and go as you wish."

"A gilded cage is still a cage."

He tilts his head, "Not if you're safer within the walls than outside."

"Is that what you think?" I scoff, "That I am safer inside here?" I shovel more of the pancake inside my mouth.

"Considering the last time you managed to find a way out, probably not." His lips quirk, "It's why I have taken certain precautions."

"Precautions?" I narrow my gaze, "What precautions?"

"There's still time to discuss that." He nods at my plate, "Finish your food."

I scowl at the remnants of the food on my plate, "I am full."

"Only one more bite," he coaxes me. "Come on, you can do it."

I blow out a breath, "Oh, okay." I scoop up the last mouthful, chew on it, swallow. "Happy?" I place my knife and spoon in the plate.

"Finish your juice."

"But—"

"Karma," his voice lowers to a hush, "do as you are told."

"Fine, fine, I'll do it." I squeeze my thighs together. "No need to go all alpha on me."

"You like it when I do."

"That's what you think." I toss my head as I grab the glass of juice and sip from it.

He merely arches an eyebrow, indicating he knows that I am lying. Hell, I know I am lying. But so what? It's either that or confess that I want him to own me, to possess me, to wrap his arms around me, before he grabs my throat, pushes me up into the wall, then shoves his thigh between mine and sinks his— I cough and sputter as the juice goes down the wrong way. Damn it. I place my glass back on the table.

Once the coughing subsides, I frown at him, "So, what are the stupid precautions you wanted to talk about?"

"I'll tell you when the time is right." He rises to his feet. "Meanwhile, I have something I want to show you."

20

Michael

I had woken up in the early hours of the day to find her thrashing about and screaming, trapped in the throes of a nightmare. I had brought her to the island because it's the only place where I can control everyone's comings and goings…After making sure that the boathouse no longer holds any boats that she could use to get away from me again…that is. Then I'd taken her to my bedroom…

There is no question in my mind that she belongs here. Not that I am going to touch her. She needs time and space to mend from what happened, not just physically but also emotionally. And clearly, I had been right in bringing her here, for she'd jack-knifed up in bed panting, no doubt, from the images of the debacle she'd been through… Which had been my fault. Because I'd let her leave… I'd told her to leave... Something I am not going to do again… And…

I am going to makes sure that if, for some reason, she does... Or if, somehow, someone else dares to take her away from me, I'll know where to find her.

All of those thoughts had run through my head as I had reached over to her side of the bed and drawn her close to me. I had made sure to sleep on top of the covers, putting as much distance as possible between us. Because, truly, I don't want to be tempted to touch her. But comforting her? That's completely different. She needs me and I am not going to let her down. Not when she, clearly, aches for comfort.

I had wrapped my arms around her, pulled her close, and tucked her head under my chin as I had tried to soothe her. She'd cried in my arms, until finally she'd quietened and fallen asleep. I had held her through the night, and sworn that I'll never allow her to be in this situation again, where she's helpless and a victim.

It's my fault she was kidnapped. By taking her, I had drawn the attention of all of my enemies to her. By keeping her and deciding to marry her, I had proclaimed to the world that I have a weakness—her. I had given those who hate me an opportunity to get to me... Through her. It's why it's doubly important to keep her safe. And there is only one way to ensure this. I'm not egoistical enough to think I can keep her 100% protected all the time.

Sooner or later, if someone wants to get to her, they will. And while I will do my utmost to ensure that won't happen... If... In the event that, God forbid, someone else does get to her again, I have to ensure that I will be able to track her down.

I was lucky this time that Seb had heard about the guy who had seen her being taken and put two and two together. Next time, I may not be this fortunate. She may not be this fortunate. Which means I have to tip the odds in our favor...

There is only one way to ensure that I never lose sight of her, no matter what happens. And while it's not something I want to do... It's something I have to do... Something for which she is going to hate me... Something she'd never agree to... Something I don't have a choice but to impose on her. Something which will make her loath me... That is inevitable.

So, before that happens, I have to sweeten her up to me... Hey, I'm only human, after all. And while I can live with her hate—as long as she is safe, that is—I can, at least, try to get into her good books beforehand, right?

At least, that is my reasoning as I push open the door to what had been her room previously. She walks inside, then halts. Her gaze widens as she takes in the space. Where her bed had once been is a sleek sewing machine. I had bought her a sewing machine to sew her wedding dress, but I decided to replace it with a state-of-the-art, most expensive model on the market. Next to it, the yards of fabric that she had purchased from the fabric shop, along with the various sewing tools that she'd bought that day, are neatly folded and organized. And, yeah, I had added to it by asking that *stronzo* Giorgio to bring in anything that she had left behind, just to be safe.

"Wh…what is this?" She blinks rapidly, as she turns to survey the space. "You changed the room completely?"

"It would seem that way, yes." I watch closely as she takes in everything in the space.

She walks over to the worktable next to the sewing machine, opens a sewing kit. She stabs her thumb into a thimble then holds it up, "I see you've been shopping."

"Do you like it?"

She drops the thimble back in the kit, then folds her arms around her waist. "When," she says without turning to face me, "when did you manage to do all of this?"

"Don't worry about that." I take in her flushed features, her bright eyes, "I take it that you *do* like it then?"

"I… I am not sure what to say." She shuffles her feet.

"Everything you might possibly need to create is here."

"I can see that," she murmurs, still not meeting my gaze. She walks over to the mannequin in the corner, and runs her finger along the curve of the figure. "I don't think this is enough."

"It isn't?" I frown as I take in the mirror on the opposite side, the adjustable shelves with cubbyholes, the rectangular table in the center of the room with enough surface area for her to work on.

"Nah," she turns to me, "I think you left out something very important."

"Eh?" I run my fingers through my hair, "What did I miss? I swear, I bought out that entire blasted shop."

"Clearly, you didn't research what goes into making a design studio."

Heat flushes my neck. Truth is, I had merely told Giorgio that I wanted everything that she'd possibly need to create in her studio. I hadn't exactly researched it myself though. *Merda!* Typical, that she had to catch me out on that, huh?

"So, what's missing?" I scowl, "Tell me and I'll make sure to get it for you."

"You sure about that?"

"Of course, I am."

Her lip curves, "No backing out after I tell you what it is."

I plant my palms on my hips, "Try me."

"Last chance," her smile widens.

I draw in a breath, "Do you want me to get it for you or not?"

"A cat."

"What?" I blink.

"A cat." She saunters over to me. "C-A-T, cat. You know, the furry thing that says 'meow'?"

"I know what a cat is."

"Good." She flicks some imaginary dust off my collar, "Now you can get one for me too. Make sure it's cute."

I gape as she sashays over to the fabrics and begins to examine them.

"Let me get this right, you want a cat to complete your studio?"

"Do I need to repeat myself?"

What the—! That little thing; she dares to talk that way to me? I take a step forward, then pause. Of everyone I have met, she is the only one who doesn't take shit from me. It takes some guts to stand up to me too… Especially after everything that we've done to each other. But then, Beauty, isn't just anybody. She's special. She's always known which of my buttons to press to get a reaction from me.

I thought I'd surprise her, but yet again, she's managed to throw me for a loop. A chuckle rumbles up my chest, turns into a full-blown laugh. I throw my head back and guffaw until tears run from my eyes. I wipe them away, then straighten to find her watching me.

"You okay?" she asks, her tone hesitant. "Not coming down with something, are you?"

"No," I shake my head, aware I am still wearing a smile on my face, but fuck, there is no one else here. Only this pint-sized woman who always knows how to put me in my place. "Why do you ask?"

"Never seen you laugh like that before. Hell, I've never seen you smile properly, let alone…give in to a full belly laugh like that."

"I've never been asked to buy a cat before."

"Never?" Her forehead creases.

"Never."

"Oh," she raises a shoulder, "guess there's a first time for everything."

She turns back to playing with the fabrics, before reaching for the sheets of paper next to them. She picks up a drawing pad, and a pencil, then turns to glance at me over her shoulder.

"What are you still doing here?" She scowls, "Leave, so I can work."

<h1 style="text-align:center">21</h1>

Michael

And I had obeyed her. Fuck me, but she had asked me to leave—not very politely either—and I had turned on my heel, skulked out of there, and left her in her studio. Me, the Capo with enough kills under my belt to warrant most people in Sicily warning their children at night that if they don't go to sleep, I'll kidnap them… Yeah, that's the kind of myth that accompanies my reputation… And I had simply acquiesced and left her to work. Maybe it's because she had seemed so happy to find herself surrounded by things that bring her pleasure. Maybe I had seen the sheer joy in her eyes in finding a space where she can work to her heart's content?

She had been taken aback, but also, there had been relief in her eyes. Has she missed her art that much? I raise the glass of whiskey to my lips and take a sip as I stare out of the double doors of the living room, which are flung open to face the sea. The evening sun slants its rays, lighting up the waves. The colors of the impending sunset bleed across the skies. Reds, pinks, golden hues… As pretty as her eyes. As gorgeous as her lips. No… She's more beautiful than nature's treasures. *Che cavolo…* Now I am waxing poetic about her while watching a sunset? Next, I'll be writing odes in her honor.

I left her room a few hours ago, and haven't seen her since. Cassandra had informed me that she had taken lunch up to Beauty's room and that she had eaten it all, as evidenced by the empty tray that had been deposited outside the door. Which is progress. At least, she is eating and happily ensconced in her studio. Which is more than I can say for myself. I glare at the fast-sinking sun on the horizon. Damn it, why is it that my thoughts are still on her?

A knock on the door interrupts my thoughts, and I confess, it is with relief that I turn to find Christian walking in. I nod to my brother, then turn to the woman at his heels.

"Doc," I jerk my chin, "he's briefed you on what I need?"

She draws herself up to her full height, "I have been told what you'd like me to do, but I must record my complete disagreement with what you have proposed."

"I wasn't asking for your opinion."

"I am giving it to you anyway," she firms her lips. "As a health care provider, as a professional, and as a woman, I must protest in the harshest of terms."

"Noted." I tilt my head, "If there's nothing else then—"

"I have something to say as well." Christian folds his arms across his chest. "You know I would never interfere with your personal relationships. I respect you too much for that, *fratellone…*"

"But?"

"But," he shuffles his feet, "I have to say that this is taking things too far."

"You think so?"

He nods, "I definitely do. Why not just speak to her first? Why not tell her what you have in mind?"

"And if she refuses—and you know she will—what then?"

"Then," he rubs the back of his neck, "then maybe you find another way to reach your goal without having to hurt her along the way."

"If this is what is needed to keep her safe, then I am not sorry."

"What if you are afterward? What if she hates you so much that your relationship with her breaks down completely?"

"It's not like the relationship between us is all that healthy right now."

"But at least, there is some semblance of one, isn't there?"

"Is there?" I rake my gaze over his features, "I'll take the risk, if it means I can keep her safe."

"I take it that's the most important thing for you, her safety?" the doctor murmurs and I turn to her.

"What did you say your name was again?"

"Aurora." She tightens her fingers around the sleek briefcase-like bag that she holds, "Doctor Aurora Garibaldi. My father is unwell, so I am here in his stead."

"I assume you are reliable?"

"My father wouldn't have sent me if I weren't."

I arch an eyebrow, "You do realize who you are talking to?"

"To the Capo of the Cosa Nostra," she says in a tone that is respectful, while her gaze is anything but.

"Everything you say and do here is confidential," I murmur. "If I hear of anyone getting wind of what you did, you are dead. You realize that."

"It won't come to that," Christian angles his body, half-blocking her from my view. *Interesting.* "I vouch for her, *fratellone,*" he adds.

The woman jerks her head in his direction. She firms her lips but doesn't say anything. *Very* interesting.

"Do you now?" I stroke my chin. "Can I trust you to keep an eye on her?"

"I don't need anyone to keep an eye on me," she snaps at the same time that his features brighten.

"With pleasure." The bastard all but rubs his hands together.

"Meet me in my office in ten minutes." I walk past them and to the exit.

As I leave the room, I hear her say, "I don't need you to vouch for me." Her tone is so chilly that it could freeze a gelato in seconds.

I can't stop the smirk that curls my lips. This, whatever it is between them, is going to be fun to watch. I head up the stairs and to Beauty's room.

I walk into her room and find her bent over the table. Her back is to me and that gorgeous peach-shaped behind of hers wriggles as she focuses on whatever it is that she is working on. Around her, there are crumpled pieces of paper on the floor. More paper is strewn all across the table. As I watch, she straightens, then balls a piece of paper and tosses it over her shoulder. I reach forward, snatch it up and out of the air. I straighten it out, take in the half-sketched design which looks like the outline of a woman with the dress sketched on her.

"It's called a croquis."

"Whatquis?"

"A croquis," she replies without turning around. "A quick sketch of a human body that serves as a template for a fashion designer piece of clothing."

"I knew that."

"No, you didn't."

"You're right," I agree and she turns to scowl at me over her shoulder.

"What are you doing here?"

"Glad to see you are enjoying yourself." I toss the wadded-up piece of paper in the general direction of the piles of paper she's abandoned on the floor. "We do have a wastepaper basket in the room."

"I'll clean up the room once and for all at the end."

"What are you drawing?" I step behind her, try to peer over her shoulder. She moves to block my view.

"None of your business."

"Everything about you is my business."

"Don't you ever give your alphaholeness a rest?" She huffs.

"Do you want me to give it a rest?"

She raises a shoulder, "I am not sure I'd recognize you if you ever started conversing like a normal person."

"Normal is boring, Beauty. No-one understands that more than you."

"Oh?" She turns to shoot me a glance over her shoulder, "How do you know that?"

"Haven't we established many times over that I know you better than anyone else?"

Her forehead furrows. "It's true, actually," she concedes. "Only, I don't understand how someone like you can be intuitive enough to understand what I like."

"I know what you don't like, too."

She arches an eyebrow, "And what would that be, Mr. Capo of all he surveys?"

"I know that you don't like to be manhandled, for one." I wrap my fingers around her nape, and she shivers. "I know that you don't want to be urged to bend over your drafting table." I apply enough pressure that she lowers her upper body to the surface. "That you don't want me to palm your butt." I do just that as I place my palm against the curve of her denim covered backside, "And that you don't like being spanked." I bring my palm down against her ass and she draws in a sharp breath. "And that you don't like being spanked again," I slap her other asscheek, "and again." I smack both her asscheeks, alternating between them, and she groans. Her entire body shudders.

She slaps her palm onto the paper strewn the table, "Bloody hell." She groans, "Oh, my bloody God."

"And you don't like your pussy being fingered either, do you now, *tesoro mio*?"

I step behind her, fit my tented crotch against the valley between her butt-cheeks. She huffs, then parts her legs further— so I can push my throbbing shaft into her butt. I reach around, to lower her zipper, then slide my fingers inside the seam of her panties.

I brush against her pussy lips and she whines. "Oh, Mika, please… please—"

I slip one finger inside her sopping wet channel and she moans, then clamps down on my digit with her inner walls. The blood rushes to my groin. I thrust a second finger, then a third inside her, as I lean over to press my chest into her back, then bite down on the skin between her neck and the curve of her shoulder.

She yells, "Ouch, you neanderthal, what the hell was that for?"

I lick the abraded flesh and a whine spills from her lips. Moisture drips from between her legs and my cock instantly lengthens. Fuck, I had come here because I need to complete the one thing that will keep her safe, but one look at her, one glance at her delicious behind, one whiff of her sugary scent, and hell, if I can keep away from her. I hesitate with my fingers still inside of her when she frowns at me as she gives me side-eye.

"Either put it in or get away from me, you ass."

A chuckle rumbles up my chest. "Challenge accepted, *piccolina*." I pull my fingers out of her and she scowls, "What the hell, you horrible man, why do you have to tease me so, why—"

I yank her jeans down to her mid-thigh. I reach for the thimbles in her sewing kit, slide one onto my middle finger—thank the *Vergine Maria* that they fit—then another onto my forefinger, and she blinks, "What the hell are you doing?"

"What the hell does it look like I am doing?"

"I don't know. That's why I am asking you...oh!" She gasps as I shove the gusset of her panties aside then play with her pussy lips. "Oh, my," she gasps, "wha...what are you up to?"

"Shh." I finger the opening of her pussy, then slide my thimble-wrapped middle finger inside her channel.

"Gah!" She opens and shuts her mouth, "You didn't just, you didn't—"

"Oh, I most certainly did, my little wife." I add my thimble-wrapped forefinger, then my ring finger, and stretch her channel. She trembles, then clamps down on my fingers and I feel the pull all the way to the tip of my cock. "*Gesü Cristo,* you can take everything I can give you, can't you? You'll take it and you'll ask for more. Your greedy pussy will never have enough. It wants to be fucked and torn into. It wants every filthy thing I can do to it. It wants my cock and my fingers in at the same time so I can stretch it and fill you up until you have no idea where I begin and where you end, isn't that right?" I pant... "Beauty?"

She moans loudly and the sound snaps something inside of me. I release my hand on her neck, spit on my fingers, then slide one inside the opening of her backhole.

"Fuck you," she growls, even as she parts her legs even more, giving me better access. I add a second finger to her back channel, then begin to move my fingers in and out of her. At the same time, I fuck her pussy with the thimble-covered fingers of my other hand.

"Oh, hell. Oh, my bloody hell!" she yells as her entire body shudders. Her shoulders snap back, she thrusts back with her hips, trying to take more of my fingers inside her, then propels her hips forward, chasing her climax. "Mika, Mika," she chants, "I am going to—"

"Come for me, Beauty; come all over my fingers."

22

Karma

His command cuts through the thoughts in my head. Something primal inside of me rushes to obey him, and the vibrations which had been threatening at the base of my spine gallop out and up my back, to spark behind my eyes. I throw my head back, open my mouth and a soundless cry emerges. The climax crashes over me, and seems to go on and on. When I open my eyes, I am in his arms and being carried to the bathroom.

He seats me on the sink, pulls off the thimbles from his fingers before he reaches over to wash his hands.

"Guess it's a good thing that you ordered leather thimbles big enough to fit your fat fingers, eh?"

"You weren't complaining when I had said fat fingers inside you," he chuckles.

Heat sears my cheeks again. Can't believe I let him fuck me with thimbles. OMG, I let him fuck me with his thimble-wrapped fingers. Ugh, and I also enjoyed it. Double ugh. I glance away from him, reach down for my jeans, which are down around my ankles, but he grips my wrist. "Let me," he murmurs, and I straighten.

I watch as he wets a towel, then presses it between my legs.

Heat sears my cheeks, "You don't have to."

"I want to."

"None of this will change how I feel about you."

"I don't expect it to."

"If you think setting up a studio for me will get you into my good books...then you are... " I hesitate and he peers up at me from under those thick eyelashes.

"I am..."

"You are absolutely right," I mumble under my breath.

He smirks, then urges me down from the sink. He turns me to face the mirror then drags the washcloth between my arsecheeks.

"Oh, geez," I squeeze my eyes shut, "you really don't have to do that."

"Let me take care of you," he murmurs as he pats me down once more, then throws the towel aside. He reaches for the cabinet over the sink, opens it and grabs an ointment.

"What's that?" I ask, then gasp when he applies it to my smarting backside. Coolness soothes the skin instantly. I glance over my shoulder to find him administering more of the soothing ointment to my other butt –cheek.

"It's aloe vera," he replies as he continues to massage it slowly into my arse. The rhythmic movement sends pulses of awareness up my spine.

My core stutters, my belly flip-flops, and I squeeze my thighs together, chew on the inside of my cheek to stop myself from moaning aloud. *Down, slut, down. How much more will you humiliate yourself today, hmm?* I choke down all possible sounds of pleasure that threaten to spill from my lips. Watch as he finishes his task, then caps the ointment and places it aside. He pulls up my panties, then bends and yanks my jeans. He turns me around and I glance away as he zips up my jeans. He fits a knuckle under my chin, and angles my face toward him. "Of all the things I have done to you, you find this embarrassing?"

"Of all the things you've done to me, this is the most intimate," I shoot back. "You really didn't have to."

"I really did have to." He leans in closely enough for our eyelashes to tangle. His breath merges with mine; his lips almost brush mine. Those blue eyes of his seem to come alive with an emotion I don't dare put a name to.

Shit, of all the things that have taken place between us so far, this… This is, by far, the most threatening. My heart rate spikes and my pulse thuds at my temples. Heat from his body slams into my chest, and I gasp. The force of his personality is a heaviness that pushes down on my shoulders and holds me in place. It's a kind of safety blanket, like one of those weighted-down duvets that hold you in place, that keep you secure, that envelop you with a sense of safety which lulls you into a state of contentment. The hair on my forearms rises.

"What are you going to do?" I whisper, "Why are you being so nice to me?"

His features freeze for just a millisecond, then he brings his big palm up to cup the nape of my neck. "So fucking intelligent, my Beauty. You make a worthy opponent, you know that?" His fingers are long enough to meet around the front of my throat.

I bring my hands up to grab his thick forearm. "Please," I murmur, "don't."

"Do you trust me?" He lowers his forehead to mine, "Do you, Beauty?" He peers into my eyes, holds my gaze with those hypnotic depths of his. "Do you?" He asks again, "Do you trust me?"

"Yes." I whisper, and in that moment, I know I do. Damn it, why do I have to give him this part of myself too?

His fingers around my neck tighten, specks of black flicker at the edges of my eyesight, I draw in a breath and my lungs burn, then everything goes dark.

I hear voices as if from far away. "What did you do to her?" A man's voice—not Michael, one of his brothers maybe—asks.

"It's for her own good. I told you already," Michael rumbles back. "Don't question me again, *fratellino*."

"I must warn you again that what you are doing is unethical, and goes against everything my profession stands for." A woman's voice, this time. Her tone is filled with concern. For me? What's happening? What is he doing to me?

I try to stir, and must succeed, for the next moment, Michael's breath brushes my cheek. His scent fills my senses as he presses a kiss to my forehead. "Shh, baby," he murmurs, "you're safe with me."

I shouldn't believe him. Why the hell do I *want* to believe him? Why do I still trust him? I swallow, try to ask him…but can't seem to string the words into a sentence. I turn my face toward him, and his warmth envelops me. His arms come around me and he hauls me close to his chest. I try to open my eyes, but my eyelids are weighed down.

"Go on, Doc," his voice rumbles, "don't delay further."

"I must formally record the fact that I am doing this under duress."

"You are boring me, Doc." Michael's voice is impatient, "If it weren't for the fact that my brother, here, seems to have taken a shine to you, I'd have killed you by now."

I sense the woman stiffen in shock. Huh? You'd think she'd be used to the ways of the Mafia if she works for them? Or maybe she doesn't? Is that why she sounds so...above-board...so normal? Enough to protest against whatever it is that Michael wants done to me? Holy shit, what does he want her to do to me? Whatever it is, it can't be good. But I do trust him, don't I? I had told him so... So why is it that all my instincts insist that I don't want whatever it is that is going to happen? I try to push against him, but his arms tighten.

"Doc," he growls, "do it now."

Wh-a-t the— I open my mouth to protest, but his mouth covers mine, and the kiss... OMG, his kiss is soft, tender, sweet... WTF? Michael Byron Domenico Sovrano can kiss with so much emotion? So much tenderness...so much...devotion? He swipes his tongue across the seam of my lips and I open my mouth. He slides his tongue over mine, deepens the kiss, opens himself up so his presence seems to invade my mouth, my throat, my chest... Every cell in my body is filled with Michael. Michael. Michael. I sink into the kiss, surrender to his strength, his complete dominance, that absolute force that is my husband. I push into him, aching to be near him, wanting to be closer to him, needing to feel his skin on mine. He brushes the hair away from my ear, holds it to the side, then grips my jaw, holding me in place.

Something—no, someone—pulls back my ear... The same ear from which he had brushed away my hair. Something pricks me behind my ear. I stiffen, try to turn, but his grip on my jaw tightens. He licks into my mouth and my belly trembles. My pussy clenches, my thighs spasm, and I moan deep in my throat, thrust up and into him. He drags his arm over my butt, grasps the curve of my hip and holds me immobile as he thrusts his tongue in and out of my mouth, in and out. His complete mastery over me something I cannot deny as my head lolls back and I surrender to him, as he deepens the kiss even further. Even as I sense another prick behind my ear...this one a pin-prick that I might have missed if it were not for the fact that a part of me is still resisting him, the part that has allowed me to survive thus far. The part that insists I give in to his ministrations now — or at least, pretend to. That part insists that I close my eyes and drift with the warmth, the comfort that he provides. I allow his presence to engulf me, let the darkness pull me under.

When I awake, I am in his bed and it's dark outside. I sit up, and when a shape looms over me, I scream.

23

____

Michael

"It's only me." I hold up my hands.

She draws in a breath, "Michael?" Her hushed voice shudders across my skin, and a shiver runs down my spine. My nerve endings pop. The blood drains to my groin as I lean forward in my seat.

"How are you feeling?"

"A little dazed," she yawns, then looks around the room, "Where am I? What happened?" She runs her fingers through her hair. "One moment you were kissing me, the next moment, I think I blacked out..."

"You were out for a little while," I concede.

"Why are you sitting in darkness?" I sense rather than see her scowl. She reaches over, flicks on the light next to the bed, then winces. She blinks her eyes as her eyesight adjusts, then glances over at me. "You going to tell me what happened?" She folds her arms about her waist.

I rise up to my feet and walk over to her. Sink down next to her on the bed. Reach for her, but she pulls away.

"Oh, no," she shakes her head, "no, no, no." She throws up her hands. "Keep your distance, buster..."

"Or what?" I smirk.

"Or… " she glances about the room, then grabs the book next to the bed, "or I'll throw this at you."

"You sure you want to do that?"

"Why wouldn't I?"

"Have you seen what the book is about?"

She frowns at me, then lowers the book, "It's a fashion sketchbook." She turns it over, then flips the pages. "With readymade templates I can use to sketch my fashion designs…"

"And…"

"And plan my outfits; and for my illustrations; also, a diary to take notes when inspiration strikes." She lowers the book, "If you think you can distract me that easily—"

"That's not all," I nod toward the side table.

She glances down and her gaze widens. She places down the sketchbook, then picks up the other slim volume, *"25 Cats Named Sam and One Blue Pussy."* Her voice hitches. "Am I the *Blue Pussy?* Is that why you bought this for me?"

"You're my pussy, regardless of the color, *Bellezza.*"

"Ha, you're funny." She laughs nervously as she swipes her palm across the book.

"I mean it."

She peers into my face. "You really do mean it, don't you?" she says in a low voice.

"You know, I do." I jerk my chin toward the book, "Open it."

"Is it what I think it is?" she murmurs.

I chuckle, "Only one way to find out."

She flips open the cover and draws in a breath. "It's the original illustrated manuscript by Andy Warhol." She glances up at me. "It *is* the original illustrated manuscript, isn't it?"

I arch an eyebrow, and she blows out a breath. "Shit, it really *is* the original manuscript." She glances down at the book again, "I didn't think this was available to buy."

"It wasn't."

"Then, how—?" She glances up at me, "I have a feeling you may have had to spill a little blood to get a hold of this."

I stare at her and her gaze widens. "In fact, I am *sure* that you had to spill more than a little blood to get ahold of this, but you know what…?"

I tilt my head.

"In this instance, murder may have been justified."

I blink. "Say that again?"

"I said, you may have had to commit—"

"I heard you." I reach for her, and this time, she doesn't shy away. A hot sensation stabs at my chest. I push a strand of hair behind her ear. "I had a dream, which was not all a dream..." I whisper.

She swallows, "The bright sun was extinguished, and the stars..."

"Did wander darkling in the eternal space..." I lean in close enough for us to share breath.

Her pupils dilate, "Rayless, and pathless, and the icy earth..."

"Swung blind and blackening in the moonless air," we say in unison.

"Byron," she murmurs.

"Lord-fucking-Darkness himself."

"What is with you and Byron?" She peers into my face, "Why do I get the feeling that there's more to why you recite him than what meets the eye?"

I pull away, then stand up, "Because there is."

I turn to walk away, and she grabs my wrist, "That's it? That's all you are going to give me?"

I glare down at her fingers and her grip tightens. "You can scare your men with that Michael Byron stare, but it doesn't do anything to me."

"Is that right?"

She stares at me with a strange look on her features.

"What?" I scowl, "What is it?"

"Michael Byron," she murmurs.

"Yeah, that's my name."

"Were you named after Byron, as well?"

I drag my fingers through my hair, "It's also my father's name."

"The two of you share more than your first name, huh?"

"Cursed to have not one, but all four of my names in common," I reply bitterly.

"You don't like him, huh?"

"Did you like your father?"

She shakes her head.

"There you go."

"Still, you are following in his footsteps, so I assume it's not all bad when it comes to the relationship between the two of you?"

"Some things I do only because it's tactically the right thing."

"You love plotting your moves, huh? You love to move people

around like they are pawns on a chessboard, and only you have control over their futures."

"I am the only one who has control over the destinies of my clan."

"And that includes me?"

"You're my wife, so you're part of the clan; ergo..." I raise a shoulder.

"That's why you did whatever it is you did earlier?"

"What did I do earlier?"

"Don't bullshit me, Michael." She places the book back on the side table with care, then throws off the cover and rises to her feet. "What did you do, earlier? Tell me."

"I don't think you want to know."

"You mean, *you* don't think I want to know," She scoffs.

"Getting sassy, Mrs. Michael Byron Domenico Sovrano?"

"I didn't say that I have accepted being your wife yet."

"Not giving you a choice, Beauty."

"There's always a choice." She tosses her head, "Also, if you really did think of me as your wife, you'd tell me what happened earlier." She scowls at me, and there's something in her eyes, some kind of knowledge...a suspicion, maybe, of what happened earlier.

Merda, I ball my fingers into fists at my sides. Why the hell am I second guessing myself here? Why can't I just tell her what I did? Since when have I become so...worried about someone else's response? She's my wife. She'll damn well take whatever I do to her... And if I had wanted someone meek and servile, I'd have married someone from my clan a long time ago. Maybe I had been holding out for someone like her, and I hadn't even been aware of it. I shake my head to clear it. And since when have I begun thinking in such emotional terms about her? Love is for fools and poets, neither of which I am.

"You going to tell me about it, yet?" She scowls.

"Do you want me to tell you about it?"

She throws up her hands, "What else have we been talking about all this time?"

"Okay, then."

"What does that mean?"

"It means, okay. I'll tell you about it."

"So, what are you waiting for?"

There's a knock on the door and I smirk at her, "This." I pivot, walk over to the door, and open it just enough to accept the covered basket that Seb hands over to me.

"You owe me, *fratellastro*." He scowls.

I nod, "I won't forget this." I shut the door on him, then turn back and prowl over to her. I plant the basket at her feet.

"What's that?"

"Open it."

She hesitates and I chuckle, "Not like you to be uncertain."

"Hmm, let me see... A surprise given to me by the Capo himself," she jabs a finger in her cheek, "why does that not reassure me?"

I laugh, "I promise, this one won't bite you... Well, not unless you provoke it."

"Huh?" She scowls, "Now *that* has piqued my curiosity."

Bingo! I can't stop the smile from curving my lips as she bends, then grabs the cloth and whisks it off.

Stunned, she stares into the basket. "What...what is that?" she splutters.

"What do you think?"

"I... I..." she reaches for the tiny creature that stretches and yawns. "It's a...cat?"

"A kitten," I correct her.

"Oh!" She rubs the forehead of the little thing that mewls pitifully. "Oh, you beautiful, beautiful creature." She scoops up the kitten and holds it against her chest. The animal nestles against her breasts. What the fuck? When I had bought her a pet, I hadn't anticipated competition for her attentions. I scowl at the beast, which nuzzles into her palm.

"What's your name, you sweet little thing?"

"He doesn't have a name, yet" Shit should have bought a female kitten. Now, I have another male in the house who is closer to her than I am.

"Andy," she murmurs.

"What?"

"His name is Andy."

"Because I bought you a book by Andy Warhol?"

"D-u-h!" She smiles without look at me. "Are you hungry, Andy? Do you want something to eat?"

"There's cat food in the kitchen, if you want to feed him."

She stares at me, and I scowl back, "What?"

"You bought cat food?"

"I got you a kitten. Of course, I also bought cat food." I shrug. "Well, kitten food, to be exact."

Her gaze widens.

"What?" A flush heats my neck. "I am not completely heartless, you know?"

"Hmm." She bites down on her lower lip, and hell, my groin instantly hardens.

"How did you know that I wanted a Savannah?" she murmurs.

"Lucky guess?"

"And how did you find out that Andy Warhol is one of my fave artists ever?"

I raise a shoulder, "His style of expression seemed closest to how I see you."

"How do you see me?"

"You don't get to ask me the questions." I scowl and her smile widens.

"Humor me on this, Capo."

Fuck, when she calls me that, I'll do anything for her. Good thing she doesn't realize that.

"So," she urges, "how do you see me?"

"I see you as being original, unique, someone who stands apart just by being herself."

"Wow," she breathes, "that's a huge compliment."

"Saying it as it is, Beauty."

The kitten mewls again and she frowns, "I think he's getting hungry."

"Why don't I call Cassandra and ask her to feed it."

"What?" she cries. "No way. " She pulls the creature closer to her chest, "No one feeds my baby except me."

Ten minutes later, I am seated at the table in the kitchen, nursing a glass of whiskey as she watches the kitten eat from his bowl. Yeah, I bought not just cat food, but also all of the shit that the beast would need — bowls to eat from, more bowls to drink from, a basket in the corner of the kitchen with the softest blankets that can be used for his bed. She kneels down next to the kitten, pets him as he eats. She makes little cooing noises and I stare. Her entire attention is focused on the creature. I take another drink of my whiskey, place the glass down on the table with a *thwack* that echoes around the room. She doesn't even look up.

Gesu Cristo, maybe this hadn't been a good idea. On the other hand, she hasn't breathed a word about what had happened earlier, so there's that.

"Don't think your buying me a kitten has bought you into my good graces," she murmurs at me over her shoulder.

"Me?" I raise my hands, "I'd never think that."

"Ha," she scoffs, "why don't I believe that? Speaking of," her forehead furrows, "I only told you that I wanted a cat last evening, and you've managed to get me one in what...twelve hours?"

Nine, but who's counting?

"How did you do that?"

I smirk and she rolls her eyes, "Why do I even bother to ask these questions?"

She continues to pet the creature and it's like I have been dismissed. *Che cazzo?* Have I been usurped by a few weeks old kitten, and in my own home? I drag my fingers through my hair. And why the hell am I even threatened by that beast? Is it her proximity that's making me weak? Is it the fact that by falling for her...

Hold on. Back up. Who said anything about falling for her? I want her to stay my wife. Doesn't mean I have feelings for her...do I? And if I do? What then? What am I going to do about that, eh? I lower my chin, narrow my gaze on her, "I chipped you."

24

———

Karma

"What do you mean, you chipped me?" I rub Andy's head. He's stopped feeding and proceeds to curl himself in my arms. Aww, sooo cute. A melting sensation coils in my chest. Just a few hours after I told him that I wanted a cat, he got me one. Not to mention, that Andy Warhol book, which was, like, totally unexpected. Okay, so he has more money and power than anyone else I've met in my life, but still… It means something that he noticed my tastes enough to actually buy me things which reflect who I am. No one else has done that before. Maybe Summer… I suppose, but she is my sister. She is supposed to know these things. This man, however, is practically a complete stranger, and in a few weeks, he has really gotten to know me well on so many levels, he— *hangonabloodysecond.* I whip my head around to face him. "You *chipped* me, chipped me?"

He nods.

"You…" I bite the inside of my cheek, "you put a GPS tracker in me?"

He nods again.

"Holy shit." I glance around the kitchen, find a basket that, no doubt,

the faithful Cassandra must have organized for the kitten. I walk over
and place him in the bedding which is of the softest cotton, by the way.
Nothing but the best for the pet of... His pet, huh?

I straighten, then turn to face him. "That's what all that activity
earlier was about, huh? I thought maybe I'd dreamed it, but I didn't."

He simply holds my gaze.

I slide a finger behind my ear, feel the slight bump. "Holy hell," I
burst out. "It's true; you actually put a tracker in me."

"Told you I did."

Anger surges through my veins. My heart slams against my rib cage.
"Why would you do that?" I cry. "And you didn't even ask my permission to do so, you asshole!"

"I don't need your permission. Have you forgotten?" He looks me up
and down. "You are my property — mine."

"I am my own person. I don't belong to anyone else, least of all, you."

"Then why did you come back?"

"That was only to make sure that you were actually dead...you... you
bastard."

He laughs, "That's a lie and you can do better than that insult,
Beauty."

"Don't call me that," I snarl. " I should have known there's an ulte-
rior motive behind everything you do. The studio, the books, the
kitten... It was all so...what? So you could distract me? Or maybe, you
thought that you could buy me off with expensive gifts?"

"Maybe, it's because I want you to be happy?"

"How can I be happy when you chipped me like.... I am an animal?"

"Did it ever occur to you that I did it because I don't want to lose
you again?" The skin around his eyes tightens. For a second, I am sure
he's afraid... Of what? He's the bloody Capo of the Cosa Nostra. What
could he possibly be afraid of, eh?

"You could have told me that's what you intended to do," I snap.

"You wouldn't have agreed."

"You don't know that."

"Would you have?"

I look at him, then away.

"That's what I thought." He pushes back his chair, then rises to his
feet. He prowls over to me, pauses when he's right in front of me. "Look
at me, Beauty."

I scoff.

He notches his knuckles under my chin and raises my head, so I have no choice but to meet his gaze. "Maybe I put a tracker in you because you are what's most precious to me."

"Maybe I don't care why you did it," I try to pull away from him, but he tightens his grip.

"Maybe you need to care more. Maybe you need to come clean about the fact that whatever is between us is not going away any time soon."

I stare into those blue eyes of his. He holds my gaze, and in them I see…the same helplessness that I feel.

"You know, I returned because I couldn't believe that I had killed you. I prayed that you were still alive, that there had been a mistake. I had hoped that if you were… Perhaps, we could find a way to be together. But all you were interested in was revenge. Then, when I was taken from you, I guess you had a change of heart or something. And just when I think that perhaps I can find a way of being with you, after all… You do this." I wave a hand in the air, "You chip me, without batting an eyelid, like I'm your pet. This is not normal behavior, Michael."

He opens his mouth, but I shake my head. "No, don't give me your bullshit about me not being normal. I know I am not. It's why, all my life, I've hoped to find someone who could give me the kind of normalcy that I have missed all my life."

"You don't mean it," he growls.

"Oh, but I do." I swallow. "All this time we were together, not once, did you ask me what I wanted."

"I didn't need to," he jerks his chin toward where Andy is sleeping in his basket, "I know exactly what you need."

"Maybe that is the case," I murmur and he glares at me. "Fine, fine," I pull away from him, and this time, he releases me. "I don't deny that everything you did…from refurbishing the studio, to the books to the kitten, was spot on. It's what I'd have chosen for myself… Still, it's just politeness to ask me what I want."

"You don't want me to be polite."

"See?" I turn on him, "This… this is what I am talking about. You assuming you know my mind."

"I do."

"You don't."

"Yes, I do."

"Argh," I dig my fingers in my hair and tug, "this is going nowhere."

"It can go exactly where you want it to."

"Where I want it to go is..." I tip up my chin, "far away from you."

"Don't lie to me." He scowls.

"I am not." My heart hammers in my chest. My pulse rate spikes. I square my shoulders, hold his gaze. "If you think I can forgive what you did to me, then you have another think coming. I may have been able to look past the kidnapping, even, but this...this. What you did... It's... I can't even pretend to understand it. It's the worst kind of violation, ever."

His jaw tics. A dense cloud of anger spools off of him and smashes into my chest. I gasp, take a step back.

"If you think I am letting you leave, you have another think coming," he growls.

"Fine," I snap.

"Fine."

25

Karma

That stupid conversation was yesterday. I haven't seen the alphahole since. I had wanted to leave the bedroom I've been sharing with him and move into one of the guest rooms, but he wouldn't hear of it. He had commanded me to stay and had walked out. He hadn't come to bed, so I guess he's sleeping somewhere else. Whatever. I'm not going to feel sorry for depriving him of his own bed. Not after what he did to me.

I woke up early this morning and he was gone. Good riddance! I took a quick shower, then headed down to the kitchen to check in on Andy…who had already been fed by Cassandra. I tried not to be jealous about that.

I grabbed his basket, as well as two bowls, one for his food and one for water, and a can of cat food, and brought them up to my studio with me. I settled him a corner, before continuing to work on my latest creation.

I'm not quite sure what it will be yet. I am still in the doodling stage. And yeah, I refuse to use the sketchbook he got me. I also haven't touched the Andy Warhol book because… Well, I want to spite him. Maybe I'm spiting myself. But whatever.

I draw a design, then crumple up the paper and throw it aside. Draw the design again… Ugh! It sucks. I scrunch up the paper, toss it aside. To be honest, I don't know exactly what it is that I am drawing here.

It's often like that for me. I need to doodle first, wait for the design to emerge from my subconscious mind. Often, I have to draw for days on end before the motifs begin to reveal themselves. It's like, by drawing, I plumb the images in my subconscious mind. I stare at my scribblings… The wide forehead, the hooked nose, the square jaw. Gah, it's an outline of his stupid face.

Shit. Clearly, I have his features imprinted on my brain. OMG! This is soo not happening. I design clothes. I don't draw people or profiles… but somehow, I have ended up etching his likeness instead of focusing on my new creation. I crush the paper between my palms, toss it over my shoulder.

"Ouch," a female voice protests, "I've never had a patient deck me with a paper ball, and that too, on our first meeting."

I turn to find a woman I have never seen before standing in the doorway.

"Who are you?" I scowl, "And haven't you heard of knocking before entering?"

"I'm Doctor Aurora Garibaldi," she murmurs, "and I'm sorry, we're normally not that formal in this part of the world."

"Well too-bloody-bad." I sniff, "In my part of the world, it's polite to knock and ask permission before you enter a person's room, and—" I stiffen, "did you say that you are a doctor?"

"I am." She tilts her head, "May I come in?"

My heart begins to beat faster and I don't know why. No, I do know why, but I don't want to acknowledge it. Yet.

"If I say you can't," I say in a low voice, "what then?"

She blows out a sigh, "I think you'll want to hear what I have to say, Karma. May I call you, Karma?"

"You know my name."

"Yes," she nods, "that's what I want to talk to you about."

"Oh, hell."

I stare at her, and an uncomfortable silence descends between us, broken by a soft mewling from Andy's basket.

I turn toward him at the same time as the doctor. I watch as Andy peeks over the side of the basket. He mewls again, then crawls out and my heart stutters. I walk over, lift him up in my arms.

"Oh, wow, you have a kitten?"

I don't reply. Instead, I walk over to the arm chair near the window and sit down with the kitten in my arms.

"So sweet," she murmurs, still hovering by the doorway.

"I'm not sweet," I snap.

"The kitten, she's—"

"He," I interrupt her. "It's a he; his name is Andy, and I suppose you had better come in."

She nods, steps inside the room and shuts the door behind her. She walks over to take the chair on the opposite side of the table, then places the sleek satchel she's brought with her on the floor. One thing about Italy—everyone seems to be dressed and carrying designer wear, like it's the norm. Which, I guess it is here, considering that so many well-known designers are of Italian origin. Both of us watch as the kitten purrs in my arms, then snuggles in.

"How old is he?"

"Nine weeks," I reply.

"He's beautiful," she says, her tone sincere.

I can't stop the smile that curves my lips, "He's a Savannah."

"Have you had him long?"

"No," I rub my finger over Andy's tiny forehead and he yawns, "Michael gave him to me yesterday."

She blinks rapidly, "The Capo gave you a kitten?"

"Umm, yeah." I scowl at her, and she stares at me with a strange look on her face.

"What?"

"Nothing."

"Out with it." I point a finger in her direction, "It's not nothing when you have that weird look on your face."

She tilts her head, "It's just... The Capo, getting you a kitten...is—"

"What?"

"It's out of character."

"Hmm," I bite the inside of my cheek. "Well, I am his wife, after all." Not that you'll catch me saying that to him, but he's not here in the room, so it's fine to say it aloud in front of a stranger, isn't it? Speaking of... "Why are you here, Doc?"

"Call me Aurora." She half smiles. "I came to check on you, Karma."

It's my turn to blink, then I square my shoulders. "You're the one who did it." I touch the slight bump behind my ear which, while I had managed to push it to the back of my mind, in all honesty, I haven't forgotten about. "I heard your voice last night. I thought maybe I had dreamed it, but guess I didn't."

"I was there," She folds her hands in her lap. "It's why I had to come and check on you today."

"You were there and you didn't stop him from tagging me?" I say in a low voice. "What kind of a doctor are you that you were actually part of this process? Isn't this going against the Hippocratic oath or something?"

She glances away, then back at me, "You have to understand that this is the Capo you are talking about. I am but a lowly doctor. I have to do as he says, else—"

"Else?"

"He'll kill not just me, but every member of my family. He'll wipe out all trace of us if we defy him."

I take in her wide gaze, the white skin around her lips. "Wow, you really do believe that, don't you? You are afraid of him."

"He's the Capo," she says simply. "His word is law."

"And I am his wife. Supposedly." I scowl, "And this is what he does to me." I rise to my feet with the sleeping Andy in my arms, then walk over to the basket. I place him in it, soothe him when he wakes up so he falls asleep again. If only it were that easy for me to forget everything he's done to me. I turn to face her. "You know this is wrong... So wrong," I ball my fists at my side. "He tagged me like I am some... some...animal with no rights."

"He," she clears her throat, "he only wants to keep you safe."

I stare at her, "I can't believe you are taking his side."

"I am not really." She swallows. "If I were, I wouldn't have risked his anger and insisted he allow me to come check on you this morning."

"Fat lot of good that will do." I begin to pace. "You were there and you didn't stop him."

"I tried, believe me. His brother and I begged him not to do it, but he was most insistent. I got the impression that he—"

"What?" I scowl, "Say it."

"That he's afraid for your safety. That he'd do anything to protect you. That he doesn't want you out of his sight. That he wants to make sure that if, for whatever reason, you are separated from him, he'll know where to find you."

"Ha," I scoff. "All this is just a power play. It probably turns him on to know that he can do anything with me. That he could even…even…put a bloody tracker on me so he'll know exactly where I am every minute of every day."

"And you like that?"

"What?"

"That he's so…focused on you. That all of his attention is targeted on you."

I flush. Honestly, there's a part of me that revels in it…but damn, if I am going to admit that aloud. "Frankly, I don't care for it. Especially not, if it means that he virtually has me on a leash here… Besides, it's wrong. Can't you see that? You don't go around tagging another human being just because of your own insecurities."

"You're right," her shoulders slump. "It's not the 'done' thing. But then, when have the Capo and his brothers ever conformed to the 'done' thing?"

"You sound like you know them well."

"No one knows them well." She half smiles. "They are a force all their own. I went to the same school as them, though they are all much older than me. All the boys wanted to be them and all the girls…couldn't take their eyes off of them." She adds, "Even our teachers were afraid of them in school. They could do pretty much whatever they wanted and no-one would dare stop them."

"Sounds like nothing has changed." I scowl, "Once a bully…"

"They weren't all bad though."

"No?"

"They helped my father when he needed money the most."

"Oh? How did they help?"

"The Capo paid off his mortgage, paid for me and my sister's education."

"Only so he could buy your father's loyalty."

"That may be the case," she raises a shoulder, "but just the threat of his power would have been enough to have my father fall in line. He needn't have done everything else that he did. I know he comes across as gruff and uncaring —"

"You have no idea."

"—But that's just the persona he's had to create to survive in the Mafia world."

Maybe I did guess that. Maybe a part of me has hoped that's true. Maybe, in the moments that we had been intimate, I had glimpsed the tenderness that he is capable of... But then he had gone and chipped me, and without even asking me. He may claim that it's to keep me safe, but surely, I should have a say in it too?

"I am afraid I don't buy it." I square my shoulders. "Why are you here anyway? If you came to make sure that I am alive, then you can rest assured that I am."

"It's not only that." She bites her lower lip, "I guess, I just wanted to make sure that you are okay."

I scoff.

"Maybe I just want to help?" she offers.

"You can help me by getting rid of this microchip."

She shakes her head, "I am sorry but I can't do that."

I push my hair back from my face, "Then get me out of here."

"What?" she says in horror. "I... I can't. If I go against the Capo, he will have me killed."

I can't stop the smile from curving my lips, "You owe me, Doc."

She shakes her head, "No, please don't ask me to do that." She rises to her feet and picks up her bag, "I guess it was a mistake coming here. I should have realized there was nothing to be gained from it."

"Sit down," I say in a hard voice. Shit, some of Michael's assertiveness is rubbing off on me. Hell, I even sounded like him there for a second.

She blinks, but sinks back slowly into the seat. "You are not letting me leave without some kind of a deal, are you?"

I smile wider, "You guessed right, Doc. You can make up a little bit for what you were part of."

"How?" She swallows. "He has you chipped. Even if you did manage to escape, he'd be able to track you."

But if I manage to get to a phone and call Summer first, she'll be able to help. "Let me worry about that," I murmur. "Your role is only to get me out of here."

She locks her fingers together, "The moment you go missing, Michael will suspect me. Also, I was checked thoroughly on the way in, and they are bound to repeat the procedure on the way out again."

"Hmm," I tap my finger against my chin, "you're a doctor, right?"

She frowns, "You know I am."

"So, if I were unwell enough that you couldn't treat me here, you'd have to take me out of here to a hospital, right?"

She peers into my face, "You really are a devious woman, aren't you?"

"You have no idea."

"Does he know that you can run circles around him?"

"*He* has no idea." I chuckle and a reluctant smile curves her lips.

"So, I was thinking…"

"Stop," she throws up her hand, "whatever it is you're thinking, don't tell me. I trust you to plan the events. Then, I'll be called in and when I am, I'll simply be the concerned doctor who insists on doing the right thing by you."

She rises to her feet, "Now, may I check you out, to make sure the wound behind your ear is healing properly?"

"That was like barely a prick."

"Regardless, Capo's orders."

I take my seat again and she checks me out. When she's satisfied, she packs her bag, and straightens, "Right then, I'll leave you here." She glances around the studio, "The Capo had this set up for you, didn't he?"

"Are you surprised?"

"Not anymore. When it comes to his wife, I am realizing, the Capo will do just about anything for you."

She heads toward the door. Somehow, I get the feeling that my only friend in the entire world is leaving. Not that I know Aurora that well, but with some people you just know that you can trust them, right? Maybe it's because she's a doctor… A doctor who is in his employ, who was the one who implanted the tracker. But still… She's also a woman. Surely, she understands why it's important for me to leave here?

"Aurora!"

I call out and she stops. She turns to me, with a quizzical look on her face.

"Thank you."

She tilts her head. "Don't thank me, yet," she murmurs, "you don't know if this plan of yours is going to succeed."

26

Michael

"Goddamnit, missed again," I straighten, then slam my cue against the edge of the billiards table. It promptly snaps in two. "*Che cazzo!*" I glower at the half-broken cue in my hand, then raise my hand to hurl it.

Seb steps aside. "Watch it, Mika," he murmurs. "Your temper is getting the better of you."

"There should be a rule that you cannot defeat the Capo at a game," I lower my arm and glare at Massimo—the *pezzo di merda* who smirks at me from across the table.

"Giving up so easily, *Padrone*?"

"*Vaffanculo!*" I growl as I fling the broken half of the cue on the floor. It's her fault that I am in this state. Every night I sleep next to her... No, not sleep. I lay awake next to her, breathing in her sweet scent, aware of her luscious curves next to me on the bed. And the little noises she makes sometimes in her sleep, or the way she sometimes turns over and snuggles into me. The first time that happened, I tried to move away— yeah, me, the man who never denies himself pussy, tried to put distance between himself and his wife... So, yeah, tell me again, how that happened?—and she simply followed me, insisting on cuddling into my side, as I lay there with a fast-thickening erection, that I had to jerk off to in the bathroom, trying not to make too much noise before leaving before dawn. And even after leaving and trying to get some work done in my study, the scent of her followed me. Images of her assailed me, as if determined to burn right into my brain.

Che cazzo! I am really losing it. I glare around at the faces of my brothers. "What?" I growl at Christian who's staring at me over his knitting needles. What the— I do a double take. "Is that what I think it is?"

"You mean this?" He holds up the knitting needles, and nope, na-a-h I wasn't imagining things. *Stronzo* actually does have a pair of—you heard that right—knitting needles, held between his fingers.

"What are you doing?" I snap.

"What do you think I'm doing?"

"I am not sure." I rub my eyes, "Tell me you are not knitting."

He glances down at the needles. "I am…not…knitting." The clackity-clack of the needles fills the space.

"Shit, he's actually knitting," Massimo turns to gawk at him.

"Why the hell are you knitting?" Seb mutters from his position against the wall—he's put a fair distance between us, I notice, *bastardo*.

"Maybe he's trying to get in touch with his feminine side?" Xander offers.

"That's the kind of shit we expect you to pull," Adrian retorts, "But Christian? Naw." He scratches his chin, "It must have something to do with a chick."

"A chick?" Seb scoffs, "If that were the case, surely, he'd need to be using a completely different kind of needle?"

Adrian shoots him a sideways glance, "Was that a joke? Because I don't get the joke."

"You wouldn't get the joke because you have no sense of humor."

Adrian laughs, "So speaks the most serious of all the men in Sicily."

"I'm not serious; you are serious."

"I'm afraid, in this regard, I have to side with Adrian," I state. "You are going to make a very effective Capo, but you could do with a little bit of loosening up."

"Yeah, you take everything too seriously," Christian drawls from his position in the armchair. Fucker is sprawled out, and with the reading glasses he has on… He resembles a more serious version of the brother I know.

"Not all of us can be happy-go-lucky and waste time trying to explore our feminine side or some such shit," Seb growls. "Some of us have had to fight for everything that comes our way."

"Here we go again," Christian mutters, "like we haven't already heard about how your being the half-brother means you always get the raw deal. When you know it's not true. Not only did our mother embrace you as her own son, but she also worked herself to an early grave taking care of the both of you, in addition to her own five sons."

"And look where that got her," Seb pushes away from the wall. "Her own son, your own brother turns on his own flesh and blood and helps his Capo's wife escape... Now, that's something to make her turn in her grave, for sure."

"Don't talk about her that way." Christian rises to his feet, still holding those goddamn knitting needles. He takes a step forward and the ball of yarn falls to the floor next to him.

"I ain't telling a lie here and you know that," Seb scoffs. "Ask *fratellone*, here, and he'll only confirm it."

"Don't bring me into this, you guys," I mutter. "Luca has his punishment coming to him, when I finally catch up with him. So, whatever this unresolved business is between the two of you, it's up to you guys to sort it out."

Christian glowers at Seb, "You've always had a chip on your shoulder about being the illegitimate bastard. Time you moved on from that, don't you think?"

"Who are you calling a bastard?" Seb prowls toward Christian, who takes a step forward as the yarn winds around his ankle. He takes another step, stumbles, then rights himself. *"Che cazzo!"* He glares at the ball of yarn, "Why is it that the shit that seems so easy is the most difficult to master?"

"Is that a rhetorical question?" I ask.

"Are you sure you're talking about the knitting, or is this about women?" Massimo arches an eyebrow.

"You mean 'are you talking about one particular woman,' right?" Xander inserts.

"Shut the fuck up." Christian glares at Xander.

"You're twisting yourself up in knots." Seb smirks.

"No, I am not." Christian scowls at Seb, "And what the fuck are you smirking at?"

"Me?" Seb's grin widens, "I am not smirking."

Christian throws up his fist, "You laughing at me, *stronzo?*"

"You talkin' to me, *stronzo*?" Seb retorts.

"*Vaffanculo, testa di cazzo.*" Christian lunges forward. This time, he does actually trip on the yarn. He crashes down, just as Seb gets out of his way.

"Shit, you're a mess," Seb shakes his head. "Alas, poor Christian, he did mean well."

Christian pushes up to his feet. He grabs his now crooked reading glasses and flings them on the table. "First, you quote *Taxi Driver*, then Shakespeare. Make up your mind, asshole." He swipes out his fist; Seb ducks. Christian hurls his fist again. This time, Seb steps aside. Christian stumbles past him. Seb's on him in a flash. He steps up behind Christian, wraps his arm around his neck, and yanks. Christian growls. He grips Seb's arm, bends forward, heaves, and Seb goes flying over his shoulder. He lands on his back with a crash that seems to reverberate through the room. Christian rushes forward, only his foot slips on the damn ball of yarn again. He falls over and hits the ground next to Seb. The two lay there, chests having, breaths coming in pants.

I swallow my laughter, walk over to stand between them. "You guys done, yet?" I hold out both of my arms.

Christian grabs my left hand, and I pull him up. I stare down at Seb, who glowers at Christian. "This is not over yet," he growls as he grabs my hand. I haul him to his feet, as well.

"You two need to sort out your shit before we meet the Kane Company. I can't have bad blood between the two of you weakening our position."

"I am not the one with issues; he's the one with issues," Christian glowers back.

"No bad blood here." Seb shrugs. "Only a man pretending to be bad, when he'd rather be playing doctor with a certain...doctor."

"Doctor, huh?" Just as I thought. I jerk my chin toward Christian, who glares at Seb.

"I have no idea what you're talking about."

"Don't think I haven't noticed how you keep finding excuses to see the doctor. She's something, eh? That figure, that fair skin, those tits..." Seb cups his palms below his chest, and Christian's features harden.

His nostrils flare, and a growl rumbles up his chest. "Stop talking about her, you *pezzo di merda*." He starts to dive toward Seb, only I slap my palm in Christian's chest.

"Back off, you complete idiot. He's trying to get under your skin."

"Oh, he's succeeding, all right." Christian lunges forward, and this time, Massimo grabs him from behind.

"Shit, you're pussywhipped. You haven't even slept with her and you're already protecting her honor?"

Christian struggles against Massimo's hold. He manages to break free, but Adrian grips his other shoulder. "Chill the fuck down, *stronzo*," he snaps. "Asshole's simply trying to make a point."

"I'll make a point all right, with him." Christian rolls his shoulders. His biceps bulge, he rolls his neck, and his shoulders seem to grow even more massive. He's not the tallest nor the broadest of all of us. That honor belongs to Massimo. But Christian also never gets angry enough to lose his cool and fight, so guess this is a first, all around. He rushes forward, with both Massimo and Adrian still holding onto him, before Massimo throws his arm around Christian's chest, and manages to halt him.

Seb laughs, "That all you got in you, you pathetic piece of—"

I turn and sink my fist in his face.

"What the fuck?" he roars as he stumbles back.

"Back the fuck off, Seb. Stop trying to bait him." I turn on Christian, "And that goes for you too, Christian. Get a grip on your dick, or your emotions, or both."

"You mean like you have?" Christian mumbles.

I freeze.

So does every other person in the room.

"*Minchia,*" Christian swears. "I'm sorry, I shouldn't have said that."

I glare at him, and he holds my gaze, "No, seriously, *fratellone*. I didn't mean it."

"Sure, you did," I glance around at the rest of them. "Is that what this is about? Is that why there's unrest among you lot? You think I've lost control of my personal life; that's why you bastards are picking fights with each other, as well?"

The guys look at each other, the expressions on their faces ranging from embarrassment to unease to discomfort.

"*Che cazzo!*" I growl, "This is about me, eh? You guys don't trust me to figure out my own shit?"

"It's not that, Mika," Xander murmurs.

"Then how do you explain that your twin, who is normally as even-tempered as you, lost his cool today?"

"It's to do with a woman," Massimo offers.

"Bull-fucking-shit," I snap. "You going to feed me that line, as well?" I scowl at Massimo, "You, who is the most straight-talking of all of us?"

Massimo's face reddens. He glances away then back at me, "You're right." He adds, "It is about you… Partly." He raises a shoulder, "Okay, it is definitely… Probably…only about you." He releases Christian; so does Adrian. Christian straightens his collar, as Massimo steps back. "Look, Mika, you've just been a different man, is all. You've, uh, changed, since you met her."

"Changed?" I scowl, "How have I changed?"

"For one, you're wearing jeans," Massimo points out.

I glance down at my clothes, then swear aloud. Fuck, if I am not wearing jeans. "What's wrong with wearing jeans?" I glare at him, "You wear jeans. Hell, we all wear jeans."

"But not you, Mika." Adrian shuffles his feet, "You hate being dressed in anything except formal pants, and that too, only made by our family tailor."

"These are stitched by our family tailor." I glance around at their faces again. "*Porca miseria.* These aren't stitched by our family tailor?"

Xander shakes his head, "Sadly not, *fratellone*. They're off the shelf, *Levi's*."

I wince. How the hell had I gotten hold of them? How the hell do I even own a pair? "I had no idea…" my voice tapers off. "It's only jeans." I scowl at Xander, "It's not like it's the end of the world."

"To quote you, *fratellone*," he smirks, "wearing jeans is the end of the world."

I glower at him and he raises his hands, "At least, that's what you said not too long ago."

"*Merda*," I run my fingers through my hair, "I'll fix it." I scowl down at the offending garment I have on. "Still, it's hardly a sign that I don't have things under control."

That's when there's a knock on the door. I frown. The staff knows not to disturb me when I am in here with my brothers. It's a billiards room, but the rest of my team knows that this is where I discuss business. So, they wouldn't disturb me, unless… I stiffen. My heart begins to race. I pivot, head for the door and pull it open. "Is she all right?"

Cassandra peeks behind me and her lips firm. I glance over my shoulder to find Adrian hovering behind me. I turn back to her, "Well," I snap, "is she okay?"

Cassandra pulls her gaze back to my face. "She fainted."

27

Karma

I hear the door open and I squeeze my eyelids shut. My heart begins to race and my pulse pounds at my temples. In all honesty, I don't have to pretend that I am unwell. The sheer nervousness of what I am trying to pull off here has me feeling faint. Oh, also the fact that I haven't eaten in nearly a day. It's been twenty-four hours since Aurora left. I'd told Cassandra to leave my meals outside my door and she had obliged. I had then flushed the food down the toilet... Ugh, I know, one shouldn't waste food. But it was either that or involve Cassandra in my scheme. And while I had been tempted, I hadn't wanted to put that heavy of an onus on her. It would have meant putting my trust in her, and while I sort of do trust her, especially since she helped me the last time around... But this...this is different.

I am throwing everything I have behind this. This time, I am going for broke in trying to escape, and if Michael ever found out that Cassandra had helped me, he wouldn't hesitate to kill her, and honestly, I can't live with her death on my conscience. This is what I get for becoming close to her. Damn it.

Guess that's why Michael prefers to keep his emotions bottled up inside and not get too involved with anyone…Except for his brothers, of course. The way those men look out for each other, it totally reminds me of Summer and me and our relationship.

Shit, Summer. I really do miss my sister. Hopefully, though, I'll be out of here and with her very soon. If everything goes well, that is. Footsteps approach and the heavy tread, the even gait, proclaims it's his. I sense him sink down to his knees next to me… Yeah, I had pretended to faint in front of Cassandra, and hit the floor…which had hurt, but it had been worth it.

Fingers touch my cheek and my pulse rate spikes again. I flutter open my eyelids, gaze into his burning blue eyes. "Mika," I whisper, "you came?" Ugh, drama much? But Michael doesn't seem to suspect a thing. His features pale. A groove appears between his eyebrows as he scoops me up in his arms. His heartbeat thunders against my cheek, in synchrony with mine, as he walks over to place me on the bed.

He sits down next to me, leans over, and place his palm on my forehead. "What happened?" he murmurs. His voice is so soft, so gentle, so unlike how he's ever spoken to me before that a tear squeezes out from the corner of my eye. Shit, shit, shit. Why the hell am I feeling so weak in front of him? And all because he showed me a little tenderness.

"Shh!" He leans over and kisses my forehead, "Are you okay? When I saw you collapsed on the floor I…" His shoulders seem to shudder. Umm… What? Is he faking it? But why would he? On the other hand, why does he seems so upset that I am unwell?

He pulls back and I clutch at his arm. "Michael," I cough, "I…I don't feel so well."

He frowns, then places a palm against my forehead, "You do seem warm. Is that why you fainted?" He glances around the space, "Is it too stuffy in here? Should I change the location of my bedroom?"

Eh? He'd change his bedroom to another room in the house, rather than just move *me* to another room? Hold on, he's offering to change rooms because he thinks I'm uncomfortable in this room? In his room? "You'd do that for me?" I whisper.

"Of course." He cups my cheek, "I'd do anything for you, *amore mio*, don't you know that by now?"

"Only, you won't release me."

His jaw hardens, "You know I can't do that, *tesoro mio.*"

I swallow. Bloody hell when he uses those gorgeous Italian words on me, words which I now know the meaning of, then he completely slays me. I bring my hand to my chest and press it against my heart thumping against my rib cage.

"What's wrong?" He scowls, "Are you okay?"

"I..." I clear my throat, "I... I am fine." I only partly lie. Truth is, my stomach has tied itself up in knots, and a coldness has wrapped itself about my shoulders. I glance away from him, as I bite the inside of my cheek. "I... I am sure it's nothing."

His frown deepens.

"I am sure I will be okay," I cough. "I just need to... Maybe close my eyes for a little bit." I do just that, allow my shoulders to shudder.

I hear him inhale a sharp breath. "You are definitely not fine," he growls. He places his palm on my forehead, and honestly, it feels cool against my skin.

Shit, I am not really running a fever, am I? A shiver grips my body. I turn over on my side, curl into myself. "I... I'll be okay," I whisper.

"Bull-fucking-shit," he growls, then grips my shoulder. "You're not okay at all. What's happening? Talk to me, baby."

I freeze. Baby? He called me baby? Shit, why does he choose now to call me baby? Now, when I am trying to pull another fast one over him. Deceive him. Try to escape him. NOW is when he decides to show that humane part of him hidden behind that mafiahole facade?

I cough, try to swallow it, and end up choking. That sends him into a veritable tizzy.

"*Che cazzo!*" he swears, his voice almost hoarse with panic. I sense him pull out his phone, dial a number. The phone rings once, then a male voice says, "*Pronto?*"

"Sebastian," he snaps, "ready the chopper! I need to take my wife to the hospital."

My muscles freeze. Chopper? He has a bloody helicopter on the island? Of course, he has a bloody helicopter on the island. But why hadn't he mentioned it to me so far? Not that I can fly a helicopter or anything. Not that he's had any reason to tell me. So, if he hadn't mentioned it to me, does that mean he was hiding it from me? What else has he conveniently failed to tell me? My stomach twists. Bile bubbles up my throat. I sit up so suddenly that my head bumps his chin. Pain whispers down my spine. The phone slips from his grasp and hits the bed. I slide down the bed, then around him and swing my legs to the floor.

"Where are you going?"

I point in the direction of the bathroom as I take off toward it. I dive across the floor to the commode, then bend over it as the contents of my stomach gush out. Gross. I puke what little food I have left inside, considering I haven't eaten for the last twenty-four hours. A cool hand grips my forehead. He gathers the hair back from my face as I continue to dry heave. My head spins and darkness laces the edges of my vision. I blink it away, reach for the toilet-paper, but he's already there. He rips off a few sheets, hands them over to me, and I clean my mouth. He reaches over, flushes away the evidence of my being sick. I wince as I slump down onto the tiled floor, but of course, he catches me.

He swings me up and into his arms, and I turn my head away from him. How embarrassing. He saw me being sick. Can things get any worse from here? He carries me over to the sink, then lowers me to the floor. "Rinse your mouth," he orders, and I lean over and do as he commands. This once, I have no strength to disobey him, and not only because I need to get rid of the funny taste in my mouth.

Also, what's wrong with me? In pretending to be sick, I seem to be honestly coming down with something. That's all I need right now, some stupid virus to get a hold of me. I shut off the faucet, and he hands me a towel. As soon as I pat my mouth dry, he, once more, scoops me up in his arms. He carries me out into the bedroom, then out of the door.

"I can walk," I mumble. My voice trembles, and shit, I wasn't even pretending that time.

"I don't know what's wrong with me," I say truthfully. "One minute I was fine, the next..." I swallow down the rest of the words. Can't really tell him that I started out pretending to be sick, only to find out that I am really sick, can I?

"Don't worry, Beauty." He tucks my head under his chin, "You'll be fine, I promise. Once you are at the hospital—"

"No," I turn to him, only half-faking the alarm. I really do hate hospitals. So, it's not a complete lie when I say, "Why don't you simply fly the doctor here, instead?"

"I'll call ahead when we are on the way and have her meet us there."

"But Michael, please, I don't wanna go to the hospital," I whine.

"When it comes to your health, I will not take any risks," he says as he stalks down the stairs. When he reaches the bottom of the steps, Seb joins him.

"How is she?" he murmurs.

"Not good," Michael replies without glancing down at me once.

"Christian's readying the chopper for us." Xander joins us as Michael continues without pausing. He reaches the main door and Cassandra pushes it open. We walk down and Massimo turns to us. "Christan's already called for the doctor to meet us at the hospital."

"Of course, he did." Seb smirks, and Michael glares at him. "Sorry, Boss," he mimes zipping his lips, "won't mention it again."

"You better not," Michael growls. "Things are complicated enough without you and Christian coming to blows over something that, clearly, hits a nerve with him."

I glance between them. *What the hell are they talking about?*

"It hits something," Seb agrees, then quietens when Michael shoots him a glance.

"I won't warn you again, Sebastian," he says in a soft voice. It's his 'killer' voice, the one that says that he means business, that he won't hesitate to take action if anyone dares go against him or his orders. The one he'd probably use with me if he found out just how I am double-crossing him...again.

I shudder and he pulls me closer to his chest. "You okay, *Bellezza*?" His voice is soft again...but in a different way. It's more tender, more caring. More...everything. Everything I've wanted from him, he's now willing to give to me. If I asked him now, I have no doubt, he'd hand over his very business to me. Not that I'd want that. In fact, the opposite. Given a choice, I'd put enough distance between me and his Mafia state of affairs... Only, I can't separate the made-man that he is from the man who is my husband.

I curl my fingers into a fist. He hasn't returned my ring yet. I had returned it to him, but he hadn't trusted me enough to put his ring back on my finger. That's my fault though. I had felt the need to rub it in when I had left him the last time. If only I hadn't, I'd have the ring still with me, when I walk out on him again. A part of him would, at least, stay with me. Not that I need that to remind me of him. His scent, his heat, his sheer dominance...and his unexpected tenderness... All of it has spoiled me for anyone else.

Once I leave him... I'll probably spend the rest of the days trying to fill the void that his lack of presence in my life will create. My heart begins to race and the band around my chest tightens. I cough again, and this time, he hurries his pace until he's almost running. The guys follow us. As we reach the helicopter, Antonio reaches for him, but he declines, holds onto me as he navigates the steps. Once inside the chopper, he sinks into a seat with me in his lap. Seb reaches over to buckle both of us in. Xander and Massimo slip into the seats behind us as Christian readies for take-off.

"You sure you don't want me there, Boss?" Antonio hesitates and his features wear a worried look. "I'd feel much more comfortable knowing I'm there with you."

Michael chuckles, "I have my brothers with me; I will be more than fine."

Antonio frowns.

"Stay with Adrian, hold down the fort here."

Antonio looks like he's about to refuse when Michael jerks his chin, "You're delaying us from taking off."

Antonio nods, then steps off the helicopter. Seb shuts the door behind him and straps in, and the chopper instantly lifts into the air.

28

Michael

I pace the corridor outside the hospital examination room. What the hell is taking them so long? We'd made it to the hospital in Palermo in under fifteen minutes, thanks to Christian's expert flying skills. A team had been ready and waiting for us when we'd landed on the makeshift helipad next to the hospital. One that Christian had organized at the same time as he'd called ahead to alert the medical staff. They'd rushed her over in a stretcher, and all through, she hadn't let go of my hand. She'd also seemed to grow paler by the second. Even more than when we'd been in the air. Throughout the trip she'd clung to me, her shoulders shaking every time the helicopter had banked. I had yelled to Christian to take it easy with the chopper and he had managed to smooth out the helicopter and still get us here in record time.

I owe him for that. Hell, I owe all of them for dropping whatever is important in their lives and coming over with me. Not that I didn't expect it, considering I am the Capo. But still... They are also human. They have their own lives, their own...women?

Holdonasecond. Not one of my brothers... Not even Seb or Adrian have ever introduced me to any of their women... Or ever been serious with anyone, so far, as far as I know. Xander has his childhood crush... but he is far from admitting his feelings for her. Then there's Adrian. He seems to have noticed Cassandra; and Christian seems to be taken in by the doctor...but that's just speculation on my part. None of them have ever confessed to ever being in love...

Cazzo! What am I doing thinking about my brother's love lives? Sure, I want to see them settled and have families... And not just because it is important to ensure continuity of power, but also because I want them to be happy. So why is it that not once in all these years, have any of my brothers ever mentioned anything about finding someone special?

A touch on my shoulder and I turn to find Sebastian at my elbow. He hands me a paper cup filled with a dark brew. I take a sip and the liquid warms me. I toss the rest of it back, feel it rejuvenate me somewhat. I crumple the cup in my fist, walk over to the waste paper basket and deposit it. I turn to find the four of them watching me. Xander is sprawled out in a seat that looks too small for him. Christian is seated opposite him, his elbows digging into his thighs. Massimo leans his hip against the wall, watching me. Seb stands where I had left him, his gaze ticking my progress as I walk over to them.

"Why the hell haven't any of you married before now, huh?"

"Eh?" Massimo blinks, "What kind of a question is that?"

"A straight one." I scowl, "It's not normal that none of you have even brought a woman home to meet the rest of us."

"And risk scaring her away?" Xander snorts, "Not likely."

"But that isn't why you haven't brought anyone special over to introduce her to us, is it?" I scowl between them, "It's because none of you have anyone important in your lives."

Massimo raises a shoulder. "I haven't met anyone. Not that I was looking. Besides," he narrows his gaze on me, "since when did you decide it's important to find out about our personal lives?"

"Guess because he's married now, for better or for worse; he's hooked and he wants the rest of us to be balled and chained too," Seb murmurs.

I frown at him, "That's not why I asked."

"It's the first time you've bothered to ask about our personal lives," Christian points out. "Like I said earlier, you have changed."

"Huh," I rake my fingers through my hair, "just because I thought to ask after my brothers doesn't mean I have changed."

The four exchange looks.

"You also haven't asked us once if we've made any progress on finding Luca," Seb points out.

I glare at him. "Speaking of," I look him up and down, "your time is almost up on that, so have you any inkling on his whereabouts yet?"

"He's in —"

The sound of the door opening has me jerking toward it. The doctor steps out. She walks over to us and Christian instantly rises to his feet. His gaze eats her up as she comes to a stop in front of me. Yeah, there's definitely something there… I glance from him to the doctor who shoves her hand into the pocket of her scrubs.

"How is she? Is she okay?"

"She's fine, but we need to keep her overnight under observation."

"But she's not in any danger, is she?"

"She's exhausted, a little dehydrated; Also, her blood pressure and pulse rate are elevated. While she's not in any immediate danger —" She hesitates and my pulse rate instantly spikes.

"What is it?" I snap.

She stares at the rest of the men, then back at me.

"These are my brothers; you can speak in front of them."

"This may be something you want to hear in private?"

"Tell me, woman," I burst out, "or I swear —"

There's a touch on my shoulder. I turn to find Christian right behind me. He jerks his chin toward the doctor, then shakes his head. *Che cazzo!* Of course, he has to come to her rescue. Did I say that I wish my brothers would find their own women and settle down? Guess I wasn't aware of exactly how that would change the dynamics between us when that happens. I glare at him and he holds my gaze. Shit, he's serious about her? When the hell had that happened, eh? I shrug off his hand, turn to her.

"Look, Doc, I appreciate your being sensitive about the situation, but right now, I only want to find out what's wrong with my wife, so if you can just spit it out —"

"She's pregnant."

Next to me, Christian inhales. A pulse of shock runs through the assembled men. "What did you say?" I growl.

"She's pregnant," the doctor repeats herself.

"She's…." I swallow, "She's…"

"Pregnant." The doctor nods, "Your wife is pregnant, Capo."

"My wife is pregnant?" I open and shut my mouth, "She's having my child?"

A small smile curves her lips, "It would seem that way, yes."

My knees seem to give way from under me.

Christian grips my shoulder. "Steady, Capo," he murmurs.

I blink to clear my vision, then focus my gaze once more on the doctor.

"She's fine, other than that?"

The doctor nods, "Like I mentioned, it would be best if we kept her under observation overnight."

I nod, "Of course, whatever you think is best for her."

"Also," she glances to the side, "there was—ah— Something else that I think you should know."

"What is it?"

"I…ah…" She shuffles her feet, "It's just that—" She straightens her shoulders, "She needs to take better care of herself. She needs to eat well, sleep well, make sure she's getting her vitamins."

"I'll make sure of that." I run my fingers through my hair. "Anything else?"

She seems like she's about to say something, then shakes her head.

"Can I see her now?"

"Of course."

She turns and I follow her inside. I walk into the room, almost bumping into the doctor who's come to a halt inside the threshold. She's staring at the bed. The empty bed. I glance around the space. The entire room is empty. I stalk toward the door on the far side, peek inside. There's no one in the bathroom either.

"What the hell?

A draft blows in through the open window. I lunge toward it, glance down at the ground which is maybe five or six feet away. Not too close, but not too far either. Could she have jumped? The hair on the back of my neck rises. She did jump. She managed to get away. My pregnant wife managed to escape. Is she strong enough to have made the jump? How far can she go in the condition she is in? I had found her collapsed on the floor of the room, and now she manages to jump out of the window and leave? My guts twist and my stomach ties itself in knots. I bunch my fists at my side, "What the hell is happening here? Where is she?"

"She… I…" the doc's voice trembles. I glance at her, find her features have lost all color. She has her fingers gripped together in front of her; the skin over her knuckles is white.

Minchia! Why is she so nervous? I close the distance between us, and glare at her, "Something you want to tell me, Doc?"

"I... " she shakes her head, "it's my fault; I agreed to help her. I had no idea she was pregnant. As soon as I found out, I—" I raise my hand and she flinches. *Damnit!* I lower my arm, brush past her, then out the door. My brothers crowd around me.

Seb takes in my features and his own harden, "What's wrong, Boss? What happened in there?"

"She did," I point a thumb over my shoulder, "she helped my wife escape."

"Karma's gone?" Christian glances between me and the doctor who's standing behind me.

I pull out my knife from the small of my back, "I am going to kill her for it." I am about to turn, when Christian closes the distance between us.

"Leave her to me."

"What do you mean?"

"Don't waste your time on her. I've got this."

I peer into his eyes, then jerk my chin, "I am going after my wife."

29

Karma

When I'd been brought to the hospital, Aurora had examined me thoroughly, not just going through the motions, as I'd thought she would.

I had protested and she'd said it had been to make things look authentic. Authentic? When no one was around to see her? Hmm. When she'd completed her examination, she'd told me that she needed to run a few more tests. I'd asked her if something was wrong and she'd said, not really, it was just a precaution. But the look on her face.

Seriously, it reminded me of the time when the doctor had told me that I have a hole in my heart—that it wasn't dangerous yet, but that it needed to be fixed. Clearly, this was something similar. Either her examination had revealed my condition… Or it was something else. And either way, I was not staying to find out more.

I'd asked her if she had changed her mind about helping me and she had said, of course, not. That she'd do everything in her power to help me. And somehow, it had been the way that she'd said it, how she had avoided looking at my eyes when she said it, that had caused me to mistrust her. Something was up with her. Maybe she was getting cold feet, or an attack of conscience. Or perhaps, she had realized she could not go up against the Capo. Either way, I wasn't waiting around to find out. She had told me that she needed to access a few more things to run some more tests on me, and that's when I had decided, no way, was I going to stick around to find out what those tests involved. Likely, she was going to tell the Capo that I was planning on escaping. I had been sure of that. So, when she'd left the room, I had promptly pulled my clothes and shoes back on and rushed to the window.

The ground hadn't seemed too far, until I had jumped, that is. I had landed with a thump that had sent pain slicing through my body. I had picked myself up, then broken into a run. I hadn't dared to look back for fear that he'd have already discovered my absence. I'd raced out of the hospital complex, up the road, until I had reached a junction. I had glanced around, wondering which way to go, then decided to keep straight. I was on a road that was busy enough that I felt safe. If I was in a crowd, he wouldn't do anything, would he? He couldn't just drag me off kicking and screaming if he managed to track me down, could he?

I had taken off up the pavement, trying to not hurry too much, trying not to attract too much attention to myself. All the while my heartrate had skyrocketed; my pulse had kicked up...

Shit! Once more, I am pushing myself too much. My breath comes in puffs. I can feel my heart slamming against my rib cage. Sweat pools under my armpits, and overall, I don't fell so well. I slow down to a normal walk, but that doesn't help. My head spins and the edges of my vision flicker with dark spots. Shit, what the hell is wrong with me? Why am I feeling so woozy? I've never fainted in my life... Not counting the fake fainting spell earlier, which is how he had found me.

I hope this isn't my heart acting up. It can't be my heart acting up. It had better not be my heart acting up. I press my knuckles into my thundering heartbeats that vibrate through my chest. Shit, shit, shit, this is not good! I glance about the space at the people engaged in their day-to-day lives. The woman scolding her child, who seems to be on the verge of tears. The men crowded around a table outside a coffeeshop. A couple of boys on their electronic scooters driving by on the pavement. The man and woman holding hands as they peer into the shopfront. The image fades back and forth as I take a step forward, and another. My knees wobble. I throw out a hand as the ground comes up to meet me, stops, as arms grasp me. The scent of testosterone envelops me. Musky, like leather, with a hint of woodsmoke. The heat of his body envelops me as he swings me up in his arms.

"Foiled, again," I murmur. "I tried to run, I tried to leave you, but—"

"I found you." His blue eyes bore into mine. "I'll always find you, no matter how far you go. I'll always track you down, no matter how far you flee. You can try to escape me, but I'll never let you."

"Michael."

"Beauty?" He rakes his gaze across my face, "You should have planned better. I gave you more credit than this half-brained escape attempt."

"It wasn't half-brained. I had—" I chew the inside of my cheek. No way, am I going to give up Aurora, no matter that she had abandoned me at the last minute. Guess she's entitled. I would be worried for my skin, too, if my family was answerable to the Capo.

"You had help," he states.

"No, I didn't."

"I know it was the doctor," he says as he turns and begins retracing our steps. The smattering of people on the pavement glance at us, then away. No one tries to stop him. Not that I am struggling or anything. Still, apparently, it's normal for a man to carry a woman through the streets here...

Not that he is just any man. He is the Capo. *Their* Capo. Guess none of them would have stopped to help me even if I had been struggling to get away from him...which I am not, anyway. I snuggle into his chest, push my cheek against where his heart thuds steadily. It's beat slower than the organ that pounds away against my ribcage.

"I have something to tell you," I say at the same time as him.

He glances down at me, "You first."

"You first," I murmur as I reach up to touch his cheek. *So bloody gorgeous. Why couldn't you have been, at least, ugly looking?*

He chuckles and I realize that I have spoken the words aloud. Heat sears my cheeks.

"What did you want to tell me?" I ask, more because I want to divert his attention from my earlier faux pas. That's all I need, voicing my thoughts aloud... I mean, if he could read what my thoughts are when I am normally around him...then he'd know that I'm fighting a losing battle when it comes to him.

OMG, why are all of my thoughts so muddled? Why does my brain feel as if it's turned to mush? Why do my arms and legs feel so heavy? I squint up at him through the sunlight that pours over him, bathing him in a golden glow that brings out the hollows under his cheeks, the shadows under his eyes, the grooves on either side of his mouth. That stern mouth, those lips that had brought me so much pleasure, every time he's kissed me, every time he's sucked on my nipples, bit me on my pussy. I clench my thighs together, drag my fingers to his mouth, as his lips move.

"You're pregnant, Beauty."

I still, "Wh… what?"

"You're with child," his arms tighten around me, "my child."

"It's not possible."

"It's very possible."

"I… I mean. I can't be pregnant."

"You are."

"Who told you?" I firm my lips. "The doctor?"

He nods.

So that's why she had stepped out of the room to talk to him? To alert him first? Why hadn't she told me? This is what I get for trusting someone who is one of them… Clearly, they owe their loyalties only to each other, and I am not one of the Mafia. No wonder, she had pretended to be my confidant, only to betray me. It wasn't even the fact that she had mentioned it to him first. Why hadn't she shared it with me when she had found out? Because then she knew, I would never have allowed myself to be caught by him. No bloody way. I begin to struggle, but his grasp tightens about me.

I wince, "You're hurting me."

He eases his hold just a fraction, but keeps me plastered to his chest.

"Is that why you came after me? Because I am carrying your heir?"

"I came after you because you are mine."

And this child…would also be his. Shit, this is what I had been afraid of. That if I became pregnant, I'd never be able to leave him. That he'd become even more possessive, and stake his claim on me even more firmly.

Oh, hell. "Let me go," I say in a harsh whisper, and he shakes his head.

"You know I can't, especially not now that —"

"That I am carrying your precious child."

"Your child too."

No kidding. My stomach ties itself up in knots. The band around my chest tightens. "I… I don't want this child," I lie.

"Too bad, you don't have a choice."

I stare up at what I can see of his face. "Fuck you," I snap and he chuckles.

"I'd love to, but we may have to exercise caution until you are stronger."

"Nothing is wrong with me."

"Other than your being pregnant with my child, that is."

His child. His wife. What about me? What about what I want? I dig my fingers into the front of his shirt, "I can't do this."

"Yes, you can."

"I don't want to do this."

"Yes, you do."

"Are you hearing anything I am saying?"

"You're afraid," he murmurs. "It's normal."

"I am not afraid, you prick."

"Is that any way to speak to the father of your child?"

Oh, my god! I am pregnant with his child. Our child. Oh god, oh god. My stomach seems to coil in on itself. "I think I am going to be sick again."

He glances down at me as we reach the entrance to the hospital. He shoulders his way inside, then makes a beeline past the reception down the corridor. He shoves open the door, races to a bathroom stall and deposits me on my feet. I sink to my knees, and for the second time in twelve hours, I puke my guts out in front of him.

30

Michael

She sinks down onto the floor of the bathroom next to the commode. I place the wet cloth on her forehead, "How are you feeling?"

I had brought my wife home from the hospital two days ago, and since that vomiting bout at the hospital bathroom she hasn't stopped puking.

"How do you think?" She scowls back at me, before launching up again on her knees and hanging over the bowl. When she finishes retching, she collapses against the wall. "I am dying," she groans, "I am never going to make it through the next few months."

I flush away the evidence of her being sick, then gently pat her mouth, "The doctor said the morning sickness should fade by the end of the first trimester."

"Considering I am only a few weeks along, that doesn't comfort me very much." She scowls, "Besides, I don't trust him or his diagnosis."

When Aurora's role in my wife's escape had emerged, I'd wanted to make her pay for it. I'd come very close to pulling my gun on her, except Christian had stepped in. He'd insisted I spare her life, which I had. He'd wanted me to let her return to her previous life, which I had decided was unacceptable. The result is that she's currently locked up in a room in one of my safe houses while I figure out what to do with her. I can't simply let her go; that would weaken my reputation and my ability to stake my claim as Don when the time comes. On the other hand, I can't kill her, since I promised Christian I won't. However, there is no way I am letting her treat my wife. I've lost my faith in Aurora and I can't imagine any circumstance under which I would allow her anywhere near Beauty. The result is that I had a specialist flown in from Rome—had ordered him to relocate to be near us so he can come when needed.

"He's a perfectly capable doctor."

"I prefer Aurora."

"Considering she let you down when you needed her help to escape, I am surprised you want to be treated by her."

Beauty hesitates, "I admit, I was pissed off at her, at first, but I guess I do understand why she did it. I just don't understand why she didn't tell me I was pregnant, as well."

"Maybe she was trying to protect you and the child?" I raise a shoulder. "Frankly, I don't give a rat's ass about her intentions. She alerted me in the nick of time. Else not only would we not be here having this conversation, but I doubt she'd have made it out of that hospital alive."

She pales further and I curse myself. I really need to curb my vocabulary when I am around her in this state. Since finding out she's pregnant, Karma has done an about face. It's as if all of her hidden emotions and sensitivities have come to the fore. She's become needy, absent-minded, and also, possessive. None of which I mind. She's also been very sick. Enough to make me think she might need to be admitted to the hospital a couple of times. Except, no way, am I letting her out of my sight.

Instead, I had arranged for the hospital to come to her. I had a complete suite in my home converted to a hospital room...which will also serve as the birthing room, when the time comes. Yeah, also a team of doctors and nurses are on-call around the clock, in case of any emergency. No, I am not being over-the-top about this... I am just being safe. No way, am I taking any chances when it comes to my wife's health or of that of my unborn child. I reach forward and push the hair away from her forehead. "How are you feeling now?"

"Hungry." She scowls. "I wish my body would make up its mind.

One minute, I am puking my guts out; the next moment, I am starving like I haven't eaten in days."

"Well, you are eating for two."

"More like I am eating for a crowd," She pouts as she pushes up to standing. Her color is better and she definitely seems stronger than even a few seconds ago. Her ability to recover from these bouts of puking never ceases to amaze me. All in all, since discovering she's pregnant, she's been too preoccupied with trying to keep up with the changes to her body to think of trying to escape… Or at least, I hope so.

I reach for her and scoop her up in my arms. She frowns, "I can walk, you know."

"Indulge me," I murmur as I walk out of the bathroom, past the bed in our bedroom, and down the stairs to the kitchen. When I found out she was pregnant, I moved her to my house on the outskirts of Palermo. Not the one I normally use, but the one I bought many years ago, with the hope of, one day, using it as a base for my family. The location of this place is known to only my brothers, and the closest members in my clan.

It's away from the city, which means she's also out of reach of our rivals. Not to mention that with the security I have placed about it, we'd spot anyone coming from a mile off.

Once in the kitchen, I place her at a chair at the dining table, then busy myself making breakfast. I sense her gaze on me as I move around, popping the bread in the toaster and whipping up the eggs for an omelet. I plate out the toast and the omelets for both of us, place them on the table, then pour her a glass of orange juice.

When I slip into the seat in front of her, she stares at me.

"What?" I arch an eyebrow, "Everything okay?"

She nods, "Everything is fine. Maybe too fine."

"What do you mean?" I jerk my chin at her plate and she begins to butter her toast before cutting a piece of her omelet and bringing it to her mouth. She finishes almost all of the food on her plate before she leans back and surveys me with a gaze.

"I don't understand why you are being this nice to me."

"I am always nice to you, Beauty."

"You weren't very nice to me when we first met."

"I didn't know you as well as I do now."

"You think you know me well?" She arches an eyebrow, mirroring my earlier gesture.

I smirk as I cut into my omelet and continue eating.

"Well?" She prods, "Do you think you know me well?"

"I think…" I pause as I survey her features, "I know you well enough, to allow you access to your phone again."

She huffs, "That doesn't mean anything. You allowed me access to my phone earlier, as well."

"Until you insisted on showing me that you couldn't be trusted," I glower.

"So, you trust me now?"

"Nope."

She gapes, "So you don't trust me now?"

"Not an inch, my darling Beauty." I place my knife and fork on the plate, before I push my chair back, "However, I do trust you enough to give you…" I slide my palm inside my pocket, pull out her ring.

"Oh," her chest heaves.

I go down on one knee in front of her—only because it's the only way to reach for her fingers as I slide the ring onto her left ring finger.

She draws in a breath. "I really don't understand you," she murmurs as she raises the fingers of her left hand.

"What do you not understand?" I push back a strand of her hair behind her ear.

"You say you don't trust me, yet you give me back my ring… I mean, your ring." She glances up at me, "Why would you do that?"

"Because you are my wife?" I cup her cheek, "And the mother-to-be of my child."

"This child means a lot to you, doesn't it?"

I tilt my head, "As do you."

"Do I?"

"Do you doubt my word?"

"You just said that you don't trust me…so…"

"I don't have to trust you to—" *love you*. Shit, did I almost say that aloud? I rise to my feet, and she grabs my hand.

"To—?" She tips up her chin, "What were you going to say?"

"To acknowledge you as my wife," I reply and her features fall.

"Oh, right."

I pull my hand away from her grasp, then nod to her plate, "You didn't finish your breakfast."

"I…I'm not hungry anymore."

"Have you told your sister yet that you are pregnant?"

She whips her head around to stare at me, "You'd be okay with that?"

"Of course."

"As well as if I told her that I am married?"

"Wouldn't expect you to say one without the other."

She screws her features, "See, this is what I mean?"

"What?"

"You being nice to me... It's weird."

"I don't see why that should surprise you so much."

"It's just..." She waves her hand in the air, "All this conversation, your cooking meals for me, taking care of me when I am sick... It's just..."

"Normal?"

She frowns, "In a way, and that weirds me out even more."

"So, you find it weird that we are actually getting along, and that you are not trying to escape me anymore?"

Her shoulders slump and I curse myself. Why the hell did I have to bring that up? Just as I was thinking that she was settling in here and she also seemed content, I had to go and spoil it all, eh? *Che diavolo!*

"I am not trying to escape you because, for some reason, I seem to be forgetting exactly why I wanted to get away from you in the first place."

My heart begins to race. "You are, eh?" I say softly.

"It's all your fault," She lowers her chin as she proceeds to polish off the remaining food on her plate. Then she takes a couple of sips of the orange juice from her glass before turning to me. "You're making me too comfortable here."

Good.

"You're spoiling me by how you take care of me."

That's the idea, tesoro mio.

"You're..." her chin wobbles, "you're confusing me, you know that? You're tying me up in knots, you're messing with my head, you...you..." her voice catches, tears slide down her cheeks, and my heart stutters.

It fucking stutters. I squat down in front of her, frame her cheeks with my hands, "Don't cry, Beauty."

She sniffles, even as she turns her head away from me, "You think I want to cry, you ass? It's these stupid hormones. They are all over the place, and half the time, I can't even understand why things set me off when they do, without any warning. I am making a fool of myself in front of you, and I still can't stop bawling, damn it." She balls her fingers into fists as I pull her into my arms. She stays rigid as I rub her back. She refuses to unbend as I haul her into my chest.

I hold her there until her muscles slowly unwind, one by one. When her breathing has evened out, I finally pull away from her. "Better?" I ask as she blinks away her tears.

"Sort of," she mumbles, as she reaches for the tissues on the table in front of her and blows her nose. I rise to my feet again, and keep a hand on her shoulder as she pushes back her chair and gets up as well.

"So, you going to call your sister?"

She shakes her head.

"Why not?"

"I am not ready to talk to her about...," she gestures to the space between us.

"Why not?"

"Hell, I am still digesting the fact that I am not only married but already pregnant, so please..." she tosses her hair. "Just give me a little time, okay?"

"Hmm." I stare into her features and she scowls back at me.

"I hate the sound of that hmm!"

"Hmm..." I scratch my chin. "Is it just time you need, or is it something else?"

"Like what?" She brushes past me, then heads out of the kitchen and down the corridor to the study, which is where she spends a lot of her time these days. When I had furnished the space with all of my favorite books, I'd had no idea then that my wife, the mother-to-be of my child, would love the space so much. If I'd known, I'd have made sure to have books which were more to her liking on the shelves... Not that she has complained about my taste in literature so far.

I follow her down the hall and watch as she sinks down onto the settee in front of the fire, then pulls her legs up under her.

"What else would I need?"

"You tell me," I murmur as I lean a hip against the back of the chair near her.

"No, why don't *you* tell me?" She scoffs, "Since you seem to think that you can read my mind or something." She sniffs.

"Maybe you are ashamed to be married to the Mafia? Maybe you don't want to tell your family that you are carrying the child of a criminal?" I lower my chin, "May...be...you are hoping that if you wait long enough, things will go back to the way they used to be?"

She flushes, then glances away from me, "Honestly, I want to deny all of that, but—" She raises a shoulder. "I won't deny that all of those thoughts have gone through my mind," she murmurs, "but I also know things aren't just going to go back to being what they were."

"Do you?" I cross the floor to stand in front of her, "Do you understand that you are my wife and I am not letting you go? Ever? That this child is the one thing that can ensure that my bid for Don is sealed?

She starts, "So that's the only reason you want this child? Because he or she guarantees your position as the head of the Cosa Nostra?"

I stare into her now flushed features, "What other reason could there be?"

31

Michael

I can't believe I actually said that. *What other reason can there be?* What other reason can there *not* be? Why is it that when it comes to the crunch, I'm unable to tell her how I feel? Why is it that when she looks at me with her big green eyes, I feel myself sinking into them, feel the barriers around my heart melting away, realize that somewhere along the way I've developed feelings for her, that I want her in my life, and not only because she is the mother of my child? I need her because she makes me feel... And maybe that's the problem.

Once you start developing an emotional connection to someone else, once you make yourself vulnerable in that way, you're opening yourself up to being hurt. Once my rivals discover that she and the child are the chinks in my armor, they'll never stop, until they've hurt both of them. They'll use them to get to me... Just as they had already tried once before.

Only now, the stakes are higher. She is pregnant. *Dio santo!* She is going to give birth to my child. A hot sensation stabs at my chest. I stare out of the window of my home office, where I had returned after hurting her with that last comment. I had wanted to hurt her. I had wanted her to feel a little of the agony I am going through, to understand how powerless I had felt in that instant when I had realized that I would do anything for her…for the both of them. I would give up my claim to being the Don if it meant that I could keep them safe…

And that…is non-negotiable. I owe it to myself to see this through. After coming this far, after taking on my own father, and facing my worst nightmares, I deserve to be the head of the *Cosa Nostra*. This is what I was born for. This is what my mother sacrificed herself for. To ensure that I, one day, displace my father and changed the face of the *Cosa Nostra*; modernize them so there will no longer be victims like my mother. And I thought I had been on track… Until she had come along and exposed just how frail my beliefs are.

I had thought I was not like my father, that all I needed was to seize power and I could wipe out all traces of how he had run our clans… But she'd shown me just how similar to him I am… When it comes to her… to my child. When it comes to what really mattered to me, I am as possessive as my father, if not more so. I am as controlling, as dominating, as hellbent on taking control and getting things done my way, no matter that it hurts the people I love most… *Che cazzo!* There is that word again.

Love; fucking love! I am in love with her; if only I could tell her that. Maybe then she'd understand why I act so over-the-top possessive with her? Why I want to stalk her, to ensure that she is safe. Why I want to follow her every move. Why I cannot bear to have her out of sight. Why I want to direct what she wears, who she meets, what she eats, where she lives… Why I put that stupid tracker in her… Because I want to take care of her. To protect her. To make sure that all of her needs are met. That she is provided for and happy and…

That will never work. F-u-c-k. I grip the edge of the window sill. That will only suffocate her. She is a wild thing, a woman who needs freedom to flourish. An artiste who needs to explore the world and take risks in order to create. Her imagination needs new experiences so she can reinvent herself. And me? I need her to be by my side, where I can keep her out of harm's way.

I curl my fist and punch it down into the window sill. Pain shoots up my arm. Good. This is tangible, this is real, this…pain I can deal with. But if anything happened to her or to my child… I would—

"Mika, you, okay?"

Xander's voice interrupts my thoughts. If it had been anyone else,

I'd have told them to fuck off, but Xander… Well, when he speaks, you listen. Doesn't mean that I have to come across as welcoming though, right?

His footsteps sound as he approaches me. There's a touch on my shoulder and I know he's paused beside me.

"Contemplating the view, eh?"

"I'm contemplating, something, all right," I mutter.

For a few seconds, he stands there without speaking. That's the thing with Xander. Unlike my other brothers, who prefer to voice their concerns through speech, he prefers to use silence to convey his worry instead.

"It's normal, you know," he finally says, "to feel insecure."

"Me, insecure?" I chuckle, "Now I know I've heard everything."

"Even big bad Capo's have an Achilles heel."

"I didn't think I had one until..." I pause, not sure how, exactly, to voice the words in my head without giving myself away completely. And some things…a man has to keep close to his chest. Not even for my favorite brother, am I willing to lay my feelings out there completely.

"Until her?" Xander says softly.

I blow out a breath, "This…sucks."

"You mean, you're finally realizing that you are not as invincible as you thought you were?"

"Is that what this is?"

"It's…something you are lucky to face, *fratellone*."

"Eh?" I shoot him a sideways glance, "I don't feel lucky."

"That's only because you haven't acknowledged the true extent of your feelings for her."

"That fucking 'f' word."

"Yep," he laughs, "the one and only one that has brought the strongest of men to their knees, so you don't stand a chance."

I turn to face him, "What are you trying to say?"

"That," he glances at me, "you are fighting too hard. Putting too much pressure on yourself and her. You're allowing the past to dictate your future, brother, and that's only going to lead to misery."

"You have no idea how it feels to find out that your wife is pregnant, that you are going to bring a child into this world. How am I going to protect him or her from the evils out there? How am I going to protect all of them from what I am?"

"Ah," he nods, "I see now."

"See what?" I scowl, "I hate it when you are so cryptic."

"You're scared, *fratellone*."

"Me, scared?" I scoff, "What do I have to be scared of?"

"Yourself?"

I laugh, "Now you're taking the piss, as the Brits say."

"You're worried that you won't measure up to the needs of being a husband and a parent. You are unsure if you will be able to meet the demands made of you. You think you are not good enough to be either. You are afraid that—"

"Stop," I growl, "just shut the fuck up, Xander."

He tilts his head, "Hurts to hear the truth, eh?"

I push away from the window and begin to pace. "Why is it that this feels so..difficult…so monumental? Like something that cuts through all the bullshit I have been spewing all this time, something that slices me to the core, and cuts me off at the knees? Something that makes me feel so exposed that I am sure I am going to be sick?"

"Welcome to the human race," he murmurs. "It's not all fun and games when you begin to experience the emotions, but with great vulnerability, comes the gift of extreme joy."

I wince, "Doesn't sound like my cup of espresso."

"It's good, what you are going through."

I laugh as I rub at my chest, "If you say so."

"I know so." He walks over to me and grips my shoulder, "This is all good, brother. This, what you are going through, will make you stronger, more powerful, more resilient to face what is to come. Your ability to be a little more sensitive will only make you a more insightful leader."

"When did you become this wise?"

He smirks, "I was born wise, big brother."

I ruffle his hair, "Don't let my praise go to your head."

"Not likely," he snorts, "considering you are only telling me what I already know."

"Right," I murmur, "so what now?"

"Now you go back and apologize to her."

"Apologize?" I lower my hand, "What do I need to apologize for?"

"For whatever it is you did?"

"Why is it something I did?" I frown.

"It's always the man in a relationship who is wrong. Time you accept that."

"So, you admit that you are the one who's in the wrong when it comes to not acknowledging your feelings for Theresa?"

His features tense, then he forces his expression into a semblance of a smile, "You got that right."

"What are you going to do about it?"

"Nothing."

"What?" I gape, "You give me all this sage advice, and when it comes to confessing your feeling for your childhood friend, you get cold feet."

"It's not cold feet."

"What is it then?"

"It's just..." he rubs his fingers across the back of his neck, "it's complicated."

"And you sound like a cliché."

He stares at me and I raise my hands in the air, "Okay, all right, I admit I sounded like one too, earlier."

"See how much easier it is when you simply own up to your faults?"

I laugh, "Don't kid yourself, *fratellino*." I ruffle his hair, "Just because you happen to be right about some things doesn't mean you're right about *everything*."

He chuckles, "I wouldn't dare claim that." He punches me lightly in the shoulder, "Now, go back there and talk to your wife."

32

Karma

I rub Andy's forehead and he purrs, then snuggles closer into my chest. When Cassandra had arrived with him, I had been so damn happy that I had almost shed a tear. Gosh, I'd missed the little guy, and also her, if I am being honest. I've never had any close friends, mainly because Summer has always fulfilled that role. But since she is not here with me right now, and since Cassandra is really the only other woman around now, I find myself turning to her more and more.

I glance up as the door to my bedroom opens. After that last conversation of ours, I'd told Michael that I preferred to stay separately from him. He hadn't seemed happy about it, but he hadn't pushed it either. Maybe he thought it was best not to push me further in the condition I am in. Of course, he'd insisted that Cassandra check in on me every hour to make sure I was okay and, while it's annoying, I'll take that any day over having to sleep next to him at night. Which, unfortunately, also means that I miss him at night. Gah, there really is no winning for me, right? Now, his shoulders fill the doorway and I stiffen. Think of the devil…and there he is.

He hovers at the threshold of the room, glances about the space before his gaze finally alights on mine. "May I come in?" he asks and I blink. *What the — ? Did he just ask my permission?*

"Umm… Excuse me?" I blink rapidly, "I don't think I heard that right."

He flushes, then draws himself up to his full height, "I asked if I can come in?"

"If I say no, would that stop you?"

"No?" He smirks, then sobers, "If you'd rather that I not come in then just say the word. I'll leave."

I take in his gorgeous features, the hint of something like…indecision in his eyes, the way he holds himself stiffly, like he's about to face an exam or do something that he's not completely comfortable with… Shit, the very fact that he did not barge in like he owns the place, but opted to wait for my consent before he walked in is…surprising enough that I want to find out what's on his mind. I blow out a breath, then jerk my chin, "You can come in, on one condition."

"Oh?"

I nod, "I'll tell you what it is, as long as you agree to it."

"Come now," he tilts his head "that's no deal at all."

"I'm not negotiating at all."

"Hmm," he looks me up and down, "fine, then tell me what it is."

"A Christmas party."

"Eh?" He seems taken aback, "A Christmas party?"

"It is the second week of December already," I point out. "Isn't it traditional in Italy for Christmas decorations to go up by December 8?"

"You've been researching Italian customs?" He smirks.

Cassandra had mentioned it to me, but I am not going to tell him that. "All I'm saying is that it's time we start planning for Christmas."

We? Shit, I said *'we.'*

He doesn't seem to notice though. "You want to start planning a Christmas party?" He rubs his jaw.

I nod. To be honest, I am not huge on Christmas gatherings, as such. But maybe I am lonelier than I thought… Or m-a-y-b-e, finding myself pregnant makes me want to surround myself with more people, I guess? Andy wriggles in my arms and I place him on the floor. He instantly pads over to Mika who picks up the kitten. He cuddles Andy who coils up against his chest. *Traitor.* And I thought he owed his allegiance to me. Apparently, not even kittens are exempt from the Capo's charm.

"I also want to invite Aurora to the Christmas party."

"No," his lips firm, "I can't allow that."

"Why not?"

"She conspired with you."

"She told you I was pregnant so you came after me."

"She—"

"Deserves another chance," I cut in. "Come on, she's a doctor, and she's helped you out when you needed her services, hasn't she?"

He hesitates.

"Also," I bat my eyelashes at him, "I really am starved for feminine company."

He tilts his head, "If feminine company is all you want, I could invite my Nonna..."

I gape at him, "You're kidding me, right?"

He frowns, "Why would I do that?"

"Your Nonna hates me. The last time she saw me, she slapped me."

"Only because you stuck a knife in me."

"Can't promise not to do that again," I mutter under my breath.

"What's that?"

I swear, it looks like he's repressing a smirk.

"Nothing." I clear my throat. "So, about the party—you'll let me invite Aurora to it?"

He grimaces. He bends and places Andy on the floor. The kitten walks toward the basket that has been made up for him in the corner of the room. He climbs in, turns around and begins to wash himself.

"Aww come on, Mika." I turn my gaze back on the glowering man, "It's Christmas! Isn't this when you forget the sins of your enemies and all that stuff?"

"I'll invite her, on one condition."

I scowl, "Thought this was my gig?"

He raises a shoulder, and I draw in a breath, "Fine, tell me your condition."

"You promise not to sulk in your room, and to eat well, and to get plenty of fresh air."

"If you think your fake concern for me is going to help you wheedle your way into my good books then..." I tilt my head, "you're going to have to try harder."

"So, you will eat well, get plenty of fresh air, take your vitamins and—"

"—yes, yes," I mutter, "I will."

"Promise?"

I throw up my hands, "I told you I will."

He prowls across the room to stand in front of me. Gosh, he is so big, his shoulders so massive, that he blocks out the sight of everything else. It's as if he's absorbed all of the oxygen in the room. I try to breathe and drag in his dark, edgy scent. The heat of his body curls around me, envelops me. The force of his dominance holds me immobile as he bends his knees and peers into my eyes. "There's one more thing I want."

"Wh…what?" I clear my throat, "What is it?"

Ask me to move back into your bedroom, ask me to throw myself down on my back on your bed, part my thighs and invite you to bury yourself inside me again. My core clenches. I tip up my chin, part my lips as he leans in close enough for his chest to brush mine. My nipples harden; my belly flip-flops. Those cold blue eyes of his flare with an inner fire as he drops his gaze to my mouth.

"Promise me you'll create your own Christmas dress?"

"What?"

He raises his gaze to mine, "I want you to start creating again, starting with the dress you'll wear to the Christmas party."

"That's what you wanted to ask me?"

He straightens, then kisses me on the cheek. His scent deepens, then fades as he takes a step back from me. "What else did you think?" he says, his voice so bloody innocent. Argh! I set my jaw and a low chuckle rumbles up his chest. "Wait... Surely, not..." he clicks his tongue and slowly shakes his head, "you didn't think I was going to fuck you, did you?"

Hearing him say that four letter word? OMG, it's so hot, so erotic. Not like he hasn't said that before. But considering I almost came just from hearing him do so... Hell... Is this a side-effect of pregnancy hormones? When I am not sick, I want to either eat or have sex. Is that how it's going to be from now on?

"Of course not," I sniff. "I thought no such thing."

"Good." He notches his knuckle under my chin, "Because I am not taking any chances with this pregnancy."

He turns to leave, and I call out, "Wait, what do you mean by that?"

"By what?"

"By not taking any chances with this pregnancy?"

He pauses at the door, "Just that." He turns to face me, "As long as you are pregnant, I don't plan on fucking you."

"Eh?" I open and shut my mouth, "Why the hell would you do that?"

"You need to rest and take care of yourself. Besides, I don't want to do anything to endanger the baby."

"You wouldn't be endangering the baby if you shagged me."

"Still, there's a chance that it would be uncomfortable for you."

"I am willing to take that risk," I cry.

He clicks his tongue, "It's noble of you to offer to do that, but I will not allow the mother of my child to be inconvenienced in any way."

I take in his determined stance, the set of his jaw, and blow out a breath, "Bloody hell, you're serious about this, aren't you?"

"Deadly."

I take in the set of his features, then scowl, "Wait, are you thinking of fucking someone else, maybe?"

"Do you think that I am going to fuck someone else?"

His blue gaze bores into me. I shuffle my feet, then glance away, "You tell me."

"Look at me, Beauty."

I hesitate.

"Now," he orders.

I find myself turning to face him. Dammit, what power does he hold over me that I can't disobey him.

He rakes his gaze across my face, then steps closer to me. He bends his knees, then peers into my eyes, "I am not going to fuck anyone else Karma, *caspice*?"

"Hmm," I twist my lips, "what about Larissa or that...that stewardess on the plane? You're not going to see them on the side, are you?"

His features harden, "I am not. Going to fuck. Anyone else. I take my vows to you very seriously. You understand?"

I nod.

"Say it aloud," he commands.

"I understand." I blow out a breath, "So, this means, you and I will continue to stay in separate rooms, until the baby is born?"

"Isn't that what you wanted?"

No.

No.

"Yes," I nod.

His features brighten, "Good." He curves his beautiful lips in a smile. "See? We are already getting along so well."

He straightens, turns to leave, then pauses once more. "One more thing, Beauty."

"Now what?"

"We may have arrived at a temporary truce, of sorts—doesn't mean I am not watching you."

33

Karma

If he's watching me, it's not because he has cameras in this room. I glance around the space again, taking in the light fixtures, the air vents, the shelves in the room—hell, even the corners of the ceilings, where a camera would have most likely be hidden—but can't see anything. Which is not to say that there can't be cameras in the mirror that is pushed up against one wall, or even embedded in a piece of furniture or something, but somehow, I doubt it. In the few days since Michael had made that statement, I had slept well, hadn't had the sensation of being watched in any way—not in my room, definitely not when I go walking in the large garden that surrounds the house, or even on the beach, for that matter.

A few hours after Michael had left, Cassandra had hauled in yards of different fabrics. Then Antonio had shown up carrying a sewing machine—a new one, by the looks of it—followed by a drafting table, and all of the other instruments I need for sewing.

The result is that half of my bedroom has been transformed into a studio, and honestly, I am not complaining about it. I had also asked Cassandra to fetch me additional supplies that I'll need for the creation I have in mind, and she had done it very happily. Andy is now a permanent fixture in my room and he keeps me company as I sew.

I've taken to having my meals with Cassandra in the kitchen, and while I have not seen Michael on any of those occasions, she has assured me that he is very much around, and working hard, both in his study as well as at meetings that he has had to attend out of the house. Something to do with a flare up of tensions with a rival clan. Which is none of my business, really.

I have less than two weeks to come up with a creation which will blow his socks off, and I intend to make the most of that time. I have also drawn up a guest list for the event, which is beginning to look like an evening party, which is good. It means there's no need to sit around a table and endure uncomfortable silences. No, for my Christmas party, which is going to be goth themed—surprise!—there are going to be lights and music...and a DJ. Yep, definitely need a DJ to get the crowd going.

I run into Michael briefly in the hallway and ask him who he wants to invite, and he says I can decide. When I tell him I want to get in a DJ, he flat out refuses, though. No strangers are to be allowed. Only close family i.e. his brothers, and yeah, unfortunately, that also includes extending an invitation to his father and his Nonna, I guess. So much for getting to decide who to invite.

I head back toward my room, grumbling under my breath. I don't want to. But clearly, the man is close to his grandmother... As for his father... Well, he is family...so it makes sense to have him. And his brothers...of course. Not that I have a problem with any of them. Speaking of, I wonder what's going on with Luca? Anyway, we'll invite Antonio, Cassandra, and Aurora, as well. Which still leaves the question of the DJ. Damn it! I reach my room and start slamming things around on my work table. "What's a party without a DJ?" I muse aloud.

"Someone mention a DJ?"

I jerk my head in the direction of the voice and find Xander, standing in the open doorway.

"Didn't realize I had mumbled that aloud." I redden.

"I heard you were organizing a Christmas bash and figured you could do with a hand." He ambles in. "Mind if I take a seat?" He nods toward the chair by the window, then before I can agree, he wanders over and sits down on it. Apparently, all of the Sovrano brothers are confident enough that no one will refuse them. Of course, whether that confidence is a result of respect or fear is another story. Oh, well.

He kicks out his long legs, clad in tailor-made slacks, no doubt, cut by the same family tailor who creates Michael's clothes. He taps his long fingers on his thigh, "So, you need a DJ for the party, huh?" Xander asks.

I nod.

"And I guess my brother did not want anyone from outside our immediate circle of family and friends at the party?"

"You know your brother well," I mutter as I place my scissors down by the cloth that I had been cutting earlier. I lean a hip against my work-table, "Do you have any ideas? I mean a party without a DJ is like a rose without thorns."

"Or the sixties without the Beatles," he smirks.

"Or *Apocalypse Now* without music by the Doors," I chuckle.

"Or like *Harry Potter* without Draco Malfoy," he offers.

"OMG!" I gasp, "Seriously though, sometimes I am sure I am more of a Dracohead than a Potterhead."

"You always fall for the bad boy, huh?"

I firm my lips, "You have no idea."

He raises his hands, "I didn't mean anything by that statement."

"I know you didn't," I murmur, then hunch my shoulders. "How are you in here anyway? I thought the Big Bad Capo had forbidden even his brothers from coming in here."

"Not me, though."

"Not you?"

"The rules don't apply to me." He grins and whoa, his charm hits me full whack, like the fireworks over the Thames on New Year's Eve. Jesus, these Sovrano brothers sure pack a punch. Each of them is deadly in his own right. Though Michael is, by far, the most dominant, the most mesmerizing of all of them.

"Is it because Michael doesn't consider you a threat?"

He blinks then chuckles, "You think fast, don't you?"

I raise a shoulder, "You're here, so yeah, it's not rocket science."

"Let's just say, Michael is aware that I'd never do anything to hurt him."

"You care for him deeply," I murmur.

"I'd give up my life for him."

"Oh," a ball of emotion sticks in my throat. "It's what I'd do for my sister Summer."

"She's older than you?"

I nod, "We only had each other growing up, so we learned to take care of each other."

"You miss her?"

I nod again.

"Have you called to let her know that you are here?"

I hesitate, then walk over to sit down in the chair opposite him. "I've been texting her regular updates, enough so she does not worry about me."

"But she's not aware that you are married."

"Or that I am pregnant."

I follow his gaze to my stomach and find I've placed my palm against my belly, as I seem to do so often nowadays.

"Why is that?" His voice is gentle and when I look up, the look in his eyes is even gentler.

A thickness clogs my throat and I swallow it away. "I just wasn't sure where to start, really." I wring my fingers together, "I am not sure she'll really understand what happened. More likely, she's liable to fly down here and demand that I return with her—"

"And you don't want to?"

"No," I say so softly that I can barely hear myself, but he catches it.

He leans forward and grips my shoulder. "You are not alone. We're your family now, and we are all here for you."

I sniffle.

"And Michael, regardless of his growly, grumpy nature... He does care for you, in his own way."

"That almost makes it worse." I sigh and lower my chin. "I think the two of us have grown to care for each other, yet we seem to not have a single conversation without getting angry with each other."

"Maybe it's how the two of you communicate, you know?"

"What, by sparring with words?"

"And with weapons." He waggles his eyebrows and I laugh.

"Yeah, I know, I can't believe I pulled a knife on him. Not to mention, you know—" I mime whacking someone on the forehead.

He winces, "That was quite an escape you made there, young lady."

"I ended up driving a wedge between Michael and Luca because of that, didn't I?"

"Luca did that all by himself, by betraying Mika."

I wince, "I played a role in it though. If I hadn't wanted to leave, Luca wouldn't have found the opportunity to do so."

"You just happened to be there. If it hadn't been you, it would have been something else. Luca was waiting to undermine Michael. It so happened that you came along first."

"Right." I blow out a breath, "Not sure if that makes me feel better at all."

"I know what will make you feel better."

"What?"

"Finding you a DJ."

"You know someone?"

He spreads his arms, "You're looking at one of the best DJs in Palermo."

"Which is not saying much, given the size of the city," I snicker.

"Hey," he thumps his chest, "you disparaging our fair city?"

"Not at all." I chuckle, "Besides, not like I have a choice."

"Jeez," he shakes his head, "you sure know how to trample all over a man's ego."

"I have been practicing." I tip up my chin, "Can you tell?"

"I can see why my brother likes to verbally spar with you."

"More like we can't stop fighting when we are in the same room."

"It's another way of showing how much you two care about each other."

"Oh, I am not sure about that."

"I am." He lowers his arms to his side, spears me with a look. "I have never seen Mika look at anyone the way he looks at you."

My heart begins to thud. My belly flip-flops. I push my hair over my shoulder, then pretend to study the pattern on the pile of fabric on the opposite side of the room. "You must be mistaken; it's really not like that."

He laughs, then throws back his head and laughs harder. "You can try to say otherwise, but you and I both know, you have Michael tied up in knots."

"Who's tied up in knots?"

I jerk my chin in the direction of the doorway.

34

Michael

She glances in my direction, and the expression on her face is laced with guilt. I prowl toward her and she tips up her chin. "Were you talking about me, Beauty?" I murmur and she huffs.

"My every conversation is not about you."

"What were you two talking about, then?"

"None of your business."

"Everything about you is my business," I pause in front of her, "and you'd do best not to forget that."

Xander clears his throat, and I shoot him a sideways glance.

"We were discussing the Christmas bash," he explains.

"Is that right?" I turn to her, "That what's got you tied up in knots, huh?"

"Exactly," she snickers, "*I* am the one tied up in knots." She exchanges a glance with Xander who chuckles.

"She's been worried about finding a DJ for the party. It's why I offered my services."

"You're going to DJ?" I scowl.

"Sure," he raises a shoulder, "it's no biggie. I did it at many of the parties during my university days."

"And here I thought you spent most of your time painting."

"Hey, we artists need to blow off some steam too, you know? Besides, music is a form of art, and DJing is simply a matter of arranging tunes into a pattern."

"Whoa, you a poet too?" she comments, her tone filled with admiration.

I scowl.

"I have been known to write a poem or two," Xander smirks.

I glower at him, "If you two have had enough of this mutual admiration society you've got going on here —"

Something brushes my leg. I glance down to find her kitten walking past me.

The beast heads over to Xander, who scoops him up. "Who do we have here? What's your name, little fella?" he croons as he tickles the kitten under his chin.

"His name's Andy," she replies with a big smile.

"Hello Andy, what a fine-looking kitty you are, too."

Andy purrs loudly, then rubs his head against the *stronzo*'s shirt. *Traitor.* Not only is my wife taken in with Xander, but her cat… The cat that *I* got for her seems to prefer his company to mine.

Good thing I trust Xander the most amongst all of my brothers; enough to not chew him out for spending time with her. Also, I can't exactly keep her hidden away forever, much as that would be my preference. If there is anyone other than me that I'd choose for her to spend time with, then it would be him.

So, I content myself with simply glaring at Xander, who smirks back at me.

"*Te ne devia fare in culo,*" I growl and he laughs. The bastard *laughs* as he rises to his feet. He pats the kitten once more, then hands Andy over to me. As he leaves, I pull the beast closer to me. The animal strains in my grasp, and glances over at her. It mewls pitifully, and I frown.

"Aww," she walks over to me and holds out her arms. The kitten promptly jumps onto her chest. She closes her arms about him, and he cuddles up against her breasts. I scowl at him, watch as he rubs his head up against the swell of her curves.

Only when her chin jerks up do I realize that I have growled aloud. *Porca miseria!* Apparently, I am jealous of a kitten?

I glare at the animal and she hugs him tighter to her chest. "Stop that," she orders, "you're scaring him."

"Scaring him, my ass! He's play-acting, just so he can get your sympathies."

"Play-acting?" She laughs, "Animals don't play-act. They are not like humans, who'll stoop to any level to get their way."

"Who are you talking about?"

"Who do you think?" she snaps

I fold my arms across my chest, "I have never play-acted."

"Haven't you?" She tosses her head, "You keep acting all tough and surly, but inside, you are as soft as…as that slushy thing which I had for breakfast.

"It's called a *granita*," I murmur, "and you must be mistaken. I don't play-act, and I am definitely not soft inside."

"Yes, you do, and yes, you are."

"Not." I harden my jaw

"Are." She juts out her chin.

And why can't I stop myself from rising to her bait, eh? I drag my fingers through my hair, "Look. Ever since I found out that you were pregnant… It's…ah… Confused me."

"Confused you?"

I nod, "When I think about your bringing my child into this world, it makes me feel like I am the most vulnerable person on this earth. What if my enemies got to either of you? If something were to happen to either of you, I'd… I don't think I'd be able to take it."

Her expression softens, "Nothing's going to happen to either of us."

"You're that confident, eh?"

"No, I am that confident that you will take care of us."

I stare into her features, that red-tinted hair that flows about her shoulders, those green eyes that sparkle at me, that tiny upturned nose, those beautiful pink lips that beg for me to lick them, thrust my tongue in between them and tangle with hers. The blood rushes to my groin and I am instantly hard. "You trust me to take care of you."

"I trust you." She holds my gaze, "I trust you to do what's right for the two of us. I trust that you'll never allow anything to harm us."

A hot sensation stabs at my chest. I close the distance between us, cup her cheek, "When you say things like that, it completely wrecks me, you know that?" I lower my face to hers, when there's an angry hiss from between us. Something sharp stabs at my chest… This time, for real. I wince, glance down to find the kitten has dug his claws into my shirt. He's grazed the same wound—now healed—that his mistress had bestowed on me not too long ago.

"Oh, sorry, Andy," she laughs. "Didn't mean to crush you there."

Wish I could say the same. I scowl down at the animal that glares back at me. Jesus, the cat has almost as much attitude as her. She reaches down, gently disentangles his claws from my shirt, then bends down to place him on the floor. He shakes his entire body, as if he's tossing off any residue of my touch, then struts off toward his basket in the corner of the room.

She straightens, then peers up at me from under her eyelashes. I hold her gaze and her cheeks pinken.

"Why are you looking at me like that?" she murmurs.

"Like what?"

She raises her shoulder, "Like you've never seen me before?"

"Maybe I haven't. Maybe I have underestimated you all along. Maybe, if I had known how you were going to turn my life upside down, I'd have run from you the first time I laid eyes on you."

She blinks, "Is that a compliment? Because I am not sure."

"It is," I push the hair off of her forehead, "a compliment. It takes a lot to surprise me, and I can safely say that you have done so at every turn, my Beauty."

"And you, my Capo," she goes up on her tip-toes and presses a kiss to the side of my neck, which is all she can reach, "constantly challenge me. You make me want to push myself to keep up with you. You make me want to reinvent myself so I can hold my own against you."

"Is that good or bad?"

"I am not sure," she says with a gleam in her eyes, then yelps when I pat her behind.

"What was that for?" She frowns.

"Couldn't help it. Your posterior is so beautifully rounded, that when I am near you, I have to squeeze it."

She reaches behind and grabs a hold of my butt, "Now we're even." She pouts, "Don't expect to cop a feel without—" She stutters as I grip her under her ass and hoist her up. She wraps her legs around my waist.

"Now we are even," I smirk.

She scowls, "That's not fair."

"Life's not fair, baby." I pivot, head for the door, and she peers up at me.

"Where are you taking me?"

"To dinner."

"Dinner, but—"

"Aren't you hungry?"

"It's not that. It's just..." She hesitates and I pause glance down at her.

"If we stay here, I am going to fuck you and that's not what I want."

"Why not?"

"I don't want to hurt you, not when you are in this condition."

"I am pregnant, not unwell."

"Exactly," I nod, "this early in the pregnancy, it's best to be safe."

"Is that what the doctor said?"

I hesitate and she huffs, "See? That's what I mean; I don't know where you got it into your head that just because I am pregnant, you can't make love to me."

"I'd rather wait until it's completely safe to do so."

"But the doctor never said any such thing."

"It's what I am saying."

"So, now you know better than the doctor?"

"Let's just say that when it comes to your well-being, I am taking no chances."

"This is ridiculous." She pouts. "I want you to fuck me and you are turning me down?"

"Oh, trust me. There's nothing I'd rather do more, but in this case, there's something more important than you and me at stake here."

She frowns, "You mean the baby?"

"Our baby." I nod, "I'd rather you feel better before I fuck you again."

She throws up her hands, "I've never heard anything crazier than that. I mean, are you hearing yourself? You're all worried for no reason."

"I'd rather be more careful than not."

She blows out a breath, "I am not changing your mind on this, am I?"

I shake my head.

"Fine, whatever," She folds her arms across her chest, stares straight ahead, as I head out of the door. I walk down the stairs and to the terrace on the first floor. I cross the breadth of it to a sheltered alcove and she draws in a breath, "What's this?"

35

Karma

"This is where we're having dinner," he murmurs as he lowers me into a chair. I take in the crisp white table cloth that covers a table that has been set with silverware for two. The alcove is sheltered from the breeze by a screen on one side. The view itself is undisturbed though, and I glance out at the sea that stretches out into the distance. A cool breeze tugs at my hair. I tuck the strands behind my ear, turn back to the table arrangement. There's a vase in the center of the table with one single perfectly formed black rose, the edges of the petals a blood red. It's a perfect bloom, unlike anything I have ever seen. He reaches for a blanket that has been placed on a stool by the side. He places it over my lap, then tucks it at the sides.

"How does that feel?"

"Good," I murmur.

"Not too cold? Not too warm?" He nods toward the patio heater, "Should I turn that off?"

"No," I pat the edge of the blanket, "I am comfortable, as is."

"Good." He reaches for a napkin, shakes it out, then places it on my lap over the blanket, before pushing my chair in, just so. Then he walks around to take his seat on the other side.

"What's all this about?"

"Can't I have dinner with my wife?"

"Hmm," I frown, "not that I don't appreciate it, but if you want to take me to dinner, why can't we go out?"

He tilts his head, and I scowl. "You don't want to take me out, is that it?"

He gazes at me steadily and I blow out a breath, "Since you found out I was pregnant you haven't let me out of the house. In fact, you've barely let me out of your sight, and it's really beginning to grate on my nerves."

He merely reaches for the jug of water and pours out a glass. "Drink," he orders, "you need to make sure that you are hydrated."

I open my mouth to refuse and he gives me a stern look. "Drink your water, baby," he winks at me, and bloody hell, when he calls me by that endearment, my heart seems to melt. I can't refuse him anything when he looks at me with that mix of dominance and lust and tenderness all entwined in the depths of those hypnotic blue eyes. I raise the glass of water, sip from it, and his gaze falls to my mouth. His pupils dilate and his nostrils flare. I lick my lips, scooping up a drop of water from the corner of my mouth, and his throat moves as he swallows. His chest rises and falls, he leans forward, reaches for me, when the sound of footsteps approaches.

Momentarily distracted, we look toward Cassandra, who makes her way over to us to place a basket of bread between us. "The chef will be along shortly with your main courses. Enjoy." She glances between us, then backs away without another word.

Steam rises from the bread. Whoa, have they been freshly baked? I mean, of course, they have to be freshly baked. Nothing but the best for Michael, after all. I reach for a roll, then gasp and pull back, "Ouch, it's too hot."

"Here, let me." He reaches for a roll, breaks off a piece. Steam rises from it as he offers me a bite-sized piece.

I glance at the piece of roll then back at him, "It may be too hot."

"It's not."

"What if it is?" I frown.

"And here I thought you trusted me, hmm?"

Well, he does have a point there. I open my mouth and he pops the piece of bread inside. I chew on it, and the strong, tangy, yeasty flavor of the freshly baked roll explodes on my palate. "Oh, yum!" I finish chewing, swallow the piece, then open my mouth again. He pops another piece of bread inside and I chew on that as well. "This is really good," I admit as I swallow it down as well.

He butters the remaining piece, offers it to me and I eat that too. The flavors only seem to multiply, thanks to the butter. "I have never tasted anything like it," I confess.

"The chef is the best in Europe," he confirms to me.

"It's not what's-her-name, Marissa, is it?"

"You mean Larissa?" He smirks.

I frown. "Don't flaunt your floozies in front of your wife," I snap.

He raises his hands. "*Scusa*," he murmurs, "*mi sono sbagliato*. I promise, I won't speak of her again."

"Or see her," I add, causing him to nod in agreement. *Wait a minute. What is he up to?* I stare, "You are being awfully conciliatory?"

"I admit my mistakes when I am wrong," he peers into my eyes, "but only for you, Beauty."

My stomach flip-flops; I clench my thighs. Gosh, can he be any hotter? Especially when he's being so nice to me? I push back my seat, rise to my feet, place my blanket and napkin on my chair, then walk around the table. His forehead quirks as I raise his arm then sink down in his lap.

His gaze heats as I twine my fingers with his, then reach up and brush his lips with mine. "This is nice, isn't it?" I murmur, and his breath catches. I press tiny kisses down the sharp edge of his jaw, to the hollow at the base of his throat. I lick the skin there and his hardness stabs into the side of my thigh. I bite down and a low growl ripples up his chest. He wraps his fingers around the back of my neck and tugs. I tip up my chin, stare into those blue eyes that blaze back at me.

He rakes his gaze down my features, to my lips, then back up to my eyes, "The answer, Beauty," he whispers, "is still no."

I scowl, "I didn't ask for anything."

"But you were going to."

"No, I wasn't."

One side of his lips curls, "Still lying to me, darlin'?"

I try to pull away, but he tightens his grip. Goosebumps pop on my skin, my pussy trembles, and moisture laces my core. Shit. Why is it that when he begins to get rough with me, my body responds with such ardor?

"Let go of me," I say in a low voice and his grin only widens.

"That's not the message you were conveying a few moments ago, Beauty." He brings his hand up to cup my breast, and a moan bleeds from my lips. His gaze sharpens. "Your breasts are more tender, more sensitive than they used to be," he murmurs as he brushes his thumb across my nipple. Heat races down my spine and I shift in his lap. His thickness seems to lengthen against my thigh as he leans in closer, closer...

He brushes his nose against my throat and inhales deeply, "You smell of moonflowers, with a hint of something deeper, more complex." He sniffs me again, then glances up at me, "You smell the same, and yet, different." He peers into my features, "Like you are changing, even while, at heart, you are the same girl you once were."

"Wow," I swallow, "you can sense all that?"

A crease appears between his eyebrows. "Only with you, apparently."

He leans in, nuzzles my cheek, "You smell like you are mine."

My stomach flutters and my toes curl. Oh, my God, if anyone could bring me to orgasm just by his words, it would be this man. I turn my face toward him and our lips meet and... It's unlike any of our previous kisses. It's soft and tender, with just a hint of that unleashed dominance that is so very Mika; and yet, he's holding back the full force of his personality, which thrums in the background. And that only turns me on further.

I lean into the kiss, but he tightens his grip on my neck and holds me in place. He proceeds to leisurely nibble on my mouth, lick my lips, brush his mouth over mine again and again, until our breaths mingle and our chests rise and fall in unison, until the evidence of his arousal seems to grow so solid between us that I am sure his shaft is going to stab through his pants. My core clenches and moisture trickles down the inside of my thigh. I grind my butt into his thickness and a groan vibrates up his chest.

"Fuck," he murmurs, "you are killing me, Beauty."

"You are doing it to yourself, Capo," I bite down on his lower lip and he visibly jerks.

He pulls away, stares into my features, "You're tempting me to break my self-imposed abstinence."

"Why don't you?" I scowl at him, "This entire no-sex thing is ridiculous."

"You're cute when you are angry," he chuckles.

I open my mouth to tell him off, only he's already there. He kisses me. I part my lips and he sweeps in, thank god! He sucks on my tongue, sips from me, consumes me, devours me like he is hungry and I am his last meal. My head spins and my toes curl; he pulls away from me and I slump.

I hear footsteps behind me but don't turn.

"You okay?" he murmurs as he tucks a strand of hair behind my ear in a gesture that is becoming familiar to me.

I hear the sound of plates being placed on the table and the spicy scent of food tickles my nose. I turn to find two steaming dishes placed on the table.

"*Come va, principessa*?" a familiar voice asks.

"Paolo!" I cry in delight. "What a pleasure to see you here."

"And you." His rosy cheeks widen in a big smile.

"What are you doing here?"

"I was asked to come and cook my favorite dishes for you," he nods his chin toward the plates.

"So, you left your restaurant and came over to cook dinner for us?"

He jerks his chin toward Michael, "What the Capo wants, the Capo gets."

Of course, he does.

I shoot a sideways glance at Michael. "There was no need to have Paolo shut down his restaurant and come here to cook for us. We could have gone to him."

"And you know my thoughts on that already." Michael tilts his head. His gaze clashes with mine and those blue eyes of his—damn! It's like they can see my deepest thoughts, suss out my innermost fears. Like they are aware that underneath all the protests, I am secretly flattered that he did this for me. My cheeks heat and his smirk widens. Gah, can I not even glance at him without getting turned on?

I flip my hair over my shoulder, turn to Paolo, "Well, I, for one, don't take your coming here for granted. I hope the Capo, at least, compensated you for the lost business."

He laughs, "He did, and even if he hadn't, I promise you, it would have been my honor and my pleasure to cook for the both of you. Someone in your state needs to eat well, signora, and I have made sure that my dish is perfectly balanced, with all the nutrients you and your growing child need.

"Oh," heat sears my cheeks. Guess I am still not used to the fact that I am pregnant, especially not when someone else mentions it to me.

"I told him; I hope you don't mind?" Mika whispers. "He's like family."

"It's fine, "I murmur, then turn to Paolo again. "Thank you for coming out to cook for us." I hold out my hand and he takes it, then kisses it on the knuckles, before stepping back.

He glances at the food, then at Michael, "You need to eat the food before it grows cold."

"Oh, we will." Michael gestures to the plates, "Could you place her plate in front of me before you leave? I plan to feed her."

Paolo moves the plate over so it's front of us, then he retreats.

I turn to protest and Michael shakes his head. "Indulge me, Beauty," he implores in a soft voice and my heart stutters. It bloody stutters.

This man... All he has to do is glance at me with tenderness and I'll throw myself down at his feet and be ready to do his every bidding. Oh, who am I kidding? When he orders me, it turns me on even more. But there's something about Mika being so attentive to my wishes which is simply…completely…arousing, and which also makes me giddy with happiness.

My heart begins to thud in my chest and my pulse rate ratchets up. OMG, the way he's looking at me… It's as if he loves me, and like he's beginning to realize it himself.

"Beauty, I…" he searches my features, then hesitates, "I…"

"What is it?" I whisper, "Tell me, Mika, what do you want to say?"

He seems to get a hold of himself, then reaches past me for the fork. He twirls some of the pasta, then offers it to me, "I think you need to eat."

"But—"

"Later," he murmurs, "let's enjoy our food first, hmm?"

I want to push it, but something in his gaze warns me that it's time to give in. I nod, allowing him to feed me. The pasta is a simple dish made with vegetables and a sauce that is absolutely flavorful. Mika insists on feeding me, and I tell him he needs to eat as well. We compromise when he agrees that I can feed him too.

When both of our plates are empty, I lean into him with a sigh.

"Now what?" I murmur.

"Cassandra," he calls out, "make sure that we are not disturbed."

Cassandra pops her head through the doorway. She nods, then shuts the door on us.

I turn to him, "What's that all about?"

"That," he smirks, "means it's time for dessert."

36
____

Karma

"Dessert?" I blink rapidly. "Is Paolo going to serve us dessert?"

"He offered to make dolce for us, but I told him to wait. We'll have it after."

"After?" My cheeks heat, "After what?"

"After..." He lifts me up onto the table, then pushes my legs apart. The dress I'm wearing is pushed up to above my knees. He slides his fingers up my thighs, and I try to squeeze them together.

"Relax," he murmurs, "I am going to make this so good for you."

That's what I am afraid of.

I peer at him from between my eyelashes. "I thought you weren't going to shag me?"

"Doesn't mean I can't pleasure you," his eyes gleam, "while I feast on you."

A pulse flares to life between my legs. It mirrors the beat of my heart, the thud-thud-thud of the blood roaring in my ears as he rises to his feet. Without taking his gaze off of mine, he leans over and shoves the rest of the crockery aside. The dishes and remaining cutlery hit the ground with a crash that sweeps through me. I shudder, partly from lust, partly from the adrenaline that sweeps through me. Jesus, is that hot or what? And so damn erotic.

He eases me onto my back, then peers into my eyes as he slides his hand up my thigh. When he reaches my panties, he brushes my core through the drenched fabric and flickers of heat ladder up my spine. Oh, my god, he is going to torture me with his touch, his kisses, the way he cups my pussy as he brushes his lips over mine.

"Who does this belong to?" he whispers against my mouth. "Tell me, Beauty, who do you spread your legs for?"

"You, Capo," I murmur and he draws in a breath. He hooks his fingers in the delicate lace of the panties and tugs. The material snaps. Goosebumps pop on my skin. I gasp as cool air assails my heated core. He pulls off my panties, pockets them, then places his fingers on the pulse that gallops at the base of my throat.

"You're turned on, *amore mio*," he says in a low voice. "You like it when I surprise you like this?"

I nod, not trusting myself to speak. My ability to formulate sentences flees as he pulls his knife from where he carries it tucked into the waistband at the small of his back. He holds it up. The blade gleams and I gulp. He slides it under the the neckline of my dress. I gulp. He tugs, the fabric tears down the center and I yelp.

The front falls open, exposing me to him. He sticks the blade of the knife into the wood of the table, then cups my breast. "Who does this belong to, *amore mio?*" he asks. "Tell me."

"You, Michael," I whisper. "It belongs to you."

He brushes his finger across my nipple, and my breast trembles. He brings his mouth down, sucks on my nipple, and a groan spills from my lips. I writhe under him as he curls his tongue around the pebbled bud, as he brings his other hand up to cup my other breast, as he bites down on the nipple gently, and oh, with so much care that my entire body seems to catch fire. I push my breast up and into his mouth. "Please, suck harder," I beg. "Please, Michael, please."

"I don't want to hurt you," he murmurs. "Your breasts feel heavier and your nipples are swollen. I want to make sure you enjoy this as much as possible."

"Oh." I blink as he tugs on my nipple, then blows on it. I shiver, arch my spine, chasing the suction I so crave, even as he drags his finger across my other nipple. I moan as he turns his attention to my other breast. He bites gently on the nipple, then lathes it with his tongue, before blowing on it. And my breasts are so tender that even that slight breeze sends ripples of sensations crawling down my spine. My core clenches and my toes curl as I raise my arms and throw them about his shoulders as he kisses his way down to my stomach.

He presses his lips to my belly as he grips my hips, then glances up at me, "Who does the child you carry in your womb belong to, *Tesoro Mio*?" He curls his tongue inside my belly button and I groan. "Tell me."

"You, Mi-kah," I gasp, "the child belongs to you."

He rewards me with a kiss, as he cups my swollen pussy. "Who does your cunt belong to, *Contessa*?" He whispers against my throbbing flesh, "Tell me."

"You, Mika." I push my hips forward, aching to feel him inside of me. "It belongs to you, only you."

He slips his finger inside my aching channel and I groan.

"More," I pant, "please, I want more."

I sense him smirk as he adds a second finger, then begins to work his fingers in and out of me, gently, oh so gently.

"Oh, my god," I moan. "Mika, please, fuck me with your tongue, please."

He pulls out his fingers, only to replace them with his tongue.

I writhe as he slurps his way up my pussy lips, and again, before he swirls his wicked tongue around my clit. And that's when I cry out. I dig my fingers into his hair and tug as he gently bites down on the engorged bud.

"Mika!" I yell as he grips my legs above the knees, wraps my legs about his neck. I lock my ankles, press my thighs into either side of his head and he laughs. The vibrations coil in my core, setting off a surge of heat that zings up my spine as I arch my back up and off the table.

"Ohgod, ohgod," I chant, "ohgod, please, Mika, please—" I scream as he thrusts his tongue inside my channel. In and out, he fucks me with his tongue just as I asked. He squeezes my butt, then slides a finger inside my backhole, working it in and out of me before adding another as he continues to plunge his tongue in and out of my pussy.

The vibrations scream out from my core, spreading to my extremities as my entire body bucks.

"Mika, I am going to—"

He pulls his tongue out of me, only to replace it with the fingers of his other hand as he leans over me and presses his lips to mine. "Come for me my Beauty, come right fucking now—" he growls and I shatter.

He closes his mouth over mine as he fucks my pussy and my ass with his fingers.

I scream but he swallows the sound. The climax pours over me, then fades away, leaving me shaking as I collapse against the table. The thud-thud-thud of his heartbeat against mine is reassuring, the heat of his body that envelops me is a beautiful reminder that I belong to him. I open my eyes, gazing into those blue eyes, as he licks my mouth. The sweet taste of my cum mixed with the darker taste of him fills my mouth as he holds my gaze.

"Mika," I bring my hand up and drag my fingers across his lips, "will you fuck me in the arse?"

"Eh?" He blinks, "Excuse me?"

"You told me you are not comfortable shagging me because you think it might hurt me or the baby." I raise a shoulder. "I figure this way you can shag me without worrying about any of that."

"You don't have to do that." He scowls, "I can go without sex for a little while, you know."

"I want to."

"You don't need to do this, Karma." His frown deepens, "I want you to be comfortable, and relaxed."

"And I can't be either of those when I am horny as hell."

"Woman, you just came." He arches an eyebrow, "Are you telling me that wasn't enough?"

"It wasn't enough."

"And you want me to take your ass because—"

"Because," I swallow, "I want you to own me completely, I want you to imprint your mark in every part of me, I want you to…possess me so absolutely that I can't think of anyone else but you."

Michael

This woman... The things she says... She never ceases to surprise me. I grip her shoulders to pull her up and she wraps her arms around my neck. "I mean it, Mika," she murmurs, "I want you inside me, one way or the other."

"I don't want to hurt you." I wrap a strand of her gorgeous hair around my fingers, "Right now, your comfort is more important than anything else to me."

"And I already told you that I want you."

I peer into her face, take in her flushed features, her gaze wide with anticipation; those green eyes stare back at me and in them is a look of feverish need. I wrap my fingers about the back of her nape and bring her forehead to mine, "Any other time, if you weren't pregnant, I'd not deny this to you, but right now, given your condition, it's not something I can give you."

"Michael," she pleads, "this is no time for an attack of conscience."

I laugh, "Trust me, if it were up to me, I'd be inside you so often you wouldn't be able to walk straight, but this is not just about you and me now, is it?"

She scowls.

"Think about the baby."

"I'd rather think about..." she places a hand on my crotch and squeezes her fingers around my already engorged cock, "this."

My groin hardens. I huff out a breath as she drags her fingers down my thick column. *Gesü Cristo*," I growl, "what are you doing to me, woman?"

"You said that you won't fuck me, but there's no rule against my going down on you, is there?" She pushes at my shoulders and I resist.

"Come on, Mika," she pleads. "Don't deny me this. At least, let me get off on getting you off."

I stare into her eyes.

"Please," she licks her lips, "please, Mika." She shoves at my shoulder and I sit back. She presses down and I sink back into my chair. She slides off the table and onto her feet and her already torn dress flutters down her arms. She shrugs it off, then slides down to her knees. She runs her hand up my thigh and my focus zeroes in on her. She holds my gaze as she outlines the length of my arousal. She rubs her fingers up and down the column and my balls harden. I part my thighs wider and she moves in closer. She brushes her fingers across my waistband and her fingertips graze my belly. My muscles jump, I roll my shoulders as I lower my chin.

"Take it out," I growl and a smile curves her lips.

"Oh, no, if we do this, we do it my way."

Che cazzo! How dare she try to direct the proceedings? "Is that right?" I reach down, curl my fingers around the nape of her neck. The column of her throat is so slender that my fingers meet around the front. "It doesn't work that way, Beauty."

She peers up at me from under half-closed lids, "Would you deny me this, Mika?"

I draw in a breath. Damn it. When she gazes at me with that beseeching look in her eyes, how can I deny her anything? I release my hold, lower my hand to my side.

Her smile widens as she unhooks my belt buckle. She lowers my zipper, then pulls down my boxers, and my cock springs free.

"Oh," she blinks, as she lowers her gaze to my throbbing shaft. She licks her lips and I swear I could come right then. She squeezes my shaft all the way up to the crown, then drags her fingers across the tip. Goosebumps pop on my skin.

Goddamn! "Your touch is killing me, Beauty," I growl and her smile widens. She lowers her head, licks the head of my shaft. Her pink tongue curls around the rim of the crown and the sight of it has my muscles tensing. I lean forward and she brings her hand up to cup my balls. She squeezes and a groan rumbles up my chest. She drags her other hand down to the base of my shaft, then up again.

"Oh, fuck," I swear as I curl my fingers into fists at my side. I glare down as she licks the tip of my cock again. I jerk my hips forward, chasing the suction I crave, and her eyes gleam. She massages my balls and I dig my heels into the ground. She licks her tongue down the length of my shaft and up again, and fuck if I don't almost come right then. "If you don't take me down your throat this instant, I'm going to—"

She closes her lips around the head of my cock. I grit my teeth as I watch my dick disappear inside her mouth. Fucking hell, if that isn't the ultimate description of erotic, I am not sure what is.

She peers up at me, holding my gaze as she pulls back, leaving a trail of wetness on my shaft. Only to dip her head and move forward, and this time, she does take me down her throat.

"F-u-c-k." I grab hold of the armrests as she proceeds to swallow. My groin tightens, my balls swell, and the tension at the base of my spine curls into a ball. She pulls back until my dick is poised at the edge of her lips, then she closes her mouth around me again. Heat flushes my skin as she drags her teeth across the underside of my shaft. My muscles tense and the ball of tension at the base of my spine explodes out. "By the *Santa Maria,*" I snap, "I am going to come all over your face, Beauty."

I pull out and grab my dick and position it as the climax grips me. The heat vibrates out, my cock jerks and I come, shooting a stream. I paint her face, her hair, position my cock to eject across her creamy breasts. By the time I am done, streaks of white crisscross her hair, her features, curve across her nipples.

I shove my fingers through her hair, grip the nape of her neck, haul her up, and fasten my lips on hers. I swipe my tongue across her teeth, tangle my tongue with hers as I grab her hip with my other hand. I squeeze and she moans into my mouth. And fuck, if that doesn't send the blood emptying to my groin again.

I reach between her legs and the wetness welcomes me. I slide my fingers inside her melting pussy, as I kiss her and finger fuck her, and she trembles, and writhes under me, but I don't stop. I shove four fingers inside her and she gasps. I continue to kiss her as I move my fingers in and out of her, in and out. I press my thumb into her clit and her entire body bucks. She grips my shoulders, holding on as I continue to finger fuck her. I tilt my mouth, suck on her tongue, bend her back as I curl my fingers inside her. Her body jolts and a trembling grips her. A moan bleeds from her and I swallow it down. Her body shudders, her pussy clamps down on my finger and I know she is going to— I tear my mouth from hers. "Come," I order, and she shatters.

38

Karma

We didn't get to the dessert, after all.

After I came, he'd taken off his shirt and made me wear it over my torn dress. Then he'd scooped me up into his arms and carried me to his bedroom. We hadn't encountered anyone on the way. Not Cassandra, not Paolo. Apparently, his staff knows when to make themselves scarce. And, yep, he broke his own rule for us to have separate bedrooms. Score!

I had fallen asleep promptly. When I woke up, he was gone. I had spent the rest of that day working on my dress, with Andy for company. Oh, also I'd moved my things into his room, and he hadn't said anything.

It might be because I didn't see Michael all that day, or for that matter, on any of the days that followed our reconciliation. Cassandra mentioned to me that he has been deep in negotiations with rival clans to restore some semblance of peace in the country.

This means that the security around the house has been tripled… Or so she tells me. Not that I can tell the difference. For all practical purposes, I am still a prisoner of sorts in the house.

At least, I have the preparations for the upcoming party to keep me distracted. At some point though, I know I have to pick up the phone and call Summer. At some point, she is not going to be happy with just the text messages that I send her.

She has promptly replied to all of them, and by all indications, she seems deliriously happy in her marriage to Sinclair Sterling... So that lessens the guilt somewhat.

Still, I suppose I'll have to tell her the truth of my condition at some point. Just not yet. Maybe after the party...? Maybe once I've gotten to know my husband a little better? Okay, so they are excuses, but once the party is over, I'll have time to think and decide what I want to tell her, you know?

I sit back, taking in the creation I have been working on, then stretch. Just one more week to go. It will be touch-and-go, but hopefully, I'll be able to complete it.

The morning sickness has abated somewhat, and I am finally getting my taste back. So, I can actually taste what I am eating, which is a relief. There's a knock on the door, and I turn to find a familiar figure at the entrance.

"Oh, my gosh!" I jump up, "Aurora, is that really you? How did you get here? Are you okay?"

She nods, then smiles uncertainly, "Can I come in?"

"Of course," I admonish her, "you don't need to ask me that."

She walks over to me, her doctor's satchel in her hand. I meet her half way, hug her, and she feels thinner, frailer than before. I step back, take in her pale features.

"You've lost weight," I murmur. "What did they do to you? They didn't mistreat you or anything, did they?"

She shakes her head. "They didn't do anything to me. Actually, that's the problem."

"Huh?" I step back, "What do you mean? I was so worried about you. When I realized that Michael knew about your part in helping me escape, I was so worried. I know it's not something that he would forgive easily, and he refused to tell me what had happened to you." I peer into her features, "You are okay, aren't you?"

She nods, a ghost of a smile on her lips, "Physically I am okay." She swallows, "But emotionally, mentally... I... I am in a kind of limbo."

"Tell me everything." I lead her to a chair and she sits down, places her bag on the floor.

"They have me put up in a safe house, not far from the city. I can't leave, can't see anyone else. This is the first time I have been out since I went to the Capo and told him that you were pregnant."

I lean back in my seat. "What I don't understand is why you didn't tell me."

"I wasn't sure how you would react. And," she glances away, "I didn't want you to do anything rash and hurt yourself or anything, you know?"

"As if." I huff, "I have more sense than that."

"Well, you were in an emotionally vulnerable state, and I guess, I wanted to protect you."

"So, Michael was telling the truth," I murmur.

She jolts and I explain, "That's what he told me, as well." I frown, "Which still doesn't answer the question of what you are doing here."

"I was told that I am going to be your doctor until the birth of the child."

"You are?" I murmur. Apparently, Mika agreed to my demand, after all. I lean forward, taking her hand in mine, "I am so pleased about that."

"So am I." She smiles, and this time, her eyes light up with genuine pleasure. "And not only because it means I'll be allowed out of the house, but because I do actually like you."

I laugh, "I like you too." I rub her slightly chilled hand between mine, "When was the last time you ate? Why don't I get you something? I—"

There's a knock and Cassandra shoulders open the door. In her hands, she carries a tray piled with plates of food. "I thought the two of you could do with some refreshments.

"You're a mind reader," I exclaim, "and the food is most welcome."

She walks in, places the tray on the table, then removes the covers. Delicious smells fill the room and my stomach growls. She steps back, "Enjoy." She smiles and turns to leave.

"Cassandra," I call out, "why don't you join us?"

She turns and glances between us, "Oh, no, I couldn't."

"Oh, please," I wave a hand in the air, "there's no one else in the house—"

"Except Christian," Aurora corrects me.

"Christian?"

Aurora nods, "He picked me up and dropped me off at the door. He'll wait for me to finish and accompany me back."

"Wow, so they really are making sure that you don't escape."

"I have no intention of even trying," she mutters. "If I did, the Capo would not spare my family."

I bite the insides of my cheeks. She's talking about Michael, my Capo. The father of my child… The man who has pleasured my body and brought me to orgasm countless times. The man who is so concerned about the wellbeing of my child that he refuses to have sex with me. The man who puts my needs before his. The same man who, I know, is also capable of killing if the need arises.

Yeah, Michael wouldn't spare her family. He won't take betrayal of any kind lying down. That, I know, first-hand. I blow out a breath. "Well, I am glad he allowed you to come see me."

Aurora glances at the food and her stomach rumbles loudly.

I chuckle.

She laughs, "Oops, sorry. Not that they are not feeding me. Actually, I've been quite comfortable where I am, except for the fact that I can't leave the place or see anyone."

"I know how that feels," I murmur as I reach for a plate and offer it to her. "Please, help yourself." I turn to Cassandra, who's still standing, "You are joining us, aren't you?"

"Um," she shuffles her feet, "I—"

"Please," Aurora glances up at her, "it will be so nice to listen to the voices of others instead of those in my head."

Cassandra laughs at that. "Fine, but just until lunch is over."

"And then, I still have to examine you." Aurora looks me up and down, "Not that you don't look good. In fact, you are positively glowing, but I need to make sure that you are completely okay."

"There'll be time after we eat."

Just then, Andy slips through the half open door and patters over to me, purring loudly. He brushes his body against my leg and I laugh, "You just ate, and this food isn't good for cats, I promise."

He tosses his head, and walks away toward his bed.

"The life of a cat," Aurora muses. "If only we could all be as single-minded about our needs."

"Speaking of," I turn to the food, "I know what I am going to be single-minded about for the next little while." I reach for a plate and pile mine high with helpings of *Arancini* (creamy risotto rice), *Caponata* (fried eggplant filled with celery, onion and tomatoes, and flavored with capers, pine nuts and raisins), and *Busiate al pesto Trapanese* (a fusilli-like pasta with pesto). I reach for another pasta dish and pause, "What's this?"

"Pasta a la *Norma*," Cassandra explains. "It's one of Sicily's most famous pasta dishes. It's made with local tomatoes, eggplants, garlic, basil and *ricotta salata*, or salted ricotta cheese. It's called *Norma* after the nineteenth century opera of the same name. Both the dish and the music are regarded as true masterpieces."

"You really like to cook, don't you?" I observe.

She laughs as she places minuscule portions of the food on her plate, "It's the one thing that I can rely on. Food. It can't hurt you or break a promise to you…" Her words trail off. She blinks rapidly, then smiles a little too brightly, "I love cooking, and I love feeding people. It fills something inside of me to see them enjoy what I make. After all, we are what we eat, right?"

"Right," I murmur, exchanging glances with Aurora, who shakes her head. Yeah, she's right. This is not the time to delve into those cryptic comments. "So," I train my gaze on her, "did you always know that you wanted to become a doctor?"

Aurora tilts her head, "Actually, yes."

"You did?" Cassandra's gaze widens, "Like when? I mean, how did you know that was your calling?"

Aurora glances down at her plate, then at us, "My mother was sick a lot when I was growing up. I accompanied her on her hospital visits, saw how the doctors helped her. In the end, they couldn't save her, but I knew then, one day I was going to do my best to help other people too."

"I am so sorry for your loss," I reach for her hand and squeeze it, "I lost my mother when I was very young too."

"I lost a husband," Cassandra murmurs, then bites her lips. She turns back to the food and I glance at her shuttered face. Yeah, there is a lot of grief hidden under there, all right.

"Do you want to talk about it?" I venture, and she shakes her head.

"What about you?" she asks, "Fashion designing is obviously your passion."

"Yes, it is," I nod. "I became a fashion designer because it feels like a link to my mother."

"Was she a designer too?" Aurora asks.

"Not professionally, but from what my sister tells me, she loved experimenting with colors and patterns and styles. She stitched all of her own clothes, and my sister's clothes. I never really knew her, but when I'm creating a design, when I am lost in the palettes and textures and immersed in images of what the finished product is going to look like, that's when I am truly happy. That's when I feel closest to her."

"You miss her?" Cassandra's voice is soft.

"I never knew her," I glance down at my food, "but there was always a mom-shaped hole in my life; always will be."

"The pain never goes away." Aurora draws in a breath, "It just becomes a shadow that settles in your heart, one which you are not really conscious of, but which is always there when you look inside."

"And how does it feel now that you are going to become a mother, yourself?" Cassandra tilts her head at me, "Does it fill the hole in your heart somewhat?"

I start, shoot her a glance, but see only genuine curiosity on her features. Her choice of words though... It reminds me of the one secret that I am keeping from all of them...including myself. A secret which I hope I never have to acknowledge. Maybe if I ignore it long enough, it'll stop being real. At least, I can hope.

"You okay?" Aurora puts down her plate of food, then reaches over to take my hand, "Maybe we should carry out that examination now?"

"Let's finish our food first." I nod at her plate, "Please, I am completely okay, and I really want us to do justice to this tasty food that Cassandra has made for us."

"Speaking of," I frown, "it is you who cooked this food, right?"

She shoots me a curious glance, "Who else would cook?"

"Not that Larissa woman, who I met on the island, and who Michael introduced as his chef, I hope."

"He let go of her, shortly after," she replies.

"He did?" I blink.

"Yep, told her to pack her bags and leave the very next day."

"Oh, wow!" Another thing he'd done... For me? Because he knew I couldn't stand the sight of her? I bite the inside of my cheek. Had I judged him that harshly? And this was even before I had become pregnant... Had he actually already begun to develop feelings for me then? I shake my head. Either way, it's clear that he wants to make up for how things started between us. It's why he's allowed Aurora to resume her duties as my doctor. Something for which I am very grateful. Something which I hadn't thought he'd do in a million years. He actually compromised on some of his beliefs for this… And that is huge. And I want to show him how much I appreciate it, in my own way. I turn to the both of them, "You are both coming to my Christmas party, obviously."

"We are?" Aurora frowns.

"We are?" Cassandra gapes.

"Of course, you are," I tell Aurora. "And you," I scowl at Cassandra, "you'd better be there, no excuses.

39

Michael

"I hear your wife's throwing a Christmas party?" JJ Kane, the head of *The Kane Company*, tilts his head, "That's the thing with women. They have to make their presence felt, don't they?"

I curl my fingers into fists at my sides. How dare he talk about her? And how the hell does he know about the Christmas Party? Invitations had only been extended to my brothers, my father and my Nonna. And yeah, Beauty had insisted that Cassandra and Aurora be included.

Initially, I had refused her and she had pleaded with me. She had batted those big, green eyes at me and I had been a goner. Of course, I had agreed. Cassandra is loyal, no question. And Aurora? She knows better than to open her mouth about anything she sees and hears. There's no way either of them would have spoken to anyone about the event. My brothers wouldn't have breathed a word to anyone... Nor would Nonna. As for the Don... Well, much as I don't trust him, given he knows that Karma is pregnant with his grandchild, not even he would endanger her life...

I hadn't wanted to invite him but Nonna had insisted. He's family. And family sticks together. We look out for each other, no matter what.

Within the four walls of our home, we may turn on each other... Like my father had on my mother. Nonna's reasoning is flawed, and yet, it makes sense. It helps us put up a unified front against our enemies. Like the Kane Company, the leader of whom graces my dinner table. I had invited him and Nikolai Solonik, the head of the Bratva for a three-way talk.

If you had asked me a few weeks ago if I'd ever think of negotiating a truce with my rival clans I'd have laughed. Yet that's exactly what I am doing. That's what having a baby on the way does to you, apparently. You have to try to make the world he or she is arriving into a better place. It's the least you can do, really. If I manage to take away any possible motives for my most dangerous enemies to come after my family, I reason, I am, at least, buying us some peace...some level of safety, during which time I can devote myself to being a husband and father, spend time with my wife and child, and bond with my new family as we find ourselves?

Besides, if, indeed, it was JJ who was behind her kidnapping, that's all the more reason to keep him close, until I find a way to kill him... Without drawing attention to myself. I'd sworn to hunt down whoever was behind the kidnapping and kill him... But the fact that I am going to be a father has put things in perspective. Don't get me wrong; I still want my revenge. Only, I want it in a way that it doesn't leave my child without a father.

"Michael?" JJ's voice interrupts my thoughts, "are you inviting us to this Christmas party too?"

"It's family only," I train my gaze on him. Besides, I don't trust the guy. The only reason I have him here is because it's easier to keep an eye on him when I know what he's up to. It's why I am proposing an alliance with JJ and Nikolai... On the face of it, at least, it's a business deal, but really, it's so I can understand JJ's...and Nikolai's weaknesses. The only way a man survives in my cutthroat world is to keep one step ahead of his rivals.

"And here I thought you consider us to be as close as your blood relations?" Nikolai drawls. "Not that I'd want to be there. It's bad enough that I have to spend Christmas with my entire extended family, of which there are way too many people."

I turn to him, accepting the diversion in the conversation. I owe Nikolai for getting the bastard JJ's attention away from the topic of the Christmas party. *My wife's* Christmas party. If he thinks I am going to invite him to be anywhere within a mile of her, he has another think coming.

"Are you returning to Russia for Christmas?" I ask Nikolai.

"I'm going home," he nods.

"To Russia?"

"To Los Angeles," He scowls at me.

I raise my hands. "Apologies, when you said home, I just assumed—"

"Yeah," he snorts, "of course, the man with the foreign sounding surname has to be from an exotic land, eh?"

I redden. "An honest mistake," I murmur.

"You can make up for it by giving me control of the gun smuggling routes through Latin America."

"No chance," I smirk. "I am sorry, but not that sorry."

"What about the cybercrime syndicate you control?" JJ growls. "That's something we are—"

"Nope."

JJ frowns, "So, what's in it for me? Why should I agree to any kind of peace treaty?"

"Because it's the only way for you to grow your reach in the rest of Europe. I am the key to your expanding outside the UK, and you know it."

JJ's features harden, but he doesn't deny what I said outright. He can't, because I have pointed out his weakness. The reason that has brought him here to the negotiating table, in the back office of Paolo's restaurant. We, each of us, have left our men and teams behind. It's just the three of us at this table, and the talks so far have been interesting, to say the least.

"So," JJ leans back in his chair, "I repeat, what's in it for me?"

"Money, power—"

"What are you specifically offering me, Michael?"

I raise an eyebrow at his usage of my name. He's testing me by not using my title, calling me by my name and implying a familiarity which we don't share currently, nor at any point in the future, if I have my way.

"Real estate scams."

"Excuse me?" He blinks.

"Real estate," I murmur, "it's where there's lot of money to be made in Europe."

"You're kidding me, right?" He leans forward, his hard British accent growing more pronounced, "If this is why you called me all the way to a back office behind a smelly restaurant then—"

"Cryptocurrency," I throw out and he blinks again.

"Cryptocurrency?" he says slowly.

I nod, "The two of you…" I glance between the two clan leaders. "Partner with us in the deals we have going there. Nikolai, you bring the cyber experience. We bring the contacts of those at the highest echelons in the top 100 investment firms in Europe. JJ, you bring the contacts of those in the UK and together, we'll all be able to walk away much, much richer."

"Hmm," JJ strokes his chin, "how much richer?"

"Molto più ricco."

He frowns, "I'd prefer you be specific."

"Take a number, triple it, and I guarantee, the three of us will come into enough money to increase our sphere of influence on a global scale."

JJ's eyes gleam. His right eyelid twitches. He taps his fingers on the table, before he stops… And bingo, the guy is interested, all right. I turn to watch Nikolai surveying me with a shrewd look in his eyes.

"It's going to be a challenge," Niko murmurs. "No one knows exactly how cryptocurrency reacts to worldwide influences. Hell, we know far less about it than we know about the weather or the stock market. It's a big risk."

"The higher the risk…" I raise a shoulder.

"You getting cold feet, Solonik?" JJ smirks, "You can opt out of the deal. More for the two of us."

Nikolai's gaze narrows. He tilts his head, a question in his eyes, one he's not going to voice because he's not going to give away his hand. He's smart. I respect that. And he abides by the same kinds of laws that we do. Family first and last, and above all, keep your enemies close at hand. It's why he's sitting here at the negotiating table.

"Perhaps it's you who's getting cold feet at the thought of keeping pace with the both of us?" Niko murmurs.

JJ's features harden and a nerve throbs at his temple. "That's enough of pleasantries," he growls, then turns to me. "The money we make is split three ways."

"Sixty, twenty, twenty, is more what I had in mind—"

He opens his mouth to protest.

"But I can work with fifty, twenty-five, twenty-five," I add.

"Split three ways evenly," JJ snaps "and not a penny less."

"You think the same way, Nikolai?" I turn to him, "A three-way split, I presume."

Nikolai drums his fingers on his chest, "You know what they say about three being a crowd."

"Are you saying you are not interested?"

"I am..." he glances from me to JJ, then back at me, "interested."

"Well then," I knock my knuckles on the table, "gentlemen, let's drink to our new business partnership, shall we?"

The door opens and a woman walks in with a bottle of Macallans whiskey and three glasses. She retreats, but not before JJ has looked her up and down. "Part of your crew?" he asks, "Is she—"

"No," I pour out a shot of whiskey into each of the glasses before sliding one over to Nikolai. "She's part of my clan and off limits to anyone except her fiancé."

"Take care of your own, eh?"

I raise my glass, "Always."

JJ glances down, spies the glass still on the tray. He leans over and picks it up. "Now, that's not being very polite," he arches an eyebrow, "but to each their own." He raises his glass.

"I don't like this," Christian mutters.

After the two other men leave, the rest of my crew walks in. They hadn't been in favor of this meeting. Definitely not that I go in unarmed and without any of them as back up. But it was something that had to be done, and by me.

"What guarantee do we have that they don't renege on their agreement?" He scowls.

"What guarantee do we have that we are all going to be alive tomorrow?" I widen my stance from the position at the head of the table. I had opted to stand, too keyed-up from the earlier meeting. Normally, I wouldn't tolerate this kind of post-meeting analysis of my actions, but if the alliance with the rival clans is going to work, then I need my crew behind me... And currently, they, clearly, are not.

"That's a rhetorical question, and you know that." Christian runs a finger around the collar of his shirt. "Forming an alliance with the enemy is only going to come to bite you in the ass if we're not careful."

"Much as it pains me to admit it, in this instance, I agree with Christian." Seb glowers. "Nikolai, maybe, I understand. Not that I'd trust the

Bratva, but at least, they'd come at you from the front. With the Kane Company? Those asshole Brits are going to stab you in the back, make no mistake."

I roll my shoulders, glare at the faces around the table.

"You know I don't give a toss about your alliances," Massimo murmurs, "but in this case, I have to admit, I don't quite understand the reasoning behind this move. It reeks of desperation, Michael." He leans forward in his chair, "And that's not like you. You always plan each and every move. You strategize for months, sometimes years, before you decide to act. This time, you're just jumping in, without any due diligence." He drums his fingers on the table, "It's not like you, Michael."

"You're right," Xander drawls from where he's sprawled out in a chair in a far corner of the room.

"I am?" Massimo turns to him. "So, you agree that this is Michael acting out of character?"

"It is." He rises to his feet and prowls over to us. "This is not the Michael we know anymore."

I glare at Xander as he comes to a halt at the table.

"It's not?" Christian stares at his twin, "What the hell are you talking about?"

Seb curls his fingers into a fist, "Do you know something you haven't shared with us yet?"

"Maybe."

"This is not the time for one of your artistic jokes," Seb growls. "Not that I could ever understand them, but if you have to say something, then now is the time."

"Back off, Seb," Adrian says mildly. "Have you ever known Michael to do anything that could jeopardize our future?"

"I am afraid this time he has," Xander comes to a halt at the table.

I draw in a sharp breath, glance at him. "What are you trying to say, Alessandro?" I say in a soft voice.

"Just that you are no longer Michael, the Capo of the Cosa Nostra."

"I'm not?" I frown.

He nods, "You are a husband and a father-to-be, too... Roles which you, clearly, place a lot more importance on than just being the leader of our clan."

I blink, "If you mean I am neglecting my duties as the head of the clan—"

"I mean that you are taking a bigger picture into view. You are looking to the future, and for the first time, you are planning with peace in mind, rather than a short-sighed chance to gain the upper hand."

I rub the back of my neck, "Is that a backhanded compliment? If so—"

"It's not a compliment. It's a fact." He folds his arms across his chest. "You want to ensure that you neutralize any possible threats against your family. It's understandable. It's why you went ahead and met with two of our fiercest rivals. It's why you didn't breathe a word about it to anyone before-hand. You were going to do it anyway; nothing would have deterred you. And you know this is also for the good of all of us... Even though there is a very good chance that this tactic could backfire on all of us."

I lower my hands to my sides.

"So yes, you did put us all in jeopardy, but not without reason. And I, for one, support you in this tactic."

There's silence around the table. The rest of the guys turn to me. Seb and Christian wear twin expressions of surprise. Xander's lips stretch in a smile. Massimo looks like he is taking it all in. Adrian rises to his feet and walks over to me. "I am also with you. It's time to give peace a chance. If we can grow our business and do it without bloodshed, I am totally behind you."

"You are?"

"You bet." He holds up his hand and I fist bump him. "It couldn't have been an easy decision to make, Capo. It took guts to go through with it. Courage that you have. And while it could just as easily come back to haunt us, I am willing to give this tactic a chance."

Adrian backs away a few steps and stands behind me. He's the quiet one, but his loyalty is unshakeable. I admit, I have taken him for granted sometimes, but it's clear that when I need someone in my corner, Adrian will always be there.

Xander's face splits in a smile, "I am glad that Karma came along." He plants his palms on his hips, "You've been a changed man since you met her. Hell, sometimes I can't even recognize you anymore, and in a good way."

I scowl, "Now, *that* is definitely not a compliment, though I appreciate your sticking up for me, *fratellino.*" I glance around at the rest of them, "You all do realize I don't need approval from any of you to go ahead with this alliance. But given a choice, I'd rather you be behind me, than not."

Christian rises to his feet. He rounds the table and grips my shoulder, "I can't claim to understand how it feels to know that you are about to have a child, but I get the rationale behind what you did. And in all honesty, I can say that I am for it."

Massimo raps his knuckles on the table, "Count me in, *fratellone*, I trust you to keep all of our interests at heart, with whatever action you take."

"And you, Seb?" I glance toward the man at the foot of the table. "As my possible successor what do you think?"

"I still wish there was another way out." He folds his arms across his chest, "I can't, in all fairness, say that I agree with this alliance, but," he raises a shoulder, "I understand why you did it. And I hope, for all our sakes, that it works out."

So, do I. I tilt my head, "Fair enough, Seb." I narrow my gaze on him, "You still owe me information."

"Luca," he exhales a breath.

I nod, "Your time is running out to track him down."

"He's being more elusive than I gave him credit for." Seb rubs the back of his neck. "Give me until Christmas to track him down, Capo."

"That's—"

"A week away," he murmurs.

"Seven more days," I look down at him, "and not a minute more."

40

Karma

It's six days to the Christmas party, and I am almost done with the projects I have undertaken. My dress is done. So is the other outfit I have been working on. My morning sickness is also almost gone. And if I have to stay another day cooped up in here, I am going to go stark, raving mad. Argh! Andy saunters over to me. He winds his way around my legs and purrs loudly. I scoop him up, pet him, but he glances the other way. He's one demanding cat. As demanding as the other man in my life… That is, he used to be demanding...and mean…and growly… And now? He's just grouchy.

Clearly, the lack of sex is getting to him. Since our tryst on the terrace, I have not seen him at all. If he does sleep at night… It, clearly, isn't in the bed next to me, as his side of the bed remains untouched when I awake in the mornings. He hasn't been in the room, as far as I can tell. Which means he is sleeping somewhere else. Likely, in his office at *Venom*. Is he also sleeping *with* someone else there? But he said that he wasn't fucking anyone else. That he wouldn't fuck anyone else. He wouldn't lie to me, would he? I tighten my fingers and Andy yowls in protest.

He flicks out his baby claws and I yelp as he scratches me. I release him and he jumps down to the floor, then walks away with his tail high in the air. I glance down at the streak of blood across the back of my palm. Shit! I walk over to the bathroom, and hold my hand under the running water at the sink. Then raise my hand to check the scratch. Blood begins to drip out again. Oh, damn. I reach for a tissue when, "What are you doing?" His voice interrupts me.

I yelp, lose my grip on the tissue which flutters to the ground. "You scared me," I mumble.

He prowls into the bathroom, wearing his well-fitted suit—all black, of course. With a tie that's blue enough to bring out the blue in his eyes. His jaw is clean-shaven, and when he leans in close, his dark, spicy scent envelops me. My nipples pebble and my belly flutters as he extends his hand. I draw in a breath, freeze, and he switches off the tap.

Jerk.

His lips curl in a smirk, then he glances down at the still-bleeding scratch on the back of my hand. His eyebrows draw down. "You're hurt?"

"It's only a scratch," I reply, "Andy... I may have scared him."

"If I had known that the cat was going to wound you—"

"Seriously, he barely broke the skin," I glare about, spot the tissue on the floor and go to pick it up.

"Leave it," he orders as he snatches up a fresh one. Then circles my wrist with his fingers and presses the tissue to the scratch. He presses down and I hiss out a breath. "Did that hurt?" He scowls at me.

"No," I lie.

He shoots me a glance and I redden, "Just a little, but it's nothing."

"Let me be the judge of that." He grabs another tissue, holds it over the previous one, then brings my other hand down on it, before lifting both to my chest. "Hold it there, above your heart, and apply pressure," he commands.

Before I can protest, he turns away. He reaches up to pull open a door near the sink, then pulls out a first-aid kit. He pulls out cotton balls, antiseptic, and bandages, lays them out near the sink, then turns to me. He throws away the bloodied tissues, then proceeds to dab the antiseptic onto the scratch. I wince and he blows on it to cool down the injured skin. Then he places a band-aid over it. "There," he steps back, "all done."

I glance down at the neatly bandaged wound. "Thanks," I murmur as he puts away the first-aid kit.

"Where have you been all these days?" I burst out when he straightens. "I haven't seen you at all."

"Did you miss me?" He smirks, and a ripple of heat runs down my spine. Man, that smirk of his... It's sooo hot. Even when he's being a jerk, it turns me on. Clearly, I am fighting a losing battle against his charm.

"Of course, not." I toss my head, "It's just colder at night when you are not in bed with me."

His grin widens, "So, I am just a substitute for an electric blanket, huh?"

"Yep," I nod, "that's all you are. A warm body to keep my toes from getting cold at night."

"And here I thought you had other uses for me."

"If you mean as a sperm donor, well, that ship has already sailed."

I scowl, and he chuckles. "You always have been able to match me word for word, wife."

Wife. Hell, I still can't get used to him calling me that. And he's been so tender to me, taking care of me. Tears prick the backs of my eyes. Oh, hell, and now these stupid pregnancy hormones have my insides all twisted up.

I turn my head away, but he catches my chin. "Hey," he murmurs, his voice soft, "what's this all about?"

"Nothing." I sniffle, "Everything. It all just seems too much."

"The party?" He frowns, "We can call it off."

"No, not the party," I respond. "I am looking forward to it. It's the one time I'll get to visit with other people, other than you or Cassandra or the occasional visit from Xander."

"Xander's been coming by, eh?" He scowls, "He hasn't been troubling you, has he?"

"Oh, please." I roll my eyes. "At least, he keeps me company, unlike his oldest brother who's, clearly, been avoiding me."

"I haven't been avoiding you."

"Oh?" I shoot him a look from under my eyelashes, "So you haven't been keeping away from me over the last week."

He has the grace to flush. "M-a-y-b-e." He shuffles his feet.

"See?" I point my finger at him, "I knew it." I pivot away from him and walk toward the door.

"Beauty?" he calls out and I ignore him. I reach the doorway of the bathroom and step out, then cross the floor.

"Stop," he commands.

"Oh, F' off," I hold my middle finger up, above my shoulder, head for the door to the room.

"Karma!" He commands, "Stop."

I freeze. Damn, I want to disobey him, but of course, my body responds to his orders. It's as if he has a direct line of communication to the most primal part of me that will bend to his every will. Damn it. And soon, I'll have a child and he won't need me anymore. Then what? Will he keep me imprisoned here for the rest of my life? Hidden away for fear of his enemies getting to me? Despite the fact that he, clearly, has feelings for me, he hasn't even been able to tell me that he loves me. And damn it, I hate these histrionics. I am used to fending for myself, to finding my way out of tough spots. But the very fact that he is there for me, has weakened me. He's coddled me, and turned me into this blubbering mess who I don't recognize anymore, frankly.

More tears squeeze out from the corners of my eyes as I hear his footsteps approach. "Hey," he steps around, and notches his knuckles under my chin. "Don't cry, *Bellezza*," he murmurs. "Please don't. When I see your tears, I swear, it hurts me so fucking much."

"Does it?" I sniff.

"You bet." He drags his thumb across my lower lip, "I'd kill anyone who caused you pain, my Beauty. I'd change anything to see you smile again."

"Would you?" I peer up at him.

"No doubt about it."

"A car."

"What?"

"I want a car and I want lessons to learn to drive it, so I can drive myself around the city."

"No way." He lowers his hand and steps away. "No fucking way, am I allowing you out on your own."

"I'll be in a car, Mika," I snap. "Surely, that would be safe. Besides, I don't know how to drive yet—"

"You don't know how to drive?"

I shake my head.

"How do you not know how to drive?"

"Because I grew up in a city with good transport links so I never needed to learn how to drive. Also," I scowl, "I didn't exactly have an overabundance of money so I could buy a car, you know?"

"So why do you want a car, if you don't know how to drive?"

"So I can learn how to drive?"

He shakes his head, "Your logic, as always, is irrefutable."

"Thank you," I mutter. "So can I get a car?"

He seems like he is about to refuse.

"Please, Mika, please," I wheedle. "It would, at least, give me an illusion of being in control, and I'd love to have some semblance of freedom."

"Hmm." He scowls.

"Also, surely, being stuck in here is not good for my mental health. And I do need to stay happy if I want the kid to be born healthy, right?"

He blows out a breath, "Fine."

"Yay!" I throw my arms about his neck, and rise up on tip-toe to kiss him.

"On one condition."

I pause before my lips touch his, "What?" I scowl, "What is it?"

"I'll teach you how to drive."

"You are too busy," I roll my eyes. "I mean, I'd love for you to teach me, but seriously, when have you been able to tear yourself away from your work to spend time with me?"

"You're more important than any job," he retorts.

"Really?"

"Have I ever given you reason to doubt that?"

"Umm, yeah?" I scoff. "I mean, if I'm more important, wouldn't you have spent more time with me over the last month?"

"That was only so I could keep distance between us so I wasn't tempted to —"

"I know," I say hastily, "Still, you have to admit, from where I am, it seems that your work takes priority."

"Well, I am going to prove to you that it doesn't." He grips my cheek, "Tomorrow, after lunch, be ready."

41

Karma

At least, last night, he had come to bed at midnight, and I had woken up enough to wrap myself around my husband and fall asleep. He'd kissed me tenderly, had run his hands down my body, aroused me to fever pitch, only to slip my nightgown and my panties aside and slide his fingers into me. He'd slid down my body, eaten me out, then he'd risen over me and pinched my clit as he'd commanded me to come. And I had. I had shattered right there, and then, promptly fallen asleep, sated.

It was almost noon when I woke up to find a letter on his pillow, asking me to peek out of the window. I had, and had cried out when I had seen a car... Not just any car, a Maserati. A twin of his...but in black, with a red line running across its side, and wrapped up in a bow. It's my car. My car! OMG! I had showered, changed, eaten a late breakfast, then rushed down to examine my new toy.

It is beautiful, with sleek lines that remind me of him, a color dark enough to hint at his growly personality, and a motor under the hood that is powerful enough to outpace any other car on the road. A bit like him, really... And also, like me, if I am being honest. It's a twin of his car, and he sees me as his equal enough to gift it to me.

Now, I stand staring at it when my phone rings. I glance at the screen then answer it, "Hey," I say softly.

"Hey, yourself." His deep voice sends shivers down my back. "What do you think?"

"What do I think of what?"

"You know what," he laughs, "do you like it?"

"I... I love it," I blubber as a tear streaks down my cheek. "When are you coming to teach me how to drive it?"

"About that, ah," he sighs, "something came up."

"Knew it," I hunch my shoulders. "So, you can't come?"

"I can't, but Xander will."

"But I wanted to have the first lesson with you."

"I know, baby," he murmurs. "I am so sorry, but I'll make it up to you."

I hang up, and am about to turn away, when a Ferrari drives up. A red Ferrari that screeches to a halt right behind the Maserati. Xander pushes open the door and steps out. He swaggers over to me and I burst out laughing. "Oh, my god, you sure do know how to make an entrance."

"Nice wheels, eh?" He flicks a satisfied glance over his shoulder, "Not that yours isn't almost as good..."

"Almost, eh?" I chortle as he runs his finger down the lines of the Maserati. "Nice one, what say we inaugurate this baby, eh?"

I laugh, "Well, why not?" The last thing I want to do is go back inside and hide myself away, moping. Not when I really, really do want to drive this car. And I do want to learn how to drive. That is one more step toward leading some kind of a normal life... Or as normal as it can be, being the wife of a Capo.

I step forward, grab hold of the ribbon that's stretched across the car, and pull at it. It falls away and I walk around to the driver's seat. I step in and Xander slides in from the other side.

"Ready?" He turns to me, "First, let's adjust the seat so you are able to reach for the accelerator and the brake with ease." He helps me do so, then sets about pointing out the pedals for the accelerator and the brake, as well as the various buttons on the dash all of which seems like an exact twin to the one I had seen in Mika's car. But really, when you have to operate it, it becomes an entirely new ball game. "This is an automatic car, so it's really very easy."

He shows me how to adjust the mirrors, then points out the additional buttons on the console for the headlights, the wipers on the windshield, the taillights, the buttons to be used to signal that I am going to turn, etcetera.

He makes me run through the entire routine twice. Then, when he is satisfied that I know my way around the console, he leans back. "Well, that was the first lesson."

"What?" I stare, "It's over already?"

"Yep."

"But I want to take the car out."

"You never do that on the first lesson."

"But I want to," I scowl and he laughs.

"Just kidding, let's do it."

"Ass." I swipe at his shoulder. Xander is every bit the brother I never had.

I reach for the ignition button when a movement catches my attention from the corner of my gaze. I look up to find my husband's Maserati screeching to a halt in front of us. He shoves open the door and jumps out. Michael isn't wearing his suit jacket and his tie is askew. He races toward us.

"What is he doing here?" Xander scowls.

Michael raises his arm. I see his mouth move. I am not sure what he's trying to say, but I want to show him how much I love this car, and how I am already able to drive it.

Xander turns to me, his face pale. "Don't do it," he yells, but I've already touched the ignition button. For a second nothing happens, then the entire car seems to erupt.

I glance up, see Michael's face, as if from a distance, then everything goes dark.

AND NEXT MAFIA WAR

PART III

MAFIA WAR

1

Michael

"You are bleeding."

Massimo's voice cuts through the silence in my mind. I raise my hand to my brow and my fingers come away wet. "It's nothing." I stare at the redness. The same blood that runs through her veins. The scarlet that had pooled around her body which had been thrown clear of the car in the blast.

Thank *Santa Maria* I had insisted on installing an ejector seat, as well as a protective shell around the driver's seat which would deploy in case of something just like this.

I had ordered the specially-made Maserati for myself, but had gifted it to her when she had asked for a car. Thank god I had. For when I had seen her trapped under the ejector seat, something inside of me had awakened. I've never been a believer in god, but at that instant, as I had jumped to my feet from where the blast had knocked me down and raced over to her, a part of me had reached out to that higher power. I had beseeched him, had pleaded with him, had asked him with every breath that I had drawn to spare her. To let her live. To allow her to survive this incident, one that I could have averted by being more vigilant. As long as I live, I'll never forgive myself for what happened.

I had leaped across the distance, reached her, sunk to my knees, and released the seatbelt. I had caught her, then lowered her gently to the ground. I had touched her brow... Cold; she had been so cold. Dirt smeared her face, her hair was in a cloud about her shoulders, and she seemed uninjured, as if she were simply sleeping, except for a cut on her arm that was bleeding. I had held her close, turned toward the car to find the flames leaping from the vehicle. That was when Christian had driven up in his car, followed by Massimo and Seb.

Christian had jumped out of his car, taken one look at us, then at the burning car, then back at us.

"Xander," I'd croaked, "Xander."

Some of the sparks had rained down on my Maserati, and Massimo had jumped into the Maserati and driven it a safe distance away. Meanwhile, Christian and Sebastian had run to the burning car. They had dragged Xander out and stamped out the fire on his coat, but it had been too late. The blast had dislodged a piece of metal which had struck through his heart. My *fratellino,* my youngest brother with the face of an angel, the talent of a genius and the disposition of a man who was so good that no-one could come in contact with him without being affected by his charm, his humor, his good nature... And his smile... The sheer goodness of it would melt the most hardened of hearts, would make all of the women around him swoon and want to throw themselves at him willingly and ask him to bed them... That man will no longer tease me in that drawling voice of his, he'll no longer be around to banter with his twin, and be the voice of reason that the rest of us most often need.

Xander, my brother, is gone and she... I had glanced down at her still form in my arms. She'd seemed to have gone paler in the last few minutes, her eyelashes a dark fan against her cheeks. The circles under her eyes had seemed so much more prominent. She'd seemed too fragile, so breakable. My heart had thundered in my chest and my stomach had been in knots as I had surveyed her features. She'd seemed still, too still...but she couldn't die. No way, was I going to let her leave me.

The wail of an ambulance had sounded in the distance. Seb had walked over to me. He'd told me that he'd called the ambulance. He'd stayed with me as I had held her, never taking my gaze off of her features, as first one ambulance, then another had pulled up the driveway.

I had watched as they'd checked Xander, declared him dead. They had placed a white sheet over the body and... My brain had frozen. My brother...was dead? My little brother was gone?

I had held onto her. I had refused to let go of her, until Seb had gripped my shoulder. He'd reminded me that they needed to get her to the hospital. I'd managed to loosen my grip on her enough for the paramedics to sweep into action. They'd placed an oxygen mask on her face, checked her vitals, run an IV into her vein, even as they had strapped her into a stretcher. They'd carried her into the ambulance and I had paused. Torn between wanting to follow her and to stay with Xander, I had paused. That's when Seb had told me that they needed to keep Xander here until the cops—who are on our payroll— had time to gather evidence. He'd reassured me that Christian and Adrian would stay with Xander while he and Massimo would follow us as I rode with her to hospital. Only then, had I gotten into the ambulance. I'd clasped her hand in mine for the entire journey.

Within seconds of reaching the hospital, she had been admitted and a team of doctors and nurses had swarmed over her. I had followed until a nurse had stopped me, told me they needed to operate on her.

I had raged and asked her if she'd recognized who I was. That I had half the hospital on my payroll. That I was not letting go of her. That's when Sebastian and Massimo had burst into the hospital with Antonio hot on their heels. They had stopped me, reasoned with me to let her go. I had watched in a haze as she had disappeared, with the doctors in tow, behind the double doors. Someone had pushed me into a chair in the waiting room across from them, and there I had sat and waited. Someone had pushed a cup of coffee into my hands. And I had drunk it. At some point, I had torn my gaze from the double doors long enough to ask them about Christian.

Christian, who had lost his twin, the soul who had been with him from the moment he'd been conceived. Sebastian reminded me that Adrian was with him. The two of them had accompanied Xander to the mortuary, where his body had been taken for a post-mortem.

"They need to release the body." I had risen to my feet, only for my legs to give way, and I had slumped back in my chair. "I need to go to Christian," I had murmured, and tried to stand up again, but Seb had stopped me.

"You need to stay here with her," he'd told me.

"She'll want to see you when she regains consciousness," Massimo had added, and I'd known that they were right. I wanted to be here with her, but at the same time, I wanted to be able to comfort my brother, to mourn my youngest sibling Xander. I had balled my fingers into fists as I had stared at the double doors. I could not allow her to also leave me. I would not allow the same fate to befall her.

I continue to stare at the doors, willing them to open. I lean my head back against the wall. Every time my eyes close, I jerk myself awake. Antonio gets all of us coffee, which I sip before placing the half-filled cup aside. At some point, Sebastian brings me something to eat, and my stomach lurches. I refuse the food, lean forward in my seat as I keep my eyes glued to the door.

Suddenly, the sound of the doors opening has me snapping my eyes open. I spring to my feet and my head spins. I square my shoulders, dig my booted feet into the floor, and track the progress of the doctor who walks toward me. Around me, my brothers, too, stumble to their feet. Massimo and Seb flank me as the doctor halts in front of me. His scrubs are blood splattered, his hair awry and shadows encircle his eyes. His jaw is set and his features wear an expression of stoic patience? Of resignation?

I falter and Seb grips my shoulder. "Steady, *fratellone*," he murmurs, "stay strong."

"How is she?" I croak, then clear my throat. "Tell me," I demand, "how is my wife?"

"She's still unconscious." He holds my gaze, "It's difficult to say anything until she is awake."

The next thing I know, my fingers are wrapped around his collar and I have hauled the doctor up to his tiptoes. "She has to make it," I growl. "She cannot die."

"We are doing everything we can," he says in a calm voice.

Anger thuds at my temples. "Do better," I snap. "If anything happens to her, I will not let you live."

He doesn't blink. Either the man's a fool or he's got the balls to face up to my anger. "Do you hear me?" I demand.

He holds my gaze, then nods.

I tighten my hold on his collar, and Massimo touches my shoulder. "Not going to help if you kill him, brother. He's treating her; he's on your side."

I glare at the doctor, then release him. He steps back, his features impassive.

"I'm sorry," he murmurs, "but we couldn't save the child."

The child. My child. Our baby. A hot sensation stabs at my chest. The pressure behind my eyes builds. I swallow down the ball of emotion that clogs my throat. "I don't need your sympathy," I growl. "If she dies, you die; remember that."

Seb shuffles his feet next to me.

"Do you understand, *doctor*?" My eyes bore into his before I turn away, stalk toward the door at the end of the corridor.

"Don't you want to see her?" the doctor calls after me. "It would help her if you sat with her for a little while, maybe spoke to her."

I set my jaw. It's because of my negligence that she is in this situation. How can I stand in front of her, when I have failed her? I failed to protect my own wife. She deserves so much better than this. Since I first saw her, all I have done is screw up her life. She's better without me.

I slow my steps, then glare at him over my shoulder. "No," I snap, "I don't want to see her." I turn to Massimo, "You stay here with Antonio. Make sure you protect her."

"With my life, *fratellone*," Massimo replies.

I wince, then set my jaw, "Seb, with me."

I stalk out of the hospital, Seb on my heels. He doesn't say anything as I head for my Maserati, which one of my clan must have parked in the hospital parking lot. As I approach it, Seb hands over the key fob. I beep the car to unlock it, open the door and slide inside. I glance around the car, a twin to the one that she had been in.

One in which her blood had been spilled. Xander is dead, my child is no more, she is injured and I... I am responsible for all of it. I tighten my fingers around the steering wheel, press the ignition button, shift into gear, and the car jumps forward. I slam on the brake and the car stops millimeters from crashing into the wall in front.

"You okay, brother?" Seb turns to me, "Maybe I should drive."

"No," I throw the car in reverse, peel out of the parking lot.

We drive in silence for a few minutes, then he glances sideways at me, "Why didn't you want to see her, brother?"

"None of your business."

"You can't blame yourself for what happened to her."

I step on the accelerator and the car leaps forward.

"It was because you had a protective plate installed around the driver's seat and it worked like an ejection seat, that she survived."

"I should have known that it was too risky to gift her the car. I shouldn't have tempted fate by giving it to her. I should have, at least, test driven it first before allowing her to climb into it."

"Your actions saved her, Michael," he insists.

"It's my actions that put her in danger, in the first place... If she had not survived...I..."

"But she did."

"Whoever rigged that car got past me," I growl. "I'll never forgive myself for that."

"The bomb was rigged wrong. Only the ignition blew; she survived, Michael."

"We lost our brother, Seb," I take the next corner without decreasing speed and the tires screech in protest. "Xander's no longer with us and it's my fault." I slam my fist into the steering wheel and the car fishtails. The back of the vehicle rises off the road as the Maserati circles in a wide arc, once, twice, before I slam on the brakes and come to rest on the side of the road.

A truck blows it horn as it whizzes past, then silence descends.

I grip the steering wheel, staring ahead as my chest heaves.

Seb sits silently as more vehicles pass us at a more sedate speed.

"Not seeing her is only going to make it worse, Michael."

"You don't understand," I growl.

"Oh?" He turns on me, "Make me. Tell me what you're thinking, Mika. This once, confide in me so I know what's going on in that screwed up mind of yours."

I shake my head, "You won't get it."

"Try me."

"I love her," I snap. "Do you understand? I love her, and already, I have put her at risk. The only way to protect her is if I keep her away from me."

2

———————

Michael

Twenty minutes later, we are parked outside the building that houses the mortuary. I stare at the door that leads inside. If I get out of here and walk in, if I see his face, then nothing will ever be the same again. *Nothing is ever going to be the same again.*

"Michael," Seb murmurs, "you don't have to do this."

I stare straight ahead, unable to take my gaze off the goddam door. Another door that leads to another loved one who is lying there...stretched out...cold. Another of my flesh and blood I have failed. Another sorrow that I will carry around for the rest of my life. Oh, Xander, why did it have to be you? Why couldn't I have protected you? How could I have allowed this to happen to you?

"Michael?" Seb touches my shoulder and I jerk. I shove the door open, climb out of the car. I step into the coolness of the building and a shiver runs down my spine. I walk down the corridor, turn right... knowing where I have to go.

This is not my first visit to the morgue; it's the first time I am here to identify the body of someone I loved like he was my own child. Xander was born when I was nine years old, and I had felt more like his parent than his older brother. And Christian? Even though Christian was only a few minutes older, it was Xander who had been the cheekiest, who could get away with anything. Who is now dead... Because I hadn't been able to protect him. It should have been me.

My footsteps echo in the empty corridor. The two men at the end of the corridor turn to watch me approach. Christian's gaze tracks me as I walk toward him. I stop in front of him, reach out for him. He evades me, then swipes out and buries his fist in my face. I absorb the hit, and the next, as he sinks his fist, this time, into my shoulder, then on the other side. He raises his arm again and his big body sways. He crumples and I catch him. I wrap my arms around him, rock him as his shoulders shudder. His chest rises and falls, as he tightens his hold on me and weeps. I rock him, even as the band around my chest tightens. The burning sensation behind my eyes intensifies and my nose starts to run. Adrian and Seb flank us as I squeeze my arms around my brother. I stay that way until he calms down somewhat, then step back.

Christian rises his red rimmed eyes, and I hold his gaze. "We'll find who did this," I vow, "and when we do, I will wipe out his entire bloodline."

Christian swallows, then steps back and wipes his face.

Footsteps approach us. I turn as a man pauses in front of us, "Who's going to identify the body?"

"I will," I brush past him, heading for the doors that lead to the morgue, when a woman bursts into the corridor.

"Xander," she gasps, glancing between us. "Is it true, what I heard about him?"

She glances between us, then her gaze settles on me. She marches over to me. "Xander," she swallows, "I need to see him."

"I don't think that's advisable." The coroner scowls, "He's not in good shape."

"Yes." She shudders, then shakes her head as tears squeeze out of the corners of her eyes, "I must see him with my own eyes. I don't believe you."

"Theresa?" Sebastian murmurs. "It's not a good idea."

Xander's childhood friend sets her jaw. "I don't care. I am going to see him, whether you like it or not. Xander... He...he can't leave me like this." She turns to me, "Michael, please." Her voice cracks.

I peer into her features, take in the determination reflected in her eyes, then jerk my chin.

"Thank you," she whispers as she wipes the tears from her face.

I move forward and she follows me. The coroner marches forward and falls in step with me. He leads us down another corridor and pauses in front of double doors.

He opens it, and next to me, Theresa stumbles. I grab her arm and steady her. "Easy," I murmur.

She squares her shoulders, then nods, "I am ready."

We step in together and the doors snicks shut behind us. The scent of antiseptic, combined with a sickly-sweet scent that I can't identify, overpowers me. My hackles rise and my pulse begins to race. Theresa's steps falter and she tightens her grip on my arm. There is a big glass window which separates us from a smaller room in which there is a covered body on a gurney.

Theresa must spot it at the same time as I do, for she draws in a breath. I sense the nervousness vibrating off of her as I steel my shoulders. The coroner asks us to wait while he goes to the other room. He walks around and stops behind the gurney. "Are you two ready?"

His voice sounds over the speakers.

Theresa flinches, then nods. So do I.

The coroner raises the sheet on the face of the body. My heart seems to stop for a second. I take in the pale features, the wide forehead, the high cheekbones, the dark hair that curls about his shoulders. It's my little brother. It's Xander, all right, and yet... It isn't.

Gone is the life that animated his every movement. Aside from sleep, which he never seemed to require much of, I've never known him to be still for a second. Not when he was a child; not when he was older... Nor even when he was painting, when he seemed to use his entire body as he dragged his brush across a canvas. He focused on the colors he chose to animate his art, focused on his plate as he relished his food, on women...and men...as he danced with them, flirted with them... As he fucked them... Even as he held back his emotions and how he felt from the woman who clings to my arm like it is a lifeline. Her body grows heavy and she slumps. I catch her before she can hit the floor.

I scoop her up in my arms, jerk my chin at the coroner, then walk out.

Adrian straightens as I stalk over to him and hand Theresa over. "Take care of her. Xander felt...something for her, so she is under our protection."

I turn to Seb, "We need to find those behind the explosion that killed him and my child, and wounded my wife. Pull out all stops. Ask our men to hunt down every single one of their contacts to find out who is behind it."

"Is that wise?" he asks.

Christian turns on him. "How could you even ask this question?" He snarls, "Someone killed our brother, and instead of seeking out vengeance, instead of returning that favor a million-fold, you choose this time to question why we'd do it?"

"Michael's spent his life building up his reputation among the five families. He's worked his entire life to attain the position of Don," Seb retorts. "If he screws it up, he'll only regret it later."

"Are you saying that you'd rather he not do anything about what those *stronzos* did to him...to our family? Our brother is dead, Seb. Dead." Christian's chest heaves, "Or is it because Xander wasn't your brother, that he was only your half-brother, that makes you so uncaring about his death?"

Seb pales. "Take that back," he growls.

"That's it, isn't it?" Christian peers into his face, "You've always wanted to be one of us. You couldn't stomach the fact that you were a bastard. That no matter how much you tried, you'd never be a true heir to the Don. It's why you don't care that our brother's body lays there lifeless. Instead, it's why you are more concerned with avoiding vengeance... Which, by the way, would mean that we also lose face with the rest of our clan, you—"

Seb rears forward and smashes his head into Christian's face. Blood blooms from his nose, and with a roar, Christian charges him. He shoves Seb into the wall, gets an upper cut in. Seb's body jerks and his head snaps back. He growls, grabs at Christian's shoulders and I snap, "Stop."

Seb glares at Christian, who glowers back at him.

"Back the fuck up, the both of you," I order.

Seb pauses; Christian snarls. The two stare at each other, anger pouring off of both of them in waves.

"Control yourselves. I won't remind you again."

Seb shakes his head, seems to get a hold of himself. He releases Christian, who takes a step back.

"Sorry," Seb rubs the back of his neck, as he shoots me a sideways glance and mumbles, "you know I mean well."

Christian turns to me. "So, what's it going to be, Capo?" he says through gritted teeth. "You going to let this go, or you going to hunt down the men who did this?"

I jerk my chin in Seb's direction, "I appreciate your counsel. I know you only have the best interests of the Cosa Nostra at heart, but you know what I have to do."

Seb jerks his chin, "I am with you whatever you decide, Boss."

I turn my attention toward Christian. "Shake hands with Seb," I order and Christian glowers at me.

"Now," I snap.

He stiffens, then turns and holds out his hand and Seb shakes it.

Christian instantly pulls back his arm, then brushes past me, "I am going in search of the motherfuckers."

"You are not going anywhere on your own."

He stalks forward and I call out, "I've lost a brother. I don't plan to lose another."

Christian pauses; his shoulders heave. I stalk forward, wrap my arm around his neck and pull him to me. "I know it hurts," I swallow, "I know how much he meant to you... To all of us. We won't let this go unpunished."

Christian tries to shake off my arm, but I don't let go. "Cry, go punch a bag, do what you need to do to let off steam. Then, when you're thinking straight, come find me and we'll finish this."

Christian avoids eye contact. He pulls away and I release him. He stalks off and I turn to Adrian, "Stay with him. See that he doesn't hurt himself... Or get himself killed."

Adrian follows him while Seb draws abreast with me. "What now, Capo?"

"Now we track down the bastards," I square my shoulders, "but first, I need to see my wife."

"You took off without seeing her, now you want to go back?" Seb shoots me a sideways glance, "What's happening with you, brother?"

"None of your bloody business," I growl at him.

He frowns at me and I blow out a breath. "I wanted to get here and make sure that Xander was..." I squeeze my eyes shut, "that he was okay. That Christian was able to deal with the grief. That he..." I swallow down the ball of emotion in my throat, "wasn't going to do something crazy."

"You mean, like kill himself?" Seb says in a low voice.

I turn on him. "Don't fucking say that aloud; don't even go there," I warn him as I try to deny my own fears. I bunch my fingers into fists, "I will do everything in my power to keep my brothers, my family...to keep all of you safe, you feel me?"

Seb jerks his chin, "You're a good Capo, and an even better brother and husband, but—"

"But?"

"You can't control everything, Mika. Not even you can cheat death. When it's time to go, it's time to—"

I grab his collar and shove him against the wall, "The fuck are you getting at, Seb?" I thrust my face into his, "You trying to tell me I couldn't have saved him? Or my unborn child? Or prevented my wife from getting hurt? Is that it?"

"I'm trying to tell you that it's not your fault, Capo."

He holds my gaze, his own calm and steady. Somehow, in the last few weeks he's grown more mature, more patient, able to keep a clear head while I am on the verge of losing my shit.

It comes from being too close to a situation. I understand it. Hell, I have seen men crack when tragedy came knocking on their doorstep. I'd always thought I was above that. I thought I was invincible, that even if something happened to me or mine, I'd be able to deal with it, to find a way through it. Yet here I am, unable to face my own wife, which is what had sent me running from her in the first place. And now, I can't wait to see her again, to make sure that she is safe. Apparently, I can't make up my mind about something as simple as, do I want to stay with her or stay away from her? And there is only one way to find out. By going back to her. By being in the same room as her. By finding out how it feels to hold her again, to breathe in her scent, to take in her gorgeous features, to look into her eyes and apologize for not having been able to protect her from what happened.

I release Seb, then step back. "I'm sorry," I roll my shoulders, "I know you mean well."

"And I know you love your family and her more than anything else in this world."

"Like that made a difference when it came to their welfare." I rub the back of my neck, "I am aware that not even I can cheat death." I bare my teeth, "Doesn't mean I am not going to try my damnedest."

Turning, I stalk toward the exit.

3

Karma

Thump, thump, thump. The muffled sound reaches me, then fades away. I glance around at the white space that envelops me. I am floating on a cloud of nothingness. It's peaceful here and so…so lonely. A chill grips me. I glance around, take in the white space that envelops me. Where am I? I try to move but my limbs feel too heavy. I try to put one foot in front of the other but my legs don't seem to obey me. The scent of something dark and edgy teases my nostrils. His scent. I glance up, spot a man walking away from me.

"Capo," I try to reach for him, but am not able to move. Thump, thump, THUMP. The sound grows louder. More persistent. It mirrors his steps as he stalks away from me. His broad shoulders, that narrow waist, those powerful thighs that flex as he puts more distance between us.

"Capo," I yell, but he doesn't look back.

"Michael," I scream as I push myself forward, but am not able to move. *Why can't I move?* "Mika, stop, don't go, Mika!"

"Beauty?"

"Mika," tears flow down my cheeks, "oh, Mika, where are you?"

"Here." Warm fingers twine with mine and I force my eyes open. Blue eyes meet mine, a burning white in their depths that echoes the white I had been surrounded by.

"No," I grip his palm, "Mika, no." A sinking sensation coils in my chest. The hair on the nape of my neck rises, "Mika, please," I whisper, my voice hoarse, my throat dry.

He leans in closer. "What's wrong?" He peers into my features, "Are you in pain?"

"No," I shake my head as I glance around the space. The scent of antiseptic assails my senses. I take in the white walls, the fluorescent lighting, the equipment pushed up against the wall, "Am I in the hospital?"

He nods, holds up a cup of water and places the straw between my lips. "Do you remember what happened?"

I pause to collect my thoughts as I swallow. "I remember seeing you..." I scrunch up my eyebrows. "Then I reached for the ignition, and the car," I swallow, "the car...it..."

"The ignition blew. The bomb placed in the vehicle was faulty. You were thrown free."

"Thrown free?" I raise my free hand to my forehead and wince.

"I had a jump seat installed, so if anything ever happened to the vehicle, the roof would open and the ejector seat would activate."

"So, I was...ejected out of the vehicle, along with the seat?"

He nods.

"And Xander?" I frown. "I remember seeing you say something to us. I couldn't understand what it was, but I think Xander did, because he turned to me, and then... I don't remember anything after that."

"I was speaking in Italian." He sets his jaw, "He probably realized that I was warning him."

"Where is he?" I glance around the room. "Is he okay?"

Michael glances away, then back at me. My heart begins to race, a bead of sweat slides down my back.

"Mika," I whisper as I tighten my hold on his fingers, "Xander... Is he..."

Michael holds my gaze, "He didn't make it."

"No." My heart feels like it's going to break and a ball of emotion blocks my throat. I shake my head back and forth, intensifying the pounding. "No, Mika, no," I gasp.

A vein throbs at his temple. I take in his mussed-up hair, the hollows under his eyes.

"It wasn't your fault, Mika," I whisper.

"Wasn't it?" He holds my gaze and his features seem to settle into a mask. I sense him withdrawing from me and my stomach drops.

He tries to pull his hand free and I hold onto him. "Michael, don't do it."

"Don't do what?"

"Whatever it is you're thinking about, don't do it."

"You're distraught," he murmurs, "still dazed from the…the incident."

"No." I swallow and try to sit up, but he places his hand on my shoulder.

"Don't try to move yet."

"I am fine." I glance between his eyes, "Thanks to you, Michael. Don't you see? You had the foresight to ensure that the car would hold up to something like this."

"I failed you," he says in a hard voice. "I couldn't protect you and our child."

"Child," I stare at him. "The baby." I release his hand and place both of my palms against my stomach. My flat…empty stomach. How could I have forgotten? Or had I already subconsciously known and hadn't been able to face up to it? "My baby," I whisper as I glance down at myself, "he's gone."

The tears that I had been holding back well up. My face crumples and he moves forward. He wraps his arm around my shoulders, pulls me close. I bury my face in his chest and allow the shock, the sorrow, the disappointment to well up and overwhelm me. I dig my fingers into the front of his shirt and allow myself to cry. He holds me, rocks me, runs his fingers down my hair. I sense his chest planes flex under my cheek and glance up. His features are hard, but his eyes? Those blue eyes of his blaze with an inner emotion… Grief? Anger? A mix of the two, maybe? He holds my gaze, neither of us speaking as I reach up and flatten my palm against his cheek. "Mika," I swallow, "I'm so sorry."

"I am the one who should be sorry." A nerve flares at his temple, "I'll never forgive myself for this."

"It's because of you, I am alive, Mika." I frame his face with my palms, "It's because of your foresight that I am here."

"But he isn't." His voice is dull, "Xander is gone, and so is our child.

I should have seen this happening. I should have known that as soon as I allowed myself to feel for you, that as soon as I fell in love with you —"

He firms his lips, attempts to pull away, but I grip his lapels. "You love me?" I whisper. "Of course, you love me. I knew it, Mika. I knew it...even before you told me."

"Past tense," he grabs my fingers and detaches them from his shirt, "I loved you."

"Wait, what?" I blink. "You don't mean it."

"Don't I?" His lips twist, "Now that you're no longer the mother of my child, I don't see any reason for this arrangement to continue."

Something hot stabs at my chest. I gaze into his features, and of course, he stares back. He allows me to read the intention in his eyes. The decision he's made is clear in the cut planes of his face.

"Don't do this, Mika. Don't push me away. Not now; not when I need you; not when we need each other."

"I don't need you." His fingers squeeze mine as if he's imprinting the sensation of my skin against his, then he releases me.

"I don't believe you," I reach for him and he steps back.

"Believe it, Karma." He straightens. "I never should have taken you from London, should have never married you. If I hadn't, you wouldn't be in this situation today."

"You need to let go of the guilt, Mika, and look forward. Xander is gone, but I am still here and I love you, Mika; I do."

He winces, then squares his shoulders. "It doesn't matter anymore." He balls his fists at his sides, "All that matters is tracking down the men who did this and making sure that they pay for it."

"You need revenge. I understand," I tip up my chin, "but that's not going to bring back Xander or our child."

"A few weeks of being with me and you think you know me?"

"I know what's going to hurt you, Mika, and this...this quest for vengeance will destroy whatever you have left. It will destroy us."

He chuckles, "There is no more us, Karma, can't you understand that?"

"No," I tuck my elbows into my sides, "but what I do understand is that you are hurting and lashing out. And you think if you sever your connection with me—which, by the way, you can't—but you think if you cut all ties with me, I am going to be safe, and you're wrong."

"Oh?"

I nod, "It doesn't work that way, Mika. It's not you, it's the lifestyle you are in that was bound to backfire on you some day. And it did."

He scoffs, "You going to lecture me about my beliefs and my values now?"

I shake my head, "No, of course, not. If anyone can understand the pull of the dark side, it's me, Michael. It's why we are so well-suited."

"It's why you are lying here on a hospital bed, having lost our child."

I squeeze my eyes shut. "You are trying to hurt me, Michael, and it's because you are in so much pain right now. Why can't you share it with me? Why can't you lean on me? Why can't you allow me to lean on you, when I need it the most right now?"

"Because. I. Can't." His voice is so anguished, so full of torment that I snap my eyes open.

"Michael, please don't do this," I beg. "Don't leave me; not now."

"You are free to go back to your family." He looks everywhere but at my face. "I'll make sure to tell Antonio to help you with any arrangements."

He turns to leave and I call out, "I am not going anywhere."

He freezes.

"You heard me, Michael. This is my home, I am your wife, and I am not leaving. Not when you need me more than anything. Not when we need each other."

He shakes his head, "Your choice. If you prefer to stay in Palermo, that can be arranged too."

He stalks forward, and I stare at his retreating back. Shit, shit, shit, what do I do now? How can I make sure to have some form of contact with him? What can I do to make sure that he doesn't just disappear after this?

"The Christmas party," I cry out, "I want to go ahead with the event."

He turns abruptly and his gaze bores into me. "Xander is gone and you want to go ahead with the festivities?"

I flinch. "He'd have wanted it. He'd have hated for us to be unhappy and mourning him."

He hesitates. "In Sicily, we mourn for at least a month in the period following a death. Celebrations are normally cancelled, or at the very least, conducted in a somber setting."

"I understand," I glance away, then back at him. "We needn't have a party on the scale I'd planned for, but maybe something in a smaller setting? Xander would have wanted us to celebrate his life." I tip up my chin, "You know I am right, Mika."

Michael jerks his chin. "Fine," he tilts his head, "you can stay until the Christmas party, and then I am sending you back home."

And then he's gone.

4

Michael

What the hell is wrong with me? I had wanted to haul her into my arms, comfort her about our loss, hold her close and tell her that it was okay, that she was still alive and that's what really mattered. But something inside of me had hardened, and I hadn't been able to lower the barriers enough to tell her.

It's as if Xander's death crushed every last emotion that had sprung to life since I met her. He is gone, my child will never be born, and the only thing that matters to me now is to make sure that she is safe. It's why I want to send her away, far from here, away from my influence, where my presence can't taint her, where the company I keep can't endanger her. Where my way of life will no longer cause her harm. It is the only way to ensure that she will never have to go through this kind of loss again.

She deserves better than me. She deserves someone who is on the right side of the law, who can give her security and safety, and keep her shielded from the darkness in which I spend so much of my time. She deserves more, so much more. Everything that I can't give her. It's why I have to let her go.

And yet, when she'd asked me about the Christmas festivities, I hadn't been able to refuse her. She'd been right—Xander would not have wanted us to grieve his absence. He'd have wanted us to remember him with happiness, wanted us to have a good time as we indulge ourselves in his memory. It's why I had given in to her request, and the Christmas party will take place as planned...

First though, I have to get through the funeral.

It's been three days since I left her at the hospital and returned home. I'd gotten on the phone and made arrangements for Xander's funeral. My brothers had offered to help but I had refused. This is something I have to do by myself.

Despite all of my influence within the police department, I hadn't been able to prevent them from conducting an autopsy on the body, which had delayed the funeral by a few days. But it had also given me the time to arrange for a funeral of the kind that befits Xander.

I straighten my cuffs, stare at my reflection in the mirror.

The eyes that look back at me, the features that fill the mirror are so like Xander's. It should be me in the casket... It should have been me in that passenger seat and not him.

The only way to get through this tightness that claws at my chest is to find the bastards who did this and kill them... That is one thing on which I will not compromise. That is the only thing that keeps me focused... Avenge him, that's the only thing that can restore the balance...somewhat. I knot my tie around my neck, tug on it until it hangs straight down. Then I turn and head for the doorway to my bedroom.

Her door opens at the far end of the corridor and she steps out. Clothed completely in black, from the veil that flows over her eyes and covers the bandage on her forehead, to the gown that draws across her narrow shoulders and down to her feet, which are clad in black stilettoes, she resembles a goddess who has come to stake her claim on the souls of us mortals.

She approaches, her movements slow enough to indicate that she is not completely healed from the incident.

The day on which I had lost, not one, but two of my children. If something had happened to her as well... I never would have been able to live with myself.

As she walks toward me now, all the pent-up emotions threaten to boil over. My fingers tingle and I want to wrap them around the nape of her neck, haul her close as I lick her lips, slide my fingers up her skirt and shove aside her panties to cram them inside her channel, which I have no doubt will be soaking wet.

She comes to a stop in front of me, and her scent... That luscious scent that is so Beauty fills my senses. My cock swells and the blood rushes to my groin. I widen my stance, glare at her as she tips up her chin. Her lips tremble as she parts them, and damn, if I don't want to lean down and thrust my tongue inside her mouth and feast on her, and draw from the comfort that she can offer me.

But I won't. I owe it to Xander to hold back. Xander, who is dead and who will never know what it is like to be married, to father a child, to see his paintings displayed in the best museums in the world, to grow old with his woman by his side, to see us take over the Cosa Nostra, to feel the wind in his hair as he drives with the top of his car down, to cuddle up with his wife, to hold his newborn... Fuck. I close my eyes, fold my fingers at my side. *Oh, Xander, how am I going to get through the next few hours? How am I going to bury you...my heart?*

Soft fingers curl around mine, and I glance down to find Beauty has clasped her fingers around mine. She flattens my hand between her much smaller ones. They almost seem like a child's in comparison to the width of mine. Her pale skin is like ivory against my tan. I stare at the contrast. So fragile, yet so strong. So breakable, yet so... Tenacious. She is a study in contrasts. The yin to my yang. The other part of me... and yet...

I can't keep her with me. This one time, I need to be selfless. I need to let her go so she can survive. So I know that she is safe... Wherever... Whoever... She is with.

The breath hisses out of me and I hear her intake of breath. I glance down to find I've wrapped my fingers around hers and have squeezed. I loosen my hold, but she doesn't let go.

"You didn't hurt me," she insists.

"You shouldn't come to the funeral," I snap.

"We've been through this, already." She firms her lips, "Now is not the time to pull back. Now is when I appear by your side. Now is when we show the world that they didn't strike us down. That I am still alive."

"And mark a target on your head again?" I growl.

"I'll be safe as long as I am with you."

"You'll only be safe when you are away from me."

"I beg to differ."

"Why are you so stubborn?" I growl.

"Why are you so...so...pigheaded?" she snaps back.

I scowl at her and she flushes, but doesn't look away. Her eyes blaze with that inner fire that has attracted me to her from the beginning. That I need to resist if I have any hope of letting her go. I take a step back. "Just this once, I am allowing you to have your way," I set my jaw, "but make no mistake, once Christmas has passed, you will return home to London."

I release her, begin to walk away.

"Twice," she calls out behind me. "That's twice you've let me have my own way."

I stiffen. *Minchia!* She's right. First, I allowed her to continue with the Christmas festivities, and now, I've acquiesced and allowed her to come to the funeral. Goddamn it, she's getting to me and I am not even aware of it. The faster I get her out of my sight, the faster I can go back to being how I was.

Alone. Focused. This time, on revenge. It's the path I have chosen for myself; the path I should have never allowed her to sway me from.

I turn away from her, then walk down the stairs and open the door for her. We step outside where Antonio, Sebastian, Christian, Adrian and Massimo wait for me. I slide into the driver's seat of my Maserati. Sebastian holds the passenger door open and she slides in next to me. He slips into the back seat, along with Antonio.

Massimo follows behind in his car with Christian.

We complete the fifteen-minute drive to the chapel in silence. The last time I was here, I had faked my own funeral. This time… It's real… More than real.

I ease the car into a parking space in front of the chapel, push open the door and step out. I walk around to open Beauty's door. I hold out my hand and she places her palm in mine. I tuck it into the crook of my elbow, then walk forward. Sebastian follows me, and within minutes Christian, Adrian, Massimo and Antonio fall into line behind me. We walk into the chapel and every person turns to watch us. The place is packed, as is to be expected. I walk to the front row, guide her to our seats, when she stiffens. I glance over as Nonna rises to her feet. She closes the distance between us and holds out her hand.

"Nonna," I take her hand and kiss her fingertips. Her fingers tremble. I glance down into her face, take in her anguished eyes. Her features are composed though. I wouldn't have expected anything else.

She grips my fingers as she gazes up at me. "Mika," she swallows, "I hope you are going to hunt them down and teach every last one of them a lesson."

I bend my head, and she kisses my forehead. She releases me and turns to Beauty. Something unspoken seems to pass between the two women. My Nonna nods. She steps back, takes her place next to my father, who turns his face away from me.

Typical. In times of crisis, you can count on my father to retreat into that stony place inside of him where none of us can reach him. *Like me. Che cazzo.* Where did that thought come from? I am nothing like him.

I will not let myself become like him. I am far more focused, have more empathy for my brothers, for my clan. Hell, if it weren't for that, I'd have gunned down every single head of our rival clans, and all of the other families. I'd have shot first, then asked the questions.

Instead, I have my men searching, identifying who was behind it… Then, I'll begin the killing. Which is only fair. An eye for an eye; a tooth for a tooth. The death of their entire family for the death of my brother and my unborn child. Yeah, that's only right.

There's a commotion behind me. I turn to find Luca prowling up the aisle.

5

Karma

I glance around to find Luca stalking over to Michael. What the hell? What is he doing here? Michael stiffens, his nostrils flare, and color suffuses his features. His shoulders seem to grow even bigger in size, stretching the material of the suit-jacket. He pivots, closes the distance to Luca, then smashes his fist into Luca's face.

There's an audible gasp from the congregants as blood spurts from Luca's nose and drips to the floor. He staggers back, then straightens. He makes no move to defend himself as Michael plants his fist in his left shoulder, then his right, then slams it into his stomach. The breath whooshes out of him and he drops to his knees. He bunches his fists at his sides, bows his head almost in supplication as he waits...and waits.

Michael raises both of his fists as if to bring them down on him and I scream, "Stop!" I lunge forward and every bone in my body seems to protest. My head spins at the abuse I am subjecting my already battered body to, and I grab hold of Michael's jacket. "Stop," I pant, "please, don't do this."

There are more gasps from the mourners. Behind me, I sense Nonna and Michael's father rising to their feet, but I ignore them.

"Get away from me, Karma," he growls. "Get out of my way before I hurt you."

"You said you'd never hurt me, Michael," I hiss. "You promised you'd never allow anything to happen to me."

His shoulders bunch. Thick waves of tension vibrate off of him and his muscles jump under his skin. His entire body tenses and I am sure he is going to shake me off and complete what he'd set out to do, but he pauses. One by one, he forces his muscles to unwind. He lowers his arms to his sides and I release the breath I'd not been aware I was holding.

"Karma," Nonna calls out to me in a low voice. I turn to her and she glances at Michael, then back at me. She shakes her head. Something in her gaze reaches out to me. I can't understand what she's trying to tell me…but something inside me insists that I obey.

I release my hold on Michael and stumble. Michael pivots so quickly that he seems to blur. He grips my shoulder, holds on until I have regained my footing. He eases me back into my seat, then points a finger at me. "Stay," he growls, before he stalks over to where his brother has risen to his feet.

The two men glare at each other. Luca's features are pale but his gaze is clear. Defiance is evident in his stance, but his eyes reflect regret and hope and love… I swallow, turn to Michael, take in the hard set of his features.

He jerks his chin and Luca holds up his hands. "I am sorry," he says in a voice low enough that only Michael and his family can hear. "I am truly sorry, brother."

Michael blinks and his features twist as if he's torn between forgiving him and hitting him again. Then he seems to compose himself.

"I forgive you," he snaps, "but you will have to pay your dues, Luca. What you did can't go unpunished."

Luca draws himself up to his full height, "I would expect nothing less."

Michael nods, "Then welcome back, *fratello*."

Luca holds out his hand. Michael ignores it and winds his arm around his brother's neck. Luca grips his shoulder and the two embrace.

A palpable murmur runs through those assembled as Michael claps Luca on his back. Luca does the same, then both step back.

"I am so sorry," Luca murmurs. "It was my mistake to go after something that belongs to you."

"And mine that I never trusted you enough to let you in on our inner workings." Michael steps back. "But let's discuss that later." They both turn to look at the open casket.

"Fuck," Luca swears, "fuck, fuck, fuck." He balls his fists at his sides, "I should have been here protecting our family. I failed you, brother, and for that, I will never forgive myself."

Michael stays silent. The two stare at Xander's body for a few seconds more. Then, Luca walks around and to the other side of the pew. He sits down next to Christian who glares at him before he looks away.

Michael walks toward the front of the church, then turns to face the audience. A frisson of fear runs through the gathered people who instantly fall quiet.

It's unusual that he'd be the first to speak. I'd have thought the priest would read from the Bible, but he's the Capo, so I guess Michael makes his own rules, even at a funeral.

He glances around the assembled people and silence envelops the space.

"Alessandro Donatello Domenico Sovrano was more than my brother. In many ways, he was my son. My flesh and blood. The child I brought up and protected and made sure he never went to bed unhappy. He was the most talented of us. He had the face and the heart and the temperament of an angel. He was the youngest, and yet, he was the thread that held our family together. Now that thread has snapped and it falls to me to avenge whoever took him from us." Michael glances around the room.

I don't need to look over my shoulder to know that he's making eye contact with the different heads of the families who've gathered there. I imagine the leaders of rival clans are also there. At least, I think I saw Nikolai among them.

The silence stretches as Michael continues his silent assault on the audience. Someone coughs, someone else shuffles their feet, a baby cries and is shushed. The sound of someone sniffing reaches me. I glance over to the other side of the aisle, and find a girl clutching a handkerchief in her hand as she glances in the direction of the coffin. Her shoulders shudder, her features seem to crumple. She jumps to her feet and runs out. I spring up to go after her, but Nonna grips my arm and hauls me back.

"Leave her be; she needs time to come to terms with what has happened," Nonna murmurs.

I sink back onto the seat, "Who is she? Did she know Xander well?"

"Her name is Theresa," Nonna replies, "she is Alessandro's childhood friend."

Just then, a book drops to the floor with a thud that echoes around the room. I jump and Nonna places her hand on my leg. Her touch is reassuring. I glance toward the front where Michael hasn't moved from his earlier stance. The silence stretches once again, a beat, then another.

"What is he doing?" I whisper. "Why isn't he speaking?"

"He's making sure he gets his message across to all those who are present, making sure they'll take the message out to whoever was responsible for what happened."

Nonna firms her lips. She pulls her hand away and I stare straight ahead.

Michael sweeps his gaze over the audience, then nods. "I will hunt down the murderer who was responsible for my brother's death, and when I catch him... Not even God will be able to save him from what I have planned."

Goosebumps pop on my skin. He returns to his seat and the priest takes his place to read from the Bible.

Two hours later, I glance around the living room of my husband's home.

For all practical purposes, we are still married and I am still in the role of the Capo's wife... A role I am hoping to keep for a long time, despite Michael's insistence to the contrary. Fact is, I can't see myself anywhere else; can't see myself with anyone except him.

If I'd had any doubts about this... If I'd held onto any notion of escaping from him before... The car incident completely wiped all of it out of my mind. Somewhere between sleep and wakefulness, where I had floated after being ejected from the car... When all my barriers had dropped and I had sunk into the depths of my subconscious mind... At that point, I had shed all of my inhibitions, all of my fears, all of my insecurities, and I had embraced what I truly want. Him. I need him as much as I need the air I breathe. I yearn for him as much as I wish for a place to belong. I hunger for him, thirst for him, covet him with a passion that comes from somewhere deep within.

I ache to know him fully, completely. I hanker to have a family with him, to carry his children, to envelop myself in that sensation that I only get when I am with him. When I am secure in the knowledge that he belongs to me and I to him… That our darkness cancels out that of each other, that our hearts and minds and intentions are in sync… Maybe because I had lost the child I had briefly carried, because I had almost lost my own life, I know now what I am meant for. To not only embrace my art as a fashion designer, but to also embrace my heart's calling to be a mother, to embrace my soul's purpose to be his other half, to be the Beauty to his Beast, to be his.

There's a touch on my shoulder, and I turn to meet Nonna's shrewd gaze.

"You're in love with him," she declares.

I half smile, "Am I that obvious?"

"You wear your heart on your sleeve." She peers into my face. "It's why you took a knife to him… It's why you now follow him with your gaze, in the hope that he'll recognize what almost anyone else can read from your expression."

Shit. My shoulders slump, "I *am* that obvious."

"Except to him," she glances toward where Michael is speaking with Seb.

Christian and Luca are glowering at each other, while Massimo is speaking with a woman I don't recognize.

In another corner, Nikolai Solonik, stands quietly sipping his vodka —yes, Michael had provided for everyone's tastes. Nikolai's two brothers stand on either side of him. None of the three are speaking. With their imposing height and wide shoulders, not to mention the tattoos that peek out from under their collars and from the edges of their shirt sleeves, they should seem threatening… But somehow, the feeling that emanates from them is more of curiosity as they follow the proceedings.

In a third corner, a tall, broad-shouldered man sips his whisky. His lean features are striking, and there's a tightly leashed sense of power about him.

"That's JJ Kane, head of the Kane Company," Nonna offers.

"The Kane Company?" I wrinkle my nose, "Why do they sound familiar?"

"They are the most powerful organized crime syndicate in England."

Of course. I have read about him in the news. "And he's here, why?"

"He wants an alliance with the Cosa Nostra to grow his presence beyond the UK."

"I thought Mafia men don't share their business dealings with women?"

Nonna chuckles, "But then, I am not just any woman. I am the Nonna of the Capo and the mother of the Don." She turns to me, "Besides, I have my sources."

"You mean you have spies within the clan?"

"Also, people who owe me who keep me informed of all important developments." Her eyes gleam, "Of course, if I were to ask my son and grandson, they wouldn't refuse to share information with me, but this way is more interesting, don't you think?"

"Interesting?" I open and shut my mouth, "You really are quite a woman, you know that?"

After the funeral, Michael had driven me here. We hadn't exchanged one word the entire way. Hell, he hadn't even directly looked at me for the duration of the trip. It's almost as if he's trying to avoid me.

"So why is he avoiding you?" Nonna's voice interrupts my thoughts.

What the—! Is she reading my mind or what? I blink, turn my attention to her, "Who's avoiding me?"

She clicks her tongue, "Don't try that with me. You know who I am talking about."

I blink rapidly, then bite the inside of my cheek. If I thought the Sovrano men were overwhelming… Well, Nonna is, undeniably, far ahead of them. "If you mean Michael, it's because he feels responsible for the explosion and for…" I clutch at my glass of wine, "And for the baby, and for what happened to Xander."

"Ah," she takes my arm and guides me to a chair, "sit."

"I am fine." I frown.

"You're not fine. You just left the hospital and you've been through an emotional rollercoaster, not to mention the physical impact of the car blowing up."

I flinch.

"It hurts to hear it, huh?"

"You know it does."

"It's better to talk about it than to keep it all bottled up inside."

"Is that what you did with them when they were growing up?"

She draws in a breath, then urges me to sit down. I sink into the chair, then glance up at her, "Did you?"

"I wish I had," She straightens, and glances across the room at the faces of the Sovrano brothers. "I wish I had been more open with them. Wish I had taken them from under their father's care earlier…but I was weak."

"You, weak?" I laugh, "Not quite how I see you, Nonna."

She glances down at me. "I come from a traditional Sicilian family. I was married at sixteen, pregnant at eighteen with my first child."

"Don Sovrano?"

"Don Sovrano," she nods. "I had four other miscarriages after him. Gave birth to a girl who didn't live."

"I am so sorry," I whisper.

Her lips twist, "It was a long time ago."

"Does the pain…ever go away?"

"It…fades a little with time," she draws in a breath, "but it never leaves you. It settles in your heart, becomes a part of it, so you occasionally take it out and glance at it. You try to get over it but it doesn't really leave you. It becomes a part of you. And much as you want to take the story out of you… Some resonance of it always remains."

"Oh," I blink back my tears, "that's…profound."

She glances away, then back at me, "I know you've been through a lot in the short time that you've known Michael, but the two of you are lucky."

"We are?" I stare, "How can you call us lucky? He kidnapped me. I tried to kill him. He married me because my father promised me to him and he… Ah…hasn't exactly been nice to me since."

"He saw you, saw something in you that he wanted; he took you, wedded you, and despite the fact that you stabbed him at his wedding, did not kill you."

I bite the inside of my cheek.

"You escaped him, only to return to him."

"Only because I thought he was dead."

"He faked his own funeral, knowing it would entice you to come back to him."

I shuffle my feet. "I still wanted to escape him," I whisper.

"Only you were foiled by the car-bomb."

"Now he doesn't want to acknowledge me anymore. He is convinced that my being with him puts me in danger. He wants me to return to London."

"Are you going to?"

"No," I swallow. "No," I say with more vehemence, "if he thinks he can snap a finger and I obey him, then he has another think coming."

"If that isn't true love, what is? He is worried about your safety and you are worried about him. The two of you found each other." She raises a shoulder, "The circumstances were a little, what you English might call dodgy, but that only adds to the excitement, I am sure."

"Nonna," I open and shut my mouth, "you can't say things like that to your granddaughter-in-law; and at a funeral too."

"You're right."

"I am?"

"I am not nearly as drunk as I should be at the funeral of one of my favorite grandsons." She glances around and a waiter materializes with a tray of drinks. She snatches up a snifter of whiskey, then holds it up to me, "To Alessandro."

I opt for the wine, then raise my wineglass, "To Xander."

She drinks from her own glass, then stares into the depths of her whiskey, "He wasn't what he seemed you know?"

"Xander?" I frown, "Are we talking about the same laid-back man who loved to paint and who was the most charming of all the brothers?"

"He was all that, and brilliant at his painting too. A genius ahead of his time, some would say." She takes another healthy swig of her whiskey. "I loved him more than anyone else, maybe even Michael sometimes." She glances around the room, "And the boys know it. But what they didn't realize was that he was also confused."

"Confused?"

She glances at me, "Let's just say, he felt something for Theresa, but never told her so. Not because he couldn't, but because he wasn't sure if he loved her. Because she wasn't the only one he was interested in."

I straighten in my seat. "You mean there was someone else he loved?"

"Not one..." She stares at me meaningfully.

"Oh, so you mean he slept around?"

"He did," she glances away, then back at me, "and not only with women."

"Oh," I take a sip of my wine, "which is normal, right? People are attracted to both men and women sometimes."

"Not in Sicily, they aren't."

"Oh, please," I scoff. "Sicilians are not exempt from who they are drawn to, and I don't understand why you are speaking like this about Xander, considering we've just come from his funeral."

"When you are old like I am, you are always only one step ahead of death, and you never know when it's going to catch up with you."

A shiver runs down my back. "That's…"

"The truth," she cuts in. "I've learned it's best not to fuck around when you have something to say."

I laugh, then turn it into a cough, "Didn't expect you to use that word." I take in her determined features, "You're a force to be reckoned with, Nonna."

"So are you."

"I am?"

She tilts her head, "You'd have to be for the Capo to marry you. You do realize that he broke the norm when he did so."

"And that's a problem…?"

She raises a shoulder, "I'd have been happier if he'd married a nice Sicilian girl, who'd have stayed home and given him kids, but it wasn't to be."

I glower at her.

She raises her hand, "I hope you don't mind I'm being honest with you. I feel like we've gone beyond the need to hide things from each other, don't you think?"

"By all means," I tighten my hold around the stem of my wine glass, "go ahead and tell me what you're thinking."

"Ultimately, though, I am coming around to the fact that you are good for him."

"You are?"

She nods, "Clearly, the two of you are in love with each other, and as I said, it's rare to find that, so…"

"So?"

"So, you'd better play your part and make sure he comes around to accepting you now. And I do hope and pray that you get pregnant quickly again. Nothing like having a man's child to completely change things and ensure that your marriage is on rock solid ground."

"And here I thought you were ahead of your time."

"I am." She smiles sadly, "It's why, after going against my son and ensuring that I moved the boys to LA and took them out of his grasp, and after holding my own against the men of the Cosa Nostra, one thing

I have realized is that it's best not to make things too difficult for yourself."

I frown, "I am really not sure what you are trying to tell me."

"That what you did earlier, when you tried stopping Michael from attacking Luca in front of everyone else... Don't do it again."

"Excuse me?" I snap. "I'll do what I want, when I want with him. He's my husband."

"And the Capo of the Cosa Nostra."

"I know that," I scowl.

"Do you, though?" She looks me up and down, "You are the wife of the most powerful man in Europe. Which means your position comes with certain responsibilities."

"Oh, please," I scoff. "It's not like I am married into the bloody British royal family."

"Isn't it?" She arches an eyebrow.

I blow out a breath, "Can you please stop playing games and just tell me whatever it is that you are trying to say?"

"You tried to stop your husband from beating up his younger brother in front of his rivals and in front of the people who look to him as their leader. The same brother who helped you escape earlier. At the worst, it looks like you were trying to cuckold the Capo—"

"Oh," I gulp.

"—at the best, it looks like you were trying to defy him."

"O-k-a-y," I flush.

"Either way, you made him lose face in front of his clan and his business rivals. And the fact that he didn't turn on you, but actually listened to you, revealed that he places a lot of faith in you."

"What's wrong with that?"

"Haven't you been listening to anything I have been saying?" She scowls, "You showed yourself as being his weakness—"

"—which means I made myself a target all over again? And that it's probably only a matter of time before they try to get to him through me again." I slump my shoulders.

Nonna half smiles, "Knew you were smarter than you look."

"Gee, thanks." I twist my fingers together. "So, what? I need to be more careful how I come across with him in public."

"Among other things." She purses her lips, "Can I share something else with you?"

"Please," I raise my hand, "don't stop now."

"I didn't get along with my mother-in-law, at all, god rest her soul," Nonna crosses herself, "but she did give me one piece of advice which stood me well."

I eye her warily, "And that is?"

She leans in closer, "You need to be a feminist at heart and an independent woman to the outside world, but when it comes to your husband, you want to be his mistress in daily life, and his whore in bed."

6

Michael

I look over to find my Nonna engaged in conversation with my wife. They seem to be getting along. Nonna says something and Karma chokes on her drink. I take a step forward when she places her drink on the table and composes herself. She glances at Nonna, who smiles at her. The old bat actually smiles… And it's one of her rare genuine smiles, too. What the hell?

What are they talking about? And why do I care about it, anyway? I turn my attention back to Sebastian, "It's time." I jerk my chin at him, then pivot and walk out of the living room, down the corridor to my study. My father follows me and closes the door after him. I walk to the bar in the corner, pour whiskey into two glasses. My father walks over and accepts a glass from me.

We each take a sip in silence, then my father turns to me, "It's a mistake, accepting Luca back. He's turned on you once; he can do so again."

"Didn't ask for your advice, father."

He bares his teeth, "She's making you weak. This is what happens when you think with your dick. If you'd only killed her as you'd originally planned instead of marrying her, Xander might still be alive today; she—"

"That's enough," I snap.

My father's eyebrows rise up. "Don't raise your voice," he growls.

"Don't talk about my wife. Not now, not ever. Next time you do so, I'll—"

"What, kill me?" He bares his teeth, "You'd kill your own father over a whore?"

"Shut up," I snarl, "shut the fuck up."

He laughs, "You're losing your ability to think straight."

"And you…" I tighten my grip around my whiskey glass, "are overstepping the line."

"I am your father." He chuckles, "I am meant to overstep the line."

"You're nothing to me," I growl. "The day I consolidate my power with the rival clans, I will take over as Don, and then… You will be nothing to anyone in the Cosa Nostra."

"I look forward to that day."

I snort, "You expect me to believe that?"

He looks me up and down. "You may find it difficult to believe this, but I am your father, and nothing would give me more pleasure than my oldest son succeeding me."

I place my glass on the bar counter, "If that is all—"

"Xander was a liability."

"Excuse me?"

"He wasted all his time painting."

"He had a gift."

"He fucked men."

"I am aware."

The Don stiffens, "You knew it and you didn't do anything about it?"

"He was entitled to do as he pleased."

"Not when he was my son."

"I am not going to stand for you talking shit about him," I growl.

"He's better off dead. At least, his funeral provides a stage for you to turn up the pressure on our rival clans. Now is the time for you to act, to take assertive action that will allow you to consolidate this hold over our rivals, to increase the influence of the Cosa Nostra, to—"

I throw up my fist and catch him in the jaw. He stumbles back, and the glass slips from his grasp and crashes to the floor. "The fuck?" he growls. "How dare you raise your hand to me?"

"I'll do more than that." I straighten as the door to my study flies open. Seb rushes in, followed by Massimo, Christian, Luca, and Adrian. They pause when they notice the Don bleeding from his mouth.

He levels his gaze on me. "You are making a big mistake, boy," he murmurs, "you don't want to make an enemy of me."

"You became my enemy the day you raised your hand to me."

"It was the only way to ensure you grew up to be a man."

"I grew up, all right… To hate you. I don't want you anywhere near my wife or my brothers."

"They are my sons, too."

I turn to the men. "Choose, then," I snap, "him or me."

They glance at each other, then Seb turns to me, "We're with you *fratellone*. You've been more than a father to us, more a parent than the Don has ever has been."

My father chuckles. He glances over the faces of the men, then laughs again. "You leave me no choice then."

"Leave, father," I jerk my chin toward the door, "you have your answer."

"You are going to regret this, each one of you."

Seb walks over to the door and holds it open. The Don turns and stalks over to the exit. He pauses, then turns to glare at us, "When you need help, don't bother coming to me. When you lose everything, including that pretty new wife of yours, you remember that it was I who was behind it."

Turning, he leaves.

The door snicks shut.

"What the fuck?" Christian explodes. "What the hell was that about?"

"He wasn't very complimentary about Xander," I rub my fingers across the back of my neck, "It was inevitable."

"I mean, what did he mean by that threat?"

"That?" I raise my shoulder, "Who the fuck cares?"

"He's not one for idle threats, brother," Massimo cautions.

"Neither am I." I snatch up my glass, drain it, top it up again, then walk over to take my seat behind the desk.

"Out," I jerk my chin at the door, "it's time to cut this bullshit short."

. . .

Ten minutes later, I lean back in my chair as I take in Nikolai and JJ. The silence stretches as none of us speak. Neither JJ nor Nikolai shuffle in their seats nor look uncomfortable. Their faces wear the same expression of patience that I assume my features reflect... At least, I hope it does. I glance between them, then consider my drink.

"Revenge," I finally say, "is a powerful emotion. It can make or break a man. It can galvanize you to do the kinds of things you didn't think you were capable of."

"And you need revenge," JJ ventures. "Hell, I would too if it were my brother who was killed in an explosion, and my wife who was hurt."

"She was pregnant," I growl. "My wife was pregnant."

Silence descends, then Nikolai murmurs, "I am sorry, brother. How can we help you?"

"By helping me track down the bastards behind this."

"I'll spread the word... Hell, if your speech earlier hasn't gone viral within the underground network...in a manner of speaking, that is," JJ offers, "I'll make sure I alert all of my sources. It's only a matter of time before the perpetrators are found.

I jerk my chin, "And you, Nikolai?" I train my gaze on him, "What are you thinking?"

"Whoever did it was, clearly, after your life."

"That's no secret. He's the Capo. Hell, they want him to step down from becoming the Don." JJ frowns. "They were trying to finish him off before he took the position."

"Is that all it was?" Nikolai drawls.

"What else could it be?" JJ replies.

"You tell me," Niko holds my gaze, "you sure you're looking in the right place, Michael?"

My heart begins to race and my pulse pounds at my temples. I lean back into the chair, and the handle of my knife that's tucked in at the small of my waistband digs into my back. "You're implying—"

"That it may have been one of your own." Niko nods. "Don't tell me the thought hadn't occurred to you?"

It had, but I am not going to own up to it. "You let me take care of what happens with my clan." I tip up my chin. "I simply need you to spread the word among your men and their contacts. I want the culprits to be brought to heel before Christmas."

JJ whistles, "That's only a few days away."

"More than enough time, if the two of you get behind the effort."

"You threatening us, Michael?" Niko asks in a soft voice.

"I am..." I glance between them, "reminding you that when we embarked on this partnership, it meant that you prioritize my...request before anyone else's."

"Your brother was killed; it's like my own was taken from me." JJ raps his knuckles on the table, "Consider it done."

I turn to Niko whose gaze narrows. He seems like he's about to say something, then changes his mind. "I'll get my men on the job."

I rise to my feet and so do they. JJ turns to leave and Niko follows.

"Nikolai," I call out and he pauses, "I am counting on you."

He glances at me over his shoulder, "Partnerships are almost as important to me as family." He touches his forefinger to his forehead then stalks out.

I walk toward the bar and pour the rest of the whiskey into my glass. The door opens and her scent reaches me. I stiffen, then place the now empty whiskey bottle down on the counter. The door snicks shut and footsteps approach. I sense her pause behind me. She touches my arm and I pull away. I walk over to my chair and sink down into it.

"What are you doing here?" I ask as she stands there, still dressed in that black dress that outlines her every curve. She reaches up, removes her hat with the netting and places it on the bar counter. Instantly, my gaze is drawn to the wound on her forehead. Her features are pale, her frame too slim. There are dark shadows under her eyes, and fuck, if she doesn't look like she's going to collapse any moment. As if on cue, she sways and I curse. I slam my glass down on the table, then lunge forward. I reach her just as she puts out a hand to steady herself.

I swing her up in my arms and she protests, "Put me down, Michael."

"Not a bloody chance."

She chuckles, "You're swearing like a true Brit."

"God forbid," I snap as I walk toward the door.

"Where are you taking me?" she asks in a soft voice.

"To bed, which is where you should have been all day."

"I couldn't have missed the funeral, Michael," she protests. "Xander was my friend... maybe one of the only friends I have made since I came to Sicily."

"What about Cassandra and Aurora?"

"They are my friends too, but Xander... He was special, you know?"

A ball of emotion clogs my throat. I increase my pace, until I reach the steps. I take them two at a time and reach the landing. I stalk down the corridor to her room, then shoulder my way inside. Her cat meows, then brushes past my legs. I stumble, right myself. "Bloody cat," I swear, and she laughs.

"Yep, my influence is rubbing off on you, Capo."

I reach the bed, lower her down onto it, then reach over and pull off her stilettos. "What was the need to wear these god-awful things? You could have worn something that did not put so much pressure on your back."

"Worried about me, Capo?"

Her soft voice coils in my chest. My heart stutters and my groin hardens. Every sense in my body seems to focus in on her. I straighten, take in her pale features. "Painkillers," I growl. "Where are your painkillers?"

She nods toward the bath and I walk over, rummage around in the shelves behind the mirror until I find them. I walk over, hand them over to her, then pour a glass of water from the carafe on the bedside table. She swallows down the pills with the water, then sinks back. I take in her dress-covered body, "Why don't you take that off? You must be uncomfortable in that."

She hesitates and I scowl, "I've seen everything there is to see, Karma."

She looks like she's going to protest, then nods. She sits up and I grip the hem of her dress. I drag it up and she raises her hips, then her arms so I can pull it up and off of her. I drape the dress over the chair, then take in her pale body. She's wearing a black bra and panties, and I take in the marks on her shoulders, across her chest, the small bandage across her belly button where they'd had to perform a keyhole surgery to stop the internal bleeding. My heart thuds in my chest. My gut twists. I sit down next to her on the bed and touch the bandage. She flinches and I pull back. "Does it hurt?"

"No," she whispers, "it's...just difficult seeing it, that's all."

I flatten my palm across her belly and goosebumps pop on her skin. "Are you cold?"

She shakes her head. The cat pads over to me, brushes against my leg again and mewls. "He wants to come up on the bed." Karma says softly. I bend, pick him up, place him next to Karma. The cat instantly curls into her side and purrs. She drags her fingers down his fur and smiles. I take in the way her fingers slide across his skin, how he stretches, then coils in on himself and closes his eyes. Lucky cat, to be able to press into her body and fall asleep with not a care in the world. Fuck, how can I be jealous of a bloody cat? And since when have I started using 'bloody' to swear? Maybe she is right. Maybe more of her influence has rubbed off on me then I'd care to admit. I rise to my feet and she reaches up and grabs my wrist.

"Stay, Michael," she implores. "Please, just for tonight. I don't want to be alone."

I glance away, then back at her. "You need to leave, Karma," I finally say. "I can't do what's needed if I'm constantly worried about you. It's best you return to London, to your family."

"You're my family, Michael. You and your brothers. I am one of you now."

I shake my head, "I can't justify putting you in so much danger."

"If you think my leaving you will help lessen it, then you are wrong." She sits up and the cat protests, then rises up on its feet and stalks away to the other side of the bed. "You know I'm safest when I am with you."

"I know no such thing."

"Why are you being so cold, so withdrawn? Why can't you see what's in front of your eyes?"

"Karma," I warn her, "I don't want to argue with you about this."

"Then don't." She stares at me and I hold her gaze. The silence stretches, then she sighs, "There's no talking you out of this, is there?"

I shake my head.

"Fine, then." She glances away and her chin wobbles. A tear slides down her cheek and my chest tightens. I sink back onto the bed, gather her close. She coils into me much like the cat had done earlier and sniffs. "I wish I hadn't lost the child, Michael. I hadn't thought I was looking forward to the birth of the baby, but I was, more than I'd ever imagined. I mean, I'd never thought I'd become a mother, and now it's all I can think of."

I wrap my arms around her, pull her closer. A shudder grips her as I run my hand in circles over her back. "I'm sorry, Beauty. Truly, I am."

The tears drip from her face, wet my shirt as I hold and rock her.

"I... I am also sorry that I interfered earlier today," she hiccups.

"Interfered?" I scowl, "What are you talking about?"

"When you went after Luca, I tried to stop you. I swear, I had no idea how that could be interpreted by the guests. I simply wanted to ensure that you wouldn't hurt yourself."

"I can take care of myself, Beauty," I press my lips to her forehead, "but your concern is much appreciated."

"Oh," she peers up at me, "so you're not pissed off that I made you lose face in front of everyone?"

"Maybe a little," I lie. "As you're aware, I don't take kindly to being told what to do."

"Not even by your wife?" She flutters her eyelashes, still spiky from her tears, and my heart stutters.

I peer into her face, then half smile, "You're learning how to get your way with me, hmm?"

"Me?" she sniffles, "I'm doing no such thing," She snuggles into me, "I simply want to make sure that I am not treading on anyone's toes without realizing it."

I draw in a breath, "Nonna's been talking to you, I take it?"

"A little bit," she mutters. "She does have a point. I really don't want you to lose face because of me."

I notch my knuckles under her chin so she has no choice but to meet my gaze, "I'll never lose face because of you, Beauty. And you don't have to change yourself in order to be by my side..." I hesitate.

She frowns, "But? There is a but isn't there?"

"But, you still can't defy me—not in public, and not in private. I am not a man who can be ordered around."

"You don't say?" She widens her gaze, "I really hadn't noticed that about you, Capo."

I can't stop the chuckle that rumbles up my chest. I grasp the nape of her neck, bring my forehead to hers, "So damn sassy." I brush my nose against hers, then press a kiss to her mouth, before tucking her head under my chin.

She nestles against me, as I rub circles over her back.

Her body twitches, and I glance down to find her eyes shut. I hold her a little longer, until her breathing deepens. Then I place her onto the bed. I pull the sheets up and tuck them under her chin. I glance at the cat, who pads over and settles in beside her. "Keep watch over her," I murmur as I bend and kiss her forehead.

I straighten and watch her a few more seconds. I take in her now flushed features, those slightly parted rosebud lips, the slender length of her throat. When I leave, I know what I must do next.

7

Karma

A knock on the door wakes me up. I open my eyes and grimace. A dull headache knocks at my temples, and my eyes feel swollen. I turn over on my back, and glance around the shadowed room. The curtains have been drawn... and I normally leave them open before I go to bed. That way, I know approximately what time it is when I wake up. Which means someone else must have drawn them... Michael... He must have done it before leaving. Had he stayed last night? Had he watched me sleep? I remember clinging to him, asking him to stay and then I had started to cry, damn it. I had clung to him and wept, and he had drawn me close to him and held me, and then, I don't remember anything. I must have fallen asleep in his arms. When had he left?

Next to me is Andy. He walks to the edge of the bed, jumps off, then pads over to the door. He turns to me, then glances back at the door. I swear, that cat can talk without saying a word. He's way too smart for his own good.

The knock sounds again. I sit up, call out, "Come in."

Cassandra shoulders open the door and Andy darts to the side. She walks in holding a breakfast tray. Andy follows her. She places the tray on the table near the window, draws the curtains open. The sunlight streams in and I wince.

"Good morning," she choruses as she looks me up and down. "How do you feel today?"

"Sore," I cough, then throw my legs over the side of the bed. I stand up, and every muscle in my body feels like it has been put through the wringer.

Andy walks over purring loudly; he brushes against my calf. I glance down, remember I am still in my bra and panties. I glance around for a robe or something to cover myself with.

"Here," Cassandra hands me the robe she grabbed from the chair near the bed. Andy prances away as I walk slowly into the bathroom, feeling every bit of the hard fall I took when I was ejected from the car. To think, I could have very easily died... Like Xander... Poor Xander... Like my child.

A shudder grips me. I walk over to the sink in the bathroom and grip the edge, take in a deep breath. Another. I need to stop circling back to what happened. Need to somehow focus on the now, the present... On proving to my husband that I would be safest by his side. I open the faucet, hold my palms out under the flowing water. I splash the water onto my face, brush my teeth, comb my hair back. By the time I step out, I am feeling a little better... At least, more collected, at any rate. I walk over to the tray of food on the table and take a seat. Cassandra pours a mug of coffee for me.

"Why don't you join me?" I ask.

She seems like she's about to refuse and I shake my head, "Please, I insist. I really could do with some company right now."

She hesitates, then nods. Pouring herself a cup of coffee, she sits down opposite me. I reach for one of the plates that had covered the dishes. I turn it over, pile it with scrambled eggs, toast and bacon, and push it toward her.

"Oh no, I can't," she protests.

I scowl. "I bet you haven't eaten breakfast today."

She blinks.

"Well, have you?"

She shakes her head.

"Come on, then." I nod toward her plate.

"There's only one set of cutlery," she points out.

"We can share," I reach for a fork and push my spoon toward her.

She grabs it and for a few seconds the sound of cutlery hitting the plate fills the space. When I have polished off almost everything on my plate, I place my fork down, "Is the Capo working from his home office today?" I ask.

"He left very early and told me he wouldn't be back for dinner."

"Oh," I blink, "guess he's working from his office at Venom, then."

She glances up at me, "He told me to help you in any way needed with the Christmas party."

I hold her gaze, "Guess you're thinking that it's in bad taste to hold a celebration so soon after a funeral?"

"I think it will help bridge the rift between the brothers."

"You mean between Michael and Luca?"

She nods, "And Sebastian and Christian."

"What's up between those two?"

She raises a shoulder, "I am not sure, but they seem to always be fighting."

"Hmm," I toy with my fork, "I'm hoping some kind of event to commemorate Xander's memory is what they need to lower the barriers between them and talk."

"More like talk with their fists," she snorts. "Those brothers have been known to fight at the least provocation."

"Really?" I frown. "They always come across as so suave and sophisticated."

"It's all a front." She shrugs. "When they were younger, they got into scraps all the time. It drove Nonna crazy."

"Nonna," I chuckle, "that woman is formidable. I guess she'd have to be to survive so long in this family of men, but still... I don't know whether to be in awe of her or to hate her."

"The former." Cassandra reaches for her coffee. "You have her on your side and it will be easier to win over everyone else in the family."

"Not that I want to have anything to do with Michael's father." I shiver. "That man gives me the creeps."

"The Don is dangerous," she admits, "but I don't think you have anything to worry about from him. Michael will make sure that the Don keeps his distance."

"I sure hope so," I murmur, "especially since they are both coming to the Christmas party."

"You also need to reach out to Theresa."

"Xander's friend?"

She nods, "If it's an event to celebrate Xander's life, it would be incomplete without her."

"Can you help me reach out to her?"

"Better than that, I've already asked her to come to meet you later today."

"Why can't I go to meet her?"

"Because the Capo has left instructions that you are not to leave the house."

I blow out a breath. He doesn't want me to leave the house and yet...he doesn't want me to stay with him. The man is seriously making my head spin.

"What's wrong?" Cassandra peers into my face, "Everything okay?"

"Peachy," I murmur, "what time is Theresa coming?"

8

Michael

"Capo."

I glance up as Luca strides into the room. He glances around at the assembled faces. Sebastian and Christian are sprawled in chairs in front of my table; Adrian leans against a wall; Massimo is seated in the middle of a settee on the far side, with his bulk taking up most of the space. All of them stalk him as he comes to a halt in the middle of the floor. He meets my gaze head on. "Is this going to be an inquisition?" he murmurs.

"What do you think?" I lean back in my chair. "Our father thinks it's a mistake that I took you in."

"And you?" He folds his arms across his chest, "What do you think?"

I rise to my feet, lean forward and place my palms flat on the table, "I think it would be a mistake if I didn't."

His chest rises and falls, "I am sorry, Michael." Luca looks around at his brothers. "I never meant to hurt any of you."

"And yet, you did." I curl my lips, "I am not interested in your apologies, Luca."

"What then?" He shuffles his feet, "What else do you want from me, Michael."

"Information."

"Ah," his forehead smoothens, "of course, you do. I should have known that this, too, would be a transaction for you."

"You didn't think I would simply let you walk back into the *famiglia* without paying a price for your indiscretions."

"Of course, not." He chuckles, "There's more of the old man in you than you'd like to admit, Michael."

I set my jaw, "Who was behind the attack, Luca?"

He blinks. "You think I know who was behind it? Don't you think I would have stopped him, then?"

"I don't know, Luca, would you have stopped him?"

He shakes his head, "Do you really have to ask me that question, Michael?"

"You tell me, Luca." I look him up and down. "Last I knew, you were helping my wife escape. You watched, you even encouraged her to take the oar to my forehead."

"I saw my opportunity and took it, Michael."

"Why would you do that?" Christian springs to his feet, "Why would you go against one of us? You showed our enemies that we are not invincible. You exposed a chink in the armor. It's why they dared place a bomb in the car. It's why they dared try to harm us. You are responsible for Xander's death as much as the person who actually planted that bomb."

Luca's jaw tics. He lowers his arms to his sides, "I would have done anything to protect Xander. I never would have hurt him, or one of you."

"And what do you call what you did to Michael?" Christian glares at him. "How can you stand there and claim what you did wasn't to hurt us when all the evidence points to the contrary? In fact, how dare you think you can simply walk back in and pick up where you left off, after everything that happened?" He lunges toward Luca, but Massimo jumps up to his feet, and with a litheness that belies his bulk, Massimo grabs Christian around his chest and yanks him back. Christian growls, strains in his hold, but Massimo doesn't let go.

"Take him out, until he's cooled down," I order and Christian snarls.

"Let me get my hands on the bastard. It's he who's responsible for what happened to Xander. When I get hold of you, I am going to kill you, you motherfucker!"

Massimo tries to steer Christian away, but Christian resists. The two grapple. Adrian leaps to his feet and grips Christian's shoulder. Between him and Massimo, they manage to maneuver Christian out of the room. The door snicks shut and I turn to Luca.

"Who were you working with?" I snap. "This is your chance to come clean, Luca."

His shoulders flex. He uncurls his fists at his sides and lowers his chin. "The Kane Company," he says in a hard voice. "My plan was to join forces with them, and try to take you down."

"Motherfucker," Sebastian growls. "Fucking *Cani*," he grumbles, alluding to the Italian pronunciation of the word that translates to dogs.

"So were they behind the rigging of the car."

He frowns, "I honestly don't know."

I scowl, "You'd better know."

"I swear upon our mother," Luca thumps his chest, "I have no idea who's behind it. When I heard what had happened, all I knew was that I needed to be with my family. That I had to help you track down who did it and ensure they realize that they can't fuck with us again."

I drag my fingers through my hair. "Fuck," I hiss. "This is bloody unhelpful." I walk around the table, then stalk over to him. "What else can you tell us? What else is the Kane Company up to? You'd better have something for me, Luca, if you want to rejoin."

Luca shuffles his feet. "JJ exploited the fact that I wanted to be Capo. He offered me the chance to be his second-in-command with the understanding that I'd take over from him."

"And his son?" Sebastian frowns, "Wouldn't his son be next in line for succession?"

"His son's a tech wiz. Runs a multibillion-dollar tech start-up in Silicon Valley. He's hardly interested in following in his father's footsteps."

"JJ's not that old, though," Seb scowls. "He's what, forty-nine?"

"If that," Luca retorts. "Look, I didn't really want to take over as the head of the Kane Company. I just wanted to send a signal to you guys that you were not the only fish in the sea. That if I could not become the Don of the Cosa Nostra, there were other places I could go."

"Fuck, Luca," I glower at him, "all you had to do was talk to me, brother. We could have figured something out."

"The way you did when you went off to LA, leaving the rest of us behind?"

My heart thuds in my ribcage. "I am sorry for that; I truly am. If I could do it all over again, I wouldn't have left until I had a chance to take the rest of you with me."

"Save it, Mika." He cracks his neck. "It's water under the bridge."

"Fuck, brother, I would have done anything to ensure all of you were safe. If I had had any inkling that he'd come after you, Luca, I would have…"

"Killed him?" Luca says softly, "There's still time."

"He's our father." I roll my shoulder. "As much as I hate to say it, he is our sperm donor."

"And he'd be happy to kill any of us if he could hold onto his position as Don."

"What the fuck are you talking about?"

"Do you really think our 'dear father' will let go of his power that easily?"

I squeeze my fingers into fists, "Are you saying he was behind what happened to Xander and my wife?"

"I wouldn't put it past him."

Fact is, after how he beat our mother and drove her to an early death, I wouldn't be surprised either. And yet, I can't quite accept it. Maybe a part of me still clings to the hope that there is some modicum of love in him toward his own children? Despite what he said about Luca and Xander on the day of the funeral…

I curl my fingers into fists, "He's a bastard, and granted, he fucked up our lives…but family is the one thing that is important to him." I roll my shoulders. "He's always been clear that he wanted me to succeed him. Hell, he's the one who nominated me for Capo. It's thanks to his vote of confidence that I took over this role."

"You'd have become the Capo with or without his help, Michael." Luca's lips twist. "You have the leadership qualities, the ability to influence people, the determination and motivation to become a Don, before anything else."

Until I met her. Now all that matters is keeping her safe. No matter that it means I am going to do something that's going to make her hate me. It's better that way though. It'll make it easier for her to walk away from me.

"Michael?" Seb's voice cuts through the thoughts in my head. I turn to him and Seb takes in my features. "You okay?"

I jerk my chin, "Have we had any other information from any of our sources?"

Seb scowls, "Nothing, Michael. It's like whoever did it has buried himself in a hole and pulled the hole in after him."

Fuck, every day that goes by without us tracking down those responsible, the more the danger grows. And if it's our father who was behind it… It means she isn't safe, even in my home. It means he might still go after her, and if anything were to happen to her… This time… I would not be able to get over it. There is only one way out. To expedite my plan.

9

Karma

The sound of footsteps reaches me and I glance up from the outfit I've been working on.

After breakfast, I had taken a nap, then woken up refreshed. I had met Theresa, Xander's friend, and it had been clear that she had been in love with him. He'd never mentioned anything to her, and she hadn't exactly confessed her feelings to him either. She had broken down during the course of the meeting and had been so regretful about the fact that she'd never gotten to tell him how she felt.

It certainly put things in perspective. It was a poignant reminder that you have only one life and you'd better go after what you want in the time you have... Like him.

I had been emotionally drained after the meeting and had ended up eating lunch and taking another nap, from which I had woken up disoriented a few hours ago. I'd grabbed some tea, then decided to start working on this outfit—the idea had been bubbling in my mind since I had woken this morning.

It's a good thing I slept a lot today, because I feel stronger and more alert. I am determined to stay awake until Michael gets home, and God knows, I'll need all of my faculties for what I have in mind. I mean, I am going to confront him again. No way, am I giving up and allowing him to send me away. He needs to understand that it really is safest for me with him and there is no way I am leaving him… Not now, when he needs me most. So, I've been focused on my creation while keeping my ears peeled for him. Until, I hear the sound of footsteps in the corridor.

I rise to my feet, and walking over to the door, I peer outside into the corridor. Another sound reaches me from the direction of Michael's room. I step out into the corridor, reach his door, and push it. It swings open to reveal Michael sprawled out at the foot of his bed. His tie is off, his shirt sleeves rolled up. His legs, still clad in his pants, are spread out…and between them is a woman.

She's kneeling, her back to me, her hair flowing around her shoulders as she leans forward. Her shoulders move and her head bobs… What the hell? I glance up to find Michael staring at me. His features are unperturbed, almost as if he expected me to walk in on him.

Hell, he expected me to walk in on him, all right. It's why he brought her here. My heart begins to thud and my pulse rate ratchets up. I take a step forward and my knees seem to buckle. I grab the door frame and steady myself. Watch as he buries his fingers in her hair and begins to move her head forward and back, and forward. She moans and the sound snaps me out of the weird haze I'd fallen into.

"What are you doing, Michael?" I snarl. "How dare you…you…?"

"Shove my cock down another woman's throat?" He smirks, and his blue eyes seem to gleam with suppressed mirth.

"What the fuck, Mika?" I take another step forward and he chuckles.

"Do you want to join us, wife? I wouldn't say no to a threesome."

I pause, "Why the hell are you trying to put distance between us Michael? After everything we've been through, I thought you'd realize that my place is with you."

"Your place is…" he glances down at the woman between his legs, "where I tell you to be."

"Fuck this," I growl. "This is not you, Michael. You are not the macho, overbearing, chauvinistic man you try to portray yourself as."

"No?" He tilts his head, "Pray, enlighten me then about my qualities."

"You care about people, your family, your brothers. Hell, you even care about your lousy father."

He stiffens.

"You care about me, Michael. You love me."

"So?" He raises a shoulder. The woman begins to lean back and his muscles bunch as he grips her hair tighter. He pushes his hips forward and my stomach knots. A cold sensation pools in my chest.

"Stop it," I say in a low voice. "Stop it, right now."

"You don't give me orders, Beauty."

"Don't call me that."

"How about I call you the love of my life, hmm?"

"Am I, though?" I swallow, "I am beginning to think you don't really understand the meaning of the word love."

"And you do?"

I nod. "It's what I felt for the child I carried," I press my fingers against my stomach. "It's what I feel for you, Michael."

"Love," he smirks, "is overrated. It's sex that matters, and the ability to fuck who you want, when you want. Speaking of…do you want me to fuck you, Beauty?"

"I lost our child not four days ago. Do you think I want to be fucked, asshole?"

"I think," he looks me up and down, "I could take your ass. That wouldn't hurt any of the other parts now, would it?"

I snap my head back, "Fuck you, Michael. Don't do this to us, please. Just tell me all of this is an act, that you are simply doing this to piss me off so you can get me to leave."

"This," he yawns, "is me, Beauty. The real me. The man you married."

"The man I married was not only in touch with his emotions, but he also had the courage to express them. He wouldn't have put me through this…" I wave a hand at the space between us, "whatever this is."

"This is called scratching an itch. Speaking of," he cracks his neck, "you joining us or what?"

"No."

"Then you may as well leave, babe."

"You sure, Michael?" I wipe the tear that has somehow squeezed out of the corner of my eye. "Once I am gone, I won't return."

"Don't take this too badly," he gestures to the woman between his legs. "It's normal for us Mafia guys to have women on the side, you know. It had to happen sooner or later. Best you see it now, so there are no more illusions."

"You told me that you wouldn't fuck anyone else. You swore that you took your vows to me seriously."

He shrugs. "Guess I lied."

Anger thrums at my temples. I draw in a breath and my lungs burn. I take a step forward and that's when she grips his thighs, tips her head, and I can all but sense her taking him down her throat. My heart squeezes in on itself. My stomach seems to bottom out and specks of darkness blink at the corners of my vision. Damn, if I am going to faint here, in front of him and that…that…whoever that is. I spin on my feet, stagger to the door, then step out.

"Shut the door behind you, would you?"

His voice follows me out as I slam the door shut behind me. I lean against it, drawing in a breath, then another. Force myself to put one foot in front of the other. I reach my room, manage to shut the door behind me. Andy walks over and purrs as he weaves between my legs. I sink down, gather him close, and burst into tears. Fuck him, fuck the Mafia, fuck this bloody town. I am getting out of here, before he does something else that's going to humiliate me further.

His fingers had tightened on the back of her head, his biceps bulging with the effort. He dared allow her to feel the thickness of his cock? He dared let her kneel in front of him, allowed her to take the position that belongs only to me? He dared…let another woman close enough to smell him, to put her lips on him, to wind her fingers about his massive thighs? To touch what is mine?

Fuck. This. Shit.

I rise to my feet and begin to pack. Ten minutes later, I am done. I've only packed a couple of dresses, underwear, the essentials, and that's it. I am not going to take anything else that…that bastard bought for me. Andy rolls around on the carpet, then springs up to chase a ball of yarn that I had tossed his way earlier. How the hell am I going to carry him, though? Of course, he was given to me by Michael too, but no way, am I going to leave him behind.

There's a knock on the door and before I can call out, it opens. Cassandra walks in carrying a pet carrier with her. She holds it out to me without saying anything.

"He told you, eh?" I swallow back the anger that clogs my throat. Asshole couldn't wait to get me out of his home, apparently. I walk over, grab the pet carrier and place it near Andy who, of course, decides that's the moment he wants to run away. He darts into the bathroom and I blow out a breath.

"I'll get him, while you get dressed," she murmurs.

She walks toward the bathroom and I change into a pair of jeans and a shirt, both of which had appeared in the closet, along with a pair of sneakers. All of these things which Michael had gotten for me, in my size, and without my having to ask for anything. He'd known how much I needed to feel comfortable in those early days of my pregnancy. It was as if he'd read my mind and gleaned exactly how I wanted to be taken care of...without smothering me. And now...

He was getting a blow job from another woman? Fuck. Why the hell did he have to do that? Even if it was all an act... But it wasn't. It had seemed all too fucking real from where I was.

There's another knock on the door. I snarl at the back of my throat. What the hell is this? Paddington station, where everyone comes and goes as they want? The knock comes again and I call out, "Come in."

Adrian opens the door. He glances past me to where Cassandra has stepped back into the room. She falters and the air seems to buzz with some unsaid emotion. I glance between them, am about to speak, then change my mind. Whatever. I have enough of my own shit to deal with.

"Believe you need a ride?" Adrian murmurs.

"Took him no time to alert his cronies to the fact that I am leaving, huh?"

"The chopper is waiting."

I blink. "The chopper? That's how fast he wants me out of here?"

Adrian merely stands there without speaking.

"Not that it matters. And yeah, I'll take the chopper ride. Why not?"

Cassandra walks over to the pet carrier with Andy. She sinks to her knees, coaxes him inside. I get a glimpse of the compartments inside which carry collapsible bowls and food, water, there's even a compartment with kitty litter. Wow, that's one top-of-the-line carrier that Mika has sprung for. How can a man who takes such good care of my pet, also turn out to be so unfaithful? It doesn't make sense.

Cassandra locks the door and rises to her feet, "I'll come with you, until the chopper."

"No, thanks." I reach out and she hands the pet carrier over to me. I grab my bag in my free hand, then pause. I nod to her. "Thanks Cassandra," I murmur, "you've been a good friend."

"I am so sorry, Karma," she whispers, then steps forward and hugs me. Andy mewls and I step away from her.

"Maybe I'll see you at some point, huh?" I turn away, then pause, "Tell Aurora I'll try to reach her once I've figured out what I am going to do next."

She nods and I turn away. I follow Adrian down the corridor, past *his* closed bedroom door, down the steps, out of the house and to the chopper. The helicopter's rotors begin to whir as we approach it. Adrian opens the door, helps me up, then deposits my bag and Andy's pet carrier next to me.

Massimo looks up from the controls, "Where would you like to go?"

10

Michael

After she walks away from the door, I wait for a few minutes, just to make sure she's not in hearing range, then I push Larissa away.

She falls back on her ass. "Hey," she protests, "I haven't even started."

"It doesn't matter." I zip up my pants and stand up, move past her and head to the door. I grip the handle, only to stop myself. *Let her go; let her leave.* That's what you wanted, and that's what you are getting. She is leaving you, and it's the only way for her to be safe.

I sense Larissa stand up and move toward me. She places her hand on my shoulder and I shake it off.

"Let her go," she murmurs. "You and I can have a lot more fun together, like we used to. The bitch has no idea how lucky she was to have had you even for a little time. Now that she's gone —"

"Shut up," I turn on her and she stumbles back. "Shut the fuck up."

She pales. "I… I…only meant —"

"Get out," I jerk my chin toward the door, "and make sure she doesn't see you or hear you." She nods, then rushes to the door. I push the door shut, then walk to the bathroom. I glance at myself in the mirror, stare into my reflection. *You asshole. You complete idiot. What have you done?*

I blew any chance of her ever being with me again. I shattered her heart... And so soon after the loss of our child. What is wrong with me? In one swoop, I had broken her trust in me... A trust I'll never be able to rebuild. I've ensured that she'll hate me, and treat me as what I am: her kidnapper, her captor... Her husband, who had cheated on her with another woman.

"Minchia!" Only when my fist connects with the mirror do I realize that I have swung at it. The pain slices up my arm as blood drips down and splatters on the sink and down on the floor. I gaze at the fragments of my reflection in the shattered mirror.

An hour later, Seb and Christian arrive with Aurora in tow. When I had finally pulled my head out of my ass, I had called Seb who'd, in turn, contacted Christian, and the two had turned up with her. Christian hands the medical bag over to Aurora and she approaches me. She pulls up a chair, then unrolls the towel I'd wrapped around my hand and grimaces." I'll need to stitch this."

"Do it." I turn my attention to where Christian is positioned by the doorway watching her. She cleans and disinfects the cuts. "This will hurt," She glances up at me. "Do you want an anesthetic to numb the area before I —"

"No," I growl, "just get on with it."

Christian shuffles his feet. I stare at him and he glares back. *Stronzo* seems to have taken a shine to the fair doctor. At least, it seems to have taken his mind off of Xander. Xander...

The band around my chest tightens. The needle digs into my skin and I wince. The doctor peers up at me, and I jerk my chin at her to continue stitching. She firms her jaw, focuses on the stitching once more.

I sense Christian scowling at me, and I arch an eyebrow. He seems like he's about to say something, then firms his lips. He watches as she stitches me up. When she's done with her task, she cuts the last thread. She bandages my right hand, then begins to pack up her things.

"Thank you," I mutter.

"Try and keep it dry, and I am giving you a prescription for antibiotics to prevent any infections." She hands over a sheet of paper, then rises to her feet. "May I speak with Karma before I leave?"

"No," I say in a hard voice, and she blinks.

"No?" She scowls, "Why not?"

"Because she's not here."

"Not here?" She searches my features, "She's recovering from a serious accident, and she's not here? Where did she go? She should be resting, she—"

"*Basta,*" I raise my hand, then turn to Christian, "get her out of here."

"Get me out of here?" She firms her lips, "I am not some piece of luggage that he owns, that you can command him to move me around, you know."

"Not yet," Christian drawls.

She turns on him, "What's that supposed to mean?" She scowls, "If you think you have any claim on me, you are sadly mistaken."

"It's because of me that you and your family are still alive, make no mistake," Christian retorts.

Her face pales. She draws in a breath as he walks over and snatches up her bag, "Let's go, Doc."

She scowls at him, then back at me, "Not until I am sure that Karma is safe."

I glare at her, "She's my wife. Of course, she's safe."

"She's your wife. That's why I am worried about her."

I rise to my feet and she takes a step back. She bumps into Christian, who reaches out to steady her. She pulls away from him, tucks her elbows into her sides and tips up her chin, "What did you do to her?"

"I told you, woman. I didn't do anything to her. She's safe—much safer than she was here."

"What's that supposed to mean?"

I drag my fingers through my hair, "Look, she left for her own good. If she were here, she'd only be a target for our rival clans, or whoever it is that was behind the blast that blew up her car."

She swallows, "You…you think they are going to target her again?"

"I have no doubt they are going to strike again, and as long as she was here with me, she would have been their focus."

"That's why you let her go?"

"I told her to leave because we're done."

"Done?"

"Our marriage is done, over, *finito,* kaput," I slice my hand through the air, "and that is all I am going to say about that particular topic."

She opens her mouth, then shuts it. "How can I reach her?"

"You can't."

"She's my friend. I want to get in touch with her and make sure that she is safe."

"If you reach out to her, you'll only draw attention to where she is. Do you understand that?"

She blows out a breath, then wraps her arms around her waist, "You were wrong to let her go."

Don't I know it? I jerk my chin at Christian and he grips her shoulder. "Let's go, Doc," he says, his voice gentle. "As soon as I get any word about her, I'll let you know."

She turns to him, "Promise?"

He nods. Their eyes meet, hold. A flush tinges her cheeks. She pulls away from him, then walks to the door, leaving him staring after her.

Seb snorts, "Go on then. You've been called to heel, *coglione.*"

Christian scowls at him, "Shut the fuck up, *testa di cazzo.*"

Seb laughs and Christian turns to me, "You'd better know what you are doing, brother." With a last glare in Seb's direction, he follows Aurora out.

I drag my fingers through my hair, then wince when a flash of pain slides up my arm. And this is from just a cut. How much pain was she in after what she had been through? Had I been wrong to break up with her in that fashion and send her on her way? It was for her own good, after all.

So why is there a sinking sensation in the pit of my stomach? Why does my chest feel heavy? I'm rubbing the skin above my heart when Seb's phone rings.

He pulls it out, answers it, then turns to me. "We have a suspect."

Half an hour later, I enter the basement that's two stories down in the house. Luca stands facing a man who's been strung up from the ceiling. Antonio walks out to stand guard by the basement door. Purely a precaution, as the staff have been forbidden from coming down here, and the only woman who would have been nosy enough to find her way here is gone.

I clench my fingers at my sides. Fuck, I have to stop thinking about her and get on with the job at hand. The sooner I can track down whoever was behind the explosion, the sooner I can try to earn her forgiveness. Which, given how she'd left me, would be a complete miracle. What a bloody mess.

I roll my shoulders and glare at the man who watches me without any change in expression. He's in his late thirties, well built, dark-haired, and he meets my gaze. Interesting. None of my own men would have the courage to do that, which means he isn't from around here. I walk over to him, pause when I'm a couple of feet away. "You have something to tell me?" I ask.

The man's features harden. He clears his throat, then spits. The glob of saliva narrowly misses me and falls to the ground between us.

"*Figlio di puttana*!" Luca growls as he lunges forward and slams his fist into the man's side. The stranger groans and sways. Luca hits him again and the sound of ribs cracking fills the space. The man gasps, and blood drips from his mouth.

"Enough," I say mildly. "Good to know your anger issues haven't diminished in the time you were away."

Luca steps back and shakes out his hand. "Motherfucker, that hurts like a bitch."

I turn back to the man. "You have something to tell me?"

He glares at me. Sweat pours down his face, and blood blotches stain his shirt. He lowers his chin and firms his lips.

"No?" I pull out my knife and the overhead light bounces off of it. He blinks, lowers his gaze to the knife, then back at me. I close the distance between us, until the smell of his fear envelops me. He glances at Luca, then back at me, but doesn't say a word.

"Last chance before I cut off your ear, or maybe your nose... What do you say? You'll live, but look a lot like Voldemort. That might work for Halloween, but not sure you'd be a hit with the women when you resemble He-Who-Shall-Not-Be-Named, *tu mi capisci?*"

He swallows, glancing around the room again.

"No one's going to save you." I peer into his features, "Start talking or I'll start cutting."

He presses his lips together. I slash the knife down the front of his face and he screams. Blood pours out from the cut on his cheek. His gaze widens until I can see the whites of his eyes.

"Wait," he blubbers, "wait, I'll tell you."

I pause. "I'm listening."

"It was the Kane Company."

"The Kane Company?"

He nods, "I... I owed them. And the man who approached me said if I rigged the car, my debts would be forgiven."

"Who?" I thrust my face into his, "Who asked you to do this? What's his name?"

"I don't know."

"What did he look like?"

"I don't know," the man gasps out, "he...he wore a mask. I couldn't see his features."

"Fuck!" I hold the knife to his neck and he stiffens. "You're not helping me, asshole." I dig the knife into his neck and blood drips from the cut.

He swallows. "Wait," he pleads, "please wait." He licks his lips as he darts his gaze left, then right. I press the knife deeper and he wheezes, "Stop, please." He squeezes his eyes shut, "I have a daughter. I can't leave her orphaned."

"We'll take care of your daughter."

He snaps his eyes open, "Don't you dare touch her."

"Start speaking," I growl. "You have three minutes."

"He was tall, as tall as you, and spoke with a British accent."

"As does half the population of Britain," Luca snarls. "Was he old, young? How did he walk? Any tattoos? Jewelry? Anything that stands out?"

"Wait," he freezes and glances into the distance, "he had a tattoo of a flower that peeked out from under his sleeve."

Seb swears aloud, "Fucking *cani*! I knew it was them. I knew it was a mistake to be working with them."

I hold up my hand and he falls silent. "Are you sure?" I peer into the man's face. "If you are lying...." I let the words hang there.

"I'm not," he beseeches, "I swear on my daughter, I am not."

I nod, then step back, "You do realize, I can't let you go after this though."

"Please," he begins to sob. "Don't do this. I am all my daughter has."

"All I can promise is that she will be taken care of." I hesitate. If I had had a daughter, and if it were me about to die, would I regret the kind of life I had led? Given that I have lived by violence, am I bound to have a violent end? Is this how I would go too? At the hands of an enemy? Worried about my family...my wife and children, and wondering who would take care of them? Is there a way out of this for me? Do I want to leave this life of crime behind?

"Capo?" Seb murmurs and I tip up my chin. I swipe out my hand and bury my knife in the man's chest.

11

———

Karma

"Whiskey, please," the man a few chairs down from me at the bar orders, "Macallan's reserve."

It's the same whiskey that my Capo favors. I glance down at my own drink. A glass of wine. I had arrived yesterday at the Four Seasons, checked in, and slept away most of the day. I'd woken up, only to get myself a quick dinner and feed Andy—who had been provided with his own food and water bowls and a designated litter area in the corner of the vast bath. Guess that's what money can get you. The red carpet treatment, not only for you, but also for your pet.

The man glances around and spots me. His face lights up with interest. His eyes gleam—brown eyes, interested gaze. "Hello, you staying at the hotel too?" He nods toward me, and honestly, he seems all right. Not creepy or anything. Only I'm not in the mood to strike up a conversation with a stranger, and certainly not, in a hotel bar. Not that I am in the mood for speaking with any man right now. Strike that... Perhaps one man would fit the bill, one alphahole whom I want to strangle; one bastard whom I hate…and love… Damn it, I am still in love with him.

Enough to still wear the wedding ring he gave me. The man's gaze lowers to my left hand and his features close.

Good. At least, it's serving some purpose, considering I had come this close to taking it off so many times since I had arrived in London. Massimo had flown me to the Capo's personal private plane in Rome. Initially, I had refused to board it, but he had persuaded me. He'd told me this was the easiest and fastest way to get out of Italy. The 'fastest' part of it had done the trick. Not to mention, the fact that Andy could travel in relative comfort had helped.

Massimo had produced a passport for Andy, and when I had thanked him, he'd said it had been Michael who had seen to it. What the —? Had he been planning this for a while then? Before I could come to grips with that thought, Massimo had handed me a check. Which I had refused… And he'd said, it was only right that I be compensated for what I had been through. That had pissed me off. I mean, could my time and emotions actually have a price put on them?

Then, he had told me not to be stubborn. That I was going to need it to get back on my feet—which was true. He said I could put it toward my fashion designing business, to think of it as seed capital, and a loan which I could return to the Capo when I was up and running.

In all honesty, I had wanted to refuse it. I didn't want anything to do with my husband's money, but Massimo had been insistent. He'd told me to accept it, that I owed it to myself. After all, I had lost time, which I would have used to grow my business, and this was compensation for that.

Well, the £100,000 check was much more than what I would have made in the past month if I had focused on growing my business. But I had decided not to argue that point. Instead, I had torn up the check He hadn't been very surprised, which had surprised me, until he'd said that Michael had warned him that this would be the probable response.

He'd pulled out an envelope stuffed with money. I had stared at it, and he had insisted I take it. When I'd refused, he'd simply said that I'd need it to feed Andy, if nothing else. And of course, he'd been right.

I'd wondered, then, if this was the reason that Michael had given Andy to me… As a means of manipulating me… But it couldn't be that, could it? Still, he'd made sense, so I'd accepted the cash… Also, I had run out of energy by then, wanting nothing more than to grab a drink — at least, I can drink now, so that's a silver lining, eh? —and crawl into some dark corner where I wouldn't have to think or do much.

Then Massimo had sprung the third surprise. He'd said there would be a car waiting for me in London and that it would take me to a flat where I could live until I found one of my own. That… I had vehemently refused. No way, was I going to stay in a place owned by my husband. Not after what he'd done to me. Asshole.

If he thinks he can still try to control my life…even when he's not in it, he has another think coming. Why would he do that anyway, though? He's the one who wanted me out of his life, so why is he now concerned about me, huh?

I had been firm on that point and Massimo had finally given up. He'd left and I had boarded the plane. I'd turned down the prosecco the stewardess had brought me, and instead, turned to vodka… It had seemed like a drink I could drown myself in. I had managed to down a couple, then taken a brief nap on the short flight to London, where I had disembarked and walked out of the airport…

And that's when the enormity of what I had done…of what lay ahead of me had hit me. I'd wondered, then, if I should have accepted that offer of a car ride and an apartment to rent, but no… I'd made the right choice. If I had ended up in an apartment that he owned, then I would have never been able to meet my own gaze in the mirror again, if I'm being honest.

Which is how I'd come to stay at the Four Seasons. I'd woken up this morning and spent the day finding a flat for myself and Andy. I could have phoned my sister and gone over and met her… Only, I'm not ready.

Damn it. At some point, I am going to have to call her… But not today. I still need some time to come to grips with everything that happened. Also, in all honesty, I can't bear to tell her that I've been married, lost a child, and separated from my husband, all in the matter of a month.

I swallow down another sip of wine, ignore the man who's still glancing at me from the corner of his eye. Maybe it had been a bad choice to come down to the bar on my own, but I couldn't stay in the room for another night on my own. Good thing I am moving out the day after Christmas though. I had managed to not only find a flat, but with the money I had accepted from Massimo, I had also paid an advance to secure the place for the next three months. At least, it gives me enough time to figure out what I want to do next, you know?

I place my half-filled drink on the bar counter, then leave. I take the elevator up to my room and use my keycard to open the door. Andy greets me with a loud purring. I sink down to my knees to pet him, and that's when my phone rings.

12

Karma

"Aurora?" I stare at the woman whose face appears on the screen.

"Karma!" She smiles. "How are you? Where are you?"

"I'm in London."

"London?" She frowns. "What are you doing there?"

"This is my home, you know?" I retort. "More to the point, how did you get to a phone?"

"Ah," she glances to the side, then back at me, "the phone is Christian's."

"Christian's, huh?" I tilt my head, "Are you and he—"

"No," she says, horrified, "of course, not. He, ah, came by to check how I was doing—"

"Did he now?" I smirk.

She scowls. "It's not like that. He just wants to be sure I don't escape or anything. He's responsible for me."

"Responsible for you?"

"I mean, he's taken charge of me. I mean..." She throws up her hands, "You're twisting my words all around the wrong way, and I wasn't calling about me, I was calling to find out how you are."

"I am fine," I sink down onto a chair near the window and Andy jumps onto my lap. He meows, I pat him, and he stretches up to try and peer into the phone. Funny cat. He purrs at the screen.

Aurora laughs. "Hey, Andy," she calls to him, and he blinks at the screen. "Whatcha doin', boy?" she coos.

I blink, "I thought you'd speak to him in Italian."

"Well, he's your cat," she pushes out her chin in a very Italian gesture, "so I see him as English."

Andy yawns, then leaps down onto the floor and flounces away.

"Guess he isn't impressed by our discussion," Aurora chuckles.

"At least, he travelled well. I thought he'd have trouble on the flight, but nope. We strapped his pet carrier to a seat for takeoff and landing and he was fine. He's also not had any problem adjusting to his new surroundings."

"And you?" She peruses my features, "How are you?"

"Honestly, I don't know." I rise to my feet and begin to pace. "I am still trying to adjust to everything."

"Hold on," she murmurs. "Don't say anything more until I dial in Cassandra."

"Cassandra?" I frown. "How did you—" Before I can complete my statement, Cassandra pops up in a window on the screen.

"Karma," Cassandra exclaims, "how are you?

"Not too bad," I raise a shoulder. "Are you at the house?" *Is he there?* That's what I want to ask, but I don't.

"He's not here," she says softly.

"Who?" I arch an eyebrow.

"You know who I am talking about."

"If you mean the man who cheated on me—"

"Cheated on you?" Aurora bursts out. "No, really?"

"Yeah," I hunch my shoulders. "I walked in on him with another woman, and they were... Let's just say, they were quite intimate."

"Oh, Karma," Aurora cries, "I am so sorry."

"Yeah, well," I flick my hair over my shoulder, "what can I say? Guess I overestimated him, eh?"

"You sure he cheated on you?" Cassandra frowns. "The Capo is not the kind of man who takes his promises lightly."

"Yeah, well... In this case, he broke his vows, all right."

"Are you sure?"

"I was there, remember?" I scowl.

"Maybe you were mistaken?" Cassandra posits. "Maybe it's not what it seems?"

"You don't think I've been trying to convince myself of that? But not only was he engaged in the action of getting his dick sucked, but when I confronted him, he told me to leave."

"Oh, Karma," Cassandra bites her lips, "I am so sorry. I wish things had worked out differently."

"Yeah, me too." I roll my shoulders. "But enough about me. What are the two of you up to?" I turn to Aurora, "When are you going to tell Christian that you have a thing for him?"

"I don't have a thing for him."

"Ha, if the sparks between the two of you were any hotter, you'd set the room on fire," Cassandra laughs.

"And you, girl," I narrow my gaze on her, "you and Adrian."

"Wha—" She opens and shuts her mouth, "Me and Adrian, what?"

"There's something there." I waggle my eyebrows.

"But—"

"Don't bother denying it, missy, I've seen how he follows you with his gaze when he thinks no one is looking, and how you steal glances at him on the sly."

"I don't steal glances at him," she protests.

"Oh, yeah, you do." Aurora laughs, "I noticed it too."

"Right?" I crow, before redirecting my attention toward Aurora. "So, when are the two of you getting on and doing something about it?"

"Somehow I don't think that's a good idea, considering I am still the captive of the Mafia."

"Some captive," Cassandra says with a wicked gleam in her eyes. "From what I've seen, you are getting the royal treatment. You have Christian hovering around you. Any excuse he has to come see you, he takes it. If ever there is a need for a doctor, and given these Mafia guys are constantly involved in some scrap or the other, there is a need a lot of times… Guess who volunteers to go get you?"

"Suppose there's something to be said for having a doctor in the house huh?"

"I'm sure it's very convenient for them," Aurora huffs. "Guess it suits them to have me locked up in here."

"You don't seem to be too put out by it, you know?" I observe.

"What am I going to do, protest?" She scoffs, "Like that will do any good. At least, I know that my family is taken care of."

"How can you be sure of that?"

"It's an unspoken promise among the Cosa Nostra," Cassandra explains. "If one of us is injured or dies in the line of duty, so to speak, then the family is taken care of."

"Huh," I blink, "I didn't know that."

"The Cosa Nostra takes care of their own," Aurora says in a soft tone.

"Their influence within the city and the community is all pervasive. They are linked into the police, the judiciary, and with the heads of Fortune 500 companies." Cassandra begins to pace the room she is in. "And of course, they rule the underworld. It's why, if you have a problem with anything, you go to them."

"With anything?" I frown. "What do you mean, anything?"

"Meaning, *anything*." Cassandra raises a shoulder, "If you have a problem with your husband cheating on you, you go to the Cosa Nostra. If you have a problem with your business being in debt, you go to them. If you have a problem with the plumbing in your house, you go to them. Hell, if you have a problem with dog shit littering your street, you go to—"

"—them," I finish her statement. "Though I don't understand why. I mean, it seems so archaic. Like you guys live in some kind of feudal country."

"We do, for all intents and purposes." She laughs. "Remember, this is the country whose prime minister, at one point, owned the biggest media company in the country, effectively controlling the media itself, and who was responsible for some of the worst scandals we have seen."

"And the only organization who could stand up to him was—"

"—the Cosa Nostra?"

She nods.

"Thanks for the history lesson," I lower my chin to my chest. "Still... not sure where I fit in with all of this."

"You are one of us, Karma," Aurora states. "You are married to the Capo of the Cosa Nostra."

"The most-wanted man, internationally."

"What...what?" I gape. "I mean, I know he is not on the right side of the law...He is a..."

"Criminal?" Cassandra suggests.

"Most people would call him that, but here in this country, he is...

second, only to the Don, in terms of the sway he holds over most people's lives." Aurora seems to carefully watch my reaction.

"You make him sound like God or something." I laugh nervously.

"Close." Aurora nods.

"Jeez, if I had known all this before-hand—"

"—you wouldn't have married him?"

"Not like I actually had a choice." I drag my fingers through my hair, "You girls have given me a lot to think about."

"Don't tell me you didn't realize all of this already, Karma?" Cassandra peers at me through the screen.

"I guess, I was aware subconsciously, but honestly, to hear it from the two of you... Well, it kind of makes a bigger impact on me."

"You okay?" Cassandra half smiles. "Hope we didn't scare you with the conversation. We only wanted to make sure that you were okay."

"I will be," I say with more confidence than I feel.

"Stay in touch, eh?" Aurora smiles at me, "Let us know what you plan to do next."

"I will, as soon as I figure things out myself."

We hang up and I walk over to the window and gaze down at the garden. What the hell am I doing here? Am I really going to have to spend Christmas Eve on my own? I ponder my options, then mind made up, I head out of the room.

13

———————

Michael

I glance at the sea in the distance. Clouds are rolling in, which is not unusual for late December. It's the day before Christmas and I am on my own. Not for long, as my brothers are going to arrive soon, as will Nonna.

My Beauty may have left me, but the party she organized to celebrate Xander will go on. It feels only right to do so, considering she made all of the arrangements. I have to believe she'd have wanted it to go on even though she is not here with me. Hell, I want the event to take place so I can feel close to her. So I can finally try to put what happened to Xander behind me... Not that I will ever be able to make peace with it. But mulling over it is self-defeating. I need to function at peak efficiency, to focus all of my efforts at taking down the Kane Company.

Bastards are clever. Have to be careful in how I trap them and rein them in so I can have my revenge. Right after the Christmas event today.

Do criminals take time off for Christmas too? I never have before, but this time...just for her...because she'd have wanted me to if she were here... For Beauty, I'll be present. For Xander, I'll be there to celebrate his life.

I raise the glass of whiskey and sip from it. This is bullshit. Me on my own here. My wife in London. My brother dead... Not to mention, the child I never had, the one whose absence I feel more keenly than before. Is it possible to miss something that you never had? The notion of a family, of a child I'd hoped to hold in my arms. Maybe I had counted on it more than I had realized. Maybe, I had already foreseen a future for us. Maybe I had just not acknowledged it, and it took the lack of a child, the lack of *her* in my life, to bring it all to the fore. Pain shoots up my arm and I glance down. The skin over my knuckles is white and I force myself to loosen my grip. I bring the glass up to my lips, drain it and turn; just as Massimo walks onto the terrace.

"*Fratellone,*" he jerks his chin.

"How is she?" I snap.

"She?"

"You know who I am talking about."

"The last I saw of her, she was pissed at you. I don't think that has changed."

I scowl, "Not asking your opinion on her state of mind. I mean, how is she physically? Is she safe?"

"As safe as she can be in a five-star hotel."

"And there are guards posted around her, day and night?"

"There are people who have her in their line of sight, twenty-four-seven. If they move any closer, she'll trip over them."

"Good."

He stares at me steadily and I glare at him, "What?"

"Are you sure this is a good idea?"

"Like I said, not asking your opinion," I snap.

"I am going to give it to you anyway."

"Of course, you are."

"Not sure why you think it's a good idea to pretend to break up with her, but —"

"Nothing pretend about it," I insist.

He laughs. The *testa di cazzo* laughs.

"*Vaffanculo,*" I glower at him.

He raises his hands, "So you broke up with her, sent her on her way, and now you have people watching her. I fail to understand the logic in this."

"The logic in what?" Seb walks in and glances down at my whiskey. "You need a refill."

I hand the glass over to him and he stalks over to the bar. He snatches up a few more glasses, then proceeds to fill them up.

He walks over, hands a glass to Massimo and one to me. "*Salute,*" he clinks the glass with both of ours. "What were you talking about?" he asks.

"Just how the Capo is tying himself up in knots." Massimo smirks.

"He hasn't been the same since he fell in love."

"Love," Massimo shakes his head, "it's been known to gut the fiercest of people. You'd have thought *il nostro fratellone,* here, stood a chance, eh? Considering he's, on the face of it, at least, the toughest of all of us."

"You know what they say, the stronger they are…the harder they fall." Seb chuckles.

Massimo rises his glass, "I'll drink to that."

"*Che cazzo!*" I glare at the two of them, "Since when did my love life —"

"Or the lack thereof," Massimo points out.

"What-fucking-ever. Same thing —"

"Not." Seb shakes his head. He turns to Massimo, "Ever known the Capo to be this short of words."

"Never," Massimo laments.

"He'd best get used to this state of affairs, eh?"

"*Basta,*" I growl. "Shut the fuck up, you two."

"You losing your temper again?" Adrian stalks in, heads straight for the bar. He bypasses the already poured glass of whiskey, leans over and grabs a Macallan thirty-year-old. He hefts it onto the counter and proceeds to open it.

"Thanks for checking in with me." I try to infuse sarcasm into my voice and fail. *Merda.* I am growing soft, all right. Or maybe not, considering I killed a man in cold blood yesterday. I'd hesitated, though, which had been a first for me. And now, I am unable to muster enough anger at my brothers and stepbrothers as they swarm all over my expensive liquor. I drain my glass and hold it out. Massimo grabs it from me, walks over to the bar and places it on the counter. Adrian opens the bottle and tops me up, then Massimo's glass, then his own. He pours liquor into three more glasses, then pauses.

I stare at the glasses. So do Massimo and Seb.

Christian walks onto the terrace. He bumps into the back of a chair,

"Oops!" he apologizes to no one in particular, then weaves over to the bar. He snatches up a glass of whiskey and sniffs it. "This is *eccezionale*." He tosses it back, then slams the glass onto the counter. "Top me up," he commands Adrian, who hesitates.

"Come on, *brother*." Christian hiccups, "It's Christmas after all, and you know this is Xander's favorite festival. Even though the man's grown up, you'd think he was a kid the way he looks forward to the festive season. It feeds his creativity, he says, and—" Christian's voice tapers off. "Fuck," he growls, "fuck, fuck, fuck." He grabs the bottle from Adrian, tops up his own glass. That's when he spots the two other glasses. He freezes, then spinning around, carries the bottle and glass with him to a table in the far corner. He slaps them both on the table, before pulling out a pack of cigarettes. He lights one, blows out smoke.

"When did you start smoking?" I scowl.

"Don't nag, *fratellone*," he takes another puff of his cigarette.

That's when Luca enters the terrace. He glances between us, his gaze cautious. "I assume I have been invited to this?"

I nod my head at the same time that Christian growls, "Get the fuck out of here. You don't deserve to be here, *faccia di merda*."

Luca doesn't respond. He marches over to the bar, snatches up the glass of whiskey. That's when he notices the last glass that's topped to the rim with the amber fluid.

He pales. "Fuck," he growls as he keeps his gaze focused on the glass.

I stalk over to stand next to him. Seb prowls over to flank me on the other side, with Massimo next to him. Adrian falls in line next to him. Christian draws in a breath. He stabs out his cigarette on the bar counter, stumbles across the terrace, and comes to a halt next to Seb. Christian sways; Seb steadies him, but Christian pulls free. He fixes his gaze on that full glass on the counter.

For a few seconds, all of us stare at the glass, then I raise mine. "To Xander." I swallow down the ball of emotion in my throat. "Rest in peace, brother."

"To Xander." Seb raises his glass, "I'll miss your easygoing nature, little brother."

"And your humor," Massimo jerks his chin, "not that I understood all of your jokes."

The rest of us chuckle.

"You were way too much of a nerd... But I'll still miss the jokes that I did not understand." Massimo's lips kick up in the semblance of a smile.

"I'll miss how you always made everyone feel like you were giving them your complete attention. You actually cared for others..." Adrian draws in a breath, "unlike the rest of us reprobates, who swear by violence; you were the good one among us."

Luca goes still. He seems like he's about to say something, then shakes his head. "I'm sorry," he squeezes his eyes shut, "I am so sorry. You had the best of us all—the most goodness, the most talent, the most warmth... It should have been me, not you, *fratellino.*"

"It should have," Christian says through gritted teeth. "Why don't you fuck off and off yourself, eh? Why don't you leave and never return, you *testa di cazzo!*"

"Christian," I growl.

"Don't tell me you don't agree." The skin across his knuckles whitens as he squeezes his fingers around the glass. "This asshole, here, is responsible for your child being killed. I'm sure you've thought of that."

"Christian," I snap. "Shut the fuck up."

"I am only saying what everyone is thinking," he growls. "This asshole is responsible for everything that happened. If he hadn't helped Karma leave, she'd still be here and so would your child, and Xander would not be lying in a coffin six feet under and—" he draws in a breath and his features seem to crumple. He manages to get a hold of himself, only for a tear to run down his cheek. "F-u-c-k," he cries, "fuck, this shit." He tosses his drink back, turns to leave, but Luca grabs his shoulder.

"I am sorry, brother. I really am sorry for what I did. I swear, I had no idea it would turn out like this."

"Didn't you?" Christian tries to pull away but Luca doesn't let go.

"I really didn't. I messed things up, I know that, but I am here now, aren't I? I am going to help you guys take revenge on the Kane Company. This, I promise."

"Fuck that." Christian swings, Luca ducks, and Christian's glass crashes to the floor as Luca wraps his arms around him. "Let the fuck go of me, man."

"No," Luca says in a hard voice, "This family has been fractured enough. The rest of us need to stick together now. It's the only way we are going to survive."

"And what if I don't want to survive?" Christian glares at him, "What if I don't want to go on living? What if I—"

Luca slaps his face.

"What the—!" Christian gapes. "How dare you?" He tries to head-butt Luca, whose still-full glass hits the floor and rolls away.

Luca wraps his arms around Christian and holds him immobile. "How dare you talk about dying, you asshole? If anything, Xander's death should have taught you how lucky you are; how lucky we all are to be alive. We love you, Christian, don't you get that?"

"Yeah," Adrian, nods. He moves around, throws his arms around the both of them. "We need you with us, bro."

"Totally," Seb walks over to them and hugs the lot of them.

Massimo heaves a sigh, "Can't believe I am going to do this," He tosses back his drink, glances around for somewhere to place it. Then, still clutching the glass in his gigantic hand, he closes the distance to them, and enfolds his big arms around the group.

He glares at me over the heads of our brothers. I glance away, stalk over to the bar and place the glass on the counter. I draw in a breath, square my shoulders, then turn and prowl over to the group where I wrap my arms around all of them.

For a few seconds we stay that way, then Christian grumbles, "Enough of this emo shit."

Instantly, I step back. So does Massimo, then Adrian, Seb, and Luca.

Christian rubs the back of his neck. "I need another fucking drink."

"And I," I roll my shoulders "have something I need to do."

14

Karma

I stand at a distance from the penthouse, not far from Tower Bridge in London. The place belongs to Dr. Weston Kincaid, one of the Seven, as they like to call themselves. Seven billionaires who co-own 7A, one of the leading financial companies in the country. Weston is a friend of Sinclair Sterling, another of the Seven. Sinclair is married to my sister Summer. The one whose wedding I had attended before I had run into my Capo.

I had gone to Summer and Sinclair's townhouse on Primrose Hill, just as they had been leaving the house. I had grabbed a taxi and followed them here. I had jumped out of the cab and walked toward them as they had left their car and approached the entrance of the building. They had paused halfway and Sinclair had hauled my sister close to him and kissed her… Okay, he had practically devoured her face, if you want to know the truth. The heat between them had been palpable enough that my face had reddened. My toes had curled, and gah! That's wrong. This is my sister and brother-in-law, for chrissakes! Still, the way they had been going at it, in the open… It had reminded me of how it was with my Capo… My cheating Capo—*the asshole who'd decided to have his dick sucked by another woman, making sure that you'd see it, remember?*

Ahead, Sinclair had finally released Summer, who'd laughed. She'd reached up and rubbed the lipstick off of his mouth. "Your friends are going to know what we have been up to."

"Like I bloody care?" Sinclair had snorted. "Honestly, I'd rather have stayed home with you, but I couldn't pass up the opportunity to surprise the twat, Weston in his love nest."

That's when I'd realized where they were going.

"You'd have hated it if they had done the same to us." She'd giggled.

"All the more reason to spring the surprise on him." He'd smirked.

Another car had driven up, and that's when I had fallen back. I had darted away behind a parked van. Then peeked around it in time to see Saint, another of the Seven, get out of the driver's seat. He'd walked around to open the door to the passenger's side and Victoria had gotten out. Huh? I guess Victoria is with Saint now? What else have I missed in the time that I have been away?

Clearly, the entire group is converging at Weston's. Of course, they are. It's Christmas, right? They want to be together to celebrate.

I'd peeked around the side of the van again and seen Summer moving forward to greet Victoria with a kiss. Guess my sister has found her tribe. Her people. Her husband…

And me? Shit, I'd had it all…and lost it… I flatten my palm against my stomach and tears slide down my cheeks. I have to stop breaking down at the least provocation. I can't go through life always thinking of what I could have had. I need to focus on the now, on what I still have. Myself… My health… And I still have my new friends, Aurora and Cassandra…who know what I have been through. And I have Andy, of course.

I wipe away my tears, glance around the van just as another car draws up. Jace and his wife Sienna, both friends of Sinclair, step out. Then Jace reaches into the back seat, and a few minutes later, emerges with a baby carrier.

The group exchanges greetings, the women kiss, they coo over the baby, then all of them enter the building. I take a step forward, then stop. If I go in there now, I'll have to confront all of them, and honestly, that's the last thing I want to do right now. Guess I'll just have to find another time.

I hunch my shoulders, turn away and begin walking down the road.

The hair on the back of my neck rises. I glance around. What the hell caused that feeling? Am I being watched? I look up and down the road. The sensation fades and I start walking again. I reach the end of the road, glance around for a cab, but can't see any. I hear a noise behind me and stiffen. My heart begins to race; my pulse pounds at my temples. Shit, where's a taxi when you need it, eh? I increase my speed and head for the tube station that I remember passing on my way here. Footsteps sound behind me, and I break into a run. I race down the street, turn another corner and see the entrance to the tube station ahead. Thank god! My breath comes in huffs as I run toward it. I am almost there when someone grabs my shoulder.

"No," I yell as I try to pull free, "let me go. Now!"

"Beauty?"

"No, no, no," I struggle wildly, "don't fucking come near me."

"Language, Beauty."

I blink, then pause. I am turned around and find myself staring at a broad chest, clad in a plain white T-shirt that outlines the sculpted planes. A black jacket that has seen better days clings to his broad shoulders. The dark, masculine scent that could only belong to one man envelops my senses. I swallow, refuse to look up. He notches his knuckles under my chin and applies pressure. I tilt my chin up and meet his cold blue gaze.

"You?" I whisper. "What are you doing here?"

"I came to see you."

"No," I try to pull away, but his grip tightens. "You told me to leave, remember?"

"And I came after you."

"You cheated on me."

He shakes his head, "I only pretended to."

"A likely story," I snap. "I was there, buster. I saw you, remember?"

"You thought you saw her going down on me—" I wince and his jaw hardens. "The mind can play tricks on you, so you think you see what you expect to see."

"Your pants were unzipped."

"I had my boxers on."

"I saw her bob her head."

"Larissa's a good actress."

"Larissa!" I spit out. "That woman again? You let her touch you? You let her put her hands on you again?"

He frowns, "She doesn't mean anything to me."

"You wrapped her hair around your fingers and pretended you enjoyed what she was doing to you."

"I did what I thought was right."

"Well, this is me doing what I think is right, too." I try to knee him in the groin but he swerves. My knee brushes against his hard thigh instead and I stumble. His grip tightens. He pulls me toward him so I fall against his chest.

"Listen to me, Beauty," he growls.

"Don't call me that you...you asshole."

"Beauty," his voice lowers to a hush, "just give me a chance to explain."

"No."

"I had a reason for what I did."

"Nothing you say can justify what you did to me."

"I did it to save your life."

"Ha!" I scoff, "That's how men justify getting away with dipping their dicks in other vaginas."

"The only vagina I want to dip my dick in is yours."

"I don't believe you."

"How can I make you believe it?"

"You can't."

"I can, and I will." He hauls me to him and my breasts flatten against his chest. "I sent you away because I needed the word to spread that we had separated."

"Uh-huh, sure." I turn my head so I don't have to gaze into his eyes. If I do, I'll be lost. Asshole will use his charm, his ability to influence me to get me to do what he wants.

"Don't you see? After what happened, after almost losing you... And our child. After losing my brother, I couldn't...risk anything else happening to you."

My pulse rate ratchets up and my ribcage tightens. I try to draw in a breath and my throat burns. My head spins and flickers of black dot the edges of my vision. To think, I went through the car blast and the surgery without it coming to light, only for my heart to act up now. Of course, no-one in Italy had access to my medical records, and unless I had revealed it, the doctors would not have had any way to know. Still... This is so not the time for my ailment to make itself known. Sweat beads my forehead and a black hole opens up where my heart should be.

"What's wrong?" He scowls down at me, "What's happening, Beauty?"

I shake my head, try to regulate my breathing. In-out-in, I will my heartbeat to slow down, for my pulse to stop hammering in my wrists.

"Karma?" He cups my face and turns me to face him, "Talk to me, baby. Are you okay?"

"Y…yes," I cough.

His features pale. "*Cazzo*, you're definitely not okay."

I sway and he makes an angry noise at the back of his throat. He scoops me up in his arms and I slap my hand against his shoulder.

"Put me down."

"No." He turns, walks back the way we came.

"Where are you going?" I glance up the street. "Why are you going this way?"

"I am taking you to my car." He walks faster.

At least, we are not on the same street as Weston's penthouse. So, there's less of a chance of running into my sister or any of the Seven. He reaches a black Maserati—of course, it's a Maserati that he's driving, even in London—and unlocks it. He opens the passenger door, slides me onto the seat, then leans over me. He buckles my seatbelt and his big body dwarfs mine for a few seconds. The scent of him intensifies, my core clenches, and my mouth waters. Then he moves back and I sag against the seat. I wipe my damp palms on my thighs and try to fight the weakness that grips my limbs. I draw in another deep breath and my nostrils flood with the dark, edgy scent that is so very Mika. My toes curl, even as my heart refuses to let up its relentless hammering. Shit, shit, shit. Even stuck in the middle of these heart palpitations, I can't stop myself from being aroused.

Apparently, being away from him has only made the yearning I feel for him so much worse. He walks around to take his place behind the wheel. He starts the car, eases it onto the road. There's silence as he drives forward.

I close my eyes, focus on my breathing, on willing my muscles to relax, on bringing the trembling in my arms and legs under control. My body slowly responds, and by the time I feel like myself again, a good ten minutes must have passed. I finally open my eyes, take in the familiar surroundings of Park Lane. "Where are you going?" I turn to him.

"To your hotel."

"To my hotel?" I frown. "You know where I am staying?" I shake my head, "Of course, you know where I am staying."

We don't speak for a few more seconds, then I burst out, "Why did you come after me, Michael?"

"Because I had to."

"Bullshit," I wrap my arms around my waist, "you asked me to leave, then not even forty-eight hours pass, and you turn up after me." I rake my fingers though my hair, "I mean, this is just…crazy."

"What is?"

"This entire, elaborate, set-up — you breaking up with me — "

"Pretending to break up with you."

"Then putting me on your plane and getting me out of there, only to follow me."

"I hadn't intended to come," he says in a low voice, "but I couldn't help myself."

"Gee, thanks," I murmur.

"That was a compliment," a thread of humor runs through his words.

I shoot him a sideways glance, "I still don't believe that you fabricated that entire scene."

"Sure, you do."

"Eh?" I turn to him, "Care to explain yourself?"

"In your heart of hearts, you knew that I wasn't capable of cheating on you."

I scoff, "I am not a mind reader."

"You know me Beauty. You know how much I care for you."

"If you did, you would have taken me into your confidence and explained your plans. But you didn't."

He stays quiet.

"If you did actually consider me your wife — "

"Which I do."

"If you considered me your partner, you'd treat me as your equal. You'd share your plans with me…not… Pull that stupid shit like you did…where you upset me so much that I leave you."

"I needed it to look authentic."

"To whom? The only people there were you, me and…"

He nods.

"Oh," I blink rapidly. "OH! You mean Larissa… She…"

"Is enough of a gossip that, by now, all of Palermo knows that my wife has left me."

I think for a minute. "But if you were pretending, she knows that too."

"As far as she knows, I just wanted her to pretend so that you would leave. I implied there might be room for her after you were gone, but..." he shrugs.

"Hmmm. Do they know that you've come after me?"

He shoots me a glance and I raise my hands. "Hey, I'm only asking. I mean, you took the plane—"

"A private plane."

"Landed in London, and now you are driving around in this Maserati—"

"I cleared immigration through a private channel, whose agents are sworn to secrecy, and do you know how many Maseratis are in London?"

I shake my head.

"Let's just say that, while it's not my favorite city, god knows the Brits are too uptight for me, still, one advantage of being here is that it's difficult to track anyone."

"Yeah, but you with your bodyguard and your brothers... You guys draw attention wherever you go..." my voice trails off. "So, you ditched your bodyguard?"

He nods.

"Do your brothers know where you are?"

He doesn't answer.

"So, they don't know you are here, either?"

He continues to focus on the road and I turn on him, "Michael, is that wise? You here on your own, without any security?"

"You worried about me?"

I snort, "Not that you can't take care of yourself, but I am told that you are an international fugitive, so..."

He shoots me a glance, "How did you find out about that?"

When I stay quiet, he frowns, "Who have you been talking to?"

"No one."

"You're not a good liar." He scowls as he navigates the road, "Was it one of the women? Cassandra? Did she tell you?"

"You leave her out of this, okay?"

He glances at me again, "I am not going to hurt her. You know that, right?"

"I don't know much about you at all, Michael."

He smirks, and my cheeks heat. "I mean, I know you in *that* way... But as for how your mind works or what motivates you... Well, I am only slowly coming to grips with that."

"I'd rather come to grips with you."

"If you think you can simply barge back into my life and into my bed, think again."

His features soften, "I wasn't planning on that, Karma. I merely wanted to see you. It's Christmas, and I missed my wife. I wanted to be with you."

"So, you hopped a flight —"

"I flew the plane."

"Of course, you did." I resist the urge to roll my eyes. Is there anything this man can't do? "You flew the plane, and tracked me down —Shit!" I slap my forehead, "The stupid tracker. Of course, you tracked me down. You knew exactly where I was all this time."

He doesn't reply.

Damn it... Somehow, the fact that he had tagged me, so all he had to do was literally look at a screen and find me... Makes everything somewhat less than what it should be.

"What are you thinking?" he asks softly.

When I don't reply, he shoots me a sideways glance, "I know you hate the fact that I could find you so easily..."

I don't reply and his jaw tics. A pulse flares to life at his temple and he seems like he's about to slam on the brakes and tell me off, but he doesn't. Instead, he turns the corner and the hotel looms in front of us. He eases into a slot at the entrance, then shuts off the engine. He reaches behind his seat, grabs a duffel bag, then gets out. He slings the bag across his chest, then walks around, to open my door. I slide out, then brush past him and head for the hotel entrance. Behind me, I hear him speaking to the valet who agrees to park the car and deposit the key with the concierge.

We enter the elevator, and damn him, but his size dwarfs the space. "If you think you are staying the night, you have another think coming."

"Ask me to stay," he growls.

"That's never happening." I swipe my hair over my shoulder. "What's with the get up anyway?"

"Get up?"

"The jeans and jacket and boots thingy you have happening?"

He glances down at himself, then back at me. "What's wrong with it?"

"Nothing's wrong with it." It's perfect, actually. That entire mussed-up, sexy look he has going on is bloody hot. It makes me want to throw myself at him and wrap my legs around his waist. "If you think that's going to help you blend in with the crowds, you thought wrong."

"I was trying to dress down, yes," he raises a shoulder, "was trying for a casual look, I suppose."

Only, he'd never blend into a crowd. Hell, my Capo will always stand head and shoulders above anyone else. He'll always command attention, always suck up the oxygen in any room that he walks into. He'll always be a leader, and no matter how much he tries to disguise that part of himself, it won't work.

"Next time, don't try so hard," I drawl.

"Next time, don't lie."

"Ha," I snort, "I am not lying.

"You are."

I shrug, turn away, and he makes a sound deep in his throat. "Don't look away when I am talking to you," he snaps.

"A-n-d there he is." I throw up my hands, "If you think you going all macho on me is supposed to make me all hot and bothered, you are wrong."

He closes the distance between us so quickly that I yelp. He backs me up into the wall, then slaps his hand on the stop button. The elevator jolts to a halt and I gasp.

"Wh…what are you doing?" I squeak.

"You may deny that you still have feelings for me, but your body says otherwise."

"It…it… Doesn't."

"Oh?" His lips twist and my pussy spasms. He thrusts his face into mine, holds my gaze as he raises his hand and pushes away a lock of hair that has fallen over my eyebrow. I shudder and his mouth curves. The tenderness in his touch is so at odds with how intense his gaze is that moisture laces my panties. His nostrils flare, and I swear, the man knows exactly how turned on I am. He drags his finger down the side of my throat and I shiver. He reaches my breast, circles one taut nipple. The hair on my forearms rises. He continues the journey until he reaches the waistband of my jeans. A moan bleeds from me. He slides his hand between my legs and cups my pussy. "If I cram my fingers inside your pussy, will I find you wet and needy and aching for my cock, Beauty?"

Yes.

Yes.

"No," I shake my head.

He laughs. "Liar."

He stays there, holding my gaze, the heat from his large palm sinking through the crotch of my jeans, through my panties. My belly clenches and the flesh between my thighs throbs, yearns…for more, so much more. I jerk my pelvis forward, wanting to feel him squeeze my throbbing core, and his smile becomes a full-blown grin.

"I rest my case." He raises his hand as he pushes his face into mine, his mouth positioned just over mine, his eyelashes entangled with mine, and I pant. *Please, please, please.* I close my eyelids. The next moment, the heat of his body moves away, and the elevator jerks as it starts its journey upward. I snap my eyes open to find him leaning against the opposite wall.

"Asshole," I say in a low voice.

"That's alphahole to you, darling wife." He smirks, and goddam him, why does he have to look so goddam hot when he's being all antagonistic to me? I open my mouth to tell him off, and that's when the elevator dings. The door opens and he beckons me to exit first.

Jerk.

I exit the elevator and he follows me to my room. I open the door, and with a loud meow, Andy immediately brushes past me.

"Hey, cat!"

I sense him bend down to pick up Andy. By the time I drop my keys on the table and turn, he has Andy nestled against his chest. The cat purrs and snuggles in. Lucky cat. I frown as he pets the animal, then carries him inside the suite. He glances around the large space, then walks over to Andy's basket. He places the cat down and Andy settles in. Michael straightens, then stretches. The jacket pulls across his shoulders as he raises his arms above his head. His T-shirt lifts and I catch a glimpse of that flat stomach. It would be rock hard, if I touched his belly. I wouldn't be able to make out an ounce of fat. And if I touched the space between his legs, that part would be even harder. And long and thick and fat and —

"Beauty?"

"Eh?" I glance up in time to see him smirk. "What?" I scowl, "What is it?"

"Can I use your bath? I'd like a shower."

"A shower?" I ask with suspicion, "You want to take a shower?"

"I've been on the road for more than half a day; I just wanted to freshen up."

"Hmph," I purse my lips and he holds up his hand.

"Just a shower; that's all."

"No hanky-panky from you, okay?"

"Hanky-panky?" He chuckles, "You're adorable, you know that?"

"Whatever," I huff, "go take your shower, but be quick about it."

"Will you come in and check in on me if I am gone too long?"

"Of course, not." I scowl, "See? This is what I mean. No innuendos, no sexy smirking, no—"

"You think my smirk is sexy?" He smirks at me again and my stomach flip-flops. My pussy flutters.

Argh! What's wrong with me? So, he's my husband and I know exactly how his muscles feel under my fingers, and yeah, he's the hottest man I've ever met... But he also kidnapped me, married me against my will, tagged me, then pretended to have his dick sucked off by someone else... All so he could try to protect me... Or so he says. *And he did cross countries to see you; now, you don't have to be lonely on Christmas.* I jerk my chin toward the door of the bathroom, "Ten minutes."

15

───────

Michael

Ten minutes, and five seconds later, I walk out with a towel around my waist. If she thinks she can order me around, she has another think coming. I walk over to where I'd dumped my duffel on a chair and pull out a pair of sweatpants.

"Hey," she protests, "don't get too comfortable. You're leaving, you—"

I turn around, whip my towel off and she opens and shuts her mouth and I suppress a smirk.

"Wha...what..." She lowers her gaze to my crotch, and her breathing quickens. Her chest rises and falls, and the almost imperceptible motion of her thighs signals that she's squeezing them together.

"You were saying—"

"I was—" she clears her throat, "I was..." She swallows, licks her lips. "I...ah... I mean..."

"I was going to wear my sweatpants, but if you'd rather I not—"

"I'd rather you not—" She scowls, "I mean, don't wear your sweatpants. I mean..." Color suffuses her cheeks. She raises her hand, seems like she is about to speak, then pivots and heads for the bathroom.

I chuckle. "You sure about that?" I call after her as she slams the bathroom door behind her. I turn back to survey the contents of my duffle bag. This is a temporary reprieve. And it had been an under-handed move, maybe, to drop my towel... But hey, it had been a surefire way to grab her attention. Don't judge. I pull on my pair of sweats.

By the time she returns, having scrubbed her face clean and wearing a nightshirt that I recognize as one that I bought for her, I am settled on one side of the bed. I take in the hem of the shirt, which hits somewhere above her knees, revealing a portion of her creamy thighs, her calves, her tiny feet with toenails painted—black, of course—and the blood rushes to my groin. *Santa-Maria*, those toes of hers. I'd love to suck on them, run my tongue between them and down across the sole of her foot, over the arch and down to her heel, before I retrace my steps and nip on her toes again. She digs her toes into the carpet, then clears her throat.

I glance up as she stomps over to me, then dumps my jeans and T-shirt on my chest. "You left your clothes all over the bathroom floor."

"Thanks, honey." I smirk as I pull out my secure phone—the only reason I carry it is because not even the FBI should be able to break into it, at least, in theory. Ideally, I shouldn't be carrying a phone at all. It does make me more vulnerable to being tracked, but I have to stay in touch with my brothers.

I wasn't lying when I told her I had slipped into the country without informing anyone, but at least, my brothers know how to get in touch with me. Also, the security detail I have on Karma is sure to have seen me, so it's not like I am completely unprotected.

When I check my phone, there's a message from Seb asking me to let him know when I decide to head back and that they'll be holding down the business in my absence. Goddam!

I drag my fingers through my hair. Had I been that transparent to them about where I was headed? I could have sworn I hadn't mentioned anything to them. Then again, I guess it wouldn't take a rocket scientist to figure out where I could have disappeared to. Guess my brothers know me too well.

I put my phone aside as she scoffs, "If you think acting all nice and domestic is going to make me take you back, you're wrong."

"Hey, only being myself, sweetheart."

"Argh." She throws up her hands and stomps around the bed to the other side. She slips under the covers, then turns over on her side facing away from me.

I turn off the lamp, and bend my arm behind my head. For a few seconds, there's only the sound of us breathing. Then she wriggles around, making herself comfortable.

"How are you feeling now?" I murmur. "No pain or anything?"

She draws in a breath and the silence stretches. I am almost sure she isn't going to answer me when she sighs. "I am okay. I guess, I am surprised at myself as to how fast I've recovered. I was lucky, I suppose, that I wasn't hurt more."

I curl my fingers into fists. "You shouldn't have been hurt at all," I say in a low voice. "If I could do anything to go back and prevent what happened—"

"Don't beat yourself up over what happened, Michael... It's just one of those things that we need to move on from."

"Have you moved on from it yet?"

I sense, rather than see her shake her head.

"Me neither," I murmur. "I wanted to take you out somewhere nice for dinner, but it's Christmas Eve, and everything is closed."

"It's fine." She moves around, tugs the sheets in her direction, then quietens.

"I thought you'd have spent the evening with your sister and her new husband?"

She blows out a breath, "I thought about it... Even went to their house, then I changed my mind."

"You did?"

"Yeah," she half laughs. "Don't know why I am telling you this because I don't really see you as my friend right now."

"You're right."

"I am?"

"Yeah, I am your husband, your dom, and your master... Certainly not, your friend."

"Seriously?" She switches on the lamp and sits up. "You're going to pull that line on me, now?"

"What's wrong with it?"

"You'd think you'd try to grovel, at least a little, if you wanted to get into my good graces."

I smirk, "Why should I grovel when I have something far more lethal that you'd prefer?"

She narrows her gaze on me, "Do I even want to know what that is?"

I hold up my fingers and wiggle them, "How about these?"

Her gaze falls to my fingers and her eyes widen.

"Or this?" I drag my tongue across my lips. Her breathing grows ragged.

"Or..." I slide my hand under the sheet and down my sweatpants, "this?" I grip my cock, and despite the sheet over my crotch, it's clear what I am up to.

She swallows, the sound audible in the silence.

"You have a preference, *piccolina*?"

Her gaze is fixed on the movements visible through the sheet. Her chest rises and falls, she licks her lips, and the blood drains to my groin. My dick lengthens and I swipe my fingers around my thickness and drag them up the length. A growl rumbles up my chest and she shivers.

"What are you doing?" She clears her throat, "Are you touching yourself?"

"Would you rather touch me instead?"

"I..." she draws in a breath, "I...I'd rather that we go to sleep." She tears her gaze away, turns on her side, facing away from me.

I continue to drag my fingers up my shaft, and again. A groan rumbles up my chest, and she wriggles around on her side of the bed. I throw off my cover, shove my sweatpants down, then begin to jerk myself off in earnest. Not what I had planned, damn it. I had come here simply to spend time with her. I couldn't keep away, and I hadn't really thought if it meant that I was going to fuck her... But considering everything she's been through, I wasn't going to do that... Not unless she asked me to... But just being near her is enough for my dick to swell, my balls to throb, and my groin to harden and knot until I have to relieve myself. So what, if it means I am lying next to her in bed, wanking off.

Che cazzo! Get a grip on yourself, stronzo. I squeeze my shaft tighter — exactly what I am doing...not what I meant...but no matter. If this is the only way of getting off...then so be it.

I increase my pace, squeeze my dick from base to crown, again and again. My shaft thickens and my balls harden as the sound of flesh hitting flesh fills the space. The tension at the base of my spine coils, the blood pounds at my temples, and a bead of sweat crawls down my spine. I throw my head back as I squeeze my cock and yank on it again and again. The pressure in my groin increases and I groan as my balls draw up. That's when she throws off the sheet and crawls over to me.

16

Karma

I had tried to go to sleep. I swear, I had shut my eyes and tried to forget that he was lying in bed next to me, dressed in nothing but that pair of low-hung, grey sweatpants. Argh! Why did he have to wear grey sweatpants? I mean, it's good that he wore them, rather than not wearing anything... Like when he had dropped that towel. OMG... I had seen his perfect arse followed by that full-frontal view of him, his thick cock which had stood to attention the crown leaking precum, and that vein that ran up the underside of his length, and my heart had almost stopped.

Not that I haven't seen him naked, but it has been a while since I've seen all of him, every single inch of his gloriously-sculpted form show-cased in the light from the lamp on the bedstead...and... I'd almost sunk to my knees and crawled over to him, and raised myself until I was at eye level with him, and opened my mouth and taken him down my throat, and sucked him off. I had barely managed to tear my gaze off of his gorgeous cock and stagger to the bathroom to wash up. So, when he'd begun to get himself off and the wet sound of flesh hitting flesh had filled the space... My pussy had clamped down so hard, I'd had to stuff my knuckles in my mouth to stop myself from moaning aloud.

I had resisted. I swear, I had tried so hard to resist, had tried to shut out the sounds as he'd dragged his fingers up his shaft, and increased the pace with which he'd fucked his own palm. I'd tried to squeeze my eyelids closed and my thighs together, and tried to pretend that it didn't matter that he had thrown off the covers and was now beating himself off and was so close to coming... But when he'd gasped and I'd known that he was almost there, I hadn't been able to stop myself. My mouth had watered, my fingers had tingled, and in something resembling a dream or a trance... I find myself crawling over to him.

I swing my leg over his thigh, then nestle between his legs, and he glances up as I wrap my fingers over and around his. He pauses mid-motion and I hold his gaze as I lower my head to his crotch. Without breaking the connection between our eyes, I lick the head of his cock.

His jaw tics and a pulse leaps to life at his temple. The blue in his eyes deepens until it's almost black in color. I have never seen him this turned on... This...almost beside himself with desire. I close my mouth around the tip of his cock and a growl rumbles up his chest. He pulls his hand out from under mine, folds his palms behind his neck and leans back. The expanse of his chest stretches out in front of me. Acres of cut planes, of sculpted muscle and hewn flesh that ripple as he glares down at me.

"Suck me off," he growls and I swallow. The suction on his dick has the muscles under his skin jumping. His biceps twitch, his nostrils flare, and he fixes his gaze on my mouth, watches as I swirl my tongue around the head of his shaft. His chest rises and falls, his scowl deepens, and I bob my head. I open my mouth, swallow down on his length, and he groans. I pull back, until my mouth is once more fitted around the crown of his length. He thrusts his pelvis forward, chasing the suction that only I can provide, and I can't stop my lips from curling. I lick around the circumference of the head, then drag my tongue down the length of his shaft and his shoulders flex. His gaze intensifies, he sets his jaw, and a bead of sweat slides down his temple. I lower my head and take his cock in my mouth and he hisses.

"Fuck," he growls and I hold his gaze as I swallow. Color flushes his cheeks. The next moment he leans forward, wraps my hair around his fingers. "You little tease," he says in a hard voice. "Are you wet yet, Beauty? Is your pussy clamping down, imagining my fat cock is inside of you? Stretching you, thrusting into you, cramming your hole as I squeeze your ass cheeks, and driving up and into you, hitting that place deep inside of you that only I know, that only I can reach every time I fuck you... Are you empty and needy and straining for my fingers in your asshole as I tear into your swollen channel?"

The moan vibrates up my throat and his shoulders go solid. He wraps the fingers of his free hand around my neck as he begins to fuck my mouth in earnest. He pulls my head forward and I choke. Tears slide down from the corners of my eyes, saliva drools from my mouth, and his gaze intensifies. "Do you know how it is to feel my cock down your throat?" he says in a hard voice. "Do you know what it does to me to see you all messed up as you swallow around my shaft, Beauty?"

I press my tongue against the column of his thickness and his features contort. "F-u-c-k, Beauty, you are killing me." He pulls me up until the crown of his dick is poised between my lips, then thrusts me down so his cock impales my throat. I swallow and his jaw tics. He continues the movement, down-up-down, and again. His chest muscles bunch, his shoulders flex, his jaw hardens, and I know he's close again. I grip his thighs as he pulls me up, then thrusts me down so I take him down my throat again. His stomach muscles ripple and he throws his head back.

"Fuck, I am coming," he growls as his hips jerk and he shoots his load. His cum fills my mouth and I swallow, and yet, he keeps coming. Drops dribble down my chin, onto his thigh, splashing on my chest. He pulls out, and at the same time, he hauls me up and locks his mouth over mine. He thrusts his tongue in between my lips and I can taste his cum, and his lips, and that essence that is so dark and so him, and my pussy clenches. I moan deep in my throat and it's like a signal, for he flips me under him.

He settles between my thighs, then deepens the kiss as his still turgid cock stabs into my lower belly. I knot my arms around his neck as he continues to kiss me and suck on my tongue, before he licks my lower lip. He breaks the kiss, only to kiss my chin, nibble his way down my throat. He grips the bottom of my sleep shirt, pushes it up so its above my breasts. He squeezes my tits together then bites down on one nipple. I yelp, then moan when he licks the engorged flesh, then repeats the action with the other. He blows on the flesh and I shiver. He works his way down to kiss my belly button, then kisses the flesh between the waistband of my panties and my navel.

"How do you feel down there? Are you still sore?" He gazes up at me, "Are you, Beauty?"

I shake my head and he holds my gaze. He pushes aside the gusset of my panties, then lowers his chin to my center. Without taking his gaze off of mine, he licks my clit. A whine bleeds from my lips. His lips curve up and he drags his tongue between my pussy lips. I shiver, then bury my fingers in his hair as I try to coax him down to the opening of my channel. He swipes his tongue down the length of my core, then up to my clit again. A shiver runs up my spine, as he wraps his fingers around the tops of my thighs and pries them apart, his touch still gentle as he buries his nose in my core.

"Oh," I moan as he presses his lips to my throbbing clit. "Oh, my god, Mika." I lean my head back as he licks his way down my pussy, then up again and again. He doesn't thrust his tongue inside my channel though. I jerk my pelvis forward, chasing the intrusion I need—that rough tongue of his as he licks inside me, the thickness of his fingers as he stretches me, the hardness of his dick as he crams it into me... And it would hurt... Not gonna lie, but I want that hurt. I need it, I need... "You, Mika, I need you."

"Don't want to hurt you, babe," he murmurs, his breath hot against my tender flesh. "Don't want you to feel sore again."

"I won't," I insist, "I'll be fine."

He scowls up at me, "Are you sure?"

I hesitate and he tilts his head, "Doesn't mean I can't make you come."

"Oh?" I blink, "I..." I gasp as he buries his face in my pussy again and closes his mouth around the flesh. With his tongue, he strums my pussy lips, with the roughness of his whiskered jaw, he scrapes the tender flesh, with his teeth, he bites down on my clit, and I explode. The climax vibrates out from my center, gathering speed as it roars toward my extremities. My arms and legs tremble, my entire body shudders as I try to close my thighs and end up capturing his head between them. I release his head, grab hold of the headboard behind me as he thrusts his tongue inside my channel. He curves his tongue and the orgasm continues to explode deep inside of me. The moisture gushes out from between my thighs and he laps it up. He licks my pussy lips, and my clit again and again, as if he can't get enough. I sense him move up my body and open my eyes to find his face in front of mine. He presses his lips to mine, and our combined essences fills my palate.

The taste of him, the scent of him, the heat of him overwhelms me. I press myself closer to him as my eyelids flutter down.

When I awaken, the room is dark. I try to move, but a weight around my waist pins me down. I try to turn and realize that Michael is holding me close, his chest pressed to my back, his leg flung over me. The man gives off so much heat that even though the cover is thrown off, sweat beads my brow. I wriggle my butt into him so I can turn, and a thick column stabs into the valley between my arse cheeks. "Oh." I freeze. I draw in a breath, another, then push my butt back again and the thickness hardens. I bite the inside of my cheek, manage to wriggle my hand free from under his arm. I try to turn my torso and his grip tightens. He pushes his pelvis forward so every last ridge of his dick is imprinted into the curve of my hip. My pussy spasms, my nipples harden, and moisture laces my core. I gulp, wriggle my backside again, and this time, his cock seems to stab through the thin material of my underwear. I begin to move my butt against the column. Back and forth, back and forth. That's when he shoves me onto my front.

17

Karma

"What the," I protest, "what are you doing, Michael?"

"You started this, Beauty." He lowers his face so his cheek is pressed into mine. "Don't think I didn't notice you wriggling your little tush against my cock." He presses said cock into the curve of my hips and I can't stop the moan that wheezes out.

"Michael," I whisper. "Oh, Michael."

"Do you know how much it turns me on to hear my name from your lips?"

I swallow, "I… I didn't mean to wake you up."

"Liar," he murmurs without heat as he licks the shell of my ear. He sucks the earlobe and I feel the tug all the way to my core. My pussy clenches and I dig my fingers into the bedspread. "Mika, please," I implore. "Please, Mika."

"Tell me what you want, Beauty," He flicks his tongue inside my ear and goosebumps pop on my skin. Who'd have thought that could be so sexy, him licking, nibbling, biting down on my earlobe and every part of my being responding to that action. I wriggle under him and he slaps my butt. "Stop that."

"Wha—" I splutter, "what was that for?"

"For causing me so much distress that I had to fly across three countries to see you."

"Hey," I scowl, "I am not the one who put on that stupid show then asked me to leave."

"I'm sorry about that."

He kisses the side of my temple and I blink. "You apologized?"

"I've been known to do that," I sense him smirk, "on occasion. Just don't get used to it."

"Like I would dare?" I peer up at him from the corner of my eyes. "Are you going to use your monster dick, or what?"

He pauses, then laughs. The rich sound fills the space, and my heart stutters. It bloody stutters. Will I ever get used to this man's magnetism, his sheer charisma, his preening, the force of his personality, his allure that draws me to him constantly, until I am sure I'll never be able to live separately from him? Tears prick the backs of my eyes and I blink them away. Or I think I do, but his gaze narrows. He bends, licks up the lone tear that has escaped from the corner of my eye. "What's wrong?" he murmurs, and I shake my head.

"Nothing."

"Don't lie," he admonishes me. "Tell me what's on your mind."

"Nothing." I scowl back.

"It's something that when I am plastered to you, you are crying." He pulls away, "Is it me or—?"

"No," I protest. "No, come back."

He chuckles, "You're fucking adorable, wife."

"Yeah, yeah," I mumble, "what-bloody-ever."

"Love it when you talk dirty, babe."

"Oh, for fuck's sake," I push up and into him, only to be met by that thick hardness between his legs which, on its own, is enough to pin me down. "Let me go."

"Thought you wanted me to use my monster cock on you?"

"Well, are you?"

He sobers, "I'm still not sure if you are fully healed, baby."

My heart melts a little. Fuck, all he has to do is call me baby, and I'll throw myself at his feet panting. Hell, I'll throw myself at him anyway, as I have been doing since practically the first time I met him. I squeeze my thighs together, and scowl up at him. "I really am fine, promise."

"I am not convinced."

"The doctor said it was okay to start having sex when I felt ready."

"And do you feel ready?"

"I told you I do."

"Hmm." He pats the curve of my arse and my belly flip-flops.

"What?" I scowl.

"Given you're so horny, and since I don't feel comfortable shoving my monster shaft inside your pussy—"

"Y-e-s," I frown, "what is it you're thinking?"

"We could, of course, satisfy ourselves with sex of the non-penetrative kind—"

I shake my head, "I want to feel you inside of me, Mika."

"Hmm." His eyes gleam, "There is, of course, another way for me to be inside of you."

"Oh." I blink rapidly, "OH!" I swallow, "You mean?"

He nods.

"You mean you want to come in by the backdoor, again?"

He stares at me, then throws his head back and laughs, a full belly laugh.

"What the hell?" I grumble as I try to wriggle out from under him and he merely leans more weight on me, so I can barely move. "Let me move, you oaf."

"No."

"Why are you laughing like a hyena?"

"Because you are so fucking cute."

"Argh," I growl, "I hate it when you use that bloody 'c' word."

"What do you say, Beauty?"

"I have to admit that the thought of you putting the python between your legs in my arse again doesn't exactly fill me with joy."

"Didn't hear you complaining about it the last time." He smirks.

I redden, "That...that was different."

"Oh, yeah?" He leans in close enough for our breaths to mingle, "How was it different?"

"Umm," I blink rapidly, "I don't know, it was just different."

He stares at me and I raise my shoulders, "It was in the heat of the moment, okay? That first time, at your fake funeral, I figured I might as well do it because it would please you."

"So, it didn't please you?" He frowns.

"It...it did." I try to shift my body, but again, I'm pinned in place. "It was a bit painful, at first, but then, you know, once I got into the uh, swing of things, it actually did accentuate the pleasure," I admit. "And then, of course, there was that second time at your place..." I glance at him, then away.

"And," he prompts me, "how was that for you, Beauty?"

"It was..." I shake my head. "It was when you took me against the wall of your room," I whisper.

"And?" He nuzzles at my temple, "Do you remember what I did to you then?"

I draw in a breath, "You..." I clear my throat, "you pounded into me so hard that I felt you all the way down to the tips of my toes. You breached me with such force that I was sure that you were going to split me in two. It...it was..."

"It was?" He peers into my face. "Complete the sentence," he insists when I hesitate.

"It was intense and filthy and indecent and yet," I swallow, "there was something deeply satisfying about it. Like we were communicating on a different level. Like we were arguing without words. Like our bodies were straining to push away, and yet also, come closer. It felt like we were fighting more than fucking. It was..." I tip up my chin, "it was the most erotic experience of my life, okay?" Heat flushes my cheeks, and I am sure that I am blushing even more.

"Only," he searches my gaze, "you still have doubts about doing it again."

"I didn't say that."

"It's written all over your face."

"And when did you become so good at reading my mind?"

He tilts his head and I blow out a breath, "Yes, okay, I admit, I am still not a big fan of anal sex."

"I am sorry if you weren't completely comfortable with it earlier, which is why..." He releases me, then rolls off of me and pads over to his duffel bag. He squats and rummages around, then straightens. He turns to walk over to me and I take in the three packages he holds. One is a small square and another is rectangular in shape. Both have ribbons tied around them. The third one is not wrapped and he sets it down on the side table.

"Oh," I turn over, then sit up. "You bought gifts?"

"For you, and for that beast," he nods toward the sleeping cat. He hands the rectangular one over to me. "That's for Andy," he adds. I pull off the cover, then open the box and pull out a plush toy in the form of a mouse.

"You bought him a cat toy."

"Apparently, I did." He shakes his head.

"Aww," I coo, "sooo sweet."

He grimaces, "You make me sound like I've lost my mind."

"Or found your heart."

His features tense. "No emo shit, okay?"

"Can I kiss you to show my gratitude?"

"You can kiss my cock, instead, and I would be most grateful."

I huff, "Do you always have to equate everything with sex?"

"Is there any other way?"

I nod toward the other package, "What's that?"

"That—" he hands it over to me, "is for you."

I tear off the wrapping, then stare at the square velvet box. "Oh," I swallow, "what is it?"

"Open it."

I pull off the top, then stare at the short, ribbed column which tapers on one side, before broadening out, then narrows into a notch before it flares out into a heart shape. A tiny black stone is set into the center of the heart around which is set a circle of red stones. I stare at it, "Is that a…?" I blink rapidly, "That is a…"

"A butt plug," he supplies helpfully, then picks it up and hands it to me, "for you."

"For me?"

"It's going to make the entire experience of our fucking even more pleasurable."

"Oh." I swallow. I glance from the sparkling plug thingy to his face, then back at it. "You sure about this?"

"Very," he promises me. "I promise you that it'll make your orgasms even more intense."

"I don't know about that," I laugh, "they've been plenty intense with you already."

"This will make it even better for you, baby." He leans over and presses a kiss to my temple, then to my cheek, then to the corner of my lips, "Go on. Let me put it in."

"You really want this, eh?"

"I want to imprint myself on every part of you. Own every cell of your body. Rub my cum into every inch of your skin. Kiss every curve, every finger, every toe, every piece of your flesh, so you never forget who you belong to."

I gulp.

"I want to own every inch of you, Beauty," he peers into my eyes. "All of you." He places his lips over mine, "Only you. Just as you own me, completely."

My toes curl and my pussy clenches. I squeeze my thighs together, already wanting him inside me, in me, filling every hole in my body, goddamn! I draw in a breath, then place the velvet box on the side table. "Fine."

"Good girl." He kisses me hard and heat flushes my skin. He takes the jeweled plug from me, then presses on my shoulder and I turn over on my front.

He sweeps my hair aside and presses a kiss to the nape of my neck and I shiver. He kisses his way down my spine and I swoon. OMG, I almost swoon as he presses his lips to the hollow of my back. He peels back my panties, kisses the curve of my arse, then yanks down my underwear until it's just above my knees. He reaches over and I turn my head to find him flipping open the third box. He extracts a bottle of lube, and pours out a little of the liquid in his palm. He warms it between his hands, then leans over me again. He kisses first one arse cheek, then the other, then slides his finger inside my backhole.

18

———————

Karma

Too much, too thick. His fat digit stretches my butthole. I huff, try to pull away and he flattens his palm on the small of my back. "Relax," he murmurs as I clench down on his finger. "Draw in a breath," he instructs me.

I do.

"Now hold it."

I hold the breath in my lungs.

"Now release," he exhales and so I do.

He guides me through the next few breaths and at the end of it, to my surprise, I find that my muscles have, indeed, relaxed. I exhale again and his finger slips inside. "Oh," I gasp as he allows me to adjust to the intrusion.

He leans down and presses another kiss to the nape of my neck, "Okay?"

"Y…yeah," I swallow.

"How does it feel?"

"It feels…strange… And yet, it also feels, weirdly, good."

"Good," he nips the curve of where my shoulder meets my neck and heat tugs at my lower belly. He curves his finger inside of me and tendrils of sensation crawl up my spine. I bite the inside of my cheek to keep from crying out. He pulls out his finger, slides it back in, repeats the action until it feels much more normal.

The next time he withdraws his finger, he replaces it with something cold, metallic. Oh, I clench down and he bends to place his cheek next to mine. "Trust me, *Bellezza*," he murmurs. "You do trust me, right?"

"I.." I swallow, then nod. "Yeah, I do." And I mean it. Despite everything that has happened, despite the fact that he had staged that scene which had almost shattered my heart, despite the fact that our entire relationship had started in the most unorthodox of terms... I do trust him. More than anybody else.

"Beauty?" He nuzzles the space behind my ear. "Eyes on me." He pinches my chin, turns my head toward him. I raise my gaze to his and he nips on my lower lip. I open my mouth and he swoops in. He slides the butt plug in past the tight ring of my sphincter at the same time.

"Oh," the breath whooshes out of me and he inhales it. He sucks on my tongue, kisses me with such passion, such intensity, that my head spins. I lean into him, try to flatten myself against him, but already, he is moving back. "Wha—?" I open my eyes to find him sliding off of the bed. "What are you doing?"

I turn my head in his direction as he holds out his hand, "Come on, we have to leave."

"We...do?"

He nods. "I may have risked being detected by coming to this country, but I don't take unnecessary chances."

"You don't?"

He wiggles his fingers and I automatically reach for them. He grabs my hand, tugs me up and off the bed. I stand before him, tip my chin up, "Where are we going?"

"You'll see."

Half an hour later, I stare out of the window of the plane. Below me is a void of darkness which I have been told is the sea. Michael had barely allowed me to get dressed as he'd coaxed Andy into the pet carrier. I'd packed fast, and then he'd ferried me out of the room, down a private elevator, to a side entrance where his Maserati had been waiting. He'd driven us through the almost empty streets, to a private airport in the heart of the city. The same airport at which I had arrived. To the same plane that had dropped me off, or at least it seemed like the same one. Do all luxury private aircrafts look the same? The interior had seemed the same but the crew was different.

After takeoff, I had let Andy out of the carrier. He had retreated to a corner of the cabin and hadn't been particularly happy. That was, until the steward had fussed over him. Turned out, Michael had also sprung for a comfortable cat-cave like bed for him, and Andy had been some-what mollified when he'd discovered it.

Meanwhile, Michael had guided me to a seat near the window and taken the one next to me.

I've just dozed off when something buzzes right between my legs. I yelp, then realize the source is the butt plug which is still firmly wedged in my back entrance. I turn to find Michael watching me with a smirk.

"Wh…what are you doing?" I stutter. "More to the point, how are you doing it?"

He holds out his palm, uncurls his fingers, and I spot the little remote control. He presses down on the button on the remote and the thing in my backhole vibrates again. My thighs quiver and my pussy spasms. The vibrations seem to go on and on, and by the end of it, I am gasping. Heat flushes my cheeks and a bead of sweat slides down my spine.

He smirks, then lean in to kiss me. "Happy Christmas and Happy Birthday," he whispers as he tucks an errant strand of hair behind my ear.

"How did you know it's my birthday?"

"I know everything about you, *piccola*," He brushes his lips over mine. Then, the asshole leans back in his seat and closes his eyes. Letting me stew in my own juices… Literally. I clench my thighs together, try to block out the gnawing ache that flares between my legs, and turn to glance out of the window.

The cabin is silent, and I take in the dawn breaking over the horizon. The pinks bleed out across the skies, darkening into blues and golds as the sun rises. I glance below to see the waves stretching out before me, and in the distance, I sight land.

Next to me, he stirs. Then heat envelops me as he leans in to peer over my shoulder. "Almost there." His dark voice rumbles up his chest. My nerve-endings instantly flare to life. Goosebumps pop on my skin and I shiver. "You cold?" he nuzzles the hair at my temple and I shake my head. "Here," I turn to find him shrugging out of his leather jacket.

I slide it on, and have just finished zipping it up when the steward comes over with Andy back in his traveling case. She places Andy in the seat opposite us and secures the seatbelt over the case.

Within minutes, we have begun our descent. I glance down to find the flight circling what appears to be a small island.

"Oh," I blink as the pilot brings the flight over the water and onto a landing strip that seems to be surrounded by water. The flight comes to a halt, and Michael unsnaps his seatbelt and rises to his feet. He helps me up, then grabs Andy's traveling case. He swings his duffel bag over one shoulder, snatches up my suitcase in the other hand and heads out. I follow him down the steps and up the path that leads away from the airstrip. We have barely made it behind the trees that line the space, when the plane's engine revs up. I turn to find it taxiing up the runway, then turning around to take off.

"The plane's leaving," I remark.

When he doesn't respond, I increase my pace to catch up with him, "Is there another way off of the island?"

"I do have a motorboat in the boathouse and a jetty, in case of contingency; but yeah, outside of that, there's no other way off of the island. If anyone approaches the island, either by plane or by boat, I'll hear them."

"Oh," I open and shut my mouth. "Guess this is as safe as it gets?"

He jerks his chin and I follow him up a path that leads another half a mile upward before we reach a plateau that looks out over a beach that abuts the sea. There, in the middle of the space, is a two-story, Greek-style bungalow. The walls are white-washed, and the cube-shaped building's smooth-edged corners lend a sense of space and freedom to the structure. The sun shines down on us, bathing the entire area in a golden glow. A bead of sweat trickles down my temple and I unzip his jacket.

"Where are we, anyway?" I glance around the space, "It's much warmer than London."

"I should hope so," he laughs. "We are on an island off the coast of Malta that has its own microclimate."

"Microclimate?"

He nods, "We are about two and a half hours away from London, but as you can see, the weather here is infinitely better."

"You're not a big fan of London, huh?"

He raises his shoulder, "It has its charms."

"But you prefer Sicily?"

"For the food, absolutely. For the weather, normally, except when it gets too hot at the peak of summer. That's when I normally escape here."

"On your own?"

"Mostly; I've had my brothers over on a few occasions."

"And girlfriends?" I force the words out, "Have you brought them over as well?"

"And if I have?" I can't see his face, but hell, if I don't hear the smirk in that voice of his.

I pause and he walks forward for a few seconds before he pauses. He places my suitcase and Andy's case on the ground, then turns to glance at me over his shoulder, "What?"

"So, you have brought women here before?"

"I haven't not brought them here."

"Argh!" I plant my hands on my hips, "Michael Byron Domenico Sovrano, if you're taking me to your love nest, then I have absolutely no interest in going there."

"Are you jealous?"

"Of course, not," I sniff, "and you haven't answered the question."

"I've brought…" he walks over to me, "no other woman here before."

"Oh," I bite the inside of my cheek.

He pauses in front of me, then notches his knuckle under my chin. He peers down into my features, "You are the first woman to have set foot on this island."

"Not even Nonna has come here?"

He laughs, "Nonna hates traveling. She hasn't left Sicily in, maybe, twenty years."

"Ah," I murmur, "okay."

"Okay," his lips kick up, "now, can we go inside?"

19

Karma

The inside, as it turns out, is not exactly the rough-and-ready holiday getaway bungalow I had envisioned. From the exterior, the place is whitewashed, and the lines are that of a structure that had been built to blend in with the island's surroundings.

Inside… Well… I follow him through the wide doorway and take in the large space. One entire wall is made of glass, beyond which, is the beach, and then an uninterrupted view of the sea. Facing it is a large sectional in the center of which is a coffee table. A fireplace is set into one wall. Diagonally opposite is a kitchen separated from the main area by a breakfast bar. In the other corner is a dining table with four chairs. He walks past the kitchen and down the short corridor into a bedroom….which is also massive. High ceilings, one wall made of glass through which the same uninterrupted view of the sea spreads out before us. A king-sized bed is set against a wall. I assume the double doors opposite the bed lead to the ensuite. Another set of double doors must lead into a closet.

He places Andy's pet carrier down next to a large cushion in the form of a cave.

"The litter box is in the bathroom," he murmurs.

I walk over, open the door to the carrier and coax Andy out. He mewls and I carry him in my arms. I cuddle him as Michael carries the bags inside. I walk into the bathroom, place Andy down near the litter box and allow him to get acquainted with it. Then walk out and across the bedroom to the large glass wall to take in the view. I hear his footsteps approach.

The next second, he wraps an arm about my shoulders, pulls me back to rest against his chest. He tugs my head under his chin, and for a few seconds, we stand there admiring the view.

"So, this is the kind of privacy money can buy, eh?"

"Or notoriety."

"You know," I tip my chin up, "that is the first time I've heard you refer to your profession honestly."

"I am on the wrong side of the law; I was born with that knowledge. It's who I am."

The band around my chest tightens. I am not sure why, but hearing him put that out there so baldly...sends a shiver of apprehension down my spine. Not that I didn't know about his vocation... I mean, from the very first time we met, it was clear that he wasn't an ordinary, law-abiding citizen. It's just, maybe somewhere, I'd held onto the hope that he might change. *And yet... It's the darkness within him, that edginess, that cloak of danger that clings to him that you find so attractive.*

"I can hear you thinking, *Bellezza.*" His grip around me tightens, "Want to tell me what's on your mind?"

I turn to face him, "I was thinking of the cat cave."

"The cat cave?"

I jerk my chin toward the cushion shaped like a cave, which I know Andy is going to love. "You got that for Andy?"

His features smoothen out, "And if I did?"

"So, you were that sure I was going to come with you?"

"Let's just say, I can be persuasive."

"And you had enough time to have someone come in and place the cat cave here?"

"And place the litterbox in the bathroom, as well as make sure there's enough food to last us for, at least, a week."

"A week?" I blink.

"If not more."

"Guess even mob bosses take time off over Christmas and New Year, eh?"

"Not usually," he smirks. "But this year I've asked my men to spend time with their families, so yes, things will be quiet."

"How convenient for you." I brush past him and walk over to the cat cushion, just as Andy pads out of the bathroom. He prances over to the cat cave then jumps onto the cushion. He tips his head up and mewls at me. I scowl at him as Michael walks over to me.

"Not sure why you are angry, but I think the beast needs to be fed."

"You're not sure why I am angry?" I straighten, "And I am sure your minions ensured the place is stocked with cat food."

"I did tell them to make sure to do so, yes," he admits.

I turn on him, "Well, don't let me keep you from whatever it is you normally do when you come to your uppity island retreat." I stalk off in the direction of the kitchen. I know I am being unreasonable, but really, the fact that he could fit me so neatly into his schedule rankles a little bit… Okay, a lot. Also, I don't want to admit it, but the fact that he's been so thoughtful about making sure that Andy is taken care of… It paints him in a favorable light…which I am not happy about. He could try a little harder to be unlikeable, right? It doesn't help that he's decided to sweep me off to an island for some time off. An island that I am dying to explore. Gah!

I reach the kitchen, yank open the nearest shelf. Spices. This one is packed with spices. I slap it shut, pull open the next one. Dried pasta, loaves of bread, risotto rice, other packs of products with Italian names that I am not familiar with. I slam it shut, open the next one. This has pots and pans. The next one has plates and mugs. I yank open the drawer below it and find cutlery. "Argh!" I step back, survey the room. "Where the hell have you hidden it?"

He pulls open the door of the shelf closest to him, then reaches in and extracts a pack. I flounce over and grab it from him. Glancing around, I spy the bowls set out for food and water on the window ledge. "Of course, you'd even have his name engraved on the bowls, right?"

I stomp over to it, pour out the food, top up the water bowl. Before I can turn to call for Andy, the bloody cat pads over to me. He leaps onto the ledge and laps up the water. I watch him to make sure he's happy to eat the cat food, then turn, brush past Michael and back to the bedroom.

"I think it's presumptuous that you thought I'd share the bedroom with you."

"You're my wife; of course, you'll share my bed."

"And if I don't want to?"

"You will."

"But I don't."

"You do."

I throw up my arms and turn on him, "And if I refuse?"

"Then I'd—"

"What?" I snap. "What would you do? Tie me to the bed until I agree to cooperate?"

"That's not a bad idea." He tilts his head, "But I have a far simpler method."

"What?"

He slides his hand inside his pocket. The next moment, the plug between my arse cheeks vibrates.

20

Michael

I press down on the button of the remote control and she stiffens.

"What the—" she gapes. "You... I... Ahhhh!"

She looks about ready to strangle me and I smirk. I hadn't meant to, but…it had been the easiest way to shut her up. Not that I don't find the fact that she's having a meltdown attractive. Hell, I love every mood of hers… None more so than when she's angry enough that her green eyes dart sparks at me and color fills her cheeks. But when I slid my hand in my pocket, my fingers brushed over the button, and I couldn't resist. I simply wanted to see what her reaction would be.

And I am not disappointed when she sputters, "How…how dare you? That's so underhanded of you."

"You think?" I allow my smile to widen and she plants her hands on her hips.

"Argh, you are so damn annoying."

"Admit it. You like it, though."

"The only thing I admit is that I am going to take that goddam butt plug out right now." She pivots, marches toward the door.

I call out, "Stop, Beauty."

She holds up her middle finger as she reaches the door, and I press down on the button again. And keep it pressed. She gasps, stiffens, then clutches the frame of the doorway.

"Oh, my god," she moans. "Oh, god." She squeezes her thighs together, presses her cheek against the wooden frame.

I turn a dial to increase the intensity. Instantly, she rises up on her tiptoes, throws up her hand, and grips the door. "Jesus," she huffs, "this…this thing is—"

"Turning you on?" I reach for her, grasp her shoulder and turn her around.

Her breath comes in short gasps, her chest rises and falls, sweat beads her upper lip, and she swallows. I turn the button further to the right and she groans, thrusts out her luscious breasts.

If I move the jacket—my jacket, that she's wearing—out of the way, I am sure I'll see her pebbled nipples. The blood rushes to my groin, and fuck, if my balls don't throb.

I turn the button even more, as far as it will go, and she throws back her head. "Oh, bloody hell," she groans as she bites down on her lower lip. She throws out her hand, as if looking for support, and I grab it. I release my hold on the button and she slumps. I catch her around the waist, then throw her over my shoulder. She half protests and I slap her butt. Which must send vibrations through her aching backhole, for she moans again.

She wriggles around and I squeeze her butt. She chafes her thighs tighter, and fuck, the scent of her arousal seeps into the air. My vision tunnels. My blood begins to thud in my veins. I increase my pace until I am half jogging toward my bedroom.

I reach my bed and lower her to the mattress. She sprawls on her back, dark hair spread out about her shoulders, cheeks flushed, pupils dilated until there's only a circle of green around her pupils. I rake my gaze down her chest, her narrow waist, her generous hips and thighs, those tiny feet clad in the sneakers she'd worn when she'd left my home in Palermo. I sink down to my knees, untie her shoes and pull them off, then her socks.

"What are you doing?" she mumbles.

"Making you more comfortable." I smirk as I rise up to my feet. I tear off my own shoes and socks, then plank my body over hers. "You're fucking gorgeous, Beauty."

She swallows as she stares up into my face. I lean down, brush my lips over hers once, twice, thrice. A moan bleeds from her lips and she flutters her eyelids shut. I press kisses over each eyelid, then to her nose, to her chin. To the hollow at the base of her throat. I inhale that moon-flower scent of hers, and my balls harden. An urgency grips me.

I lean back on my knees, grab her hands and haul her up. She blinks as I divest her of the jacket, then unbutton her shirt and pull it off. I glance down at her lace bra and the dark nipples that are visible through it. I lower my head and kiss her in the valley between her tits. She shudders, and the drumbeat of her heartbeat against her ribcage ratchets up. I pull back, then reach behind her to unhook her bra. It falls down her shoulders and I pull it down her arms and fling it aside. She stares at me, holds my gaze as she thrusts out her breasts proudly.

"Minchia," I growl, "you're a fucking goddess."

Her cheeks heat as she glances away, then back at me. I reach for the waistband of her jeans, unhook the button and pull down the fly. I step back onto the floor, pull her up to her feet. Then roll her jeans down her thighs, along with her panties as I drop to my knees. She steps out of them and I throw them aside. Then glance up to find her gaze on me. Her lips are parted, her elbows tucked into her sides as she watches me from under hooded eyelids.

I grip the tops of her thighs, pull her close as I reach in and bury my nose in her pussy. The scent of her, sweet and sexy and fucking erotic, fills my senses. I draw her essence into my lungs, until it feels like it's invading every pore in my body. I thought I'd wanted to imprint myself on her, but the fact is, she's already stamped her impression onto every part of me. I'll never be the same, never be able to go back to being the emotionless, focused, tunnel-visioned man who'd only wanted one thing. Power.

With her, I feel vulnerable, yet alive… I felt like I can experience the highs of life…and the lows… She made me real, human… She makes me *feel*. It won't help me to do my job better. To become emotional is the beginning of the end for any made man. It has caused the downfall of too many of them to count… And yet… It feels right. Being with her feels right. It feels like the only thing worth living for. What is this life if I can't open myself to her, allow her to see what she does to me, allow her to invade my secrets, to see my weaknesses. To strip myself bare as I've stripped her.

I rise to my feet, reach for the back of my T-shirt and pull it off. She stares at my chest, drags her gaze down the planes to my waist. I lower the zipper on my jeans and step out of them. Then straighten once more. I widen my stance, hold my arms at my sides, and allow her to take in every part of my body. Naked. Open. At her mercy.

Her breathing grows ragged, her lips part, and when she raises her gaze to mine, the look in her eyes is hungry, horny, and so needy that my breath hitches. I turn around, walk over to my duffel, remove the box I've been carrying, and return to place it on the nightstand.

She glances at it, then at me, and grows a shade paler.

"Shh," I reach over and kiss her, wrap my arms around her, and hold her close so every inch of her body is plastered to mine. I massage her shoulders, rub circles over her back, and bit by bit, the tension seeps out of her. I step back, turn her around then push her onto the bed.

"On your hands and knees, baby." I place my palm flat on the small of her back. She shivers but complies as she bends over, beautifully. I take in her heart-shaped behind, arched up, showing the valley between her ass-cheeks, the glittering butt plug, and finally, the pink of her pussy, already glistening with her arousal. I move in closer and she shudders. I grip her hip, then grasp the heart-shaped head of the butt plug and work it out of her. She groans as it comes free and the sound coils somewhere deep inside of me.

The blood drains to my groin and I have to widen my stance to accommodate my cock, that twitches and throbs and insists that I get inside of her. I lean over, grab the lube, then pour it into my palm. I warm it up, then rub it over my shaft before I move in and slide a finger inside of her. A moan tumbles from her lips as I add a second finger, and curve it. Her entire body jerks and I grab her to keep her from falling. I slip a third finger inside, and she throws her head back, "Oh, my god, Mika, that feels—"

"Good?"

"It feels..." she seems to search for the right word, "it feels like you're stretching me apart...but in a good way."

I pull out my fingers, then fit the swollen crown of my cock to her back opening. "I am going to fuck you now."

21

Karma

I draw in a breath and before I can protest, he breaches me. A groan wells up and my knees tremble. Shit, shit, shit… This…feels…different. He feels so big, so hard, so thick as he stretches me. He pauses to allow me to accommodate his girth, and as he leans over me, he grips the back of my neck and a shiver runs down my spine. To be at his mercy like this, as he impales me and holds me captive, as he massages the curve of my arse, as his cock twitches inside of me, as he pushes forward, sinks deeper into me, as his thickness distends my backchannel so I can feel every millimeter of his throbbing cock… OMG… It's filthy and erotic and forbidden and… So bloody good.

I taste something metallic on my palate and realize that I have bitten down on my tongue. I swallow down the coppery taste, turn to glance over my shoulder and freeze.

He's gazing down, watching the place where he's entered me, watching as he thrusts forward, this time, with enough force that my body jerks. He slips inside and sheaths himself completely. He grits his teeth, and I can't stop the gasp that slips from my lips. He glances up and his blue gaze locks with mine. His jaw flexes, a look of controlled restraint on his features as his chest heaves. He holds my gaze as he pulls out, slowly, so slowly, leaving me strangely empty and craving more. He slides his hand around to play with my pussy lips gently, so gently, then lunges forward and impales me. His balls slaps against my inner thighs. A whine bleeds from my lips, he bares his teeth. He touches my clit, just a brush of his fingertips, and a trembling grips me. He rubs his fingers through my pussy lips and I moan.

"Please," I huff, "more; I want more."

He slides one finger inside my soaking pussy. I squeeze my eyes shut. "Sooo good," I moan as he pulls out his finger, then pushes it back in, and again. I clamp down on his finger, clenching around his cock, and a growl rips from him.

"You're killing me, *Bellezza.* I can barely hold back as it is."

He withdraws his dick, only to push forward inside me again, at the same time he works his finger in and out of my soaking cunt.

"Please," I mutter, "please, Mika, add another finger."

"You sure?" I sense the hesitation in his tone, and reach down between my legs. I slide my finger inside my pussy next to his and he hisses. "Fuck me," he says in a hard voice, "that's hot, Beauty."

I pull back my finger then hold it out to him. He leans over and wraps his mouth around it. He sucks on it and my pussy clenches. His cock throbs inside of me and I groan. "Mika, please…" but before I can complete the sentence, he's added a second finger inside my cunt. He moves it in and out of me as he thrusts his dick inside me again and again. Then he pulls out, and at the same time he withdraws his fingers from my pussy.

"Wha—" I protest as he flips me over on my back. He slides his arms under my knees, throws my legs over his shoulders, then holds my gaze as he notches his cock against my puckered hole. He slides in easily, filling me, stretching me again, and I sigh and he groans.

"*Cazzo!*" He swears aloud. Seriously, why does 'fuck' in Italian sound so damn erotic? He reaches between us, strums my pussy lips as he thrusts in and out of me again and again. He hits a spot deep inside me and a whine bleeds from my lips. He pushes into me, hitting that spot again as he grinds the heel of his hand into my clit, and that's when it hits me.

"Mika I'm—"

"Come," he growls, "come for me, *Beauty.*"

The climax rips through me, smashes into me and I scream. I swear I see sparks behind my eyes as I collapse. I am aware of him continuing to plunge in and out of me, before he growls as he comes inside of me. Hot spurts of his cum bathe me. He drags his fingers across my clit, then holds them up to my lips. I lick them and the taste of myself, mingled with him, sinks into my blood. Lust twangs my underbelly and I stare up at him.

He lowers his head and licks my lips. "So gorgeous," he rumbles, "so damn sweet."

He pulls out and I wince.

"Does it hurt?" he murmurs and I nod.

He scowls and I smirk, "In a good way."

"Brat." He falls onto his back and gathers me onto his chest. I cuddle into him as he runs his palm across my back. "Sleep," he kisses my temple, "I've got you."

I wake up sprawled on my front. The sheets tangled around my legs. Through the undrawn curtains, the evening light pours in to bathe the bed. A touch on my lower back makes me shiver. I glance over my shoulder to find him staring at my back. He touches the letters that he carved into me, and another shiver runs down my back. I squeeze my thighs together as he bends and traces the letters with his tongue. He bites down the curve of where my back meets my arse and I moan. "Michael?"

"Hmm?"

"What are you thinking?"

"Did it hurt when I wrote this into your skin?"

I lower my cheek to the pillow. "A little…but it was also, strangely, erotic."

He pauses and I sense him staring at what he can see of my face. "Erotic?"

I swallow, "Yeah… I knew you were angry and that you needed to mark me in some form."

"You knew that, huh?"

I nod, "Well, knowing how possessive you are, and I had left with your brother."

He stiffens and I try to turn on my back but he stops me, "Go on… Complete what you were going to say."

"It's not like it wasn't a shock when I realized what you had done, but at the time, when you were marking me… It made me feel close to you. It was one way for you to show me that I couldn't do that again."

"And now?" His voice lowers to a hush, "Now, how do you feel about it?"

"Knowing that I am your whore, you mean?"

"My whore," his voice thickens, "my slut, my wife…mine to do with as I want."

I turn over and this time he lets me. He bends and kisses my belly, swirls his tongue in my belly button and my goosebumps pop. "I am sorry you lost the baby," he continues to kiss his way down to my pussy. "I am sorry you got hurt," he presses a kiss to my still swollen clit. "I am sorry you were in that car." He crawls up my body until his lips are over mine, until his nose bumps mine and his eyelashes tangle with mine. "But I am not sorry for kidnapping you."

I swallow.

"Or forcing you to marry me."

I bite the inside of my cheek.

"Or tagging you, or marking you with my knife."

He brushes his lips over mine.

I reach down between us, wrap my fingers around his cock. He hisses out a breath, but doesn't break my gaze. I notch his dick against my pussy and his gaze intensifies. "You're sure?"

I nod.

"I won't hurt you, will I?"

"I want you to hurt me, Mika. I want you to show me how it is to be yours wholly, completely, and —"

He thrusts his hips forward and impales me. I gasp, grip his biceps as he stays there, holding most of his weight off of me. I wrap my legs around his waist, tilt my hips up, and he slips in further. I moan, and he grits his teeth.

"Cazzo!" He growls, "So wet, so tight, Beauty." He grinds his hips against mine, breaching me further, deeper, hitting that spot deep inside of me again. A whine spills from my lips as I grind my heels into his arse. I dig my fingernails into his back, wanting to mark him as he did me. He wraps his fingers around my throat, pressing down slightly. I draw in a breath, and my lungs burn. I open my mouth and he kisses me. He plunges his tongue in between my lips, mirroring the way his cock saws in and out of me. He increases the pressure on my throat, cutting off my airflow, then raises his head to peer into my eyes. I gasp,

tears squeezing out from the corners of my eyes as he pulls back, then slams into me. My entire body jerks as he begins to fuck me in earnest. I can feel every ridge, every striation of his dick as he shoves into me. At the same time, he releases his hold on my throat. "Come," he growls, "come all over my shaft."

The climax slams into me as I draw in a breath, then darkness overwhelms me.

When I wake, I am alone.

22

Michael

I sip from the cup of espresso as I stare out at the sea from the patio outside the living room. I'd left her asleep... Okay, I had watched her sleep before I'd slipped out and made us both dinner. I'd even fed and replenished the water for the cat, who had followed me into the kitchen. The beast had lapped up the water and finished off his food as if he hadn't just been fed a few hours ago. Hell, we had forgotten to eat but we had fed him.

To be fair, we had been otherwise occupied. I hadn't been able to keep my hands off of her, or my dick out of her. I had intended to take out the butt plug and give her time to adjust to the trip, the fact that I had whisked her away without giving her time to mentally adjust to it. But the moment I had touched her, I had lost all sense of control. I had needed to claim her all over again, possess her completely. Ensure she understood who she belongs to. That she is mine, only mine.

I hear footsteps behind me, then she wraps her arm around me, and presses those full tits up and into me.

"You smell good." She presses her nose into my bare back.

"Do I now?" I chuckle.

"You smell of the salt air, and yourself and... Something else..." She sniffs me again. "Food," she says in a surprised voice, "you've been cooking?"

"I've been making dinner, yes."

"You cooked breakfast for me." She slides around to face me. "Now dinner too?"

"I am a good Italian boy. I learned cooking from my Mama when I was very young."

"I thought Italian men were fussed over by their mamas, who made sure they didn't have to lift a finger around the house?"

"Not my mama," I laugh. "She made sure we could hold our own in the kitchen. She may have been weak when it came to standing up to our father, but she made up for it by showering us with love." Some of the heaviness fades from my chest, "She said she wanted to make sure that we would be good husbands. Unlike her own."

She places her palm against my cheek, "You loved her?"

"Very much." I turn away.

She grips my chin, "Tell me about her."

"What's to tell?"

"Everything. Do you look like her? What else did you do together?"

I peer into her eyes, "You really want to know?"

"Of course, I want to know. It's why you brought us here, right?"

I tilt my head.

"So we could get to know each other. This is a kind of delayed honeymoon, isn't it?"

"Am I that transparent?"

"No," she chuckles, "normally, you are very hard to read."

"But not right now?"

She half smiles, "Something about being here... You are so much more relaxed, and you've lowered your barriers. You're not wearing that tough Capo look anymore."

"What's my tough Capo look?"

She rises up on her tip-toes, raises her arm then frowns "Bend your head," she instructs. And because it's Beauty asking me to do it... And only because yes, I want to indulge her, I lower my head. She traces the lines between my eyebrows. "Normally, you have a groove between your eyebrows and," she touches the skin around my eyes, "lines at the edges of your eyes, and," she drags her fingers around my mouth, "the skin around your lips is stretched."

I turn my head, pretend to bite her fingers, and she yelps.

"Do I now?"

"Mmhmm." She wraps her arms about my waist. I'd pulled on my sweats before heading to the kitchen and now she slides her fingers under the waistband, "These sweatpants are something else."

I chuckle, "I take it you like them?"

She grips my ass and I raise an eyebrow, "Correction. I take it you really like them."

"They're bloody hot on you."

"You mean it's the way I wear them, isn't it?"

She rolls her eyes, "Yes, yes. It's the way they hang low on your waist, then cling to your butt and mold your powerful thighs, and of course," she slides a hand between us and traces the outline of my cock, which is already standing at attention, "highlights just how much you are packing."

"Didn't hear you complain about that when I was inside you."

She bats her eyelids, "Were you, now? I hadn't noticed."

"Excuse me." I step back from the circle of her arms, place the cup on the table, then straighten. "You were saying—"

"Was I?" She bites down on her lower lip.

"Something about not having noticed I was in you?" I take a step forward and she skitters back. I lunge for her and she screams. I move toward her again. She pivots, runs forward, jumps off of the patio, and races ahead. She turns, panting, then screams when she realizes I am right behind her. I grab for her and she ducks, then takes off running, throwing up sand in her wake. The T-shirt that she's pulled on, my T-shirt, flaps about her thighs. The fabric clings to her shapely butt that twitches as she runs. She glances over her shoulder, "What? Can't keep up, old man?"

"Who are you calling old man?" I sprint toward her and she squeals. She puts on a burst of speed and she dashes toward the water's edge. I dart toward her, closing the distance between us. I tackle her around the waist and she yells as she hits the ground. I clamber over her, flip her over, then pin her down to the sand with my hips. She flails around with her arms and I grab them and hold them above her. I wrap my fingers about her wrists and shackle them. "Do you submit?"

"No!" She spits out sand, "No way."

I begin to tickle her under her arms and she screams, then begins to shake with laugher. "Stop," she gasps, "stop, please."

"Submit to me, Beauty."

"No!"

I release her arms, only to tickle her down both sides of her body. She laughs and chokes, "Fine," she gasps between bouts of laughter that make her entire body shake, "fine, I submit."

I lean back, "Good."

I pin her arms on either side of her as I straddle her. There's sand on her cheek, on her throat, in the valley between her breasts. I lean down and bury my face there and she moans. "Oh, Mika!"

I slide down until I am positioned over her core. I shove my sweatpants down, notch my dick against her pussy, and in one thrust, impale her.

She gasps, "Oh, god, Mika!" She wraps her legs around my waist, and in that move which always drives me crazy, pushes her hips upward so I slide further inside her.

I stay there, allowing her to adjust to my size as I gaze into her green eyes. Pupils blown, color flushes her cheeks as I begin to move inside her. Once, twice, thrice, I release her arms then yank down the neckline of her T-shirt. I squeeze her nipple and she sucks in a breath. I twist it and a whine bleeds from her lips.

"The noises you make, *Bellezza*... They drive me fucking crazy." I lower my head to her breast, bite down on her nipple, and she screams. Her body bucks. I straighten, hold her gaze as I begin to fuck her in earnest. Once, twice, thrice, I slam into her with such force that my balls slap against the insides of her thighs. Her entire body goes rigid, her eyes roll back in her head, then she wheezes, "Oh, my god, I am going to —"

"Come, Beauty," I growl, and her features twist as she cries out. Moisture bathes my cock as her body spasms. I plunge in and out of her, in and out. My balls draw up and I empty myself inside of her.

Twenty minutes later, I glance up from the tub I've run for her. "What?" I murmur as she watches me with a strange look in her eyes.

I'd carried her inside and run a bath for her while she'd discarded the now sodden shirt that she'd been wearing. I'd divested myself of my sweats as well and poured in the bath salts I'd specially ordered for her.

The scent of moonflowers fills the air and she starts. "That...that's my favorite fragrance."

"I know," I murmur as I rise to my feet. She runs her gaze down my chest to my crotch, where she takes in my already semi-aroused state.

"Again?" she murmurs "You're already hard?"

"Seems to be my constant state around you." I walk over to her and push a strand of hair out of her eyes. "What was that earlier look for, hmm?"

"I am still getting used to seeing you so relaxed, is all."

"It helps that we are on an island, and no one can get on it without my noticing."

A purring sound reaches me and I glance down to find the cat brushing up against my leg.

"I think he's beginning to grow on you."

"Feed the beast a couple of times and he thinks he owns you."

"And this beast?" She grips my cock and squeezes, "Do I own him, now that I've fed him a few times?"

"Why, Beauty, where have you been hiding this filthy mind of yours?"

She chuckles, "It's one of the things you like about me; admit it."

"I like everything about you. Haven't you realized that?"

"Oh, my god!" She pretends to be shocked, "Who are you and what have you done to my alphahole Capo?"

I grin as I smack her butt, "Into the water, before it gets cold."

23

Karma

Five days. We've been here five glorious days, where we've fucked. A. Lot. And everywhere. Against the kitchen counter, on the kitchen floor, in the tub, in the shower, on the beach—many times. And of course, in the bed. Tonight, being New Year's Eve, Michael wants us to dine out on the patio.

I've decided to dress up a little. Well, a little more than the last few days when I've walked around almost naked. It had seemed ridiculous to be putting on clothes when all Michael would do was to pull them off. He, himself, had taken to wearing a pair of shorts that he'd pulled out from the clothes that had been there in the closet.

While he is off setting the table, I take in the dress I've chosen. He's refused to let me cook in all the time that we've been here. Which is good, considering my cooking skills are nowhere close to the level of expertise he's showed. The man is not only good in the bedroom, but also in the kitchen... How the hell have I gotten so lucky, eh?

This dress is one of the few I had packed when I left his home—an alternative version of my wedding dress that I had stitched before I'd left. It's in the form of a sheath with the skirt cut high over one thigh and low at the breast line. The dress is sleeveless with halter neck that I've tied around my neck, leaving most of my back bare.

It's the kind of dress that could be worn for a formal occasion but would look as good on a beach. There had been so much material I hadn't used for my wedding dress that I had managed to cut a second dress from it. I consider my light make-up—just eyeliner and lipstick; it hadn't felt like I needed anything more for this evening—then turn and head out to the patio.

In the kitchen, I find Andy already eating his food. The cat seems to have taken to Michael a lot more than when we had been in his house. Guess he really does know who is responsible for the food he is getting here.

I walk toward the patio, then pause when I see the table laid for two. There are plates, silverware, even starched white napkins, and a bottle of prosecco chilling in a bucket. Beyond that, the sea forms the perfect background.

"Wow," I breathe as heat envelops me. I lean back and into his hard chest, and Michael wraps his arm around my waist.

"Like it?"

"I love it," I say simply, then turn to face him. "I love you."

He glances down at me and his lips kick up in a real smile. "I..." he hesitates, "I know." He leans down to brush his lips over mine. The kiss is soft, tender... So different from the Capo I knew when we were in Italy.

Was he going to say 'I love you'? Why had he stopped himself? I open my mouth to ask, and he thrusts his tongue inside. He deepens the kiss, and all thoughts drain from my mind. I press into him, revel in the hardness of his sculpted chest, the thickness between his thighs that reveals how much he wants me.

He must love me. All of his actions say so. So what, if he hasn't said those three words to me yet?

He seems to tear his mouth away with reluctance, his breathing heavy, color flushing his cheeks. "*Cazzo,*" he growls, "I can't get enough of you."

"Then don't," I lean up on my tiptoes, wanting to kiss him.

He evades me. "First food," he counters.

"First sex," I insist.

"I've created a sex maniac!" He chuckles, "I can't have you wasting away. Besides, you need your energy for when I am going to have my wicked way with you." He slaps my butt, then steps back, "Come on, sit down."

Once I am seated, he makes sure that my chair is pushed in properly. Then he opens the prosecco and pours out a glass for me and one for himself. He sits down and I raise my glass, "To us."

"To you," he clinks his glass with mine, "my sexy, smart wife whose darkness matches mine."

I laugh, "Only you'd compliment me on that."

He takes a sip of his prosecco, then glances at me, "It's what attracted me to you. I saw you…and I knew there was something inside of you calling out to me. That you would be as depraved as me. That I could bare my soul to you and you wouldn't be afraid."

"But I was," I take a sip from my glass, then peer up at him from under my eyelashes. "I was afraid that once I fell for you, I'd never be able to leave you."

"And that's bad?"

I tilt my head, "I am still making up my mind about that."

"Now that, I hadn't anticipated… That you'd turn out to be this bratty. Clearly, I haven't been punishing you enough."

"Please, Daddy," I flutter my eyelashes, "will you spank me?"

His nostrils flare and his shoulders flex. He places his glass on the table, then rises to his feet. He walks around to tower over me. He holds my gaze as he lowers his head to mine, "Only if you ask me nicely."

Heat flushes my skin and my belly trembles. A gust of wind blows my hair across my cheek and he pushes it aside. His touch sends a pang of need shooting through my veins. I part my lips. He drops his gaze to my mouth, "And only after we've eaten."

He straightens and stalks away.

"Asshole," I yell after him and he laughs.

"Jerk," I murmur to myself, then snatch up my flute of prosecco and toss it back. I grab the bottle and am about to top up my glass, then change my mind. He wants me? He can come get me.

Walking out to the patio, I shut the door…to make sure Andy can't get out, then walk out onto the beach, then away from the house toward the jetty I'd seen earlier.

The setting rays of the sun bathe me in their warmth. The heat from the cooling water seems to rise in the air. I stand at the edge of the jetty, raise the bottle to my mouth, and drink the sparkling prosecco. It slides down my throat and cools me enough that goosebumps pop on my skin.

The waves lap at the edge of the jetty as I tilt the bottle to my mouth and take another sip.

The hair on the back of my neck rises. I turn to find Michael is silhouetted against the window of the kitchen. I raise my hand and wave at him and he waves back. This man… He's the best thing that has ever happened to me. To think, I'd thought the opposite when I had met him. Guess love can come in so many different ways, eh? And he does love me. So what, if he hasn't told me so?

It's there in his every gesture, in how he takes care of me and of Andy. He's so gentle with my pet… Always taking care of his needs first. If he can be so tender with that kitten… Surely, he'd be a wonderful father, too. And I am not on birth control, so maybe I'll leave this island pregnant. I slide down to sit at the edge of the jetty, with my legs hanging over. I take another sip of the prosecco and set it aside. Then stretch my arms above my head.

I circle my head once, then glance down to find waves rippling out from a spot in the water. Huh? I lower my arms, glance at it, not sure what I am looking at. A black shadow appears under the water, and before I can pull up my legs, it swoops up, grabs my leg and tugs. I yell, but I am already falling.

<h1 style="text-align:center">24</h1>

Michael

She is going to love this dish. I slide the roast back into the oven, then straighten and turn my attention to the salad that I am assembling. Andy prowls into the kitchen and brushes against my leg. I smirk as he glances up at me, then at the dish I am cooking.

"No food for you yet, boy." I chuckle. "Your mother's gonna be pissed if I feed you between meals. But if you are a good, little kitten, I might sneak you a little snack to keep you going."

The beast blinks at me, then with a huff, turns and walks away. I swear, that cat can understand me. And here I am, talking to it. I shake my head.

That's the kind of magic she has woven over me, my Beauty. My *piccola*. Mine.

I glance through the window and find she's not at the jetty. Huh? I peer through the pane, take in the surroundings. There is no sign of her. What the hell?

Maybe she just went for a walk. Yea, that's all it is. She just walked out of sight of the house. I glance down at the salad, then back at the now empty jetty. The hair on the back of my neck rises. I place the knife on the counter, turn and head for the doors that lead to the patio. I throw open the door, rush out…then pause.

"Cazzo!" That cat needs to stay inside. If he wandered out and something happened to him, she be beyond pissed-off about it. I retrace my steps, close the door behind me, then take off again. Around the house, across the sand that surrounds the house, toward the jetty. I reach it, and there's still no sign of her. I glance around at the water and freeze. A figure dressed all in black, tows another figure that is prone and on her back. Ahead of them is a motorboat, manned by a second man.

Che diavolo! Who'd dare come to my island and try to take my wife from right in front of me? My heart pounds in my chest and adrenaline laces my blood. I dive into the water and swim toward them. Every time I surface for air, the distance between us seems to have shrunk, but it's not fast enough. Once they reach the boat, I'll lose them and not be able to find out their identity.

Oh, I'll be able to track her down, thanks to the tagging device, but damn, if I am going to let them get their hands on her. I increase my pace, propel my body, and cut through the waves. I kick and move forward bit by bit.

When I surface again, it's in time to see the diver handing the prone figure to the man on the boat. *How dare he touch her! How dare they take her from me? I am not going to lose you, Bellezza; not this time.* I thrust forward through the waves, just as the sound of the motor starting reaches me.

Fuck, fuck, fuck! I push forward and reach the boat just as it takes off. I lunge up, grab at the boat. My fingers graze the side of the boat but it leaps forward. Bloody fuck! I fall into the water, then begin to swim in the wake of the boat. I kick and propel forward, almost reach the boat again, only it pulls forward.

I watch helplessly as the distance between me and the boat grows. Motherfucker! This can't be happening. My heart pounds so hard in my chest that I am sure it's going to leap out of my rib cage.

I had gotten swayed by my Beauty. So immersed in her that I had gotten sloppy again. I hadn't been able to protect her. It's my fault that they got to her. I should have stayed in Sicily and focused on tracking down the men responsible for rigging the car that caused my brother's death. Instead, I had given in to my need to see her and I had put her in danger. Again. But this time, I am going to find them and put an end to this. Never again, will they be able to harm me or what's mine. I am going to reveal the true wrath of what it means to cross the Capo of the

Cosa Nastro. And when I am done... No one will ever defy me. Ever again.

Turning, I begin to swim toward the island.

Fifteen minutes later, I pull up the app on my phone that allows me to track her. *There.* I see the blue dot moving across what appears to be the expanse of the sea. They are heading toward England... What the hell? It has to be the Kane Company who took her. Fuck.

I had known who it was, and yet, I hadn't moved in on them. If I had, they wouldn't have been able to take her. *Stop that.* I shake my head. *Focus, I need to focus. I need to get to her.* I strip out of my wet clothes, pull on jeans securing them with a belt, then a T-shirt, and the jacket that I had loaned her earlier. I reach for my knife and slip it into the sheath at my waist. If only I had brought my guns. I drag my fingers through my hair. The, one time in my life I had lowered my guard and she had been taken from me. It's dangerous to go in without my weapons but fuck that, my knife will have to do.

I turn off the oven, top up the food and water in the cat's bowls, then race for the door. Andy darts out from under the settee and I sidestep him. He races for the door, plants himself squarely in front of it and stares up at me.

"Out of the way, cat. I need to get to her."

He blinks, and I swear, he is aware that something has happened to her. I bend down, grasp him gently by the nape of his neck and move him to the side. He tries to dart past me, and I manage to hold him in, then shut the door before he can leave the house. I hear the angry hisses as he scratches at the door. I dial Seb's number as I race toward the boathouse where I have the motorboat stored.

"*Fratellone?*" Seb answers on the second ring. "Where are you?"

"Enroute to her." I slow down a little so he can hear me speak "They took her again; motherfuckers snuck up on me on the island and took off with her."

"I don't understand," his voice is puzzled, "how did they reach you without your noticing their arrival?"

"They swam underwater, got to her when she was on the jetty." I growl, "*Maledizioni!*" I raise the phone, ready to bring it down and smash it, then draw in a breath. Another. Force my muscles to relax as I lower the phone to my ear.

"Get the plane, then get to the island and arrange to have her cat taken to safety," I order.

"A plane? Just for the cat?"

"It's *her* cat," I growl. "Just do it, Seb."

"Got it, Capo, and what about you?"

"I am going after her."

"Alone?" His voice grows concerned, "Wait for us, Mika. We'll be there soon with back up."

"Fuck that. If you think I am going to wait around here not doing anything while my wife is in the hands of my rivals, then you are mistaken."

"So, you are going to barge in, knowing that this is what they want? That they want you to lose your composure enough to walk into a trap?"

"Fuck that!" I bark. "Of course, it's a trap. Likely, I'll be overpowered the moment I get there, but at least, I'll be there with her. At least, she'll know that she is not alone."

"Mika, you're making a mistake. You're the Capo; you—"

"You'll be able to see her location on the app; get there as soon as you can."

I cut the call, then squeeze my eyes shut. *Fuck, fuck, fuck.* I pull up the app, focus on the dot again. *Wait for me, Beauty. I am coming after you as soon as I can.*

25

Karma

I cough, sputter, then sit up with a gasp. I glance around the room I am in…which is empty, save for the bed I am on… Well, calling it a bed is giving it too much credit. It's some kind of bunk built into a wall. Starlight slants in through the only window, which is high up in the wall. *Shit, where the hell am I?* One second, I had been sitting on the jetty, sipping my prosecco and planning my future with my Capo. The next, something… No, someone had swooped up from out of the water, grabbed my leg and pulled. I had screamed… Or tried to scream, but I had hit the water and swallowed a few mouthfuls before remembering to hold my breath.

The guy had started towing me away. I had resisted and he had cuffed me on the side of the head. He'd stunned me enough that I didn't resist as he towed me along the surface, then hauled me onto the boat. Then, I had pretended to lose consciousness while they fired up the engine and set off.

I'd stayed still, in the hopes that I'd hear the men speak and give me some clues of who they were and where they were headed. But they had, annoyingly, spoken very little to each other.

When they cut the engine, I peeked through half-closed eyelids to find that they were docking the boat. One of the men reached for me and I lost it then. I struggled, tried to evade him, and he hit me on the back of the head. And then I found myself here.

A headache builds behind my eyes. I touch the back of my head and wince at the bump there. Damn it, I am tired of being kidnapped and used as a pawn in this stupid game that the Mafia seems to want to play with their rival gang. It has to be a rival gang holding me, right? The same one who had kidnapped me the last time. The same one who had planted the bomb in my car. The one that killed Xander and my unborn child. I squeeze my fingers at my sides. This time, I am going to have my revenge. No way am I going to let them get away with this a third time.

The door to the room opens and light streams in. I throw my hand over my eyes to protect them from the glare, when footsteps sound. The light bulb overhead is switched on and I wince.

"Come on," a woman's voice says in precise English, "he is waiting for you."

I lower my hand, stare at the middle-aged woman wearing a black dress that comes to her knees. Her hair is black and pulled back in a bun. She wears minimal makeup and has the kind of looks that would help her blend into the background anywhere. It's almost as if she's trying not to draw any attention to herself, and succeeding quite nicely, by the looks of it—no pun intended.

I snort to myself as I rise to my feet. My knees threaten to give way and I have to dig my feet into the ground for purchase. I tip my chin up, walk to the door. She steps out of the room and I follow her. She leads me to an elevator…and I blink. Of course, there is an elevator. Not sure why, but I imagined this was a room in a place where such modern trappings would be nonexistent. I watch her profile, but she gives nothing away.

The car ascends two floors, then jolts to a halt. She heads out and I follow her up the corridor and into a room. She beckons me to enter. I walk in, turn to find her standing at the entrance to the room. "You are to get dressed and come down to the dining room for dinner in an hour."

"An hour?"

She nods.

"And how do I tell the time?"

She points to a small antique alarm clock on the dresser.

She turns to leave and I yell out, "Hey, you do realize that I have been kidnapped right?"

She closes the door in my face.

I walk toward it, and open it, to find she's striding away. "One hour; you don't want to keep him waiting," she calls over her shoulder.

I take a step forward, then hesitate. Guess it's not going to help if I follow her now. She'll probably just call one of those two idiots who grabbed me earlier to come get me. Also, I want to take something for this headache that has been growing in intensity.

By the way, I am taking all this rather calmly, aren't I? I mean, I am tagged, so he is going to come after me. Bet he's already on his way. All I have to do is sit tight, and make sure I don't get myself killed in the meantime.

Half an hour later, I step out of the shower. The hot water has taken the edge off of my headache and made me feel almost human. I walk into the bedroom and find a simple black dress, underwear made of white cotton, still in its packaging, and a pair of sneakers laid out for me. Did the same woman place it here? Probably.

I pull them on and they fit. So, whoever took me had anticipated that I'd need clothes, but he or she isn't going to keep me here for too much longer? And given the utilitarian feel of the clothes, he or she doesn't have a romantic interest in me... At least, I don't think so.

I dress quickly, then dry my hair with the hairdryer provided. I head for the door when it opens. I pause as the same woman from earlier beckons me. I follow her. This time, down two flights of stairs. So, we are back on the same floor as the room where I had been kept earlier.

I follow her down a long corridor with closed doors leading to other rooms. Each of the doors are ornate. There are paintings on the walls depicting scenes from the English country side. "Are we in England?"

"Yes," she confirms.

"In the countryside?"

She doesn't say anything, but I am sure we are.

"Whose clothes are these?"

"They were purchased for you."

O-k-a-y. Not what I was expecting.

She reaches the door at the end of the corridor, and pushes it open. I walk in to find a long table with places set for two at the head of the table, facing each other. I walk toward it, when the door on the opposite side of the room opens.

A man prowls in. He is tall, broad shouldered, dressed in a black suit that clings to his shoulders. His features are hard, his gaze intelligent as he takes me in. Gray threads the hair on his temples, hinting that he is in his early forties, maybe? It's difficult to say, because with his trim build and the obvious muscles that stretch his jacket, he could be anywhere from late thirties to early fifties.

"Finally, we meet, Signora." His voice is very cultured, very British.

"You?" I frown, "I know you."

"We haven't been formally introduced though, have we?" He prowls over to me. "JJ Kane, at your service."

I glance down at his hand and hesitate. The man looks like Daniel Craig toward the end of his career as James Bond — cynical, hardened, and I hate to admit it, but he radiates raw sex appeal that fills the space between us. He's not as sexy as my Capo, but this man... He's as dangerous.

"Why did you kidnap me?" I demand.

Amusement lurks in his gaze. He doesn't seem to be offended by my obvious snub. "Not my style, but something I couldn't avoid."

"Were you also behind the rigging of my car that killed Xander?"

"I heard about that." He tilts his head, "Sad affair. But no, also not my style. Too messy."

I glower at him, "What's your game anyway?"

"No game," he holds up his hand, his gaze steady, and his tone reeks of sincerity. All the more reason I don't believe him.

"I am simply inviting you to lunch."

"Oh, so that's why you took me from my husband's island, because you wanted to have lunch with me."

"Indeed," he gestures to the table, "and because I wanted him to realize that he shouldn't underestimate me."

"You couldn't have told this to him directly? Honestly, this entire 'being a pawn in the games that you made men play' is proving to be a little tiresome."

He laughs, "You don't mince words do you?"

"Please," I hold up my hand, "enough with the false praise; I can do without it."

I walk over to the chair at the head of the table and drop into it.

His features go solid. A pulse flares to life at his temple, then he throws back his head and laughs. It's a full-bodied laugh that comes from the pit of his belly and makes him seem younger than his years. He stalks over to the chair on my left and slides into it. "You have balls, *signora*."

I sniff, "Lady balls, don't you mean?"

"Precisely," he glances at me closely as if noticing me for the first time, "so this is why Michael is so taken with you."

"Aren't you his arch rival or something?"

"Rival?" He frowns, "I wouldn't use such a common word. More like we are two players who are competing for the same thing."

"And what is that?"

"Power."

"Of course, it is." I roll my eyes and notice a man walking through the door. He's followed by a second man holding a tray on which there are two steaming bowls of soup. Both men are dressed in uniforms, clearly indicating that they are staff.

They retreat and JJ gestures to the food, "Please, eat."

"Don't mind if I do." I reach for the soup spoon then hesitate. "This doesn't have any seafood in it does it?"

He shakes his head and I scoop up some of the broth.

The scent of coriander and ginger fills my senses. And the taste? Whoa, creamy and light at once, spicy and nourishing, and yet, there are traces of some ingredient that I can't identify but which adds such depth that the taste lingers in my mouth long after I've swallowed it. "Wow," I stare at the food, then back at him, "that is good."

"Indeed, it is." He chuckles, "Gordon is the best chef right now on the entire continent."

"And he's cooking this meal for you?"

"A favor." He inclines his head, "It's not every day that I have such a distinguished guest."

I stare at him. Should I believe him? Why would I? The way he had me brought here shows that he has something up his sleeve. But what?

I turn my attention back to the soup and don't stop until I've swallowed down most of it. I lean back with a sigh and find JJ watching me with a pleased expression.

"And she also doesn't stint when it comes to eating well. You are, indeed, a catch, signora."

"*Grazie*," I murmur as I pat my mouth with my napkin.

The next course is a fragrant rice dish with vegetables and pieces of chicken that have been marinated so well, they melt in my mouth. And the dessert… Chocolate mousse, with a vanilla ice-cream that is so fresh I can taste the vanilla pods.

"I'm stuffed," I admit when the last dish has been cleared.

JJ pushes back his chair and stands up. He comes around and holds out his arm, "May I escort you into the library for an aperitif?"

"Why not?" I rise to my feet and allow him to guide me out of the room, down the corridor, and to a room whose door is now open. I walk in and take in the floor-to-ceiling books that fill the wall opposite the fireplace. In between is a bank of windows that looks out over the grounds, and above the fireplace, is a portrait of a family.

He catches me staring at it. "My family," he says simply as I take in the likeness of a younger JJ, a woman who is seated, and next to her, a teenaged boy who resembles both JJ and his wife.

"That's your son."

He nods.

"I saw him at Xander's funeral."

"Indeed."

"Is he here?"

A shadow crosses JJ's features. "He's back in LA. He seems to prefer the US to our country."

"Oh." I sense something else he's not telling me, but I am not going to ask him to explain that.

He guides me to a chair in front of the fire. "What will you drink? Coffee? A brandy maybe?"

"A brandy sounds good."

He moves to the bar, pours out two snifters of brandy and walks over to hand one to me. He seats himself then holds up his glass, "To you, *Signora*."

I raise my glass and take a sip. The taste is exquisite. "To what do I owe this wining and dining?" I fix my gaze on him.

He laughs, then contemplates his drink, "My father, rest his soul, was not a very empathetic man. Well, that's putting it mildly. He was a complete villain."

"Coming from you, I'd better believe it."

He chuckles. "There was only one piece of advice he gave me which I adore, to this day."

"Which is?"

"He told me to always keep one step ahead of the enemy. To never show him your cards, and to surprise him when he least expects it."

"So that's why you decided to take me from the island; so you could show my husband that you're better than him?"

"Not just better, but faster, more lethal, more dangerous, more unpredictable, more everything…"

"Never."

"Excuse me?" He frowns. "Would you mind repeating yourself?"

So polite. Fuck, this guy's a joke. "I said that you couldn't hold a candle to him."

"Is that right?" He stares at me, then breaks into a laugh that sends shivers down my spine. This guy…he's certifiable. He straightens, and just like, that all mirth is wiped from his face. He leans forward, his movements careful, precise, as he places his glass on the table in front of us.

"But then, you are biased." He strokes his chin, "You would be; you are his wife."

"Why have you brought me here?"

"You are a clever girl; haven't you figured it out by now?"

"To hold me as ransom?"

He clicks his tongue, "How pleb would that be? No, nothing like that… I am simply going to use you as a negotiating tool to get what I need from him."

"Like I said, a ransom."

"A simple give and take. He has what I want, and I have something that is very precious to him. All he has to do is give me what I want, and in return, he can take what's his."

"Michael will never forgive you for this."

"Not doing this to win friends."

"He is going to kill you."

"Love a challenge."

"So, if you didn't rig the car, then who did?"

"That's something he'll need to figure out himself, won't he?"

"So, while we wait for him, we are simply going to sit here and shoot the breeze?"

"Probably, but to be fair, I don't think we need to wait that long either."

"You're that sure that he'll come for me?"

"Surely, he must be able to keep track of you wherever you are?"

I frown, "How would you know that?"

"You are important to him—probably more than anything else he owns at the moment. Of course, he'd find a way to track you even when you are not in his line of sight."

I shake my head, "You Mafia guys."

"Not Mafia. I'm simply the leader of an organized crime group."

"Gosh, is that a posh way of saying you are a crook, or what?"

"Never claimed to be on the straight and narrow."

"No one would ever mistake you for that." I take another sip from my glass. "So, how long do you think I have to make conversation with you?"

"Surely, it's not that much of a chore."

I glance at him, then away, "If you want me to be honest—"

"Always."

"I'd much rather be back on the island. But considering you took me from there, I doubt I'll ever be going there again," I say glumly.

He chuckles, "Now, young lady, never say never again. If there's one word of advice, I can give you it's that…"

"That?"

He leans forward and touches my arm, "That you never know what's going to happen next."

That's when the door to the library is pushed open with such force that it slams against the wall. "You *testa di cazzo*!" a familiar dark voice growls, "I am going to kill you."

26

Michael

I lunge inside the room, spot the man seated opposite my wife. My wife… who seems to be in good shape overall, and he has his hand on her. He has his hand on her. JJ. Has. His. HAND. On. Her. Fuck. Anger thrums at my temples. My vision tunnels. I pull out my knife and throw it at him. The asshole ducks. She screams. The sound slices through the noise in my head. I jerk my head in her direction, in time to see her features pale. She jumps to her feet, takes a step in my direction, but JJ grabs her. The next moment he has a gun in his hand that he's pressed into her temple.

I freeze. Glare at the traitor, who smiles. He gestures toward the chair he's just vacated. I growl, deep in my throat, take a step in his direction. That's when three men burst into the room.

Two of them grab me by my shoulders, the third pushes the butt of a gun into the back of my head. Anger suffuses me, pours thorough my blood. My stomach ties itself in knots as I take in the fear in her gaze.

FUCK! I had sworn to myself that I'd never allow her to be afraid. Never need for anything else. And I had broken my promise in a matter of days. Why am I unable to hold myself back when it comes to her? Will nothing I do ever be enough to protect her?

I had made it here as fast as I could, following the tracking device. Then had searched the house until I had found them.

The men push me toward the chair. She follows me with her gaze as they apply pressure on my shoulder so I sink down into it.

The man behind me removes his gun. He proceeds to pat me down, then when he finds me clean — not that I didn't want to carry weapons, but if I had any chance of getting close to her, I knew that I had to be clean — he pulls out a length of rope. He proceeds to run it around my arms and chest and tie me to the chair. He also knots it around my ankles. I flex my muscles, hoping to get some slack as he does so. I don't take my gaze off of her. She swallows, and I shake my head. *Don't be afraid, my love. I won't let anything happen to you.*

Almost as if she can read my mind, she jerks her chin in a downward direction. If I hadn't been paying such close attention to her, I'd have missed it.

Their job complete, the men holding me back away. They leave the room and the door snicks shut.

"Sit down, *Signora*," JJ murmurs. He slides the gun back into the waistband at the small of his back. Karma doesn't move and he touches her shoulder.

I growl, lunge forward again and the chair shifts. The scrape of wood against wood sends a screech through the space.

JJ glances at me. "Impressive," he tilts his head, "but unnecessary. I have no wish to hurt her."

"That's why you took her." The blood pounds at my temple, my pulse rate ratchets her. "How dare you touch her?"

"Calm down." JJ arches an eyebrow, then turns to Karma, "You'd better get your husband in hand, *Signora,* else I won't be responsible for my actions."

Karma swallows.

"Do it," he snaps, and her lips tighten.

A growl rips from me as she moves forward. She closes the distance between us, then sinks to her knees in front of me.

"Capo," she whispers, "my Capo." She places her palm against my cheek and every pore in my body seems to pop. I stare into her green eyes, take in the golden sparks that flash there. I hold her gaze as she leans up and presses her lips to mine. "I love you," she murmurs, "only you, Capo." The sound of my title from her lips... Fuck, but right now, I'd tear the world apart, just to hear her say it again.

She peers into my face and an expression of hope, of anticipation laces her features. I hold her gaze...knowing what she wants to hear. Wanting to say it. Wanting her to feel it. I try to form the words, but my tongue doesn't seem to work. I don't glance away, allowing her to read my expression, the raw need I feel right then, the helplessness. Do I have any right to love her, if I can't even protect her?

She moves back and I spring forward. I smash my lips to hers and kiss her and kiss her. I lick her lips, thrust my tongue inside her mouth and absorb her. I kiss her until someone taps me on my shoulder, "That's enough, ol' chap."

JJ's voice cuts through the haze in my head. I tear my mouth from hers and survey her flushed features. She licks her lips as if absorbing my taste within her before she rises to her feet.

JJ walks around and pats the chair opposite me. "Please, *Signora*," he says in a casual tone, "do take a seat."

With a last glance at me, she heads over and sits down.

JJ picks up the snifter of brandy on the table between us. He takes a sip as he glances first at her, then at me, "Now where were we?"

"What the fuck do you want?" I snap.

He smiles. "You know what I want."

"The cybercrime syndicate," I say in a low voice. "That's what this is about?"

"Right on one." His smile broadens. "Now that I have your attention on it, what say you?"

"What do you want with it?"

"I don't want you to hand it over to me."

"You don't?"

He shakes his head, "That would mean getting in the trenches and monitoring the day to day, which wouldn't work for me."

"You simply want to share in the profits," I surmise.

"Right again," he says in a pleased tone. "Look at that, *Signora*. Your husband is being exceptionally cooperative. Makes me think that I should have tried this tactic earlier."

"You rigged her car with an ignition bomb, you *pezzo di merda*!"

"Now, now, that wasn't me."

"You think I am going to believe you?"

"That's not my style. If I wanted to kill your brother, I'd have done it to his face. And yours."

Anger sears my blood. I attempt to jump to my feet, only to be restrained by the ropes. I growl as the bonds cut into my arms and my ankles.

"Don't talk about my brother, you bastard."

"I had nothing to do with his death," he insists. "Whether you believe it or not, that's not my problem."

"By bringing her here, you've brought an entire shitload of problems to your doorstep, you *carogna!*"

"Nothing I can't face," he drawls.

"You sure about that?"

The door flies open, and he jerks his head toward it.

Sebastian prowls forward, his gun trained on JJ. Luca follows, then Massimo and Antonio. All three of them have their guns drawn. Christian brings up the rear; he drags the man by his collar—the one who'd restrained me—and throws him on the floor. Then levels his gun at the temple of the guy and fires.

Karma shudders, glances away as the man's body jerks. He slumps to the floor and Christian slams the door shut behind him. He takes his position in front of it.

JJ takes a sip from his brandy. The man's one cool customer; I'll give him that. Seb keeps his gun trained on JJ as he jerks his chin in Luca's direction. Luca stalks over to where the knife is embedded in the wall next to the fireplace. He grunts as he works it out, then pivots and walks back to me. In two strokes, he's cut through the ropes. I rise to my feet and he hands the knife back to me, handle first. I snatch it from him, stalk over to where JJ is seated. He raises his tumbler to his lips and I press the knife to his throat. "I am going to kill you," I growl.

That's when the windows explode.

27

Karma

The panes of glass explode and the pattering of what sounds like hail stones fills the space. My throat hurts, and that's when I realize, I am screaming. The sound of my own voice echoes in my ears. The next second, I am pushed to the ground; a big body covers me. The scent of leather with a hint of woodsmoke. Fresh snow fallen on the earth… His scent envelops me. The heat from his body pours over me, cocoons me. I push up and into him, trying to get as close to him possible; to touch as much of my body to his as I can. Even though we are in the middle of what sounds like a gunfight, I can't help but exult in the fact that he's near me, on me, around me. I turn my head and push my cheek into his T-shirt covered chest. I draw in deep lungfuls of Michael, and my head spins. His chest heaves, the hard planes digging into my breasts as he gathers me even closer.

His arm moves and I realize that he's holding the knife out and over me. Guarding me, protecting me. My own personal bodyguard. My champion. My knight… Stop… Clearly, I am in shock. That is the only reasonable explanation for why my thoughts are in such free fall.

I draw in a breath and my lungs burn. My stomach twists, my arms and legs tremble, and I squeeze my eyes shut. Shit, shit, shit. Not the time to be going into shock.

The silence lengthens, I sense him move, then he grips my chin. I feel his gaze peruse my features, and crack my eyelids open. His blue gaze burns into me. In their depths, there's so much fire, so much concern... So much everything. I open my mouth, but my brain seems unable to put the words together. I draw in another breath, feel a tear run down my cheek.

Stop that. Why am I acting like such a weakling? I can get through this. I've survived this far; hell, I've faced the biggest transformation possible and come through the other side. I lost my child, almost died, lost a man who I had grown to love like a brother in such a short time, and I am still here, aren't I?

So why is my heart racing, my pulse pounding, my arms and legs trembling like I am in shock...? *Um, it's because you are in shock?* Because I may be married to a Mafia Capo but I am still not used to being shot at. Hell, I may never be used to being shot at, truth be told. Because as much as there is darkness at my core... I am also a creature who craves the life I once had?

A home, a career, a focus on creating art through my designs. Producing clothes that will bring my visions to life, and getting them out in the world. Where does all of that fit in with this life that I have been thrust into? Where do I fit in with this world that is Michael's life? This is where he came from and this is where he will always be. And if I want to live with him, I'll have to fit in. Do I want to fit in with this life that he has chosen for me? Do I want to walk away from everything I have spent my life working toward...to be with him?

So far, he has led and I have followed. Since I met him, it's been a roller coaster ride, and I've been happy to go along for the ride. But now... It's as if I am waking up from a long sleep and realizing that I have a choice.

I hear the sound of someone moving and glance around to find JJ belly-crawling forward toward the doorway. He reaches it, straightens, keeping as close as he can to the wall, and hits the light switch.

Gloom descends on the room. The rays from the sun slant into the room, but I guess switching off the lights makes us less of a target? Maybe? JJ's eyes glitter as he glances toward Michael, who nods. Something silent passes between the men. That's when another burst of shots rings out, and JJ drops to the floor again.

"Merda!" Michael swears as he throws his body over mine again. This time, the shots seem to go on and on. Things hit the floor around me. People? Or pieces of the furniture that the bullets have ripped out? Or bits of the wall that the bullets have loosened and which are now hitting the floor? A moan wells up and I swallow it down. My entire body trembles.

Michael seems to sense my anxiety, for he presses me into the floor. Thump-thump-thump; his heartbeat pounds against my back. Strong, steady…grounding me. I focus on it, on him. Strange, even though I know that our time together is, surely, drawing to a close, I still can't stop myself from leaning on him. Another tear runs down my cheek and I try to swallow the ball of emotion that clogs my throat.

Silence descends and I realize the shooting has finally stopped. No one moves, then something else crashes to the floor.

I turn to find Seb and Massimo have upturned the table so it's another barrier between us and the windows. While Luca keeps his gun trained on JJ, Seb and Massimo use the edge of the table to balance their guns and return fire. The sound of gunshots fills the room again. It's so loud, so close... Too close.

A tremor runs up my spine. I am not a weak person, but my daily life and my fashion designing business seem so far away right now. One wrongly– or rightly-directed bullet, and I'll be dead. Gone. A soft moan leaves my lips before I can stop it.

"Shh," Michael presses his lips to my temple, "you're safe, *Bellezza*. I promise, I won't let anything happen to you."

And you? Who will ensure that nothing happens to you? Will we spend our lives always worried about the next bullet that's going to kill one of us, or our loved ones?

I bite the inside of my cheek, knowing there are no answers to these questions. He'd never leave the Mafia… He wouldn't want to, and even if he did, they'd never leave him. Besides, what would he do? Work in an office behind a desk? Ha! As if he'd ever be able to fit into an ordinary lifestyle.

Michael is too big. Too vital. Too real… Too much everything. Maybe he's always been too much for me, but I haven't wanted to see it. I've been too consumed by his larger-than-life image, his sexiness, his over-the-top attractiveness, his dominance which consumes me, overpowers me completely.

I had lost myself in him… And now, I am finding myself again…

And I am not sure whether I want to be this woman I've become being with him.

The firing ceases.

The room plunges into silence again.

"*Fratellone,* we need to get out of here," I hear Luca murmur. I peer from the corner of my eye to find he still has his gaze on JJ. Guess they weren't taking any chances with the boss of the Kane Company.

"I am not sure that's a good idea," Seb's voice protests. "We leave here, and whoever is shooting at us will kill us."

"We stay here and we are sitting ducks," Luca hisses back.

"I vote we fight back," Christian interjects.

"With what?" Massimo growls, "We'll be out of ammo very soon."

"I have guns in the basement," JJ speaks up.

Silence, and I imagine all of them are glaring at JJ. I push at Michael's chest and he rises to his feet.

"Stay down." He bends low and I follow suit.

He guides me toward the back of the room. I step over pieces of wood, pieces of paper that have been torn out of the books that the bullets hit. I try to avoid stepping on them but there's too much of it. That, combined with the bits of plaster from the ceiling that have fallen to the floor, have turned the once beautiful room into a war zone.

Michael urges me behind the settee. He pushes down on my shoulder so I have no choice but to sink to my knees behind the sofa. It's some kind of protection, in case the shooting starts again, I suppose. I stare up at him and for a second, it's so erotic, so hot to have him looming over me, the breadth of his shoulders shutting out the sight of everything else, his gaze on me as he reaches down and cups my cheek. "You okay?" he asks in a soft voice.

I swallow, not trusting myself to speak, then nod.

He holds my gaze a second longer before glancing toward JJ. "Weapons," he snaps, "how many guns do you have?"

"You're going to take his help?" Christian glowers, "You're going to take the help of the man who murdered our brother."

"I didn't kill him," JJ retorts and Christian lunges for him. He brings the butt of his gun down on JJ, who ducks, but not fast enough. The butt smashes into the side of his temple and blood spurts from the wound. JJ grabs Christian's arm and twists it. His gun falls to the floor. Both leap for it, only someone fires a shot in the air. It hits the ceiling and chunks of rubble pour down in the center of the room. Neither JJ nor Christian move.

Massimo stalks forward. He grabs JJ by his collar, hauls him to his feet, then presses a gun to his temple. Christian picks up his gun and straightens. He brushes off the dust that has settled on his jacket. "Thanks, bro," he jerks his chin at Massimo.

"You have something to say, Christian?" Michael demands.

Christian stares at him, then at JJ. "I understand why you think we need to take his help," Christian growls, "but as far as I am concerned, he is guilty of our brother's murder until proven otherwise."

"And this…is why the Mafia is struggling to hold onto their position as the most notorious of all the organized crime bodies in the world." JJ smirks, "You guys are too emotional."

"No one asked you for your opinion, *stronzo.*" Christian's shoulders tense and anger vibrates off of him. His jaw is clenched so tightly, I wonder if he's going to pop a blood vessel any second.

"He's right, though," Michael says slowly, and Christian turns on him.

Michael raises a hand, "I understand how much you miss Xander. We all do. And if he is, indeed, the person responsible for his death, then trust me, I'll ensure that he dies in the most painful way possible. But right now, we need to find a way out of here."

"And quickly," Luca adds. "They've stopped shooting, but this is only a temporary reprieve. They must be reloading their weapons and planning their next move."

"Agreed," Seb nods his assent.

Michael glances between them, then at Christian, who glowers back. "How about we kill the *bastardo* first, then head down to get his weapons?"

"Won't work, ol' chap," JJ drawls. "You need my retinal scan to get through."

"We could always cut off his head and take that to unlock the door," Massimo offers.

Luca chuckles, "Now that's something I have been looking forward to."

"Cutting off his head?" Seb asks.

"Specifically, the heads of our rivals and parading them around the streets of the city to teach our enemies that they can't fuck with us," Luca retorts.

Seb scowls at him, "This is not an episode of *Game of Thrones*, you ass!"

"More's the pity; I always did prefer a sword to a gun." Luca raises a shoulder.

"You always did like to overcompensate," Seb chuckles.

Luca's frown deepens. He points his gun toward Seb, then blows out a breath, "Pity, I can't shoot you for that."

"I'd like to see you try," Seb waves his own gun in the air.

"Gotta say, your brothers make for a fascinating comedy act." JJ trains his gaze on Michael, "And these are the jokers you count on to have your back in a sticky situation?"

"Asshole," Luca trains his gun in JJ's direction, "one more word and I won't hesitate to shoot."

JJ firms his lips. The bastard still doesn't seem to be put out by the fact that he's surrounded by men who would not hesitate to kill him if he breathed too hard. Jesus, the man has nerve, all right.

He trains his gaze on Michael, who jerks his chin, "Let's go get those guns."

28

Michael

Am I a fool to trust JJ—the man who stole her from my island, under my watch, and brought her here? Am I totally *stupido* to follow him as he walks us down another flight of stairs to the basement?

He reaches a closed door, presses a code into the keypad, in the space next to the doorframe. He places his eye in front of the retinal scanner which glows green, and the door buzzes open. I shoulder open the door, Karma at my side.

Luca, who's taken great pleasure in holding a gun to JJ's head during the entire trip, brings up the rear. He pushes JJ through the now open door, then follows him in, along with Seb and Christian.

Massimo stands guard outside the door.

I take in the row of guns on the opposite wall.

Sebastian whistles, "He wasn't kidding when he called it an armory." He grabs a gun, then the ammunition next to it. He checks the gun, loads it, slides it into his waistband at the small of his back. Christian glares at JJ before arming himself. I reach for a gun, slide it into the empty holster at my ankle, then under my bicep, a third in my waistband at the small of my back.

Karma slips away to stand at the side. She folds her arms about her waist, a haunted look on her features. I glance at her, then snatching up one more gun which I slide into the front of my waistband, I walk toward her and she glances away.

"What's wrong?" I murmur and she bites down on her lower lip. I glance at the glistening flesh and my cock twitches. Fuck, this is not the time to be turned on...but with Beauty, just being close to her makes me want to throw her down and bury myself inside her again.

"Tell me, Karma," I insist.

She tips up her chin, "It's nothing."

"It's something." I bend my knees, peer into her face. "What is it?"

"I was wondering..."

I tilt my head.

"Is that a gun or are you happy to see me, Capo?" She shoves her hand down my pants and pulls out the gun.

"Know how to use that?"

"Aim and shoot?" she ventures.

I smirk, "First thing I am gonna do when we get out of here is teach you how to use a gun."

Her forehead crumples.

"What?" I search her features, "What is it?"

"Nothing."

"Don't lie," I growl, "tell me what's bothering you, Beauty. If not—"

"You two love birds ready to leave before whoever is shooting at us starts up again?" Seb's voice cuts through the space, and she glances past me.

"We have to leave," she murmurs and I know she is hiding something. "This is not over, Beauty," I warn her as I cock the gun and hand it to her. "Take care with that," I murmur.

"Always," She stares into my features, then reaches up and presses a quick kiss to my lips. My heart begins to thud against my ribcage. What is she hiding from me? What is she not telling me? *What are you up to, Beauty?* I deepen the kiss, thrust my tongue in between her lips, and kiss her with everything I feel for her.

"Michael," Seb's urgent voice reaches me, "we need to go, *fratellone*."

I straighten, then step back from her, "Stay close."

I pivot and head for the door, Karma right behind me.

"What about him?" Luca jerks his chin toward JJ, "What do we do with him?"

"Give me a gun and let me fight with you."

I hold his gaze.

"Not the time to think with your heart, Capo." JJ tilts his head, "You need men on your side. You need *me* on your side to fight your way out of this one."

Fuck this, but he's right. If I let my ego get in the way and don't give him a gun, and if whoever is attacking us manages to hurt us… I'll never be able to forgive myself about it.

I close the distance between us and bury my fist in his face. JJ rears back. Blood streams from his nose and spills onto his shirt.

He shakes his head, then curls his fingers into fists. "The fuck was that for?" He scowls.

"That," I growl, "was for taking my wife to get my attention."

He rolls his shoulders, then uncurls his fists, finger by finger. "Fair enough," he rumbles.

"Don't fucking touch what's mine again, you hear me?"

"And you keep your hands off of what's mine," he growls.

We glare at each other, then I jerk my chin toward the array of weapons, "Now, you may grab a gun."

"No fucking way!" Christian explodes. "You're going to give him a gun?"

I turn to him, "Not the time to debate this, *fratellino*."

"You can't give him a gun, Capo," he insists.

"That's my final decision," I say in a hard voice. Christian holds my gaze, then turns away. He marches toward the door and I watch him go with mixed feelings. "Fuck," I growl, "fuck, fuck, fuck."

"You're doing the right thing, if it's any consolation," JJ pulls out a pristine white handkerchief and dabs at his face. "And to prove it to you, I'm going to take you to a place from which we can return fire in relative safety."

"And you are telling us this now?" I arch an eyebrow.

"Had to make sure that I could trust you, first."

"Don't trust him, Capo," Luca growls. He grabs a few more firearms for Massimo, then turns and marches off after Christian.

JJ grabs the guns and arms himself, then turns to me, "Follow me."

I hold his gaze, trying to read the expression on his face. Next to me, Beauty shifts her feet, while Seb glares at JJ, before turning to me. "You going to trust this motherfucker, boss?"

I scowl at JJ, then nod, "Lead the way."

. . .

Five minutes later, we are in the room next to the library, and surprise—we used a hidden door from the armory that had a staircase that led directly up to this room.

"The walls are made of reinforced cement, and the windows," he jerks his chin toward the panes "are made of reinforced glass."

"You have a regular Fort Knox here," I say mildly.

"Never can be too prepared in our line of business." He shoves his gun in the opening between the panes.

Seb follows suit, and so do I.

Karma hunkers down behind me, that same distant look on her face. The one that makes my gut churn every time I glance at her. I want to talk to her, to reassure her that everything will be okay. That I will not let anything happen to her. I reach for her, and that's when the first shots ring out.

Seb returns fire, as does JJ.

The shots die away. In the silence that follows, my phone buzzes. I put it on speaker, "Massimo?"

"There's an entire group of them." He speaks rapidly from his perch up on the top floor of the house. Along with Christian and Antonio, he'd headed there to take stock of how many people we're up against. Additionally, they were going to try to take down as many as they could from their vantage point. "I count at least fifteen men surrounding the house and closing in on the grounds," he adds.

"Fuck," Luca swears from the other side of Karma. I had asked her to stay in the corridor, out of the line of fire, but is the woman having any of that? Of course, not. In this, she was as adamant as ever. She'd insisted that she'd be here with me. When I had protested, she'd said that she felt safer with me. And how could I argue with her after that?

JJ stiffens on the other side of me. "This would be a good time to have more of my men," he mutters.

I growl.

He raises a shoulder, "Not putting the blame on you for offing them. It's merely a fact that we need more men on our side."

In their zeal to get through to us, Seb had gunned down JJ's men. The only people who remain are the household staff, and JJ had instructed them to stay in the kitchen and not come out. They had been more than happy to oblige us. Not that I blame them. It's going to get a lot uglier here before it gets better.

"You sure you don't want to join the rest of the household staff?" I ask Karma.

She shoots me a scathing glance, "And leave you here on your own?"

"I am quite good at surviving tricky situations."

"This time, I am going to be with you every step of the way."

I glance into her green eyes that are dilated…with fear? With the adrenaline of the fight. Her lips part and my cock thickens.

"I don't want to sully your hands with blood," I murmur. "You don't have to do this, Beauty."

"But I do." She stares back, "I want to see what it is about fighting with a gun that gives you such a hard-on, Capo."

"Nothing and no one gives me a hard-on as much as you, Beauty."

Seb groans next to me, "Can you guys keep it down? Some of us here are trying to focus on not getting killed."

Karma flushes, then rises to her feet to peek through the windows.

A shot rings out again and Seb instantly returns fire as well.

I pull her down. "What the hell do you think you are doing?" I hiss.

"N…nothing," she blinks rapidly, "uh, just wanted to see what was happening out there."

"What's happening is that, unless we do something fast, they are going to start shooting and there are more of them."

"We have more ammunition," Seb reminds us.

"Five of us —" JJ begins and Karma interrupts him.

"Six of us."

He inclines his head, "Six of us, and fifteen of them."

"The odds are not good," Seb blows out a breath.

"But not impossible, either." I am not going to let whoever they are get the better of us. I am going to bring them down and find out who's at the bottom of this attack…and likely, the attack on Karma's car, as well.

"It's time we go on the offensive," I crack my neck.

Seb scowls, "That would not be advisable —"

"I agree with the Capo," JJ interrupts him. "Let's take this situation by the horns and surprise them."

I exchange glances with JJ, who jerks his chin. Apparently, the two of us think more alike than I'd have expected. And somehow, I am not sure if that's a good thing. It means he's more astute than I'd given him credit for. It also means that I have underestimated him all this time.

Holding the gun with one hand, JJ slides the other inside his pocket.

Seb swoops down to grab his arm. "What do you think you are doing?" he growls.

"Relax," JJ drawls, "I'm only going to call for additional men."

Seb glances at me. I nod; he releases JJ's arm.

JJ pulls out his phone, his fingers fly over the keys as he shoots off a message. Then he pockets his phone again, "They should be here in the next half an hour. Think we can hold them off until then?"

Seb scowls, seems about to say something, then thinks the better of it. "What do you think, Capo?"

"I think," I bare my teeth, "that we don't have a choice."

29

Karma

Is this me or is it a dream? Am I really standing here next to my gangster husband holding a gun? A weapon I have never held before, and which I have no idea how to use...but which already feels familiar in my hands. The metal seems to draw warmth from my skin as I clutch it.

I should be more scared of the power I hold in my hands. The ability to play God, to fire this gun and snatch someone else's life... It's both worrisome, but also, strangely, empowering. That dark core of me is thrilled at the force I hold in my hands. With this, I could make others obey me. I could control people. I could get my way. I could—

"Beauty?" His soft whisper cuts through the noise in my head, "Are you okay?"

"What?" I blink at him, "Did you say something?"

"I asked if you were okay."

"Yes, of course." My palms sweat and I tighten my grip on the gun.

He stares at me a little longer and I tip up my chin, "I am fine, honestly."

"Good." He rakes his gaze across my features, "You sure you don't want to go inside, and get out of the line of fire?"

"And miss all the fun?" I allow my lips to curl in a poor attempt at mirroring his smirk.

He chuckles, then kisses my forehead, "I knew I was obsessed with you for a reason."

He's obsessed with me. He's. OBSESSED with me. OMG, did he just say that? I peer up at him from under my eyelashes, but he doesn't seem to be aware of the ramifications of what he just said.

He reaches for his phone and dials a number. When Massimo answers it, he glances first at JJ, then Seb, before fixing his gaze on me. "Open fire," he commands.

Instantly, shots are fired from above, and returned. Each time a bullet hits the glass, it's deflected, but the sound of the bullet bouncing off makes me wince.

The splattering sound of the bullets rebounding off of the glass increases in intensity. It feels like we are in the middle a hailstorm, only deadlier.

All through it, Michael, JJ and Seb continue to return fire, adding another layer of noise to the sound of bullets being deflected.

I thought I was prepared. I thought I could face this barrage of gunfire, but I had mistaken just how intense it was to be in the line of fire. The shooting seems to rise to a crescendo. The shots come so thick and fast that it's like the popping of corn, at the height of when you are zapping it in the microwave, only much bigger, much larger than life, much more in your face... Much more lethal.

I know I am not in direct danger, yet I can't stop myself from flinching. I hunch my shoulders and wish I could cover my ears to lessen the intensity of the sound. I sense Michael glancing at me. He puts his arm around me, pulls me closer. I huddle into him, still holding the gun in my hands. My fingers tremble to pull the trigger, to answer back, to do something... Anything, except sit here with only a wall of glass separating us from the bullets that never seem to stop coming.

The shots go on and on. My heart beat ratchets up, my pulse rate accelerates, sweat pools under my arms, and black spots flicker at the corners of my vision. My heart seems to palpitate with such intensity that I can hear the blood thud in my ears. "Bloody hell," I gasp as my knees seem to buckle.

I lean heavily into Michael, who grips my shoulders. "You okay?" he yells, close to my ear so I can hear him above that never-ending barrage of bullets. A bullet rain. I am stuck in a monsoon of ballistic proportions with my very own avenging devil. A shiver runs down my spine. My heartbeat seems to grow louder, bigger, expanding until it fills my entire chest.

Over us, the hail of bullets reaches a crescendo, then stops. The sound ricochets through the corners of my mind, then fades away. I draw in a breath, another, then gasp when he hauls me to him, "You okay, baby?" he asks in a harsh voice.

"I am fine." My voice quivers and I clear my throat. Goddammit, I am not going to act like a wimp. Not now.

He searches my face and swears, "You're pale."

"It's the light." I attempt a weak smile. "I'm fine; honest."

He nods, then turns back to the window and shoots. JJ, Luca and Seb follow suit.

I'm fairly certain Christian, Massimo, and Antonio open fire from above, for once more, the air is thick with the sound of bullets being shot. The vibrations from the recoil slam into my chest, echo through my mind, press down on my stomach, my womb. My knees give way and I sink down to the floor.

I sense Michael glance down at me but he doesn't stop shooting. I coil into myself, still holding onto the gun, as pain slices through my chest. Sweat pours down my temples, drips down my chin. Shit, shit, shit. This is it. It's my heart... It's finally giving out. How poetic that it had to be when I am holding a gun, and next to my gangster husband, in the middle of a gun fight. Am I going to die, not struck by a bullet, but because my heart finally chose this moment to show that I don't belong with a Mafia guy, after all? Something I had already realized but which the events of the past few seconds have brought home even more firmly?

I shudder and curl into myself as the firing continues on and on. The spent cases from the used bullets hit the floor in front of me, a constant stream of metal clinking...

Like the coins in my pocket when I had walked home from school and stopped to buy my favorite candy at the corner shop. It had been during the time we had been with one particular foster family who had been so good to us. We—Summer and I—had fit in so well with them, we'd thought we had found our forever family. They'd give us pocket money we could use to buy candy, a huge treat. Something we had never been able to do before. One day, we'd reached the shop, and I'd chosen my candy and brought it to the till to pay. Then I had reached for the coins, which had slipped from my hands and hit the floor and rolled away. I'd managed to gather them back. At least, I'd thought I had, but when I had handed them over, some had been missing. I hadn't had enough to pay for the candy. Summer had stepped in and bought me the candy. She had skipped her treat that day and shared mine, and I had been so happy. The jingling of coins would always be associated with that particular memory and now with this…

The constant barrage of bullets that my husband and his brothers fire at those who are trying to kill us. A chill grips me and my teeth chatter. I grasp the gun, drawing on some of the residual warmth from the metal. *I am not weak. I will not give in to the frailty that envelops me. I am not going to just sit here and allow the men to fight while I play the role of a woman who needs to be protected all the time.* I push myself up to my feet, place my gun on the barrier and fire.

30

Michael

One minute, she's trembling on the ground; the next, she is on her feet and firing off the gun as if she's done it her entire life. She holds her finger down on the trigger and fires. Her body shudders with the recoil. She pauses, changes her stance, then grips the gun tighter and fires again, and again.

Each time she fires, her body shakes with the recoil. Each time the gun spits out a bullet, she winces, but she doesn't stop. She keeps her finger glued to the trigger, long after the rest of us have stopped.

Her features are contorted, her cheeks flushed; her chest rises and falls as she widens her stance to better support herself and the weight of the gun she holds. At some point, I realize the rest of the men have stopped shooting and are watching her. But she still doesn't stop.

The skin across her knuckles stretches white, but she keeps the trigger depressed, keeps shooting, until the empty clacking of the chambers fills the space. Tears run down her cheeks, drip from her chin. She sways, her legs seem to give way from under her, and I catch her as she crumples.

The gun slips from her fingers, and Seb snatches it up. I lower her to the floor, take in the sheen of sweat on her forehead, the trickle of sweat that runs down her temples, and my heart stutters.

"*Bellezza!*" I haul her close as I peer into her features, "You are not feeling well."

"I am fine," she insists, and her voice cracks.

"You are not fine."

"I..." she swallows, and more color leaches from her features, "I am fine, really, I am."

Seb drops down to one knee next to us, "What's wrong? How is she?"

"We need to get out of here." I glance up at him, "I need to take her to a doctor."

"No!" She rears up, "No doctor."

"You need to see someone to find out what's wrong with you."

"I... I know what's wrong with me."

I blink, "You do?"

She nods.

"Are you going to tell me?"

"I..." she glances away, "it's nothing, really."

"It's something if it has you jumping to your feet to fire off your gun, only to collapse in the next instant."

"Michael..." she opens and shuts her mouth, "it'll pass."

"What is it?"

"Honestly, it's nothing that you need to concern yourself with."

"Everything that concerns you concerns me."

"Argh!" She makes that sound deep in her throat that she does when she is frustrated, and fuck, if my cock doesn't instantly twitch. Everything about this woman is designed to drive me mad, surely?

She glowers at me, "You're impossible!"

"And you are beautiful."

Her lips tremble, "Don't say that." She glances away from me.

"Why not?" A cold sensation coils in the pit of my stomach. "I'll say it as many times as I want to you. You're my wife, after all."

"Am I?" she muses in a low voice, but I catch it.

"What the hell is that supposed to mean?"

She doesn't reply and that knot in my stomach pulls tighter. "Karma, what's going on in that head of yours?"

"If we don't do something about those men shooting at us, nothing is going to go on, because we'll all be dead," JJ interjects.

I jerk my chin up in his direction. "Don't you dare interrupt when—"

"He's right," Seb says in a hard voice. "We're stuck in the middle of a gunfight."

"You don't say?"

"What do you want to do, Capo?"

I glance down at Karma, then at Seb, "We need to—"

"We're going to stay and fight it out," Karma retorts.

I glare at her, "Now, you're going to make my decisions for me?"

"She's right," JJ cuts in. "Try to leave here and you will be gunned down."

Seb nods, "Our only hope is to stay and fight and take down those shooting at us."

"We have the weapons needed to outlast them," JJ reminds me.

Karma grimaces. If possible, she turns even more pale. Sweat dots the front of her dress, which clings to her chest. Her chest rises and falls and her lips twist. She's in pain. She's not admitting to it, but she's in pain.

"No," I say in a cold voice.

"What?" Seb stares. "What do you mean, no?"

"I mean, no." I glance down at Karma, "I am going to find a way to get her out of here and to a doctor."

"Fuck," Luca swears from above us, "that's suicide."

"We'll survive. I'll make sure we survive."

"*Cazzo!*" Seb growls, "*Fratellone,* that is not a good idea."

"I'm going to do it anyway."

"Think of her, if not yourself; you don't want to put her life in danger."

"I am thinking of her," I say in a low voice. "If I don't get her out of here, her life will be in danger."

"But—"

"Let him go," JJ murmurs. "You can take her to my doctor; I'll text you the address. I'll call him and let him know to expect you."

"*Grazie,*" I jerk my chin at him.

"You're welcome." JJ pulls out his phone and walks away to make a call.

Just then, footsteps sound outside. The door flies open and Christian, Massimo, and Antonio burst through the door.

"What's wrong?" Christian sinks down to his knees next to Seb, "What's happening?"

"Karma is not feeling well, and the Capo has decided he is going to make a run for it to get her to a doctor."

"You are both going to die," Christian says flatly. "There are still, at least, ten people out there, and probably more on the way."

"I am not going to let my wife suffer. I am going to get her to a doctor."

"And how are you going to do that?" Christian growls, "I assume you parked your car a distance from the house so you could approach without being discovered?"

"*Cazzo!*" I swear aloud, "It's not going to be easy to get to it without being spotted."

"You can use my car," JJ pockets his phone as he prowls over to us. "It's in the garage and it's bullet-proof."

"No vehicle is completely bullet-proof." Christian snaps. He turns on me, "I speak the truth and you know it. Try to take her out of here and you endanger both of your lives."

I hesitate. Do I want to be more beholden to one of my enemies...more than I already am.

Making my decision for me, Beauty gasps. She grips my hand and I glance down to find her eyes closed. Her chest rises and falls; her breathing is shallow. Fuck this. "Fine," I snap, "I'll take the car."

"What the—!" Christian explodes, "How can you willingly put yourself in danger, and after what happened to Xander—"

"It's because of what happened to Xander that I can't allow anything to happen to her." I scowl up at him.

He holds my gaze and whatever he sees on my face must convince him, for he blows out a breath. "Fuck," he growls. "Fuck, fuck, fuck." He rises to his feet, then stares down at us, "I am coming with you."

"No, you're not," I snap.

"If you are putting yourself in danger—"

"Nothing is going to happen to us."

"Then let me come with you."

"No," I say in a low voice.

He opens his mouth to protest and I slice the air with my palm, "This is not open to debate."

"*Cazzo!*" He sets his jaw. "We'll cover you. We'll fire at the mother-fuckers and make sure they are so occupied that they won't be able to stop you."

"Good plan," JJ remarks.

Christian glares at him. "We're out of ammo."

"You know where to find it," JJ replies.

"Don't we need your iris scan to unlock the door?"

"Do you?" JJ smirks.

Christian's face suffuses with color.

He jumps up to his feet, swoops out and jams his gun into the side of JJ's temple. Everyone freezes as the two glare at each other. JJ doesn't flinch, doesn't lower his gaze. The staring match goes on and on, then Christian nods. He slowly lowers the gun, pivots and walks out.

"I'll come with you." Antonio follows him.

A bead of sweat slides down JJ's temple. "The boy has balls," he concedes, "and he's hurting."

"We all are." It's not lost on me that in the space of a few hours I've gone from wanting to kill the motherfucker to trusting him...albeit grudgingly. Perhaps it's because of the life and death situation in which we currently find ourselves. It's what happens when you are under pressure. You need to make snap decisions, and trust your instincts. And right now, my gut says JJ is on our side. Temporarily. Until we find out who the hell is after us.

"You'll need this," JJ holds out his phone, "I've deactivated the lock and the doctor's address is already keyed into the GPS."

I slide the phone into my pocket.

"Garage is at the back of the house, through the kitchen," he adds, as he hands over the key fob. I take it, then rise to my feet and scoop Karma into my arms. She protests and I scowl at her. "Don't even think about it."

"But—"

"I am not going to let you walk."

"I was going to ask for my gun back."

I scowl at her, she tips up her chin. "My gun, Michael."

I nod at Seb, who reloads her gun, then holds it out. She accepts it, and cradles it close to her chest.

"Don't shoot me with that thing."

"Don't insult me." She purses her lips. "I may not be used to holding a gun, but I can hold my own with it."

"That you can," Seb concedes.

I glance around, take in the faces of my brothers, then turn to JJ. "Thanks," I say grudgingly. "This doesn't mean that I trust you."

"Same." He jerks his chin.

Seb picks up my gun from where I had placed it on the floor. He loads it, then slides it into my waistband at the small of my back.

I head for the door and he follows me.

"Where are you going?" I frown at him over my shoulder.

"Going to get you guns so you can defend yourself."

"I'll stay here," Massimo rumbles. He glares at JJ and it's clear he doesn't trust the other man to leave him on his own. Good call.

I head down to the ground floor, then out of the back door, and into the garage. The lights flicker on, revealing six parked cars. I press the keyfob and the Mercedes in the corner lights up. As I head toward it, Seb pulls out his phone, calls Christian and asks him to come to the garage with the ammo. We reach the car and Seb opens the passenger door; I place Karma inside. Then walk around to the driver's side.

Christian and Antonio join Seb, and together, they pile guns and boxes of ammo on the floor in the back of the car.

"You realize, if any one sees this, they are going to report you to the police immediately, right?" Karma grumbles.

"Will they?" I take in the pile of weapons.

"Maybe not in Sicily, but not too many people know you here," Karma insists.

"I'll make sure not to draw attention to the car."

"And the doctor?" She frowns. "Won't he get suspicious about it?"

"It's JJ's doctor; I assume he's used to seeing guns," I retort.

"Guns are not as common in England as in Sicily."

"More's the pity." I shake my head, "Never understood the appeal of a stiff upper lip, when you could simply leave a stiff behind that wouldn't talk."

"Is that a joke?" She scowls, "That *is* a joke. OMG, Capo, you made a joke?"

"Your English sense of humor must be rubbing off on me." I smirk.

"Here," says Christian as he lays a dark blanket over the guns. "Done."

The guys slam the back doors shut.

"Wait for the diversion, then drive," Christian orders.

"Don't worry about us. Don't stop for anything; you just keep going," Seb adds.

"I wish you'd let me, at least, come with you." Antonio scowls, "I am your bodyguard. It's my responsibility to make sure that nothing happens to you."

"And I want you to stay with my brothers and fight back."

With a last glance at the men, I slide into the car.

"Arrivederci," Christian calls out. *Until we meet again.*

They turn to leave, and I snap my seatbelt into place at the same time as she does.

"Now what?" Beauty lays the gun across her lap, then looks at me expectantly.

I reach over, wrap my fingers around her neck and bring her close. I kiss her, then thrust my forehead into hers. "Now we wait."

"And what do you suggest we do while we wait?"

"What do you have in mind?"

"What do you think?"

"You're not well." I scowl and she raises an eyebrow.

"Let me be the judge of that."

She reaches over and grips my crotch and my cock instantly hardens.

"Karma," I scold, "now is not the time."

"Now is exactly the time." Her eyes twinkle. Color seeps back into her face and she doesn't seem to be sweating anymore.

"You're feeling better, I take it?"

She massages my crotch, "I am now." She winces again and I glare at her.

"You lying to me again?"

"I…" She scowls, then pulls her hand back. "Fine, fine," she glances to the side, "have it your way."

I blow out a breath, "Baby, I know you want me, but your health is more important."

She scoffs, "What would make me feel better is if you eat me out."

"And get you overexcited again?" I shake my head, "not that I don't want to, but I am worried about you Karma, and I'd rather play it safe until we have you examined by a doctor."

That's when shots ring out.

31

Karma

"Fuck," he swears under his breath, "it's beginning." He rakes his gaze across my features, "You ready for this?"

No.

No.

"Yes," I jerk my chin.

He holds my gaze a second longer, then turns and puts the car in gear. He eases the car toward the garage door which rolls up, revealing the driveway. He revs the engine, peers through the glass as he waits... waits...

I search the driveway and what I can see of the grounds up ahead. "Shouldn't all the shooting have attracted cops by now?"

"It would have if we'd been in London."

"We aren't?"

"We are on the outskirts, and the grounds are so big that there are no neighbors around for miles."

"So, he lives close to one of the most expensive cities in the world and his estate is so big that he could literally commit murder and go undetected?"

He shoots me a glance and I raise my hands. "Just saying. I guess crime does pay, eh?"

"Does that bother you?"

"It's your world."

"And yours," he points out.

"Not yet."

"That's the second time you've come up with a cryptic remark in the past twenty minutes." He scowls.

Ahead, there's a muffled boom, then a section of the trees catches fire. Instantly, he puts the car in gear and roars forward. A creaking sound reaches me. I peer through the windshield, then gasp. "Mika!" I point to where the tree on the side of the driveway in front of us begins to topple over. He accelerates with such speed that I am pushed back into the seat. The Mercedes leaps forward, and the tree misses the tail of the car and hits the ground. The crash seems to resound through the space. The dust from the impact flows over the car.

Mika slaps on the wipers and their rhythmic *whoosh-whoosh* fills the car. He keeps his foot pressed on the accelerator as he races up the driveway, past the trees that surround the house on either side.

More shots ring out, bullets pepper the sides of the car, slam into the windshield. I scream and throw up my arms, only to realize that the bullets are bouncing off the car. Each bullet embeds into the windshield, and on the glass of my door, leaving a star shaped crack on impact. More shots ring out and I flinch with each impact. I glance sideways to find Mika focused on the road ahead.

The shooting seems to go on and on, there's a yell, then all noises fade. Except for the *whoosh* of the wipers, which he switches off as the car hurtles forward. Silence fills the car, for a beat, another. We continue up the driveway, and the gates to the estate loom in the distance.

"The gates are open? Was it JJ who...?" I shoot him a sideways glance in time to see him nod.

His jaw is hard and a nerve pops at his temple. His muscles seem to have turned to stone as he keeps his gaze focused forward.

Less than a mile now to the gates, three-fourths of a mile, half a mile... He leans forward as if urging the car forward with his entire being.

I draw in a breath, hold it. Twist my fingers together in front as I part my legs, push my heels into the floor of the car and brace myself. Adrenaline pours through my veins, and the blood pumps at my temples, thrums at my wrists. My heart beat ratchets up again, and this time, I don't care. I feel the flush that stains my cheeks, that sensation of the pulse flaring to life in my stomach, between my legs, as I stare through the windshield and the scenery zips by. I am excited and turned on. I shouldn't be, but I am.

Speed... Goddamn, I love speed, even though I've never had the chance to indulge in it. Not unless you count the video games I'd managed to play with one of my foster siblings. It had been only for a few months, but it had been long enough to give me a taste of what it would be like to take on an opponent, to race forward, eyes on the prize, as you mowed down anyone who dared to come in your way. As I hope Mika will do too. I shoot him another sideways glance and find his gaze completely focused on the road forward.

He presses down on the accelerator and the car seems to fly forward. Less than fifty feet to the gates...forty...now, thirty... That's when a car shoots out from the undergrowth and onto the center of the driveway in front of the gates. Then a second car from the other side. They park nose to nose in the center.

"Cazzo!" Mika growls, and for a second, I am sure that he is going to crash into the cars, but he slams on the brakes with such speed that I am slammed against the restraint then back against the seat. A scream boils up, even as a part of me relishes the adrenaline rush that builds within me.

Even as I turn to him Michael is already out of the car. He pulls out his gun as he fires at the man getting out of first car. Blood gushes from his chest and he drops to the ground. Michael continues to fire at the second man who's come around from the car, then at the driver from the second car, who's stepped out, and the other men who pour out from the second car.

He runs out of bullets, flings the gun aside, grabs another from the holster under his arm, and continues firing in such a smooth move that I blink. The men fire at him, he drops to the ground, rolls, comes up firing. It's like a dance, a much-practiced, smooth motion which he's rehearsed so many times, it's a part of him. *Of course, it's a part of him.* He was born into this world. The sound of bullets echoes in his cells, the scent of ammunition is steeped in his veins, this...weaving, ducking the shots that come his way, as he returns fire, taking out man after man who dares to threaten him... This is Michael at his rawest, truest, stripped-to-the-bone naked. This is Michael unadorned. Just how I like him. How I like the darkness that clings to his core. This…feeling of danger that surrounds him is what I crave, and what I worry may consume me until I can't differentiate right from wrong.

It's why I know I can't be with him.

It's also why I will not be a woman who cowers in the background while her man is fighting a war.

I snap my seat belt open, grab the gun from the floor, push open the door and step out, still holding the gun. I raise my gun, depress the trigger, and it doesn't fire. What the hell? I apply pressure on the trigger, again and again. Still, nothing happens. What the—! The breath whooshes out of me. Michael switched on the safety. That's why I am not able to fire. I reach for the safety, when the barrel of a gun is pushed into the back of my head.

32

Michael

"Stop or I'll shoot her."

A familiar voice rings out. I keep my finger pressed down on the trigger, take the last man out, then pivot, gun pointed toward the man who has his weapon trained on her.

"*Cazzo!*" I growl as my gaze collides with a pair of blue eyes so similar to mine.

"Don," I growl, "What the hell are you up to?"

"Sorry it had to come to this, Capo," he says without any change in expression, "but I have to protect what's mine."

"You wanted me to become the Don."

"Correction," he looks me up and down, "I wanted you to think that I wanted you to become the Don."

"Why," I shake my head trying to understand what his intentions are, "Why would you do this?"

"Why would I hold a gun to your wife's head?" His lips curve, "You know why. You let it become personal, Capo. You allowed her to get to you. You went against everything I taught you."

"Everything you taught me?" I explode, "You didn't teach me shit, you bastard."

"Technically, I am not a bastard. Neither are you, for that matter." He shakes his head, "American insults; they're so predictable, don't you think?"

"There's enough American in me to use the insult when it fits the occasion."

"That was my first mistake. Agreeing to let you go to the US to study. You came back, not just with an American accent, but with their sensibilities as well, which don't fit in with our way of life."

"What doesn't fit in with our way of life is you."

"And you?" His lips kick up, "You are going to modernize the ways of the Mafia, eh? Bring us into the digital age with your virtual businesses? The very nature of which has resulted in this mess."

"It did," I agree. "The virtual businesses which you mock are so profitable that it led to my partners trying to betray me to get a hold of it, but thanks to you," I allow my own lips to curve in a smile, "I've not only sorted that out, but at the same time, I've made allies of our closest rivals."

"You'd engage in a partnership with our enemies?" My father's features harden. "That is a recipe for disaster."

"What is a recipe for disaster is that you still have your gun trained on my wife."

"What are you going to do about it?"

I curl my fingers around the trigger and the Don shakes his head, "Don't do it; not unless you want to see your wife's brains all over the ground."

Karma pales and her fingers holding the gun tremble. He leans around, grabs the gun from her. I stiffen, take a step forward, but he wiggles his gun in my direction. I pause, take in Karma's features. Her chin wobbles, but her gaze never wavers. Magnificent woman. She squares her shoulders and firms her lips. She's scared, but she's trying her best not to show it. I hold her gaze for a second longer, then turn my attention to my father. "What do you want?"

"You. Dead," he points her gun at me, then releases the safety. The sound is loud in the silence, broken only by the sound of the hot metal of the cars contracting as they release some of their heat into the air.

She winces, but doesn't give any other sign of the fear I am sure grips her right now.

"I thought you wanted your legacy to continue."

"It's why I have five sons."

"Four," I say in a low voice, "you have four sons left."

"Too bad about Alessandro," he raises a shoulder, "but the way he was going... He wasn't worth the Mafia name."

"You?" Anger clouds my brain and my pulse rate ratchets. Something hot stabs at my chest. "You?" I manage to form the word with my tongue. "You were behind the rigging of the car? You killed him?"

"An accident." For a second, he seems almost contrite, then his features smooth out again. "I hadn't meant for the bomb to kill him."

My gut clenches and my vision tunnels. He killed him? My father killed my brother? He killed Xander? I clench my fingers around the trigger of my gun. I am going to kill the bastard myself. But I don't yet have a clear shot. *Merda!* I glare down the barrel of my gun at him, force my muscles to relax, "But you did intend to kill her?"

"Something to distract you from your path to taking over as Don."

"I don't understand." I shake my head. "You encouraged me to become Don; you are my father."

"So?" He raises a shoulder, "Doesn't mean I ever have to step down. I intend to stay at the helm of the Mafiosa for a long, long time...but you, were becoming too great a threat."

"You'd kill me, rather than see me succeed?"

"And then I'd still have three sons." He raises a shoulder, "Enough to continue my lineage, when the time comes."

"You've lost it," I growl.

"You're the one who's lost the fight." He narrow his gaze on me, "Lower the gun, son."

Son? He dares call me son after everything he's done to our family? Bile bubbles up my throat and I swallow it down. I glance from him to her, then back at his face.

"Do it," he warns. "If you want her to survive this, you'll lower the gun."

"If you let her walk away, I'll hand myself over."

"No, Michael," Karma bursts out, and he must push the gun into her head, for she winces again.

Anger coils in my belly, my vision narrows, adrenaline laces my blood, and I force myself to uncurl my fingers from where they have pressed down on the trigger. "Let her walk away, now," I insist, "and I won't fight this."

"Lower your gun first," he says in a cold voice. "Don't forget, I am the one who taught you the game that you now insist on playing."

I glare at him and he doesn't blink. My father's features are set in lines that I find familiar. He means it. He won't hesitate to shoot her. The only way out is to show him that I am willing to comply, for the moment. I lower my gun, and he jerks his chin. "Place it on the ground."

I follow his instructions, then straighten.

"Now kick it toward me."

I do so, and he nods.

"Now let her go."

"No," he drawls, "I am going to shoot her, then you."

"Wait," I burst out, "the man I interrogated and who said that it was the Kane company who'd put him up to rigging the car, was that your doing?"

His lips twist, "What do you think?"

"I don't know..." I draw in a breath. *Delay him, delay him.* Just until I've gathered myself together. Just until I find a way to get him to release Karma. "If it was, then that was sheer genius. It derailed us from going after the real culprit."

"Me," he bites out the word with satisfaction writ into his features.

He holds my gaze and I can read the intent. I know he's going to do it. He's going to pull the trigger on her, on my Beauty, my soul, my wife. My everything. All of my muscles tense and I lean forward on the balls of my feet, ready to throw myself at him, when the screech of brakes sounds from behind me.

He glances past me and I yell, "Hit the ground, Karma."

I lunge toward my gun, but before I can reach it, a shot rings out.

There's a hoarse cry. I grab the gun, raise it to find Karma is on the ground, her arms over her head and smoke rising from a hole in the center of my father's chest. It's smoking, but there's no blood. Motherfucker. He's wearing a protective vest. Of course, he is. There's only one way to kill this guy.

He raises his gun, fires, and something slams into my left shoulder. Pain slices through me, burns a path down my arm. I raise the gun with my other arm, pull the trigger, and again.

Blood blooms from a hole in the center of his forehead, and a second from the hole in his throat. He seems almost surprised. Then his body begins to tumble forward. I race toward Karma, grab her under my arm, swing her up and to the side. My father's body crashes to the ground where she was.

A trembling grips her and I pull her close as I stare at the man who was my father.

He betrayed me… Hell, he had been betraying me my entire life. At each turn, I had forgiven him, because he was my blood. Was he right? Was it because I am too emotional that I couldn't see what he really was? Is that why I couldn't stop him before he killed my brother?

A coldness grips my chest. I stare at the fallen body of my father and a buzzing sound fills my senses.

"Mika, are you okay?"

Specks of black infiltrate the corners of my vision as I gaze down at her.

"Karma?"

She glances at my features, then down to my left shoulder.

"Oh my god, Mika," she gasps, "you are hurt."

"Just a scratch," I smirk… Then cough, and blood drips from the corner of my mouth.

Her gaze widens, "It's not just a scratch. The bullet... It hit you; you are bleeding out." She presses her hand to where the blood pulses from the wound, trying to stem the flow, and pain shoots up my neck. It explodes behind my eyes, and I grunt as my legs seem to fold in on themselves. I try to straighten myself, waver on my feet, and Karma tries to support me. "Help," she screams as footsteps sound behind me, "help me."

Strong arms grip me, then lower me to the dirt. I glance up into Nikolai's face.

"Sorry, I got here a little late." He grimaces. His face fades in and out of view.

"You were…not late," I force out the words. A coldness grips me and I shudder.

More footsteps sound, then suddenly, Christian is there. He takes one look at me and his features go solid. He pulls off his jacket, sinks to his knees, and hands it to Karma. "Use this to apply pressure," he growls.

Sirens sound in the distance, and I frown.

"Ambulance," JJ's voice seems to come from far away, "I called an ambulance."

I grasp Karma's hand in mine. "Don't leave me," I whisper. "Don't leave me, Karma."

"Don't talk," she swallows, "save your energy."

Darkness pulls me under, but I fight it off.

"Promise me that you'll be there when I wake up."

She moves her mouth but I can't hear her.

"Andy," I murmur.

"You're dying," she bursts out, "and you're worried about my cat?"

"I am not dying," I insist, "and you love your cat, so of course, I am worried about him."

"Please, don't exert yourself," she pleads. "Please, Mika, just focus on staying alive."

"I am not going anywhere," I smile. "Not as long as I have you by my side."

She glances away and a sick sensation twists my stomach.

"Karma, don't do it," I plead with her, or at least, I think I try to do that. Then everything goes dark.

33

Karma

"You've put yourself under a lot of pressure, Mrs. Sovrano," the doctor murmurs. "You are lucky you didn't come out of this in worse shape."

"I think you meant to say that to my husband, not me." I firm my lips, "He's the one who was shot."

The doctor shoots me a knowing glance, "I am talking about you, ma'am, not your husband."

After Michael lost consciousness, holding onto my hand, the ambulance had arrived. True to his word, it had been an ambulance to a private hospital that JJ owns in London.

He had briefly regained consciousness as they were strapping him onto the stretcher and insisted that they check me out.

I had told the paramedics I was fine, but Michael had refused to cooperate with them until they had finally given in and one of them had begun to examine me.

I had kept insisting that I was fine, but the paramedic had said that my blood pressure and my heart rate were both elevated—which I already knew, of course, but had feigned surprise when he'd said that.

They'd asked me to ride in the same ambulance as Michael to the hospital so they could check me out thoroughly. I'd wanted to leave right then. I should have left right then. But how could I until I knew that Michael was really okay? So, I had agreed.

Michael had flitted in and out of consciousness, and each time he was lucid, he'd ask for me. He'd gripped my hand and not let go even when he'd lost consciousness. It was only when we arrived at the hospital and they had had to wheel him to the operating theatre that I had managed to disentangle my fingers from his.

Seb and Christian had arrived then, along with Massimo and Antonio. Christian had insisted that I have myself checked out. I had refused, wanting to stay and wait for news of Michael, but my protest fell on deaf ears.

Within minutes, I was being ushered into an examination room. Just as I had changed out of my bloodied clothes and into a hospital gown, a doctor had arrived. He'd already accessed my records via the National Health Service system that the hospital had access to, so of course, there had been no escape. He'd known about my heart condition, and that's what had prompted this conversation.

I set my jaw as I scowl at him. "My condition is stable," I insist.

"Only if you completed your course of medication, and only if you manage your condition properly."

"That's exactly what I did."

"Hmm," he purses his lips, "your records indicate that you started the course of medication prescribed by your specialist, but you missed your last appointment, and you also did not complete the course."

Shit. My cheeks flush.

"Also, judging by your current condition," he glances at my blood splattered clothes, "I assume the latter is not something that you are adhering to either."

Gah! Why do I feel like a student who is pulled up in front of the class for something I've done wrong? I fold my arms around my waist.

"Well, Mrs. Sovrano," the doctor murmurs, "I take it from your silence that I am right on both counts."

"Yeah, yeah," I sniff, "so what do you propose I do now?"

"I propose that I complete your check up, then restart you on your medication."

"Okay."

"Also, I am going to have to insist that you come in for your next check-up, in two weeks."

I nod.

"And," he murmurs, "you need to try not to excite yourself too much. At least, until your blood pressure and heart rate are back to normal."

I open my mouth to speak, and he arches an eyebrow, "And even after that, you need to ensure that you don't overexert yourself physically."

I snort.

"This is not a joke, Mrs. Sovrano." He frowns, "We are talking about your heart here."

"My heart is lying in the other room getting operated on," I burst out.

His features soften, "The doctors are doing everything possible for your husband."

I startle. "What do you mean by that."

He holds up his hands, "Just that he is in safe hands. The best surgeons in the country are taking care of him right now."

I swallow.

"He'd probably rest better if he knew that you are taking care of yourself too," the doctor offers.

I lower my chin to my chest and blow out a breath. "Look, I have no wish to die young, okay?" I swallow, then glance away, "It's just, sometimes I want to live a normal life. I don't want my condition to be a constant worry. I want to experience all of the highs and lows of being alive. Hell, I am barely in my twenties and I want to have first-hand knowledge of everything life can offer, you know?"

"And you will," he gives me a small smile, "provided you take your medication and your vitals return to normal. And even after that, you need to take care of yourself."

"Which I am very good at, I assure you."

He peers into my face, then nods. "You're a clever woman, Mrs. Sovrano. I am sure you understand the risks of not following professional medical advice."

"I do," I nod, "and I'll complete the course of medication this time."

"Good, the nurse will come by with your medication." He rises to his feet, "I'd also recommend that you stay in the hospital for overnight observation, and ideally, take it easy for the next few days."

"But it's not something you can force me to do, can you?"

"You're a grown woman, Mrs. Sovrano. You can make your own decisions."

He turns to leave and I call out, "Doctor, I have one more question."

He turns to me.

"Am I correct that I can still get pregnant without causing my condition to be exacerbated as a result?"

He fixes me with a shrewd glance, "There are those with your condition who get pregnant and carry their children to term, and there are those whose condition deteriorates as a result. As your physician, I should warn you that it's safer if you don't get pregnant. But the choice is yours, of course."

Right.

I bite the inside of my cheek. I knew it already. It's what my doctors had previously indicated to me. Only, I hadn't paid any attention to it. Hell, becoming pregnant had been the last thing on my mind then. But after losing my baby... Well, it's something that's so in my face right now that I couldn't help but ask the question.

The doctor turns to leave and I call out after him, "This...conversation is covered under doctor-patient confidentiality, right?"

He pauses then turns to me. "It is," he nods.

"So, I'd prefer it if you didn't say anything to my husband, or to any of his brothers out there."

He frowns then nods, "As you wish." And he leaves.

I glance around the space, then because my clothes are all bloodied, I change out of my hospital gown and into the scrubs he'd left behind for me.

After meeting with the nurse and getting my medication, I pad out of the examination room to find Antonio waiting for me.

"Are you guarding me now?" I scowl.

"It's what he'd have wanted." The big Sicilian doesn't seem put off by my irritation. He merely steps aside.

He trails me as I head toward the waiting room —which is a spacious area, with big windows through which light floods in. It's a far cry from the rooms I have seen in the government-run hospitals I've been to previously. I step on the carpeted floor and take in the scene. Christian is sprawled out in a chair in one corner. He glowers at Luca, who glowers back at him from the opposite corner. Massimo is by the window, and he turns as I approach.

"Karma," he comes forward and when he opens his arms, I walk into them. Of all the remaining Sovrano brothers, Massimo is, by far, the least threatening. Despite his height and the fact that he is the biggest of all of them... He is also the quietest and the gentlest.

"You okay?"

I nod into his chest and he leans back. "He's going to be fine," Massimo murmurs.

"Have they said anything?"

He shakes his head, "He's still in surgery."

"How much," I clear my throat, "how much longer do they think he'll be?"

"They don't know yet," Christian says. I turn to find him standing next to me. I glance at the blood on his shirt and my stomach churns. That's Michael's blood. Oh, my god, it's his blood. A sob wells up and I push my knuckles into my mouth. Christian glances down at his blood-splattered shirt and pales. "I'm sorry, Karma," he draws in a breath, "I didn't realize... I..."

"It's okay," I swallow down the ball of emotion that clogs my throat.

Luca rises from his seat and walks over to join us, and I survey their faces.

"I... I have something to tell you... I..." *I am going to leave him. I am going to walk away while your brother is still in surgery. I...*

"What is it, Karma?" Massimo says in a soft voice. "You can tell us," he glances around the assembled faces and they nod, "we're your family."

The rest of them murmur their assent, and tears prick the backs of my eyes.

"I..." I shake my head, "I am tired."

"Are you okay?" Massimo frowns, "The doctor examined you. Did he say—"

"I'm fine."

"Are you sure?" He brushes past me, "I should ask him myself, maybe?"

"Massimo," I call out and he stops. "Leave it."

He hesitates and I draw myself up to my full height. "I am okay, and anyway, I am not the one who you should be worried about. It's your brother who needs our complete attention, at the moment."

He seems like he's about to hesitate and I square my shoulders. "I am the wife of your future Don, and I order you to stay here so we can be together while we wait for news about him."

A frisson runs through the space. The guys glance at each other, as if just realizing the ramifications of the events that have taken place. Michael is going to be the new Don. And I am still his wife…which means my word carries weight yet, right?

"Where's Seb?" I ask, suddenly realizing that he's missing.

"He stayed back with JJ and Niko to ensure disposal of the evidence before the cops get wind of it."

Evidence. Oh, he means the body of their father. The man who killed Xander, who put Michael and his brothers through so much, who almost killed me. I shiver and that seems to galvanize Massimo into action. He shrugs off his jacket and walks over, places it around my shoulders. "Thanks," I murmur, "and Adrian?"

"Here I am," a voice calls out from the doorway.

I turn to find Adrian walking into the waiting room. He stalks over to me, then holds out the pet carrier.

"Is that?" I blink. *It can't be. Is it—* An angry meow sounds from the carrier as I drop to my knees. I peer into the carrier and Andy's indignant face looks back at me.

"Andy," I whisper. "OMG," I tip my chin up to stare at Adrian, "how did he get here?"

"The Capo was clear we had to take care of him. So, I waited on the island until the private jet had deposited these guys in London, then flew back to pick me up and bring me here."

"Oh," I blink rapidly, "so a private plane trip, just so you could get Andy to me?"

"Two trips, actually," he smiles, "but the Capo ordered it."

And what the Capo wants, the Capo gets. Andy peers at me through gaps in the wall of the carrier.

"How did you bring him into a hospital?" I frown. "Aren't pets not allowed in here?"

"It's a private hospital." He shrugs. "It's funded by the Mafia, so—"

So, no rules apply, I guess. I rise to my feet, grab the carrier from him. "Thank you," I say.

I bend down, take Andy out of the pet carrier, then sit down with him in my arms.

The rest of the guys disperse to different corners of the room. Antonio continues to stand by the door on the outside of the room.

Christian pulls out his phone and begins to message someone. I walk over to sit next to him and he pockets his phone again.

"Was that Aurora?" I scowl.

"What do you mean?" He asks in an a voice that sounds all too innocent.

"You were texting with Aurora, weren't you?" I accuse.

"And if I was?"

"Have you told her that you like her?"

"Like?" He smirks, "That's not the world I'd use."

"You going to marry her, or what?"

"Marry?" He looks at me in alarm, "Whatever gave you that idea?"

"Isn't that what good Italian men do when they've been struck by the 'thunderbolt'?"

"You mean *colpo di fulmine?*" He leans over and scratches Andy behind his ear. The cat purrs, then stretches his neck, inviting him to continue his actions.

"Exactly," I peer into Christian's face, "so?" I arch an eyebrow, "You going to do something about it?"

"She betrayed the Capo."

"To help me."

"Still," he hesitates, "it's not something that can be forgiven without some kind of punishment."

"But if you marry her, she becomes part of the *famiglia* right?"

He stiffens, "Marriage? Who's talking about marriage?"

"And once she is your wife, she is safe from any punishment, correct?"

He holds my gaze, "You and she have become good friends, eh?"

"She is a wonderful person, Christian," I soften my voice, "and it's clear there's something between the two of you."

"There's something, all right," he snorts, "but it's not what you are thinking."

"Oh, please, the sparks between the two of you could light up a room."

"So?"

"So, what are you going to do about it?"

He stares at me.

"What?" I frown. "Don't tell me you are going to ignore it?"

"Trust me," he says in a soft voice, "the last thing I am going to do is ignore it."

"So, you are going to talk to her?"

"Maybe more than talk." He smirks.

O-k-a-y, that doesn't sound very promising at all.

"Christian, I—"

He holds up his hand, "What's between Aurora and me is our concern and no one else's."

"But—"

"Leave it, Karma."

He glances away and I blow out a sigh.

"Fine," I murmur, "I won't push it, but you'd better not hurt her, okay?"

He simply pulls out his phone and begins to play with it again. I rise to my feet, holding Andy close to my chest with one arm. I grab the pet carrier with my free hand and walk over to a chair in an unoccupied corner.

Sitting down, I coax Andy back into the carrier. For once Andy doesn't protest, he prowls in, curls around and closes his eyes. I straighten, then take my seat. I lean my head back against the wall, and close my eyes. A touch on my shoulder jolts me awake. I open my eyes to see Massimo standing in front of me.

"What's wrong?"

He jerks his chin toward the door. I follow his glance to find a doctor standing there in scrubs. His mask is around his neck and he glances around the room before his gaze alights on me.

"Mrs. Sovrano?" he says in a neutral voice. "Please come with me."

34

———————

Karma

"What...what's wrong?" I try to stand up, but my legs don't seem capable of supporting me. I push my feet into the floor then straighten in my seat. "How..." I croak, "how is he?"

"The surgery went well; we removed the bullet."

A frisson of relief rushes through me, "Is he, is he going to be okay?" I rasp.

"The bullet missed his vital organs. He is a very lucky man."

Tension drains from my limbs, and I sink against the back of the chair, exhaling loudly.

"Is he...is he awake?"

"He's not conscious, yet," the doctor replies, "but you can see him for a few minutes, if you'd like."

I nod, then rise to my feet. Christian rises with me, but I wave him off. "I'll be fine," I tell him as I walk over to the doctor. I follow the doctor as he strides down the corridor.

He leads me to a room. "He's inside." The doctor steps aside and I push the door open and step in. The beeps of the machines monitoring his vitals fill the space. He's covered in a sheet that's tucked around his waist. The bandage that is wrapped around his chest is stark against the tan of his skin. His eyes are shut, those gorgeous eyelashes fanning in an arch against his high cheekbones. His cheeks are pale, the hollows under his eyes more pronounced than normal. I walk over to him, reach over and take his hand in mine. My fingers look tiny against his. I hold his big palm between both of mine, then bring it to my face and press it against my cheek. His skin is warm, and that dark, edgy scent of his is tempered by the scent of antiseptic. It's still him, though. My Capo. Mine.

Only, he'll never leave this life. I couldn't ask him to leave it. Which means he'll always be in danger. Maybe a part of me has always known that. It's why I had been attracted to him, after all… But now, with the evidence of how it could hurt him in front of me, I am not sure I can live with it. I lower his arm, place his hand on the bed next to him. Then I lean in and kiss his cheek. I push away the strand of hair that has fallen across his forehead, take in the whiskers that have grown across his jaw, the rise and fall of his chest, the sculpted planes still visible, despite the bandage that swathes him.

This man… Even unconscious, he's lethal. Even with his charisma dimmed, he's potent. I lean down and brush my lips over his. Soft lips, that could kiss so hard I could feel it all the way to my toes. I share his breath, revel in that unique maleness of his that is a combination of everything he is.

I am sorry, my Capo, but I am leaving. Sorry that I can't stay with you and tell you so in person. If I did, you'd stop me and I'd never be able to refuse you. I'd give in to your dominance and stay… And then I'd never know if it was because I really wanted to stay, or if it was because I couldn't turn you down. That's why I am leaving now. Do you understand?

I turn to go and something tugs at my hand. I look down to find his fingers are wrapped around my wrist. I glance up at his face but his eyes are shut. Peer down at where he still holds onto me. I reach for his fingers and peel them off, one by one.

Tears pricks the backs of my eyes. *Don't cry, damn it. This is the right thing to do.* If I have any hope of living life in a way that is true to myself, then I need to do this. It's the right thing for both of us.

Just as I'd never ask him to leave the Mafia, he too should never force me to do something that I don't want. And that was how our relationship started. With him taking me against my wishes.

Lots has changed since then, though. We know each other so much better. He knows what I am all about, what I like, and don't like. Surely, he'll understand?

I turn to leave, and this time, nothing stops me. I pause at the door, turn to look at him one last time. Then I head back to the waiting room. "Does anyone have a pen and paper?"

The guys look at each other, then Massimo reaches inside his jacket. He pulls out a small diary and a pen, before walking over to hand it to me.

I glance at it, then up at him, "Molesekine?"

He flushes, "I, uh, doodle a bit when I have time."

I open the book filled with pages of his surprisingly neat handwriting, until I find a clean page. I start to write and he turns his back to me. "Use me as a table," he tells me.

I balance the diary against his back, and start writing. When I am done, I tear out the page. As he straightens and turns to me, I slip off my ring, wrap it in the page and hand it over to him. "Give it to him when he wakes up," I tell him.

"Karma" he whispers, "what are you doing?"

"What is right for both of us."

"He took a bullet for you," Christian walks toward me, "and you are leaving him?"

"Just give him the letter, Massimo," I plead, "please."

Massimo hesitates.

Christian glares at me.

Seb and Luca walk over to surround me.

I firm my lips, "Your new Don will not be happy that you refused to help his wife."

"Our new Don will be even less happy if we let his wife leave," Christian points out.

I turn on him, "What's between my husband and me is our concern and no one else's."

He winces, "Karma, don't do this."

I turn back to Massimo. "Take it." I jut out my chin, "It would be a lot worse if I left without his having this letter. He needs to read this, Massimo."

He draws in a breath, then reaches over and takes the letter and the ring from me.

I move back a few steps, take in their faces. These men whom I have come to regard as family. I glance at Luca, who jerks his chin in my direction. Even Luca, who helped me escape…then helped me return to my husband…Yeah, they are each impressive in their own right. And together like this…it brings home just how strong they are as a unit. The strongest, most impressive of them all is my husband—the one who I am going to leave.

A hot sensation stabs at my chest…and it's nothing to do with my heart condition. Damn it, I am going to miss them. Guess I didn't realize how much I've come to regard myself as one of them, and now, I am going to have to leave them. Tears prick the backs of my eyes and I turn away.

"What about Andy?" Adrian calls out after me.

I pause, "Tell Michael to take care of him."

Turning, I walk out of the room. Out of the hospital. Out of his life.

35

Michael

"You let her what?" I try to sit up but pain lances through my wounded side. I gasp, lay back. Sweat beads my temples, and my muscles protest. *Cazzo!* I am as weak as a newborn. I draw in a breath, then another, wait until the pain subsides somewhat.

"You could take painkillers," Christian points out.

"And allow myself to be knocked out again?" I snap, "No, thanks." Besides, it's better this way. The pain keeps me from slipping back into the tiredness that threatens my limbs. I glare at the faces of my brothers. "Not one of you thought of stopping her?"

"Of course, we did," Seb retorts. "Not that she was going to listen to us."

"Besides, as she took great pains in pointing out, she is the wife of a Mafia Don, who wouldn't take kindly to us using coercion to have held her back," Massimo adds.

"So, you let her walk?"

"We didn't have a choice, *fratellone*," Luca murmurs.

"*Cazzo!*" I glare at the lot of them. "Five grown men, and she found a way to outwit the lot of you?"

"She also left this," Massimo pulls out something wrapped in a piece of paper and hands it over.

I take the paper, unwrap it and find her ring. *"Che cazzo!"* I stare at the ring, then notice the writing on the paper. I straighten it out, and begin to read.

Capo (or should I call you Don?),

I know you are going to be angry when you read this, but please, can you give me a chance to explain? I am leaving you, not because I don't love you. Not even because you haven't yet told me that you love me, which you do (and which I know, by the way, even though you've been adamant not to admit it to me so far). I am not leaving you because our relationship started out in the most unorthodox way, or because you'll never leave the Mafia. Okay, that last thing... Maybe that has somewhat to do with it.

But, Capo, when that bullet hit you... It also hit me. It hurt me when it sliced through your flesh. I bled when you did.

I feel everything you do, Capo, just as I know you do too. I'd never ask you to give up your way of life... It's what makes you who you are. It is a part of you. It's even one of the things that attracts me to you, to be honest. But... I also can't stand the thought of you being hurt again.

The thought that one day there'll be a knock on the door and someone will tell me that you are gone... Like Xander... Like how I almost died... It would be much, much worse if it were to happen to you, Capo. I don't think I could survive it, actually.

And...I know, being a Don's wife means I need to be prepared for the worst. A bit like being a soldier's wife, you know? You just have to always be ready to have the rug pulled out of from underneath you. And maybe I will be... Maybe I won't... But I need to arrive at that conclusion for myself.

As long as I am with you, I can't think. When you touch me, I lose sight of everything else except wanting to throw myself at your feet and allow you to have your way with me... There you have it—the 'naked' truth. Pun intended.

So, I ask you to give me this time away, so I can think for myself. So I can figure out if this is how I want to spend the rest of my days...as the wife of a Don...or...or... I can't even contemplate the other scenario...but it's something I need to be open to, at least, considering.

If you love me at all, and I know that you do, I ask that you not track me. Do not come in search of me. Please, give me this space to figure out what I truly want for myself.

Yours,

Beauty aka Bellezza aka Karma

P.S. How is it that you have so many nicknames for me and I haven't even thought of one for you?

P.P.S. I am leaving Andy to keep you company.

I glance up as Adrian walks in holding the pet carrier. He holds it up and Andy's baleful gaze greets me. He glares at me, then retreats to the side of the cage. Fuck, the cat is moping, all right. Probably misses her.

If she thinks that she can flounce out of my life like that, she has another think coming. I sit up, ignore the pain that grips my side. I grab the IV and yank it out of my arm, wincing as the tape used to hold it in place tears off some of my skin, Blood drips down my arm and onto the floor. I swing my legs over the side of the bed and rise to my feet, only to fall back against the bed frame.

"*Cazzo!*" I growl, try to straighten again and my head spins.

"What the fuck are you doing?" Christian growls.

I straighten again, manage to take a couple of steps before my knees threaten to give way. Massimo grabs my unhurt shoulder and I shake him off, "I am going after her."

"And I assume she specifically asked you not to?" he retorts.

I turn on him, "Did you read my note, asshole? If you did—"

"You really think I'd read the note that your wife entrusted to me before she left?"

I glare at him, then shake my head. "Forgive me," I mumble. "I'm, clearly, losing perspective."

"And she needs to gain perspective." Massimo lowers his chin, "Clearly, that's why she left. I assume she also asked you to give her space?"

When I glare at him, he raises a shoulder, "You need to respect that."

"And you are an expert on relationships now?"

"No," Seb interrupts, "none of us are, but we've seen the two of you engaged in this push-pull of a relationship, and even to jerk-faces like us

— and I say that in the most loving way possible — it's clear that both of you need to sort your own shit out first."

"And that's exactly what she's doing," Luca adds.

"How? First, by taking your help to run away from me, and now, by leaving me?" I scowl.

"You know that old adage about letting someone you love go and if they love you, they'll come back?" Christian drawls and I turn on him.

"If you dare tell me that's what I have to do... Then I'm going to deck you, right now."

"You're too weak to deck me." His lips tilt up slightly, "And no, that's not what I was going to tell you...but," he raises a shoulder, "I have to admit, that statement seems to carry a modicum of truth right now."

I glare at him, then at the note in my hand. *Fuck. Fuck, fuck, fuck.* I sit down heavily on the bed, stare at her ring. Where are you, Beauty? Did you think that I'd actually allow you to leave and not track you? Did you think that the better part of me would prevail and that I'd actually let you go? I crumple the piece of paper in my palm, close the fingers of my other hand around the ring.

36

One month later

Karma

"How much is this dress?"

I glance up from arranging the outfits in my stall in Camden Market. When I'd walked out of the hospital, I'd headed to the flat that I'd arranged to rent before I'd left for the island with Michael. Then, I'd focused on getting my little fashion designing business up and running. I'd managed to wrangle back my place in the market and had gone to work creating outfits in the style I love. I'd poured all of my efforts into it, in an attempt to drown out thoughts of Michael and the life I had decided to leave. I'd been diligent in taking the medicines that had been prescribed to me by the specialist at the hospital and have already been back for a follow-up.

I had insisted on paying for my treatment with the money in my bank account. Technically, it was still Michael's money... Except, well, in a way, I had earned it for the time I had been his wife. I shouldn't have used the money at all, actually…but I didn't have any other means to live on. And I didn't want to take a loan from Summer… To do so, would have meant I'd have to tell her everything I'd been through, and honestly, I am still not ready for that. To be honest, I am not ready for any kind of company. Which is why I'd simply stuck to the flat, set up my studio in the spare bedroom and worked my ass off to get enough outfits ready for market day—which is today.

It also means I've gone an entire month without communicating with anyone. Except for the visits to the shops to choose my fabrics and to order what I needed to set up my studio, that is. I haven't spoken to any of my friends since moving to the flat.

I'd also messaged Summer to let her know that I was doing fine, but that I needed more time to figure out the status of my relationship with my 'guy.'

I know it's selfish of me, not speaking with Summer for so long, or meeting her now that I am in London. But I really do need to figure out where my head's at regarding the status of my marriage.

Besides, she is busy with her husband and the circle of friends she's built, thanks to being married to one of the Seven. So, although it hurts that we've gone this long without communicating… It's also a relief that I am not answerable to anyone else. Not my sister, not my husband… Not even, to my cat. I miss Andy almost as much as I miss him…

Okay, I miss *him* a lot more…when I allow myself to think of him. Which is…most nights. In those moments before I fall asleep, and those early morning moments before I wake up, when my guard is down and I am at my most vulnerable, that's when thoughts of him crowd in on me. Is he still tracking me on a screen somewhere? A blue dot that he can't reach out to but which indicates to him exactly where I am? Does he miss me as much as I miss him? The feel of me. The touch of me. The scent of me. Does he miss being inside of me as much as I miss the girth of him thrusting into me, stretching me, filling me. My toes curl. Heat flushes my skin.

I glance up to find the woman who'd been interested in buying the dress I'd created staring at me strangely.

"Are you okay?" She frowns, "You look flushed."

Which is saying something, considering it's freezing right now, at this outdoor stall where I am.

"I'm fine." I jerk my chin toward the dress she's holding, "There's only one of those in existence, you know?"

She glances at the dress, then back at me, "Really?"

I nod, "It's a Karma original. A unique dress handcrafted just for you."

She runs her fingers over the purple collar, "It has a certain *je ne sais quoi* feel about it, for sure." She rubs her palm across the embroidered vest that constitutes the top half of the dress. "And these colors... They are gorgeous."

"They are," I agree, "inspired by the colors of Sicily."

"Sicily?" Her eyes gleam. "Now the red and black mixed with the ochre yellow makes sense."

"It does, right?" I take in the dress with pride. "I tried to bring to life all of the smells and tastes and textures I found when I was there."

"Oh, did you live there?"

"Yes," I murmur, "I've only been back a month."

"Were you there on work?"

"Eh?" I frown. "No, not really, I was..." *married* is what I am going to say, then change my mind. "Uh, I was there on unfinished business."

"And did you complete it?"

I frown. "Complete what?"

"The business that took you there?"

"No," I lower my chin to my chest, "not yet."

"So, are you going back then?"

A hot sensation coils in my chest. I glance away, then back at her, "Not sure yet."

"Pity, for the place, clearly, inspires you." She digs into her purse, then hands me her credit card.

"I haven't even told you how much it costs."

"It doesn't matter." She smiles. "I'll pay whatever price you ask."

"Wow," I blink, "really?"

"You bet," she massages the fabric of the dress like it's already hers, "this is perfect for a wedding I am going to attend."

"A wedding?"

"Not mine," she laughs, "but a friend's. This will suit the occasion very well. It's unique, but it won't take attention away from the bride. It's perfect, really."

I charge her credit card, then hand over the machine for her to key in her pin. She taps in her pin without protest. One-thousand pounds. Hell, I charged her one-thousand pounds and she was happy to pay that for a Karma original. Wow!

I wrap the dress up for her, place it carefully in a cloth bag that has my brand proudly displayed on it. She thanks me with a big smile, then slings it over her shoulder and leaves. That is the single, biggest sale that I have ever made. It's a new record. It means I am good. That people will pay what I ask for my creations. That I can finally charge what I am really worth. I make ten more sales, all in the three-figure range, and by the time I close for the day, it's a record day of sales for me.

I pack up the remaining dresses, then haul the merchandise into the van that I have rented for the day. I drive home, lug the clothes back into my flat, then walk back down and return the van. I take the tube back home, and by eight pm, I am parked in front of the TV with a glass of wine.

I finish my dinner, have an early night, and I'm up by five am. By six, I have drunk my coffee and paced the floor of the living room end to end, at least twenty times. I really need to get started on creating more outfits, but don't feel like it.

I change into my yoga pants, a tank top, and throw a sweatshirt on top. I lace up my running shoes. Then, picking up my phone, my keys and my earphones, I set out to run. I keep my pace leisurely, just a little above a fast walk. I run through my neighborhood, across the road that leads to the next block. The one where I used to share a flat with Summer when I lived with her.

I am almost not surprised when I run up the road that takes me to Waterlow Park. Maybe I've known I was heading here. Maybe I've been biding my time since I walked out of the hospital. Maybe I am still finding myself... Maybe I am done searching for what makes sense. Ten minutes of half-walking, half-jogging up the incline, and I reach the park. I slow to a walk, continue up the familiar path. I pick up speed again, as I jog around the perimeter of the space, then up the hill-side. I reach the top, and turn to face the vista that stretches out in front of me. The rays from the rising sun bathe the trees and the city in dappled gold. The breeze lifts the hair from my forehead and a bird calls out nearby. Another returns its call. Its mate probably. Does nature really want us to be in pairs? Is this why we are so hung up on finding our soul mates? Had I found my mate and decided to leave him behind?

To Michael's credit, he hasn't called me, or touched base with me, or tried to reach me in any way since I left. It's nerve-wracking, really, because I don't entirely trust the man. No way, could he have stayed away all this time. And yet, since I left, I've never had the sensation of being watched. Or of being in any danger.

Likely, his alliance with JJ and Nikolai means neither of those clans are out to harm me in any way. I sink down on the grass, draw up my knees to my chest.

Has he taken over as Don? How is he finding it? He's gotten what he wanted, so he must be happy, I suppose. Does he miss me, though? My scent, my touch... *Stop.* I lean my chin on my knees and stare forward.

Something brushes against my leg and I find myself staring down at a cat... A Savannah with gleaming spots, pointed ears, a delicate face, and golden eyes that glare at me.

"Andy?" I cry. "Oh, my god, Andy. Where did you come from?"

I gather the cat close and he meows, rubs up against me again. I lower my knees and place him in my lap. I rub his head and he blinks, soaking up every second of the attention.

"I missed you boy, you know that?" I tickle him under his jaw and he yawns. He wriggles in my grasp and I allow him to jump down. He prowls away, to the side, to where a man is standing.

A tall man, with wide shoulders that shut out the scenery behind him. A man with cold, blue eyes fringed by the most beautiful eyelashes I have ever seen. His features are harsh, his nose hooked; his square jaw might as well be hewn from the rocks that are set into the side of the lawn I am seated on.

His chest is so wide that his suit jacket stretches across the front; a lean waist, trim hips that lead down to powerful thighs, clad in pants that are, surely, tailor-made for him. On his feet, he wears Italian loafers that have been polished to within an inch of their life.

The cat brushes up against him and he bends and picks up the animal. He cuddles it against his gorgeously cut jacket as he approaches me. Closer, closer. When he reaches me, he sinks down to sit next to me. He's careful enough to not touch me, keeping enough space for the breeze to fan the gap between us.

He places the cat down, and Andy pads over to lay down on the grass in front of us.

We sit there, quietly watching the sun come up over the city. Andy yawns and stretches. I reach out to pat him at the same time as the man next to me. Our fingers brush and goosebumps pop on my skin. The hair on the nape of my neck rises. I keep my hand where it is, and so does he. Neither of us moves. Then he curls his little finger around my thumb. The width of his digit is wider than mine. A shiver runs up my spine.

He waits, as if expecting me to move away. As if giving me time to retreat, but I don't. I stare at the contrast between the tan color of his skin and my much paler one.

He whispers his finger over to the center of the back of my hand, and my toes curl. He wraps his fingers around mine and my entire body seems to shudder. My stomach flip-flops, and every cell in my body seems to stretch and come alive as if they've been exposed to a jolt of electricity. He brings our joined hands up to his face. I follow the length of my arm to where he kisses the tips of my fingers, then raise my gaze to meet those searing, blue eyes.

"Karma," he whispers, "I love you."

37

Michael

Her features crumple and tears run down her cheeks. My heart stutters and the pulse pounds at my temples. I reach for her at the same time that she throws herself at me. I pull her into my lap, wrap my arms around her, yank her into my chest, as I surround her with every part of me I can.

"*Bellezza*," I murmur, "my Beauty, I missed you, my love."

She only cries harder and my heart feels like it's about to crack open.

"Please, Karma, don't cry," I plead. "I can't stand to see you like this, *piccola*."

She turns her face into my shirt, grabs handfuls, and holds on as if she can't bear to be parted again. I rock her and run my fingers across her hair, say words to soothe her that make no sense, but it doesn't seem to help.

I tuck her head under my chin, glance out at the now awakening city. "*She walks in beauty, like the night,*"

I begin to recite.

. . .

"Of cloudless climes and starry skies;
And all that's best of dark and bright."

Her sobs quieten.

"Meet in her aspect and her eyes;
Thus mellowed to that tender light
Which heaven to gaudy day denies."

She hiccups, then seems to compose herself.

"One shade the more, one ray the less,
Had half impaired the nameless grace
Which waves in every raven tress,
Or softly lightens o'er her face;"

I glance down to see her eyes closed as she listens.

"Where thoughts serenely sweet express,
How pure, how dear their dwelling-place."

I continue.

"And on that cheek, and o'er that brow,
So soft, so calm, yet eloquent,
The smiles that win, the tints that glow,
But tell of days in goodness spent,
A mind at peace with all below,
A heart whose love is innocent!"

. . .

She draws in a breath, then rubs her cheek against my shirt. We sit there in silence as the sun rises overhead. Finally, she stirs and looks up at me. Her eyes are swollen, her nose reddened by her crying jag. Her beautiful lips are pink and moist. I catch myself leaning in toward her and pull back. I tuck a strand of hair behind her ear and she shivers.

"Are you cold? I can give you my coat—"

"No," she shakes her head, "the heat of your body is all I need to keep warm. The scent of your skin is all I need to turn me on. The fire in your eyes..." she swallows, " is all I need to consume me. To take me. To mark me as your own. The darkness inside of you," she pushes her palm into my chest, "is my own. I know that now."

I tip her chin up, "When did you get so poetic?"

"Says the man who quotes Byron," her lips tremble in a ghost of a smile. "Why are you named after him?"

"It's a family tradition." I peer into her features, "Every first-born takes it as one of the given names."

"That whole four name thing... It's daunting." She blows out a breath, "Imagine giving birth to a baby and saddling him with a name that long."

"Would you have minded if I had done that with our child?"

She blinks rapidly and a lone tear slides down her cheek.

"*Cazzo!*" I didn't mean to bring that up.

"No, it's good," she swallows, "we should talk about it. It's healthy to talk about it, rather than hiding it away and pretending it didn't happen."

"I miss him" I murmur. "I miss our baby, and I never even knew him or her."

"Me too," she glances away, "sometimes I wake up from my sleep and am sure that I can hear the patter of a child's footsteps outside my bedroom door."

I draw in a breath. "Beauty," I cup her cheek, "I am so sorry for what happened."

"It's not your fault," she tips up her chin, "it is one of the reasons I felt like I had to leave, though."

My heart begins to race. Subconsciously, I had been aware that she may well blame me for the loss of our child, but hearing her say it aloud, makes my stomach knot.

"What were the other reasons?"

"Seeing you almost killed in front of me."

I open my mouth and she shakes her head, "I know, that's rich coming from someone who almost killed you." She raises a shoulder, "But things change. I stopped trying to get at you, but I forgot that there's an entire world out there who is out to get you."

"He's gone," I say in a low voice. "My father, who was the culprit behind everything that happened, is dead."

"The rival gangs—"

"I have made my peace with JJ and Nikolai. The Kane Company and the Bratva have proved themselves as my allies."

"There will be other gangs," she murmurs. "There will always be someone who'll want to get to you, who'll try to use me to get to you."

"That's the price I pay for my past." I square my shoulders, "It's where I come from, but..."

"But?"

"But it needn't be the future that we bring our children into."

"What are you saying?" she whispers, "Do you mean that—"

"With my father no longer involved in the Cosa Nostra, I have the chance to change the course of what is to come. I plan to legalize our businesses, something I have been working on for a while now."

"You have?"

I nod, "I have created a framework that I can use to capitalize both the real-world operations and the virtual businesses."

"But won't that counter the ground you have gained with the rival gangs? Surely, they are not going to be on board with that plan?"

I narrow my gaze on her. Beautiful and clever. This woman is more than capable of holding her own against my brothers, of going toe-to-toe with me, of partnering with me in the truest sense.

"Not if I show them that the legal businesses can be as lucrative as our illicit ones."

"Oh," she swallows, "you'd do that for me?"

"It won't be easy. And it will take some time to unravel the intricacies of our businesses, and a hell of a ton of paperwork to figure out the best way to legitimize them. But yeah," I nod, "I'd do it for us, for our children, for my brothers, so they have a chance to live life to the fullest. Without having to constantly protect themselves and their loved ones from the threat of danger."

"Mika," she whispers, "please don't think that I am forcing you to do this. I know I left you, but I never meant for it to act as some kind of coercion to make you give up your way of life."

"I am merely changing lanes." I rub my thumb across her cheek. "I am smart enough to know when I need to adapt and change with the times. It's something my father wasn't good at, and look where that got him."

"I am sorry you had to..." she swallows, "that you had to..."

"Kill him?" I blow out a breath, "Me too. I am probably going to hell for it, but... I am going to hell anyway, so..." I raise a shoulder.

"It's something you are going to have to come to terms with. He may have been responsible for so much evil, but he was still your flesh and blood."

"So was Xander." I firm my lips. "It's because of my father that my mother died so early. He is the one who kidnapped the Seven when they were boys."

"That... I suspected."

"You did?"

She nods. "When Summer told me that I needed a bodyguard because the Mafia may be after me...? Well, initially, I thought it was because my father had betrayed you guys, but then I realized, there was more to it than that." She tips up her chin, "Then, I met your father and realized just how evil he was. That he was capable of doing things that were so morally wrong... The kinds of things you and your brothers wouldn't be involved in. I guessed, then, that there had to be more of a connection between the Mafia and the Seven. That, possibly, the Mafia was behind their kidnapping when they were children. I couldn't reconcile you doing that. But your father? Now, he could be capable of anything."

"Including emotionally and physically abusing me and my brothers." I roll my shoulders, "It's because of him that we are so fucked up inside."

"You're not...fucked up." She bites the inside of her cheek, "Well, not completely, anyway."

I chuckle, "Is that a compliment?"

"Would it be terrible if I admitted that your twisted-upness is what attracted me to you in the first place?"

"Is that right?" I can't stop the smirk that curls my lips.

She glances away, "This doesn't mean I have forgiven you for everything you did, or that I am returning to you."

"You are, though."

"I am?" She frowns.

"You bet." I slide my hand inside my pocket and withdraw her wedding ring. I slide it onto her left ring finger and we both stare at it. "Admit that you missed the weight of it on your finger, that you —" I lower her onto the grass, on her back, and push my body between her legs, "miss the weight of me between your thighs?"

Her pupils dilate as I push the evidence of my arousal — which has been stretching my crotch since I sat down next to her — into her center.

I grind into her and she moans. I begin to dry hump her and she shudders. I press my thumb in between her lips and thrust it inside her mouth in an action that mirrors what I want to do to her when I am finally inside her. Her entire body shudders. She sucks on my thumb and the blood rushes to my groin.

"Fuck," I growl. "F-u-c-k, *Bellezza*, what you do to me with your little cries, your moans, the way you wriggle your body against mine, in a sign that you are aroused."

"I am not aroused," she protests.

"Is that right?" I slide my finger down her waistband, inside her panties and thrust my finger inside her.

She gasps. "Oh, hell," she warbles, "oh, bloody hell."

"Indeed." I pull out my finger, glistening with the evidence of her arousal, and bring it to my mouth. I suck on it and a whine bleeds from her.

"What do you want, Beauty?" I lower my voice to a hush, "Tell me."

"You," she swallows, "I want you."

That's when Andy prowls over to us.

38

Karma

Andy crawls onto my chest. He coils between my breasts and tips his head up. He must glare at Michael, who glowers back at him. "You and I need to have a talk, buddy. You don't interrupt when your parents are in the middle of an important discussion."

"Is that what this was?"

He scowls at me over Andy's head, "It was a very important discussion." His gaze intensifies, "Come home with me, baby."

I swallow.

"I've been lonely without you. Andy has been lonely without you."

"Andy seems fine to me." I arch my eyebrow at him. "You, however," I tilt my hips forward so I push into the bulge between his legs.

Color smears his cheeks. "You still punishing me? Even after everything I said I'd do for you?"

"Not what I expected to hear from you, Don." I rake my gaze across his features, "You are the Don now, aren't you?"

"Only if I can have you by my side. I need your sass, your shrewdness, your ability to think fast on your feet so you pick up anything that I may have missed. I need you, Beauty, only you."

He holds my gaze and in his blue eyes I see…love, lust…and sincerity. An honesty that had been missing before, a vulnerability which I'd never thought that I'd glimpse in my Don's gaze.

"Okay," I blow out a breath, "okay."

Two days later, I rub Andy's forehead as I glance out at the sea that stretches out in front of me. Michael had taken me from the park, straight to his private jet. He'd flown me to Palermo, and to a new home that he'd purchased on the island on the opposite side from where his home used to be.

A fresh start, he'd said. A new chapter in our lives. He'd also arranged for a doctor to come and remove the tracker from behind my ear. I had protested and told him that, in retrospect, it actually made me feel safe to know that no matter what happened he'd always be able to find me.

He'd told me that he'd feel better if he had it removed, especially since he wanted us to try for a child right away, and he didn't want anything to interfere with that.

So I had agreed.

Truth is, I want to try to get pregnant straight away, too. Guess this is when I should have come clean to him about the doctor's warning that it could be dangerous for me to get pregnant. On the other hand, the doc had also said that many women carried their babies to term without any problems, despite having a hole in the heart. And I know if I mention it to him, he won't want to take the risk. And honestly, I feel it in my guts that everything will be fine. That things will work out. So, I haven't said anything to him.

Yes, I know, I should be honest with him... But if I were...he'd never agree to my having a baby. He'd never allow me to get pregnant. He'd be willing to go without an heir, and that's something I will not allow.

Besides, I can do this. I can get pregnant and carry the baby to term and nothing will happen to me. I am confident of that.

Meanwhile, he's already set up a full-fledged studio for me in the house, where I can start working on my masterpieces. All, in less than forty-eight hours. The man is relentless when it comes to making sure that all of my needs are taken care of.

And when I had suggested we have the long overdue Christmas party, combined with a New Year's Eve one—he had agreed to it.

I'd also messaged Summer to let her know that I was fine, but that I needed a little more time to figure things out. Summer was initially upset about it. She'd insisted that I return to London or she'd be on the next flight to Sicily and drag me home.

I'd told her not to do that. Begged her to give me a little more time. I'd told her that I am in love with this guy. I'd wanted to tell her that I'd already married the man. Honestly, it had been on the tip of my tongue to tell her, but then I had chickened out. Because I know that she'll be upset to find out that I got married without telling her. And then she'll want to know everything and …

I'm still not ready to share with her all that has happened. No, I want to tell her everything in person. And yes… I am also a little worried about her reaction. She's never going to forgive me for embarking on this adventure on my own, and without keeping her completely in the loop… And I know, the more I put it off, the worse it's going to get…so… Yeah, for the moment, at least, I am okay with her. But at some point, I am going to have to tell her everything. Soon. Just not today.

Footsteps sound behind me. The scent of fresh snow, of darkness, of edgy testosterone, washes over me a second before his arms come around my waist. Andy wriggles in my arms, then digs his claws into my shirt as he attempts to climb up my chest. He peers over my shoulder, growls at my husband. Michael growls right back. Andy stiffens, then hisses at him. He turns his head away, wriggles in my arms, then proceeds to jump out and onto the wall of the terrace.

"That cat is the most fickle creature I have ever met." His dark voice coils in my ear.

I shiver, then turn in the circle of his arms, "He's my cat; of course, his loyalties lie with me. Speaking of," I frown, "did you just growl back at him?"

"He needs to learn that he can't monopolize my wife's attention."

"Are you jealous of a cat, Michael Byron Domenico Sovrano?"

"Uh, oh," he smirks, "do you know how much of a turn on it is when you say my complete name?"

I slide my hand between us and cup the bulge at his crotch, "I am beginning to guess."

He pushes into me and my hips touch the wall behind me. He tilts his hips so I can feel every single ridge of his length against my palm. Heat coils in my belly and moisture laces my panties.

"You're so damn sexy, you know that?"

"I am, aren't I?" He smirks.

I laugh, "And not modest at all."

"Can't afford to be, in my line of work, baby."

My smile promptly vanishes. "How are the talks going with JJ and Nikolai? Are they agreeable to legitimizing the businesses?"

"Not completely," he raises a shoulder, "but I am sure I'll win them over."

"Like I said, not modest at all."

"They'll come around. They'll have to, when they see that the figures make sense. This is an opportunity for them to carve out a future that is safer for their families too, after all."

"You think they'll agree to that?"

"They will, once we've figured out the practicalities of how to manage the transition."

"Meanwhile," he lowers his head so his eyelashes entangle against mine, "where were we?"

He drags his palms up my hips and his fingertips brush against the bandage across my lower back.

I freeze; so does he.

"What's this?" He scowls, "Did you hurt yourself?"

"N...no," I tip up my chin, "I, ah, wanted to add something to what you marked on my back earlier.

"Can I see?"

I nod, then turn my back on him. He raises my shirt, stares down at the strip of clear plastic which covers my lower back.

His breath catches. "Beauty, you..." his voice cracks. "you wrote my name on your body?"

"I wanted to..." I glance at him over my shoulder again, "I wanted to find a way to ink your name into my skin and this seemed fitting.

"Mika's whore," he reads out aloud. "You shouldn't have hurt yourself further, this way."

"It's a hurt that I gladly bear," I say softly. "I needed to show you that I meant it, that this time, I am not leaving you. That you are stuck with me, Don."

He swivels me around in the circle of his arms. "My whore," he kisses my forehead, "my slut," he kisses me on one eyelid, "my pussy," then the other. "My Beauty," he kisses me on the tip of my nose. "Mine." He presses his lips to mine. "Only mine."

I share his breath, drag his scent into my lungs, and my entire core clenches. I lean in to deepen the kiss when.

"Get a room, you guys!"

Seb's voice sounds behind us.

Michael groans. "Ignore him," he murmurs as he presses his lips to mine. I open my mouth and his tongue sweeps in. He deepens the kiss and my belly trembles. He hauls me up against him, and I pull my hand out from between us and wind it about his shoulders. He pushes his hips forward and the thickness between his legs stabs into my core.

A whine bleeds from my lips and he swallows it down. He grabs my arse, squeezes, and heat jolts up my spine. I press myself into him and my breasts flatten against his chest. He nibbles on my lips and I can't stop the moan the spills from my lips.

"Michael," I gasp, "we need to stop. Your brothers... Your family will be here soon."

"The fuck I care?"

"Michelangelo!" Nonna calls out, and both of us freeze.

Michael steps back, peers into my face. "To be continued," he smirks.

Then, as if he can't stop himself, he leans down and presses a hard kiss to my lips. He slides around to stand behind me, then places his hands on my shoulders. I glance toward the entrance where Nonna stands, a knowing look on her face. Seb and Massimo flank her. Seb smirks. Massimo looks like he's about to say something, then seems to change his mind.

Nonna walks toward us and I stiffen. Not that I am afraid of her, but I am definitely wary of her. Despite the fact that the last time we met, she seemed almost friendly. And of course, I am the Don's wife now... But she's the Don's grandmother, so in that sense, she still has influence over my husband. Still, I know Michael's too smart to let his grand-mother manipulate him into anything, but Nonna's w-a-a-y too astute. It's why I am not sure what to make of her yet.

Michael wraps an arm around my waist, still keeping the lower part of his body hidden behind mine.

"What are you doing?" I hiss. "Why don't you walk forward and meet her?"

"Because if I did that, everyone would know just how aroused I still am from kissing my wife."

"Oh." Heat flushes my cheeks.

"Exactly," he chuckles and the sound pulls at my nerve endings. My toes curl and I have to glance away. Damn it, I am turned on and his Nonna is watching us with a curious gaze as she approaches us.

She pauses in front of us, then takes my hand in hers, "Thank you for organizing this delayed Christmas get together." Her lips tilt in a smile that is—dare I say, quite genuine?

"Thank you for coming, Nonna." I step forward. Michael removes his hand from around me and I kiss Nonna's cheek. Her skin is papery thin, and she seems more fragile than when I last saw her.

Guess burying a son can do that to you? Michael had decided to bury his father with full honors. I hadn't been in Sicily to attend it, but I'd heard that the funeral itself had been attended by all the clan leaders. Cassandra had mentioned to me that Nonna had been pale-faced and ashen throughout the funeral, but she had managed to stay dry-eyed until the end. Maybe she had shed her tears in private. She seems genuinely pleased to be here though, so that's something.

"You don't think that this was too soon after what happened with Xander do you?"

She pauses, a considering look on her face, "Perhaps for a more traditional person it might seem that way," she murmurs. "And it's not that I don't mourn him," she swallows, "but I also know that Xander would not have wanted us to dwell on the past. He was an artist, a dreamer, a visionary, even. He would have wanted us to celebrate his life and look to the future."

I peer into her features, take in the intent expression on her face, "You mean it, don't you?"

"I never say anything I don't mean, Karma." She smiles. "In fact, I am going to follow your example." Her eyes gleam with that devilish glint that is so familiar. Something I have seen in Michael's eyes, too.

"You are?" I frown.

"Absolutely." She glances between us, "This family has been through so much, we need a fresh start. A chance to know each other all over again."

Oh, hell, do I even want to know where this is going?

"What are you thinking of, Nonna?" Michael asks.

"A Christmas getaway."

"Christmas is over," Michael points out, "and we're already having this delayed Christmas get together to make up for not being able to celebrate Christmas."

"It's not enough." Her lips firm. "It will take more than a few hours to mend the fractures left behind by your father. It's time we came together and found a way to heal, don't you think?"

Michael blows out a breath, "Are you sure about this?"

"Are you questioning me, Michael?" she asks in a deceptively soft tone that mirrors the one Michael often uses to get his way.

Michael stiffens, then a reluctant chuckle rumbles up his chest. "You are one hell of a woman, Nonna." He reaches around me to take her hand, "If it will make you happy..."

"It will." The older woman nods her head as a smile forms on her face. "Now that you are married," she glances between us, "it's time for me to focus on getting the rest of your brothers hitched, too."

Michael groans, "I'm glad I am no longer in the line of fire."

"You were smart enough to snap up your soulmate when you met her. Now, I need to make sure your brothers follow your lead. Also," that same wicked gleam reappears in her eyes, "I'm hoping that spending a few days in each other's company will help us strengthen our familial ties... If we don't kill each other first, that is."

I chuckle, Michael laughs, and Nonna's face lights up with a proper smile. "Now, where's my drink?"

As if summoned, Cassandra walks toward us with a tray of prosecco flutes. I take a glass and hand it to Nonna. She accepts it, sniffs it, then raises her eyebrows at me. "Is this — ?"

I nod, "It's your favorite."

I take a glass for myself, then smile my thanks at Cassandra. She turns, then stops when Adrian walks onto the terrace. She seems to steel herself, then walks past him. He turns and his gaze tracks her until she disappears from sight. He turns, catches me staring and a small smile tugs at his lips. He walks over to the bar just as Luca steps onto the terrace. He glances around and his gaze collides with Michael's. The tension in the air ratchets up. I glance over my shoulder to find Michael scowling.

"Be nice, Don," I murmur.

He blows out a breath. "It's going to take some getting used to, but family is family after all, eh?" He walks past me and meets Luca halfway on the terrace. The two men murmur in low voices, then Michael jerks his chin. "Get us some Macallan," he calls out to Massimo, who's behind the bar. Massimo raises his thumb in a 'will do' gesture, then goes back to pouring.

"Good to see Michael making an effort," I remark.

Nonna turns to me, "You're good for him."

"Oh?" I meet her gaze, "Are you being sarcastic?"

"Do I look like I am being sarcastic?" She tilts her head. Her faded blue eyes twinkle, and again, I see so much of Michael in her that I can't stop the smile that curves my lips.

"No," I chuckle, "that sounds like a real compliment."

"It is." Nonna raises her glass, and so do I. We clink, and I take a sip. Notes of cherry and vanilla pop on my palate as the crisp taste of the Prosecco slides down my throat.

"Mmm," I lick my lips, "that's so good."

"My husband used to get me a bottle for every celebration." She stares at her flute with a soft look in her eyes. "Roberto was a typical Mafioso, as macho as they come, but he always remembered what I liked."

"He loved you?"

"He did," she raises her glass to her lips, "in his own way." She glances past me and frowns. "Who is that with Christian?"

I turn to find Christian walking into the family gathering, Aurora's arm tucked into his, his hand on hers. Either in a soothing gesture...or in one meant to control her, maybe?

He pauses a little way inside of the entrance. When Cassandra walks over with a full tray of Prosecco, he picks up a flute and hands it to Aurora, who accepts it. She's also wearing a beautiful silk dress that clings to her curves and flows to below her knees. On her feet are six-inch heels which are very different from the sensible wedges I normally see her in. She seems...different... Like a mafioso's woman. She glances at me, then away.

Huh? What's happening here?

Aurora downs the prosecco in one go. She places the glass back on Cassandra's tray, reaches for another, but Christian wraps his fingers around her wrist and stops her. He leans in, whispers something in her ear as Cassandra walks away.

Aurora shoots him a glance full of hatred; Christian chuckles.

What the hell? What's happening between these two?

Christian straightens, then he turns and walks toward us.

"Christian Roberto Domenico Sovrano," Nonna narrows her gaze on him, "just the person I am looking for."

Christian frowns, "I am?" He comes to a stop in front of us, Aurora in tow.

Nonna's eyes gleam, "I am an old woman, Christian, I don't know how long I have left on this earth."

"Nonna, please," Christian holds up his hand, "you are going to outlive us all and you know it. So why don't you come to the point, hmm? What's on your mind?"

"What's on my mind is that I am worried about you Christian."

"You are?"

She nods, "It's high time you got married and settled down."

"Michael just got married," Christian points out.

"And now I can't wait for you to settle down."

"What about Massimo?" Christian scowls, "he's older than me. Shouldn't he get married before I do."

"Massimo didn't lose his twin, you did."

Christian pales, "Nonna, what are you trying to say?"

Nonna narrows her gaze on him, "Since before you were born you had Xander by your side. Now he's gone and you are on your own."

Christian's jaw tics, "your point being?" He finally says through gritted teeth.

"I don't want you to be alone. In fact I have someone who would make you the perfect wife, I —"

Christian holds up his hand, "Let me stop you right there, Nonna."

Nonna scowls, "Let me complete what I am going to say."

"I know what you are going to say, and I am a step ahead of you." His lips curl.

Uh-oh! I am not sure I like the expression on his face. He seems too confident, too sure of himself. He releases his hold on Aurora only to wrap his arm around her and pull her close.

"Nonna," He tilts his head, before he locks his gaze with Michael's. "Don Sovrano," his smile widens, "meet the woman who is going to be my wife."

To find out what happens next read Christian & Aurora's story HERE.

Read an excerpt

Aurora

"Open the door!" The banging on the main door reaches me. I stare at the coffee-table wedged against it. It'll hold the door, surely, won't it? I glance around the living room space, but can't see any means of escaping. Not that I haven't checked every inch of this house in the last few weeks that I have been held here as a prisoner. Every window is barred and the door to the terrace on the first floor is sealed tight. The only way in or out of this house is through the front door. The door on which the man who is trying to enter is currently leaning his weight.

Shit!" The double doors creaks as he puts his shoulder to it.

"Open the fucking door, Aurora, or else I'm gonna break it down."

"Who—" My voice cracks, and I clear my throat, "Who's there?"

"You know who it is. Who else comes to this house, except me?" Christian's voice lowers to a growl, "When I get through, I am going to teach you such a lesson, you are not going to be able to sit down for days."

"Oh?" My stomach trembles. "OH!" I blink as the full meaning of his words sinks in. My heart rate ratchets up and moisture laces my core. I should not find that so hot. Why do I find that such a turn on?

"How can I be sure who it is, if you don't tell me who you are? Not like I can recognize your voice or anything, you know."

"Is that right?" His tone is almost lazy now.

Like he's realized I am playing a game and has decided to go along with it. My belly twists. I rub my damp hands on my thighs. Why the hell did I decide to stop him from coming in? I should have known it was going to be futile, that nothing I say or do would deter him.

The door creaks again, pushes against the coffee table, which moves forward by an inch.

"Oh, hell!" I race toward the coffee table, push against it to hold it in place. Something slams into the door from the other side, and again. The double doors shudder, the bolt across the door shivers, and the coffee table moves forward by another inch. I yelp, take a step back.

"Don't fucking make me wait, Aurora," Christian growls.

I shiver. Even through the heavy wood of the double doors, the menace rolls off of his voice. Goosebumps pop on my skin. My toes curl. Shit, this should not turn me on so much.

That...that mean edge to his tone, the promise of punishment when he finally gets through... I shouldn't want it so much.

"Last chance, Aurora. Open the door or—"

"Or," I call out, "what are you going to do, eh?"

"Do you really want to find out?" He lowers his voice to a hush, but I can still hear him. "Do you, Aurora?"

Yes.

Yes.

"No," I yell back, "I am tired of being kept a prisoner here. Tired of being held without anyone telling me how long I am going to be here."

There's silence for a beat, then another.

"It's why I've come here," he retorts, "to tell you what's going to happen next."

"Do you think I am going to believe you?"

"I hope you are standing clear, Aurora," he says in a low pitched voice. "I am coming through."

I straighten, stare at the door. He's joking. He's not really going to batter down that door, is he?

"Get back, Aurora!" he growls. "Now!"

I jump, stumble back, just as he smashes into the door. The wood creaks, groans. The coffee table I've wedged against the door screeches forward. I yelp, slide back a few more steps. Just in time. For there's another crash.

The entire door whines, then the doors fly off the hinges.

I scream, turn and race toward the bedroom, then close the door and bolt it. I sink down against it, and my shoulders shudder.

Shit, shit, shit. What is wrong with me? Why did I try to shut him out? I should have known I couldn't win, that he'd find a way to come inside. But the truth is, I am tired of sitting here in this house, trying to figure out what is going to happen to me next. Tired of not knowing my fate. Tired of being punished for helping out my friend Karma. She'd wanted to escape her husband, the then Capo—now Don Michael Sovrano, and of course, I couldn't say no to helping her.

I'd known how dangerous it was to do so. To go against the leader of the Cosa Nostra is to bring death to yourself and to your family… I'd known it, and yet, something in me had not been able to turn her down. I'd recognized another woman in need and something in me had snapped.

Maybe it's all the time spent as a woman in the heart of the Mafia. Knowing that we are often seen as disposable. Interchangeable. Good only to procreate, as wives as mistresses, as objects to be lusted after, but never respected as individuals with our own minds, who could control our own destinies.

And you know what? I, sure as hell, am going to control my future… At least, that's what I had thought… That's what I had aimed for during all of my years growing up. And while the Capo had paid off my father's debts and paid for me to go to medical school in London, and I had accepted it then...because it had seemed like the only way to find my way out of the situation that I had been born into — I don't owe him anything. Right?

Clearly, he'd done it so he could indenture my family, ensure that he'd bought our loyalty and those of any future generations. Only I am not going to accept my fate.

It was this streak of defiance in me that had urged me to help Karma. I had treated her when she'd been brought into the hospital in Palermo. She'd been faking the illness, of course, as she'd warned me she would. I had examined her, nevertheless, so the situation would appear as genuine as possible — and discovered that she was pregnant.

I hadn't been able to stop myself from revealing that to her husband. We had returned to her room and found her gone... And the Capo would have killed me on the spot except... His brother, Christian had intervened. He'd saved my life that day, and I suppose, I should be grateful for it.

Only, I am not sure about his intentions toward me. Since that day, he's shadowed me wherever I go. Oh, he hasn't made a move on me or anything like that... I wish he would. That way, I'd know what he wants from me. No, he simply watches me with that gray-blue gaze of his that seems to peer into my soul.

He's the person who accompanied me when I went to see Karma while she was pregnant.

She'd lost her child in an unfortunate incident when her car had been rigged with a bomb which, luckily for her, had turned out to be a defective. Although it had killed Xander, Christian's twin. Turned out, it was their father who was behind it. Michael had ended up killing his father, and becoming Don, and Christian is now even more firmly entrenched in the inner circle of the leader of the Cosa Nostra. So the question is, why is this man, who can have any woman in the city — hell, on the continent, even — beating down the door to my bedroom?

"Go away," I yell as I slap my hands on my ears. "Get the hell away from me...you...you asshole!"

"Now, play nice, Flower," Christian drawls. I can hear him from the other side of the door. Hell, I can all but feel the heat of his body as it permeates through the wood, which is likely my imagination. But every time I've been near him, it's as if I've stepped past a furnace. The man has so much vitality, he can probably light up an entire Christmas tree by his proximity. I snort.

That's fanciful thinking. Probably because I spent Christmas Day shut up in here, feeling sorry for myself. Hell, even criminals in jails get to celebrate Christmas. I had spent it locked up here, and except for the brief time on Christmas Eve when Christian had come in to check on me and had lent me his phone so I could call Karma, I had been alone. At least, I hadn't starved. The fridge had been full of food, as had the pantry, so there was more than enough to eat. Still, it didn't fill the void left by being alone, on the one day of the year when every family is together.

Karma had wanted to organize a Christmas gathering, but Xander's death, and then her losing her baby, had put paid to that. Christian had updated me that she was spending time in London, had even given me his phone so I could speak with her. A favor I hadn't wanted to accept, but which I didn't turn down, starved of company as I had been.

But everyone has a limit, and I have reached mine. No way, am I going to allow myself to be shut up inside here. I want to leave this prison, go see my family, lead a normal life...or else... I am willing to die. Yeah, not being dramatic here...

When you live in the heart of the Mafia community, death is as much a part of life as going out to dinner is. And I...like it or not, am one of them.

I grew up surrounded by macho guys who think they own the world. And you know what? I have spent enough time among them to be able to play them at their own game. I am not going to let one of them scare me, no matter that he happens to be big, brooding and growly, and sexy and...hot...and that he turns me on by just a glance. I am not going to let my attraction to him get in the way. No. I am going to tell him exactly where he can shove this awareness he seems to have for me, the one which has him pushing his shoulder into the door and applying his weight so the entire barrier shakes.

"Open the door, Flower," he rumbles, "or I am going to break this down and come inside and then you are going to regret shutting me out."

Is that right? I jump up to my feet, tuck my elbows into my side.

"Last chance," he warns. "Open. The. Door."

I spin around, unlock the door and yank it open. Just as he lunges forward.

Christian

I dive forward just as she pulls the door open. I careen through the doorway and toward her, managing to swerve at the last minute. Still I don't avoid her completely, and my shoulder brushes hers. She yells out in surprise and her body hurtles toward the floor. I grab her, manage to get my body under hers as we hit the floor, with her on top of me.

The back of my head hits the floor and the breath rushes out of me. Or it may be because of the soft curves that tremble against my chest, her breath that shivers against my throat, her sweet scent like honey-suckle and crushed rose petals that teases my nostrils and goes straight to my head. The blood rushes to my groin, my cock thickens. She pushes off of me, or at least tries to, for I've thrown my arm around her waist and held her in place.

"Let me go," she snarls.

"No," I sit up wince when the bump on the back of my head protests. I ignore the pain, push myself up to standing, still holding her close."

"What the hell are you doing?" She hisses as I head further into the house with her in my arms.

"Let me the hell go," she slaps her palm against my chest, "Right now."

"Fine." I lower my arms and she hits the floor on her ass.

"Ow!" She grunts, then stares up at me, a shocked expression on her face. "You... you dropped me?" She stutters, "Like honest to god, you allowed me to crash to the floor?"

"You asked me to let you go," I remind her, "I was only obliging you."

"Asshole," She snaps, then pushes up to stand to her full height, which still means she hits somewhere below my breastbone.

Gesü Christo, but she's tiny, and also very angry right now. Her cheeks are flushed, her hair awry about her features. She pushes a strand away from her face and scowls at me, "you're a dick, you know that?"

"Glad you recognized that."

"Argh!" She makes a noise at the back of her throat, "and insuffer-able, not to mention you're so full of yourself that if anyone were to prick your skin, you'd take off."

"Take off?"

"Yeah, all that hot air which you carry around would catapult you into the stratosphere, no doubt."

I glare at her, then can't stop the surprised chuckle that rumbles up my chest, "You're funny," I murmur.

"You're annoying."

'You're on my turf."

"You're in my house," She shoots back.

"A house you're in thanks to my having intervened on your behalf. If not you'd be dead by now."

Her features flush further, "should I be grateful to you for that? I bet you have your reasons for having stepped in."

"At least you are smart," I curl my lips, "So you'll realize that I am being very serious when I said that I am going to punish you."

"Whatever," She huffs, "Why are you here anyway?"

"It's my place remember? I can come and go as I want."

She seems like she is about to say something, then changes her mind. She pivots and walks into the room. I shut the door and follow her into the kitchen. She reaches the *Bialetti* - the espresso maker, tops it up with coffee powder and places it on the stove. She reaches for two cups and saucers, places them on the counter, then turns to me. "What do you want from me?"

"Marry me."

"What?" Her gaze widens, "What did you say?"

"Marry me," I allow my smile to widen, "not for real, of course."

"Of course," She nods, "So you want me to pretend to marry you?"

"For 30 days."

"What happens in thirty days?"

"I am able to convince my older brother and my Nonna that we are really serious about each other. After which time, you are free to go your own way."

"So if I leave after that how can you convince them that we are serious about each other."

"You're right."

"I am?" She scowls.

"Sixty days," I cross my arms over my chest.

"What the--!" She gapes, "you added on an entire month?"

I raise a shoulder, "It's going to take that long for us to convince them that we are in love with each other."

"But we are not," she points out.

"Given that I am incapable of falling in love, that's a foregone conclusion."

"Is that right?" Her gaze narrows.

"Which is why when we decide to separate, no one will raise an eyebrow. In fact given that by the we'd have proved to be incompatible it will be all too believable that," I peer into her face, "our marriage was a complete mistake."

"And what's the benefit of that?"

"That they won't bother me about getting married to anyone else for a long time after that."

She purses her lips, "Somehow I can't see you being bothered by anyone about being married."

"Have you met my Nonna?" I tilt my head, "She's been planning our weddings from the moment each of us were born, and now that Michael's married and with Xander's passing..." I firm my lips.

"You were saying?" She prompts.

"Nothing," I straighten my spine, "fake marriage, you and I, that's all you need to know."

"Hmm," She takes in my features, "and what's in it for me?"

I glare at her, "Really?" I snap, "you dare ask me that?"

She pales, but doesn't glance away, "yes," she says in a firm voice, "I need to know what's in it for me."

I take a step toward her and she leans back, only there's nowhere for her to go for she presses back and into the counter. I close the distance between us, plant my hands on the counter and cage her in.

"You were saying?"

"I was asking a question actually," she tips up her chin, "what's in it for me, Christian?"

I peer into her features, and her pupils dilate. Her brown eyes lighten until they seem almost golden in this light. I lean in closer until my breath raises the hair other forehead. I run my finger down the side of her cheek and she shivers, "Don't," She murmurs, "Don't try to distract me."

"Oh, so I do distract you?"

"Don't change the topic."

I step back and the breath rushes out of her, "your life, Aurora, you get a new lease of life."

"So," she furrows her forehead, "if I acted as your fake wife for sixty days, I'll be free to leaves and live as I want."

No.

No.

I nod, slowly. "If you fulfill all the conditions and if you put up enough of a performance that my Nonna and my brothers are convinced of the veracity of our relationship."

She bites down on her lower lip and hell if my gaze isn't drawn to her glistening flesh. Why the hell does this woman affect me so? She's only a convenience after all? Someone to use and discard. So I can go back to the life I prefer to lead. To be surrounded by enough pussy so I can forget the I lost my twin brother. The other half of my soul. The one who's been with me since before we were born. Xander and I were so different yet so alike. He was the artist, and I was the numbers guy. It's why steering the finances of the Cosa Nostra fell to me.

If there's one thing I am good at, it's getting the numbers to speak to me. Numbers don't lie. They can't hide. They can't hurt you like our father had. After our oldest brother Michael had left to study in the States, my father had turned his anger on our mother, and onto us. Luca our second oldest brother got the brunt of it. Massimo our middle brother was already getting to the big and tall enough that our father didn't dare hurt him. But me and Xander? We were still small and young enough, that he knew he could hurt us without fear of retaliation.

I had been older had tried to protect him from being physically beaten up by our father and I had mostly succeeded. I still had the scars to show for it too… I had saved him then, but when he was targeted by the car bomb that our own father had rigged his car with… I hadn't been able to go to his rescue then. The car bomb had been faulty but a piece of metal had embedded in his chest and killed him on the spot. Michael's wife Karma had been in the car and she had managed to escape, but she had been pregnant and lost her child. We had all suffered… but losing Xander, it was a trauma that haunted me, that stuck to me, that accompanied me day and night like a shadow which refused to peel away from me. I'd never be the same again, never be able to see myself in the mirror without seeing my twin brother. Never be able to experience life without thinking that he'd never be able to see, smell, taste life. It should have been me who died in that incident, not him.

Me who was buried under the earth, not him.

I didn't deserve any happiness, not when Xander wouldn't get to experience it.

I should turn away from life itself... except that's not Xander would have wanted. It's for him that I will continue living... didn't mean I had to let myself feel though. It's for him that I would support my family, help Michael consolidate his position as the new Don of the Cosa Nostra. Michael had killed our father... too bad I hadn't had the opportunity to do so. I should have felt some level of satisfaction considering it was our father who had been behind rigging the car, the reason that Xander had died... but all I feel is a numbness. Like I am not in my body. Like nothing else matters except, trying to get through life. Trying to swallow down the grief the threatens to overwhelm my every waking moment. And her... how dare she try to infiltrate the nothingness that I have surrounded myself in since Xander died? Why is it that thoughts of her occupy my mind when I should have only space to mourn Xander?

"And if I don't?" She tips up her chin. "What if I disagree?"

I move so fast that she flinches. I wrap my fingers around her throat and haul her up to her toes. "I don't recall giving you a choice, Flower."

She swallows and I feel the movement against my fingers. Such a slender throat. How would it feel to have my cock sliding down it, hmm?

I tighten my grip and the color fades from her cheeks. A soft sound emerges from her mouth. She parts her lips and I take in her flushed features, the contours of her pouty lower lip and my balls throb. Fuck this, why the hell should I deny myself when I am going to marry her anyway... only temporarily of course. Still... soon she will be my wife and I am going to take full advantage of it. I pull her even closer until her breasts are flush against my chest, then I lower my mouth to her's.

To find out what happens next read Christian and Aurora's story in A Very Mafia Christmas HERE

Want to be the first to find out about L. Steele's new release? Join her newsletter here

Read an excerpt from Summer & Sinclair's story in The Billionaire's Fake Wife

Summer

"Slap, slap, kiss, kiss."

"Huh?" I stare up at the bartender.

"Aka, there's a thin line between love and hate." He shakes out the crimson liquid into my glass.

"Nah." I snort. "Why would she allow him to control her, and after he insulted her?"

"It's the chemistry between them." He lowers his head, "You have to admit that when the man is arrogant and the woman resists, it's a challenge to both of them, to see who blinks first, huh?"

"Why?" I wave my hand in the air, "Because they hate each other?"

"Because," he chuckles, "the girl in school whose braids I pulled and teased mercilessly, is the one who I—"

"Proposed to?" I huff.

His face lights up. "You get it now?"

Yeah. No. A headache begins to pound at my temples. This crash course in pop psychology is not why I came to my favorite bar in Islington, to meet my best friend, who is—I glance at the face of my phone—thirty minutes late.

I inhale the drink, and his eyebrows rise.

"What?" I glower up at the bartender. "I can barely taste the alcohol. Besides, it's free drinks at happy hour for women, right?"

"Which ends in precisely" he holds up five fingers, "minutes."

"Oh! Yay!" I mock fist pump. "Time enough for one more, at least."

A hiccough swells my throat and I swallow it back, nod.

One has to do what one has to do... when everything else in the world is going to shit.

A hot sensation stabs behind my eyes; my chest tightens. Is this what people call growing up?

The bartender tips his mixing flask, strains out a fresh batch of the ruby red liquid onto the glass in front of me.

"Salut." I nod my thanks, then toss it back. It hits my stomach and tendrils of fire crawl up my spine, I cough.

My head spins. Warmth sears my chest, spreads to my extremities. I can't feel my fingers or toes. Good. Almost there. "Top me up."

"You sure?"

"Yes." I square my shoulders and reach for the drink.

"No. She's had enough."

"What the—?" I pivot on the bar stool.

Indigo eyes bore into me.

Fathomless. Black at the bottom, the intensity in their depths grips me. He swoops out his arm, grabs the glass and holds it up. Thick fingers dwarf the glass. Tapered at the edges. The nails short and buff. *All the better to grab you with.* I gulp.

"Like what you see?"

I flush, peer up into his face.

Hard cheekbones, hollows under them, and a tiny scar that slashes at his left eyebrow. *How did he get that?* Not that I care. My gaze slides to his mouth. Thin upper lip, a lower lip that is full and cushioned. Pouty with a hint of bad boy. *Oh!* My toes curl. My thighs clench.

The corner of his mouth kicks up. *Asshole.*

Bet he thinks life is one big smug-fest. I glower, reach for my glass, and he holds it up and out of my reach.

I scowl, "Gimme that."

He shakes his head.

"That's my drink."

"Not anymore." He shoves my glass at the bartender. "Water for her. Get me a whiskey, neat."

I splutter, then reach for my drink again. The barstool tips, in his direction. This is when I fall against him, and my breasts slam into his hard chest, sculpted planes with layers upon layers of muscle that ripple and writhe as he turns aside, flattens himself against the bar. The floor rises up to meet me.

What the actual hell?

I twist my torso at the last second and my butt connects with the surface. *Ow!*

The breath rushes out of me. My hair swirls around my face. I scrabble for purchase, and my knee connects with his leg.

"Watch it." He steps around, stands in front of me.

"You stepped aside?" I splutter. "You let me fall?"

"Hmph."

I tilt my chin back, all the way back, look up the expanse of muscled thigh that stretches the silken material of his suit. *What is he wearing? Could any suit fit a man with such precision?* Hand crafted on Saville Row, no doubt. I glance at the bulge that tents the fabric between his legs. *Oh!* I blink.

Look away, look away. I hold out my arm. He'll help me up at least, won't he?

He glances at my palm, then turns away. *No, he didn't do that, no way.*

A glass of amber liquid appears in front of him. He lifts the tumbler to his sculpted mouth.

His throat moves, strong tendons flexing. He tilts his head back, and the column of his neck moves as he swallows. Dark hair covers his chin —it's a discordant chord in that clean-cut profile, I shiver. He would scrape that rough skin down my core. He'd mark my inner thigh, lick my core, thrust his tongue inside my melting channel and drink from my pussy. *Oh! God.* Goosebumps rise on my skin.

No one has the right to look this beautiful, this achingly gorgeous. Too magnificent for his own good. Anger coils in my chest.

"Arrogant wanker."

"I'll take that under advisement."

"You're a jerk, you know that?"

He presses his lips together. The grooves on either side of his mouth deepen. Jesus, clearly the man has never laughed a single day in his life. Bet that stick up his arse is uncomfortable. I chuckle.

He runs his gaze down my features, my chest, down to my toes, then yawns.

The hell! I will not let him provoke me. Will not. "Like what you see?" I jut out my chin.

"Sorry, you're not my type." He slides a hand into the pocket of those perfectly cut pants, stretching it across that heavy bulge.

Heat curls low in my belly.

Not fair, that he could afford a wardrobe that clearly shouts his status and what amounts to the economy of a small third-world country. A hot feeling stabs in my chest.

He reeks of privilege, of taking his status in life for granted.

While I've had to fight every inch of the way. Hell, I am still battling to hold onto the last of my equilibrium.

"Last chance—" I wiggle my fingers, from where I am sprawled out on the floor at his feet, "—to redeem yourself…"

"You have me there." He places the glass on the counter, then bends and holds out his hand. The hint of discolored steel at his wrist catches my attention. Huh?

He wears a cheap-ass watch?

That's got to bring down the net worth of his presence by more than 1000% percent. Weird.

I reach up and he straightens.

I lurch back.

"Oops, I changed my mind." His lips curl.

A hot burning sensation claws at my stomach. I am not a violent person, honestly. But Smirky Pants here, he needs to be taught a lesson.

I swipe out my legs, kicking his out from under him.

Sinclair

My knees give way, and I hurtle toward the ground.

What the—? I twist around, thrust out my arms. My palms hit the floor. The impact jostles up my elbows. I firm my biceps and come to a halt planked above her.

A huffing sound fills my ear.

I turn to find my whippet, Max, panting with his mouth open. I scowl and he flattens his ears.

All of my businesses are dog-friendly. Before you draw conclusions about me being the caring sort or some such shit—it attracts footfall.

Max scrutinizes the girl, then glances at me. *Huh?* He hates women, but not her, apparently.

I straighten and my nose grazes hers.

My arms are on either side of her head. Her chest heaves. The fabric of her dress stretches across her gorgeous breasts. My fingers tingle; my palms ache to cup those tits, squeeze those hard nipples outlined against the—hold on, what is she wearing? A tunic shirt in a sparkly pink... and are those shoulder pads she has on?

I glance up, and a squeak escapes her lips.

Pink hair surrounds her face. *Pink? Who dyes their hair that color past the age of eighteen?*

I stare at her face. *How old is she?* Un-furrowed forehead, dark eyelashes that flutter against pale cheeks. Tiny nose, and that mouth— luscious, tempting. A whiff of her scent, cherries and caramel, assails my senses. My mouth waters. *What the hell?*

She opens her eyes and our eyelashes brush. Her gaze widens. Green, like the leaves of the evergreens, flickers of gold sparkling in their depths. "What?" She glowers. "You're demonstrating the plank position?"

"Actually," I lower my weight onto her, the ridge of my hardness thrusting into the softness between her legs, "I was thinking of something else, altogether."

She gulps and her pupils dilate. *Ah, so she feels it, too?*

I drop my head toward her, closer, closer.

Color floods the creamy expanse of her neck. Her eyelids flutter down. She tilts her chin up.

I push up and off of her.

"That... Sweetheart, is an emphatic 'no thank you' to whatever you are offering."

Her eyelids spring open and pink stains her cheeks. Adorable. Such a range of emotions across those gorgeous features in a few seconds? What else is hidden under that exquisite exterior of hers?

She scrambles up, eyes blazing.

Ah! The little bird is trying to spread her wings? My dick twitches. My groin hardens, *Why does her anger turn me on so, huh?*

She steps forward, thrusts a finger in my chest.

My heart begins to thud.

She peers up from under those hooded eyelashes. "Wake up and taste the wasabi, asshole."

"What does that even mean?"

She makes a sound deep in her throat. My dick twitches. My pulse speeds up.

She pivots, grabs a half-full beer mug sitting on the bar counter.

I growl, "Oh, no, you don't."

She turns, swings it at me. The smell of hops envelops the space.

I stare down at the beer-splattered shirt, the lapels of my camel colored jacket deepening to a dull brown. Anger squeezes my guts.

I fist my fingers at my side, broaden my stance.

She snickers.

I tip my chin up. "You're going to regret that."

The smile fades from her face. "Umm." She places the now empty mug on the bar.

I take a step forward and she skitters back. "It's only clothes." She gulps, "They'll wash."

I glare at her and she swallows, wiggles her fingers in the air, "I should have known that you wouldn't have a sense of humor."

I thrust out my jaw, "That's a ten-thousand-pound suit you destroyed."

She blanches, then straightens her shoulders, "Must have been some hot date you were trying to impress, huh?"

"Actually," I flick some of the offending liquid from my lapels, "it's you I was after."

"Me?" She frowns.

"We need to speak."

She glances toward the bartender who's on the other side of the bar. "I don't know you." She chews on her lower lip, biting off some of the hot pink. How would she look, with that pouty mouth fastened on my cock?

The blood rushes to my groin so quickly that my head spins. My pulse rate ratchets up. Focus, focus on the task you came here for.

"This will take only a few seconds." I take a step forward.

She moves aside.

I frown, "You want to hear this, I promise."

"Go to hell." She pivots and darts forward.

I let her go, a step, another, because... I can? Besides it's fun to create the illusion of freedom first; makes the hunt so much more entertaining, huh?

I swoop forward, loop an arm around her waist, and yank her toward me.

She yelps. "Release me."

Good thing the bar is not yet full. It's too early for the usual office-goers to stop by. And the staff...? Well they are well aware of who cuts their paychecks.

I spin her around and against the bar, then release her. "You will listen to me."

She swallows; she glances left to right.

Not letting you go yet, little Bird. I move into her space, crowd her.

She tips her chin up. "Whatever you're selling, I'm not interested."

I allow my lips to curl, "You don't fool me."

A flush steals up her throat, sears her cheeks. So tiny, so innocent. Such a good little liar. I narrow my gaze, "Every action has its consequences."

"Are you daft?" She blinks.

"This pretense of yours?" I thrust my face into hers, "It's not working."

She blinks, then color suffuses her cheeks, "You're certifiably mad—"

"Getting tired of your insults."

"It's true, everything I said." She scrapes back the hair from her face.

Her fingernails are painted... You guessed it, pink.

"And here's something else. You are a selfish, egotistical jackass."

I smirk. "You're beginning to repeat your insults and I haven't even kissed you yet."

"Don't you dare." She gulps.

I tilt my head, "Is that a challenge?"

"It's a..." she scans the crowded space, then turns to me. Her lips firm, "...a warning. You're delusional, you jackass." She inhales a deep breath, "Your ego is bigger than the size of a black hole." She snickers, "Bet it's to compensate for your lack of balls."

A-n-d, that's it. I've had enough of her mouth that threatens to never stop spewing words. How many insults can one tiny woman hurl my way? Answer: too many to count.

"You—"

I lower my chin, touch my lips to hers.

Heat, sweetness, the honey of her essence explodes on my palate. My dick twitches. I tilt my head, deepen the kiss, reaching for that something more... more... of whatever scent she's wearing on her skin, infused with that breath of hers that crowds my senses, rushes down my spine. My groin hardens; my cock lengthens. I thrust my tongue between those infuriating lips.

She makes a sound deep in her throat and my heart begins to pound.

So innocent, yet so crafty. Beautiful and feisty. The kind of complication I don't need in my life.

I prefer the straight and narrow. Gray and black, that's how I choose to define my world. She, with her flashes of color—pink hair and lips that threaten to drive me to the edge of distraction—is exactly what I hate.

Give me a female who has her priorities set in life. To pleasure me, get me off, then walk away before her emotions engage. Yeah. That's what I prefer.

Not this... this bundle of craziness who flings her arms around my shoulders, thrusts her breasts up and into my chest, tips up her chin, opens her mouth, and invites me to take and take.

Does she have no self-preservation? Does she think I am going to fall for her wide-eyed appeal? She has another thing coming.

I tear my mouth away and she protests.

She twines her leg with mine, pushes up her hips, so that melting softness between her thighs cradles my aching hardness.

I glare into her face and she holds my gaze.

Trains her green eyes on me. Her cheeks flush a bright red. Her lips fall open and a moan bleeds into the air. The blood rushes to my dick, which instantly thickens. *Fuck.*

Time to put distance between myself and the situation.

It's how I prefer to manage things. Stay in control, always. Cut out anything that threatens to impinge on my equilibrium. Shut it down or buy them off. Reduce it to a transaction. That I understand.

The power of money, to be able to buy and sell—numbers, logic. That's what's worked for me so far.

"How much?"

Her forehead furrows.

"Whatever it is, I can afford it."

Her jaw slackens. "You think… you—"

"A million?"

"What?"

"Pounds, dollars… You name the currency, and it will be in your account."

Her jaw slackens, "You're offering me money?"

"For your time, and for you to fall in line with my plan."

She reddens, "You think I am for sale?"

"Everyone is."

"Not me."

Here we go again. "Is that a challenge?"

Color fades from her face, "Get away from me."

"Are you shy, is that what this is?" I frown. "You can write your price down on a piece of paper if you prefer," I glance up, notice the bartender watching us. I jerk my chin toward the napkins. He grabs one, then offers it to her.

She glowers at him, "Did you buy him too?"

"What do you think?"

She glances around, "I think everyone here is ignoring us."

"It's what I'd expect."

"Why is that?"

I wave the tissue in front of her face, "Why do you think?"

"You own the place?"

"As I am going to own you."

She sets her jaw, "Let me leave and you won't regret this."

A chuckle bubbles up. I swallow it away. This is no laughing matter. I never smile during a transaction. Especially not when I am negotiating a new acquisition. And that's all she is. The final piece in the puzzle I am building.

"No one threatens me."

"You're right."

"Huh?"

"I'd rather act on my instinct."

Her lips twist, her gaze narrows. All of my senses scream a warning.

No, she wouldn't, no way—pain slices through my middle and sparks explode behind my eyes.

To find out what happens next get The Billionaire's Fake Wife HERE

Read about the seven in the Big bad Billionaires series

US

UK

Other countries

Each of the sovrano brothers gets his own story. Read the entire Series

US

UK

Other countries

Claim your FREE copy of Mafia Heir the prequel to Mafia King

Claim your FREE billionaire romance boxset

Claim your free paranormal romance

Follow L. Steele on AMAZON

Follow L. Steele on BookBub

Follow L. Steele on Goodreads

Follow L. Steele on Facebook

Follow L. Steele on Instagram

Join L. Steele's secret Facebook Reader Group

More books by L. Steele HERE

Join L. Steele's Newsletter for news on her newest releases

FREE BOOKS

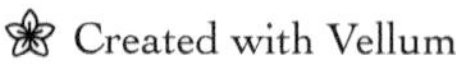 Created with Vellum